I0561701

THOMAS ADOLPHUS TROLLOPE.

From a Painting by Maria Taylor.

WHAT I REMEMBER

BY

THOMAS ADOLPHUS TROLLOPE

AUTHOR OF

"LINDISFARN CHASE" "A SIREN" "DURNTON ABBEY" ETC.

NEW YORK

HARPER & BROTHERS, FRANKLIN SQUARE

1888

OMNIBUS WICCAMICIS

T. ADOLPHUS TROLLOPE

B. M. DE WINTON PROPE WINTON COLL.

OLIM ALUMNUS

GRATO ANIMO

D. D. D.

CONTENTS.

CONTENTS.

WHAT I REMEMBER.

CHAPTER I.

I HAVE no intention of writing an autobiography. There has been nothing in my life which could justify such a pretension. But I have lived a long time. I remember an aged porter at the monastery of the "Sagro Eremo," above Camaldoli, who had taken brevet rank as a saint solely on the score of his ninety years. His brethren called him and considered him as Saint Simon simply because he had been porter at that gate for more than sixty years. Now my credentials as a babbler of reminiscences are of a similar nature to those of the old porter. I have been here so many, many years. And then those years have comprised the best part of the nineteenth century—a century during which change has been more rapidly at work among all the surroundings of Englishmen than probably during any other century of which social history has to tell.

Of course middle - aged men know, as well as we ancients, the fact that social life in England—or, rather, let me say in Europe — is very different from what it was in the days of their fathers, and are perfectly well acquainted with the great and oftentimes celebrated causes which have differentiated the Victorian era from all others. But only the small records of an unimportant individual life, only the memories which happen to linger in an old man's brain, like bits of drift-weed floating round and round in the eddies of a back-water, can bring vividly before the young of the present generation those ways and manners

1

of acting and thinking and talking in the ordinary, every-day affairs of life which indicate the differences between themselves and their grandfathers.

I was born in the year 1810 at No. 16 Keppel Street, Russell Square. The region was at that time inhabited by the professional classes, mainly lawyers. My father was a barrister of the Middle Temple to the best of my recollection, but having chambers in the Old Square, Lincoln's Inn. A quarter of a century or so later all the district in question became rather deteriorated in social estimation, but has, I am told, recently recovered itself in this respect under the careful and judicious administration of the Duke of Bedford. The whole region appeared to me, when I was recently in London, about the least changed part of the London of my youthful days. As I walked up Store Street, which runs in a line from Keppel Street to Tottenham Court Road, I spied the name of "Pidding, Confectioner." I immediately entered the shop and made a purchase at the counter. "I did not in the least want this tart," said I to the girl who was serving in the shop. "Why did you take it, then?" said she, with a little toss of her head. "Nobody asked you to buy it." "I bought it," rejoined I, "because I used to buy pastry of Mr. Pidding in this shop seventy years ago." "Lor', sir!" said the girl, "did you really?" She probably considered me to be the Wandering Jew.

I remember well that my father used to point out to me houses in Russell Square, Bedford Square, and Bloomsbury Square in which judges and other notable legal luminaries used to live. But even in those days the localities in question, especially the last named of them, were beginning to be deserted by such personages, who were already moving farther westward. The occasion of these walks with my father through the squares I have named —to which Red Lion Square might have been added—was one the painful nature of which has fixed it in my memory indelibly.

"Infandum *memoria* jubes renovare dolorem."

For the object of these walks was the rendering an account of the morning's studies. I was about six years old

when, under my father's auspices, I was first introduced
to the "Eton Latin Grammar." He was a Wykehamist,
had been a fellow of New College, and had held a Vine-
rian fellowship. And his great ambition was that his eldest son, myself, should tread in his steps and pursue the
same career. *Dis aliter visum!* as regards at least the
latter stages of that career. For I did become, and am, a
Wykehamist, as much as eight years at *Coll. B. M. Winton prope Winton* can make me.

Of which more anon.

For the present I see myself alone in the back drawing-
room of No. 16 Keppel Street, in which room the family
breakfast took place :— probably to avoid the necessity of
lighting another fire in the dining-room below—at 7 A.M.,
on my knees before the sofa, with my head in my hands
and my eyes fixed on the "Eton Latin Grammar" laid on
the sofa-cushion before me. My parents had not yet come
down to breakfast, nor had the tea-urn been brought up
by the footman. *Nota bene.*—My father was a poor man,
and his establishment altogether on a modest footing.
But it never would have occurred to him or to my mother
that they could get on without a man-servant in livery.
And though this liveried footman served a family in which
two tallow candles, with their snuffer-dish, supplied the
whole illumination of the evening, had the livery been an
invented one instead of that proper to the family, the circumstance would have been an absurdity exciting the
ridicule of all the society in which my parents lived.
Tempora mutantur! Certainly, at the present day, an
equally unpretending household would be burdened by no
footman. But on the morning which memory is recalling
to me the footman was coming up with the urn, and my
parents were coming down to breakfast, probably simultaneously; and the question of the hour was whether I
could get the due relationship of relative and antecedent
into my little head before the two events arrived.

And that, as I remember it, was the almost unvaried
routine for more than a year or two. I think, however,
that the walks of which I was speaking when this retro-
spect presented itself to me must have belonged to a time

a little, but not much, later; for I had then advanced to
the making of Latin verses. We used to begin in those
days by making "nonsense verses." And many of us
ended in the same way! The next step— *Gradus ad Par-
nassum* — consisted in turning into Latin verse certain
English materials provided for the purpose, and so cunningly prepared as to fall easily and almost inevitably into
the required form. And these were the studies which, as
I specially remember, were the subject of rehearsal during
those walks from Lincoln's Inn to Keppel Street.

My father was in the habit of returning from his chambers to a five-o'clock dinner — rather a late hour, because
he was an industrious and laborious' man. Well! we, that
is, my next brother (not the one whose name became subsequently well known in the world, but my brother Henry,
who died early) and myself, used to walk from Keppel
Street to Lincoln's Inn, so as to arrive in time to walk
back with my father. He was a fast walker; and as we
trotted along, one on each side of him, the repetition of
our morning's poetical achievements did not tend, as I
well remember, to facilitate the difficulty of "keeping our
wind."

But what has probably fixed all this in my mind during
nearly three quarters of a century was my father's pat application of one of our lines to the difficulties of those per-
ipatetic poetizings. "*Muse and sound of wheel do not
well agree,*" read the cunningly prepared original, which
the *alumnus*, with wonderful sagacity, was to turn into,
"*Non bene conveniunt Musa rotæque sonus.*" "That,"
said my father, as he turned sharp round the corner into
the comparative quiet of Featherstone Buildings, "is exactly why I turned out of Holborn!"

I do not know whether children of eight years old, or
thereabouts, would at the present day be allowed to range
London so freely as we were. But our great amusement
and delight was to take long exploring walks in as distant
parts of the huge (though then comparatively small) city
as could be compassed within the time at our disposition.
One especially favorite excursion, I well remember, was
to the White Horse Cellar in Piccadilly to see the coaches

start or arrive. I knew all their names, and their supposed comparative speed. By this means, indeed, came
my first introduction to English geography. Formal lessons on such a thoroughly "commercial academy" subject
were not, of course, thought of for an aspiring Wykehamist. But for the due enjoyment of the White Horse Cellar spectacle it was necessary to know the whereabouts of
the cities, their distance from London, and the routes by
which they were reached. It thus came to pass that our
geographical notions were of a curiously partial description—tolerably copious and accurate as regards the south
and west of England, far less so as regards the north; for
the north-country coaches did not start from Piccadilly.
On the opposite side of the way to the White Horse Cellar
there was another coaching inn, the White Bear, on which
I remember we used to look with much contempt, from
the belief, whether in any degree well founded I know not,
that the coaches which stopped there on their way out of
town, or arrived there, were mainly slow coaches.

One does not traverse well-nigh fourscore years without having experienced longings for the unattainable on
several occasions. But I have no remembrance of any
such eager, craving longing as the chronic longing of those
days to make one of the great-coated companies who were
departing to their various destinations by those "Telegraphs," "High-Flyers," "Magnets," and "Independents."
(The more suggestive names of the "Wonder," and its
rival the "No Wonder!" once celebrated on the north-
western road, belonged to a later day.) Had I been offered
a seat on any of these vehicles my choice would have been
dictated solely by considerations of distance — Falmouth
for choice, as the westward Ultima Thule of coaching experience. With what rapture should I have climbed, in
my little round jacket as I was, and without a thought of
any other protection, to the roof of the Falmouth mail
— *the* mail for choice, the Devonport Quicksilver being
then in the womb of the future—and started to fetch a
forgotten letter (say) of the utmost importance, with strict
injunctions to bring it back by the returning coach! I
don't think my imagination had yet soared to the supreme

glories of the box-seat. That came later. To have been
a booked passenger, that that horn should have sounded
for me, that I should have been included in the guard's
final and cheery assurance that at length all was "right"
—would have been ample enough for an ecstacy of happiness. What an endless vista of ever-changing miles of
country! What an infinite succession of "teams"! What
a delicious sense of belonging to some select and specially
important and adventurous section of humanity as we
should clatter at midnight, or even at three or four o'clock
in the morning, through the streets of quiet little country
towns, ourselves the only souls awake in all the place!
What speculations as to the immediate bestowal and occupation of the coachman, when he "left you here, sir!" in
the small hours! What a delightful sense of the possible
dangers of the undertaking as testified by many eagerly
read narratives of the disasters of the road. Alas! I had
no share in it all, save to stand on the curbstone amid the
crowd of Jew boys selling oranges and cedar pencils sixpence a dozen, and hurrying passengers and guards and
porters, and look on them all with envious longing.

Nota bene. On such an occasion at the present day—if
it be possible to conceive such an anachronism—the Jew
boys above referred to would be probably Christian boys,
and the object of their commerce the evening papers.
But I have no recollection of any such element in the scene
at the White Horse Cellar some sixty-eight years since.

Occasionally when a holiday from lessons occurred—I
am afraid most probably in consequence of my father
being confined to his bed with headaches, which even at
that early day, and increasingly, as years went on, afflicted
him—we, my brother Henry and I, obtained permission
for a longer ramble. I have no recollection that on these
occasions either the parks (unless, perhaps sometimes St.
James's Park), or Kensington Gardens, or Hampstead, or
Highgate, or any of the places that might be supposed to
be attractive, had any attractions for us. Our faces were
ever turned eastward. The city with its narrow, mysterious lanes, and still more mysterious wharves, its quaint
secluded churches, its Guildhall, and its Gog and Magog,

the queer localities of the halls of its companies, and specially the abstruse mystery of that venerable Palladium, the London stone, excited in those days an irresistible influence on my imagination. But above all else the grand object of a much-planned eastern pilgrimage was the docks!—with the outgoing ships bearing, tied to their shrouds, boards indicating their destinations. Here again was unsatisfied longing! But it was a longing more tempered by awe and uncertainty. I am not sure that I would, if it had been offered to me, have stepped on board an East Indiaman bound for Bombay as eagerly as I would have climbed a coach starting for the Land's End. But it was a great triumph to have seen with our own eyes the *Agra* (or some other) *Castle* majestically passing through the dock gates, while passengers on deck, men and women, whose feet would absolutely touch land no more till they stopped at far Bombay on the other side of the world, spoke last farewells to friends standing on the dock walls or even on the gates themselves.

But I can recall no less vividly certain expeditions of a kind which appeared to our imaginations to be—and which, perhaps, really were in some degree—fraught with a certain amount of peril. Stories had reached us of sundry mysteriously wicked regions, where the bandit bands of the great city consorted and lived outlaw lives under circumstances and conditions that powerfully excited our young imagination. Especially accounts of a certain lane had reached us, where it was said all the pocket-handkerchiefs stolen by all the pickpockets in London were to be seen exposed in a sort of unholy market. The name of this place was Saffron Hill. Whether any such place still exists, I know not. It has probably been swept away by the march of recent improvement. But it did in those days veritably exist. And to this extraordinary spot—as remote and strange to our fancy as the realms of Prester John—it was determined, after protracted consideration by my brother and myself, that our next long ramble should be devoted. We had ascertained that the dingy land of our researches lay somewhat to the westward of Smithfield—which had already been the object of a most successful, adventurous, and delightful expedition, not without pleasurable perils of its own from excited drovers and their dogs—and by dint of considerable perseverance we reached it, and were richly rewarded for our toil and enterprise. Report had spoken truly. Saffron Hill was a world of pocket-handkerchiefs. From every window, and on lines stretched across the narrow street, they fluttered in all the colors of the rainbow, and of all sizes and qualities. The whole lane was a long vista of pennon-like pocket-handkerchiefs! We should have much liked to attempt to deal in this strange market, not so much for the sake of possessing any of the articles, as with a view of obtaining experience, and informing ourselves respecting the manners and customs of the country. But we were protected from the possibly unpleasant results of any such tentative by the total absence from our pockets of any coin of the realm. We doubtless had pocket-handkerchiefs, and I have no recollection of their having been stolen. Probably it was ascertained by the inhabitants that they were not worth their notice.

But the subject reminds me of an experience of the pocket-picking world which occurred to me some twenty years later. It was at Naples. People generally in those days carried silk pocket-handkerchiefs instead of the scraps of muslin which are affected nowadays. And five silk pocket-handkerchiefs were abstracted from my pockets during my walks abroad in as many days. I then took to wearing very common ones, and lost no more! An American then at Naples, whose experiences of the proclivities of that population had been similar to mine, was not so fortunate in the result of the defensive measures he adopted. He sewed strongly into the interior of his pocket a large fish-hook. The result which he anticipated followed. The thief's hand was caught, and the American, turning sharply, seized him by the wrist and held him in a grasp like a vise till he could hand him over to a gendarme. But within a fortnight that American was stabbed to the heart one night as he was going home from the theatre. The light-fingered fraternity, it would seem, considered that such a practice was not within the laws of the game; whereas my more moderate ruse did not offend their sense of justice and fair-play.

My brother and I reached home safely enough after our expedition to thief-land; and were inexhaustible in our accounts of the wonders we had witnessed. For it formed no part of our plan, and would not have been at all in accordance with the general practice of our lives, to conceal the facts from our parents. Probably we had a sufficient suspicion of the questionable nature of the expedition we contemplated to prevent us from declaring it beforehand. But our education and habits would have forbidden any dream of concealing it.

As far as my recollection serves me, our moral and religious education led us to consider the whole duty of boy to be summed up in the two precepts "obey" and "tell no lies." I think there was a perfunctory saying of some portion of the catechism on a Sunday morning. But I am very sure that in our own minds, and apparently in those of all concerned, the vastly superior importance of the Virgil lesson admitted of no moment's doubt. But it must not be imagined from this that my parents were more irreligious people than their neighbors; still less that they were not most affectionately and, indeed, supremely solicitous for the well-being and education of their children. My father was the son of a priest of the Church of England, and my mother the daughter of another, the Rev. William Milton, Vicar of Heckfield, a New College living not far from Reading. Their associates were mainly barristers or clergy. My father was wholly and absolutely free from the prevailing vice of the time, and I never remember to have seen him in any slightest degree the worse for drink. And in the whole *manière d'être* of the house and home there was no note or symptom of any life save one of the most correct respectability and propriety, fully up to the average of the time. But my parents were by no means what was called in the language of the time "evangelicals." And in the social atmosphere of those days, any more decided and marked amount of religious instruction and teaching would have unmistakably indicated "evangelical tendencies." Moreover, though I can-

1*

not remember, and it is exceedingly improbable, that any ideas were directly instilled into our minds on the subject, it certainly is the fact that I grew into boyhood with the notion that "evangelicalism," or "low churchism," was a note of vulgarity—a sort of thing that might be expected to be met with in tradesmen's back parlors, and "academies," where the youths who came from such places were instructed in English grammar and arithmetic, but was not to be met with, and was utterly out of place, among gentlemen and in gentlemanlike places of education, where nothing of the kind was taught.

All this to mark the change of *tempora* and *mores*, in these as in so many other respects, since George the Third was king.

Among the few surviving remembrances of those childhood's years in Keppel Street, I can still recall to the mind's eye the face and features of "Farmer," the highly trustworthy and responsible middle-aged woman who ruled the nursery there, into which a rapid succession of brothers and sisters was being introduced in those years. Farmer, as I remember her, inspired more awe than affection. She was an austere and somewhat grim sort of body. And somehow or other the obscurely terrible fact that she was an Anabaptist (!) had reached the world of the nursery. I need hardly say that the accusation carried with it no sort of idea whatever to our minds. I don't think we had any knowledge that the mystic term in question had reference to any forms or modifications of religious belief. But we were well assured that it implied something mysterious and terrible. And I am afraid that we gracelessly availed ourselves of what we should have considered a misfortune, if we had at all known what it meant, to express, on occasions of revolt against discipline, our scorn for an individual so disgraced by nature. I have still in my ear the lilt of a wicked chorus the burden of which ran:

> "Old Farmer is an Anabap*tist!*
> When she is gone, she will not be missed!"

I remember, in connection with poor Farmer and her heresies, an incident which must have been ridiculous enough to the adult actors in it. Dr. Nott, one of the prebendaries of Winchester, was an old and intimate friend of my mother's—had been such, I believe, before her marriage. The mention of this gentleman recalls to my mind —but this recollection dates from a later day—that it used to be said satirically, with what truth I will not attempt to guess, that there was a large Chapter at Winchester and *Nott*, one of them, a clergyman: the intention being to insinuate that he was the only properly clerical character among them. At all events, Dr. Nott was an exemplary dignitary of the Church, not only in character, tastes, and pursuits, but in outward presentment also. I remember well his spare figure, his pale and delicately cut features, his black gaiters to the knee, and his elaborate white neckcloth. He was a competent, and what would have been called in that day an "elegant," Italian scholar. It was wholly under his supervision that, a few years subsequently, the extensive restoration and repair of Winchester Cathedral was executed; a supervision which cost him, in consequence of a fall from a ladder in the nave, a broken leg and subsequent lameness for life. He had, if I mistake not, been one of the tutors of the Princess Charlotte.

Well, upon one occasion of a visit of Dr. Nott's in Keppel Street, we children were summoned to the drawing-room for his inspection; and in reply to a variety of questions as to progress, and goodness in the nursery, etc., I, as the eldest, took courage to reply that if we were not always as good and obedient in the nursery as might be desired, the circumstance was to be attributed to the painful fact that our nurse was an Anabaptist! Whether Dr. Nott was selected as the recipient of this confidential communication because I had any vague idea that this disgraceful circumstance had any special connection with his department of human affairs, I cannot say. We were, however, told that the fact was no wise incompatible with Farmer's character as an excellent nurse and good servant, and least of all could be considered as absolving us from the duty of obedience. I remembered that I wondered then—and I wonder still—what passed upon the subject between my mother and the doctor after our dismissal to the nursery.

Another intimate friend of my mother's and frequent visitor in Keppel Street was Lady Dyer, the wife, and subsequently widow, of General Sir Thomas Dyer. Sir Thomas resided on his estate of Ovington, near Winchester ; and I take it that my mother's intimacy with Lady Dyer had been brought about by the friendship existing between both ladies and Miss Gabell, the eldest daughter of Dr. Gabell, the head-master of Winchester College. Lady Dyer, after several years of widowhood, married the Baron de Zandt; and I remember, very many years subsequently to the time that I am here writing of, visiting her with my mother at her *schloss*, near Bamberg, where she lived in the huge house alone after losing her second husband.

I fancy it was mainly due to her intimacy with my mother during those years in Keppel Street that the house was frequented by several Italians ; exiles from their own country under stress of political troubles. Especially I remember among these General Guglielmo Pepe, subsequently the hero of the hopeless defence of Venice against the Austrians. Of course I was too young to know or see much of him in the Keppel Street days; but many years afterwards I had abundant opportunities of knowing Pepe's genuine nobility of character, high honor, and ardent patriotism. He was a remarkably handsome man, but not a brilliant or amusing companion. I remember that his sobriquet among the three ladies mentioned together above was *Gâteau de Plomb!* But none the less was he highly and genuinely respected by them. He had a kind of simple, dignified, placid manner of enunciating the most astounding platitudes, and replying to the laughter they sometimes produced by a calm, gentle smile, which showed how impossible it was for his simple soul to imagine that his hearers were otherwise than delighted with his wit and wisdom. How well I can remember the pleasure his visits were wont to afford in the nursery by reason of the dried Neapolitan figs and Mandarin oranges, which he used to receive from his brother, General Fiorestano Pepe, and never failed to distribute among his English friends. His brother, when Guglielmo threw in his lot with the "patriots," never forfeited his allegiance or quarrelled with the King of Naples. Yet the two brothers continued on affectionately fraternal terms to the last.

The quiet course of those Keppel Street years was, as I remember, once or twice broken by the great event of a visit to Heckfield to my maternal grandfather, the Rev. William Milton, a *ci-devant* fellow of New College. He had at that time married a second wife, a Miss Partington, his first wife, a Derbyshire Gresley, my maternal grandmother, whom I had never seen, having died young. As my grandfather Milton was the son of a Bristol saddler (who lived to the age of ninety-nine), I suppose his marriage with a Gresley must have been deemed a *mésalliance* for the lady. But her death having occurred before my time, I never heard anything of this.

The Vicar of Heckfield held the adjoining chapelry of Mattingly, at which place the morning service was performed on alternate Sundays. He was an excellent parish priest after the fashion of his day; that is to say, he was kindly to all, liberal to the poor to the utmost extent of his means, and well beloved by his neighbors, high and low. He was a charming old man, markedly gentlemanlike and suave in his manner; very nice in his person; clever unquestionably in a queer, crotchety sort of way; and thoroughly minded to do his duty according to his lights in that state of life to which it had pleased God to call him. But he would have had no more idea of attempting anything of the nature of active parochial work or reform, as understood at the present day, than he would have had of scheming to pay the national debt. Indeed, the latter would have been the more likely to occupy his mind of the two, for he was crotchety and full of schemes. Especially he was fond of mechanics, and spent much money and much labor during many years on a favorite scheme for obviating the danger arising from the liability of a stage-coach to be upset. He published more than one pamphlet on the subject, illustrated—I can see the pages before me now—by designs of various queer-looking models. There was a large coach-house attached to the vicarage, and it was always full of the strangest collection of models of coaches. I remember well that they all appeared to me hideous, and as æsthetically inferior to my admired Telegraphs and High-Flyers as a modern iron-clad seems to the three-decker of his youth in the eyes of an old sailor. But, as may be imagined, I never ventured to broach any such heresy in my grandfather's hearing! I should unquestionably have done so had it been my father. But lesser acquaintanceship and the venerable age of my grandfather checked my presumption.

There was—and doubtless is—a very pretty evergreen-embowered lawn at the vicarage, and on this also there always used to be some model or other intended to illustrate the principles of traction. One I especially remember which was called (not, it may seem, very grammatically) *rotis volventibus*. This machine consisted of two huge wheels, some ten feet high, joined together by a number of cross-bars at a distance of a foot or so from each other. It will be understood what a delightful amusement it must have been to creep into the interior of this structure, and cause it to roll over the smoothly-shaven turf by stepping treadmill fashion on the cross-bars one after the other. But unfortunately in one part of the lawn there was a steep declivity, and one day, when the idea of making *rotis volventibus* descend this slope became irresistible, there was a tremendous smashing of the evergreen hedge, and a black-and-blue little body, whose escape without broken bones was deemed truly prodigious.

"Never, Tom," said my grandfather, "put in motion forces which you are unable to control!"

The words remained implanted in my memory. But I do not suppose they carried much instruction with them to my mind at the time.

I believe my grandfather spent more money on his mechanical fads than was quite prudent, and took out patents which were about as remunerative and useful as that which Charles the Second is said to have granted to a sailor who stood on his head on the top of Salisbury steeple, securing to him the monopoly of that practice!

I remember another eccentricity in which the vicar

indulged. He said the contact of a knife's edge with earthenware, or porcelain, was extremely disagreeable. He caused, therefore, a number of dinner plates to be made with a little circular depression some two inches in diameter and about as deep as a crown piece in the centre, and had some round pieces of silver to fit into these receptacles, on which he cut his meat.

He was withal a very popular man, a good scholar, with decidedly scholarly tastes, much of a mathematician, a genuine humorist, with a sort of Horatian easy-going geniality about him which was very charming even to us boys.

My brother Henry was one year my junior; my brother Anthony, with whom the world subsequently became acquainted, was five years younger than I. Henry, therefore, was the companion of all the London rambles which have been mentioned. I think we were tolerably good boys, truthful and obedient to legitimate authority. I was, however, if nursery traditions of a somewhat later day may be accepted as embodying real facts, rather too much given to yielding obedience only on reason shown; to "argify," as certain authoritarians are wont to call it; and to make plenary submission only when consciously defeated in argument.

We had little or nothing of the "amusements" nowadays so liberally supplied to children. There was the pantomime at Christmas, intensely enjoyed. And I remember well pondering on the insoluble question *why* my parents, who evidently, I thought, could, if they chose it, go to the theatre every night of their lives, should abstain from doing so.

I do not remember any discontented longings for more or other amusements than we had. I was a thoroughly well constituted and healthy child, but without the smallest pretension to good looks, either *in esse* or *in posse;* sturdily built, with flaxen head, rosy cheeks, and blue eyes; broad of hand and foot; strong as a little pony—a veritable Saxon in type. I seem to my recollections to have been somewhat bravely ready to accept a life in which the kicks might be more superabundant than the half-pence not without complacent mental reference to the moral and physical breadth of shoulders, ready for whatever fate might lay on them. The nature of my childish mind, as I remember, was to place its ideas of heroism in capacity for uncomplaining endurance, rather than in capability for mastering others.

All the usual childish complaints and maladies touched me very lightly. I was as indifferent to weather, wet or dry, wind or shine, as a Shetland pony. Feet wet through had to remain *in statu quo* till they were dry again. Assiduously taught by my mother, I read at a very early age. Her plan for teaching the letters was as follows. She had a great number of bone counters with the alphabet in capitals and small letters on either side printed on them; then having invited a charming little girl, the daughter of a neighbor (Katie Gibbon, laid to rest this many a year under the yew-tree in the churchyard of the village of Stanton, near Monmouth), who was just my own age, she tossed the counters broadcast over the floor, instituting prizes for him, or her, who should, in crawling races over the floor, soonest bring the letter demanded. Reading thus began to be an amusement to me at an unusually early age. I believe I gave early indications of possessing a certain quantum of brain power; but had no reputation for cleverness. Indeed, had my parents ever formed the opinion that any one of their children was in any way markedly clever, they would have carefully concealed it from the subject of it. I take it, I was far from being what is called a prepossessing child. I had, I well remember, a reputation for an uncompromising expression of opinion which was not altogether admirable. My mother used to tell in after-years how, when once I had been, at about four years old, attentively watching her dressing for dinner, while standing on a chair by the side of her dressing-table, I broke silence when the work was completed to say very judicially, "Now you have made yourself as fine as poso" (possible), "and you look worse than you did when you began!"

I am tempted to insert here a letter to my father from Dr. Williams, my old Winchester master, which (amusingly to me) illustrates what I have here written of my nursery tendencies. It belongs to a later date, when I was within half a year of leaving Winchester. I had not found it among my papers when I wrote the passage to which it is now appended. But I place it here in homage to the dictum that the child is father to the man.

"I have the pleasure," Dr. Williams writes, "to express my approbation of your son's conduct during the last half-year. His firmness in maintaining what was right and putting down what was wrong was very conspicuous in the early part of that time; not that I imagine it was less afterwards, but occasion did not call it forth so much."

What the occasion was I entirely forget; evidently he refers to some exercise of my power as a prefect.

"I have remarked to you before that he is *fond of having a reason* assigned for everything; but he must take care that this do not degenerate into captiousness. His temper is generally good, but a little too sensitive when he fancies a smile is raised at his expense."

I feel no confidence that years have rendered me safe from the first fault which my excellent master thus warned me against; but I am sure they have cured me of the second.

I remember, too, in connection with those Keppel Street days, to have heard my mother speak of an incident which somewhat curiously illustrates the ways and habits of a time already so far left behind us by a whole world of social changes. It was nothing more than a simple visit to the theatre to hear Mrs. Siddons in Lady Macbeth. But this exploit involved circumstances that rendered it memorable for other reasons besides the intense gratification derived from the performance. In the first place "the pit" was the destination to which my father and mother were bound; not altogether, I take it, so much for the sake of the lower price of admission (though my father was a sufficiently poor and a sufficiently careful man to render this a consideration), as from the idea that the pit offered the best vantage-ground for a thoroughly appreciative and critical judgment of the performance. For when we children were taken to see a pantomime we went,

as I remember, to the boxes. But this visit to the pit involved the necessity of being at the theatre at two in the
afternoon, and then *standing* in the crowd till, if I rightly
remember, six in the evening! Of course food had to be
carried. And each man there did his best to support and
assist the lady under his charge. But the ordeal must
have been something tremendous, and the amount of enthusiasm needed to induce a lady to face it something
scarcely to be understood at the present day. My mother
used to relate that sundry women were carried out from
the crowd at the theatre door fainting.

Before closing this Keppel Street chapter of my existence I may mention one or two circumstances of the family life there which illustrate the social habits of those
days. The family dinner-hour was five. There were no
dinner-napkins to be seen ; they were perhaps less needed
by clean-shaven chins and lips. Two tallow-candles, requiring to be snuffed by snuffers lying in a little plated
tray *ad hoc* every now and then, partially illumined the
table, but scarcely at all the more distant corners of the
room. Nor were any more or better lights used during
the evening in the drawing-room. The only alternative
would have been wax-lights at half a crown a pound—an
extravagance not to be thought of. Port and sherry were
always placed on the shining mahogany table when the
cloth was withdrawn, and no other wine. Only on the
occasion of having friends to dinner the port became a
"magnum" of a vintage for which my father's cellar was
famous, and possibly Madeira might be added.

Perhaps it may be worth noting here, as an incident
illustrating change of manners, that I vividly remember
my mother often singing to us children in Keppel Street an
old song about an "unfortunate Miss Bayly," who had been
seduced by a "Captain bold of Halifax, who dwelt in
country quarters." Now a purer or more innocent-mind-
ed woman than my mother did not live, nor one less likely
to have suffered aught that she imagined to be unfitted
virginibus puerisque to reach the ears of her children.
Nor do I suppose that we had the faintest notion of the
nature of the evil inflicted on the unfortunate Miss Bayly

by the captain bold, nor that we were in any degree scandalized by the subsequent incident of the parish priest being bribed by "a one-pound note" to accord Christian burial to the corpse of a suicide, which he had previously refused to bury. It may be feared that quite as many "unfortunates" share the fate of Miss Bayly, either in town or country quarters, at the present day as in the early days of the century. But I take it that the old-world ditty in question would not be selected for nursery use at the present day.

I could chatter on about those childish days in Keppel Street, and have been, I am afraid, too garrulous already. What I have said, however, is all illustrative of the social changes seventy years have wrought, and may at the same time serve to show that I started on my octogenarian career a sturdy, hardy little mortal, *non sine Dis animosus infans.*

CHAPTER II.

THESE fragmentary recollections of our childish days may have served to suggest some hints of the changes which have made the London of the present day almost— perhaps quite—as different from the London of the second decade of this century as the latter was from "the town" in the days of George the First. But it is difficult for middle-aged people of the present day to form any vivid and sufficient conception of the greatness of them. Of course the mere material ameliorations and extensions have so metamorphosed the localities that I, on returning after long years to the London I once knew, topographically at least, so well, find myself in a new town, of which the geography is in some parts strange to me, with just so much of the old landmarks remaining as serves to suggest false clews to the labyrinth, and render the matter more puzzling. But the changes in ways and habits and modes of living and feeling and thinking are still greater and of much more profound significance.

To say that there were in those days no omnibuses and no cabs, and of course no railways, either under ground or over it, is a simple matter, and very easily stated. But it is not easy to picture to one's self the whole meaning and consequences of their non-existence. Let any Londoner, with the exception of the comparatively small number of those who use carriages of their own, think what his life would be, and the transaction of his day's work or of his day's pleasure, without any means of locomotion save his own legs or a hackney-coach, which, at a cost of about five times the cab-hire of the present day, used to shut him up in an atmosphere like that of a very dirty stable, and jolt him over the uneven pavement at a pace of about four miles an hour. Dickens has given, in his own graphic

way, more than one sketch of the old hackney-coach. I
do not think that I ever saw a hackney-coach that had
been built for the work it was engaged in as such. They
were heavy, old-fashioned, rickety vehicles, which had become too heavy, too old-fashioned, too rickety to be retained in the service of the families to which they had
once belonged. They were built, for the most part, with
hammer-cloths, and many of them exhibited huge and
gorgeously-painted armorial bearings on the panels. (By-
the-bye, why did not the officials of the inland revenue
come down on the proprietors of these venerable vehicles
for the use of armorial bearings? I take it that the march
of modern intelligence, *acuens mortalia corda*, would impel their successors of the present day to do so.) The
drivers of those carriages were "in a concatenation accordingly"—shabby, slow, stupid, dirty, and often muddled
with drink. We hear occasionally nowadays of a cabman
"driving furiously" when drunk. The wording of the
charge smacks of another era. Not all the gin in London
could have stimulated the old "Jarvey" to drive his skel-
etons of horses furiously. He was not often incapacitated
by drink, but very frequently muddled. If it was necessary for him to descend from his hammer-cloth for the
purpose of opening the door of his carriage, which the
presence of the "waterman" of the stand for the most
part rendered unnecessary, he was a long time about it,
and a longer in clambering back to his seat, loaded as he
generally was in all weathers with an immense greatcoat
of many capes, weatherbeaten out of all resemblance to
its original color. The "watermen," so called, as we know
from high authority, "because they opens the coach-doors,"
were nevertheless surrounded by their half a dozen or so
of little shallow pails of water, as they stood by the side
of the curbstone near a coach-stand. They were to the
hackney-coachman what the bricklayer's laborer is to the
bricklayer. And a more sorry sight can hardly be conceived than the "stand" with its broken-down carriages,
more broken-down drivers, and, worst of all, broken-down
horses, which supplied us in the days when we "called a
coach, and let a coach be called, and he that calls it, let

him be the caller," as it stands written in a page almost as much (but far less deservedly) forgotten as the hackney-coach.

Already in my boyhood "Oxford Road" was beginning to be called "Oxford Street." But my father and his contemporaries always used the former phrase. At the end of Oxford Street was Tyburn turnpike ; not a mere name, but a veritable barrier, closing not only the continuation of the Oxford Road, but also the Edgware Road, turning at right angles to the north of it. And there stood *one* turnpike-man to receive the toll and give tickets in return for the whole of Oxford Street traffic ! I can see him now, with his low-crowned hat, a straw in his mouth, his vigilant eye, and the preternatural quickness and coolness, as it seemed to me, with which, standing in the centre between his two gates, he took the half-pence and delivered the tickets. He had always an irreproachably clean white apron, with pockets in front of it, one for half-pence and one for tickets.

I have spoken of my delight in the spectacle of the coaches starting from and arriving at the White Horse Cellar in Piccadilly. But there were many other aspects of London life in the days before railroads in which the coaches made a leading feature. One of the sights of London for country cousins was to see the mails starting at eight P.M. from the post-office. To view it under the most favorable circumstances, one went there on the anniversary of the king's birthday, when all the guards had their scarlet coats new, and the horses' heads were all decked with flowers. And truly the yard around the post-office offered on such an occasion a prettier sight than all the travelling arrangements of the present day could supply. Of course I am speaking of a time a little subsequent to my earliest recollections. For I can remember when the huge edifice in Saint Martin's le Grand was built; and remember well, too, the ridicule and the outcry that was raised at the size of the building, so enormously larger, it was supposed, than could possibly be needed! But it has now long since been found altogether insufficient for the needs of the service.

A journey on the box of the mail was a great delight to
me in those days—days somewhere in the third decade
of the century ; and, faith ! I believe would be still, if
there were any mails available for the purpose.   One journey frequently performed by me with infinite delight was
to Exeter.   My business was to visit two old ladies living there, Miss Mary and Miss Fanny Bent.   The Rev.
John Bent, rector of Crediton, had married the sister of
my grandmother, the Rev. William Milton's wife.   Miss
Mary Bent was his daughter by a second wife ; but her
half-sister, Fanny Bent, as we and everybody else called
her, was thus my mother's first cousin, and the tie between Fanny Milton and Fanny Bent had always, from
their earliest years, been a very close one.

And that is how I came, on several occasions, to find
myself on the box of the Exeter mail.   A new and accelerated mail service had been recently established under
the title of the Devonport Mail.   It was at that time the
fastest, I believe, in England.   Its performances caused
somewhat of a sensation in the coaching world, and it
was known in those circles as the Quicksilver Mail.   Its
early days had chanced, unfortunately, to be marked by
two or three accidents, which naturally gave it an increased
celebrity.   And, truly, if it is considered what those men
and horses were required to perform, the wonder was, not
that the Quicksilver should have come to grief two or
three times, but rather that it ever made its journey without doing so.   What does the railway traveller of the present day, who sees a travelling post-office, and its huge tender crammed with postal matter, think of the idea of carrying all that mass on one, or perhaps two, coaches ?   The
guard, occupying his solitary post behind the coach, on the
top of the receptacle called, with reference to the construc-
tions of still earlier days, the hinder *boot*, sat on a little
seat made for one, with his pistols and blunderbuss in a
box in front of him.   And the original notion of those who
first planned the modern mail-coach was, that the bags
containing the letters should be carried in that "hinder
boot."   The "fore boot," beneath the driver's box, was
considered to be appropriated to the baggage of the three

outside and four inside passengers, which was the mail's entire complement. One of the former shared the box with the driver, and two occupied the seat on the roof behind him. The accommodation provided for these two was not of a very comfortable description. They were not, indeed, crowded as the four who occupied a similar position on another coach often were; but they had a mere board to sit on, whereas the seats on the roof of an ordinary stage-coach were provided with cushions. The fares by the mail were always somewhat higher than those by even equally fast, or in some cases faster, coaches; and it seems unreasonable, therefore, that the accommodation should be inferior. I can only suppose that the patrons of "the mail" were understood to be compensated for its material imperfections by the superior dignity of their position. The box-seat, however, was well cushioned.

But if the despatches, which it was the mail's business to carry, could once upon a time be contained in that hinder boot, such had ceased to be the case before my day. The bulk of postal matter which had to be carried was continually and rapidly increasing, and I have often seen as many as nine enormous sacks heaped on the coach roof. The length of these sacks was just sufficient to reach from one side of the coach to the other, and the huge heap of them, three or even four tiers high, was piled to a height which was sufficient to prevent the guard, even when standing, from seeing or communicating with the coachman. If to the consideration of all this the reader will add (if he can) a remembrance of the Somersetshire and Devonshire roads, over which this top-heavy load had to be carried at about twelve miles an hour, it will not seem strange to him that accidents should have occurred. Not that the roads were bad; they were, thanks to Macadam, good, hard, and smooth, but the hills are numerous, and in many cases very steep.

But the journey, especially on the box-seat, was a very pleasant thing. The whole of the service was so well done, and in every detail so admirable. It need hardly be said that the men selected for the drivers of such a coach were masters of their profession. The work was hard, but the remuneration was very good. There were fewer passengers by the mail to "remember the coachman," but it was more uniformly full, and somewhat more was expected from a traveller by the mail. It was a beautiful thing to see a splendid team going over their short stage at twelve miles an hour! Of course none but good cattle in first-rate condition could do the work. A *mot* of old Mrs. Mountain, for many years the well-known proprietress of one of the large coaching inns in London, used to be quoted as having been addressed by her to one of her drivers: "You find whipcord, John, and I'll find oats!" And, as it used to be said, the measure of the corn supplied to a coach-horse was his stomach.

It was a pretty thing to see the changing of the horses. There stood the fresh team, two on the off side, two on the near side, and the coach was drawn up with the utmost exactitude between them. Four hostlers jump to the splinter-bars and loose the traces; the reins have already been thrown down. The driver retains his seat, and within the minute (more than once within fifty seconds by the watch in my hand) the coach is again on its onward journey.

Then how welcome was breakfast at an excellent old-world country inn — twenty minutes allowed. The hot tea, after your night's drive, the fresh cream, butter, eggs, hot toast, and cold beef, and then, with cigar alight, back to the box and off again!

I once witnessed on that road—not quite *that* road, for the Quicksilver took a somewhat different line—the stage of four miles between Ilchester and Ilminster done in twenty minutes, and a trace broken and mended on the road! The mending was effected by the guard almost before the coach stopped. It is a level bit of road, four miles only for the entire stage, and was performed at a full gallop. That was done by a coach called the Telegraph, which was started some years after the Quicksilver, to do the distance from Exeter to London in the day. We left Exeter at 5 A.M. and reached London between nine and ten, with time for both breakfast and dinner on the road. I think the performance of the Exeter Tele-

2

graph was about the *ne plus ultra* of coach travelling.
One man drove fifty miles, and then, meeting the other
coach on the road, changed from one box to the other and
then drove back again. It was tremendously hard work!
I once remarked to him as I sat beside him that there was
not much work for his whip-arm. "Not much, sir," he
replied; "but just put your hand on my left arm!" I did,
and felt the muscle swollen to its utmost, and hard as iron.
"Many people think," he said, "that it is easier work to
drive such a coach and such a team as this than to have
to flog a dull team up to eight miles an hour. Nobody
would think so that had ever tried both!"

I once persuaded my mother, who was returning with
me from Exeter to London, to make the journey on the
box of the Telegraph while I sat behind her. She had
been a good deal afraid of the experiment, but admitted
that she had never enjoyed a journey more.

But, having been led by my coaching reminiscences to
speak of my visits to Exeter and to Fanny Bent, I must
not turn that page of the past without dedicating a few
lines to one to whom I had great cause to be gratefully
attached, and whose character, both in its high worth and
its originality and singularity, was a product of that day
hardly likely to be reproduced in this.

Very plain in feature, and dressed with Quaker-like
simplicity and utter disregard for appearance, her figure
was as well known in Exeter as the cathedral towers. She
held a position and enjoyed an amount of respect which
was really singular in the case of a very homely-featured
old maid of very small fortune. She affected, like some
other persons I have known both in the far west and the
far north of England, to speak the dialect of her country.
Though without any pretension to literary tastes or pursuits, she was a fairly well-read woman, and was perfectly
able to speak better English than many a Londoner. But
she chose, *when in Devonshire*, to speak as Devonshire
folks spoke. She was a thoroughgoing Churchwoman
and Conservative, though too universally popular with all
classes to confine her sympathies within any party bounds.
She had a strong native sense of humor, and, despite the

traditions and principles which taught her to consider
"Peter Pindar" as a reprobate, she could not resist the
enjoyment of his description of the king's visit to Exeter.
It was a treat to hear her read the verses in her own Devon vernacular. And I shall never forget her whispering
to me as we walked up the nave of the cathedral, "*Nate,
nate! Clane, clane!* Do ye mop it, mop it, Mr. *Dane?*"
And how *Dane* Buller replied, "In all our Ex'ter shops
we do not meet with such long mops. Our mops don't
reach so high!" I quote possibly incorrectly from the
recollections of some sixty years ago; and I have never
studied Mr. Woolcott's works since. But the very tones
of the dear old lady's voice, as she whispered the words,
bursting the while with suppressed laughter, remain in
my ears.

A pious Churchwoman of these improved days would
not, I take it, select such a place and such a time for such
whisperings. But I am sure it would be difficult to find
a better or more sincere Christian than dear old Fanny
Bent. And the anecdote may be accepted as one more
illustration of change in manners, feeling, and decencies.

Then there were strawberry-and-cream parties at a place
called, if I remember right, Hoopern Bowers, always with
a bevy of pretty girls, for attracting whom my plain old
spinster cousin seemed to possess a special secret; and excursions to Marypole Head, and drives over Haldon Down.
When I revisited Exeter some months ago Hoopern Bowers seemed to have passed from the memory of man! And
whether any one of the laughing girls I had known there
was still extant as a gray-headed crone I could not learn!
Marypole Head, too, has been nearly swallowed up by the
advancing tide of "villas" surging up the hill, though the
look-down on the other side over Upton Pynes and the
valley of the Exe is lovely as ever. And Haldon Down,
at all events, is as breezy as of yore!

Dr. Bowring—subsequently Sir John—was at that time
resident in Exeter with his two daughters. The doctor
was hardly likely to be intimate with Fanny Bent's Conservative and mainly clerical friends, but, knowing everybody, she knew him too, and rather specially liked his

girls, who used to be of our Hoopern Bower parties. Lucy Bowring was some years my senior, but I remember thinking her very charming; she was a tall, handsome, dark-eyed girl, decidedly clever, and a little more inclined to be *emancipée* in matters ecclesiastical than were the others of the little world around her. Then there was gentle Rachel Hutchinson! How strangely names that have not been in my mind for half a century or more come back to me! Rachel was the daughter of a retired physician, a widower, whom I recognized as a man of elegant and refined culture, somewhat superior to the majority of the local clergy among whom he lived. I can see him now, a slender, somewhat daintily dressed figure, punctiliously courteous, with a pleasant, old-world flavor in his manner; with carefully arranged gray hair, double gold eye-glass, a blue swallow-tailed coat, nankeen trousers, and polished shoes. But he did not come to Hoopern Bowers. His daughter Rachel did; and was curiously contrasted with Lucy Bowring in every respect. She was a small, sylph-like little figure, with blue eyes, blond hair, very pretty and very like an angel. She was also very, very religious after the evangelical fashion of that day, and gave me a volume of Low-Church literature, which I preserved many years with much sentiment, but, I fear, no further profit. I think that the talks which Lucy and Rachel and I had together over our strawberries and cream must have had some flavor of originality about them. I do not imagine that Lucy thought or cared much about my soul, but I fancy that Rachel felt herself to be contending for it.

And now, all gone! Probably not one of all those who made those little festivities so pleasant to me remains on the face of the earth! At all events every one of them has many, many years ago passed out of the circle of light projected by my magic lantern!

And how many others have passed like phantasmagoric shadows across that little circle of light! It is one of the results of such a rolling-stone life as mine has been that the number of persons I have known, and even made friends of for the time, has been immense; but they all pass like a phantom procession! How many! How many! They have trooped on into the outer darkness and been lost!

I suppose that during the half-century, or nearly that time—from 1840 to 1886—that I knew little or nothing of England, the change that has come upon all English life has been nearly as great in one part of the country as another. But on visiting Exeter a few months ago I was much struck at its altered aspect, because I had known it well in my youth. It was not so much that the new rows of houses and detached villas seemed to have nearly doubled the extent of the city, and obliterated many of the old features of it, as that the character of the population seemed changed. It was less provincial—a term which cockneys naturally use in a disparaging sense, but which in truth implies quite as much that is pleasant as the reverse. It seemed to have been infected by much of the ways and spirit of London, without, of course, having anything of the special advantages of London to offer. People no longer walked down the High Street along a pavement abundantly ample for the traffic, nodding right and left to acquaintances. Everybody knew everybody no longer. The leisurely gossiping ways of the shopkeepers had been exchanged for the short and sharp promptitude of London habits. I recognized, indeed, the well-remembered tone of the cathedral bells. But the cathedral and its associations and influences did not seem to hold the same place in the city life as it did in the olden time of my young days. There was an impalpable and very indescribable, but yet unmistakably sensible something which seemed to shut off the ecclesiastical life on one side of the close precincts from the town life on the other, in a manner which was new to me. I have little doubt that if I had casually asked in any large—say—grocer's shop in the High Street, who was the canon in residence, I should have received a reply indicating that the person inquired of had not an idea of what I was talking about; and am very sure that half a century ago the reply to the same question would have been everywhere a prompt one.

The lovely garden close under the city wall on the

northern side—perhaps the prettiest city garden in England—with its remarkably beautiful view of the cathedral
(which used to belong to old Edmund Granger, an especial
crony of Fanny Bent's), exists still, somewhat more closely
shut in by buildings.   We were indeed permitted to walk
there the other day by the kindness of the present proprietor, merely as members of "the public," which would
not have been dreamed of in those old days when "the
public" was less thought of than at present.   But I could
not help thinking that "the public," and I, as a portion
and representative of it, must be a terrible nuisance to the
owner of that beautiful and tranquil spot, so great as seriously to diminish the value of it.

Another small difference occurs to me as illustrative of
the changes that time and *the rail* have brought about.   I
heard very little of the once familiar Devonshire dialect.
Something of intonation there may yet linger, but of the
old idioms and phraseology little or nothing.

But I have been beguiled into all these reminiscences
of the fair capital of the west and my early days there
by the Quicksilver Mail, itself a most compendious and almost complete illustration of the nature of the differences
between its own day and that of its successor, the rail !

To the rail is due principally much of the changed appearance of London.   Certainly the domestic architecture
of the Georgian period has little enough of beauty to recommend it.   It is insignificant, mean, and prosaic to an extraordinary degree, as we all know.   But it is not marked
by the audacious, ostentatious, nightmare-hideousness of
the railway arches and viaducts and stations of modern
London.   It is difficult to say whether the greatest change
in the daily life and habits of a Londoner has been produced by gas, by Peel's police, electric telegraphy, modern postal arrangements, or the underground railway.   Can
the present generation picture to itself what London was
and looked like when lighted only by the few twinkling
oil lamps which seemed to serve no other purpose save to
make darkness visible ?   Can it conceive a London police-
less by day, and protected at night only by a few heavily
great-coated watchmen, very generally asleep in their

"boxes," and equipped with a huge rattle in one hand and a large stable lantern in the other? The two-penny post was considered an immense boon to Londoners and their needs of quick communication between the different districts of their even then overgrown town. But what would they have thought of an almost hourly postal delivery, and of the insufficient quickness of that being supplemented by telegraphic messages, to be outstripped in their turn by telephony? And what would the modern Londoner think of doing without all these things?

But perhaps the underground railways have most of all revolutionized the London habits of the present day. Why, even to me, who knew cabless London, they seem to have become indispensable. I loathe them! The hurry-scurry! The necessity of "looking sharp!" The difficulty of ascertaining which carriage you are to take, and of knowing when you have arrived at your journey's end! The horrible atmosphere! All strong against the deed! And yet the necessities of time and place in the huge, overgrown monster of a town seem to compel me to pass a large portion of my hours among the sewers, when I find myself a dazed and puzzled stranger in the town I once knew so well.

Another very striking change in the appearance of London in the jubilee year of Queen Victoria as contrasted with the London of George the Third and the Regency, is caused by the preposterous excess of the system of advertising. Of course the practice is deeply rooted in causes which profoundly affect all the developments of social life and modes of thought, as Carlyle well understood. But I am now speaking merely of the exterior and surface effect of the ubiquitous sheets of paper of all colors of the rainbow, with their monstrous pictorial illustrations. I know that to say that it vulgarizes the town to a quite infinite degree may be thought to be mere meaningless cant, or illiberal affectation, itself truly vulgar. Yet surely the accusation must be allowed to be a just one. If brazen-faced self-assertion, frantically eager competition in the struggle for profit, and the persuasion that this can best be attained by the sort of assertions and inducements with

which the walls are covered, be not vulgar, what is? And
what of the public which is attracted by the devices which
the experience of those who cater for it teach them to
employ? I miss in the London of the present day a kind
of shop which was not uncommon in the days when I first
knew the town—shops at which one description of article
only was sold, and where that one was to be had notoriously of the best possible quality; shops that appeared to
despise all the finery of glass and brass and mahogany;
where prices were not cut down to the lowest possible
figure by the competitive necessity of underselling, but
where every article could be trusted to be what it pretended to be. Shops of this kind never advertised at all,
but were content to trust for business to the reputation
they had made for themselves. I am told that everything
is a great deal cheaper than it used to be, and truly find
that such is the case. But I am not at all persuaded that
I get better value for my money. To tell the truth, it
seems to my old-fashioned notions and habits that in commercial matters we have arrived at the cheap and nasty
stage of development. I am a poor man—far too poor
a man to drink Lafitte Bordeaux. But that need not
compel me to drink cheap claret or any abomination of
the kind! Good ale is far better than bad wine, and
good water better than bad beer! At least that is what
the experience of well-nigh fourscore years has taught
me!

One of my earliest strolls in London revisited lately
was to the old haunts I had once known so well at Lincoln's Inn. I had walked along the new embankment lost
in wonder and admiration. The most incorrigible *lauda-
tor temporis acti* cannot but admit that nineteenth-century
London has there done something and possesses something
which any city on this earth may well be proud of! And
so I came to the Temple, and, rambling through its reno-
vated gardens and courts, thought how infinitely more inviting they looked than anything in Belgrave Square or
Mayfair! *Templa quam dilecta!* Why, if only a wall
could be built around the precincts high enough and strong
enough to shut out London sounds and London smells and

London atmosphere, one might be almost as well there as in Magdalen at Oxford!

And Alsatia too, its next-door neighbor to the eastward, all ravaged and routed out, its mysterious courts and light-abhorring alleys exposed to the flouting glare of a sunshine baking a barren extent, devoted apparently to dead cats and potsherds! That Whitefriars district used to be a favorite exploring-ground of mine after the publication of "The Fortunes of Nigel." How the copper captains, if condemned to walk their former haunts, would slink away in search of the cover of darksome nooks no longer to be found! What would Miss Trapbois's ghost, wandering in the unsheltered publicity of the new embankment, think of the cataclysm which has overwhelmed the world she knew!

Then, marvelling at the ubiquitous railway bridges and arches, which seem to return again and again like the recurring horrors of a nightmare dream, I passed westward, where the Fleet Prison is not, and where even Temple Bar is no more, till I came to Chancery Lane, which seemed to retain much of its old dinginess, and passed thence under the unchanged old gateway into Lincoln's Inn Old Square, where my father's chambers were, and where I used to go to him with my nonsense verses.

Old Square looks much as it used to look, I think. And the recollection darted across my mind—who shall say why?—of a queer-looking shambling figure, whom my father pointed out to me one day from the window of his chambers. "That," said he, "is Jockey Bell, perhaps the first conveyancer in England. He probably knows more of the law of real property than any man breathing." He was a rather short, squab-looking, and very shabby figure, who walked, I think, a little lame. He came, I was told, from the north country, and spoke with a strong Northumbrian accent. "It is a dreadful thing to have to decipher an opinion of his," said my father; "he is said to have three handwritings—one when he is sober, which he can read himself; one when he is drunk, which his clerk can read; and one next morning after being drunk, which no human being can read!"

2*

And I looked for the little shabby, stuffy court in which I had so often watched Eldon's lowering brow, as he doubted over some knotty point. My father had the highest opinion of his intellectual power and legal knowledge. But he did not like him. He used to say that his mind was an instrument of admirable precision, but his soul the soul of a pedler. I take it Eldon's quintessential Toryism was obnoxious to my father's Liberalism. He used to repeat the following "report" of a case in the Court of Chancery:

> "Mr. Leech * made a speech;
> 'Twas learned, terse, and strong.
> Mr. Hart, on the other part,
> Was neat and glib, but wrong.
> Mr. Parker made it darker;
> 'Twas dark enough without!
> Mr. Cook cited a book;
> And the Chancellor said, I doubt."

Una omnes premit nox!

Of course among the other changes of sixty years language had changed. There had been a change, especially in pronunciation, a little before my time. Only very old and old-fashioned people continued in my earliest years to say *Room* for Rome; *gould* for gold; *obleege* for oblige; *Jeames* for James (one of our chaplains at Winchester, I remember, always used to speak of St. *Jeames*); a beef-*steek* for a beef-steak; or to pronounce the "a" in danger, stranger, and the like, as it is in "man." But it is a singular fact, that despite the spread, and supposed improvement of education, the literary—or perhaps it would be better to say the printed—language of the earlier decades of the nineteenth century was much more correct than that of the latter part of it. I constantly find passages in books and newspapers written with the sublimest indifference to all grammatical rules, and all proprieties of construction. A popular writer of fiction says that her hero "rose his head!" And another tells her readers that something happened when "the brunt of the edge had

---

* Subsequently Master of the Rolls.

worn off!" There are certain words, such as "idiosyncrasy," "type," "momentary," and many others which I
cannot while writing recollect, which are constantly used,
not by one writer only, but by many, to express meanings
wholly different from those which they really bear. There
is another word which is worth mentioning, because the
misuse of it is rapidly becoming endemic. I mean the
verb "trouble;" which it seems to me all the world before
the birth of the present generation very well knew to be
an active, not a neuter verb. Now scarcely a day passes
without my meeting with such phrases as "he did not
trouble," meaning, trouble himself; "I hope you won't
trouble," instead of trouble yourself. To old-fashioned
ears it seems a detestable vulgarism. But as far as I can
gather from observing books that have a greater, and
books that have a lesser, degree of success, and from the
remarks of the critical journals, a book is in these latter
days deemed none the worse, nor is at all less likely to
find favor with the public, because it is full of grammatical or linguistic solecisms. Now certainly this is an instance and indication of changed ideas; for it assuredly
was not the case when George the Third was king.

Another difference between that day and this of very
considerable social significance may be observed in the
character and development of the slang in use. There
was at the former period very little slang of the kind that
may be considered universal. Different classes had different phrases and locutions that were peculiar to them, and
served more or less as a bond of union and exclusiveness
as regarded outsiders. The criminal classes had their
slang. The universities had theirs. There was coster-
mongers' slang. And there was a slang peculiar to the
inner circles of the fashionable world, together with many
other special dialects that might be named. But the specialties of these various idioms were not interchangeable,
nor for the most part intelligible outside the world to
which they belonged. Nor—and this difference is a very
notable one—did slang phrases grow into acceptance with
the rapidity or universality which now characterizes their
advent—a notable difference, because it, of course, arises

from the increased rapidity of communication, and from the much greater degree in which all classes and all provincial and town populations are mixed together and rubbed against each other. It used to be said, and is still said by some old-world folks, that the use of slang is vulgar. And the younger generation, which uses it universally, ridicules much the old fogey narrowness which so considers it. But the truth is, that there was in the older time nothing really vulgar in the use of the slang which then prevailed. Why should not every class and every profession have its own shibboleths and its own phrases? And is there not real vulgarity in the mind which considers a man vulgar for using the language of the class to which he really belongs? But the modern use of slang is truly vulgar for a very different reason. It is vulgar because it arises from one of the most intrinsically vulgar of all the vulgar tendencies of a vulgar mind —imitation. There are slang phrases which, because they vividly or graphically express a conception, or clothe it with humor, are admirable. But they are admirable only in the mouths of their inventors.

Of course it is an abuse of language to say that the beauty of a pretty girl strikes you with awe. But he who *first* said of some girl that she was "awfully" pretty was abundantly justified by the half-humorous, half-serious consideration of all the effects such loveliness may produce. But then, because this was felt to be the case, and the *mot* was accepted, all the tens of thousands of idiotic cretins who have been rubbed down into exact similarity to each other by excessive locomotion and the "spread" of education—spread indeed after the fashion in which a gold-beater spreads his metal—imitate each other in the senseless use of it. They are just like the man in the "Joe Miller" story, who, because a laugh followed when a host, whose servant let fall a dish with a boiled tongue on it, said it was only a *lapsus linguæ*, ordered his own servant to throw down a leg of mutton, and then made the same remark!

There was an old gentleman who had a very tolerable notion of what is vulgar and what is not, and who char-

acterized "imitators" as a "servile herd." And surely,
if, as we are often told, this is a vulgar age, the fact is
due to the prevalence of this very tap-root of vulgarity,
imitation. Of course I'am not speaking of imitation in
any of the various cases in which there is an end in view
outside the fact of the imitation. The child in order to
speak must imitate those whom it hears speaking. If you
would make a pudding, you must imitate the cook ; if a
coat, the tailor. But the imitation which is essentially
vulgar, the very tap-root, as I have said, of vulgarity, is
imitation for imitation's sake. And that is why I think
modern slang is essentially vulgar. If it is your real
opinion — right or wrong matters not — that any slang
phrase expresses any idea with peculiar accuracy, vividness, or humor, use it by all means; and he is a narrow
blockhead who sees any vulgarity in your doïng so. But
for Heaven's sake, my dear Dick, don't use it merely because you heard Bob use it !

Yet there is something pathetically humble too about
a man so conscious of his own worthlessness as to be ever
anxious to look like somebody else. And surely a man
must have a painful consciousness of his inability to utter
any word of his own with either wit or wisdom or sense in
it who habitually strives to borrow the wit of the last re-
tailer of the current slang whom he has heard.

In some respects, however, this is, I think, a less vulgar
age than that of my youth. Vulgar exclusiveness on grounds
essentially illiberal was far more common. It will, perhaps, seem hardly credible at the present day that middle-
class professional society, such as that of barristers, physicians, rectors, and vicars, should sixty years ago have
deemed attorneys and general medical practitioners (or
apothecaries, as the usual and somewhat depreciatory
term was) inadmissible to social equality. But such was
the case. My reminiscences of half a century or more ago
seem to indicate also that professional etiquette has been
relaxed in various other particulars. I hear of physicians
being in partnership with others of the same profession—
an arrangement which has a commercial savor in it that
would have been thought quite *infra dig.* in my younger

day. I hear also of their accepting, if not perhaps exacting, payments of a smaller amount than the traditional guinea. This was unheard of in the old days. An English physician is a member of the most generously liberal profession that exists or ever existed on earth. And it was an every-day occurrence for a physician to think more of the purse of his patient than of the value of his own services. But he did this either by refusing to accept any fee whatever, or by declining it on the occasion of subsequent visits: never by diminishing the amount of it. In some other cases professional dignity had to be maintained under circumstances that entailed considerable sacrifices on those who were called upon to maintain it. It was not etiquette, for instance, for a barrister going on circuit to travel otherwise than by a private conveyance. He might hire a post-chaise, or he might ride his own horse, or even a hired one, but he must not travel by a stage-coach or put up at a hotel. I have heard it said that this rule originated in the notion that a barrister travelling to an assize town by the public coach might fall in with some attorney bound on a similar errand, and might so be led, if not into the sin, at least into temptation to the sin, of "huggery." I dare say many a young barrister of the present day does not know what huggery means or meant!

Among the sights and sounds which were familiar to the eye and ear in the London of my youth, and which are so no longer, may be mentioned the two-penny postman. Not many probably of the rising generation are aware that in their fathers' days the London postal service was dual. The "two-penny postman," who delivered letters sent from one part of London to another, was a different person from the "general postman," who delivered those which came from the country. The latter wore a scarlet, the former a blue livery. And the two administrations were entirely distinct. In those days, when a letter from York to London cost a shilling, or not much less, the weight of a single letter was limited solely by the condition that it must be written on one sheet or piece of paper only. Two pieces of paper, however small, or however light, incurred a double postage. I have sent for a single postage an enormous sheet of double folio outweighing some ten sheets of ordinary post paper. Of course envelopes were unknown. Every sheet had to be folded so that it could be sealed and the address written on the back of it.

Another notable London change which occurs to me is that which has come to the Haymarket. In my day it was really such. The whole right-hand side of the street going downwards, from the Piccadilly end to the Opera House, used to be lined with loads of hay. The carts were arranged in close order side by side with their back parts towards the foot pavement, which was crowded by the salesmen and their customers.

I might say a good deal too about the changes in the theatrical London world and habits, but the subject is a large one, and has been abundantly illustrated. It is moreover one which in its details is not of an edifying nature. And it must suffice, therefore, to bear my testimony to the greatness of the purifying change which has been brought about in all the habits of play-goers and play-houses mainly and firstly by the exertions of my mother's old and valued friend, Mr. Macready.

CHAPTER III.

AT HARROW.

I was, I think, about eight years old when my parents removed from Keppel Street to Harrow-on-the-Hill. My father's practice, I take it, was becoming less and less satisfactory, and his health equally so. And the move to Harrow was intended as a remedy or palliation for both these evils. My father was a very especially industrious and laborious man. And I have the authority of more than one very competent judge among his professional contemporaries for believing that he was as learned a chancery lawyer as was to be found among them. How, then, was his want of success to be accounted for? One of the competent authorities above alluded to accounted for it thus: "Your father," he said to me many years afterwards, when his troubles and failures had at last ceased to afflict him, "never came into contact with a blockhead without insisting on irrefutably demonstrating to him that he was such. And the blockhead did not like it! He was a disputatious man; and he was almost invariably—at least on a point of law—right. But the world differed from him in the opinion that being so gave him the right of rolling his antagonist in the dust and executing an intellectual dance of triumph on his prostrate form." He was very fond of whist, and was, I believe, a good player. But people did not like to play with him. "Many men," said an old friend once, "will scold their partners occasionally. But Trollope invariably scolds us all round with the utmost impartiality; and that every deal!"

He was, in a word, a highly respected, but not a popular or well-beloved man. Worst of all, alas! he was not popular in his own home. No one of all the family circle was happy in his presence. Assuredly he was as affectionate and anxiously solicitous a father as any children

ever had. I never remember his caning, whipping, beating, or striking any one of us. But he used, during the
detested Latin lessons, to sit with his arm over the back
of the pupil's chair, so that his hand might be ready to
inflict an instantaneous pull of the hair as the *poena* (by
no means *pede claudo*) for every blundered concord or false
quantity ; the result being to the scholar a nervous state
of expectancy, not judiciously calculated to increase intellectual receptivity. There was also a strange sort of as-
cetism about him, which seemed to make enjoyment, or
any employment of the hours save work, distasteful and
offensive to him. Lessons for us boys were never over
and done with. It was sufficient for my father to see any
one of us "idling," *i. e.*, not occupied with book-work, to
set us to work quite irrespectively of the previously assigned task of the day having been accomplished. And
this we considered to be unjust and unfair.

I have said that the move to Harrow was in some degree caused by a hope that the change might be beneficial
to my father's health. He had suffered very distressingly
for many years from bilious headache, which gradually
increased upon him during the whole of his life. I may
say parenthetically that, from about fifteen to forty, I
suffered occasionally, about once a fortnight perhaps, from
the same malady, though in a much less intense form.
But at about forty years old I seemed to have grown out
of it, and since that time have never been troubled by it.
But in my father's day the common practice was to treat
such complaints with calomel. He was constantly having
recourse to that drug. And I believe that it had the effect
of shattering his nervous system in a deplorable manner.
He became increasingly irritable; never with the effect of
causing him to raise a hand against any one of us, but with
the effect of making intercourse with him so sure to issue
in something unpleasant that, unconsciously, we sought to
avoid his presence, and to consider as hours of enjoyment
only those that could be passed away from it.

My mother's disposition, on the other hand, was of the
most genial, cheerful, happy, *enjoué* nature imaginable.
All our happiest hours were spent with her; and to any

one of us a *tête-à-tête* with her was preferable to any other
disposal of a holiday hour. But even this, under all the
circumstances, did not tend to the general harmony and happiness of the family circle. For, of course, the facts and
the results of them must have been visible to my father;
and though wholly inoperative to produce the smallest
change in his ways, must, I cannot doubt, have been painful to him. It was all very sad. My father was, essentially, a good man. But he was, I fear, a very unhappy
one.

He was extremely fond of reading aloud to the assembled family in the evening; and there was not one individual of those who heard him who would not have escaped from doing so at almost any cost. Of course it was
our duty to conceal this extreme reluctance to endure what
was to him a pleasure—a duty which I much fear was very
imperfectly performed. I remember—oh, how well !—the
nightly readings during one winter of "Sir Charles Grandison," and the loathing disgust for that production which
they occasioned.

But I do not think that I and my brothers were bad
boys. We were, I take it, always obedient. And one incident remains in my mind from a day now nearly seventy
years ago, which seems to prove that the practice of that
virtue was habitual to me. An old friend of my mother's,
Mrs. Gibbon, with her daughter Kate, mentioned on a former page as the companion of my lessons in the alphabet,
were staying with us at Harrow. Mrs. Gibbon and Kate
and my mother and I were returning from a long country
ramble across the fields in a part of the country my mother
was not acquainted with. There was a steep, grassy declivity down which I and the little girl, my contemporary,
hand-in-hand, were running headlong in front of our respective parents, when my mother suddenly called out,
"Stop, Tom!" I stopped forthwith, and came to heel as
obediently as a well-trained pointer. And about five minutes later my mother and Mrs. Gibbon, following exactly
in the line in which we had been running, discovered a
long disused but perfectly open and unfenced well!

If I had not obeyed so promptly as I did I should not

now be writing reminiscences, and poor "Katy 'Bon," as I used to call her, would have gone to her rest some ten years earlier than she found it. My mother always said that she could in no wise account for the impulse which prompted her to call me to stop!

The move to Harrow was as infelicitous a step in the economic point of view as it was inefficacious as a measure of health. My father took a farm of some three or four hundred acres, to the best of my recollection, from Lord Northwick. It was a wholly disastrous speculation. It certainly was the case that he paid a rent for it far in excess of its fair value; and he always maintained that he had been led to undertake to do so by inaccurate and false representations. I have no knowledge of these representations, but I am absolutely certain that my father was entirely convinced that they were such as he characterized them. But he was educated to be a lawyer, and was a good one. He had never been educated to be a farmer; and was, I take it, despite unwearied activity, and rising up early and late taking rest, a bad one.

To make matters worse, moreover, he built on that land, of which he held only a long lease, a large and very good house. The position was excellently chosen, the house was well conceived and well built, and the extensive gardens and grounds were well designed and laid out; but the unwisdom of doing all that on land the property of another is but too obvious.

The excuse that my father might have alleged was that he was by no means wholly dependent either on his profession or on his farm, or on the not inconsiderable property which he had inherited from his father or enjoyed in right of his wife. He had an old maternal uncle, Adolphus Meetkerke, who lived on his estate near Royston, in Hertfordshire, called Julians. Mr. Meetkerke — the descendant of a Dutchman who had come to this country some time in the eighteenth century as diplomatic representative of his country, and had settled here — lived at Julians with an old childless wife, the daughter, I believe, of a General Chapman — and my father was his declared heir. He had another nephew, Mr. John Young, as flourishing and prosperous an attorney as my father was an unsuccessful and unprosperous barrister. John Young, too, was as worthy and as highly respected a man as any in the profession. But my father, as settled long years before, was to be the heir; and I was in due time shown to the tenantry as their future landlord, and all that sort of thing. I suppose my grandfather, the Rev. Anthony Trollope, of Cottenham in Hertfordshire, married an elder sister of old Adolphus Meetkerke, while the father of John Young married a younger one. And so, come what might of the Harrow farm and the new house, I was to be the future owner of Julians, and live on my own acres.

Again, *Dis aliter visum!*

I well remember more than one visit to Julians with my parents about this time—visits singularly contrasted with those to my Grandfather Milton, the Vicar of Heckfield. The house and establishment at Julians were on a far more pretentious scale than the home of the vicar, and the mode of life in the squire's establishment larger and freer. But I liked Heckfield better than Julians; partly, I think, even at that early age, because the former is situated in an extremely pretty country, whereas the neighborhood of the other is by no means such. But I please myself with thinking, and do really believe, that the main reason for the preference was that the old Bristol saddler's son was a far more highly-cultured man than the Hertfordshire squire.

He was a good man, too, was old Adolphus Meetkerke; a good landlord, a kindly-natured man, a good sportsman, an active magistrate, and a good husband to his old wife. But there was a sort of flavor of roughness about the old squire and his surroundings which impressed itself on my observation even in those days, and would, I take it, nowadays be deemed almost clownish rusticity.

Right well do I remember the look and figure of my Aunt Meetkerke, properly great-aunt-in-law. She was an admirable specimen of a squiress, as people and things were in that day. I suppose that there was not a poor man or woman in the parish with whose affairs of all sorts she was not intimately acquainted, and to whom she did not play the part of an ever-active providence. She always came down to breakfast clad in a green riding-habit, and passed most of her life on horseback. After dinner, in the long, low drawing-room, with its faded stone-colored curtains and bookless desert spaces, she always slept as peacefully as she does now in Julians churchyard. She never meddled at all with the housekeeping of her establishment. That was in the hands of "Mrs. Anne," an old maiden sister of Mr. Meetkerke. She was a prim-looking, rosy-apple-faced, most good-natured little woman. She always carried a little basket in her hand, in which were the keys and a never-changed volume of Miss Austen's "Pride and Prejudice," which she always recommenced as soon as she had worked her way to the end of it. Though a very precise sort of person, she would frequently come down to breakfast a few minutes late, to find her brother standing on the hearth-rug with his prayer-book open in his hand, waiting for her arrival to begin prayers to the assembled household. He had a wonderfully strong, rasping voice, the tones of which were rarely modulated under any circumstances. I can hear now his reverberating "Five minutes too late again, Mrs. Anne; 'Dearly beloved brethren,'" —etc., the change of person addressed and of subject having been marked by no pause or break whatever save the sudden kneeling at the head of the breakfast-table; while at the conclusion of the short, but never-missed prayers, the transition from "Amen" to "William, bring round the brown mare after breakfast" was equally unmarked by pause or change of voice or manner.

The parish in which Julians is situated is a small vicarage, the incumbent of which was at that time a bachelor, Mr. Skinner. The church was a very small one, and my great-uncle and his family the only persons in the congregation above the rank of the two or three small farmers and the agricultural laborers who mainly composed it. Whether there was any clerk or not I do not remember. But if any such official existed, the performance of his office in church was altogether not only overlaid but extinguished by the great rough "view-halloo" sort of voice of my uncle. He never missed going to church, and never missed a word of the responses, which were given in far louder tones than those of the vicar. Something of a hymn was always attempted, I remember, by the rustic congregation; with what sort of musical effect may be imagined! I don't think my Uncle Meetkerke could have distinguished much between their efforts and the music of the spheres. But the singers were so well pleased with the exercise that they were apt to prolong it, as my uncle thought, somewhat unduly. And on such occasions he would cut the performance short with a rasping "That's enough!" which effectually brought it to an abrupt conclusion. The very short sermon—probably a better one for the purpose in hand than South or Andrews would have preached—having been brought to an end, my uncle would sing out to the vicar, as he was descending the pulpit stairs, "Come up to dinner, Skinner!" And then we all marched out, while the rustics, still retaining their places till we were fairly out of the door, made their obeisances as we passed. All which phenomena, strongly contrasted as they were with the decorous if somewhat sleepy performance in my grandfather's church at Heckfield, greatly excited my interest. I remember that I had no dislike to attending service either at Heckfield or Julians, while I intensely disliked making one of a London congregation.

If I remember right there were two or three Dissenters and their families at Heckfield, generally considered by their neighbors much as so many Chinese settled among them might have been—as unaccountably strange and as objectionable. But nothing of the sort existed at Julians; and I take it, as far as may be judged from my uncle's general tone and manner in managing his parish, that any individual guilty of such monstrous and unnatural depravity would at once have been consigned to the parish stocks.

Mr. Meetkerke was, as I have said, an active magistrate. But only one instance of his activity in this respect dwells in my recollection. I remember to have seen, in the nondescript little room that he called his study, a collection of some ten or a dozen very nasty-looking pots, with some white, pasty looking substance in each of them, and to have wondered greatly what mystery could have been attached to them. I learned from the butler's curt word of information that they were connected with my uncle's magisterial duties, and my mind immediately began to construct all kinds of imaginings about wholesale poisonings. I had heard the story of the "Untori" at Milan, and had little doubt that we were in the midst of some such horrible conspiracy. A few days later I learned that the nasty-looking pots were the result of a magisterial raid among the bakers, and contained nothing worse than alum.

These reminiscences of Julians and its little world recurred to me when speaking of my father's financial position at the time he took a farm at Harrow and built a handsome house on another man's land. He was at that time Mr. Meetkerke's declared heir, and would doubtless have inherited his property in due time had childless old Mrs. Meetkerke lived. But one day she unexpectedly took off her green habit for the last time, and in a day or two was laid under yet more perennial green in the little churchyard! Mr. Meetkerke was at that time over sixty. But he was as fine an old man physically as anybody could wish to see. Before long he married a young wife, and became the father of six children! It was of course a tremendous blow to my father, and never, as I can say from much subsequent information, was such a blow better or more bravely borne. As for myself, I cannot remember that the circumstance impressed me as having any bearing whatsoever on my personal fate and fortunes. In after-years I heard it asserted in more than one quarter that my father had in a great measure himself to thank for his disappointment. He was a Liberal in politics after the fashion of those days (which would make excellent Conservatism in these), while Mr. Meetkerke was a Tory of the very oldest school. The Tory uncle was very far indeed from being an intellectual match for his Liberal nephew, and no doubt used to talk in his fine old hunting-field voice a great deal of nonsense which no consideration of either affection, respect, or prudence could induce my father to spare. I fear he used to jump on the hearty old squire very persistently, with the result *à la longue* of ceasing to be a *personâ gratâ* to the old man. It *may* be that had it been otherwise he might have sought affection and companionship elsewhere than from a young wife. But . . . !

My father, as I have said, struggled bravely with fortune, but, as far as I have ever been able to learn, with ever-increasing insuccess. His practice as a barrister dwindled away gradually till it became not worth while to keep chambers; and his farming accounts showed very frequently—every year, I suspect—a deficit.

One of the reasons for selecting Harrow as his scene of rustication had been the existence of the school there. I and my brothers were all of us destined from our cradles to become Wykehamists, and it was never my father's intention that Harrow, instead of Winchester, should be our definitive place of education. But the idea was that we might, before going to Winchester, avail ourselves of the right to attend his parish school, which John Lyon bequeathed to the parishioners of Harrow.

I went to Winchester at ten years old. The time for me to do so did not wholly depend on the will of my parents, for the admission in those days, as in all former days up to quite recent times, was by nomination in this wise. There were six electors: 1, the Warden of New College (otherwise, more accurately in accordance with the terms of Wykeham's foundation, the College of St. Mary Winton *prope* Winton); 2, the Warden of Winchester College; 3, the Sub-warden of Winchester; 4, the "Informator" or head-master of Winchester; and 5 and 6, two "Posers," sent yearly by New College, according to a cycle framed *ad hoc*, to the Winchester election. It was at the election which took place in July that all vacancies among the seventy scholars, who, together with the warden, fellows, two masters, chaplains, and choristers, constituted the members of Wykeham's foundation, were filled. The vacancies were caused either by the election of scholars to be fellows of New College, or by their superannuation at eighteen years of age, or by their withdrawal from the school. The number of vacancies in any year was, therefore, altogether uncertain. The first two vacancies were filled by boys who came in as "College

Founders," *i. e.*, as of kin to the founder. Of course the bishop's kin could be only collateral; and I remember that "the best blood" was considered to be that of the Twistletons. Originally there had been an absolute preference for those who could show such relationship. But, as time went on, it became apparent that the entire college would thus be filled with founder's kin; and it was determined that two such only should be admitted to Winchester every year, and two only sent out to fellowships at New College. Even so the proportion of fellowships at the Oxford college awarded to founder's kin was large, for it was reckoned in those days that the average vacancies at New College, which were caused only by death, marriage, or the acceptance of a college living, amounted to seven in two years, of which the founder's kin took four. And this rule operated with certain regularity. For the superannuation at eighteen did not apply to founder's kin, who remained in the school, be their age what it might, till they went to New College.

These two boys of founder's kin were admitted by the votes of the six electors. After them came the boy nominated by the Warden of New College; then the nominee of the Warden of Winchester; and so on till the eighth vacancy was filled by the nominee of the junior "Poser." Then a ninth vacancy was taken by the Warden of New College's second nomination, and so on. Of course the vacancies for Winchester were much more numerous than those for the Oxford college; and it often happened that the "Poser's" second, or sometimes even third, nomination had a very good chance of getting in in the course of the year. The cycle for "Posers," which I have mentioned, allowed it to be known who would be "Poser" for a given year many years in advance; and the senior "Poser's" first nomination for 1820 had been promised to me before I was out of my cradle. He was the Rev. Mr. Lipscomb, who subsequently became Bishop of Jamaica. It was written, therefore, in the book of fate that I was to go to Winchester in the year 1820, when I should be ten years old.

That time, however, was not yet; but was looked for-

3

ward to by me with a somewhat weighty sense of the in-
evitability of destiny. And I can well remember meditating on the three fateful epochs which awaited me—to
wit, having certain teeth taken out in the immediate future; going to Winchester in the *paulo post futurum ;* and
being married in the ultimate consummation of things.
All three seemed to me to need being faced with a certain
dogged fortitude of endurance. But I think that the terrors of the first loomed the largest in my imagination,
doubtless by virtue of its greater proximity.

I remember, too, at a very early age maintaining in my
own mind, if not in argument with others, that to be brave
one must be very much afraid and act in despite of fear,
and uninfluenced by it, and that not to fear at all, as I
heard predicated of themselves by sundry contemporaries,
indicated simply stupidity. And when the day for the
dentist came my heart was in my boots, but they carried
me unfalteringly to St. Martin's Lane all the same.

At present, however, we are at Harrow, getting into my
father's new house, and establishing ourselves in our new
home. It was soon arranged that I was to attend the
school, scarcely, as I remember, as a regular inscribed
scholar attending the lessons in the schoolroom, but as a
private pupil of the Rev. Mark Drury. I was about eight
years old at the time, and I suppose should hardly have
been accepted as an admitted member of the school.

At that time Dr. Butler, afterwards Bishop of Peterborough, was the head-master. He was not the right man
in the right place. He was, I take it, far more adapted
for a bishop than a school-master. Moreover, there were
certain difficulties in his position not necessarily connected
with the calling of a head-master. He had succeeded Dr.
Drury in the head-mastership, and he found the school
full of Drurys. Mark, the brother of Dr. Drury, was the
second master; a Mr. Evans, a respectable, quiet nonenti-
ty, was the third; Harry Drury, a son of the old doctor,
was the fourth, and was the most energetic and influential
man in the place; William Drury, the son of Mark, was
the fifth; and two young men of the names of Mills and
Batten were the sixth and seventh masters. They were

all in priests' orders, and all received as many boarders as they could get. For the objectionable system, which made the fortunes of the masters far more dependent on their trade as victuallers than on their profession as teachers, had been copied from Eton, with the further evil consequence of swamping John Lyon's parochial school by the creation of a huge boarding-school. This, however eminently successful, has no proper claim to be called a "public school," save by a modern laxity of language, which has lost sight of the fact that the only meaning or possible definition of a "public school" is one the foundation of which was intended, not for a parish or other district, but for all England. If merely success, and consequent size, be held to confer a claim to the title, it is clear that there is no "private" school which would not become a "public school" to-morrow if the master and proprietor of it could command a sufficient amount of success. And even then the question would remain, *What* amount of success must that be?

The world in general, however, dislikes accuracy of speaking. And Harrow was then, and has been since, abundantly large enough and successful enough to be called and considered a "public school" by the generality, who never take the trouble to ask themselves, What makes it such?

Dr. Butler was eminently a gentleman, extremely suave in manner, gentle in dealing with those under his authority, mild and moderate in his ideas of discipline, a genuinely scholarly man in tastes and pursuits, though probably not what experts in such a matter would have called a profound scholar. But he had not the energetic hand needed for ruling a large school; and his rule was not a success. Mark Drury, though from the old Drury connection his house was always full of pupils, cannot be said to have exercised any influence at all on the general condition and management of the school by reason of the extraordinary and abnormal corpulence which kept him pretty well a prisoner to the arm-chair in his study. He had long since, at the time when I first knew him, abandoned the practice of "going up," as it was technically called, *i. e.*, of climbing the last portion of Harrow Hill through the village street. On this topmost part of the hill are situated the church, the churchyard, and the school-house, rebuilt, enlarged, beautified, since my day; and this "going up" had to be performed by all the masters and all the boys every time school was attended. But of this climb Mark Drury had been incapable for many years, solely by reason of his immense corpulence. Naturally a small, delicately-made man, with small hands and feet, he had become in old age the fattest man I think I ever saw. He used to sit in his study, and there conduct the business of tuition, leaving to others the work of hearing lessons in school.

His house had the reputation of being the most comfortable of all the boarding-houses—a fact due to the unstinting liberality, careful supervision, and motherly kindness of "Mother Mark," an excellent and admirable old lady, than whom it would be impossible to conceive any one more fitted for the position she occupied. The unstinting liberality, it is fair to say, characterized all the Drury houses; and probably the others also. But for truly motherly care there was but one "Mother Mark." "Old Mark" was exceedingly popular, as, indeed, he deserved to be, for a more kindly-natured man never existed. He had an old-fashioned belief in the virtues of the rod; and though his bodily infirmity combined with his good-nature to make him sparing in the application of it, a flogging was at his hands sufficiently disagreeable to make one desirous of avoiding it. "Your clock," he would say, "requires to be wound up every Monday morning," meaning that a Monday-morning flogging was a good beginning of the week. But the rods were kept in a cupboard in the study—how well I remember the Bluebeard-closet sort of reputation which surrounded it!—and the cupboard was always kept locked. And very often it happened that, somehow or other, the key was in the keeping of Mrs. Drury. Then a message would be sent to Mrs. Drury for the key, and very probably the proposed patient was the messenger, in which case—and it is strange that the recurrence of the fact did not suggest suspicion to old Mark

—it almost invariably happened that Mrs. Drury was very sorry, but she could not find the key anywhere! There never surely was a key so frequently mislaid as the key of that terrible cupboard!

Well, it was arranged that I was to go every day to Mark Drury's study, not, as I have said, as a regular member of the school, but to get such tuition as might be picked up from the *genius loci*, and from such personal teaching as the old man could bestow on me at moments unoccupied by his own pupils. And this arrangement, it must be understood, was entirely a matter of friendship— one incident of the many years' friendship between my parents and all the Drurys. There was no question of any honorarium in the matter.

My father's appetite for teaching was such that he would, I am very sure, have much preferred keeping my brother and myself under his sole tuition. But he used to drive up to London in his gig daily to his chambers in Lincoln's Inn, for he still struggled to hope on at his profession. (I remember that these drives down in the dark winter evenings became a source of some anxiety when a messenger travelling with despatches for the French minister, who at that time rented Lord Northwick's house at Harrow, was mysteriously murdered and his despatches stolen.) And it thus became necessary that some means should be found for preventing us boys from making *école buissonnière* in the fields and under the hedgerows.

I do not think I profited much by my attendance at old Mark's pupil-room. The boys whose lessons he was hearing stood in a row in front of his arm-chair, and I sat behind him, supposed to be intently occupied in conning the task he had set me, in preparation for the moment when, the class before him having been dismissed, he would have little me, all alone, in front of him for a few minutes, while another class was mustering.

How I hated it all! How very much more bitterly I hated it than I ever hated any subsequent school troubles! What a pariah I was among those denizens of Mark's and other pupil-rooms! For I was a "town boy," "village boy" would have been a more correct designation; one of the very few who by the terms of the founder's will had any right to be there at all; and was in consequence an object of scorn and contumely on the part of all the *paying* pupils. I was a charity boy. But at Winchester subsequently I was far more of a charity boy, for William of Wykeham's foundation provided me with food and lodging as well as tuition; whereas I claimed and received nothing save a modicum of the latter at the hands of those who enjoyed and administered John Lyon's bounty. Yet, though at Winchester there were only seventy scholars and a hundred and thirty private pupils of the head-master, or "commoners," there was no trace whatsoever of any analogous feeling, no slightest arrogation of any superiority, social or other, on the part of the commoner over the collegian. In fact the matter was rather the other way; any difference between the son of the presumably richer man and the presumably poorer having been merged and lost sight of entirely in the higher scholastic dignity of the college boy.

I remember also, more vividly than I could wish, the bullying to which I and others were subjected at Harrow. There was much of a very brutal description. And in this respect also the difference at Winchester was very marked. The theory of the two places on the subject was entirely different, with the result I have stated. At Harrow, in those days—how it may be now I know not—no "fagging" was authorized or permitted by the masters. No boy had any legitimate authority over any other boy. And inasmuch as it was, is, and ever will be in every large school impossible to achieve such a Saturnian state of things, the result was that the bigger and stronger *assumed* an authority supported by sheer violence over the smaller and weaker. At Winchester, on the other hand, the subjection of those below them in college to the "prefects," or upper class, was not only recognized, but enforced, by the authorities. It thus came to pass that many a big, hulking fellow was subjected to the authority of a "prefect" whom he could have tossed over his head. It was an authority nobody dreamed of resisting; a matter of course; not a rule of the stronger supported by violence.

And the result — contributed to, also, by other arrangements, of which I shall speak hereafter—was that anything of the nature of "bullying" was infinitely rarer at
Winchester than at Harrow.

Despite old Mark's invariable good-nature and kindness,
my hours in his study were very unhappy ones; and I was
hardly disposed to consider as a misfortune a severe illness
which attacked me and my brother Henry, and for the
nonce put an end to them. Very shortly it became clear
that we were both suffering from a bad form of typhus.
How was such an attack to be accounted for? My father's
new house was visited, and examined, and found to be
above suspicion. But further inquiry elicited the fact that
we boys had passed a half-hour before breakfast in watching the proceedings of some men engaged in cleaning and
restoring an old drain connected with a neighboring farmhouse. The case was clear! It would seem, however,
that the proper mode of treatment was not so clear to the
Harrow general practitioner—a village apothecary of the
old school, who, strange as it may seem, was the only
available *medico* at Harrow in those far-off days. He
treated us with calomel, and very, very nearly let me slip
through his hands. It would have been *quite*, but for a
fortunate chance. Among our Harrow friends was a Mrs.
Edwards, the widow of a once very well-known bookseller
—not a publisher, but a scholarly, and indeed learned,
seller of old books—who had, I believe, left her a considerable fortune. She was a highly cultured and very clever
woman, and a special friend of my mother's. Now it so
happened that a Dr. Butt, a physician, her brother, or
brother-in-law, I forget which, paid her a visit just at the
time we boys were at the worst. Mrs. Edwards brought
him to our bedsides. I was altogether unconscious, and
had been raving about masters coming in at the window
to drag me off to the pupil-room. My knowledge of what
followed, therefore, is derived wholly from my mother's
subsequent telling. Dr. Butt, having learned the treatment to which we had been subjected, said only, "No more
calomel, I think. Let me have a glass of port wine immediately." And with his finger on my wrist, he pro-

ceeded to administer a teaspoonful at a time of the cordial.
A few more visits from Dr. Butt set us fairly on the way
to recovery; and from that day, some sixty-eight years
ago, to the present, I have never passed one day in bed
from illness.

CHAPTER IV.

ANOTHER incident of these boyish years of a very different complexion has made a far deeper impression on my memory. It must have been, to the best of my remembrance, about the same time, probably some six months later in the same year, that it was decided that I was to accompany my father and mother in a "long vacation" ramble which had long been projected. My father's method of travel on this excursion, which was to include parts of Sussex, Hampshire, Wilts, Devon, Somerset, and Monmouth, was to drive my mother and myself in his gig, accompanied by a servant riding another horse, who was provided with a pair of traces to hook on as tandem whenever the nature of the road required such assistance. I think that this tour afforded me some of the happiest days and hours I have ever known. I can never forget the ecstacy of delight with which I looked forward to it, and the preparations I made—suggested probably, some of them, by the experiences of Robinson Crusoe. The distance and differentiation between me and other boys of my acquaintance, which was caused by my destination to this great adventure, I felt to be such as that which may be supposed to exist between Livingstone and the stay-at-home mortals who read his books.

We started after breakfast one fine morning, "George," the footman, turned into groom and courier, riding after the gig. I considered this a disappointingly tame proceeding. I had been up myself considerably before daylight, and considered that, looking to the arduous nature of the journey before us (we were to sleep at Dorking that night), we ought at least to have been on the road while the less adventurous part of the world were still asleep.

We had not proceeded many miles before an *amari*
3*

aliquid disclosed itself of a very distressing kind. I was seated on a little box placed on the floor of the gig between the knees of my father and mother, and was "as happy as a prince," or probably much happier than any contemporaneous prince then in Christendom, when my father produced from out of the driving-seat beneath him a Delphin "Virgil," and intimated to me that our journey must by no means entail an entire interruption of my education ; that our travelling was not at all incompatible with a little study; and that he was ready to hear me construe. It may be readily imagined how much such "study" was likely to profit me. Every incident of the road, every wagon, every stage-coach we met, every village church seen across the fields, every milestone even, was a matter of intense interest to me. Had I been Argus-eyed every eye would have been busy. I remember that my mother remonstrated, but in vain. And an hour or two of otherwise intense delight was turned into something which it is scarcely an exaggeration to call torture. I think, however, that my mother must have subsequently renewed her pleadings, for on the second day's journey the "Virgil" was not brought out. It was reserved for the days when we were stationary, but no longer poisoned our absolute travel.

If I never became a distinguished scholar it was assuredly from no want of urgency in season and out of season on the part of my poor father. But not even Virgil himself, backed by an "Eton Latin Grammar" and a small travelling-dictionary, could altogether destroy the manifold delights of that journey. I must not inflict on my reader all, or a tithe, of my topographical reminiscences; but I will relate one little adventure which went near to saving me, not only from this volume, but from all that half a century, and more, of subsequent pen-work may have inflicted on me. It was at Gloucester. My parents and I had gone to the cathedral about a quarter of an hour before the time for service on a Sunday morning. The great bell was being rung—an operation which was at that time performed by seven bell-ringers down in the body of the church. One large rope, descending from an aperture in the vault, was, at some dozen or so of feet from the pavement, divided into seven—one for each of the bell-ringers. Now it so happened that on that day one of the men was absent from his post, and one rope hung loose and unoccupied. No sooner had I espied this state of things than I rushed forward and seized the vacant rope, intending to add my efforts to those of the six men at work. But it so happened that at the moment when I thus clutched the rope thé men had raised the bell, and of course at the end of their pull allowed the ropes to fly upwards through their hands. But I, knowing nothing of bell - ringing, clung tightly to my rope, and was of course swung up from the pavement with terrific speed. Fortunately the height of the vault was so great as to allow the full swing of the bell to complete itself without bringing me into contact with the roof. The men cried out to me to hold on tight. I did so, and descended safely—so unharmed that I was very desirous of repeating the experiment, which, as may be supposed, was not allowed. I can pull a bell more knowingly now.

The charming old church at Gloucester was not kept and cared for in those days as it is now—a remark which is applicable, as recent visits have shown me, to nearly all the cathedral churches in England. I may observe also, since one object of these pages is to mark the social changes in English life since my young days, that the improvement in the tone and manner of performing the choral service in our cathedrals is as striking as the increased care for the fabrics. It used for the most part to be a careless, perfunctory, and not very reverent or decorous performance when George the Third was King. Those were the days when one minor canon could be backed to give another to " Pontius Pilate " in the Creed, and beat him! Other times, other manners!

I think that the points in that still well-remembered tour that most of all delighted me were, first of all, Lynton and Lynmouth, on the north coast of Devon; then the banks of the Wye from Chepstow to Ross; and thirdly, Raglan Castle. I had already read the "Mysteries of Udolpho," with more enjoyment probably than any other reading has

ever afforded me. It was an ecstasy of delight, tempered
only by the impossibility of gratifying my intense longing
to start forthwith to see the places and countries described.
And when I did in long-after years see them! Oh, Mrs.
Ratcliffe, how could you tell such tales! What! this the
lovely Provence of my dreams? But I was fresh from
"The Mysteries," and full of faith when I went to Raglan,
and strove to apply, at least as a matter of possibility, the incidents of the romance to the localities of the delightful ruin.

Nor was Raglan in those days cared for with the loving
care now bestowed on it by the Duke of Somerset. I have
heard people complain of the restrictions, and of the small
entrance fee now demanded for admittance to the ruins,
and regret the days when the traveller could, as in my
time, wander over every part of it at will. All that was
very charming, but the place was not as beautiful as it is
now. The necessary expense for the due conservation of
the ruins must be very considerable. And when one hears,
as I did recently at Raglan, that steam and bank-holidays
have brought as many as fifteen hundred (!) visitors to the
spot in one day, it may be easily imagined what the condition of the place would shortly become if careful restrictions were not enforced. Of lovely—ever lovely—Tintern
the same remarks may be made. Certainly there was a
charm in wandering there, as I did when a boy, almost
justified by the solitude in feeling myself to be the dis-
coverer of the spot. Now there is a fine hotel, with waiters
in black-tailed coats, and dinners à la carte! And huge
vans pouring in "tourists" by the thousand. Between
four and five thousand persons, I was told, visited Tintern
in one August day! Scott tells those who would "view
fair Melrose aright" to "visit it by the pale moonlight."
But I fear me that no such precaution could secure solitude,
though it might beauty, at Tintern in August. But the
care bestowed upon it makes the place more beautiful than
ever. The guardians, by dint of locked gates, prevent the
lovely sward from being defiled by sandwich papers and
empty bottles, as the neighboring woods are. But he who
would view fair Tintern aright had better *not* visit it on
a bank-holiday.

A similarly striking change between the England of sixty years since and the England of to-day may be observed at beautiful Lynmouth and Lynton. The place was a solitude when my parents and I visited it in, I think, 1818. We had a narrow escape in driving down from Lynton to the mouth of the little stream. A low wall of unmortared stones alone protected the road from the edge of a very formidable precipice; and just at the worst point the horse' my father was driving took fright at something, and, becoming unmanageable, dashed at the low wall, and absolutely got his fore-feet over it ! " George," riding the other horse behind, was at a hundred yards or so distance. But my father, with one bound to the horse's head, caught him by the bridle, and, by the sheer strength of his remarkably powerful frame, forced him back into the road. It was not a *mauvais quart d'heure*, but a very *mauvais quart de minute*—for it was, I take it, all over in that time. Now the road is excellent, and traversed daily in the summer season by some half-dozen huge vans carrying " tourists" from Ilfracombe to Lynton.

At the latter place, too, there is a large and extremely prettily situated hotel, where, on the occasion of my first visit, I remember that we obtained a modicum of bread-and-cheese at a lone cottage. Even the Valley of Rocks is not altogether what it was, for the celebrated "Castle Rock" has now well-contrived paths to the top of it. I wrote a few months ago in the book kept at the hotel, *ad hoc* that I had climbed the Castle Rock more than sixty years ago, and had now repeated the feat. But, in truth, the "climb" was in those days a different affair. I remember my mother had a story of some old friend of hers having been accompanied by her maid during a ramble through the Valley of Rocks, and having been told, when she asked the maid what she thought of it, that she considered it was kept very untidy ! And truly the criticism might be repeated at the present day not altogether unreasonably, for the whole place is defiled by the traces of feeding.

Truly England, whether for better or worse, " *non è piu come era prima !*"

That was my first journey! Has any one of the very many others which I have undertaken since equalled it in enjoyment? Ah! how sad was the return to Harrow and lessons and pupil-room! And how I wished that the old gig, with me on the little box between my parents' knees, could have been bound on an expedition round the world!

A leading feature, perhaps I should say *the* leading feature, of the social life of Harrow in those days consisted in a certain antagonism between the vicar, the Rev. Mr. Cunningham, and the clerical element of the school world, or perhaps it would be more correct to say the Drury element. Mr. Cunningham was in those days rather a man of mark among the Low-Church party. He was an ally of the Venns, of Daniel Wilson, and that school, and was well known in his day as "Velvet-Cushion Cunningham," from a little book with that title which he had published. He was, of course, an "evangelical" of the evangelicals; and among the seven masters of the school there was not the slightest—I must not say taint, but—savor of anything of the kind. Dr. Butler probably would have found no difficulty in living in perfect harmony with the vicar; but the latter—he and his ways and his doctrines—were especially abhorrent to the Drurys. Of course they were not High-Churchmen in the sense which the term has acquired in these latter days, for nothing of the kind was then known. They were of the old-fashioned sort, which had come to be somewhat depreciatingly spoken of as "high and dry!"—though in truth it is difficult to see with what justice the latter epithet could be applied to many of them.

Harry Drury, who was perhaps foremost in his feeling of antagonism to the vicar, was a man of decidedly literary tastes, though they shared his devotion with those of a *bon vivant*. He was a ripe scholar, and undoubtedly the vicar's superior in talent and intellect. But he was essentially a coarse man, coarse in manner and coarse in feeling. Cunningham was the reverse of all this. He was, I believe, the son of a London hatter, but in external manner and appearance he was a more gentlemanlike man than any of the Harrow masters of that day, save Dr. Butler. He had the advantage, too, of a handsome person and good presence. But there was a something *too* suave and *too* soft, carrying with it a certain suspicion of insincerity which prevented him from presenting a genuine specimen of the real article. I believe his father purchased the living for him under circumstances which were not altogether free from suspicion of simony. I know nothing, however, of these circumstances, and my impressions on the subject are doubtless derived from the flouts and skits of his avowed enemies the Drurys. There was, I remember, a story of his having, soon after coming to Harrow, in conversation with some of his new parishioners, attributed with much self-complacency his presentation to the living to his having upon some occasion preached before Lord Northwick! —a result which no Harrow inhabitant, clerk or layman, would have believed in the case of his lordship, then often a resident on his property there, if the preacher had been St. Paul. But again, *Audi alteram partem!* which I had no chance of doing, for we, though living on terms of neighborly intercourse with the vicar, were of the Drury faction.

I remember well an incident which may serve to illustrate the condition of "tension" which prevailed during those years in the little Harrow world. Mark Drury had two remarkably pretty daughters. They were in all respects as thoroughly good and charming girls as they were pretty, and were universal favorites in society. Now Mark Drury's pew in the parish church, where, of course, he never appeared himself, for the reason assigned on a former page, was situated immediately below the pulpit. And on one occasion the vicar saw, or thought he saw, the two young ladies in question laughing during his sermon, and so far forgot himself, and was sufficiently ill-judged, indiscreet, wrong-headed, and wrong-hearted to stop in his discourse, and, leaning over the pulpit cushion, to say aloud that he would resume it when his hearers could listen to it with decency! The amount of ill-feeling and heart-burning which the incident gave rise to may be imagined. Harry Drury, the cousin of the young ladies, and, as I have said, Cunningham's principal antagonist, never for a long time afterwards came within speaking distance of the vicar without growling "Brawler!" in a perfectly audible voice.

I well remember, though I suppose it must be mainly from subsequent hearing of it, the storm that was raised in the tea-cup of the Harrow world by the incident of Byron's natural daughter, Allegra, having been sent home to be buried in Harrow Church. A solemn meeting was held in the vestry, at which the vicar, all the masters (except poor old Mark), and sundry of the leading parishioners were present, and at which it was decided that no stone should be placed to commemorate the poor infant's name, or mark the spot where her remains rested, the principal reason assigned being that such a memorial might be injurious to the morals of the Harrow schoolboys! Amid all this Cunningham's innate and invincible flunkeyism asserted itself, to the immense amusement of the non-evangelical part of the society of the place, by his attempt to send a message to Lord Byron through Harry Drury, Byron's old tutor and continued friend, to the effect that he, Cunningham, had, on reading *Cain*, which was then scandalizing the world, "felt a profound admiration for the genius of the author!" "Did you, indeed," said Harry Drury; "I think it the most blasphemous publication that ever came from the pen."

The whole circumstances, object, and upshot of this singular vestry meeting were too tempting a subject to escape my mother's satirical vein. She described the whole affair in some five hundred verses, now before me, in which the curiously contrasted characteristics of the debaters at the meeting were very cleverly hit off. This was afterwards shown to Harry Drury, who, though he himself was not altogether spared, was so delighted with it that he rewarded it by the present of a very remarkable autograph of Lord Byron, now in my possession. It consists of a quarto page, on which is copied the little poem, "Weep, daughters of a royal line," beginning with a stanza which was suppressed in the publication. And all round the edges of the MS. is an inscription stating that the verses were "copied for my friend, the Rev. Harry Drury."

Of course, all this did not tend much to harmonize the

conflicting partisans of High and Low Church in the Harrow world of that day.

I may add here another " reminiscence " of those days, which is not without significance as an illustration of manners.

Among the neighbors at Harrow was a Mr. —— (well, I won't print the name, though all the parties in question must long since, I suppose, have joined the majority), who had a family of daughters, the second of whom was exceedingly pretty. One day this girl, of some eighteen years or so, came to my mother, who was always a special friend of all the young girls, with a long, eulogistic defence of the vicar. She was describing at much length the delight of the assurances of grace which he had given her, when my mother, suddenly looking her straight in the eyes, said, "Did he kiss you, Carrie ?"

" Yes, Mrs. Trollope. He *did* give me the kiss of peace. I am sure there was no harm in that !"

" None at all, Carrie ! For I am sure you meant none !" returned my mother. " *Honi soit qui mal y pense!* But remember, Carrie, that the kiss of peace is apt to change its quality if repeated !"

CHAPTER V.

AT WINCHESTER.

MEANWHILE the fateful year 1820, when I was to be translated from the world of Harrow, and know nothing more of its friendships, quarrels, and politics, was at hand. At the election of July in that year was to begin my Winchester life. I certainly looked forward to it with a feeling of awe approaching terror, yet not untempered by a sense of increased dignity and the somewhat self-complacent feeling of one destined by fate to meet great and perilous adventures, and acquire large stores of experience.

The sadness of departure was tempered also, as I remember, by the immediate delight of a journey to be performed. Certainly it was not the unmixed delight with which Rousseau contemplated his *voyage à faire et Paris au bout*. Something very different lay at the end of my *voyage*. Nevertheless, so intense was my delight in " the road " at that time (and to a great degree ever since), that the sixty miles' journey to be performed was a great alleviation.

The expedition was to be made with my father in his gig. A horse was to be sent on to Guildford, and by dint of starting at a very early hour, and there changing horses, the distance was to be performed in one day. We were to travel, not by the more generally used coach road by Hounslow and Bagshot, but over the district called the Hog's Back from Guildford to Farnham—chiefly, as I remember, for the sake of showing me that beautiful bit of country. For to my father beautiful scenery was as great a delight as it has always been to myself.

At Farnham there was time, while the horse was being baited at The Bush, for us, after snatching a morsel of cold meat, to visit hurriedly the park and residence of the

Bishop of Winchester. I, very contentedly trotting by the side of my father's long strides, was much impressed by the beauty of the park. But, as I remember, my mind was very much exercised by the fact, then first learned, that the bishop's diocese extended all the way to London. And I think that it seemed somehow to my child's mind that the dignity of my position as one of William of Wykeham's scholars was enhanced by the enormous extent of the diocese of his successor.

We reached Winchester late in the evening of the day before the election, putting up, not at The George, or at The White Hart, as most people would have done, but at the Fleur de Lys, pronounced "Flower de Luce," a very ancient, but then third-rate hostelry, which my father preferred, partly probably because he thought the charges might be less there, but mainly because it is situated in the vicinity of the college, and he had known and used it of old. We spent the evening at the house of Dr. Gabell, the head-master, an old friend of my father's, where his eldest daughter, an intimate friend of my mother's, who had often been a visitor in Keppel Street, made much of me.

And the next day I became a Wykehamist! And the manner of so becoming was in this wise. The real serious business of the six electors—three sent from New College, and three belonging to Winchester, as has been set forth on a previous page—consisted in the examination of those scholars, who, standing at the top of the school, were in that year candidates for New College. All the eighteen "prefects," who formed the highest class in the school, were examined; but the most serious part of the business was the examination of the first half-dozen or so, who were probably superannuated at the age of eighteen that year, and who might have a fair chance of finding a vacancy at New College (if there were not one at that present moment) in the course of the ensuing twelve months. And this was a very fateful and serious examination, for the examiners in "the election chamber" would, if the examination disclosed due cause, change the order of the roll as it came up to them, placing a boy who had distinguished himself, before another, who had not done so. And as the roll thus settled was the order in which vacancies at New College were taken, the work in "the chamber" was of lifelong importance to the subjects of it.

Very different was the "election" of the children, who were to go into Winchester. Duly instructed as to the part we were to play, we went marvelling up the ancient stone corkscrew stair to the mysterious chamber situated over the "middle gate," *i. e.,* the gateway between the outer court and the second quadrangle where the chapel, the hall, and the chambers are. The "election chamber" always maintained a certain character of mystery to us, because it was never opened or used save on the great occasion of the annual election. In that chamber we found the six solemn electors in their gowns waiting for us; especially the Bishop of Hereford, who was then Warden of Winchester College, an aged man who, with his peculiar wig and gown, was an object of awe. No bishop had in those days dreamed as yet of discarding the episcopal wig.

And then the examination began as follows: "Well, boy, can you sing?" "Yes, sir." "Let us hear you." "'All people that on earth do dwell,'" responded the neophyte — duly instructed previously in his part of the proceeding—without attempting in the smallest degree to modify in any way his ordinary speech. "Very well, boy. That will do!" returned the examiner. The examination was over, and you were a member of William of Wykeham's college, *Sancta Mariæ de Winton prope Winton.* "*Prope* Winton," observed, for the college is situated outside the ancient city walls.

The explanation of this survival of the *simulacrum* of an examination is that the ancient statutes require that candidates for admission as scholars must be competently instructed *in plano cantu* — in plain chant; the intention of the founder being that all his scholars should take part in the choral service of the chapel.

I and my fellow-novices thus admitted as scholars in that July of 1820 were not about to join the school immediately. We had the six weeks holidays before us, the election taking place at the end of the summer half-year. Election week was the grand festival of the Wykehamical year. For three days high feast was held in the noble old hall. The "high table" was spread on the dais, and all old Wykehamists were welcome at it. The boys in the lower part of the hall were regaled with mutton-pies, and "stuckling." That was their appointed fare; but in point of fact they feasted on dishes or portions of dishes sent down from the abundantly-spread high table, and the pies were carried away for the next morning's breakfast. I do not think anybody ate much "stuckling" beyond a mouthful *pro formâ*. It was a sort of flat pastry made of chopped apples and currants. And the specialty of it was that the apples must be that year's apples. They used to be sent up from Devonshire or Cornwall, and sometimes were with difficulty obtained. Then there was the singing of the Latin grace, with its beautiful responses, performed by the chapel choir and as many others as were capable of taking part in it. The grace with its music has been published, and I need not occupy these pages with a reprint of it. And then in the afternoon came the singing of "Domum" on the five courts behind the school, by the whole strength of the company.

Nine such election weeks did I see, counting from that which made me a Wykehamist in 1820 to that which saw me out a superannuate in 1828. I did not get a fellowship at New College, having narrowly missed it for want of a vacancy by one. I was much mortified at the time, but have seen long since that probably all was for the best for me. It was a mere chance, as has been shown at a former page, whether a boy at the head or nearly at the head of the school went to New College or not.

The interesting event of a vacancy having occurred at New College, whether by death, marriage, or the acceptance of a living, was announced by the arrival of "speedyman" at Winchester College. "Speedyman," in conformity with immemorial usage, used to bring the news on foot from Oxford to Winchester. How well I remember the look of the man, as he used to arrive with all the appearance of having made a breathless journey, a spare, active-looking fellow, in brown cloth breeches and gaiters covered with dust. Of course letters telling the facts had long outstripped "speedyman." But with the charming and reverent spirit of conservatism, which in those days ruled all things at Winchester, "speedyman" made his journey on foot all the same!

Of course one of the first matters in hand when this fateful messenger arrived was to regale him with college beer, and right good beer it was in those days. In connection with it may be mentioned the rather singular fact that, whereas all other supplies from the college buttery to the boys—the bread, the cheese, the butter, the meat—were accurately measured, the beer was given absolutely *ad libitum*. In fact, it was not *given* out at all, but taken. Thrice a day the way to the cellar was open, a back stair leading from the hall to the superb old vaulted cellar, with its central pillar and arches springing from it in every direction. All around were the hogsheads, and the proper tools for tapping one as soon as another should be out. And to this cellar the boys — or rather the junior boys at each mess — went freely to draw as much as they chose.

And the beer thus freely supplied was our only beverage, for not only was tea or coffee not furnished, it was not permitted. Some of the prefects (the eighteen first boys in college) would have "tea-messes," provided out of their own pocket-money, and served by their "fags." But if, as would sometimes happen, either of the masters chanced to appear on the scene before the tea-things could be got out of the way, he used to smash them all, using his large pass-key for the purpose, and saying, "What are all these things, sir? William of Wykeham knew nothing, I think, of tea!"

We used to breakfast at ten, after morning school, on bread-and-butter and beer, having got up at half-past five, gone to chapel at half-past six, and into school at half-past seven. At a quarter to one we again went up into hall. It was a specialty of college phraseology to suppress the definite article. We always said "to hall," "to meads" (the playground), "to school," "to chambers," and the like. The visit to hall at that time was properly for dinner, though it had long ceased to be such. The middle-of-the-day "hall" served in my day only for the purpose of luncheon (though no such modern word was ever used), and only those "juniors" attended whose office it was to bring away the portions of bread-and-cheese and "bobs" (*i. e.*, huge jugs) of beer for consumption in the afternoon.

Sunday formed an exception to this practice. We all went up into "hall" in the middle of the day on Sunday, and dined on roast beef, the noontide dinner consisting of roast beef on that day, boiled beef on Monday, Tuesday, Wednesday, and Thursday, and baked plum-pudding on Friday and Saturday. But the boiled beef, with the exception of certain portions reserved for the next morning's breakfast of the seniors of the messes, or companies into which the "inferiors" (*i. e.*, non-prefects) were divided, was not eaten, but given away. During the war Winchester had been one of the depots of French prisoners, and the beef in question was then given to them. When there were no more Frenchmen it was given to twenty-four old women who were appointed to do the weeding of the college quadrangles. It must be understood that this arrangement was entirely spontaneous on the part of the boys, though it would have been quite out of the question for any individual to say that he, for his part, would eat his own beef. How all this may be now I know not. Probably the college, under the enlightened guidance of her majesty's commissioners, have seen the propriety of provoking the youthful Wykehamists with table napkins and caper sauce, while the old women go without their dole of beef. On the Friday and Saturday the pudding was carried down out of hall by the juniors for consumption during the afternoon.

At about a quarter-past six, at the conclusion of afternoon school, we went up into hall for dinner—originally, of course, supper. This consisted of mutton, roast or boiled, every evening of the year, with potatoes and beer. But it was such mutton as is not to be found in English butchers' shops nowadays, scientific breeding having improved it from off the face of the land. It was small

Southdown mutton, uncrossed by any of the coarser, rapidly-growing, and fat-making breeds. And that it should be such was insured by the curious rule that, though only a given number of pounds of mutton were required and paid for to the contractor, the daily supply was always to be one sheep and a half. So that if large mutton was sent it was to the loss of the contractor.

Furthermore it was the duty of the "prefect of tub" to see that the mutton was in all ways satisfactory. The "prefect of tub" was one of the five boys at the head of the school; another was the "prefect of hall;" a third "prefect of school," and the fourth and fifth "prefects of chapel." These offices were all positions of emolument. That of the "prefect of tub" was far the most so, and was usually held by the senior college "founder," or boy of "founder's kin," during his last year before going to New College. The titles of the other offices explain themselves, but that of "prefect of tub" requires some elucidation.

In the hall, placed just inside the screen which divided the buttery hatches from the body of the hall, there was an ancient covered "tub." In the course of my eight years' stay at Winchester this venerable tub—*damnosa quid non diminuit dies?*—had to be renewed. It was replaced by a much handsomer one; but, as I remember, the change had rather the effect on the popular mind in college of diminishing our confidence in the permanency of human institutions generally. The original purpose of this tub was to receive fragments and remains of food, together with such portions—"dispers" we called them —of the evening mutton supper as were not duly claimed by the destined recipient of them at his place at the table, that they might be given to the poor; and the "prefect of tub" was so called because it was part of his office to see that this was duly done. It was also his duty to preside over the distribution of the aforesaid "dispers"—not *quasi dispars*, as might be supposed by those who can appreciate the difference between a prime cut out of a leg of mutton and a bit of the breast of a sheep, but "*dispers*" from *dispertio*. Now the distribution in question was effected in this wise. The joints were cut up in the kitchen always accurately in the same manner. The leg made eight "dispers," the shoulder seven, and so on. The "dispers" thus prepared were put into four immense pewter dishes, and these were carried up into hall by four choristers under the superintendence of the "prefect of tub" and distributed among the fifty-two "inferiors"— *i. e.*, non-prefects. The eighteen prefects dined at two tables by themselves. Their joints were not cut into "dispers," but were dressed by the cook according to their own orders, paid for by themselves according to an established tariff drawn with reference to the extra expense of the mode of preparation ordered. The long, narrow tables were six in number, ranged on either side of the noble hall, exactly as in a monastic refectory. The dais was left unoccupied, save at election time, when the "high table" was spread there. At the first two tables on the left-hand side as one entered the hall, the eighteen prefects dined.

This bloated aristocracy was supplied with plates to eat their dinner from. The populace—mere mutton *consumere nati*—the fifty-two inferiors, had only "trenchers," flat pieces of wood about nine inches square. These fifty-two "inferiors" were divided into eight companies, and occupied the remaining four tables. But this division was so arranged that one of the eight seniors of the "inferiors" was at the head of each company, and one of the eight juniors at the bottom of each, the whole body being similarly distributed. And each of these companies occupied a different table every day, the party who sat at the lowest table on Monday occupying the highest on Tuesday, and so on. So that when the "prefect of tub" entered the hall at the head of the procession of four choristers, carrying the four "gomers" (such was the phrase) of dispers, he proceeded first to the table on the opposite side of the hall to that of the prefects, and saw that the senior of the mess occupying that table selected as many of the most eligible dispers as there were persons *present*. If any junior were absent by authority of, or on the business of, any prefect, his disper was allowed to be taken for him. This senior of the mess, it may be mentioned *obiter*,

4

was called, for some reason hidden in the obscurity of time, the "candlekeeper." Assuredly neither he nor his office had any known connection with the keeping of candles. Any dispers remaining unclaimed at the end of his tour of the hall belonged to "the tub."

In return for the performance of this important office, the "prefect of tub" was entitled to the heads, feet, and all such portions of the sheep as were not comprised in legs, shoulders, necks, loins, and breasts, as well as to the dispers of any individuals who might from any cause be absent from college. Of course he did not meddle personally with any of these perquisites, but had a contract with the college manciple, the value of which was, I believe, about £80 a year. Such was the "prefect of tub."

Orderly conduct in hall generally, which did not imply any degree of violence, was maintained by the "prefect of hall," the dignity of whose office, though it was by no means so profitable as that of the "prefect of tub," ranked above that of all the other "officers." No master was ever present in hall.

But the most onerous and important duty of the prefect of hall consisted in superintending the excursion to "hills,"—*i. e.*, to St. Catherine's Hill, which took place twice on every holiday, once on every half-holiday during the year, and every evening during the summer months. On these occasions the "prefect of hall" had under his guidance and authority not only William of Wykeham's seventy scholars, but the whole of the hundred and thirty pupils of the head-master, who were called commoners. The scholars marched first, two and two (with the exception of the prefects, who walked as they pleased), and then followed the commoners. And it was the duty of the prefect of hall to keep the column in good and compact order until the top of the hill was reached. Then all dispersed to amuse themselves as they pleased. But the prefect of hall still remained responsible for his flock keeping within bounds.

St. Catherine's Hill is a notably isolated down in the immediate neighborhood of Winchester, and just above the charming little village of St. Cross. There is a clump of firs on the top, and the unusually well-marked circumvallation of a Roman (or British ?) camp around the circle of the hill. The ditch of this circumvallation formed our " bounds." The straying beyond them, however, in the direction of the open downs away from the city, and from St. Cross, was deemed a very venial offence by either the prefect of hall or the masters. But not so in the direction of the town. It was the duty of the three " juniors " in college—one of whom I was during my first half-year—to " call *domum.*" When the time came for returning to college, one of those three walked over the top of the hill from one side to the other, while the other two went round the circumvallation—each one half of it —calling perpetually " *Domum . . . domum* " as loudly as they could. All the year round we went to " morning hills " before breakfast, and to afternoon hills about three. In the summer we went, as I have said, every evening after " hall," but not to the top of the hill, only to the water-meads at the foot of it, the object being to bathe in the Itchen.

Many of the Winchester recollections most indelibly fixed in my memory are connected with " hills." It seems impossible that sixty years can have passed since I stood on the bank of the circumvallation facing towards Winchester, and gazed down on the white morning mist that entirely concealed the city and valley. How many mornings in the late autumn have I stood and watched the moving, but scarcely moving, masses of billowy white cloud! And what strange similitudes and contrasts suggested themselves to my mind as I recently looked down from the heights of Monte Gennaro on the Roman Campagna similarly cloud hidden! The phenomenon exhibited itself on an infinitely larger scale in the latter case, but it did not suggest to me such thick-coming fancies and fantastic imaginings as the water-mead-born mists of the Itchen!

There were two special amusements connected with our excursions to St. Catherine's Hill—badger-baiting and " mouse-digging," the former patronized mainly by the bigger fellows, the latter by their juniors. There was a man in the town, a not very reputable fellow I fancy, who had constituted himself "badger-keeper" to the college. It was his business to provide a badger and dogs, and to bring them to certain appointed trysting-places at "hill times" for the sport. The places in question were not within our "bounds," but at no great distance in some combe or chalk-pit of the neighboring downs. Of course it was not permitted by the authorities; but I think it might easily have been prevented had any attempt to do so been made in earnest. It seems strange, considering my eight years' residence in college, that I never once was present at a badger-baiting. I am afraid that my absence was not caused by distinct disapproval of the cruelty of the sport, but simply by the fact that my favorite "hill-times" occupations took me in other directions.

Nor, probably for the same reason, was I a great mouse-digger. Very many of us never went to "hills" unarmed with a "mouse-digger." This was a sort of miniature pickaxe, which was used to dig the field-mice out of their holes. The skill and the amusement consisted in following the labyrinthine windings of these, which are exceedingly numerous on the chalk downs, in such sort as to capture the inmate and her brood without injuring her, and carry her home in triumph to be kept in cages provided *ad hoc.*

There was—and doubtless is—a clump of firs on the very centre and summit of St. Catherine's Hill. They are very tall and spindly trees, with not a branch until the tuft at the top is reached. And my great delight when I was in my first or second year was to climb these. Of course I was fond of doing what few, if any, of my compeers could do as well. And this was the case as regarded "swarming up" those tall and slippery stems. I could reach the topmost top, and gloried much in doing so.

But during my later years the occupation of a hill morning which most commended itself to me was ranging as widely as possible over the neighboring hills. Like the fox in the old song, I was "off to the downs O!" As I have said, the straying beyond bounds in this direction, away from the town, was considered a very light offence; but I was apt to make it a somewhat more serious one by not getting back from my rambling, despite good running, till it was too late to return duly with the main body to college. It was very probable that this might pass without detection, if there were no roll-call on the way back. But it frequently happened that "Gaffer" (such was Dr. Williams's sobriquet among us) on his white horse met us on our homeward march, and stopped the column, while the prefect of hall called names. As these escapades in my case occurred mainly during my last three years, I, being a prefect myself, owed no allegiance to the authority of the prefect of hall; but the roll-call revealing my absence would probably issue in my having to learn by heart one of the epistles of Horace. Prefects learned their "impositions" by heart, "inferiors" wrote them.

Every here and there the sides of these downs are scored by large chalk-pits. There is a very large one on St. Catherine's Hill on the side looking towards St. Cross; and this was a favorite scene of exploits in which I may boast myself ('tis sixty years since!) to have been unrivalled. There was a very steep and rugged path by which it was possible to descend from the upper edge of this chalk-pit to the bottom of it. And it was a feat, in which I confess I took some pride, to take a fellow on my shoulders (not on my back), while he had a smaller boy on *his* shoulders, and thus with two living stories on my shoulders to descend the difficult path in question. And the boy in the middle—the first story—could not be a very small one, for it was requisite that *he* also should hold and balance his burden thoroughly well. I think I could carry *one* very *little* boy down now!

It was the "prefect of hall" who managed the whole business of our holidays—as they would be called elsewhere—which we called "remedies." A "holiday" meant at Winchester a red-letter day; and was duly kept as such. But if no such day occurred in the week, the "prefect of hall" went on the Tuesday morning to the head-master (Wiccamice "*informator*") and asked for a "remedy," which, unless there were any reason, such as very bad

weather, or a holiday coming later in the week, was granted
by handing to the prefect a ring, which remained in his
keeping till the following morning. This symbol was inscribed " *Commendat rarior usus.*"

But in addition to these important duties the "prefect
of hall" discharged another, of which I must say a few
words, with reference to the considerable amount of interest which the outside world was good enough to take
in the subject a few years ago, with all that accurate
knowledge of facts, and that discrimination which people
usually display when talking of what they know nothing
about.

It was the "prefect of hall" who ordered the infliction
of a "public tunding." The strange phrase, dropped by
some unlucky chance into ears to which it conveyed no
definite meaning, seems to have inspired vague terrors of
the most terrific kind. Very much nonsense was talked
and printed at the time I refer to. But the following simple and truthful statement of what a public tunding was,
may enable those who take an interest in the matter to
form some reasonable opinion whether the infliction of
such punishment were a good or a bad thing.

At the conclusion of the evening dinner or supper,
whichever it may be called, the "prefect of hall" summoned the boys to the dais for the singing of grace.
Some dozen or so of boys, who had the best capacities for
the performance, were appointed by him for the purpose,
and the whole assembly stood around the dais, while the
hymn " *Te de Profundis* " was sung. When all were thus
assembled, and before the singers commenced, the culprit
who had been sentenced to a tunding stepped out, pulled
off his gown, and received from the hands of one deputed
by the "prefect of hall," and armed with a tough, pliant
ground-ash stick, a severe beating. I never had a tunding; but I have no doubt that the punishment was severe,
though I never heard of any boy disabled by it from pursuing his usual work or his usual amusements. It was
judiciously ordered by the "prefect of hall" for offences
deemed unbecoming the character of a Wykehamist and
a gentleman, and *only* for such. Any such petty larceny

exploits as the scholars at some other "seats of learning" are popularly said to be not unfrequently guilty of, such as robberies of orchards or poultry-yards or the like, would have inevitably entailed a public tunding. Any attempt whatsoever to appropriate unduly, either by fraud or violence, anything sent to another boy from home—any portion of a "cargo," as such despatches were called—and *à fortiori* any money or money's value, would have necessitated a public tunding. The infliction was rare. Many half-years passed without any public tunding having been administered. And my own impression is that the practice was eminently calculated to foster among us a high tone of moral and gentlemanlike feeling.

These reminiscences of the penal code that was in vigor among ourselves are naturally connected with those referring to the subject of corporal punishment in its more official form.

On one of the whitewashed walls of the huge schoolroom was an inscription conceived and illustrated as follows: "*Aut disce!*" and there followed a depicted book and inkstand; "*Aut discede!*" followed by a handsomely painted sword, as who should say, "Go and be a soldier!" (offering that as an alternative for which no learning was needed, after the fashion of a day before examinations for commissions were dreamed of!); and then, lastly, "*Manet sors tertia cædi*," followed by the portraiture of a rod.

But this rod is of so special and peculiar a kind, and so dissimilar from any such instrument as used elsewhere, that I must try to explain the nature of it to my non-Wiccamical readers. A stick of some hard wood, beech I think it was, turned into a shape convenient to the hand, about a yard long, and with four grooves about three inches long and as large as a cedar pencil, cut in the extremity of it, formed the handle. Into these four grooves were fitted four slender apple twigs about five feet long. They were sent up from Herefordshire in bundles, cut and prepared for the purpose, and it was the duty of the "prefect of school" to provide them. These twigs, fitted into the grooves, were fixed by a string which bound them tightly to the handle, and a rod was thus formed, the fourfold switches of which stood out some foot—or more than that towards the end—from each other.

The words "flog" or "flogging," it is to be observed, were never heard among us, in the mouth either of the masters or of the boys. We were "scourged." And a scourging was administered in this wise. At a certain spot in the school—near the seat of the "*informator*" when he was the executioner, and near that of the "*hostiarius*" or under-master when he had to perform—in front of a fixed form, the patient knelt down. Two boys, any who chanced to be at hand, stepped behind the form, turned the gown of a collegian or the coat-tails of a commoner over his shoulders, and unbuttoned his brace buttons, leaving bare at the part where the braces join the trousers a space equal to the diameter of a crown-piece— such was the traditional rule. And aiming at this with more or less exactitude the master inflicted three cuts. Such was a "scourging."

Prefects, it may be observed, were never scourged.

The "best possible instructors" of this enlightened age, who never treat of subjects the facts of which they are not conversant with, have said much of the "cruelty" and the "indecency" of such infliction of corporal punishment, and of the moral degradation necessarily entailed on the sufferers of it. As to the cruelty, it will be readily understood from the above description of the rod, that it was quite as likely as not that no one of the four twigs, at either of the three cuts, touched the narrow, bare part; especially as the operator—proceeding from one patient to another with the utmost possible despatch, and with his eyes probably on the list in his left hand of the culprits to be operated on—had little leisure or care for aiming. The fact simply was that the pain was really not worth speaking of, and that nobody cared the least about it.

The affair passed somewhat in this wise. It is ten o'clock; the morning school is over; and we are all in a hurry to get out to breakfast. There are probably about a dozen or a score of boys to be scourged. Dr. Williams, as well beloved a master as ever presided over any school in the world, has come down from his seat, elevated three

steps above the floor of the school, putting on his great
cocked hat as he does so. He steps to the form where the
scourging is to be done; the list of those to be scourged,
with the reasons why, is handed to him by the prefect,
charged for the week with this duty, together with the
rod. He calls "Jones"—swish, swish, swish!—"Brown"
—swish, swish, swish!—"Robinson"—swish, swish, swish!
as rapidly as it can be done. Each operation takes perhaps twenty seconds. Having got through the list, he
flings the rod on the ground, makes a *demi-volte* so as to
face the whole school, taking off his hat as he does so, and
the "prefect of school" who has been waiting on the steps
of the master's seat, with the prayer-book open in his
hand, instantly reads the short prayer with which the
school concludes, while those who have been scourged
stand in the background hurriedly readjusting their brace
buttons so as not to be behindhand at the buttery hatch
for breakfast. Of any disgrace attached to the reception
of a scourging, no one had any smallest conception.

Of the cruelty of the infliction the reader may judge for
himself. Of the indecent talk about indecency he may
also know from the above accurate account what to think.
The degree of "moral degradation" inflicted on the sufferers may perhaps be estimated by a reference to the roll of
those whom Winchester has supplied to serve their country in Church and State.

The real and unanswerable objection to the infliction of
"corporal punishment," as it was used in my day at Winchester, was that it was a mere form and farce. It caused
neither pain nor disgrace, and assuredly morally degraded
nobody. I have been scourged five times in the day; not
because, as might be supposed, I was so incorrigible that
the master found it necessary to go on scourging me, but
simply because it so chanced. I had, say, come into chapel
"*tardè*," *i. e.*, after the service had commenced; I had omitted to send in duly my "*vulgus;*" I had been "floored" in
my Horace; I had missed duly answering "sum," when on
returning from "hills" "Gaffer" had met the procession
on his gray horse and caused the "prefect of hall" "to
call names," the reason being that I had been far away

4*

over the downs to Twyford, and had not been able to run
back in time; and an unlucky simultaneousness of these or
of a dozen other such sins of omission or commission had
occurred, which had to be wiped off by a scourging by the
"*hostiarius*" at the morning school, and another by the
"*informator;*" by a third from the former at "middle
school," when the head-master did not attend; by a fourth
from the "*hostiarius*" at evening school, and a fifth from
the "*informator*" the last thing before going out to dinner at six. But this was a rare *tour de force*, scarcely likely to occur again. I was rather proud of it, and wholly
unconscious of any "moral degradation."

I have spoken of the "*informator*" putting on his
cocked hat when about to commence his work of scourging. I am at a loss to account for his having worn this
very unacademical costume. It was a huge three-cornered
cocked hat very much like that of a coachman on state
occasions; and must, I take it, have been a survival from
about the time of Charles the Second. It has, I believe,
been since discarded.

The mention above of a "*vulgus*" requires some explanation. Every "inferior," *i. e.*, non-prefect, in the school
was required every night to produce a copy of verses of
from two to six lines on a given theme; four or six lines
for the upper classes, two for the lowest. This was independent of a weekly "verse task" of greater length, and
was called a "*vulgus*," I suppose, because everybody—the
vulgus—had to do it. The prefects were exercised in the
same manner but with a difference. Immediately before
going out from morning or from evening school, at the
conclusion of the day's lesson, the "*informator*" would
give a theme, and each boy was expected then and there,
without the assistance of pen, paper, or any book, to compose a couple, or two couple, of lines, and give them *vivâ
voce*. He got up, and scraped with his foot to call the
master's attention when he was ready; and as not above
five or ten minutes were available for the business, a considerable degree of promptitude was requisite. The
theory was that these compositions—"varying" was the
term in the case of the prefects, as "*vulgus*" in that of

the inferiors—should be epigrammatic in their nature, and that Martial rather than Ovid should be the model. Of course but little of an epigrammatic nature was for the most part achieved; but great readiness was made habitual by the practice. And sometimes the result was creditable to something more than readiness.

I am tempted to give one instance of such a "varying." It belonged to an earlier time than mine — the time when *Decus et tutamen* was adopted as the motto cut on the rim of the five-shilling pieces. The author of the "varying" in question had been ill with fever, and his head had been shaved, causing him to wear a wig. *Decus et tutamen* was the theme given. In a minute or two he was ready, stood up, and, taking off his wig, said, "*Aspicite hos crines! duplicem servantur in usum! Hi mihi tutamen nocte*"—putting the wig on wrong side outwards ; "*Dieque decus*," reversing it as he spoke the words. The memory of this "varying" lives — or lived — at Winchester. But I do not think it has ever been published, and really it deserves preservation. I wish I could give the author's name.

When at the end of the summer holidays in that year, 1820, I returned to college, again brought down to Winchester by my father in his gig, I confess to having felt for some short time a very desolate little waif. As I, at the time a child barely out of the nursery, look back upon it, it seems to my recollection that the strongest sense of being shoved off from shore without guidance, help, or protection, arose from never seeing or speaking to a female human being. To be sure there was at the sick-house the presiding " mother "—Gumbrell her name was, usually pronounced "Grumble "—but she was not a fascinating representative of the sex. An aged woman once nearly six feet high, then much bent by rheumatism, rather grim and somewhat stern, she very conscientiously administered the prescribed "black-dose and calomel pill" to those under her care at the sick-house. To be there was called being "continent;" to leave it was "going abroad"—intelligibly enough. Tea was provided there for those "continent" instead of the usual breakfast of bread-and-butter and beer ; and I remember overhearing Mother

Gumbrell, oppressed by an unusual number of inmates, say, "Talk of Job, indeed! Job never had to cut crusty loaves into bread-and-butter!"

I saw the old woman die! I was by chance in the sick-house kitchen—in after-years, when a prefect—and "Dicky Gumbrell," the old woman's husband, who had been butler to Dean Ogle, and who by special and exceptional favor was allowed to live with his wife in the sick-house, was reading to her the story of Joseph and his Brethren, while she was knitting a stocking, and sipping occasionally from a jug of college beer which stood between them, when quite suddenly her hands fell on to her lap and her head on to her bosom, and she was dead! while poor old Dicky quite unconsciously went on with his reading.

But I mentioned Mother Gumbrell only to observe that she, the only petticoated creature whom we ever saw or spoke with, was scarcely calculated to supply, even to the imagination, the feminine element which had till then made so large a part of the lives of ten-year-old children fresh from their mother's knee.

Perhaps the most markedly distinctive feature of the school life was the degree in which we were uninterfered with by any personal superintendence. The two masters came into the schoolroom to hear the different classes at the hours which have been mentioned, also when we were "in chambers" in the evening, either during the hour of study which intervened between the six-o'clock dinner and the eight-o'clock prayers in the chapel, or during the subsequent hour between that and nine o'clock, when all went, or ought to have gone, to bed; and subsequently to that, when all were supposed to be in bed and asleep, we were at any moment liable to the sudden, unannounced visit of the "*hostiarius*" or second master. The visit was a mere "going round." If all was in order, it passed in silence, and was all over in a minute. If any tea-things were surprised, they were broken, as before mentioned. If beer, or traces of the consumption of beer, were apparent, that was all right. The supply of a provision of that refreshment was recognized, it being a part of the duty of the bedmakers to carry every evening into each of the seven "chambers" a huge "nipperkin" of beer, "to last," as I remember one of the bed-makers telling me when I first went into college, "for all night." The supply, as far as my recollection goes, was always considerably in excess of the consumption. If all was not in order, "the prefect in course"—*i. e.*, the prefect who in each chamber was responsible for due order during the current week—was briefly told to speak with the master next morning. And this comprises about all the personal intercourse that took place between us and the masters.

Not that it is to be understood that any hour of our lives was left to our own discretion as to the employment of it; but this was attained by no immediate personal superintendence or direction. The systematized routine was so perfect, and so similar in its operation to the movements of some huge, irresistible machine, that the disposal of each one of our hours seemed to be as natural, as necessary, and as inevitable as the waxing and waning of the moon. And the impression left on my mind by eight years' experience of such a system is, that it was pre-eminently calculated to engender and foster habitual conceptions of the paramount authority of *law*, as distinguished from the dictates of personal notions or caprices; of self-reliance, and of conscious responsibility in the individual as forming a unit in an organized whole. Of course the eighteen prefects were to a much smaller degree coerced by the machine, and to a very great degree active agents in the working of it. And I was a prefect during three years of my eight in college. But at first, when a little fellow of, say, ten years old entered this new world, it was not without a desolate sensation of abandonment, which it needed a month or two's experience to get the better of.

All this, however, was largely corrected and modified by one admirable institution, which was a cardinal point in the Wiccamical system. To every "inferior" was appointed one of the prefects as a "tutor." It was the duty of this tutor to superintend and see to the learning of his lessons by the inferior, and the due performance of his written "prose" and "verse tasks," to protect him against

all ill-usage or "bullying," and to be in all ways his providence and friend. These appointments were made by
the "*informator*." The three or four senior prefects
had as many as seven pupils, the junior prefects one or
two only; and the tutor received from the parents of
each pupil, by the hands of the master, two guineas
yearly.

In order rightly to understand the working of all these
arrangements, it must be explained that each individual's
place in "the school" and his place "in college" were two
entirely different things. The first depended on his acquirements when he entered the college and his subsequent scholastic progress. The latter depended solely on
his seniority "in college." The junior in college was the
last boy whose nomination succeeded in finding a vacancy
in any given year; and he remained "junior" till the admission of another boy next year, when he had one junior
below him, and so on. Thus it might happen, and constantly did happen, that a boy's junior in college might be
much above him in the school, either from having come
in at a later age, or from being a better-prepared or cleverer boy. And all the arrangements of the domestic college life, the fagging, etc., depended wholly on juniority
"in college," and had no reference to the place held by
each in the school. But all this seniority and juniority
"in college" ceased to operate in any way as soon as the
individual in question became a prefect. He had then
equal authority over every "inferior," whether such inferior were his senior or junior in college.

It is evident, therefore, that the prefect's authority
was frequently exercised over individuals older, bigger,
stronger than himself; and for the due and regular working of this system it was necessary that the authority of
the prefect should be absolute and irresistible. It was
traditionally supposed in college that for an "inferior" to
raise his hand against a prefect would be a case of expulsion. Whether expulsion would have actually followed, I
cannot say, for during my eight years' residence in college I never remember such a case to have occurred. I
have heard my father and other old Wykehamists of his

day declare that no such absolute authority as that of a prefect at Winchester existed in England, save in the case of the captain of a man-of-war. It should be observed, however, in modification of this, that any abuse of this authority in the way of bullying or cruelty would at once have been interfered with by that other prefect, the victim's tutor. An appeal to the master would have been about as much thought of as an appeal to Jupiter or Mars.

CHAPTER VI.

AT WINCHESTER—(*continued*).

When I went into college in 1820, at ten years old, Dr. Gabell was the "*informator*," and Mr. (afterwards Dr.) Williams the "*hostiarius*," or second master. When I quitted it in 1828, Dr. Williams was head-master, and Mr. Ridding second master. I do not know that Gabell was altogether an unpopular man, but he never inspired that strong affection that his successor did. His manner was disagreeable. In short, he was not so completely a gentleman as Williams was.

I am tempted to give here an anecdote that was currently told of Gabell—though I cannot say that it occurred within my knowledge—because it is at all events a very characteristic one.

Some boy or other—he was, I fancy, a "commoner," or one of Dr. Gabell's private pupils—was guilty of some small delinquency which had the unfortunate effect of especially angering the Doctor, who, in his rage, without giving a second thought to the matter, wrote off a hurried letter to the boy's father, telling him that if his son continued his present conduct he was on the high-road to ruin.

Unfortunately the parent lived in one of the far northern counties. In extreme distress he at once left home and posted to Winchester.

Rushing, in agitation and anxiety, into Gabell's study, he gasped out, "What is it? Tell it me at once! What has my unhappy boy done?"

"What boy?" snorted Gabell. "What do you mean? I don't know what you are talking about!"

The father, much relieved, but more amazed, pulls out the terrible letter which had summoned him, and puts it before the much crestfallen "*informator*."

"I had forgotten all about it!" he was compelled to

own. "The boy is a good boy enough. You had better go and talk to him yourself, and—and tell him not to miss answering his name again!" The parent's feelings and his expression of them may be imagined.

It used to be said, I remember, that of the two masters of Winchester, one snored without sleeping (Gabell), and the other slept without snoring. Gabell was, in truth, always snorting or snoring (so to call it); but the accusation against Williams of sleeping was, I think, justified only by his peculiarly placid and quiet manner. He was a remarkably handsome man; and his sobriquet, among those of the previous generation rather than among us boys, was, "The Beauty of Holiness"—again with reference to the unruffled repose of his manner. We boys invariably called him "Gaffer." Why, I know not.

Gabell, I think, had no nickname; but there was a phrase among us, as common as any household word, which was in some degree characteristic of the man. Any conduct which was supposed likely to turn out eventually to the detriment of the actor was called "spiting Gabell;" and the expression was continually used when the speaker intended no more reference to Dr. Gabell than a man who orders a spencer has to the first wearer of that garment.

Mr. Ridding was not a popular master, though I do not know that he had any worse fault than a bad manner. It was a jaunty, jerky, snappish manner, totally devoid of personal dignity. It was said that in school he was not impartial. But by the time he became second master, on the retirement of Gabell, I had reached that part of the school which was under the head-master, and have no personal knowledge of the matter. I do not think any boy would have gone to Ridding in any private trouble or difficulty. There was not one who would not have gone to Williams as to a father.

But in my reminiscences of the college authorities I must not omit the first and greatest of all—the warden. Huntingford, Bishop of Hereford, was warden during the whole of my college career. He was an aged man, and somewhat of a valetudinarian. And to the imagination of us boys, who rarely saw him, he assumed something of the mystic, awe-inspiring character of a "veiled prophet of Khorassan." The most awful threat that could be fulminated against any boy was that he should be had up before the warden. I do not remember that any boy ever was. He alone could expel a boy; and he alone could give leave out from college; as was testified by the appearance every Sunday of a great folio sheet, on which were inscribed, in his own peculiar great square characters, each letter standing by itself, the names of those who had been invited by friends to dine in the town, and who were thereby permitted to go out from, I think, one to five. To go out of the college gates without that permission was expulsion. But it was a crime never committed. There were traditional stories of scaling of walls, but I remember no case of the kind.

There was one occasion on which every boy had an interview with the warden—that of taking before him the "college oath," which took place when we were, as I remember, fourteen. On a certain day in every year the "prefect of hall" made inquiry for all of that age who had not taken the oath, and required them to copy a sheet of writing handed to them. I cannot remember the words in which the oath was couched, but the main provisions of it were to the effect that you would never by word or deed do aught to injure the college or its revenues; that you would be obedient to the authorities; and that you would never in any way by word or deed look down on any scholar of the college, the social position of whose family might be inferior to your own. And I remember that there was appended to the oath the story of a certain captain in Cromwell's forces, who, when the Parliament troopers were about to invade, and probably sack, the college, so exercised his authority as to prevent that misfortune, being influenced thereto by the remembrance of his college oath. Before swearing, which we did with much awe, we had to read over the oath. And I well remember that if a boy in reading pronounced the word "revenue" with the accent on the first syllable (as it was already at that time the usual mode to do), the warden invariably corrected him with, "Revènue, boy!" It was, I suppose, an exemplification of the *dictum* "No innovation," which (with the "a" pronounced as in "father") was said to be continually the rule of his conduct.

Probably it did not occur to him that the Herefordshire people might have considered it an innovation that Herefordshire candidates for orders should be obliged to come to be ordained in Winchester College Chapel, as was the case, instead of finding their bishop in his own cathedral church !

Bishop Huntingford was a notable Grecian, and had published a rudimentary book of Greek exercises, which was at one time largely used. I take it he was not in any larger sense a profound scholar. But I remember a story which was illustrative of his grammatical accuracy. The Dean of Winchester, Dr. Rennell, was an enthusiastic Platonist, and upon one occasion, in conversation with the warden and others, quoted a passage from Plato, in which the adjective "παντων" occurred. Upon which the bishop promptly denied that any such words were to be found in Plato. The controversy was said to have been remitted to the arbitrament of a wager of a dinner and dozen of port, when the warden, who in fact knew nothing of the passage quoted, but knew that the dean had said "παντων" in the masculine, when the substantive with which it was made to agree required the feminine, said, "No! no! πασων, Mr. Dean, πασων !" and so won his wager.

The warden's nickname, borne among sundry generations of Wykehamists, was *Tupto* (τυπτω), as we always supposed from that Greek verb used as the example in the Greek grammar. But I have heard from those of an earlier generation that it was *quasi dicas* "tiptoe," from the fact of his father having been a dancing-master. The former derivation seems to me the more plausible.

"Tupto" very rarely came to college chapel, and when he did so in his episcopal wig and lawn sleeves it was felt by us that his presence gave a very marked additional solemnity to the occasion. Though assuredly far from being a model bishop according to the estimate of these . latter days, I believe him to have been a very good man. He lived and died a bachelor, having at a very early period

of his life undertaken the support of a brother's widow
and family, who had been left unprovided for. And it
was reported among Wykehamists of an earlier generation than mine that never was husband so severely ruled
by a wife as the bishop was by his sister-in-law. "Peace
to his manes," as old Cramer, the pianist, used to say, always pronouncing it monosyllabically, "mains"! His
rule of Winchester College was a long and prosperous one;
and as long as it lasted he was able to carry out his favorite maxim, "No innovation!"

But when old Tupto went over to the majority the spirit of innovation, so long repressed, began to exert itself
in many directions. I am told, for instance, that it has
been found too much for young Wykehamists of the present generation to wait for their breakfasts till ten in the
morning, and that the excursion to "morning hills" before breakfast is declared to be too much for their strength.
Well, I wish it may answer, as Sterne's Uncle Toby said.
But I do not think that the college, during the latter years
of our century, can show better bills of health than it did
in its earlier decades.

The dormitory arrangements are much changed, I believe, and it may be worth while to record a few reminiscences of what they were in my day.

The second or inner quadrangle of the college buildings
was formed by the chapel and hall and kitchen on one side,
and on the other three by the lodgings of the fellows and
the "*hostiarius*" on the first floor, and the "chambers"
of the scholars on the ground-floor. These chambers were
seven in number. They contained, therefore, on an average, ten beds each. But they were by no means equal in
size. The largest, "seventh" (for they were all known
by their numbers), held thirteen beds; the smallest, "fifth,"
only eight. A few years before my time that side of the
quadrangle under which were situated the "first" and
"second" chambers was burned. And the beds and other arrangements in these two chambers were of a more
modern model. In the other five the old bedsteads remained as they had been from time immemorial. They
were of solid oak of two or three inches thickness in every

part, and were black with age. The part which held the
bed was a box about six feet and a half long by three
wide, with solid sides some six inches deep, and supported
on four massive legs. But at the head, for about eighteen
inches or so, these sides were raised to a height of about
four or five feet, and covered in. The whole construction
was massive, and afforded an extremely snug and comfortable sleeping-place, which was much preferred to the
iron bedsteads in the two new chambers. Older bones
might perhaps have found the oak planking under the bed
somewhat hard, but we were entirely unconscious of any
such objection.

The door in every chamber was well screened from the
beds. There was a huge fireplace with heavy iron dogs,
on which we burned in winter large fagots about four
feet long. Four of such fagots was the allowance for
each evening, and it was abundantly sufficient. It was
the duty of the bedmakers, whose operations were all performed when we were in school, to put four fagots in
each chamber, which we used at our discretion; i. e., at
the discretion of the prefects in the chamber. As the eighteen prefects were distributed among the seven chambers,
there were three prefects in each of the larger and two in
each of the smaller chambers. By the side of each bed
was a little desk, with a cupboard above, which was called
a "toys," in which each boy kept the books he needed for
work "in chambers," and any other private property.
For his clothes he had also by his bedside a large chest,
of a make contemporary with the bedstead, which served
him also for a seat at the desk of the "toys." In the middle of the chamber was a pillar, around which were hung
our surplices. Over the huge fireplace was an iron sconce
fixed in the wall, in which a rushlight, called by us a
"functure," was burned all night. And the "prefect in
course" was responsible for its being kept duly burning.
The nightly rounds of the "*hostiarius*" were not frequent,
but he might come at any minute of any night. Suddenly
his pass-key would be heard in the door ; for it was the
rule that every chamber-door should be kept locked all
night; he came in with a lantern in his hand, and if all

was right, *i. e.*, if the functure was duly burning, every boy in his bed, and his candle put out, he merely looked around and passed on to another chamber. If otherwise, the "prefect in course" had an interview with him on the following morning. These chamber-doors, which, as I have said, it was the rule to keep always locked during the night, were exceedingly massive, iron-bound, and with enormous locks and hinges. Now there was a tradition in college that a certain former "senior prefect in third" (*subaudi* chamber) had carried the door of that chamber round the quadrangle. The Atlas thus remembered was a minor canon of the cathedral when I was "senior prefect in third," and the tradition of his prowess excited my emulation. So I had the door in question taken from its hinges and laid upon my bent back, and caused the door of "fourth" to be carefully placed on the top of it, and so carried both doors round the quadrangle, thus outdoing the minor canon by a hundred per cent. In due proportion the feat should surely have made me in time a canon! But it has not done so. I think, however, that I might challenge any one of my schoolfellows of the present generation, whose constitutions are cared for by the early breakfasts which we did not get, to do likewise; supposing, that is, the old doors to be still in existence, and *in statu quo*. From seven to eight we were, or ought to have been, at work, seated at our "toys" in chambers. And during that hour no "inferior" could leave the chamber without the permission of the "prefect in course." At eight we went into chapel—or, rather, into the antechapel only—for short prayers, and after that till nine we were free to do as we pleased. Some would walk up and down "sands," as the broad flagstone pavement below the chapel was called.

Each prefect in the chamber had a little table, at which he sat during the evening, and which in the morning served as a washing-stand, on which it was the duty of the "junior," who was his "valet," to place his basin and washing things. But all "inferiors" had to perform their ablutions at the "conduit" in the open quadrangle. In severe or wet weather this was not Sybaritic! But again I say that it would have been difficult to find a healthier collection of boys than we were.

The discipline which regulated that part of college life spent "in chambers" must have been, I think, much more lax at a former day than it was in my time, for I remember to have heard my father, who was in college under Dr. Warton, say that Tom Warton, the head-master's brother (and the well-known author of the "History of Poetry"), used frequently to be with the boys "in chambers" of an evening; that he would often knock off a companion's "verse task" for him, and that the doctor the next morning would recognize "that rascal Tom's work." Now in my day it would have been altogether impossible and out of the question for any outsider, however much an old Wykehamist, and brother of the master, to be with us in chambers.

There was an anecdote current, I remember, among Wykehamists of that generation, respecting "that rascal Tom," to the effect that he narrowly missed becoming head of Trinity, of which college at Oxford he was a fellow, under the following circumstances: There was a certain fellow of the college, whose name need not here be recorded, rather famous among his contemporaries for the reverse of wisdom or intelligence. Upon one occasion Tom Warton was sitting in his stall in chapel close to the gentleman in question, who was reading the Psalms; and when the latter came to the verse, "Lord, thou knowest my simpleness," he was so indiscreet as to mutter, in an almost audible tone, "Ay! we all know *that!*" But it so chanced that, not very long afterwards, there was an election for the presidentship of the college, and Warton, who was a very popular man, was one of the two candidates. The college, however, was very closely divided between them, and "that rascal Tom" had to apply to his "simple" colleague for his vote. "Not so simple as all that, Mr. Warton!" was the reply; and the story goes that the historian of poetry lost his election by that one vote.

And this college chapel anecdote reminds me to say, before concluding my Wiccamical reminiscences, a few words about our chapel-going in the olden time. In this department, also, very much of change has taken place, doubtless, here at least, for the better.

But it must be remembered that any change of this sort has been contemporaneous with change, at least as strongly marked in the same direction, in the general tone of English manners, sentiments, and habits. We English were not a devout people in the days when George the Third was king, especially as regards all that portion of the world which held aloof from evangelicalism and dissent. We were not altogether without religious feeling in college, but it manifested itself chiefly in the form of a pronounced abhorrence for those two, as we considered them, ungentlemanlike propensities. For about three weeks, at Easter time, the lower classes in the school read the Greek Testament instead of the usual Greek authors, and the upper classes read Lowth's "Prælections on the Sacred Poetry of the Hebrews," a book unimpeachable in point of Latinity and orthodoxy, for was not the author a Wykehamist? But I do not remember aught else in the way of religious instruction, unless it were found in the assiduity of our attendances at chapel.

We went to chapel twice (including the short evening prayers in the chapel) every day. On Fridays we went three times, and on Saturdays also three times; the service in the afternoon being choral. On Sundays we went thrice to chapel and twice to the cathedral; on red-letter days thrice to chapel, and as often on "Founder's commemoration" and "Founder's obit." These latter services, as also those on Sundays and holidays, were choral. We had three chaplains, an organist, four vicars choral, and six choristers for the service of the chapel. The "choristers," who were mentioned at a former page as carrying the "dispers" up into hall, though so called, had nothing to do with the choral service. They were twelve in number, were fed, clothed, and educated by a master of their own, and discharged the duty of waiting on the scholars as messengers, etc., at certain hours.

Our three chaplains were all of them, also, minor canons of the cathedral. Very worthy, good men they were; one of them especially and exceptionally exemplary in his

family relations; but their mode of performing the service
in the chapel was not what would in these days be considered decorous or reverential. Besides the chaplaincy of
the college and the minor canonry of the cathedral, these
gentlemen—all three of them, I believe—held small liv-
ings in the city. And the multiplicity of duty which had
thus to be done rendered a degree of speed in the performance of the service so often a desideratum, and sometimes
an absolute necessity, that that became the most marked
characteristic of the performers. In reading, or, rather,
intoning, the prayers, the habit was to allow no time at
all for the choir to chant their "Amen," which had to
be interjected in such sort that, when the tones of it died
away, the priest had already got through two or three
lines of the following prayer. One of our chaplains, who
had the well-deserved character of being the fastest of the
three, we called the diver. For it was his practice, in reading or intoning, to continue with great rapidity as long as
his breath would last, and then, while recovering it, to
proceed mentally, without interruption, so that we lost
sight (or hearing) of him at one point, and when he came
to the surface, *i. e.*, became audible again, he was several
lines further down the page; and this we called "diving."
It was proudly believed in college that this was the gentleman of whom the story was first told that he was ready
to give any man to "Pontius Pilate" in the Creed, and
arrive at the end before him. But, however worthy com-
petitor he may have been in such a race, I have reason to
believe that the chaplain of a certain college in Oxford
was the original of the story.

Another of our three chaplains was a great sportsman.
It was the practice that the lessons were always read in
chapel by one of the prefects.

I remember, by-the-bye (but this is parenthetical), that
one of our number was unable to pronounce the letter "r,"
and we used to scheme that it should fall to his lot to tell
us that "Ba*w*abbas was a *w*obber."

Now the boy who read the lessons, sat, not in his usual
place, but by the side of the chaplain who was performing
the service. And it was the habit of the reverend sports-

5

man I have referred to, to intercalate with the verses of the Psalm he was reading, *sotto voce*, anecdotes of his most recent sporting achievements, addressed to the youth at his side, using for the purpose the interval during which the choir recited the alternate verse.

As thus, on one twenty-eighth evening of the month, well remembered after some sixty years:

" Who smote great kings: for his mercy endureth forever."

Then aside, in the well-known great rolling, mellow voice (I can hear it now):

" On Hurstley Down yesterday I was out with Jack Woodburn " (this was another minor canon of the cathedral, but not one of our chaplains).

" Sehon king of the Amorites: for his mercy endureth forever."

" My black bitch Juno put up a covey almost at our feet."

" And gave away their land for an heritage: for his mercy endureth forever."

" I blazed away with both barrels and brought down a brace."

" Who remembered us when we were in trouble: for his mercy endureth forever."

" But Jack fired too soon and never touched a feather." And so on.

Now there would be no sort of interest in recording that we unfortunately chanced to have at one time a very graceless chaplain, if such had been the case, which it was not. The interest lies in the fact that the gentleman in question was a worthy and excellent man in all the relations of life; that he was absolutely innocent of intentional impropriety; and that, as far as I can remember, we had none of us the faintest idea that we ought to have been shocked or scandalized. Such was the state of things and men's minds " sixty years since."

The brother of this chaplain was the manciple of the college, and was known among us as " Damme Hopkins," from the following circumstance. His manner was a quaint mixture of pomposity and *bonhomie*, which made a con-

versation with him a rather favorite amusement with some
of us. Now the manciple was a very well-to-do man, and
was rather fond of letting it be known that his independent
circumstances made the emoluments of the place he held
a matter of no importance to him. "Indeed," he would
say, "I spoke to the bishop [the warden] a few months
ago of resigning, but the bishop says to me, 'No, no,
damme, Hopkins, you must keep the place.'" And I have
no doubt that the deficiency of dramatic instinct which
thus led the worthy manciple to transfer his own phraseology to his right reverend interlocutor rendered him quite
unconscious of any inaccuracy in his narration.

We used to go twice every Sunday, as I have said, to
the cathedral. But we did not attend the whole morning
service. We timed our arrival there so as to reach the
cathedral at the beginning of the Communion service, and
to be present at that and at the sermon which followed it.
We had no sermons in college chapel, save on certain
special occasions, such as 5th of November, "Founder's
commemoration," or "Founder's obit." On the former of
these occasions a sermon used to be preached with which
we had become familiar by the annual repetition of it
during a succession of years. I wonder how many there
are left who will remember the words, "A letter was sent,
couched in the most ambiguous terms, and who so likely
to detect it as the king himself?"

At the cathedral a series of benches between the pulpit
and bishop's throne and the altar were reserved for us, so
that the preacher was immediately in front and to the right
of us. The surplice was used in the cathedral pulpit at
the morning service, the Geneva gown at that in the afternoon. At the former one of the prebendaries or the dean
was the preacher, at the latter a minor canon.

I remember that we used to think a good deal of the
dean's sermons, and always attended to them—a compliment which was not often paid, to the best of my recollection, to the other preachers. Dean Rennell was a man
of very superior abilities, but of great eccentricity, mainly
due to extreme absence of mind. It used to be told of
him that unless Mrs. Rennell took good care, he was toler-

ably certain, when he went up to his room to dress for a
dinner-party, to go to bed. It will be understood from
what has been said of the accommodation provided for us
in the cathedral, that in order to face us, the preacher,
addressing himself to the body of the congregation in the
choir, must have turned himself round in the pulpit. And
this Rennell would sometimes do, when he thought what
he was saying especially calculated for our edification. He
was, as I have already mentioned, a great Platonist, and
when he alluded, as he not unfrequently did, to some doctrine or opinion of the Grecian philosopher, he would turn
to us and say, in a sort of parenthetical aside, "Plato I
mean."

Among the stories that were current of Rennell I remember one to the effect that when upon one occasion he
was posting from Winchester to London he stopped at
Egham for luncheon. A huge round of boiled beef, nearly
uncut, was placed upon the table. But the dean found it
was as he thought, far too much boiled; so without more
ado he cut the huge mass into four quarters and helped
himself to a morsel from the centre! The landlady, when
the mutilated joint was carried out, was exceedingly indignant, and insisted that a guinea should be paid for the
entirety of it. The dean, much against the grain, as the
chronicle goes, paid his guinea, but packed up the four
quarters of the round and carried them off with him.

Further indication of his eccentricity might be seen, as
I remember, in his habit of wearing in the cathedral pulpit
in cold weather, not a skull cap, but a flat square of velvet
on his head, with which occasionally he would, in the heat
of his discourse, wipe his face, then clap it on his head
again.

The cathedral, as I have had occasion to mention in a
former chapter, had been undergoing a very extensive restoration, one operation in the course of which had been
the removal of the organ from over the screen; and the
question whether it should be replaced there or be transferred to the north transept was very earnestly, and, it
was said, somewhat hotly debated by the chapter. The
dean was exceedingly vehement in supporting the latter

course, which was eventually adopted, it can scarcely be doubted by those who see the church as it now is, with entire judiciousness.

I could, not without gratification to myself, chatter much more about reminiscences of the years I passed at Winchester. But I feel that the only excuse for having yielded to the temptation as far as I have must be sought in the illustrations afforded by what I have written of the large changes in habits, thoughts, customs, feelings that have been wrought in English society and English institutions by the lapse of some sixty years.

And now the time had come when I, having attained the age of eighteen, was superannuated at the election in the July of 1828. It was not at that time certain whether I should or should not succeed to a fellowship at New College, for that depended upon the number of vacancies that might occur in the year up to the election of 1829. Eventually I missed it by, as I remember, one only. One more journey of "Speedyman" before July, 1829, announcing the marriage or the death of a fellow of New College, or the acceptance of a college living by one of them, would have made me a fellow of New College. But "Speedyman" did not make his appearance.

I left Winchester a fairly good Latin scholar, and well grounded—I do not think I can say more—in Greek; and very ignorant indeed of all else. According to what I hear of the present day, I had no scholarly knowledge whatever of my own language. I knew nothing whatsoever of Anglo-Saxon, or of mediæval English. I had never —have never, I may rather say—had any English grammar in my hand from my cradle to the present hour.

It is certain, however, that the enlarged requirements in this department, to which I have referred, have somehow or other failed to banish from the current literature of the day a vast number of solecisms, vulgarisms, and grammatical atrocities of all sorts, which defile the language to a much greater degree than was the case at the time of which I have been writing, and which would have been as abhorrent to me when I left Winchester as they are now.

Of arithmetic I knew nothing—I should write "know" —and of all that arithmetic should be the first step to, *à fortiori*, still less. In the art of writing I received the best possible instruction, for I was licked by my tutor and scourged by the masters if my writing was illegible. Of less indirect tuition I had none.

There was a writing-master—one Mr. Bower, Fungy Bower he was called, why, I know not—who sat at a certain low desk in the school during school-hours. I never received from him, or saw any one else receive from him, any instruction in writing. Nor did he, to the best of my knowledge and belief, form any part of William of Wykeham's foundation. The only purpose his presence in school appeared to serve was to mend pens and make up the weekly account of marks received by each boy which regulated his place in the class.

The register containing the account of these marks was called the "classicus paper," and was kept in this wise: All the members of each "class"—or "form" as it is called in other schools—continually changed places while proceeding with the lesson before the master, each, if able to answer a question which those above him could not answer, passing up above them. And part of the punishment for failing altogether in any lesson, for being as the phrase was "crippled in Virgil," or "crippled in Homer," was to go to the bottom of the class. Thus the order in which the class sat was continually changed. And the first business every morning was for the two boys at the head of the class to take the "classicus paper," and mark "1." against the name of the boy at the bottom, "2." against the next, and so on; so that the mark assigned to him at the head was equal to the number in the class. And this record of the marks was handed every week to Fungy Bower to be made up, so as to indicate the place in the class held by each member of it. But though this was done weekly, the account was carried on during the whole half year, so that a boy's final place in the class was the accurate result of his diligence and success during the whole "half."

Of course I was a cricketer—we all were, and were, indeed, obliged to be, whether willingly or not, until we became prefects, when, of course, those only who loved the game continued to practise it. I never was a great cricketer, but have been "long stop" quite often enough to know how great is the nonsense talked by those of the present generation who maintain that all the elaborate precautions against being hurt which are so abundantly taken by the players of these latter days are necessitated by the greater force of the bowling as now practised. In simple truth this is all *bosh!* though I can hardly expect a generation *in cute curandâ plus œquo operata* to believe a very old batter and fielder when he tells them so !

My favorite game was fives. We had a splendid fives court, and the game was played in a manner altogether peculiar to Winchester; now I believe—like so much else —abandoned. We used a very small ball, hardly bigger than a good-sized walnut, and as hard as if made of wood, called a "snack." And this was driven against the wall by a bat of quite peculiar construction. It was made, I think, of ash, and there were only two men, rivals, who could make it. It was about a yard long, the handle round, and somewhat less than an inch in diameter. It then became gradually thinner and wider, till at about the distance of six inches from the extremity it was perhaps an inch and a half wide, and not thicker than half a crown. Then it expanded and thickened again into a head somewhat of the shape of an ace of spades, some three inches across and half an inch thick. The thin part was kept continually well oiled—in such sort that it became so elastic that the heavy head might almost be doubled back so as to touch the part nearer the hand. It will be understood both that the difficulty of striking a bounding ball with this instrument was considerable, and that the momentum imparted to the small hard ball by the blow was very great indeed. It is true that accidents occasionally, though very rarely, happened from a misdirected blow. But it does not seem necessary that the old bat should be abandoned, for our judicious grandsons might play with great comfort and safety in helmets !

Of course I, like most of my contemporaries, left Winchester—and indeed subsequently left Oxford — as igno-

rant of any modern language, save English, as of Chinese!
And as for music—though Oxford and Cambridge are the
only universities in Europe which give degrees in music—
it is hardly an exaggeration to say that, with very rare
exceptions, to have taught an undergraduate, or a boy at
a public school, music, would have been thought much on
a par with teaching him to hem a pocket-handkerchief.
And here the present generation has the pull to a degree
which it perhaps hardly sufficiently recognizes !

It was during my last year at Winchester that I made
my first attempt at authorship. Old Robbins, the gray-
headed bookseller of College Street, who had been the
college bookseller for many years, had recently taken a
younger partner of the name of Wheeler, and this gentleman established a monthly magazine, called the *Hampshire and West of England Magazine,* to which I contributed three or four articles on matters Wiccamical. I have
the volume before me now—perhaps the only extant copy
of that long - since - forgotten publication. The Rev. E.
Poulter, one of the prebendaries of Winchester, who had
a somewhat wider than local reputation as a wit in those
days, was the anonymous contributor of a poetical prologue of such unconscionable proportions that poor Wheeler
was sadly puzzled what to do with it. It was impossible
to refuse or neglect a reverend prebendary's contribution,
besides that the verses, often doggerel, had some good fun
in them. So they were all printed by instalments in successive numbers, despite the title of prologue which their
author gives them.

CHAPTER VII.

I CAME back from Winchester for the last time after the election of 1828, to find a great change at home. My father, pressed more and more by pecuniary difficulties, had quitted Harrow, and established himself at Harrow Weald, a hamlet of the large parish in the direction of Pinner. He had not given up his farm at Harrow. He would have been only too glad to do so, for it involved an annual loss undeviatingly; but that he could not do, for his lease tied him to the stake. But he took another farm at Harrow Weald, on which there was an old farmhouse, which had once been a very good one, and, living there, carried on both farms. How far this speculation was a wise one I have no means of judging. Doubtless he took the Harrow Weald farm upon very largely more advantageous terms than those which he had accepted from Lord Northwick for the farm at Harrow; but having been absent all the time at Winchester, I knew so little about the matter that I do not now know even who his Harrow Weald landlord was. Possibly I did know, but have forgotten. But I think I remember to have heard my father say that the Harrow Weald farm did in some degree alleviate the loss sustained by the larger farm at Harrow, and that, could he have got rid of the latter, the Harrow Weald farm might have paid its way. The excellent house he had built at Harrow was, in the meantime, let to Mr. Cunningham, the vicar.

The change from it to the old farmhouse at Harrow Weald, as a home, was not a pleasant one ; but a very far worse and more important change awaited my home coming, in the absence of my mother. She had gone to America.

Where, or under what circumstances, my parents had

5*

first become acquainted with General La Fayette I do not know. I myself never saw him; but I know that it was during a visit to La Grange, his estate in France, that my mother first met Miss Frances Wright, one of two sisters, his wards. I believe she became acquainted with Camilla Wright, the sister, at the same time.

It is odd, considering the very close intimacy that took place between my mother and Frances Wright, that I never knew anything of the parentage and family of these ladies, or how they came to be wards of General La Fayette. But with Miss Frances Wright I did become subsequently well acquainted. She was in many respects a very remarkable personage. She was very handsome in a large and almost masculine style of beauty, with a most commanding presence, a superb figure, and stature fully masculine. Her features both in form and expression were really noble. There exists—still findable, I suppose, in some London *fonds de magazin*—a large lithographed portrait of her. She is represented standing, with her hand on the neck of a gray horse (the same old gig horse that had drawn my parents and myself over so many miles of Devonshire, Somersetshire, and Monmouthshire roads and cross roads—not that which so nearly made an end of us near Lynmouth, but his companion), and, if I remember rightly, in Turkish trousers.

But these particulars of her bodily form and presentment constituted the least remarkable specialties of her individuality. She was unquestionably a very clever woman. She wrote a slender octavo volume, entitled "A Few Days in Athens," which was published by Longman. It was little more than a *brochure*, and it is many years since I have seen it, but the impression that it was very clever abides in my mind. I remember the fact that the whole edition was sold. And the mention of this book reminds me of a circumstance that seems to show that my parents must have become to a considerable degree intimate with these wards of General La Fayette at some period preceding the visit to La Grange, which exercised in the sequel so large an influence over my own, and my mother's, and brothers' future. This circumstance is that I recollect my father to have been in communication with the Longmans on behalf of Miss Wright in respect to her work.

Be this how it may, at the time of that visit to La Grange spoken of above, Miss Wright's thoughts and aspirations were directed with a persistent and indomitable enthusiasm, which made the ground-work of her character, to doing something for the improvement of the condition of the slave populations in the southern states of the great transatlantic republic. Both Frances and Camilla Wright were ladies of considerable fortune; and I believe that General La Fayette wished much to induce his ward Frances not to employ her means in the scheme she was now bent on. But she was of age—I fancy some six or seven years more than that—and he had no authority to interfere with her purpose, with which besides, otherwise than as likely to be pecuniarily disastrous to her, he entirely sympathized.

Her purpose was to purchase a property in the valley of the Mississippi—in Alabama I think it was—with the slaves upon it, to free them all immediately, and to cultivate the estate by their free labor, living there with them in a sort of community, the principles and plan of which were, I fancy, very largely based upon the ideas and schemes of Mr. Owen of Lanark. His son, Robert Dale Owen, subsequently well known in Europe as the author of sundry works on spiritualism and political speculations, and as United States Consul at Naples and perhaps other cities, was a lifelong friend of Miss Wright's.

Now, my parents had taken with them to La Grange my next brother, Henry, who has been mentioned as the companion of my early London rambles, and who was then rapidly approaching manhood without having found for himself, or having had found for him, any clear prospect of earning the livelihood which it was clearly enough necessary that he should earn in some way; and Miss Wright proposed to my mother to bring him to America to join in her projected establishment and experiment at "New Harmony"—such I believe to have been the name which Miss Wright gave to her property. The original name, I think, was Nashoba, but my knowledge of any of these matters is very imperfect. I know that the whole scheme ended in complete disappointment to all concerned, and entire failure. To Miss Wright it involved very considerable pecuniary loss, which, as I learned subsequently from my mother, she bore with the utmost fortitude and cheerfulness, but without any great access of wisdom as regarded her benevolent schemes for the political and economical improvement of human, and especially black, society. I never saw her again; but remember to have heard of her marrying a French teacher of languages at the close of a course of lectures given by her against the institution of matrimony. All that I heard from my mother and my brother of their connection with Miss Wright, of her administration of affairs at New Harmony, and her conduct when her experiment issued in failure and disappointment, left with me the impression of her genuinely high-minded enthusiasm, her unselfishness, bravery, and generosity, but, at the same time, of her deficiency in the qualities which can alone make departure from the world's beaten tracks—mill-horse tracks though they be—either wise, profitable, or safe. She had a fine and large intelligence, but not fine or large enough for going quite unpiloted across country.

Whether my mother resided any time at Nashoba I am not sure, but I think not. At all events, very shortly after her arrival in America she established herself at Cincinnati. And when it became evident that there was no prospect of permanent work for my brother in the business of regenerating the negroes, it was determined—by the advice of what Cincinnati friends I know not—that he should join my mother there, and undertake the establishment and conduct of an institution which, as far as I was able to understand the plan, was to combine the specialties of an athenæum, a lecture hall, and a bazaar! And it was when this enterprise had been decided upon, but before any steps had been taken for the realizing of it, that I accompanied my father on a visit to America.

When I returned from Winchester, in July, there were still many months before me of uncertainty whether I might get a vacancy at New College or not, and my father, having determined on going for a short visit to Cincinnati, proposed to take me with him. After what I have written in a previous chapter of my early tastes and proclivities, I need hardly say that the prospect of this travel was in the highest degree delightful to me. I am afraid that, at the time, any call to New College, which should have had the effect of preventing it, would have been to me a very unwelcome one. Our departure was fixed for September, and the intervening time was spent by me in preparations for the great adventure, very much such as Livingstone may be supposed to have made on quitting England for the "dark continent."

I was, as it seems to me now, still a very boyish boy, all ex-Wiccamical prefect as I was, and, I cannot help thinking, younger and more childish than the youngsters of equal age of the present generation.

The voyage, however, really was a bigger affair in those days than it has become in these times, for it was before the iron horse had been trained to cross the Atlantic. And my father made it a very much more serious business still by engaging for us berths in the steerage of a passenger ship. I hardly think that he would have done so had he been at all aware of what he was undertaking. It is true that he was undoubtedly hard pressed for money, though I have not now, and had not then, any such knowledge of his affairs as to enable me to judge to what degree he was straitened. But there was also about my father a sort of Spartan contempt for comfort, and determination not to expend money on his own personal well-being, which was a prominent feature in his character, and which, I have no doubt, contributed to the formation of his resolution to make this journey in the least costly manner possible.

But, as I have said, I think that he had no very clear notion of what a steerage passage across the Atlantic implied. As for me, if he had proposed to make the voyage on a raft I should have jumped at the offer! It was, in truth, a sufficiently severe experience. But, as I was then at eighteen, I should have welcomed the chance of making such an expedition, even if I had accurately realized all the accompaniments and all the details of it.

We went on board the good ship *Corinthian*, Captain Chadwick, bound for New York, in the September of 1828. Ship and captain were American.

I confess that my first feeling on entering the place which was to be my habitation during the next few weeks was one of dismay. It was not that the accommodation was rough. I cared little enough about that, and should have cared as little had it been much rougher. But it was the first time in my life that I had had any experience of the truth of the proverb that misfortune makes one acquainted with strange bedfellows! Of course there was in that part of the vessel allotted to the steerage passengers no sort of enclosure for the different berths, some dozen or score of them, in which the steerage passengers had to sleep. No sort of privacy either by day or by night was possible; add to which, the ventilation was very insufficient, and the whole place was, perhaps unavoidably, dirty to a revolting degree. My father almost at once betook himself to his berth, and rarely left it during the entire voyage—indeed, he was for the most part incapable of doing so, having been suffering from his usual sick headache more or less during the whole time. If the voyage was a bad time for me, it must have been far worse for him. Indeed, I was scarcely ever below except when attending on him.

Before the first night came I declared my intention of making no use of the berth assigned to me. Where was I to pass the night then? I said I should pass it on deck. I had a huge greatcoat, a regular " dreadnought," so called in those days, and made with innumerable capes; and with that I should do well enough during the September night. My declared intention brought an avalanche of ridicule down on my head, not only from my fellow-inhabitants of the steerage, but from the captain and his mates. A night on deck, or at the very most two, would make me glad and thankful enough for the shelter of my berth. I did not know what I was talking of, but should soon find out, etc.

Well, the first night passed! It was a fine moonlight. And I enjoyed it and the novelty of my surroundings keenly. I slept, wrapped in my capacious greatcoat, two or three hours at a time, and morning found me none the worse. The second night was less delightful! I was weary, and began to feel the need of sleep after a fashion to which I was more accustomed. And then came bad weather, wet and cold! I got some shelter in an erection on the deck called the "round-house;" but the want of proper rest was beginning to tell upon me, and the fatigue was very severe. I think that, despite my horror of the steerage and the world that inhabited it, I should have succumbed and accepted its shelter if my determination not to do so had been confined to my own breast, and no necessity had existed for triumphing over the ridicule and the unanimous prophecies of the other passengers and the ship's officers. As it was, I was safe not to yield!

I did not yield! Our voyage was rather longer than an average one, and during all the thirty-eight days that it lasted I never passed a night below, or went there at all save for the purpose of changing my clothes or attending on my father, who lay sick and suffering in his berth during almost the whole time. It was a severer experience than it may seem, probably, to the imagination of those who never made a similar experiment. When I reached New York I felt as if it would be heaven to go to sleep for a week.

We had one short spell of very bad weather, and were, as I subsequently learned, in considerable danger for an hour or so. We had been running all day before a fair wind exactly aft, which, continually increasing in violence, assumed at sun-down the force of a gale. Nevertheless, Captain Chadwick, against the advice of an old English merchant captain, who was a passenger, could not prevail on himself to lose the advantage of so good a wind, and determined to "carry on." But as the night advanced the wind continued to increase and the sea to rise, till the danger of being "pooped," if we continued to run before it, became too great to be neglected. But the danger of putting about, "broaching-to" I believe is the correct term, was also great.

It became necessary, however, to do this about midnight, and I was the only passenger on deck during the operation. The English merchant captain mentioned above kept running up for a few minutes at a time every now and then; but he had a wife and young children aboard, and would not remain long away from them. The good ship, as she came round into the trough of the sea, lay down on her side to such a degree that my body, as I clung to the bulwark on the weather-side, swung away to the leeward in such a sort that I was for a minute hanging from a hold above my head, instead of clinging to one at my side. And I saw and heard—very specially heard— every sail blown away from the yards. I heard, too, the shout of the men on the yards, "We can't get an inch," as they strove to reef. Much danger was occasioned to the men by the block at the foot of the mainsail remaining attached to the sail, which was blown about, before it could be secured, with a violence which knocked the cook's galley to atoms.

And all this I saw to my great delight. For I considered a storm at sea as a part of the experiences of a voyage which it would have been a great pity to have missed, and was altogether unaware that we were in any real danger. Towards daybreak the gale moderated, and before noon it was perfectly calm, and all hands were busy in bending a new suite of sails.

With all this I should have enjoyed the voyage immensely had it not been for the nature of the companionship to which I should have been condemned if I had not escaped from it in the manner I have described. The utter roughness of the accommodation, the scanty and not very delicate food, would all have signified to me in those days absolutely nothing. But I could not tolerate the companionship of the men and women with whom I should have lived. I could have no doubt tolerated it some twenty years later, but it was at that time too new to me. I take it that ill-luck had given us a rather specially bad lot as our destined companions in the steerage. I had seen quite enough of the laborers on the farm at Harrow to know what a man living with his family on a pound a week was like, and I could have managed to live, if necessary, with

such men for a week or two without any insuperable re-
pugnance.   But some of the denizens of that steerage *bol-
gia* were blackguards of a description quite new to me.

Two figures among them are still, after nearly sixty
years, present to my mental vision.   One was a large,
loosely-made, middle-aged man, who always wore a long
gray-serge dressing-gown.   He was accompanied by nobody belonging to him, and I never had the least idea
what grade or department of life he could have belonged
to.   His language, though horrible, as regards the ideas
conveyed by it, was grammatically far superior to that of
most of those around him; and he was very clever with
his hands, executing various little arrangements for his
own comfort with the skill of a carpenter, and almost with
that of an upholsterer.   His face was thoroughly bad,
with loose, baggy, flaccid, pale cheeks, and a great, coarse,
hanging under lip.   He always looked exceedingly dirty,
but, nevertheless, was always clean-shaved.   He was always talking, always haranguing those who would listen
to him; always extolling the country for which we were
bound and its institutions, and expressing the most ven-
omous hatred of England and all things English.   I used
to listen to him during my hours of attendance on my father with an excess of loathing which I doubt not I failed
to conceal from him, and which, acting like a strong brine,
has preserved his memory in my mind all these years.

The other was much less objectionable.   He was a
younger man and called himself a farmer, but his farming
had evidently run much to horse-dealing, and he dressed
in a horsey style.   He had a miserable, sickly wife with
him, who had once upon a time been pretty.   She wore
the remains of dresses that had once been smart, and was
by far the most slatternly woman I ever saw.   Her husband, so far as I could observe, did not ill-treat her, but
he was constantly saying unkind things in language which
should have made her blush, if she had not left all blushes
far behind her, and at which the other worse brute used
to laugh with obstreperous approbation.   He could sing,
too, as I thought at that time, very well, and used to sing
a song telling how " The farm I now hold on your honor's

estate is the same that my grandfather held," etc. The
tune of it runs in my head to this day; and I remember
thinking that if the song related the singer's own fortunes "his honor" must have gained by the change of ten-
ant, however many generations of ancestors may have held
it before him.

By the time our voyage came to an end I was pretty
nearly worn out by want of rest and night-and-day expos-
ure of weather. But, to own the truth honestly, I was
supported by a sense of pride in having sustained an
amount of fatigue which none other in the ship had, and
few probably could have, sustained, and which I had been
defied to sustain. And after I had had a sleep "the round
of the clock," as the phrase goes, I was none the worse.
Moreover, it was a matter of extreme consolation to me to
think that I was accumulating a store of strange experiences of a kind which nothing in my previous life had
seemed to promise me. But, above all, the approach to
New York, and the sight of the bay, was, I felt, more than
enough to repay me for all the discomfort of the voyage.
I thought it by far the grandest sight I had ever seen, as
indeed, it doubtless was.

I do not remember to have been much struck with the
town of New York. I remember thinking it had the look
of an overgrown colossal village, and that it was very different in appearance from any English city. It seemed to
me, too, that there was a strange contrast between the
roomy, clean, uncity-like appearance of the place, and the
apparent hurry and energetic ways of the inhabitants. I
remember also remarking the very generally youthful appearance of those who seemed to be transacting most of
the business of the place.

We were received most kindly by an old friend of my
parents, Mr. Wilkes, the uncle, I think, or, perhaps, great-
uncle of him who as Commodore Wilkes of the *Trent* subsequently became known to the world, as having very
nearly set his country and England by the ears! How
and why old Mr. Wilkes was a friend of my father's I do
not know, but suspect that it was through the medium of
some very old friends of my grandfather Milton, of the

name of Garnet. Two very old ladies of that name, spinster sisters, I remember to have seen at Brighton some
twenty or five-and-twenty years ago. I remember that
Mr. Wilkes struck me as a remarkably courteous and gentlemanlike old man, very English both in manners and
appearance, in a blue dress-coat and buff waistcoat, and
long white hair. I fancy that he was connected in some
way (by old friendship only, I imagine) with the Misses
Wright, and I gathered that he altogether disapproved of
Frances Wright's philanthropic Nashoba enterprise, and
consequently of the share in it which my father and mother, on behalf of my brother Henry, had undertaken. Of
the wisdom of his misgivings the result furnished abundant proof.

My recollections of the journey from New York to
Cincinnati are of a very fragmentary description; those of
so very many other journeys during the well-nigh sixty
years which have elapsed since it was performed have
nearly obliterated them. I remember being struck by the
uncomfortable roughness of all the lodging accommodation, as contrasted with the great abundance, and even,
as it appeared to me, luxury of the commissariat department.

We passed by Pittsburgh and crossed the Alleghany
Mountains, the former remaining in my memory as a
nightmare of squalor, and the latter as a vision of beauty
and delight. We travelled long days through districts of
untouched forest over the often described "corduroy"
roads. I was utterly disappointed by the forests; all that
I saw of them appeared to me a miserable collection of
lank, unwholesome-looking, woebegone stems, instead of
Windsor Forest on a vastly increased scale, which was, I
take it, what I expected. I remember, too, being much
struck by the performance of the drivers of the stages
over the corduroy roads aforesaid, and often over boggy
tracts of half-reclaimed forest amid the blackened stumps
of burned trees. The things they proposed to themselves
to accomplish, and did accomplish without coming to
grief, other than shaking every tooth in the heads of their
passengers, would have made an English coachman's hair

stand on end. To have seen them at their work over a decent bit of road would, on the other hand, have provoked the laughter and contempt of the same critics. Arms and legs seemed to take an equal part in the work; the whip was never idle, and the fatigue must have been excessive. I do not think that any man could have driven fifty miles at a stretch over those roads.

Cincinnati was reached at last. The journey to me had been delightful in the highest degree, simply from the novelty of everything. As things were done at that time it was one of very great fatigue, but in those days I seemed to be incapable of fatigue. At all events it was all child's play in comparison with my crossing the ocean in the good ship *Corinthian*.

We found my mother and two sisters and brother Henry well, and established in a roomy, bright-looking house, built of wood, and all white with the exception of the green Venetian blinds. It stood in its own "grounds," but these grounds consisted of a large field, uncultivated save for a few potatoes in one corner of it; and the whole appearance of the place was made unkempt-looking — not squalid, because everything was too new and clean-looking for that—by uncompleted essays towards the making of a road from the entrance-gate to the house, and by fragments of boarding and timber, which it had apparently been worth no one's while to collect after the building of the house was completed. With all this there was an air of roominess and brightness which seemed to me very pleasant. The house was some five or ten minutes' walk from what might be considered the commencement of the town, but it is no doubt by this time, if it still stands at all, more nearly in the centre of it.

CHAPTER VIII.

My father and I remained between five and six months at Cincinnati, and my remembrances of the time are pleasant ones. In the way of amusement, to the best of my recollection, there was not much besides rambling over the country with my brother, the old companion of those London rambles which seemed to me then almost as far off in the dim past as they do now. But we were free, tied to no bounds, and very slightly to any hours. And I enjoyed those rambles immensely. I do not remember that the country about Cincinnati struck me as especially interesting or beautiful, and the Ohio, *la belle rivière,* distinctly disappointed me. But it was a new world, and every object, whether animate or inanimate, was for us full of interest.

Looking back to those Cincinnati days, I have to say that I liked the Americans, principally, I think, at that time, as far as my remembrances serve, because some quality in their manners and behavior had the effect of making me less shy with them than with others. I was then, and to a great degree have never ceased to be, painfully shy. How miserably this weakness afflicts those who suffer from it, how it disqualifies them and puts them at a disadvantage in circumstances constantly recurring, those who are free from it cannot imagine. And they glorify their superiority by saying all sorts of hard things to those who suffer from shyness—very unjustly in my opinion. Shyness proceeds in almost all cases, I should say probably in all, from diffidence. A man who thinks sufficiently well of himself is never shy. Did any one ever see a vain man shy? I do not think the Americans are an especially vain people; but there are specialties of their social condition which lead to every American citizen's estimate of himself, from the cradle upwards, being equal to his estimate of any other man. And one consequence of this is a certain frank and unconstrained manner in their intercourse with strangers or new acquaintances which is invaluable to a shy man.

I remember an incident of my first year at Winchester, when I was between ten and eleven, which is illustrative of the misery which shyness may inflict. A boy about a year my senior, and taller than I, was constantly annoying and bullying me, and one day in the presence of a considerable number of onlookers challenged me to fight him. I refused, and naturally, of course, was considered a coward, and had to endure the jibes and taunts due to one. The explanation of my refusal of my enemy's challenge, however—never offered to mortal ear before the confiding of it to this page—was not that I was afraid to fight, but was too shy to do so. It was not that I could not face all that his fists could do to me, as I shortly afterwards showed him; but I could not bring myself to face the publicity of the proposed contest—the formality of it, the ring, in the centre of which I should have to perform, and to be a spectacle, and have my performance criticised. All this was too absolutely intolerable to me. But early the next morning, chancing to catch my adversary "in meads" with only one or two others near him, I attacked him, to his utter astonishment and dismay, and without very much difficulty gave him as good a pummelling as my heart desired.

Whether this incident originated the nickname "Badger," which I bore at Winchester, as being one indisposed to fight, but likely to prove dangerous if "drawn," I do not know.

It was during our stay at Cincinnati that my father and I paid a visit to an establishment of "Shaking Quakers," as they were called, and I believe called themselves, at Mount Lebanon, about five-and-twenty miles from Cincinnati. We were hospitably received, paying a moderate remuneration for our lodging and food. Both these were supplied of exactly the same kind and quality as used by the inmates of the establishment, and were, though very simple and plain, admirable in quality. The extensive farm on which the Shakers lived, and which they cultivated by their own labor, was their own property, having been originally purchased at a time when land was of very small market value, and brought under tillage by the labor of the members. But nothing in the nature of private property was held or retained by any one.

The number of women was about equal to that of the men. But there were no children. None were born in the establishment, and no man or woman joining it was allowed to bring any. Nor was marriage nor connubial life in any sort recognized or permitted. And, of course, these conditions rendered the whole experiment wholly useless as an example for the conduct of any ordinary community, or for an indication of what may be economically accomplished for such.

We did not eat in company with the members, though faring, as I have said, exactly as they did, but we were present at their religious worship, or at what stood in the place of such. This consisted in a species of dance, if the uncouth jumping or "shaking" which they practised could be so called. The men and women were assembled and danced in the same room, but not together. They jumped and "shook" themselves in two divided bodies. Any spectator would be disposed to imagine that the whole object of the performance was bodily exercise. It seemed to be carried on to the utmost extent that breath and bodily fatigue would permit. Many were mopping the perspiration from their faces. No laughing or gladness or exhilaration whatever appeared to accompany or to be caused by the exercise. All was done with an air of perfect solemnity.

All the men and all the women seemed to be in the enjoyment of excellent health. Most of them seemed to be somewhat more than well nourished — rather tending to obesity. They were florid, round-faced, sleek and heavy in figure. I observed no laughter, and very little conversation among them. The women were almost all in the prime of life, and many young. But there was a singular absence of good looks among them. Some had regular

features enough, but they were all heavy, fat, dull-look-
ing, like well-kept animals. I could not spy one pair of
bright eyes in the place. All, men and women, were quite
simply but thoroughly well and cleanly dressed, not altogether, as I remember, in uniform, but with very great
uniformity. Gray cloth of very fair quality was the prevailing material of dress for both sexes.

Various articles useful for country life of the simpler
sort were manufactured by them for sale. And I learned
that all the articles so made had throughout the country
side a high reputation for excellence in their kinds. And
there could be no doubt that the Shaker community was
thriving and probably accumulating money. To what
object they should do so seems a difficult question.

I heard of no sickness or infirmity among them. Such
there must of course have been occasionally, and I presume
that the infirm, the sick, and the dying must have been
cared for.

These people lived in perfect equality; and their community proved that a community of men and women (un-
burdened with children) could by an amount of labor by
no means excessive, or even arduous, provide themselves
with an ample sufficiency of all things needful for their
material well-being and comfort. It is true that they paid
no rent, but I am disposed to think, from what I heard,
that they might have paid a moderate rent for the land
they cultivated, and still continued to do well. But it was
impossible to avoid the reflection that this well-being was
merely that of well-kept animals. There was an air of unmistakable stupidity over the whole establishment. Nobody laughed. Nobody seemed to converse. There was
excellent lodging, clothing, and food in plenty till they
died! And that was all. Perhaps it may be fairly assumed that no one, save people of very mediocre powers
and intelligence, had ever felt tempted to become a Shaking Quaker. But it can hardly be said that their experiment exhibited a very tempting sample of a world to be
modelled after their fashion!

It has been said by some observers that this materially
flourishing establishment has so many points of similarity

with the conventual institutions of Roman Catholicism that it may be considered as supplying the same natural want to which those institutions are supposed to correspond, an asylum, that is to say, for those of either sex, who, from various circumstances of fortune, or of temperament, are unfitted for the struggles of the world, and find themselves left stranded on the banks of the great social stream. The impressions I received from my visit to Mount Lebanon do not dispose me to accept any such explanation of the Shaking Quaker *raison d'être*. I saw no signs whatever, among either the men or the women, of individuals who had been tempest-tossed in any of the world's maelstroms, or of temperaments for which the contemplative life might be supposed to have had greater attractions than the active life of the world. The characteristics which were most notably observable were of a diametrically opposed kind. One would say that they were men and women thoroughly and unanimously minded to make for themselves in the most judiciously contrived manner a comfortable and clean sty, with abundant and perennial supply of everything needed for their bodily wants. Whether love or hatred, as they are found to exist in monastic communities, existed among them, of course I had not sufficient opportunity for even guessing. But assuredly it may be said with some confidence of not being mistaken, that neither those nor any other passions had left any of their usual marks on those sleek bodies and placid, meaningless faces. One would have said that the main and engrossing object of existence at Mount Lebanon was digesting.

I have recently learned that the community continues to exist under the same conditions as those under which I saw it.

I made acquaintance, I remember, at Cincinnati, with Mr. Longworth, who was, or became well known throughout America for his successful efforts in viticulture. He was one of those men who, being by no means entertaining companions on any other subject, become so, if you will talk to them upon their own. I have often thought that the "sink the shop" maxim is a great mistake. If I

6

had to pass an hour with a chimney-sweep I should probably find him very good company if he would talk exclusively about sweeping chimneys. Mr. Longworth was extremely willing to talk exclusively on schemes for the introduction of the vine into the Western States, and on that subject was well worth listening to. I find a note in a diary, written by me at that time, to the effect that he was then (1828) employing a large number of Germans on his estate at Columbia, near Cincinnati, at a little less than one shilling a day and their food. I remarked that this seemed scarcely in accord with the current accounts of the high price of labor in the States, and was answered that his—Mr. Longworth's—bailiff had said to him the other day, "If those men get to Cincinnati they will be *spoiled*"—a little touch which rather vividly illustrates one phase of the difference made in all things by railway communication.

But the most remarkable acquaintance we made at Cincinnati was Hiram Powers, the subsequently well-known sculptor, with whom I again fell in many years afterwards at Florence, when he was living there with his large family, having just acquired a great and lucrative degree of celebrity by his statue of "The Greek Slave," purchased by an Englishman whom my mother had taken to visit his studio. I do not know by what chance she had first become acquainted with him at Cincinnati.

He was at that time about eighteen years old, much about my own contemporary; and my mother at once remarked him as a young man of exceptional talent and promise. He was then seeking to live by his wits, with every prospect of finding that capital abundantly sufficient for the purpose. There was a Frenchman named Dorfeuille at Cincinnati, who had established what he called a "museum"—a show, in fact, in which he collected anything and everything that he thought would excite the curiosity of the people and induce them to pay their quarter dollars for admission. And this M. Dorfeuille, cleverly enough appreciating young Powers' capabilities of being useful to him, had engaged him as factotum and general manager of his establishment. Powers, casting about for

some new "attraction" for the museum, chanced one evening to talk over the matter with my mother. And it occurred to her to suggest to him to get up a representation
of one of Dante's *bolgias* as described in the *Inferno*. The
nascent sculptor, with his imaginative brain, artistic eye,
and clever fingers, caught at the idea on the instant. And
forthwith they set to work, my mother explaining the
poet's conceptions, suggesting the composition of "tableaux," and supplying details, while Powers designed and
executed the figures and the necessary *mise en scène*.

Some months of preparation were needed before the
work could be accomplished, and Dorfeuille, I remember,
began to have misgivings as to recouping himself for the
not inconsiderable cost. But at last all was ready. A
vast amount of curiosity had been excited in the place by
preliminary announcements, and the result was an immense
success. I have preserved for nearly sixty years, and have
now before me, the programme and bill of the exhibition
as it was drawn up by my mother. It is truly a curiosity
in its kind, and I am tempted to reproduce it here. But
it is too long, occupying four pages of a folio sheet. There
are quotations from the *Inferno*, translated by my mother
(no copy of any published translation being then and there
procurable), explanations of the author's meaning, and descriptions in very bugaboo style, and in every variety of
type, with capitals of every sort of size, of all the horrors
of the supposed scene.

The success was so complete, and the curiosity, not only
of the Cincinnati world but of the farmers round about and
their families, was so eager, that the press of spectators
was inconveniently great, and M. Dorfeuille began to fear
that his properties might be damaged by indiscreet desires
to touch as well as see. So Powers arranged a slight metal
rod as a barrier between the show and the spectators, and
contrived to charge it with electricity, while an announcement, couched in terrible and mystic terms and in verse,
by my mother, to the effect that an awful doom awaited
any mortal rash enough to approach the mysteries of the
nether world too nearly, was appended to the doors and
walls. The astonishment and dismay felt, and the laugh-

ter provoked, by those who were rash enough to do so, may be imagined!

Upon the whole those autumn and winter months passed pleasantly, and have left pleasant recollections in my memory. Doubtless there were many causes of anxiety for my elders; but to the best of my remembrance they touched us young people very lightly. We had many more or less agreeable acquaintances, and I have a vivid recollection of the pleasure I received from the fact that they all belonged to types that were altogether new to me—if indeed it could be said of people, to me so apparently unclassifiable, that they belonged to any type at all. The cleverest among them was a Dr. Price, a very competent physician with a large practice, a foolish, friendly little wife, and a pair of pretty daughters. He was a jovial, florid, rotund little man who professed, more even, as I remember, to my astonishment than my horror, perfect atheism. His wife and daughters used to go to church without apparently producing the slightest interruption of domestic harmony. "La! the doctor don't think anything more of the Bible than of an old newspaper!" Mrs. Price would say; "but then doctors, you know, they have their own opinions!" And the girls used to say, "Papa is an atheist," just as they would have said of the multiform persuasions of their acquaintances, "Mr. This is a Baptist," and "Mrs. That is a Methodist." And I remember well the confusion and displacement occasioned in my mind by finding that Dr. Price did not seem on the whole to be an abandoned man, and enjoyed to a high degree the respect of his townsmen.

The two pretty daughters, girls of eighteen or nineteen, used to have at their house frequent dances. We were constant and welcome guests, but, alas! I was not—either then or ever since—a dancer; the reason being precisely the same as that which prevented my fighting at Winchester, as above recorded. I was too shy! In other words, I had too low an opinion of myself, of my performance as a dancer, should I attempt it, and, above all, of my acceptability as a partner, ever to overcome my diffidence.

I was, as I have said when speaking of my earliest years, by no means a prepossessing child, and as a young man I was probably less so. I had never any sort of pretension to good looks or to elegance of figure. I was five feet eight in height, and thick, sturdy, and ungainly in make, healthy and pure in complexion and skin as a baby, but with an "abbreviated nose"—as George Eliot says of me in finding me like a portrait of Galileo—and pale-colored, lanky hair. All which would not have signified a button if I could have been as ignorant of the facts in question as hundreds of my contemporaries, laboring under equal disadvantages, were in their own case; but I was *not* ignorant of these facts, and the consciousness of them constituted a most mischievous and disqualifying little repast off the tree of knowledge. It has, among many other results, prevented me from ever dancing. I should have liked much, very much, to do so. I was abundantly well disposed to seek the society of the other sex. Though I never had a very perfect ear for tune, I had a markedly strong perception of time and feeling for rhythm, and therefore should probably have danced well. But the persuasion that any girl whom I might have induced to dance with me would have far rather been dancing with somebody else was too much for me!

I should unquestionably have been a far happier young fellow if I had undoubtingly believed myself to have been adapted in all respects to attract the favorable attention and conciliate the liking of all I met. But can I even now, looking back over the vista of sixty years, regret that I was able to see myself as others saw me, and wish that I had inhabited that fool's paradise which is planted with conceits in place of insights?

So I got no dancing with the Cincinnati girls. But there were theatricals, also, at the house of Dr. and Mrs. Price, and in those I did not refuse to join. It may seem that this would have been at least as great a trial to a shy man as any other form of self-exhibition; but it was not so. I think, so far as I am able at this distance of time to examine my mind upon the subject, it would have been impossible for me to attempt the representation of any personage intended to be attractive to the spectator, or such as to be confounded in his mind with my own personality.

But it was proposed that I should act Falstaff in the "Merry Wives of Windsor," and to this the difficulties referred to did not apply. I played Falstaff with immense success to an assuredly not very critical audience. My own impression, however, is, that I did it well. I think that I had reason to flatter myself, as I did flatter myself at the time, that all those who heard me understood the play and enjoyed the humor of the situations better than they had done before.

I have played many parts since, on various stages, in different parts of the world, but that, I think, was my sole Shakesperian attempt. And the members of that merry and kindly theatrical company! They have made their last exit from the larger boards we are all treading, every man and woman, every lad and lass of them. Not one but the old Falstaff of the company remains to write this chronicle of sixty years since!

There were very few formal meetings among the notabilities of the little Cincinnati world of that time, but there was an amount of homely friendliness that impressed me very favorably; and there was plenty of that generous and abounding hospitality which subsequent experience has taught me to consider an especially American characteristic. I have since that time shared the splendid hospitality of splendid American hosts, and I have been under American roofs where there was little save a heartfelt welcome to offer. But the heart-warming effect produced by the latter was the same in both cases. How often have we all sat at magnificent boards where the host's too evident delight consisted in giving you what you could not give him, and in the exulting manifestation of his magnificence. This is very rarely the feeling of an American host. He is thinking not of himself, but of you; and the object he is striving at when giving you of his best is that you should enjoy yourself while under his roof; that you should have, as he would phrase it, "a good time." And, upon my word, he almost invariably succeeds.

Nor were the Cincinnati girls in 1829 like the New York belles of 1887. But there was much of the same charm about them, which arises from unaffected and un-

self-regarding desire to please. American girls are accused of being desperate flirts. But many an Englishman
has been deceived by imagining that the smiles and cheerfulness and laughing chatter of some charming girl new
to Europe were intended for *his* special benefit, when they
were, in truth, only the perfectly natural and unaffected
outcome of a desire to do her duty in that state of life to
which it has pleased God to call her! Only beams falling,
like those of the sun, upon the just and the unjust alike!

There is another point on which Americans, both men
and women, are very generally called over the coals by
English people, as I think somewhat unreasonably. They
are, it is said, everlastingly talking about the greatness
and grandeur of their country, and never easy without ex-
torting admissions of this. All this is to a great extent
true; at least to this extent, that an American is always
pleased to hear the greatness of his country recognized.
But when I remember the thoroughness with which that
cardinal article of an Englishman's faith (sixty years ago!),
that every Englishman could thrash three Frenchmen, was
enforced with entire success on my youthful mind, I can
hardly find it in my conscience to blame an American's
pride in his country. Why, good heavens! what an insensible block he would be if he was *not* proud of his country,
to whose greatness, it is to be observed, each individual American now extant has contributed in a greater degree than can be said to be the case as regards England
and every extant Englishman; inasmuch as our position
has been won by the work of, say a thousand years, and
his by that of less than a century. Surely the creation of
the United States as they now exist within that time *is*
such a feat of human intelligence and energy as the world
has never before seen, and is scarcely likely to see again.
I confess that the expression of American patriotism is
never offensive to me. I feel somewhat as the old Cornish
wrestler felt, who said, with immense pride, when he was
told that his son had "whopped" the whole parish, "Ay,
I should think so! Why, he has whopped *me* afore now!"

Yes! I liked the Americans as I first made acquaintance
with them almost among the backwoods at Cincinnati sixty

years ago; and I like them as I have since known them better. For I have seen a great deal of them; far more than an Englishman living at home would be likely to do, during my many years' residence in Italy. The American "colony," to use the common, though incorrect phrase, is large both at Florence and in Rome; of late years fully as large, I think, as that from England. And not only do the two bodies associate indiscriminately with each other in perfect neighborliness and good-fellowship, but they do so, forming one single oasis in the midst of the surrounding Continental life, in a manner which makes one constantly feel how infinitely nearer an American is to an Englishman in ideas, habits, ways, and civilization than either of them are to any other denizen of earth's surface.

I was sorry when the time came for us to leave Cincinnati, though, as usual with me, the prospect of the journey, which we were to make by a different route from that by which we had travelled westward, was a joy and a consolation. My father and I returned, leaving my mother, my two sisters, still quite children, and my brother Henry at Cincinnati. The proposed institution—bazaar, athenæum, lecture-hall, or whatever it was to be, or to be called—had been determined on, and the site, to the best of my recollection, selected and purchased; but nothing had yet been done towards raising the building. Contracts had been entered into, and my father was on his return to London to send out a quantity of goods for the carrying out of the commercial part of the scheme.

He did so. But I had no share in or knowledge of the operations undertaken for this purpose, and may therefore as well relate here the upshot of the ill-fated enterprise. I learned subsequently that very large quantities of goods were sent out of kinds and qualities totally unfitted for the purpose. The building was duly raised, and I have been told by Americans who had seen it that it was a handsome and imposing one. But the net result was disaster and ruin. My father, having been educated to be a chancery barrister, was a good one. He became a farmer with no training or knowledge necessary for the calling, and it proved ruinous to him. He then embarked on this commercial speculation, which, inasmuch as he was still more ignorant of all such matters than he was even of farming, turned out still more entirely disastrous.

My father and I, as I have said, did not return from Cincinnati to New York by the same route by which we had travelled westward. We went by the lakes and Niagara, visiting, also, Trenton Falls *en route*. Had I written this page immediately after my journey, instead of sixty years after, I might have been justified in attempting—and no doubt should, in any case, have attempted—some description of the great "water-privilege," which I saw as it will never be seen again. The two great cataclysms which have occurred since that time have entirely changed, and in a great measure spoiled, the great sight. And now, I am told, this "so-called nineteenth century" (as I read the other day in the fervid discourse of some pessimist orator) intends before it closes to utilize the lake as a mill-dam and the falls as so much "power."

I remember that I enjoyed Trenton most. It appealed much less, of course, to the imagination and the sense of wonder, but far more to one's appreciation of the beautiful.

Our Niagara visit was in a great measure spoiled by my father's illness. He was suffering from one of his worst sick-headaches. He dragged himself painfully to the usual spot near the hotel whence the fall is commanded, and, having looked, got back to his bed. I had plenty of hours at my disposal for rambling in all directions, but, as usual with me, had not a coin of any sort in my pocket. The fall and its environs were not as jealously locked and gated and guarded as has been the case since; but I was assured that I should be very unwise to attempt to penetrate below and behind the fall without a guide, and I should have been most willing to employ one had I possessed the means. But to lose the opportunity of enjoying a sight to which I had so eagerly looked forward was out of the question, and I did succeed in making my way by the slippery and rather terrible path behind the fall, rewarded by an effect of the sun on the sheet of falling water as perfect and admirable as if it had been ordered expressly for me,

6*

and none the worse for the enterprise save returning to the inn as thoroughly drenched as if I had been dragged through the fall! Little enough I cared for that in those days!

I may mention here one of those singular coincidences which, though in reality so frequently occurring, are objected to in a novelist's pages as passing the bounds of credibility. Many years after the date of my visit to Niagara the mother of my present wife was there, and saw from the balcony of the hotel a boat with two rowers in it, who had incautiously approached too near the fall, carried over it! Her account of the horror of the sight, and of the sudden and evident despair of the frantically struggling rowers was very impressive, and hardly less so when I heard it for the second time from an American met by chance in Italy, who, sitting in that same balcony at that same hour, had witnessed the same catastrophe!

At New York we were again most kindly and cordially received by Mr. Wilkes, who gave my father much advice respecting his projected Cincinnati venture—advice wholly, as I take it, ignored.

Taught by experience, however, my father did not attempt a second steerage passage. We came back comfortably enough, and had an entirely prosperous voyage, the result being that my remembrances of it are very far less vivid than those of my steerage experience. We reached England in March, and again took up our abode at Harrow Weald, where I, with such very imperfect means and appliances as were at my disposition, was to employ the abundant hours in preparing, in accordance with my own unassisted lights, for the university.

Bad, however, as my father's circumstances were at this time, and little pleasant in any way as was our life in the farmhouse at Harrow Weald, I remember an excursion made by him and me, the only object of which, I think, could have been amusement. My father had an old friend named Skinner (no relative of the vicar of my uncle Meetkerke's parish of Julians, of whom I have spoken in a former chapter), who was the rector of a parish near Bath. He was a widower, living with an only daughter, and was, I remember, an enthusiastic student of ancient British history in connection with the localities around him. One of the two days we remained with him was devoted to a visit to Cheddar Cliffs. Mr. Skinner mounted us, and we rode a *partie carrée*, he and my father, Miss Skinner and I, some twelve or fourteen miles to Cheddar. She was a pretty, bright girl, and I found her a charming companion in a scramble to the top of the cliffs overlooking the gorge through which the road runs. We became, indeed, such good friends, that, on our homeward ride, we gradually drew away from our respective parents and reached home a good half-hour before they did — which procured for us both a scolding for knocking the horses up.

It was roughish riding, too, as I remember, for the road was very different from what I found it some months ago, when, revisiting Cheddar, I saw on the top of the hill a notice to bicycle riders that the descent is dangerous for them.

CHAPTER IX.

As the year wore on without any prospect of a vacancy at New College, it became necessary to decide what should be done as regards sending me to the university. My father was very ill able to support the expense of this. But I had received from Winchester two exhibitions—all that the college had in its power to bestow — and he was very unwilling that I should be unable to avail myself of them.

Concomitantly with continued increase in the frequency and intensity of his headaches, my father's irritability of temper had increased to a degree which made him a very difficult person to live with. For simple assent to his utterances of an argumentative nature did not satisfy him; he *would* be argued with. Yet argument produced irritability leading to scenes of painful violence, which I had reason to fear hastened the return of his suffering. But the greatest good, in his opinion, that could then be achieved for me, was that I should have a university education ; and this he was steadfastly minded to procure for me at any cost of pressure and privation.

And then the question arose, at what college should I matriculate ?

My father eventually selected Alban Hall — a singular and hardly a judicious choice in any case, but which under the circumstances, as they subsequently arose, proved a disastrous one. My father's financial position was at the time such that it would have seemed reasonable that he should have been in a great measure guided in his choice by the consideration of expense. But such was not the case. For Alban Hall was at that time by no means a specially inexpensive place of academical residence. No ! the ruling motive was to place me under Whately, who

had about four years previously been appointed by Lord
Granville Principal of Alban Hall. My father, as I have
mentioned, was a "Liberal," and Whately's Liberalism
was the point in his character by which he was most
known to the world in general. I do not think that any
personal acquaintance, or even contact, had ever existed
between my father and Whately. The connecting link I
take to have been Whately's friend Senior. Whately's
Liberalism certainly, and, I think I may say, my father's
also, would have made excellent Conservatism at the present day. But in those days the new principal of Alban
Hall stood out in strong contrast with the intellectual
attitude and habits of thought of Oxford. And this was
the leading motive of my father's choice.

I know not how the case may be now, but in those days
it was a decided disadvantage socially and academically
to belong to any one of the "halls," instead of to a college. But of all this side of Oxford life my father, who
had been a New College man in the days when New College exercised its ancient privilege of presenting its members for their degree without submitting them for any examination in the schools, knew nothing. In his day the
New College man before the vice-chancellor for his degree,
instead of using the formula prescribed for every other
member of the university, to the effect that having satisfied the examiners he begged his degree (*peto gradum*),
said, "Having satisfied my college, I demand my degree"
(*postulo gradum*). This has long been voluntarily abandoned by New College, which on the enactment of the
new statute for examinations, of course, saw that the re-
tention of it necessarily excluded them from "honors."
But in the old day it had inevitably the effect of causing
New College men to live very much in a world of their
own.

Alban Hall had been, previously to Whately's time, a
sort of "refuge for the destitute" intellectually, or academically; as were for the most part the other halls at
that period. This reproach Whately at once set himself
to remove from Alban Hall, and had altogether removed
by the time I joined the society. It would be difficult to

say what general operating influence had brought together the score or so of members who then constituted that society. They were certainly not intellectually superior to the average undergraduate of the time. Neither were they in any wise inferior in general respectability. But there was no cohesion, no general prevailing character. We seemed like a collection of waifs thrown together by as many different sets of circumstances as there were individuals. I suppose all had been brought there by some personal connection with, or respect for, either Dr. Whately, or for Mr. Hinds, the excellent vice-principal, who subsequently became Bishop of Norwich. There was, I remember, a knot of some three or four West Indians, who formed some little exception to what I have said of a general absence of cohesion.

The time which I spent under Dr. Whately's authority and tuition led me to form a very exalted opinion of his intellectual capacity, high principle, and lofty determination to do what he deemed to be his duty. But I do not think that he was the right man in the right place.

His daughter, Miss Jane Whately, in her excellent and most interesting life of the archbishop, published some twenty years ago, writes:

"Teaching was, indeed, the occupation most peculiarly suited to his powers and tastes. He had a remarkable faculty of drawing out the mind of the learner, by leading him step by step, and obliging him to think for himself. He used to say that he believed himself to be one of the few teachers who could train a young person of retentive memory for words, without spoiling him. The temptation to the student in such cases is to rehearse by rote the rules or facts he had learned, without exercising his powers of thought; while one whose powers of recollection were less perfect would be forced to reflect and consider what was *likely* to be written or said on such a point by the writer, and thus to learn more intelligently and less mechanically. The cure for this tendency in young persons who learned quickly by rote he effected by asking them questions, substantially the same as those in the text-book, but which they must answer in their own words, making them draw conclusions from axioms already laid down. In this manner he was able successfully to teach mathematics to many who had been apparently unable to master the first principles, and often to ground them in the elements of Euclid, better than some mathematicians whose actual attainments were far beyond his own. Both in this branch and in logic, as in all other studies, he always commenced analytically and ended synthetically; first drawing out the mind of the learner, by making him give the *substance* of the right answer, and then requiring the exact technical form of it in words."

This must strike all, who remember Whately's teaching, as evidently true. But it in no wise leads me to modify the opinion above expressed as to his adaptation for the position in which I knew him. The style of teaching described by his biographer, if ever suitable at all for a college lecture-room, could only be so in the case of a collection of pupils far superior intellectually to those with whom (with one or two exceptions, notably that of Mr. Wall, whose subsequent career at Oxford did credit to his Alban Hall training) Dr. Whately had to deal. Miss Whately describes a teacher whose influence in *tête-à-tête* teaching over a clever pupil would be quite invaluable. But he was always firing far over the heads of his hearers; and I do not think that his method was adapted to driving, pushing, hustling an idle and very backward and unprepared collection of youths through their "little-go" and "pass," *quod erat in votis*. Most of this necessary driving fell to the share of Hinds, who was fitted for far higher work, but was patient, kind, laborious, and conscientious to the utmost degree.

Miss Whately's book, mainly by virtue of the great number of the archbishop's letters contained in it, succeeds in giving a very just and vivid notion of her father's character and tone of mind. She is hardly justified, I think, by facts, in speaking of the "delicacy of his consideration for the feelings of others." A little circumstance that I well remember scarcely seems to indicate the possession of any such quality. It was about the time when the then burning question of parliamentary reform was exercising the minds of all men. A large party of undergraduates were dining at Whately's table—such invitations were usually given by him in every term—and Mrs. Whately, at the head of the long table, was asking the young man who sat next her what was the general opinion in the hall on the Reform question, when Whately, who at the bottom of the table had overheard her, called out, "Why don't you ask what the bedmakers think?" I have little doubt that the opinion of the bed-makers might have been ascertained with an equal, or perhaps greater, degree of profit. But I cannot think that the principal showed much "delicacy of considera-tion" for the feelings of his guests.

Perhaps a degree of roughness akin to this, though hardly altogether of the same sort, contributed to increase that strong feeling of dislike for Whately which, outside his own Oriel, was pretty generally felt in Oxford, and which was mainly caused by more serious objections to his political, and in some degree religious, liberalism.

I fear that I profited very little by his tuition at Alban Hall, doubtless chiefly from my own fault and idleness. But other causes contributed also to the result. The classical lectures were such as I had left a long way be-hind me. No study on my part was necessary to hold my own in the lecture-room by the side of my fellows in the team. Yet, of course, it was easy for such a teacher as Whately to perceive that I was trusting to Winchester work rather than to his instruction. And naturally this did not please him. I think, too, that he had a prejudice against public schools in general, and that for some reason or other he disliked Winchester in particular. I remem-ber his saying to me once—though I totally forget on what occasion—"We don't want any New-College ways here, sir!" I told him that I feared I did not deserve the compliment of being supposed capable of bringing any such there. And the reply failed to mollify him.

Those who are old enough to remember anything of the social aspects of Oxford at that day, and, indeed, any who have read the excellent biography of Archbishop Whately by his daughter, know that he was exceedingly unpopular among "the dons," his contemporaries. This was due partly to the opinions he held on matters social, political, and religious, partly to those which prejudiced minds far inferior to his own supposed him to hold, but partly also to his own personal ways and manners. I think I know, and indeed I think I knew when I was his pupil, enough of the fibre and calibre of his mind to feel sure that he was greatly the intellectual superior to most of those of similar position around him. And I suppose that the world in general has by this time come to the conclusion that in respect of most of those opinions, which were then most obnoxious to the world in which he lived, Whately was right and his adversaries wrong. But he was not the man to win acceptance for new ideas in any society. The temper of his mind was in a high degree autocratical. He was born to be a benevolent and beneficent despot. His daughter, speaking of the painful experiences that awaited him when he became Archbishop of Dublin, says that " opposition was painful to his disposition."

Doubtless the principal of Alban Hall, thoroughly congenial to him as was at that time the social atmosphere of the common room of his own Oriel, would have felt himself much out of his element in most of the common rooms of Oxford. I remember a dear old man, Dr. Johnson, of Magdalen, who was greatly beloved by his own society, and a universal favorite with all who knew him. He was a high, though not altogether dry, right divine man (*divino* rightly spelled, be it understood, and not with an " e," as in *jure de vino*), and used to maintain that the lineal descendants of the last Stuarts were still the rightful sovereigns of England. Sometimes a knot of youngsters would cluster around him, with, " But now, Dr. Johnson, do you really and truly believe that the present Duke of Modena is your lawful sovereign?" " Well, boy," the doctor would say when thus pressed, " *after dinner I do.*"

This was not the sort of man whom Whately would have tolerated, for though full of wit, as I have said, he was utterly devoid of any tincture of humor.

Those were the days when it used to be said that the rule at Magdalen respecting preferment tenable together with a fellowship, was, " Hold your tongue, and you may hold anything else."

It was supposed, I remember, at that day that there was to a certain special degree an antagonism and dislike between him and Dr. Shuttleworth, the warden of New College. There was a story current to the effect that the brusquerie of the principal of Alban Hall was upon one

occasion exhibited in an offensive manner in the drawing-
room of the warden of New College, when not only men
but ladies were present. Whately had a habit of sitting in all sorts of uncouth postures on his chair. He
would balance himself, while nursing one leg over the
knee of the other, on the two hind legs of his chair, or
even on one of them, and was indulging in gymnastics of
this sort when the leg of the chair suddenly snapped, and
he, a large and heavy man, rolled on the floor. He was a
man of far too much real pith and *aplomb* to be unneces-
sarily disconcerted at such an accident. But the story
ran that he manifested his disregard for it by simply tossing the offending and crippled chair into a corner, and
taking another as he proceeded with what he was saying
without one word of apology to his hostess.

If it was true that there was any such special feeling of
antagonism between Whately and Shuttleworth, it was a
pity; for assuredly there were very few, if any, men among
the heads of colleges of that day better calculated by
power and originality of mind, and in many respects by
liberality of thinking, to understand and foregather with
Whately than the warden of New College.

Shuttleworth was, and had the reputation of being, an
especially witty man. And I consider Whately to have
been the wittiest man I ever knew. But it is true that
their wit was of a very different character. Whately was
not a man fitted to shine in society, unless it were the society of those prepared by knowledge of and regard for
him to recognize his undisputed right to be the acknowledged leader of it. Shuttleworth was, on the contrary,
eminently calculated to contribute more than his share to
the most brilliant social intercourse. He had, with abundance of solid sweetmeat at the bottom of the trifle, a
sparkling store of that froth of wit which is most accepted
as the readiest and pleasantest social small change. Whately's wit was not of the kind which ever set any "table on
a roar." It was of that higher and deeper kind, which
consists in prompt perception, not of the superficial resemblances in dissimilar things, but in the underlying resemblances disclosed only to the eye capable of appreciating

at a glance the essential qualities and characteristics of the matter in hand. I have heard Whately deliciously witty at a logic or Euclid lecture.

An admirable specimen of this highest description of wit is given—among dozens of others indeed—by his daughter in her biography of him, which delighted me much when I read it, and which may be cited because it is very brilliant and may be given shortly. It will be found at the thirty-eighth page of the first volume of Miss Whately's work. The archbishop, writing of the controversy respecting the observance of the Sabbath, says, "This is a case in which men impose on themselves by the fallacy of the thaumatrope. On one side are painted (to obviate the absurdity of a probable law) the plain, earnest, and repeated injunctions to the Jews relative to their Sabbath ; on the other side (to obviate the consequence of our having to keep the Jewish Sabbath) we have the New Testament allusions to the Christian assemblies on the first day of the week. By a repeated and rapid twirl these two images are blended into one picture in the mind. But a steady view will show that they are on opposite sides of the card."

I remember a favorite saying of Whately's to the effect that the difficulty of giving a good definition of anything increased in proportion to the commonness of the thing to be defined. And he would illustrate his dictum by saying "Define me a teacup !" A trial of the experiment will probably convince the experimenter of the correctness of Whately's proposition.

Whether it may have been that any antagonism between Whately and Shuttleworth caused the former to be prejudiced against Wiccamical things and men, or whether the relationship of the two feelings were *vice versa*, I cannot say. But I certainly thought, and think still, that I suffered in his estimation from the fact that I was a Wykehamist. In writing on educational matters in or about 1839 (page 79 of Miss Whately's first volume), Whately says : "To compare schools generally with colleges generally may seem a vague inquiry, but take the most in repute of each — Eton, Westminster, Harrow, etc., *v.* Oriel, Brasenose, Balliol, Christchurch, etc., etc."

Now, I cannot but feel that so singular an omission of Winchester from so short a list of the schools "most in repute," glaringly in contradiction as it was with all that the whole English world—even the non-academical world —knew to be the fact, could have been caused only by preconceived and unreasoning prejudice. Of course to me the utterance above quoted comes only as a confirmation of what the personal observation of my undergraduate days led me to feel, for I knew nothing of it till I read Miss Whately's volumes published in 1886.

Yet I do not doubt that I may have occasionally " rubbed Whately the wrong way," as the phrase goes. He was, as I have said, a most autocratically minded man. And we Wykehamists, as the reader may have perceived from my Winchester reminiscences, were not accustomed to be ruled autocratically. We lived under the empire, and I might almost say, in an atmosphere of law, as distinguished from individual will. It was constantly in our minds and on our tongues, that the " *informator* " or the " *hostiarius* " *could* or *could not* do this or that. We lived with the ever-present consciousness that the *suprema lex* was not what this master or the other master, or even the warden might say, save in so far as it coincided with the college statutes. And I doubt not that Whately perceived and understood the influence of this habit of mind in something or other that I might have said or done. It was probably something of the sort which led to his telling me that he wanted no New-College manners at Alban Hall.

My " Winchester manners," however, enabled me, I remember, to understand him when some of his own flock could not. He would at a Euclid lecture say, "Take any straight line," scrawling, as he said the words, a line as far from straight as he could draw it, to the utter bewilderment of some among his audience, who, I believe, really thought that the principal was a shocking bad draughtsman, while the despised Wykehamist perfectly understood that his object was to show that the process of reasoning to be illustrated in no wise depended on accuracy of lines or angles.

There is another passage in one of the letters published
by his biographer which illustrates Whately's aversion
to all Wiccamical men and things, and at the same time
his utter ignorance of them. "It is commonly said at
Oxford," he writes, "at least it used to be, that it was
next to impossible to make a Wykehamist believe that any
examination could be harder than that which the candidates for New College undergo." My reader has already
been told in some degree what that examination was,
and the nature of it. It was a real and serious examination, whereas that of candidates for admission to Winchester College was a mere form; and it was certainly a
searching examination into the thoroughness with which
schoolboys had done their schoolboy work. But the supposition that any New-College man ever imagined his
examination in election chamber to be of equal difficulty
with the subsequent work at the university, or with that in
the schools for honors, is an absolute proof that the person so supposing never knew anything about them, or had
come much into contact with them.

I have said that Whately's reputation for a very pronounced Liberalism, certainly at that time unparalleled
among his brother heads of houses at Oxford, had been
my father's reason for placing me at Alban Hall. And
all that reached the undergraduate world in connection
with him was of a nature to lead the academic mind to
regard him as a phenomenon of Radicalism. And it is curious to recall such impressions, while reading at the present day such a passage as the following ("Life of Whately," vol. i. p. 302). The archbishop is writing about the
schemes then in agitation for the application of a portion
of the revenues of the Irish Church to the purposes of
national education. The italics in the following transcrip-
tion are mine.

"It is concluded, first, that in parishes where there is a
very small, or no Protestant population, the revenues of
the Church will be either wholly, or in part, as the case
may be, transferred to the education board, as the incumbents drop, their life-interests being reserved; secondly,
that in the event of an increase of the Protestant popula-

tion, such portion of the funds thus alienated as may be thought requisite shall be drawn from the education board, and restored to the original purpose; thirdly, that in the event of a further diminution of the Protestants, a further portion shall be withdrawn from the Church, and applied to the purpose of general education. This last supposition is merely conjectural, but is so strictly the converse of the preceding, that every one at once concludes, and must conclude by parity of reasoning, that it must be contemplated. Now it will not be supposed by any one, who knows much of the state of Ireland, that we contemplate as probable any such increase of the Protestant population as to call for the restoration of a considerable portion of the alienated funds. In a few places, perhaps, attempts may be made, I fear with disastrous results, by some zealous Protestant landlords to increase, with this view, the proportion of Protestants on their estates; but on the whole we neither hope nor fear any such result. What alarms us is, the holding out the principle of such a system as the apportioning the revenues of the Church and of the education board to the varying proportions of the Roman Catholic population to the Protestant; and again, the principle of making the funds for national education contingent upon the death of incumbents. The *natural* effect of the latter of these provisions must be to place the clergy so circumstanced in a most invidious, and *in this country a most dangerous situation. No one who knows anything of Ireland would like to reside here surrounded by his heirs, on whom his income was to devolve at his death. And such would be very much the case with an incumbent, who was regarded as standing between the nation and the national benefit,* viz., of provision for the education of their children. *Then in respect of the other point, every Protestant who might come to settle, or remain settled in any parish, would be regarded as tending towards the withdrawing or withholding, as the case might be, of the funds of the national education, and diverting them to the use of an heretical establishment.*

" *The most harassing persecutions, the most ferocious outrages, the most systematic murders, would in conse-*

quence be increased fourfold. Bitter as religious animosities have hitherto been in this wretched country, it would be to most persons astonishing that they could be so much augmented, as I have no doubt they would be, by this fatal experiment. When instead of mere vague jealousy, revenge and party spirit, to prompt to crime and violence, there was also held out a distinct pecuniary national benefit in the extermination of Protestants, it would be in fact a price set on their heads, and they would be hunted down like wolves. . . . Better, far better, would it be to confiscate at once and forever all the endowments held by the clergy, and leave them to be supported by voluntary contribution, or by manual labor. However impoverished, *they and their congregations would at least have security for their lives.*"

" *To seek to pacify Ireland,*" he writes a little further on, " *by compliance and favor shown to its disturbers would be even worse than the superstitious procedure of our forefathers with their weapon salve, who left the wound to itself and applied their unguents to the sword which had inflicted it.*"

Writing to his friend Senior on Parliamentary Reform, he says that a system of ten-pound qualification " could not last, but must go on to universal suffrage." His own plan would be universal suffrage with a plurality of votes to owners of property in proportion to the amount of it, and a system of election by degrees—parishes, *e. g.*, to elect an elector. " Some may," he concludes, " perhaps think at the first glance that my reform is very democratical. I think that a more attentive mind will show that it is calculated to prevent in the most effectual way the inroads of excessive democracy. I can at least say that no one can dread more than myself a democratical government, chiefly because I am convinced it is the more warlike."

Such were the utterances of an advanced Liberal in the first half of this century. Was I far wrong in saying that Whately's Liberalism would have made very good modern Conservatism?

There was a story current, I remember, not long after Whately's acceptance of the see of Dublin, which, as I do not think it has been told in print, and as it is very significant, I may tell here—observing that all I know is, that the story *was* current.

It was at the time when one of the great transatlantic passenger ships had been destroyed by fire with the loss of many lives. One of those saved was a Dublin clergyman of the Low-Church school of divinity, who, returning to Dublin, and finding himself the hero of many tea-tables, was wont to moralize down the great event of his life after the fashion of those who will have it, *quand même*, that the tower of Siloam *did* fall because of the wickedness of those whom it crushed. And one day, at one of those *levées* of which Miss Whately speaks, he was improving his usual theme, the centre of a knot gathered around him, when the archbishop strolled up to the group, according to his fashion, and having heard, said: "Yes, truly Mr. ——, a most remarkable experience! But I think I can cap it" (a favorite phrase of Whately's, who was fond of the amusement of capping verses). "It is little more than a month ago that I crossed from Holyhead to Kingston, and by God's mercy *the vessel never caught fire at all!*"

I cannot bring to an end my reminiscences relating to so remarkable a man as Whately without relating a story, which he told me, as having been told him by his old and highly valued friend and *protégé*, Blanco White, once so well known a figure among all the Oriel set of that period. The story was introduced, I remember, as an illustration of a favorite (and doubtless correct) theory of Whately's to the effect that the popular English "hocus pocus," as applied to any sleight-of-hand deception, is simply a derisory corruption of the *"hoc est corpus"* used in the Romish liturgical formula for the consecration of the eucharistic elements. It may be that the story in question has been told in print before now, but I have never met with it.

"A priest," said Blanco White, "was for some heinous crime condemned to capital punishment at Seville. But of course before he could be delivered over to the secular arm for the execution of the sentence, a ceremonial degradation from his sacerdotal character had to be performed. And this was to be done at the place appointed for his execution immediately before that was proceeded to; and for the greater efficacy of the terrible example to be inculcated on the people, the market-day at Seville had been chosen for the purpose.

"The criminal priest accordingly, as he was led to the place of execution, was still to all effects and purposes a priest, with all the tremendous powers inherent in that character, of which nothing save formal ecclesiastical degradation could deprive him. Now it so happened, or perhaps was purposely arranged, that the way from the prison to the place of execution lay through the market-place, where all the provisions of all sorts for the Sevillians for that day were exposed. And as the yet undegraded, and it must be feared unrepentant, priest passed among all the various displays of food thus spread out before him, the devil, seizing an opportunity rarely to be matched, entered into the unhappy priest's mind, and prompted him to deal one last malicious and sacrilegious blow at the population about to witness his miserable end. Suddenly, in the mid-market, he stretched out his arms, and pronounced with a loud voice the uncancellable sacramental words, 'Hoc est corpus!' And all the contents of that vast market were instantaneously transubstantiated! All the food in Seville was forthwith unavailable for any baser than eucharistic purposes, and Seville had to observe the vindictive priest's last day on earth as a very rigorous fast-day!"

Whether Blanco White told this as absolutely having occurred within his own knowledge, or only as a Seville legend, I do not know, but in any case the story is a good one.

I have said that when I entered Alban Hall I was not in a position to obtain much profit from the classical lectures, the main object of which was to drive those who attended them through the examination for the "little go." I was better able to pass that examination when I first went to Oxford than when the time came for my doing so. But the examination in question required that the candidate for passing should take up either logic or Euclid (four books only, as I remember), and of neither of these did I know anything. And there the Alban Hall

7

lectures profited me. The admirably lucid logic lectures of both the principal and vice-principal, to my surprise, soon rendered the *rationale* of the science perfectly comprehensible to me, and even Aldrich became interesting. I selected logic for my "little go," and Whately made me abundantly able to satisfy the examiners.

But, as I said a few pages back, my membership of Alban Hall was, for more reasons than those which have been already given, disastrous to me, and the disaster came about in this wise.

Whately was, rightly and judiciously enough, very particular in requiring that his men should return after vacation punctually on the day appointed for meeting. Now, unfortunately, my father on one occasion detained me until the following day. What the cause may have been I entirely forget, but remember perfectly well that it was in no way connected with any plans or wishes of mine. I returned a day late, and the penalty which Whately had enacted for this laches was the payment of a certain sum to his servant — the porter, buttery-man, and factotum at the hall. What the amount of this penalty was, and whether it were large or small, I have entirely forgotten, if I ever knew, for the whole matter in dispute passed between my father and Whately. The former maintained, whether rightly or wrongly I have not the means of knowing, that the latter acted *ultra vires* in making any such *motu proprio* edict. There was no likelihood that Whately would yield in the matter—indeed it would have been out of the question that he should have done so. My father had quite as little of yielding in his nature, and kicked against the pricks determinedly. The result was that I was one morning summoned to the presence of the principal, and told to take my name off the books! My father was at first disposed to forbid me to do so, but the result of refusal would have been expulsion, which would have entailed ruinous consequences, much worse than the already sufficiently injurious results of being compelled to quit the hall. I should immediately have lost the two valuable exhibitions which I held from Winchester, besides incurring the very damning stigma that through life attaches to a man who has been expelled. Eventually I took my name off the books under menace of expulsion if I did not.

The case attracted a good deal of attention in the university at the time, and I think the general feeling among the heads of colleges was that Whately was wrong. At all events, without going into the question as between my father and him, it was emphatically a case of *Delirant reges, plectuntur Achivi*. From beginning to end the whole matter passed over my head. I had neither fault nor option in the matter. And Whately knew perfectly well how very great was the injury he was inflicting on me. It was nearly impossible to get admission, under the circumstances, to any college. The great majority of them could not possibly, even if any one of them had wished to do so, receive a man at a minute's notice, from absolute want of room, and the wrong that would have been done to others who were waiting for admission. But it would have been entirely contrary to the rules and practice of almost, if not quite, every one of them to receive a man compelled to leave another college, even with a formal *bene decessit*. And the interval of a term (or even of a day, I take it in strictness) would have necessarily involved the forfeiture of my exhibitions. All which Whately also knew; but all of which, as he might have fairly answered, my father knew also!

Eventually I was received at Magdalen Hall, which has since that day become Hertford College, of which Dr. Macbride was then principal. Dr. Macbride was one of the kindliest and best men in the world, and he was one of those who most strongly felt that I was being very hardly used. It was with difficulty that it could be managed that I should be received into his society at a day's notice; but, looking to the urgency as well as to the other circumstances of the case, it *was* managed somehow, and I became a member of Magdalen Hall.

But the mischief done to my university career was fatal! Magdalen Hall was at that time a general refuge for the destitute! Dr. Macbride, well known for his active benevolence and beneficence in various spheres of well-doing on the outside of his academical character, was hardly well adapted for the position he held in the university. Anything of the nature of punishment seemed impossible to the gentleness of his character; and I fancy he held theoretically that it was desirable that a place such as his hall should exist in the university to serve as a refuge for those who, without being black sheep, were, for a variety of reasons, pushed aside from the beaten tracks of the academical career.

I made very little acquaintance with the men there; but I do not think there were many, though no doubt some, black sheep among them. There was another hall in the university at that time famous for the "fastness" of its inmates. But the "shadiness" of Magdalen Hall was of a different kind. There were many middle-aged men there — *ci-devant* officers in the army, who had quitted their profession with the intention of entering the Church; schoolmasters, who, having begun their career in some capacity which did not require a degree, were at a later day anxious to obtain one in order to better themselves. In general, the object of all there was not education or any other object save simply a degree needed for some social or economical purpose. "Honors" were, of course, about as much aspired to as bishoprics! And it was the business of Mr. Jacobson — the gentle, kindly, patient, and long-suffering vice-principal — to secure "a pass" for as many of his heterogeneous flock as possible.

Of discipline there could hardly be said to have been any. When other men of the kick-over-the-traces sort told their stories of various surreptitious means of entering college at all sorts of hours, Magdalen Hall men used to say that their plan was to ring at the gate and have it opened for them! I remember upon one occasion, when I had shown myself in chapel only on the Sunday morning during an entire week, the vice-principal mildly remarked, "You have reduced it to a minimum, Mr. Trollope!" I suppose that in classical attainments I was much superior to any man in the place. There were many, it is true, who were never seen at lecture at all — not, probably, from idleness, but because they were obtaining from a private tutor a course of cramming more desperately energetic than even kindly, patient Jacobson's elementary lectures could supply. For me the *res angusta domi* forbade all idea of employing a private tutor. But as for a "pass" degree, I was just as capable of taking it when I left Winchester (with the exception of logic, and what was called "divinity") as when I did take it; and as regards logic, I was sufficiently capable when I left Whately's hands. If my "divinity" examination had consisted of as searching an inquiry into my knowledge of the contents of the Old Testament as was required from many men, I should infallibly have been "plucked." But, as it chanced, it consisted solely of construing two verses of the New Testament. I remember that the examiner had been hammering away at the man next before me for an inordinate time, and as I construed my Greek Testament glibly enough he was glad to make up for lost time.

As for Jacobson's lectures, they were absolutely useless to me, and he never in the slightest degree pressed me to attend them. I remember, however, that he desired an interview with me on the morning I was to go into the schools, for the purpose of testing in some degree the probability of my passing. And it is a singular circumstance that—Horace having been one of the books I was taking up—he put me on, as a trial, at the very passage selected for the same purpose by the examiner in the schools an hour or two later! Jacobson found me able enough to deal with the passage he selected. But had it been otherwise he would have secured my passing—as far as Horace was concerned—despite any amount of ignorance of the author, if only I had the wit to remember his cramming for an hour or two.

Eventually, though I had in no wise aimed at anything of the sort, a third class was awarded to me—wholly, as I was given to understand, on account of my Latin writing. The examiners had given — hardly judiciously — so stiff a passage from one of the homilies to be translated into Latin that the majority of the men could not understand the English; which, to a certain extent, interfered with their translation of it into another language. They were "pass men"! With the candidates for honors it

would doubtless have been otherwise. But I *did* understand it, and I took it into my head to translate it twice—
once into Ciceronian and once into Sallustian Latin. And
this was rewarded by a third class. *Valeat quantum!*

And thus ended my academical career in a comparative
failure, the conclusion of which seemed to have been rather
a foregone one. I had no private tutor, and, with the exception of Whately's logic lectures, no college tuition of
any value to me at all. And in addition to all this I was
pulled up by the roots and transplanted in the middle of
my career. No doubt I was idle, and might have done
better. I read a good deal, but it was what I chose to
read, and not what I ought to have read with a view to
the schools. I had no very unacademical pursuits save
one. I used occasionally to hire with a friend a gig with
a fast horse, drive out to Witney, dine there, wait till the
up-mail came through, and then run back to Oxford, tor-
menting the coachman and his team by continually running by him, letting him pass me, and then *da capo.* But
these escapades were rare.

A great deal more wine, or what was supposed to be
such, was drunk at Oxford in those days than was desirable, or than, as I take it, is the case now. But I never
was much of a wine-drinker. I think I have been drunk
twice in my life, but not oftener. Very little credit, however, is due to me for my moderation, from the fact, which
I do not think I ever met with in the case of any other
individual, that the headache which to most others comes
the next morning as the penalty of excess, always used to
come to me, if I at all exceeded, *séance tenante,* and almost immediately. Nor did wine ever pleasurably raise
my spirits, nor did my palate care for it. To the present
day, as a simple question of *gourmandise,* I would rather
drink a glass of lemonade than any champagne that was
ever grown—lemonade, by-the-bye, not such liquid as goes
by that name in this country, but lemonade made with
lemons fresh and fragrant from the tree. Under these
circumstances I can make small claim to any moral virtue
for my sobriety.

I used to be a good deal upon the water, either alone or

accompanied by a single friend with a pair of sculls. But I was a great walker, and cultivated in those days, and, indeed, during most of the many years that have passed since, a considerable turn of speed. In those days Captain Barclay was called the champion pedestrian of England, and had walked six miles within the hour. I hear people talk of eight and even nine miles having been done within the hour, but I absolutely refuse to believe the statement. I dare say that the ground may have been covered, but not at a fair *walk*—at what used to be called, and perhaps is called still, a toe-and-heel walk, *i. e.*, a walk in performing which one foot must touch the ground before the other leaves it. I tried very hard to match Captain Barclay's feat, but my utmost endeavors never achieved more than five miles and three quarters—I could never do more; and, of course, that last quarter of a mile just made all the difference between a first-rate and a second-rate walker. The five and three quarters I have often done on the Abingdon Road, milestone to milestone. And at the present day I should be happy to walk a match with any gentleman born in 1810.

The longest day's walk I ever did was forty-seven miles, but I carried a very heavy knapsack, making, I take it, that distance fully equal to sixty miles without one. How well I remember walking, one fair, frosty morning, from Winchester to Alresford, seven miles, before breakfast. I asked at the inn at which I breakfasted for cold meat. They brought me an uncut loin of small Southdown mutton, of which I ate the whole. And I can see now the glance of that waiter's eye, accusing me, as plainly as if he had spoken the words, of pocketing his master's provisions! *Eheu! fugaces, Posthume, Posthume, labuntur anni*, and I never shall again eat a loin of mutton at one sitting! partly, though, because scientific breeding has exterminated the good old Southdown mutton.

One other reminiscence occurs to me in connection with the subject of walking. While I was living with my parents at Harrow, my mother's brother, Mr. Henry Milton, was living with his family at Fulham. And one Sunday morning I walked from Harrow to Fulham before breakfast on a visit to him. As may be supposed, I was abundantly ready to do ample justice to the very solid and varied breakfast placed before me, but, after having done so, was hardly equally ready to accompany my uncle's family to Fulham Church to hear the Bishop of London preach. This, however, it behooved me to do, not without great misgiving as to the effect that the bishop's sermon might have on me after my twelve miles' walk and very copious breakfast—especially as my uncle's pew was exactly in front and in the vicinity of the pulpit! So, minded to do my best under the difficult circumstances, I stood up during the sermon. All in vain! Nature too peremptorily bade me sleep. I slept, with the result of executing an uninterrupted series of profound bows to the preacher, the suddenness and jerky nature of which evidently betokened the entirety of my agreement with his arguments. I feared the reproaches, which I doubted not awaited me on my way home. But my uncle contented himself with saying, "When you go to sleep during a sermon, Tom, never stand up to do it!"

To sum up the story of my certainly unsuccessful but not entirely profitless life at Oxford, I may say that I was not altogether an idle man, nor ever in any degree a sharer in any of the "faster" phases of academical life. I was always a reader. But what academical good could come to a man who was reading "The Diversions of Purley," or Plot's "Oxfordshire," or Burton's "Anatomy of Melancholy," or Brown's "Vulgar Errors," when he ought to have been reading Aristotle's "Ethics"? Among other reminiscences of the sort, my diary accuses me, for instance, for having taken from the library of Magdalen Hall (and read!) a volume called "Gaffarel's Curiosities." I suppose no other living man has read it! The work contains among other "curiosities," a chapter "of incredible nonsense," as my diary calls it, on the construction and proper use of Talismans!

Alas, no "honors" were granted for proficiency in such studies!

CHAPTER X.

OLD DIARIES.

BEFORE quitting a phase of my life which many, if not most, old men are wont to look back on as their happiest time, but which I, by so considering, should grievously wrong many a subsequent period, I may string together at random a few notes from my diaries, which may seem to contribute some touch or trait to the story of the way we lived sixty years since.

The way men lived in Germany at that date I find given in a letter from the Baron de Zandt to my mother, as follows: "In many parts of Germany," says the baron, who, as I very well remember, understood what good living was, "a man may be boarded and lodged comfortably for £26 a year. If he prefers economy to comfort, it might be done for considerably less."

From the journal of a walking tour in South Devon, performed in the year 1831, I take the well-nigh incredible statement, that no tobacconist *ex professo* could at that date be found in Plymouth! "I succeeded after some research," says the diary, "in getting some tolerable tobacco from a chymist." Doubtless plenty of tobacco was to be had, *if* I had known where to look for it—at chandlers' shops and taverns. But I have no doubt that the statement in the fifty-five-year-old "text" is correct. No tobacconist's shop was then to be found in Plymouth.

In July, 1832, I was walking in Wales, and reaching Caermarthen in assize time (where Judge Alderson, as is recorded, was trying prisoners on the Crown side), found much difficulty in getting any accommodation for bed or even board. But at length a commercial gentleman at the Ivy Bush, the principal inn, "entering into conversation in a patronizing sort of way, told me it was a *h*error to suppose that commercial men were *h*adverse to gentle-

7*

men making use of the commercial room, provided they *was* gentlemen. For himself, he was always most 'appy to associate with gentlemen;" and, in fine, invited me to join their table, which I did at two o'clock. One of the assembled party—there were some fifteen or sixteen of them—was formally named president for the day, and took the head of the table. We were excruciatingly genteel. I, in my ignorance, asked for beer, but was with much politeness informed that malt liquor was not used at their table. Every man was expected to consume a pint of most atrocious sherry at 5s. 6d., which I suppose compensated the landlord for the wonderfully small price of the dinner. A dinner of three courses, consisting of salmon, chicken, venison, three or four made dishes, and pastry, was put before us. I was surprised at the gorgeousness of this feast, and began to have alarming anticipations of the *amari aliquid* which must follow. But I was assured that this was the ordinary every-day fare of the "commercial gentlemen," and the bill for the repast was two shillings! My diary records that the conversation at table in no wise savored of trade in any of its branches. Shakespeare and Walter Scott were descanted on in turn, and one dapper little man, who travelled in cutlery, averred that Sir Walter had on one occasion been exceedingly polite to him, and he should always say to the end of his life that he was a gentleman.

At Dolgelly I was struck by the practice prevailing there of tolling, after the ringing of the curfew, a number of strokes on the biggest bell equal to the number of the days which had elapsed of the current month. I wonder whether they do so still?

I went out of my way, I find, in the course of the same journey, in order to go from Liverpool to Manchester by the new railway, which to me, as to thousands of others, was an object of infinite curiosity and interest. My diary notes that there were fifteen carriages attached to the engine, each carrying twelve passengers. Two of these were first-class, and the fare for the journey to Manchester in them was 5s.; in the others the fare was 3s. 6d. The train I was to travel by was called a second-class train. The first-class trains carried no second-class passengers, and did the journey of fifty-two miles in one hour and a half. They stopped only once on the way. The second-class trains stopped frequently, and were two hours on the road. I estimated the speed at something over twenty-five miles an hour, and remark in my diary that "that immense rapidity was manifested to the senses only by looking at the objects passed."

At Manchester I find myself to have been much scandalized at a scene which I witnessed in the Collegiate Church there. There were seventeen couples to be married, and they were all married at once, the only part of the service individually performed being the "I take thee," etc., etc. I perfectly well remember at this distance of time the bustling about of the clerk among them to insure that every male should be coupled to the right female. "After this wholesale coupling had been completed," says my diary, "the daily service was begun, and was performed in a more indecent and slovenly way than I ever before witnessed, which is saying a great deal! While the Psalms were being sung the priest, as having nothing to do, walked out, and returned just in time to read the Lessons." Such were the manners and habits of 1832.

A few weeks later I find an entry to the effect that, "while my father was reading 'Grandison' to us in the evening I got M. Hervieu (the artist who did the illustrations for my mother's 'Domestic Manners of the Americans' and other books, and who chanced to be passing the evening with us *en famille*) to draw me a caricature illustrating the following passage of Beattie's "Minstrel:"

> "And yet young Edwin was no vulgar boy;
> Deep thought would often fix his youthful eye.
> Dainties he heeded not, nor gaud, nor toy,
> Save *one short pipe!*"

I possess this remarkable work of art to the present day!

At another page I stumble on the record of a conversation with the sexton of Leatherhead, whom, in one of my rambles, I found digging a grave in the churchyard there.

Three shillings, I learned, was the price of a grave of the ordinary depth of five feet. Those, however, who could afford the luxury of lying deeper paid a shilling a foot more.

One more note from the diaries of those days I will venture to give, because it may be taken as a paralipomenon to that "Autobiography" of my brother which the world was kindly pleased to take some interest in:

"Went to town yesterday [from Harrow], and among other commissions bought a couple of single-sticks with strong basket handles. Anthony much approves of them, and this morning we had a bout with them. One of the sticks bought yesterday soon broke, and we supplied its place by a tremendous blackthorn. Neither of us left the arena without a fair share of rather severe wales; but Anthony is far my superior in quickness and adroitness, and perhaps in bearing pain too. I fear he is likely to remain so in the first two, but in the third I am determined he shall not."

Thus says the yellow fifty-seven-year-old page!

And I have literally thousands of such pages; voluminous records—among other matters—of walking excursions in the home counties, in Devon, in Wales, in Gloucestershire, and on the banks of the Severn and Wye, not a page of which fails to bear its testimony to the curiously changed circumstances under which a pedestrian would now undertake such wanderings. I find among other jottings— deemed *memorabilia* at the time— that I carried a knapsack weighing twenty-eight pounds over the top of Plinlimmon, because I considered seven and sixpence demanded by the guide for accompanying me excessive.

But *ohe! jam satis.* I will inflict no more upon the patient reader—the impatient will have skipped much of what I have already given him.

Alas! the *amari aliquid* of these old records is the unblushing chronicle of *intentions,* enough to have paved all Acheron with a durability unachieved by any highway board! The only comfort for diarists so imprudently candid as to record such aspirations, and so yet more imprudent as to read them half a century after the penning of them, is the consideration that *au bout des comptes* the question is, not what one has done, but what one has become. If one could flatter one's self that one has the *mens sana in corpore sano* at seventy-seven years, one might accept and condone the past without too much regret ; and at all events it is something to have undeniably brought the latter to its seventy-eighth year.

CHAPTER XI.

I CAME down from Oxford to find my mother and my two sisters returned from America, and living in that Harrow Weald farmhouse which my brother Anthony, in his "Autobiography," has described, I think, too much *en noir*. It had once been a very good house, probably the residence of the owner of the small farm on which it was situated. It certainly was no longer a very good house, but it was not "tumble-down," as Anthony calls it, and was indeed a much better house than it would have been if its original destination had been that of merely a farmhouse. But it and "all that it inherited" was assuredly shabby enough, and had been forlorn enough, as I had known it in my vacations, when inhabited only by my father, my brother Anthony, and myself.

But my mother was one of those people who carry sunshine with them. The place did not seem the same. The old house, whatever else it may have been, was roomy; and a very short time elapsed before my mother had got round her one or two nice girl guests to help her in brightening it.

I may mention here a singular circumstance which furnished me with means of estimating my mother's character in a phase of her life which rarely comes within the purview of a son. Some years ago, not many years I think after my mother's death, an anonymous stranger sent my brother Anthony a packet of old letters written by my mother to my father shortly before and shortly after their marriage. He never was able to ascertain who his benevolent correspondent was, nor how the papers in question came into his possession. There they are, carefully tied up in a neat packet, most of them undated by her, but carefully docketed with the date by my father's hand. The handwriting, not spoiled as it afterwards became by writing over a hundred volumes, is a very elegant one.

There is a singularly old-world flavor about them. There is a staid moderation in their tone, which a reader of the present day, fresh from the perusal of similar literature, as supplied by Mr. Mudie, would probably call coldness. In the few letters which precede the marriage there are no warm assurances of affection. After marriage the language becomes more warm. I am tempted to transcribe a few passages that the girls of the period may see how their great-grandmothers did these things.

"It does not require three weeks' consideration, Mr. Trollope "—thus begins the first letter, undated, but docketed by my father, " F. M., undated, received 2d Nov., 1808 "—" to enable me to tell you that the letter you left with me last night was most flattering and gratifying to me. I value your good opinion too highly not to feel that the generous proof you have given me of it must forever, and in any event, be remembered by me with pride and gratitude. But I fear you are not sufficiently aware that your choice, so flattering to me, is for yourself a very imprudent one." And then follows a business-like statement of possessions and prospects, which the writer fears fall much short of what her suitor might reasonably expect.

But none of my father's faults tended in the slightest degree to lead him to marry a millionaire, whom he cared less for, in preference to a girl without a sixpence, whom he loved better.

" In an affair of this kind," the letter I have cited goes on to say, "I do not think it any disadvantage to either party that some time should elapse between the first contemplation and final decision of it. It gives each an opportunity of becoming acquainted with the other's opinion on many important points, which could not be canvassed before it was thought of, and which it would be useless to discuss after it was settled."

Could Mrs. Chapone have expressed herself better?

I find in another letter, dated (by my father) 6th December, 1808, the following George-the-Thirdian passage: "The most disagreeable of created beings, Col. —— by

name, by profession Sir ——'s led captain, is, while I am
writing, talking in an animated strain of eloquence to Mrs.
Milton" (my grandfather the vicar's second wife and the
writer's stepmother), "frequently seasoning his discourse
with the polished phrase, 'Blood and thunder, ma'am!' so
if I happen to swear a little before I conclude, be so good
as to believe that I am accidentally writing down what he
is saying. . . . Poor, dear, innocent Dr. Nott! His simplicity is quite pathetic! I am really afraid that he will
be taking twopence instead of two pounds from his parishioners, merely because he does not know the difference
between them. I cannot help feeling a tender interest for
such lamblike innocence of the ways of this wicked world.
I dare say the night I saw him at the opera, he thought
he was *only*" (note the distinction) "at the play, nay, perhaps believed they were performing an oratorio."

In one letter of the 9th of April, 1809, I find a mention
of "a frank" sent by Mr Mathias with a translation by
him into Italian of the "Echo Song" in *Comus*, of which
the writer says that it is "elegantly done, but is not
Milton."

In another, of the 18th of May, 1809—the last before
the marriage took place—I find the following, which may
interest some people. "I wish you could be here to-morrow," she writes, "we are going to see the prisoners of
war at Odiam (near Reading) perform one of Molière's
plays. Two years ago we attended several of them, and
I never enjoyed anything more."

More than a score of these faded eighty-year-old letters
are before me; and I might, perhaps, have gleaned from
them some other little touches illustrative of men and
manners when George the Third was king, but were I to
yield to all the temptations of the sort that beset the path
on which I am travelling, I should try my readers' patience
beyond all hope of forgiveness.

My mother had brought home with her the MS. of a
couple of volumes on America; and the principal business
on hand when I came home from Oxford was the finding
a publisher for these. In this quest she was zealously and
very energetically assisted by Captain Basil Hall, himself

the author of a work on America, and sundry other books, which at that time had made a considerable reputation. Basil Hall's book on America did not take a favorable view of the Americans or their institutions; and it had been mercilessly attacked and accused of misrepresentation by all the critics of the Liberal party. For Hall's book, and everything else concerning America, was in those days looked at from a political-party point of view. America and the Americans were understood to be anti-everything that was dear to Conservatives. They were accordingly the pets of the Whigs (Radicals and Radicalism had not yet emerged into the ken of respectable folk, either Whig or Tory), and Hall's book had been abused accordingly. He was very sore about the accusations of untruthfulness, and was delighted with a book which supported his assertions and his views. How my mother came to be introduced to him, and how it came to pass that the MS. of her work was shown to him, I do not remember, but the result was that he was zealously eager for the publication of it. The title, if I recollect rightly, was proposed by him. "The Domestic Manners of the Americans" was published, and made an immediate and great success. It was emphatically the book of the season, was talked of everywhere, and read by all sorts and conditions of men and women. It was highly praised by all the Conservative organs of the press, and vehemently abused by all those of the opposite party. Edition after edition was sold, and the pecuniary results were large enough to avert from the family of the successful authoress the results of her husband's ruined fortunes.

The Americans were made very angry by this account of their "domestic manners"—very naturally, but not very wisely. Of course, it was asserted that many of the statements made were false and many of the descriptions caricatured. Nothing in the book from beginning to end was false; nothing of minutest detail which was asserted to have been seen had not been seen; nor was anything intentionally caricatured or exaggerated for the sake of enhancing literary effect. But the tone of the book was unfriendly, and was throughout the result of offended taste rather than of well-weighed opinion. It was full of universal conclusions drawn from particular premises; and no sufficient weight, or rather no weight at all, was allowed to the fact that the observations on which the recorded judgments were founded had been gathered almost entirely in what was then the Far West, and represented the "domestic manners" of the Atlantic States hardly at all. Unquestionably the book was a very clever one, and written with infinite *verve* and brightness. But—save for the fact that censure and satire are always more amusing than the reverse—an equally clever and equally truthful book might have been written in a diametrically opposite spirit.

No doubt the markedly favorable reception of the book was what mainly irritated our American cousins. But they certainly were angry far beyond what the importance of the matter would seem to have justified. I remember that Colley Grattan, whose fame as the author of "Highways and Byways" was then at its zenith, in writing to me from Boston, where he resided for many years as British consul, inviting me to visit him there, went into the question of the reception I might be likely to meet with on that side of the Atlantic. "I think," he wrote, "that to come over under a false name would be *infra dig*. But really I fear that if you come under your own, you may be *in for a dig !*"

Whether Grattan exaggerated the wrath of his Bostonian friends for the sake of his joke I do not know. Unquestionably the Americans, even speaking of them as a nation, were made very angry by my mother's book. But the anger was not of a very spiteful or rancorous description, for from that day to this I have never met with anything but kindness and cordial friendliness from all the Americans I have known—and I have known very many.

The return of my mother, and the success of her book, produced a change in the condition and circumstances of affairs at home which resembled the transformation scene in a pantomime that takes place at the advent of the good fairy. Even the old farmhouse at Harrow Weald was brightened up physically, and to a far greater degree morally, by her presence. But we did not remain long there. Very shortly she took us back to Harrow, not to the large house built by my father on Lord Northwick's land, but to another very good house on the same farm— not above a stone's throw from the previous one, which he had made (very imprudently) by adding to and improving the original farmhouse — a very comfortable residence. This was the house which the world has heard of as "Orley Farm."

And there my mother became immediately surrounded by many old friends and many new ones. I remember among the latter Letitia Landon, better known to the world as "L. E. L." She was a *petite* figure, very insignificant-looking, with a sharp chin, turn-up nose, and on the whole rather *piquante* face, though without any pretension to good looks. I remember her being seated one day at dinner by the side of a certain dignitary of the Church, who had the reputation of being more of a *bon vivant* than a theologian, and who was old enough to have been her father; and on my asking her afterwards what they had been talking about so earnestly, as I had seen them, "About eating, to be sure!" said she. "I always talk to everybody on their strong point. I told him that writing poetry was my trade, but that eating was my pleasure, and we were fast friends before the fish was finished!" Her sad fate and tragic ending, poor soul! attracted much attention and sympathy at the time. And doubtless fate and the world used her hardly; but she was one of those who never under any circumstances would have run a straight and prosperous course.

Another visitor whom I remember well at that and other times was the Rev. Henry Milman, the third son of Sir Francis Milman, who was, if I rightly recollect, physician to Queen Charlotte. I remember hearing him say (but this was long previously) that no man need think much about the gout who had never had it till he was forty. His widow, Lady Milman, lived with her daughter many years at Pinner, near Harrow, and they were very old friends of my mother. She was a dear old lądy with certain points of eccentricity about her. She used always to carry a volume of South's sermons with her to church for perusal during the less satisfactory discourse of her more immediate pastor; and I am afraid was not sufficiently careful to conceal her preference. It must be over sixty years since, lunching one day at Pinner, I was much amused at her insisting that Abraham, the old one-eyed footman, who had lived in the family all his life, should kneel before the dining-room fire to warm her plate of pickled salmon! I remember walking with her shortly before her death in the kitchen garden at Pinner, when Saunders, the old butler, who had developed into a sort of upper gardener, was pruning the peach-trees. "Oh! don't cut that, Saunders," said my lady; "I want to see those blossoms. And I shall never see them another year!" "Must come off, my lady," said Saunders, inexorably, as he sheared away the branch. "He never will let me have my way," grumbled the little old lady, as she resumed her trot along the gravel walk under the peach wall. My lady, however, could assert herself sufficiently on some occasions. I happened to be at Pinner one day when Mrs. Archdeacon Hodgson, a neighbor, called somewhat earlier in the day than the recognized hour for morning visits. "Very glad to see you, my dear," said my lady, rising to meet her astonished visitor, who was at least twice as big a woman as herself, I mean physically, "but *you must not do this sort of thing again!*"

Her third son, Henry Milman, who, having begun his career as the author of, perhaps, the best "Newdegate" ever written, was famous during the earlier part of it as a poet and dramatist, and during the latter portion of it (more durably) as an historian, was, with his very beautiful wife, one of our visitors at this period. He was at that time certainly a very brilliant man, but I did not like him as well as I did his elder brother, Sir William. I give only the impressions of an undergraduate, who was, I think, rather boyish for his age. But it seemed to me that the poet had a strain of worldliness in his character, and a certain flavor of cynicism (not incompatible, however, with serious views and earnest feelings on religious subjects), which were wholly absent from the elder brother, who wrote neither poems nor histories, but was to my then thinking a very perfect gentleman. "*Nec vixit male qui natus moriensque fefellit.*"

I find recorded in a diary of that time (November, 1832) some notes of a conversation with Henry Milman, one evening when I, with my parents and sister, had been dining with Lady Milman at Pinner, which are, perhaps, worth reproducing here.

I asked him, in the course of a long after-dinner conversation, what he thought of Shuttleworth's book on the " Consistency of Revelation with Itself and with Human Reason," which formed the second volume of the series called the " Theological Library," and which I had recently been reading. He said the work had a great many faults, one of the principal of which was its great difficulty. On this point I find, from other entries in my diary, that my undergraduate experience fully coincided with his more valuable judgment. The reasoning in a great many places was, he said, false ; and in that part which treated of the Mosaic account of the creation of the world, the great question was entirely blinked. The abstract of moral duties appeared to him, he said, to be by far the most able part of the book. He considered Shuttleworth " a man of very limited reading." And this, perhaps, he may have seemed to one of whom it used to be said jocosely in his own family that " Henry reads a book, not as other mortals do, line after line, but obliquely, from the left-hand upper corner of a page to the right-hand lower corner of the same !"

Milman, on the same occasion, spoke much of the decay of a love of learning in England generally, and particularly at Oxford. He said that no four men could be found there who were up to the European level of the day in any branch of learning—not even in theology. And speaking of England generally, he said that in no one public library in the country could the books requisite for a man who wished to write a learned work on any subject whatever be found. Germany was, and was, he thought, likely to remain, the great emporium of all learning.

As for the Church, he said that it would never be the profession that it had been — that it would not be his choice for a son of his; and that the law was the only profession for talent in these days. He observed that it was very remarkable that no change—no revolution—had ever passed over this country without adding power and wealth to that profession.

Here, also, I may record, if the reader will pardon the abruptness of a transition that hurries him from scholarly disquisition to antipodean regions of subject and social atmosphere, an expedition I and my brother Anthony made together, which recurs in my mind in connection with those days. But I think that it must have belonged to the Harrow Weald times before the return of my mother from America, because the extreme impecuniosity, which made the principal feature of it, would not have occurred subsequently. We saw—my brother and I— some advertisement of an extra-magnificent entertainment that was to take place at Vauxhall; something of so gorgeous promise in the way of illuminations and fireworks, and all for the specially reduced entrance fee of one shilling each person, that, chancing to possess just that amount, we determined to profit by so unique an occasion. Any means of conveyance other than legs, ignorant in those days of defeat, was not to be thought of. We had just the necessary two shillings, and no more. So we set off to walk the (at least) fourteen miles from Harrow Weald to Vauxhall, timing ourselves to arrive there about nine in the evening. Anthony danced all night. I took no part in that amusement, but contented myself with looking on and with the truly superb display of fireworks. Then at about 1 A.M. we set off and walked back our fourteen miles home again without having touched bite or sup! Did anybody else ever purchase the delight of an evening at Vauxhall at so high a price?

I did, however, much about the same time, a harder day's walk. I was returning from Oxford to Harrow Weald, and I determined to walk it, not, I think, on this occasion, *deficiente crumenâ*, but for pleasure, and to try my powers. The distance, I think, is, as near as may be, forty-seven miles. But I carried a very heavy knapsack —a far heavier one than any experienced campaigner would have advised. This was the longest day's walk I ever achieved ; and I arrived very tired and footsore. But the next morning I was perfectly well, and ready to have taken the road again. Upon this occasion I walked my first stage of twelve miles before breakfast ; absolutely, that is to say, before breaking my fast. I think that not very many persons could do this, and I am sure that the few who could do it had much better not do so.

I have spoken of the immense change operated in the circumstances and surroundings of all of us by my mother's return from America and the success of her first work, the "Domestic Manners of the Americans." But, efficacious as this success was for producing so great a change, and sufficient as the continued success of her subsequent works was to rescue the whole of her family from the slough of ruin, in which my father's farming operations, and to some extent, I suppose, his injudicious commercial attempt at Cincinnati, had involved him, the results of this success were very far from availing to stem the tide of ruin as regarded his affairs. They were sufficient to relieve him from all expenses connected with the household or its individual members, but not to supply, in addition to all these, the annual losses on Harrow farm. Hence the break-up described by my brother in his "Autobiography," and my father's exodus from Harrow as there narrated.

CHAPTER XII.

OF all that Anthony there describes I saw nothing. I was attending the "divinity lectures" in Oxford. But as soon as the short course of them was completed, I left England to join my parents at Bruges. And here is the condensed record of the journey as performed in 1834. I suppose that I went by the Thames to Calais, instead of by Dover, as a measure of economy. I left Oxford by the Rocket at three in the morning on Tuesday, the 20th May, and on reaching London found that there was no packet to Ostend till the following Saturday. I determined, therefore, to go to Calais by that which left Tower Stairs on the Wednesday. It was the first time I had ever crossed the Channel. The times I have crossed that salt girdle subsequently must be counted by hundreds. I observe that having begun my journey at 3 A.M. did not prevent me from finding "Farren admirable" in both "The Minister and the Mercer" and in "Secret Service," at Drury Lane that Tuesday evening. I slept at the Spread Eagle in Gracechurch Street that night, and left Tower Stairs at 10 A.M. the next morning in the *Lord Melville*, Captain Middletown (names of ship and captain duly recorded), and had a rough passage of thirteen hours; all hands sick, "even I a little at last," says the veracious chronicle. I was taken by the victor in a sharp contest with half a dozen rivals over my body to the Hôtel de Londres, a clean, comfortable, and quiet, but, I suppose, quite second-rate inn. There was no conveyance to Dunkirk before one the next day. So, "after a delicious breakfast on coffee." (Ah! how *la belle France* has *dégringoléd* in respect to coffee and some other matters since those happy days! Then coffee really was *always* good everywhere in France. Now England has no cause whatever to envy her neighbor in that respect.) I spent the intervening hours in going (of all things in the world) to the top of the church tower. The diligence brought me to Dunkirk in time for supper at the Tête de Flandres Hôtel, at which "a Frenchman, who sat next me, insisted on my sharing his bottle of vin de Bourdeaux, and would not hear of my paying my share of the cost, saying that he was at home in his own country." I find that I went after supper "to the top of a fine tower" (my second that day ! I had a mania, not quite cured yet, for ascending towers), and started at five the next morning for Nieuport "in a vile little barge, in company with two young pedestrianizing Belgians," and arrived there about noon, after a most tedious voyage, and changing, without bettering, our barge three or four times. At Nieuport we found "a sort of immense overgrown gig with two horses, which conveyed eight of us to Ostend."

There I was most kindly and hospitably received by Mr. Fauche, the English consul, and his very lovely wife. Mrs. Fauche had been before her marriage one of my mother's cohort of pretty girl friends, and was already my old acquaintance. She was the daughter of Mr. Tomkisson, a pianoforte manufacturer, who had married the daughter of an Irish clergyman. Their daughter Mary was, as I first knew her, more than a pretty girl. She was a very beautiful and accomplished woman, with one of the most delicious soprano voices I ever heard. I was anxious to join my mother at Bruges, who, despite her literary triumphs, had passed through so much trouble since I had seen her. But it needed the reinforcement of this anxiety by a sense of duty to enable me to resist Mrs. Fauche's invitation to remain a day or two at Ostend.

I found my father and mother, and my two sisters, Cecilia and Emily, established in a large and very roomy house, just outside the southern gate of the city, known as the Château d'Hondt. It was a thoroughly good and comfortable house, and, taken unfurnished, speedily became under my mother's hands a very pleasant one. Nor was it long before it became socially a very agreeable one, for the invariable result of my mother's presence, which

8

drew what was pleasant around her as surely as a magnet draws iron, showed itself in the collection of a variety of agreeable people—some from the other side of the Channel, some from Ostend, and some few from Bruges.

All this made a social atmosphere, which with the foreign flavoring so wholly new to me, was very pleasant; but it seems not to have sufficed to prevent me from seizing the opportunity for a little of that locomotive sight-seeing, the passion for which, still unquenched, appears to have been as strong in me as when I hankered after a place on some one of the "down" coaches starting from the "Cellar" in Piccadilly, or gazed enviously at the outward-bound ships in the docks. For I find the record of a little week's tour among the Belgian cities, with full details of all the towers I ascended, observations of an ecclesiological neophyte on the churches I everywhere visited, and remarks on men and manners, the rawness of which does not entirely destroy the value of them, as illustrating the changes wrought there too by the lapse of half a century.

In one place I find myself tasting the contents of the library of a Carmelite monastery, and remarking on the strangeness of the *sole* exception to the theological character of the collection having consisted in a *Cours Gastronomique*, which appeared to me scarcely needed by a community bound by its vows to perpetual abstinence from animal food.

Some pages of the record also are devoted to the statement of "a case" which I lighted on in some folio on casuistry, on the question "whether it is lawful to adore a crucifix, when there is strong ground for supposing that a demon may be concealed in the material of which it is constructed!"

It seems to me on reading these pages (for the first time since they were written), that I was to no small degree seductively impressed by the music, architectural beauties, and splendid ceremonial of the Roman Catholic worship, seen in those days to much better effect in Belgium than at the present time in Rome. But amid it all, the sturdy Protestantism of Whately's pupil manifests itself in a moan over the pity, the pity of it, that it should "all be based on falsehood."

All the pleasant state of things at the Château d'Hondt at Bruges, described above, was of short duration, however, for disquieting accounts of the health of my brother Henry, who had been staying at Exeter with that dear old friend, Fanny Bent, to whom the reader has already been introduced, began to arrive from Devonshire.

It was moreover necessary that I should without loss of time set my hand to something that might furnish me with daily bread. So on the 21st of June I "went on board Captain Smithett's vessel the *Arrow* and had a quiet passage to Dover." On arriving there I "hastened to secure my place on a coach about to start, and the first turn for having my baggage examined at the custom-house. This examination was rather a rigid one, and they made me pay 4s. 7d. for two or three books I had with me. We reached Canterbury about nightfall, breakfasted at Rochester, and arrived at Charing Cross at six." My diary does not say "six P.M.," and it seem incredible that any coach—though on the slowest road out of London, as the Dover road always was—should have breakfasted at Rochester, and taken the whole day to travel thence to Charing Cross; but it is more incredible still that we should have stopped to breakfast at Rochester, and then reached London at 6 A.M.

It must have been 6 P.M.; but I read that "I started at once to walk to Harrow by the canal (!) where I was received with more than kindness by the Grants."

I had come down to London with the intention of giving classical teaching to any who were willing to pay about ten shillings an hour for it. I had testimonials and recommendations galore from a very varied collection of pastors, masters, and friends. Several of the latter also were actively eager to assist my object, foremost among whom I may name with unforgetting gratitude Dr. David Williams, my old master at Winchester, then warden of New College. Thus furnished, pupils were not wanting, and money amply sufficient for my immediate needs seemed to come in easily. I did my best with my pupils during the short hours of my work; but much success is not to be expected from pupils the very circumstance and terms of whose tuition give rise to the presumption that they are irremediably stupid or idle, and the hired "coach" a *dernier resort.* Such employers as I had to deal with, however, if they assigned you somewhat hopeless tasks, appeared to be satisfied with an infinitesimal amount of results, and I believe I gave satisfaction in all cases save that of a lady, the widowed mother of an only son, a very elegant and fashionable dame in Belgrave Square, who complained once to the clergyman who had recommended me to her, that I had come to her house one Monday morning "in a very dusty condition." I fear she might have said every Monday morning, for my custom was to walk up to my lesson from Harrow, where I had been spending the Sunday with the Grants, and "*immer noch stäuben die Wege*" hardly less on the Harrow road than Goethe found them to do in Italy. I had to tell her that the dust on my shoes had not reached my brain, and that I had no pretension, and entirely declined, to be an exemplar to her son in the matter of his toilet. We parted very good friends, however, at the end of my engagement. When she said some complimentary words about my work with her son, I could not refrain from saying that I had done my best to prepare myself for it by having my shoes carefully blacked. She laughed, and said, "I could not find fault with your Latin and Greek, Mr. Trollope. And would it not be better if people always confined their criticism to what they *do* understand?"

I was living during these months in Little Marlborough Street, in a house kept by a tailor and his mother. It was a queer house, disconnected with the row of buildings in which it stood, a survival of some earlier period. It stood in its own court, by which it was separated from the street. I found all the place transmogrified when I visited it a year or two ago. During the latter part of my residence there the lodgings were shared by my brother Anthony, who, as related by himself, had accepted a place in the secretary's office in the post-office. The lodgings were very cheap, more so I think than the goodness of them might have justified. We were the only lodgers; and the cheapness of the rooms was, I suspect, in some degree caused by the fact that the majority of young-men lodgers would not have tolerated the despotic rule of our old land-lady, the tailor's mother. She made us very comfortable; but her laws were many, and of the nature of those of the Medes and Persians.

Meantime matters were becoming more and more gloomy in the Château d'Hondt, outside the St. Peter's Gate, at Bruges. My brother Henry had returned thither from Devonshire; and his condition was unmistakably becom-ing worse. While I was still living in Little Marlborough Street, my mother came over hurriedly to London, bring-ing him and my sister Emily with her. They travelled by boat from Ostend to London to avoid the land journey. I take it poor Henry was led to suppose that the journey was altogether caused by the necessity of interviews be-tween my mother and her publishers. But the real motive of it was to obtain the best medical advice for him and (as, alas! it began to appear to be necessary) for my sister Emily.

All kinds of schemes of southern travel, and voyages to Madeira, etc., had been proposed for Henry, who, having himself, with the hopefulness peculiar to his malady, no shadow of a doubt of his own recovery, entered into them all with the utmost zest. A kind friend, I forget by what means or interest, had offered to provide free passages to Madeira. Alas! the first consultation with the medical authorities put an end to all such schemes. And my poor mother had the inexpressibly sad and difficult task of quashing them all without allowing her patient to suspect the real reason of their being given up.

She had to take him back to Bruges; and I accom-panied them to the boat lying off the Tower, and remained with them an hour before it weighed anchor. And then and there I took the last leave of my brother Henry, I well knowing, he never imagining, that it was forever.

And now began at Bruges a time of such stress and trouble for my mother as few women have ever passed through. The grief, the Rachel sorrows of mothers watching by the dying beds of those to save whose lives they would—ah ! how readily—give their own, are, alas, common enough. But no account, no contemplation of any such scene of anguish, can give an adequate conception of what my mother went through victoriously.

Her literary career had hitherto been a succession of triumphs. Money was coming in with increasing abundance. But these successes had not yet lasted long enough to enable her, in the face of all she had done for the ruined household to which she had returned from America, to lay by any fund for the future. And though the proceeds of her labor were amply sufficient for all current needs, it was imperative that that labor should not be suspended.

It was under these circumstances that she had to pass her days in watching by the bedside of a very irritable invalid, and her nights—when he fortunately for the most part slept—in composing fiction ! It was desirable to keep the invalid's mind from dwelling on the hopelessness of his condition. And, indeed, he was constantly occupied in planning travels and schemes of activity for the anticipated time of his recovery, which she had to enter into and discuss with a cheerful countenance and bleeding heart. It was also especially necessary that my sisters, especially the younger, already threatened by the same malady, should be kept cheerful, and prevented from dwelling on the phases of their brother's illness. This was the task in which, with agonized mind, she never faltered from about nine o'clock every morning till eight o'clock in the evening. Then with wearied body, and mind attuned to such thoughts as one may imagine, she had to sit down to her desk to write her novel with all the *verve* at her command, to please light-hearted readers, till two or three in the morning. This, by the help of green tea and sometimes laudanum, she did daily and nightly till the morning of the 23d of December of that sad 1834; and lived after it to be eighty-three !

But her mind was one of the most extraordinarily constituted in regard to recuperative power and the capacity of throwing off sorrow that I ever knew or read of. Any one who did not know her, as her own son knew her, might

have supposed that she was deficient in sensibility. No
judgment could be more mistaken. She felt acutely, vehemently. But she seemed to throw off sorrow as, to use
the vulgar phrase, a duck's back throws off water, because the nature of the organism will not suffer it to rest
there. How often have I applied to her the words of
David under a similar affliction !

My brother died on the 23d of December, 1834, and
was buried at Bruges, in the Protestant portion of the
city cemetery. Had his life been much prolonged, I think
that that of my mother must have sunk under the burden
laid upon it. I hastened to cross the Channel as soon as I
heard of my brother's death, but did not arrive in time
for his funeral.

A few days later I was, I find, consulting a Bruges physician, a Dr. Herbout, whom I still remember perfectly
well, about the health of my father, which had recently
been causing my mother some anxiety. Herbout was an
old army doctor who had served under Napoleon. It is
probable that he was more of a surgeon than a physician.
His opinion was that my father's condition, though not
satisfactory, did not indicate any cause for immediate
alarm.

I remained at Bruges till the first week in April. That
is to say, the Château d'Hondt was my home during those
months, but the monotony of it was varied by frequent
visits to Ostend, which Mrs. Fauche always found the
means of making agreeable. One week of the time also
was spent in a little tour through those parts of Belgium
which I had not yet seen, in company with my old friend,
and the reader's old acquaintance, Fanny Bent. It was an
oddly constituted travelling party—the young man full
of strength, activity, and eagerness to see everything that
indefatigable exertion could show him, and the very plain,
Quaker-like, middle-aged old maid, absolutely new to
Continental ways and manners and habits. Yet few people, I think, have ever seen the many interesting sights of
the region we travelled over more completely than I and
Fanny Bent. The number of towers (Antwerp among
them) to the tops of which I took her, as recorded in my

diary, seems preposterous. But Fanny Bent bravely stuck to her work, and where I led she followed. I have since squired many fairer and younger dames, but never one so bravely determined on doing all that was to be done. And very much we both enjoyed it.

Almost immediately after my return from this little excursion I received a letter from an old Wykehamist schoolfellow, the Rev. George Hall, of Magdalen, son of the head of Pembroke at Oxford, offering me a mastership in King Edward's Grammar School, at Birmingham. The head-master of that school was at that time Dr. Jeune, a Pembroke man, and thence a close friend of George Hall, who himself held one of the masterships, which he was about to resign. The salary of the mastership offered me was £200 a year, with, of course, prospects of advancement. I at once determined to accept it, and, with the promptitude which in those days characterized me (at least in all cases in which promptitude involved immediate locomotion), I decided to leave Bruges for Birmingham on the morrow. I slept at Ostend the next night, and the following day crossed to Dover with my friend Captain Smithett, of the *Arrow*, "the only other passengers," says my diary, "being a maniac and a corpse."

Smithett was a remarkably handsome man, and the very *beau-idéal* of a sailor. For many years he was the man always selected to carry any royal or distinguished personage who had to cross the Channel from or to Dover. He was an immense favorite with all the little Ostend world—with the female part of it, of course, especially. I remember his showing me, with much laughter, an anonymous *billet doux* which had reached him, beginning, " *O toi qui commandes la Flèche, tu peux aussi commander les cœurs,*" etc., etc. I discovered the writer some time subsequently in an extremely pretty *baigneuse*, the wife, I am sorry to say, of a highly respected Belgian banker. Perhaps all his Ostend admirers did not know that he had a charming wife at Dover. He was all the more an object of our admiration from the singular contrast between him and his colleague, a certain Captain Murch. Between them they did in those days the whole of the Ostend and Dover mail business. Poor Murch was much of an invalid, and, strange as it may seem, suffered invariably on every passage, from year's end to year's end, from sea-sickness. Think of the purgatory involved in the combination of such a constitution with such a profession ! The port of Ostend was at that time somewhat difficult to enter in heavy weather, and bad fogs were very frequent on that coast. Poor Murch was always getting into difficulties which involved "lying to," and reaching his destination long after time ; whereas we held that the dashing *Arrow* would go wherever the *Flying Dutchman* could. And indeed I have seen her come in when I could only remain at the pier-head by lashing myself to a post. So much for " *le beau Capitaine Smitète.*"

Losing no time in London, I reached Birmingham on the evening of Sunday the 5th, and found my friend Hall quite sure of my election by the governors of the school on the recommendation of *his* friend Jeune. But then began a whole series of slips between the cup and the lip. There appeared to be no doubt of their electing me if they elected anybody; but a part of the board wished, on financial grounds, to defer the election of a new master for a while. The governors, at their meeting, put off the decision of the matter to another meeting on the 24th. On the 24th the matter was again put off. I had left Birmingham on the 12th, with the promise from Jeune, in whom on that, and on subsequent occasions, I found a most kind friend, that he would do all he could to urge the governors to a decision, and lose no time in letting me know the result. On the 24th the election of a new master was again " deferred " by the governors, and the prospect of their coming to a decision to elect one shortly seemed to become more uncertain. Many other meetings of the board took place with a similar result. On one occasion Jeune told me that, had he been in Birmingham at the time of the meeting, he felt sure that he could have induced them to come to an election; but he had unfortunately been absent. At another meeting I was told that I should have been elected had not Sir Edward Thomason,

8*

one of the governors who wished to elect a master, run away to a dinner-party, thus leaving the non-content party in the majority.

Meantime I took my degree at Oxford on the 29th of April, which was needed for holding the appointment in question, and waited with what patience I could in London, dividing my time between the dear and ever-kind Grants and my brother Anthony, who was doing — or, rather, getting into continual hot water for not doing — his work at the post-office. He was, I take it, a very bad office-clerk ; but as soon as he was appointed a surveyor's clerk became at once one of the most efficient and valuable officers in the post-office.

Leaving Oxford on the night of the 29th I returned to Birmingham, and was again tantalized by repeated inconclusive meetings of the school governors, till at last, on the 6th of May, Jeune told me that he thought that they would not come to an election till midsummer, but that, in any case, there was another of the masters whose resignation he had reason to believe would not be long deferred, and I should assuredly have his place. On this I returned to London, and on the 8th of May left it for Dover, on my way to join my mother in Paris.

Having spoken of Anthony's efficiency as an officer of the post-office, I may, I think, in the case of so well-known a man, venture to expend a page in giving the reader an anecdote of his promptness, of which, as of dozens of other similar experiences, he says nothing in his "Autobiography." He had visited the office of a certain postmaster in the southwest of Ireland in the usual course of his duties, had taken stock of the man, and had observed him in the course of his interview carefully lock a large desk in the office. Two days afterwards there came from headquarters an urgent inquiry about a lost letter, the contents of which were of considerable value. The information reached the surveyor late at night, and he at once put the matter into the hands of his subordinate. There was no conveyance to the place where my brother determined his first investigations should be made till the following morning. But it did not suit him to wait for that, so he hired a horse, and, riding hard, knocked up the postmaster whom he had interviewed, as related, a couple of days before, in the small hours. Possibly the demeanor of the man in some degree influenced his further proceedings. Be this as it may, he walked straight into the office, and said, "Open that desk!" The key, he was told, had been lost for some time past. Without another word he smashed the desk with one kick, and there found the stolen letter!

I have heard from him so many good stories of his official experiences that I feel myself tolerably competent to write a volume of "Memoirs of a Post-office Surveyor." But for the present I must content myself with one other of his adventures. He had been sent to South America to arrange some difficulties about postal communication in those parts which our authorities wished to be accomplished in a shorter time than had been previously the practice. There was a certain journey that had to be done by a mounted courier, for which it was insisted that three days were necessary, while my brother was persuaded it could be done in two. He was told that he knew nothing of their roads and their horses, etc. "Well," said he, "I will ask you to do nothing that I, who know nothing of the country, and can only have such a horse as your post can furnish me, cannot do myself. I will ride with your courier, and then I shall be able to judge." And at daybreak the next morning they started. The brute they gave him to ride was, of course, selected with a view of making good their case, and the saddle was simply an instrument of torture. He rode through that hot day, and kept the courier to his work in a style that rather astonished that official. But at night, when they were to rest for a few hours, Anthony confessed that he was in such a state that he began to think that he should have to throw up the sponge, which would have been dreadful to him. So he ordered two bottles of brandy, poured them into a wash-hand basin, and *sat in it!* His description of the agonizing result was graphic! But the next day, he said, he was able to sit in his saddle without pain, did the journey in the two days, and carried his point.

But I must abstain from further anticipations of the

memoirs above spoken of, the more especially as I left my own story at the point where I had before me, like Rousseau—and probably with no less rose-colored anticipations —*un voyage à faire, et Paris au bout,* and that for the first time in my life !

CHAPTER XIII.

I OBSERVE that I left Calais in the *banquette* of the diligence at 6 P.M. on the Friday night, May 8, 1835, and reached Paris at 3 P.M. on Sunday morning—thirty-three hours. I remember my great surprise at finding the entire way paved after the fashion that I had been accustomed to consider proper only for the streets of towns. We used, for by far the greatest part of the way, the unpaved spaces left on either side of the paved causeway. But the conductor told me that in winter they were generally obliged to keep on the latter the whole way. The horses, two wheelers and three leaders abreast, were almost—indeed, I think quite—without exception gray. They were also all, or almost all, stallions. The style of driving struck me as very rough, awkward, violent, and inelegant, but masterful and efficacious. The driver was changed with every relay ; and it seemed to me very probable that it was expedient that each man should know such cattle, not only on the road, but in the stable.

We breakfasted at Abbeville and dined at Beauvais. And I find it recorded that I contrived at both places to find time for a flying visit to the cathedral, and was highly delighted with the noble fragment of a church at the latter city.

I went to bed on arriving at the Hôtel de Lille et d'Albion, which was in those days a very different place from its noisy, pretentious, and vulgar successor of the same name in the Rue St. Honoré. The old house in the Rue des Filles de St. Thomas has long since disappeared, together with the quiet little street in which it was situated. Like its successor, it was almost exclusively used by English, but they were the English of the days when personally-conducted herds were not. The service was performed by handmaidens in neat caps, and white bodices over their colored skirts. There were no swallow-tail-coated waiters, and the coffee was exquisite. *Tempi passati, perchè non tornate più?*

At ten the next morning I went to No. 6 Rue de Provence, where I found my parents and my sisters at breakfast.

The object of this Paris journey was twofold—the writing a book in accordance with an agreement which my mother had entered into with Mr. Richard Bentley, the father of the publisher, and the consultation of a physician to whom she had been especially recommended respecting my father's health, which was rapidly and too evidently declining. They had been in Paris some time already, and had formed a large circle of acquaintance, both English and French. I was told by my mother that the physician, who had seen my father several times, had made no pleasant report of his condition. He did not apprehend any immediately alarming phase of illness, but said that, had he been left to guess my father's age after visiting him, he should have supposed him to be more than fourscore, the truth being that he was very little more than sixty.

This, my first visit to Paris, lasted one month only, from the 9th of May to the 9th of June, and many of the recollections which seem to me now to be connected with it very probably belong to subsequent visits, for my diary, reopened now for the first time after the interval of more than half a century, was kept, I find, in a very intermittent and slovenly manner. No doubt I found very few minutes for journalizing in the four-and-twenty hours of each day.

I well remember that my first impression of *Lutetia Parisiorum*—"Mudtown of the Parisians," as Carlyle translates it—was that of having stepped back a couple of centuries or so in the history of European civilization and progress. We are much impressed at home, and talk much of the vastness of the changes which the last fifty years have made in our own city, but I think that which the same time has operated in Paris is much greater.

Putting aside the mere extension of streets and dwellings, which, great as it has been in Paris, has been much greater in London, the changes in the former city have been far more radical. Certainly there are many quarters of London where the eye now rests on that which is magnificent, and which, at the time when I knew the town well, presented nothing but what was, if not sordid, at least ugly. But, to those who remember the streets of Louis Philippe's city, the change, in the whole conception of city life and the *manière d'être* of the population, is far greater. With the exception of the principal boulevards in the neighborhood of the recently completed "Madeleine" and its then recently established flower-market, the streets were still traversed by filthy and malodorous open ditches, which did, more or less imperfectly, the duty of sewers, and Paris still deserves its name of "Mudtown." Wretched little oil-lamps, suspended on ropes stretched across the streets, barely served to make darkness visible. Water was still carried, at so much the bucket, up the interminable staircases of the Parisian houses by stalwart Auvergnats, who came from their mountains to do a work more severe than the Parisians could do for themselves.

But another specialty, which very forcibly struck me, and cannot be said to have been any survival of ways and habits obsolete on the other side of the Channel, was the remarkable manner in which the political life of the hour, with its emotions, opinions, and passions, was enacted, so to speak, on the stage of the streets, as a drama is presented on the boards of a theatre. Truly he who ran through the streets of Paris in those days might read, and, indeed, could not help reading, the reflection and the manifestation of the political divisions and passions which animated the reign of the *bourgeois* king, and ended by destroying it.

And in this respect the time of my first visit to Paris was a very interesting one. The Parisian world was, of course, divided into Monarchists and Republicans, the latter of whom labored under the imputation, in some cases probably unjust, but in more entirely merited (as in certain other more modern instances), of being willing and ready to bring their theories into practice by perpetrating or conniving at any odious monstrosity of crime, violence, and bloodshed. The Fieschi incident had recently enlightened the world on the justice of such accusations.

But the Monarchists were more amusingly divided into "*Parceque* Bourbon," supporters of the existing *régime*, and "*Quoique* Bourbon," tolerators of it. The former, of course, would have preferred the white flag and Charles Dix ; but failing the possibility of such a return to the old ways, were content to live under the rule of a sovereign who, though not the legitimate monarch by right divine, was at least a scion of the old legitimate race. The "*Quoique* Bourbon" partisans were the men who, denying all right to the throne save that which emanated from the will of the people, were yet Monarchists from their well-rooted dread of the intolerable evils which Republicanism had brought, and, as they were convinced, would bring again upon France, and were therefore contented to support the *bourgeois* monarchy "although" the man on the throne was an undeniable Bourbon.

But what made the streets, the boulevards, the Champs Elysées, and especially the Tuileries garden peculiarly amusing to a stranger, was the circumstance that the Parisians all got themselves up with strict attention to the recognized costume proper to their political party. The Legitimist, the "*Quoique Bourbon*" *bourgeois* (very probably in the uniform of the then immensely popular National Guard), and the Republican in his appropriate bandit-shaped hat and coat with exaggeratedly large lappels, or draped picturesquely in the folds of a cloak, after a fashion borrowed from the other side of the Alps, were all distinguishable at a glance. It was then that deliciously graphic line (I forget who wrote it) "*Feignons à feindre à fin de mieux dissimuler*" was applied to characterize the conspirator-like attitudes it pleased these gentlemen to assume.

The truth was that Paris was still very much afraid of them. I remember the infinite glee, and the outpouring of ridicule, which hailed the dispersion of a Republican "demonstration" (the reader will forgive the anachronism of the phrase), at the Porte St. Martin, by the judicious use of a powerful fire-engine. The heroes of the *drapeau rouge* had boasted they would stand their ground against any charge of soldiery. Perhaps they would have done so. But the helter-skelter that ensued on the first well-directed jet of cold water from the pipe of a fire-engine furnished Paris with laughter for days afterwards.

But, as I have said, Paris, not unreasonably, feared them. Secret conspiracy is always an ugly enemy to deal with. And no violence of mere speculative opinion would have sufficed, had fear been absent, to cause the very marked repulsion with which all the Parisians, who had anything to lose, in that day regarded their Republican fellow-citizens.

Assuredly the Conservatives of the Parisian world of 1835 were not "the stupid party." Both in their newspapers, and other ephemeral literature, and in the never-ending succession of current *mots* and jokes which circulated in the Parisian *salons*, they had the pull very decidedly. I remember some words of a parody on one of the Republican songs of the day, which had an immense vogue at that time. "*On devrait planter le chêne,*" it ran, "*pour l'arbre de la liberté*" (it will be remembered that planting "trees of liberty" was one of the common and more harmless "demonstrations" of the Republican party). "*Ses glands nouriraient sans peine les cochons qui l'ont planté.*" And the burden of the original which ran, "*Mourir pour la patrie, C'est le sort le plus beau le plus digne d'envie,*" was sufficiently and very appositely caricatured by the slight change of "*Mourir pour la patrie*" into "*Nourris par la patrie,*" etc.

To a stranger seeing Paris as I saw it, and frequenting the houses which I frequented, it seemed strange that such a community should have considered itself in serious danger from men who seemed to me, looking from such a standpoint, a mere handful of skulking melodramatic enthusiasts, playing at conspiracy and rebellion rather than really meditating it. But I was not at that time fully aware how entirely the real danger was to be found in regions of Paris and strata of its population which were as entirely hidden from my observation as if they had been a thousand miles away. But though I could not see the danger, I saw unmistakably enough the fear it inspired in all classes of those who, as I said before, had anything to lose.

It was this fear that made the National Guard the heroes of the hour. It was impossible but that such a body of men—Parisian shopkeepers put into uniform (those of them who had condescended to wear it ; for many used to be seen who contented themselves with girding on a sabre and assuming a firelock, while others would go to the extent of surmounting the ordinary black coat with the regulation military shako)—should afford a target for many shafts of ridicule. The capon-lined paunches of a considerable contingent of these well-to-do warriors were an inexhaustible source of not very pungent jokes. But Paris would have been frightened out of its wits at the bare suggestion of suppressing these citizen saviours of society. Of course they were petted at the Tuileries. No reception or *fête* of any kind was complete without a large sprinkling of these shopkeeping guardsmen, and their presence on such occasions was the subject of an un-failing series of *historiettes*.

I remember an anecdote excellently illustrative of the time, which was current in the *salons* of the "*Parceque* Bourbon" society of the day. A certain elderly duchess of the *vieille roche*, a dainty little woman, very *mignonne*, whose exquisite *parure* and still more exquisite manners scented the air at a league's distance, to use the common French phrase, with the odor of the most aristocratic *salons* of the Quartier St. Germain, was, at one of Louis Phi-lippe's Tuileries receptions, about to take from the tray handed round by a servant the last of the ices which it had contained, when a huge outstretched hand, with its five wide-spread fingers, was protruded from behind over her shoulder, and the refreshment of which she was about to avail herself was seized by a big National Guard with the exclamation, "*Enfoncée la petite mère !*"

Nevertheless, it may be safely asserted that the little duchess, and all the world she moved in, would have been infinitely more dismayed had they gone to the Tuileries and seen no National Guards there.

Among the many persons of note with whom I became more or less well acquainted during that month, no one perhaps stands out more vividly in my recollection than Chateaubriand. He also, though standing much aloof from the noise and movement of the political passions of the time, was an aristocrat *jusqu'au bout des ongles*, in appearance, in manners, in opinions, and general tone of mind. The impression to this effect immediately produced on one's first presentation was in no degree due to any personal advantages. He was not, when I knew him, nor do I think he ever could have been, a good-looking man. He stooped a good deal, and his head and shoulders gave me the impression of being somewhat too large for the rest of his person. The lower part of his face too, was, I thought, rather heavy.

But his every word and movement were characterized by that exquisite courtesy which was the inalienable, and it would seem incommunicable, specialty of the *seigneurs* of the *ancien régime*. And in his case the dignified bearing of the grand seigneur was tempered by a *bonhomie* which produced a manner truly charming.

And having said all this, it may seem to argue want of taste or want of sense in myself to own, as truthfulness compels me to do, that I did not altogether like him. I had a good deal of talk with him, and that to a youngster of my years and standing was in itself very flattering, and I felt as if I were ungrateful for not liking him. But the truth in one word is, that he appeared to me to be a "tinkling cymbal." I don't mean that he was specially insincere as regarded the person he was talking to at the moment. What I do mean is, that the man did not seem to me to have a mind capable of genuine sincerity in the conduct of its operations. He seemed to me a theatrically-minded man. Immediately after making his acquaintance I read the *Génie du Chrétienisme*, and the book confirmed my impression of the man. He honestly intends to play a very good and virtuous part, but he *is* playing a part.

He was much petted in those days by the men, and

more especially by the women, of the *ancien régime* and
the Quartier St. Germain. But I suspect that he was a
good deal quizzed, and considered an object of more or
less good-natured ridicule by the rest of the Parisian
world. I fancy that he was in straitened circumstances.
And the story went that he and his wife put all they possessed into a box, of which each of them had a key, and
took from day to day what they needed, till one fine day
they met over the empty box with no little surprise and
dismay.

Chateaubriand thought he understood English well, and
rather piqued himself upon the accomplishment. But I
well remember his one day asking me to explain to him
the construction of the sentence, "Let but the cheat endure, I ask not aught beside." My efforts to do so during
the best part of half an hour ended in entire failure.

He was in those days reading in Madame Récamier's
salon at the Abbaye-aux-Bois (in which building my
mother's friend, Miss Clarke, also had her residence), those
celebrated *Mémoires d'Outretombe* of which all Paris, or
at least all literary and political Paris, was talking. Immense efforts were made by all kinds of notabilities to obtain an admission to these readings. But the favored ones
had been very few. And my mother was proportionably
delighted at the arrangement that a reading should be
given expressly for her benefit. M. de Chateaubriand
had ceased these *séances* for the nonce, and the gentleman
who had been in the habit of reading for him had left
Paris. But by the kindness of Miss Clarke and Madame
Récamier, he was induced to give a sitting at the Abbaye
expressly for my mother. This arrangement had been
made before I reached Paris, and I consequently, to my
great regret, was not one of the very select party. My
mother was accompanied by my sisters only. I benefited,
however, in my turn by the acquaintance thus formed, and
subsequently passed more than one evening in Madame Récamier's *salon* at the Abbaye-aux-Bois in the Rue du Bac.

My mother, in her book on "Paris and the Parisians,"
writes of that reading as follows : "The party assembled
at Madame Récamier's on this occasion did not, I think,

exceed seventeen, including Madame Récamier and M. de Chateaubriand. Most of these had been present at former readings. The Duchesses de Larochefoucald and de Noailles, and one or two other noble ladies, were among them. And I felt it was a proof that genius was of no party when I saw a granddaughter of General Lafayette enter among us. She is married to a gentleman who is said to be of the extreme *coté gauche*." The passage of the "Mémoires" selected for the evening's reading was the account of the author's memorable trip to Prague to visit the royal exiles. "Many passages," writes my mother, "made a profound impression on my fancy and on my memory, and I think I could give a better account of some of the scenes described than I should feel justified in doing, as long as the noble author chooses to keep them from the public eye. There were touches that made us weep abundantly ; and then he changed the key, and gave us the prettiest, the most gracious, the most smiling picture of the young princess and her brother that it was possible for pen to trace. And I could have said, as one does in seeing a clever portrait, 'That is a likeness, I'll be sworn for it.'"

It may be seen from the above passage, and from some others in my mother's book on "Paris and the Parisians," that her estimate of the man Chateaubriand was a somewhat higher one than that which I have expressed in the preceding pages. She was under the influence of the exceeding charm of his exquisite manner. But in the following passage, which I am tempted to transcribe by the curious light it throws on the genesis of the present literary history of France, I can more entirely subscribe to the opinions expressed :

"The active, busy, bustling politicians of the hour have succeeded in thrusting everything else out of place, and themselves into it. One dynasty has been overthrown, and another established ; old laws have been abrogated, and hundreds of new ones formed ; hereditary nobles have been disinherited, and little men made great. But amidst this plenitude of destructiveness, they have not yet contrived to make any one of the puny literary reputations of the day weigh down the renown of those who have never lent their voices to the cause of treason, regicide, rebellion, or obscenity. The literary reputations both of Chateaubriand and Lamartine stand higher beyond all comparison than those of any other living French authors. Yet the first, with all his genius, has often suffered his imagination to run riot ; and the last has only given to the public the leisure of his literary life. But both of them are men of honor and principle, as well as men of genius ; and it comforts one's human nature to see that these qualities will keep themselves aloft, despite whatever squally winds may blow, or blustering floods assail them. That both Chateaubriand and Lamartine belong rather to the imaginative than to the *positif* class cannot be denied; but they are renowned throughout the world, and France is proud of them. The most curious literary speculations, however, suggested by the present state of letters in this country are not respecting authors such as these. They speak for themselves, and all the world knows them and their position. The circumstance decidedly the most worthy of remark in the literature of France at the present time is the effect which the last revolution appears to have produced. With the exception of history, to which both Thiers (?) * and Mignet have added something that may live, notwithstanding their very defective philosophy, no single work has appeared since the Revolution of 1830 which has obtained a substantial, elevated, and generally acknowledged reputation for any author unknown before that period—not even among all the unbridled ebullitions of imagination, though restrained neither by decorum, principle, nor taste. Not even here, except from one female pen, which might become, were it the pleasure of the hand that wields it, the first now extant in the world of fiction" (of course, Georges Sand is alluded to), "has anything appeared likely to survive its author. Nor is there any writer who during the same period has raised himself to that station in society by means of his literary productions which is so universally

---

* My query.

áccorded to all who have acquired high literary celebrity in any country.

"The name of Guizot was too well known before the Revolution for these observations to have any reference to him." (Cousin should not have been forgotten.) "And however much he may have distinguished himself since July, 1830, his reputation was made before. There are, however, little writers in prodigious abundance. . . . Never, I believe, was there any period in which the printing-presses of France worked so hard as at present. The Revolution of 1830 seems to have set all the minor spirits in motion. There is scarcely a boy so insignificant, or a workman so unlearned, as to doubt his having the power and the right to instruct the world. . . . To me, I confess, it is perfectly astonishing that any one can be found to class the writers of this restless clique as 'the literary men of France.' . . . Do not, however, believe me guilty of such presumption as to give you my own unsupported judgment as to the position which this 'new school,' as the *décousu* folks always call themselves, hold in the public esteem. My opinion on this subject is the result of careful inquiry among those who are most competent to give information respecting it. When the names of such as are best known among this class of authors are mentioned in society, let the politics of the circle be what they may, they are constantly spoken of as a pariah caste that must be kept apart.

" ' Do you know —— ?' has been a question I have repeatedly asked respecting a person whose name is cited in England as the most esteemed French writer of the age—and so cited, moreover, to prove the low standard of French taste and principle.

" ' No, madame,' has been invariably the cold answer.

" ' Or —— ?'

" ' No ; he is not in society.'

" ' Or —— ?'

" ' Oh, no ! His works live an hour—too long—and are forgotten.' "

Now, are the writers of French literature of the present day, whose names will at once present themselves to every

reader's mind, to be deemed superior to those of the time of
Louis Philippe, who "lent their voices to the cause of treason, regicide, rebellion, or obscenity," and were unrestrained
by either "decorum, principle, or taste?" For it is most
assuredly no longer true that the writers in question are
held to be a "pariah caste," or that they are not known
and sought by "society." The *facilis decensus* progress
of the half-century that has elapsed since the cited passages were written is certainly remarkable.

There is one name, however, which cannot be simply
classed as one of the *décousus*. Victor Hugo had already
at that day made a European reputation. But the following passage about him from my mother's book on
"Paris and the Parisians" is so curious, and to the present generation must appear so, one may almost say, monstrous, that it is well worth while to reproduce it.

"I have before stated," she writes, "that I have uniformly heard the whole of the *décousu* school of authors
spoken of with unmitigated contempt, and that not only
by the venerable advocates for the *bon vieux temps*, but
also, and equally, by the distinguished men of the present day—distinguished both by position and ability. Respecting Victor Hugo, the only one of the tribe to which
I allude who has been sufficiently read in England to justify his being classed by us as a person of general celebrity, the feeling is more remarkable still. I have never
mentioned him or his works to any person of good moral
feeling or cultivated mind who did not appear to shrink
from according him even the degree of reputation that
those who are received as authority among our own cities
have been disposed to allow him. *I might say that of
him France seems to be ashamed.*" (My italics.) "'Permit me to assure you,' said one gentleman, gravely and
earnestly, 'that no idea was ever more entirely and altogether erroneous than that of supposing that Victor Hugo
and his productions can be looked on as a sort of type or
specimen of the literature of France at the present hour.
He is the head of a sect, the high priest of a congregation
who have abolished every law, moral and intellectual, by
which the efforts of the human mind have hitherto been

regulated. He has attained this pre-eminence, and I trust that no other will arise to dispute it with him. But Victor Hugo is NOT a popular French author.'"

My recollections of all that I heard in Paris, and my knowledge of the circles (more than one) in which my mother used to live, enable me to testify to the absolute truth of the above representation of the prevalent Parisian feeling at that day respecting Victor Hugo. Yet he had then published his "Lyrics," "Notre Dame de Paris," and the most notable of his dramas; and I think no such wonderful change of national opinion and sentiment as the change from the above estimate to that now universally recognized in France can be met with in the records of European literary history. Is it not passing strange that whole regions of Paris should have been but the other day turned, so to speak, into a vast mausoleum to this same "pariah," and that I myself should have seen, as I did, the Pantheon not yet cleared from the wreck of garlands and inscriptions and scaffoldings for spectators, all of which had been prepared to do honor to his obsequies?

But it must be observed that the violent repulsion and reprobation with which he was in those days regarded by all his countrymen, save the extreme and restless spirits of the Republican party, cannot fairly be taken as the result and outcome of genuine literary criticism. All literary judgments in France were then subordinated to political party feeling, and that was intensified by the most fatal of all disqualifications for the formation of sound and equable estimates — by fear. All those well-to-do detesters of Victor Hugo and all his works, the "*Quoique* Bourbons" as well as the "*Parceque* Bourbons," the prosperous supporters of the new *régime* as well as the regretful adherents of the old, lived in perpetual fear of the men whose corypheus and hierophant was Victor Hugo, and felt, not without reason, that the admittedly rickety throne of the citizen king and those sleek and paunchy National Guardsmen alone stood between them and the loss of all they held dearest in the world. Nevertheless, the contrast between the judgments and the feeling of 1835 and those of fifty years later is sufficiently remarkable.

9

Much has been said, especially in England, of the great writer's historical inaccuracy in treating of English matters. But an anecdote which my mother gives in her book is worth reproducing for the sake of the evidence it gives that in truth Victor Hugo was equally ignorantly and carelessly inaccurate when speaking of home matters, on which, at least, it might have been thought that he would have been better informed.

"An able lawyer, and most accomplished gentleman and scholar, who holds a distinguished station in the *cour royale*" (in all probability Berryer), "took us to see the Palais de Justice. Having shown us the chamber where criminal trials are carried on, he observed that this was the room described by Victor Hugo in his romance, adding, 'He was, however, mistaken here, as in most places where he affects a knowledge of the times of which he writes. In the reign of Louis XI. no criminal trials ever took place within the walls of this building, and all the ceremonies as described by him resemble much more a trial of yesterday than of the age at which he dates his tale.'"

Georges Sand, certainly upon the whole the most remarkable literary figure in the French world at the time of my visit to Paris, *vidi tantum*. That I had an opportunity of doing on various occasions. She was a person on whom, quite apart from her literary celebrity, the eye of any observer would have dwelt with some speculative curiosity. She was hardly to be called handsome, or even pretty, but was still decidedly attractive. The large eyes *à fleur de tête*, and the mobile and remarkably expressive mouth rendered the face both attractive and stimulative of interest. The features were unmistakably refined in character and expression, and the mouth—the most trustworthy evidence-giving feature upon that point—was decidedly that of a high-bred woman.

She was at that period of her varied career acting as well as writing in a manner which attracted the attention of Louis Philippe's very vigilant and abnormally suspicious police. She had recently left Paris for an excursion in the *tête-à-tête* company of the well-known Abbé de Lamenais, who was at that time giving much trouble and disquietude to the official guardians of the altar and the throne. His comings and goings were the object of vigilant supervision on the part of the police authorities ; and it so happened by a strange chance that the report of the official observers of this little excursion, which reached the official headquarters, reached me also. And all the watchers had to tell was that the abbé and the lady his companion shared the same bedchamber at the end of their first day's journey. Now the Abbé de Lamenais was an old, little, wizened, dried-up, dirty—very dirty—priest. It is possible, but I have reason to think highly improbable, that economy was the motive of this strange chamber comradeship. But I was then, and am still, very strongly convinced that the sole purpose of it was to outrage the lady's (and the priest's) censors, to act differently from everybody else, and to give evidence of superiority to conventionality and " prejudice."

I wrote very carefully and conscientiously, some few years subsequently, a long article on Georges Sand in the *Foreign Quarterly* which attracted some attention at the time. I should write in many respects differently now. The lady in subsequent years put a considerable quantity of " water into her wine "—and though not altogether in the same sense—I have done so too.

To both Guizot and Thiers I had the honor of being introduced. If I were to say that neither of them seemed to me to have entirely the manners and bearing of a gentleman, I should probably be thought to be talking affected and offensive nonsense. And I do not mean to say so in the ordinary English every-day use of the term. What I mean is that they were both of them very far from possessing that grand-seigneur manner which, as I have said, so markedly distinguished Chateaubriand and many another Frenchman whom I knew in those days ; by no means all of them belonging to the aristocratic caste, party, or class. Guizot looked for all the world like a village schoolmaster, and seemed to me to have much the manner of one. He stooped a good deal, and poked his head forward. I remember thinking that he was, in

manner, more like an Englishman than a Frenchman; and
that it was a matter of curious speculation to me at the
time, whether this effect might have been produced by
the fact that he was a Protestant, and an earnest one, instead of being a Roman Catholic. Possibly my impression of his schoolmaster-like deportment may have been
the result of his manner to me. I was but a boy, with no
claim at all to the honor of being noticed by him in any
way. But I remember being struck by the difference of
the manner of Thiers in this respect.

All my prejudices and all that I knew of the two men
disposed me to feel far the higher respect for Guizot.
And my opinion still is that I judged rightly, whether in
respect to character or intellectual capacity. Not but that
I thought and think that Thiers was the brighter and, in
the ordinary sense of the term, the cleverer man of the
two. There was no brightness about the *premier abord*
of Guizot, though doubtless a longer and more intimate
acquaintance than was granted to me would have corrected
this impression. But Thiers was, from the bow with which
he first received you to the latest word you heard from
him, all brightness. Of dignity he had nothing at all.
If Guizot might have been taken for a schoolmaster,
Thiers might have been mistaken for a stockbroker, say,
a prosperous, busy, bustling, cheery stockbroker, or any
such man of business. And if Guizot gave one the impression of being more English than French, his great
rival was unmistakably and intensely French. I have no
recollection of having much enjoyed my interview with
M. Guizot. But I was happy during more than one evening spent in Thiers' house in Paris.

Of Madame Récamier I should have said the few words
I have to say about the impression so celebrated a woman
produced upon me, when I was speaking of her *salon* in a
previous page. But they may be just as well said here.
Of the beauty for which she was famed throughout Europe,
of course little remained when I saw her in 1835. But
the grace, which was in a far greater degree unique, remained in its entirety. I think she was the most grace-
fully moving woman I ever saw. The expression of her

face had become perhaps a little sad, but it was sweet, attractive, full of the promise of all good things of heart and mind. If I were to say that her management of her *salon* might be compared in the perfection of its tactical success with that of a successful general on the field, it might give the idea that management and discipline were visible, which would be a very erroneous one. That the perfection of art lies in the concealment of it, was never more admirably evidenced than in her "administration" as a *reine de salon*. A close observer might perceive, or, perhaps, rather divine only, that all was marshalled, ordered, and designed. Yet all was, on the part at least of the guests, unconstrained ease and enjoyment. That much native talent, much knowledge of men and women, and exquisite tact must have been needed for this perfection in the art of *tenir salon* cannot be denied. Finally it may be said that a great variety of *historiettes,* old and new, left me with the unhesitating conviction that despite the unfailing tribute to an *éclat* such as hers, of malicious insinuations (all already ancient history at the time of which I am writing), Madame Récamier was and had always been a truly good and virtuous Christian woman.

Miss Clarke, also, as has been said an inmate of the Abbaye-aux-Bois, and a close friend of her celebrated neighbor, I became intimate with. She was an eccentric little lady, very plain, brimful of talent, who had achieved the wonderful triumph of living, in the midst of the choicest society of Paris, her own life after her own fashion, which was often in many respects a very different fashion from that of those around her, without incurring any of the ridicule or anathemas with which such society is wont to visit eccentricity. I remember a good-naturedly recounted legend, to the effect that she used to have her chemises, which were constructed after the manner of those worn by the grandmothers of the present generation, marked with her name in full on the front flap of them ; and that this flap was often exhibited over the bosom of her dress in front ! She too was a *reine de salon* after her fashion—a somewhat different one from that of her elegant neighbor. There was, at all events, a greater and more *piquant* variety to be found in it. All those to be found there were, however, worth seeing or hearing for one reason or another. *Her* method of ruling the frequenters of her receptions might be described as simply shaking the heterogeneous elements well together. But it answered so far as to make an evening at her house unfailingly amusing and enjoyable. She was very, and I think I may say, universally popular. She subsequently married M. Mohl, the well-known Orientalist, whom I remember to have always found, when calling upon him on various occasions, sitting in a tiny cabinet so absolutely surrounded by books, built up into walls all round him, as to suggest almost inevitably the idea of a mouse in a cheese, eating out the hollow it lived in.

Referring to my mother's book on "Paris and the Parisians" for those extracts from it which I have given in the preceding pages, I find the following passage, the singular forecast of which, and its bearing on the present state of things in France, tempts me to transcribe it. Speaking in 1835, and quoting the words of a high political authority, whom she had met "at the house of the beautiful Princess B——" (Belgiojoso), she writes: "'You know,' he said, 'how devoted all France was to the emperor, though the police was somewhat tight, and the conscriptions heavy. But he had saved us from a republic, and we adored him. For a few days, or rather hours, we were threatened again five years ago by the same terrible apparition. The result is that four millions of armed men stand ready to protect the prince who chased it. Were it to appear a third time, which Heaven forbid! you may depend upon it, *that the monarch who should next ascend the throne of France might play at "le jeu de quilles" with his subjects and no one be found to complain.*'" (My italics.) On the margin of the page on which this is printed my mother has written in the copy of the book before me, "*Vu et approuvé.* Dec. 10, 1853. F. T."

The mention of the Princess Belgiojoso in the above passage reminds me of a memorable evening which I spent at her house, and of my witnessing there a singular scene, which at the present day may be worth recounting.

The amusement of the evening consisted in hearing
Liszt and the princess play, on two pianos, the whole of
the score of Mozart's "Don Giovanni." The treat was a
delightful one; but I dare say that I should have forgotten it but for the *finale* of the performance. No sooner
was the last note ended than the nervous musician swooned
and slid from his seat, while the charming princess, in
whom apparently matter was less under the dominion of
mind, or at least of nerve, was as fresh as at the beginning.

My month at Paris, with its poor thirty times twenty-
four hours, was all too short for half of what I strove to
cram into it. And of course I could please myself with
an infinitude of recollections of things and places, and occasions, and above all, persons, who doubtless contributed
more to the making of that month one of the pleasantest
I have to look back on than any of the celebrities whom
I had the good-fortune to meet. But it may be doubted
whether any such rambling reminiscences would be equally
pleasing to my readers.

There is one anecdote, however, of a well-remembered
day, which I must tell, before bringing the record of my
first visit to Paris to a conclusion.

A picnic party—rather a large one, and consisting of
men and women of various nationalities—had been organized for a visit to the famous and historic woods of Montmorenci. We had a delightful day, and my memory is
still, after half a century, crowded with very vivid remembrances of the places and persons, and things done
and things said, which rendered it such. But as for the
places, have they not been described and redescribed in
all the guide-books that were ever written? And as for
the persons, alas! the tongues that chattered so fast and
so pleasantly are still for evermore, and the eyes that
shone so brightly are dim, if not, as in most instances,
closed in their last sleep! But it is only with an incident
that formed the *finale* of our day there that I mean to
trouble the reader.

Thackeray, then an unknown young man, with whom I
that day became acquainted for the first time, was one of

our party. Some half-dozen of us—the boys of the party —thinking that a day at Montmorenci could not be passed *selon les prescriptions* without a cavalcade on the famous donkeys, selected a number of them, and proceeded to urge the strongly conservative animals probably into places, and certainly into paces, for which their lifelong training had in no wise prepared them. A variety of struggles between man and beast ensued with divers vicissitudes of victory, till at last Thackeray's donkey, which certainly must have been a plucky and vigorous beast, succeeded in tossing his rider clean over his long ears, and, as ill-luck would have it, depositing him on a heap of newly-broken stones. The fall was really a severe one, and at first it was feared that our picnic would have a truly tragic conclusion. But it was soon ascertained that no serious mischief had been done beyond that the mark of which the victim of the accident bore on his face to his dying day.

I think that when I climbed to the *banquette* of the Lille diligence to leave Paris, on the morning of the 7th of June, 1835, it was the first time that the prospect of a journey failed in any way to compensate me for quitting what I was leaving behind.

CHAPTER XIV.

I LEFT Paris a day or two before my father, mother, and sisters, though bound for the same destination—Bruges. My object in doing so appears to have been to get a sight of some of the towns of French Flanders by the way. But I was not many days after them in reaching the Château d'Hondt, outside the Porte St. Pierre at Bruges ; and there I remained, with the exception of sundry visits to Ostend, and two or three rambles among the Flemish cities, till the 3d of October.

One used to go from Bruges to Ostend in those days by "Torreborre's" barge, which was towed by a couple of horses. There was a lumbering but very roomy diligence drawn by three horses abreast. But the barge, though yet slower than the diligence, was the pleasanter mode of making the journey. The cost of it, I well remember, was one franc ten centimes, which included (in going by the morning barge, which started, if I remember rightly, at six A.M.), as much bread-and-butter and really excellent *café au lait* as the traveller chose to consume — and I chose in those days to consume a considerable quantity. What the journey cost without any breakfast, I forget, if I ever knew. I fancy no such contingency as any passenger declining his bread-and-butter and coffee was contemplated, and that the charge was always the same whether you took breakfast or not. It was not an unpleasant manner of travelling, though specially adapted for the inmates of the Castle of Indolence. The cabin was roomy and comfortably furnished, and infinitely superior to the accommodations of any of the Dutch *trekschuyts* of the present day. One took one's book with one. And a cigar on the well-seated cabin roof was in excellent keeping with

9*

the lazy smoothness of the movement, and the flat, sleepy monotony of the banks.

And these visits to Ostend were very pleasant. Consul Fauche's hospitable door was always open to me, and there was usually sure to be something pleasant going on within it—very generally excellent music. I have already spoken of Mrs. Fauche's charming voice. Any pleasant English, who might be passing through, or spending the bathing season at Ostend, were sure to be found at the consul's—especially if they brought voices or any musical dispositions with them. But Mary Fauche herself was in those days a sufficient attraction to make the whitest-stone evening of all, that when no other visitor was found there. *Noctes cœnæque Deûm!*

But those pleasant Ostend days were, before the summer ended, overshadowed by a tragedy which I will not omit to record, because the story of it carries a valuable warning with it.

We had made acquaintance at Paris with a Mrs. Mackintosh and her daughter, very charming Scotch people. Mrs. Mackintosh was a widow, and Margaret was her only child. She was an extremely handsome girl, nineteen years of age, and as magnificent a specimen of young womanhood as can be conceived. "More than common tall," she showed in her whole person the development of a Juno, enhanced by the vigor, elasticity, and blooming health of a Diana. She and her mother came to Ostend for the bathing season. Margaret was a great swimmer; and her delight was to pass nearly the whole of those hot July days in the water. Twice, or even thrice every day she would return to her favorite element. And soon she began to complain of lassitude, and to lose her appetite and the splendor of her complexion. Oh! it was the heat, which really only the constant stimulus of her bath and swim could render tolerable. She was warned that excess in bathing, especially in salt water, may sometimes be as dangerous as any other excess, but the young naiad, who had never in her life needed to pay heed to any medical word or warning, would not believe, or would not heed. And before the September was over we followed poor

Margaret Mackintosh to the little Ostend cemetery, killed by over-bathing as decidedly as if she had held her head under water.

This sad tragedy brought to a gloomy end a season which had been, if not a very profitable, a very amusing one. There was a *ci-devant* Don Quixote sort of a looking man, a Count Melfort, whose young and buxom wife boasted some strain of I forget what noble English blood, and who used to give the consul good dinners such as he particularly affected, which his wife was neither asked nor cared to share, though the ladies as well as the gentlemen were excellent good friends. There was a wealthy Colonel Dickson who also used to give dinners, at one of which, having been present, I remember the host fussing in and out of the room during the quarter of an hour before dinner, till at last he rushed into the drawing-room with his coat-sleeves drawn up to his elbows, horror and despair in his mien as he cried, "Great Heaven! the cook has cut the fins off the turbot!" If any who partook of that mutilated fish survive to this present year of grace (which, I fear, is hardly likely to be the case) I am sure they will recall the scene which ensued on the dreadful announcement. There was the very pretty and abnormally silly little banker's wife, who supplied my old friend, Captain Smithett, with *billets doux* and fun, and who used to adapt verses sent her by a still sillier youthful adorer of her own to the purpose of expressing her own devotion to quite other swains.

It was a queer and not very edifying society, exceedingly strange, and somewhat bewildering to a lad fresh from Oxford who was making his first acquaintance with Continental ways and manners. All the married couples seemed to be continually dancing the figure of *chassée croisez*, and I, who had no wife of my own, and was not yet old enough to know better, thought it extremely amusing.

When October came, and I had not heard anything from Birmingham of the appointment to a mastership in the school there, for which I had been all this time waiting, I thought it was time to look up my Birmingham friends and see how matters stood there.   At Birmingham I found that the governors of King Edward's School were still shilly-shallying ; but I heard enough to convince me that no new master would be appointed till the very fine new building which now ornaments the town, but was then in course of construction, should be completed.

Having become convinced of this, in which it eventually turned out that I was right, it only remained to me to return to Bruges, with the assurance from Dr. Jeune and several of the governors that I and nobody else should have the mastership when the appointment should be made.   I returned to Bruges, passing one day with the dear Grants at Harrow, and an evening with my brother Anthony in London by the way, and reached the Château d'Hondt on the 15th of October, to find my father very much worse than I had left him.   He was in bed, and was attended by the Dr. Herbout of whom I have before spoken.   But he was too evidently drawing towards his end ; and after much suffering breathed his last in the afternoon of the 23d of October, 1835.   On the 25th I followed his body to the grave, close to that of my brother Henry, in the cemetery outside the Catherine Gate of the town.

The duty was a very specially sad one.   When I followed my mother to the grave at Florence many years afterwards my thoughts were far from being as painfully sad, though she was, I fear, the better-loved parent of the two.   She died in a ripe old age after a singularly happy, though not untroubled, life, during many years of which it was permissible to me to believe that I had had no small share in ministering to her happiness.   It was otherwise in the case of my father.   He was, and had been, I take it, for many years a very unhappy man.   All had gone wrong with him ; misfortunes fell on him, one on the back of the other.   Yet I do not think that these misfortunes were the real and efficient causes of his unhappiness.   I do not see what concatenation of circumstances could have made him happy.   He was in many respects a singular man.   Ill-health and physical suffering, of course, are great causes of an unhappy life ; but all suffering invalids are not unhappy. My father's mind was, I think, to a singular degree under the dominion of his body. The terrible irritability of his temper, which sometimes in his latter years reached a pitch that made one fear his reason was, or would become, unhinged, was undoubtedly due to the shattering of his nervous system, caused by the habitual use of calomel. But it is difficult for one who has never had a similar experience to conceive the degree in which this irritability made the misery of all who were called upon habitually to come into contact with it. I do not think that it would be an exaggeration to say that for many years no person came into my father's presence who did not forth-with desire to escape from it. Of course, this desire was not yielded to by those of his own household, but they were none the less conscious of it. Happiness, mirth, con-tentment, pleasant conversation, seemed to fly before him as if a malevolent spirit emanated from him. And all the time no human being was more innocent of all malevolence towards his fellow-creatures; and he was a man who would fain have been loved, and who knew that he was not loved, but knew neither how to manifest his desire for affection nor how to conciliate it.

I am the more convinced that bodily ailment was the *causa causans* of most, if not of all, of his unhappy idio-syncrasy, that I have before me abundant evidence that as a young man he was beloved and esteemed by his contem-poraries and associates. I have many letters from college friends, fellows of New College, his contemporaries, sev-eral of them thanking him for kindnesses of a more or less important kind, and all written in a spirit of high regard and esteem.

What so grievously changed him? I do not believe that he was soured by pecuniary misfortune, though he had more than enough. His first great misfortune — the marriage of his old widower uncle, whose heir he was to have been — was, I have the means of knowing, borne by him well, bravely, and with dignity. I believe that he was destroyed mind and body by calomel, habitually used dur-ing long years.

Throughout life he was a laborious and industrious

man. I have seen few things of the kind with more of
pathos in it than his persevering attempt to render his
labor of some value by compiling a dictionary of ecclesiastical terms. He had quite sufficient learning and sufficient industry to have produced a useful book upon the
subject if he had only had the possibility of consulting the,
of course, almost innumerable necessary authorities. The
book was published in quarto by subscription, and two or
three parts of it had been delivered to the subscribers
when death delivered him from his thankless labor and
his subscribers from further demands on their purses. I
do not suppose that any human being purchased the book
because they wished to possess it. And truly, as I have
said, it was a pathetic thing to see him in his room at
Château d'Hondt, ill, suffering, striving with the absolutely miserable, ridiculously insufficient means he had
been able with much difficulty to collect, to carry on his
work. He was dying—he must, I think, have known that
he was ; he had not got beyond D in his dictionary; all
the alphabet was before him, but he would not give up;
he would labor to the last. My mother was laboring hard,
and her labor was earning all that supplied very abundantly the needs of the whole family. And I cannot help
thinking that a painful but not ignoble feeling urged my
poor father to live at least equally laborious days, even
though his labor was profitless.

Poor father ! My thoughts, as I followed him to the
grave, were that I had not done all that I might have
done to alleviate the burden of unhappiness that was laid
upon him. Yet, looking back on it all from the vantage-
ground of my own old age (some fifteen years greater than
that which he attained) I do not see or think that any
conduct of mine would have made matters better for him.

My father's death naturally made an important change
in my mother's plans for the future. The Château d'Hondt
was given up, adieus were said, not without many *au re-
voirs*, to many kind friends at Bruges, and more especially
at Ostend, and we left Belgium for England. After some
time spent in house-hunting, my mother hired a pleasant

house with a good garden on the common at Hadley, near
Barnet, and there I remained with her, still awaiting my
Birmingham preferment, all that winter and the following
spring. The earlier part of the time was saddened by the
rapid decline and death of my younger sister, Emily. We
knew before leaving Bruges that there was but a slender
hope of saving her from the same malady which had been
fatal to my brother Henry. But the medical men hoped,
or professed to hope, that much might be expected from
her return to her native air. But the mark of the cruel
disease was upon her, and very rapidly after our establishment at Hadley she sank and painlessly breathed her
last.

Poor little Emily! She was a very bright *espiègle*
child, full of fun and high spirits. There is a picture of
her exactly as I remember her. She is represented with
flowing flaxen curls and wide china-blue eyes, sitting, with
a brown holland pinafore on, before a writing-desk and
blowing a prismatically-colored soap-bubble. The writing
copy on the desk lying above the half-covered and neglected page of copy-book bears the legend "Study with
determined zeal."

Her youngest child had ever been to my mother as the
apple of her eye, and her loss was for the passing day a
crushing blow. But, as usual with her, her mind refused
to remain crushed, any more than the grass is permanently crushed by the storm wind that blows over it. She
had the innate faculty and tendency to throw sorrow off
when the cause of it had passed. She owed herself to the
living, and refused to allow unavailing regret for those
who had been taken from her to incapacitate her for paying that debt to the utmost.

And once again, as was usual with her, her new home
became a centre of social enjoyment and attraction for
all, especially the young, who were admitted to it. I do
not remember that, with the exception of the family of
the rector, Mr. Thackeray, we had many acquaintances at
Hadley. I remember a bit of fun, long current among us,
which was furnished by the reception my mother met with
when returning the call of the wife of a wealthy distiller

resident in the neighborhood. The lady was of abnormal bulk, and when my mother entered the room in which she was sitting, she said, "Excuse me, ma'am, if I keep my chair, I never *raise*. But I am glad to see you—glad to see anybody," with much emphasis on the last word. I wish every caller was received with as truthful an expression of sentiments.

Our society consisted mainly of friends staying in the house, or of flying visitors from London. As usual, too, my mother soon gathered around her a knot of nice girls, who made the house bright. For herself she seemed always ready to take part in all the fun and amusement that was going; and was the first to plan dances, and charades, and picnics, and theatricals on a small and unpretending scale. But five o'clock of every morning saw her at her desk; and the production of the series of novels, which was not brought to a conclusion till it had reached the hundred and fifteenth volume, though it was not begun till she was past fifty, never ceased.

The Christmas was, I remember, a very merry one. We were seeing a good deal of a young fellow-clerk of my brother's in the secretary's office at the post-office, who was then beginning to fall in love with my sister Cecilia, whom he married not long afterwards. He was then at the beginning of a long official life, from which he retired some years ago as Sir John Tilley, K.C.B. Among others of our little circle, I especially remember Joseph Henry Green, the celebrated surgeon, Coleridge's literary executor, who first became known to us through his brother-in-law, Mr. Hammond, who was in practice at Hadley. Green was an immensely tall man, with a face of no beauty, but as brightly alive with humor as any I ever saw. He was a delightful companion in a walk; and I remember to the present hour much of the curious and out-of-the-way information I picked up from him, mainly on subjects more or less connected with his profession—for he, as well as I, utterly scouted the stupid sink-the-shop rule of conversation. I remember especially his saying of Coleridge, apropos of a passage in his biography which speaks of the singular habit (noticed by his amanuensis) that he had of occupying his mind with the coming passage, which he was about to dictate, while uttering that with which the writer was busy, that he (Green) had frequently observed the same peculiarity in his conversation.

Some few of our guests came to us from beyond the Channel, among them charming Mrs. Fauche, with her lovely voice and equally lovely face, whose Ostend hospitalities my mother was glad to have an opportunity of returning.

Among these visitors from the other side of the Channel, I remember one elderly lady of the Roman Catholic faith, and a strict observer of its precepts, who was pleased to express a very strong approbation of a certain oyster soup which made its appearance one day at my mother's table. She was charmed at the idea of being able to eat such soup for a *maigre* dinner, and begged that the receipt might be written out for her. " Oyster soup ! Just the thing for a Friday !" So the mode of preparing the desired dainty was duly written out for her. But her face was a study for a physiognomist when she read the first line of it, to the effect that she was to " Take of *prime beef*" so much. Oyster soup, indeed !

It was a pleasant time—so pleasant that I am afraid that I did not regret, perhaps so much as I ought to have done, the continued delay of the Birmingham appointment for which I was all this time waiting. But pleasant as it was, its pleasantness was not sufficient wholly to restrain me from indulging in that propensity for rambling which has been with me the ruling passion of a long lifetime.

It was in the spring following that merry Christmas that I found time for a little tour of about three weeks in Normandy. The reader need not fear that I am going to tell him anything of all I did and all I saw, though every detail of it seemed to me at the time worthy of minute record. But it has all been written and printed some scores of times since those days—by myself once among the rest—and may now be dismissed with a " See guidebooks *passim.*" The expenses of my travel, accurately recorded, I have also before me. There, indeed, I might furnish some facts which would be new and surprising to tourists of the present day, but they would only serve to make him discontented with his generation.

There is one anecdote, however, connected with this little journey which I must relate. I was returning from southern Normandy and reached Caen without a penny in my pocket. My funds, carefully husbanded as they had been, had sufficed to carry me so far and no farther. There were no such things as telegrams or railways in those days; and I had nothing for it but to go to a hotel and there remain till my application to Hadley for funds could be answered—an affair of some ten or twelve days as things then were. While I was waiting and kicking my heels about the old Norman city, from which I had already extracted all the interest it could afford me, I lounged into the shop of a bookseller, M. Mancel. I revisited him on a subsequent occasion, and find the record of this second visit in the first of two volumes which I wrote, and entitled *A Summer in Brittany*. There I find that M. Mancel is "the publisher of numerous works on the history and antiquities of Normandy. . . . M. Mancel has also an extensive collection of old books on Norman history; but the rarest and most curious articles are congregated into a most bibliomaniacal-looking cabinet, and are *not* for sale."

Well, this was the gentleman into whose very tempting shop I strayed with empty pockets. He was extremely civil, showed me many interesting things, and, finding that I was not altogether an ignoramus as regarded his specialty, observed ever and anon, "That is a book which you ought to have!" "That is a work which you will find very useful!" till at last I said, "Very true! There are two or three books here that I should like to have; but I have no money!" He instantly begged me to take any book or books I should like to buy, and pay for them when I got to London. "But," rejoined I, "I don't know when I shall get to London, for I have no money at all. I reached Caen with my purse empty, and am stranded here!" M. Mancel thereupon eagerly begged me to let him be my banker for my immediate needs, as well as for the price of any volumes I chose to purchase. And though he had never seen my face or heard my name before, he absolutely did furnish me with money to reach home, and gave me credit for some two or three pounds' worth of books, it being arranged that I should, on reaching London, pay the amount to M. Dulau in Soho Square.

A few years ago, on passing through Caen, I went to the old book shop; but M. Mancel had long since gone to join the majority, and his place knew him no more. His successor, however, on my explaining to him the motive of my visit, remarked, with a truly French bow, "My predecessor seems to have been a good physiognomist, monsieur!"

I returned to Hadley to find my mother eagerly occupied with the scheme of a journey to Vienna, and a book as the result of it. She had had, after the publication of her book on "Paris and the Parisians," some idea of undertaking an Italian tour, but that was now abandoned in favor of a German journey, whether on the suggestion of her publisher, or from any other cause of preference, I do not know. Of course I entered into such a scheme heart and soul. My only fear now was that news of my appointment to a mastership at Birmingham might arrive in time to destroy my hopes of accompanying my mother. But no such tidings came; on the contrary, there seemed every reason to suppose that no new master would be appointed till after the following Christmas holidays. My mother was as anxious as I was that I should be free to act as her courier, for, in truth, she could hardly dispense with some such assistance; and I alone remained who could give it to her. My sister Cecilia was to accompany my mother. She wished also to take with her M. Hervieu, the artist who illustrated her former books; and I obtained her permission to ask an Oxford friend to make one of the party. We were thus a party of five, without counting my mother's maid, an old and trusted servant, the taking of whom, however, she subsequently considered so great a mistake that she never fell into it on any other occasion.

My delight at the prospect of such a journey was intense. I surrounded myself forthwith with an amazing supply of maps and guide-books, and was busy from morning to night with the thoroughly congenial task of studying and preparing our proposed route.

CHAPTER XV.

THAT I started on this occasion even more than on any other with the greatest delight "goes without saying." A longer and more varied journey than I had ever before enjoyed was before me. All was new, even more entirely new to the imagination than Paris ; and my interest, curiosity, and eagerness were great in proportion. We travelled by way of Metz, Strasbourg, and Stuttgardt, and, after reaching the German frontier, by *Lohnkutscher*, or *vetturino*—incredibly slow, but of all modes of travelling save the *haquenée des Cordeliers* the best for giving the traveller some acquaintance with the country traversed and its inhabitants.

A part of the journey was performed in a yet slower fashion, and one which was still richer in its opportunities for seeing both men and things. For we descended the Danube on one of those barges which ply on the river, used mainly for cargo, but also occasionally for passengers. When I look back upon that part of our expedition I feel some astonishment at not only the hardihood of my mother and sister in consenting to such an enterprise, but more still at my own—it really seems to my present notions—almost reckless audacity in counselling and undertaking to protect them in such a scheme.

Whether any such boats still continue to navigate the Danube I do not know. I should think that quicker and better modes of transporting both human beings and goods have long since driven them from their many time secular occupation. In any case it is hardly likely that any English travellers will ever again have such an experience. The *Lohnkutscher*, with his thirty or forty miles a day and his easy-going, lotus-eating-like habitudes, is hardly like to tempt the traveller who is wont to grumble at the tediousness of an express-train. But a voyage on a Danube carrier-barge would be relegated to the category of those things which might be done, " could a man be secure that his life should endure As of old, for a thousand long years," but which are quite out of the question in any other circumstances.

Here is the account which my mother gives of the boat on which we were about to embark at Ratisbon for the voyage down the river to Vienna.

" We start to-morrow, and I can hardly tell you whether I dread it or wish for it most. We have been down to the river's bank to see the boat, and it certainly does not look very promising of comfort. But there is nothing better to be had. It is a large structure of unpainted deal boards, almost the whole of which is occupied by a sort of arklike cabin erected in the middle. This is very nearly filled by boxes, casks, and bales; the small portion not so occupied being provided with planks for benches and a species of rough dresser placed between them for a table. This we are given to understand is fitted up for the express accommodation of the cabin passengers."

In point of fact, we had, as I remember, no fellow-passengers in any part of our voyage. I take it that nobody, save perhaps the peasants of the villages on the banks of the stream, for short passages from one of them to the other, ever thought of travelling by these barges even in those days. They were, in fact, merely transports for merchandise of the heavier and rougher sort. The extreme rudeness of their construction, merely rough planks roughly nailed together, is explained by the fact that they are not intended ever to make the return voyage against the stream, but, on arriving at Vienna, are knocked to pieces and sold for boarding.

" But the worst thing I saw," continues my mother, "is the ladder which, in case of rain, is to take us down to this place of little ease. It consists of a plank with sticks nailed across it to sustain the toes of the crawler who would wish to avoid jumping down seven or eight feet. The sloping roof of the ark is furnished with one bench of about six feet long, from which the legs of the brave

souls who sit on it dangle down over the river.   There is
not the slightest protection whatever at the edge of this
abruptly sloping roof, which forms the only deck; and
nothing but the rough, unslippery surface of the deal
planks, of which it is formed, with the occasional aid of a
bit of stick about three inches long nailed here and there,
can prevent those who stand or walk upon it from gently
sliding down into the stream. . . . Well! we have *determined,* one and all of us, to navigate the Danube between
Ratisbon and Vienna; and I will neither disappoint myself nor my party from the fear of a fit of vertigo or a
scramble down a ladder."

But if the courage of the ladies did not fail them, mine,
as that of the person most responsible for the adventure,
did.   And I find that, on the day following that on which
the last extract was written, my mother writes:

"At a very early hour this morning T. [Tom] was up
and on board, and perceiving—by a final examination of
the deck, its one giddy little bench, and all things apper-
taining thereto—that we should inevitably be extremely
uncomfortable there, he set about considering the ways
and means by which such martyrdom might be avoided.
He at last got hold of the *Schiffmeister,* which he had
found impossible yesterday, and by a little persuasion and
a little bribery induced him to have a plank fixed for us
at the extreme bow of the boat, which we can not only
reach without difficulty, but have a space of some nine or
ten feet square for our sole use, on condition of leaving it
free for the captain about five minutes before each landing.   This perch is perfectly delightful in all respects.
Our fruit, cold meat, wine, bread, and so forth are stowed
near us.   Desks and drawing-books can all find place;
and, in short, if the sun will but continue to shine as it
does now, all will be well. . . . Our crew are a very motley set, and as we look at them from our dignified retirement they seem likely to afford us a variety of picturesque
groups.   On the platforms, which project at each end of
the ark, stand the men—and the women too—who work
the vessel.   This is performed by means of four immense
oars protruding lengthwise [*i. e.,* in a fore-and-aft direc-

tion], two in front and two towards the stern, by which the boat is steered. Besides these, there are two others to row with. These latter are always in action, and are each worked by six or eight men and women, the others being only used occasionally, when the boat requires steering. It appears that there are many passengers who work for their passage [but this I take to have been inference only], as the seats at the oars are frequently changed, and as soon as their allotted task is done they dip down into the unknown region beyond the ark and are no more seen till their turn for rowing comes round again. I presume the labor, thus divided, is not very severe, for they appear to work with much gayety and good-humor, sometimes singing, sometimes chatting, and often bursting into shouts of light-hearted laughter."

It was a strange voyage: curious, novel, and full of never-failing interest; luxurious even in its way, in many respects; which may now be considered an old-world experience; which probably has never been tried since, and certainly will never be tried again, however many wandering young Englishmen (of whom there are a hundred now for every one to be met with in those days) might fancy trying it. No danger whatever of the kind which my mother appears to have anticipated threatened any of the party; but the adventure was not without danger of another kind, as the sequel showed.

Of course, all the people with whom we were brought into contact—the captain and crew of the boat, the riverside loungers at the landing-places, the hosts and households of the little inns in the small places at which the boat stopped every night (it never travelled save by daylight)—were all mystified, and had all their ideas of the proprieties and the eternal fitness of things outraged by the phenomenon of a party of English ladies and gentlemen—supposed by virtue of ancient and well-recognized reputation to be all as rich as Crœsus, and who were at all events manifestly able to pay for a carriage—choosing such a method of travelling. Nor had English wanderers at that time earned the privilege since accorded to their numerousness, of doing all sorts of strange things unquestioned on the score of the well-known prevalent insanity of the race. *All* who came within sight of us were utterly puzzled at the unaccountableness of the phenomenon. And one does not mystify the whole of a somewhat rude population without risking disagreeables of various sorts.

On looking back on the circumstances from my present lofty and calm observatory I am disposed to wonder that nothing worse betided us than the one adventure of which I am about to speak. But, as I remember, the people generally were, if somewhat ruder and rougher than an English population of similar status, upon the whole very kindly and good-natured.

But at one place—a village called Pleintling—we did get into trouble, which very nearly ended tragically. The terms upon which we were to be housed for the night and the price to be paid for our accommodation of all sorts had been settled overnight, and the consciousness that we were giving unusual trouble induced us to pay without grumbling such a price for our beds and supper and breakfast as the host had assuredly never received for his food and lodging in all his previous experience. But it was doubtless this very absence of bargaining which led our landlord to imagine that he had made a mistake in not demanding far more, and that any amount might be had for asking it from so mysterious a party, who parted, too, so easily with their money. So, as we were stepping on board the next morning, he came down to the water's edge, and with loud vociferation demanded a sum more than the double of that which we had already paid him. The ladies, and, indeed, all the party save myself, who was the paymaster, had already gone on board, and I was about to follow, unheeding his demands and his threats, when he seized me by the throat, and, dragging me backward, declared in stentorian tones that he had not been paid. I sturdily refused to disburse another kreutzer. The other men, who had gone on board, jumped back to my assistance. But suddenly, as if they had risen from the earth, several other fellows surrounded us and dragged down my friends. The old landlord, beside himself with

rage, lifted an axe which he had in his hand and was
about to deal me a blow which would probably have relieved the reading world of this and many another page.
But my mother, shrieking with alarm, had meantime be-
sought the captain of the boat to settle the matter by paying whatever was demanded. He also jumped on shore
just in time, and released us from our foes, and himself
from further delay, by doing so.

At the next place at which we could go on shore we
made a complaint to the police officials; and it is not
without satisfaction, even after the lapse of half a century, that I am able to say that a communication from the
police in an Austrian town some days subsequently, and
after we had crossed the Bavarian frontier, informed us
that the old scoundrel at Pleintling had not only been
made to disgorge the sum he had robbed us of, but had
been trounced as he deserved. I suspect that he had imagined, from the strangeness of our party and our mode of
travelling, that there were reasons why we should not be
inclined to seek any interview with the officers of the police.

With that sole exception our voyage from Ratisbon to
Vienna was a prosperous, and, on the whole, pleasant one,
varied only by not unfrequently recurring difficulties occasioned by shoals and sandbanks, when all hands, save
the non-working party in the bow, would take to the water in a truly amphibious fashion to drag the boat off.

But I must not be led by these moving accidents by
flood and field to forget a visit paid to the sculptor Dan-
necker in his studio at Stuttgardt. There is in my mother's book an etching by M. Hervieu of the man and place.
I remember well the affectionate reverence with which he
uncovered for us his colossal bust of Schiller, as described
by my mother, and the reasons which he assigned (mistak-
en, as they appeared to me, but it is presumptuous in me
to say so) for making it colossal. Schiller had been his
lifelong friend, and these reasons, whether artistically
good or not, were, at all events, morally admirable and pathetically touching, as given by the old man while looking up at his work with tears in his octogenarian eyes. I

10

do not think the reproduction of the bust in M. Hervieu's etching is a very happy one, but I can testify to the full-length portrait of the aged sculptor being a thoroughly lifelike one. It is the old man himself. He died a year or two after the date of our visit.

Uhland, too, we visited, and Gustav Schwab. Of the former I may say literally *vidi tantum,* for I could speak then no German, and very few words now, and Uhland could speak no other language. And our interview is worth recording mainly for the case of the noticeable fact that such a man, holding the position he did and does in the literature of his country, should at that day have been unable to converse in French.

Gustav Schwab, though talking French fluently, and, as I remember, a little English also, impressed me as quint-essentially German in manner, in appearance, and ways of thinking. He was one of the kindliest of men, contented with you only on condition of being permitted to be of service to you, and at the end of half an hour making you somehow or other feel as if he must have been an old friend, if not in your present, at least in some former state of existence.

My journey among these southern Germans left me with the impression that they are generally a kindly and good-natured people. A little incident occurred at Tübingen which I thought notably illustrated this. The university library there is a very fine one ; and, while the rest of our party were busied with some other sight-seeing, I went thither, and applied to the librarian for some information respecting the departments in which it was strong, its rules, etc. He immediately set about complying with my wishes in the most obliging manner, going through the magnifi-cent suite of rooms with me himself, and pausing before the shelves wherever he had any special treasure to show. All of a sudden, without any warning, just as we were passing through the marble jambs of a doorway from one room to another, my head began to swim ; I lost conscious-ness, and fell, cutting my head against the marble suffi-ciently to cause much bloodshed. When I recovered my senses I found the librarian standing in consternation over

me, and his pretty young wife on her knees, with a basin
of water, bathing my head. She had been summoned
from her dwelling to attend me, and there was no end to
their kindness. I never experienced such a queer attack
before or since. I suppose it must have been occasioned
by too much erudition on an empty stomach.

Our route to Vienna was a very devious one, including
southern Bavaria, Salzburg, and great part of the Tyrol.
But I must not indulge in any journalizing reminiscences
of it. Were I to do so in the case of all the interesting
journeys I have made since that day, how many volumes
would suffice for the purpose? When calling, the other
day, only two or three months ago, on Cardinal Massaia,
at the Propaganda in Rome, in order to have some conversation with him respecting his thirty-five years' mis-
sionary work in Africa, on returning from which he received the purple from Leo XIII., he obligingly showed
me the MS. which he had prepared from his recollection
of the contents of the original notes, unfortunately destroyed during his imprisonment by hostile tribes in Africa, and which is now being printed at the Propaganda
Press in ten volumes quarto. His eminence was desirous
that it should be translated into English, and published in
London, with the interesting illustrations he brought home
with him, and which adorn the Roman edition. But as
the wish of his eminence was that it should be published
unabridged (!) I was obliged to tell him that I feared he
would not find a London publisher. We parted very good
friends, and on taking my leave of him he said, pressing
my hand kindly, that we should shortly meet again in
heaven; which, considering that he knew he was talking
to a heretic, I felt to be a manifestation of liberal feeling
worthy of note in a cardinal of the Church of Rome.

Will the kind reader, bearing in mind the recognized
and almost privileged garrulity of old age, pardon the
chronology-defying introduction of this anecdote here,
which was suggested to me solely by the vision of what
my reminiscences would extend to if I were to treat of all
my wanderings up and down this globe *in extenso.*

The latter part of our voyage was especially interesting

and beautiful, but tantalizing from the impossibility of landing on every lovely spot which enticed us. Nevertheless, we at last found ourselves at Vienna with much delight, and our first glimpses of the city disposed us to acquiesce heartily in the burden of the favorite Viennese folk-song, " *Es ist nur ein Kaiserstadt, es ist nur ein Wien!*"

I remember well an incident which my mother does not mention, but which seemed likely to make our first *début* in the Kaiserstadt an embarrassing one. There was, in some hand-bag belonging to some one of the party, an old, forgotten pack of playing-cards, which the examining officer of the customs pounced on with an expression of almost consternation on his face.

" Oh, well, throw them away," said the spokesman of our party, airily, " or, if the regulations require it, we will pay the duty, though we have not the least desire to retain possession of them."

But this we soon found did not meet the case by any means. We had been guilty of a serious misdemeanor and offence against the law by having such things (undeclared, too) among our baggage ! There must be a report and a written petition, setting forth, with due contrition and humble *peccavi* admissions, our lamentable ignorance, and perhaps the enormity might be condoned to a foreigner ! After a little talk, however, and the incense of a little consternation on our faces, duly offered to the official Jove (who entirely spurned any offering of another sort), the said Jove wrote the petition for us himself, carried it somewhere behind the scenes, and shortly announced that it was benignly granted ; as I believe, by himself ! The accursed thing was ceremoniously destroyed before our eyes, and we were free to walk forth into the streets of the Kaiserstadt.

I revisited Vienna two or three years ago, and found that " *ein Wien* " had become at least three ! If the increase and changes of London and Paris have made my early recollections of those cities emphatically those of a former age, the changes at Vienna, though, of course, smaller in absolute extent, have yet more entirely meta-

morphosed the character of the place. The abolition of
the wall, which used to shut in the exclusive little city,
and placed between it and the suburbs not only a material
barrier, but a gulf such as that which divided Dives from
Lazarus, has changed the social habitudes and even the
moral characteristics of the inhabitants.

In the days of my first visit, now just a little more than
fifty years ago, nobody who was anybody would have
dreamed of living on the outside of the sacred barrier of
the wall any more than a member of the fashionable world
of London would dream of living to the eastward of Temple Bar. I think, indeed, that the former would have been
more utterly out of the question than the latter. I remember that, even in the case of foreigners like ourselves, it
was deemed, in accordance with the best advice we could
procure on the subject, necessary, or at least expedient,
that we should find lodgings *in the city*, despite the exceeding difficulty and the high price involved in procuring
them. The division of the society into classes, still more
marked in Vienna than, probably, in any other city of
Europe, at that time almost amounted to a division into
castes ; and, in the case of the higher aristocracy, to have
lived in any one of the suburbs would assuredly have involved a loss of social caste.

Mainly this arose, of course, from the inappellable law
of fashion that so it should be. But in part, also, it probably arose from the little social inconveniences arising from
mere distance. The society of Vienna at that day—society *par excellence*—was a very small one. Everybody knew
everybody, not only their pedigree and all their quarterings
(very necessary to be known), but the men and women
themselves personally. I forget entirely what were the
introductions which placed my mother and her party at
once in the very core of this small and exclusive society.
But we did find ourselves so placed, and that at once.
Probably the general notion in England was then, and
may be still, that the aristocratic society of Vienna would
be less likely to open its doors to one who had no title
whatever to enter them save a literary reputation than the
corresponding classes in any other European capital. But,

whatever was the "Open Sesame" my mother possessed, the fact was that all doors were open to her with the most open-handed hospitality. And, as I have said, to know one was, even in the case of a stranger, pretty nearly equivalent to knowing them all.

The by far greater number of this small society of nobles were, as was to be expected, wealthy men; some, more especially the Hungarians, were such, even if estimated by English standards. But there were some among them who were very much the reverse. And my opportunities of observation were abundantly sufficient to enable me to perceive, without any fear of being mistaken, that the terms of intimacy and equality upon which these latter lived with their wealthier neighbors were no whit affected by their comparative impecuniosity. One single lady of very noble birth I well remember, who to a great pressure of the *res angusta domi* added no small spice of eccentricity; but there was no mansion so magnificent that did not open its doors very widely to her. No *fête* was complete without her. She always wore a turban, and always carried it about with her in her pocket. And I have seen her pause in the midst of a splendid entrance-hall, with half a dozen lackeys standing around, while she took her turban from her pocket, adjusted it on her head, and changed her shoes.

The ladies of the *grand monde* in Vienna in those days had the queer habit of writing no notes. Their invitations and the answers to them, and the excuses, or any other communications arising from the social intercourse of the day, were all sent by word of mouth by footmen. Whether the highest *bon ton* required an affectation of not being able to write, I cannot say! But such was the practice.

Another specialty consisted in a practice of the young men of the same world. Every man of them retained in his special pay and service one of the (very excellent) hackney coaches of the city, which he always expected to find ready for his service, and the driver of which was trusted by him as much, or more perhaps, than a man is in the habit of trusting his own servant.

The social division between the different castes—between the noble and the non-noble—was absolute in those days; and, of course, both parties were the losers in sundry respects by such separation. But the results were not bad in *all* respects. One was an exceeding simplicity and absence of any affectation of finery or *morgue* on the part of the noble class, and a corresponding easy-going freedom from the small forms of social ambition on the part of the non-noble. There was among the latter no attempt or thought of attempting to enter the noble society. It was out of the question; and, as far as I could see, such entry did not appear to be an object of ambition, or the impossibility of it to occasion either heart-burning or jealousy. In the case of the ladies of the *deux mondes,* the separation was absolute and without exception. But I was told that in some few cases the *young* men of the upper class might be seen in the houses of certain of their non-noble fellow-citizens, but never with any reciprocity of toleration. In respect of mere wealth and luxury in the manner of living, there were many *bourgeois* families on a par, and in many cases on far more than a par, with those of the nobles. And no doubt it frequently occurred that the social law which forbade all intercourse between the two septs was felt to be as inconvenient and as much a matter of regret on one side of the barrier as on the other. But, *noblesse oblige,* and the law was not transgressed.

In the case of foreigners, however, or at least of English foreigners, we were very soon given to understand that the law in question was not applicable. We were perfectly free to make acquaintances in either world, and some of the most valued friends we made in Vienna, and some of the pleasantest hospitalities we accepted, were found in *bourgeois* houses. I remember two different instances of a very amusing curiosity on the part of certain noble ladies, which prompted them to avail themselves of our chartered liberty in the matter, for the obtaining of tidings of the ways and manners of the inmates of certain houses, which there was no possibility of their ever having an opportunity of observing for themselves. But on ransacking my memory for instances of the kind, I must say that all that occur to me refer to curiosity of the upper respecting the nether world, and that I do not recollect any *vice versâ* cases.

I have said that the rule of exclusion as regards all that part of the Vienna world not nobly born was absolute. But if absoluteness can be conceived as ever becoming more absolute, the social law did so in the case of Jewish families. These were numerous, and many of them in respect of wealth, and more in respect of culture, were on a par with the best and highest portion of the Viennese society. I remember one Jewish family in particular, consisting of a widow and her daughter and her niece, with whom we became intimately acquainted, and in whom and whose surroundings we found a level of high culture (taking that word in its largest extension to all that goes to form the idiosyncrasy of a human being), far in advance of anything we met with among their social superiors.

In fact, the *grand monde* of that far-distant day in Vienna was frivolous, unintellectual, and, I am afraid I must say, uneducated to a remarkable degree. It had its own peculiar charm, which consisted in the most perfectly high-bred tone of manner combined with complete simplicity, the absolute absence of any sort of affectation whatever, and great good-nature. But in all my experience of them there was not to be found a *salon* among them of equal social attraction to that of my above-mentioned Jewish friends.

But all this refers to the social conditions of a day which, as my recent visits to Vienna have shown me, is one passed away and gone. It belongs to the days when "Vater Franz" was, or, to be accurate, had only two years previously ceased to be, the idol of Austrian, and especially Viennese, loyalty and affection. The most striking instances of the devotion of all classes of the population to their emperor were constantly narrated to me. I specially remember the tale of one occasion, when the emperor had remained shut up in the palace for three or four days—or perhaps the period was somewhat longer—because he had caught a cold. A cloud seemed to have passed over the blue Vienna sky. The occasion of his first drive through the streets of the city after his little indisposition was an ovation. The people filled the streets, and hung about his carriage. Market-women poked their faces in at the window to assure themselves that "Vater Franz" was restored to them none the worse for his confinement. It was, to the best of my remembrance, on every Thursday, at that time, that it had been the emperor's practice to devote a certain number of hours in the day to receiving *any* one of his subjects who had notified in the proper quarter a desire to speak with him. But might not some Socialist or Nihilist, or other description of radical, have easily shot him at one of those entirely unguarded interviews? Aye! but I am writing of half a century ago, before such things and persons had appeared upon the scene. And assuredly the possibility of such a catastrophe had never entered into the brain of any man, woman, or child in the Kaiserstadt.

There was one among the many acquaintances we made at Vienna who belonged in no wise to any division of its society, but who was, like ourselves, to be met with among them all. This was old Cramer the pianist. I took a great liking to him. The mingled simplicity, *bonhomie*, shrewdness, and old-world courtesy of the old man delighted me. He was full of old-world stories, generally ending any anecdote of some one of the many notable personages he had known with a sigh, and "Well, peace to his *manes!*" pronounced as one syllable, as I have mentioned in an earlier page. For old John Cramer had lived in the days before the schoolmaster had gone "abroad" so widely as in these latter times. The old *maestro* had just written a monody to the memory of Malibran, then recently lost to the world of music prematurely. "It is full of feeling," writes my mother, "and, as I listened to this veteran pianist, as he performed for me his simple and classic little composition, and marked the delicacy and finish of his style, unencumbered by a single movement in which the conceptions of a harmonious genius are made to give way before the meretricious glory of active

10*

fingers, I felt at the very bottom of my heart that I was *rococo*, incorrigibly *rococo*, and that such I should live and die."

Another specialty, which in those days gave to Vienna much of the physiognomy which made it different in outward appearance from any other of the great capitals of Europe, and which would not be observed there at the present time, was caused by the heterogeneousness of the countries which compose the empire, and the very motley appearance of the specimens of all of them which might be found in the capital. A Parisian tells you in France that a provincial in the streets of Paris is as recognizable at a glance as if he were ticketed on the forehead. And so he may be to a Parisian. But the eccentricities of his appearance are not such as to impart any variety to the moving panorama in the streets of Paris as it appears to a stranger. The Breton, the Provençal, the Bearnais makes himself look, when he visits Paris, as much like a Parisian as he can, and flatters himself, no doubt, that he succeeds perfectly. But Croatians, Bohemians, wild-looking figures from Transylvania might be seen in the streets of Vienna, precisely as they might have been seen in their own distant homes. Strange and not a little sinister-looking groups of Hungarian gypsies, encampments outside and at the foot of the walls of Bohemian wagoners, caftaned Jews from the distant parts of Galicia, all added to the strangeness and much to the picturesqueness of the city. I remember one especial group, the extreme barbarism of whose appearance, incredible filthiness, and wild, picturesque, but very forbidding physiognomies, particularly attracted my attention. I was told that they were gypsies from Croatia.

On the whole it is—or, rather, I should say was—evident that one has travelled far eastward to reach Vienna, and the whole physiognomy of the place is modified by that fact.

I am unwilling to close this chapter of my Vienna reminiscences without mentioning a lady whose very exceptional histrionic talent had impressed me as vividly as it did my mother, who has given an honorable place in her volumes to Madame Rettich. I subsequently became intimate with her very charming daughter in Italy, and it is from her that I learned the fact that her mother had been the first actress to personate Goethe's "Gretchen" on the stage. Considerable doubt had been felt as to the expediency of the attempt. But Madame Rettich made it—not for the first time at Vienna, but at some provincial theatre—with entire success.

CHAPTER XVI.

IN AUSTRIA—(*continued*).

OF all my reminiscences of Vienna, and those I saw there, the most interesting are those connected with my introduction to Prince Metternich.

The present generation is perhaps hardly aware—or not habitually so—of the largeness of the space Metternich occupied in the political world half a century ago. It is not too much to say that Europe in those days thought as much about Metternich as it does in these days about Bismarck. Of course the nature of the two men, as of the circumstances with which they were called on to deal, is far as the poles asunder. But on the European stage—not, of course, on the English—no actor of that day could compete with Prince Metternich in the importance of the position assigned to him by the world in general, as no actor of this day can with Prince Bismarck.

It is hardly enough to say, as is said above, that the nature of the two men was as far as the poles asunder; it was singularly contrasted. To both of them the *salus patriæ* has ever been the *suprema ex ;* and both of them, with increasingly accepted wisdom, have sought that supreme end in the strengthening of the principle of authority. The history of human affairs has not yet sufficiently unfolded itself for it to be possible to say in this year of grace 1887 whether they have done so with very different measures of success. But it is very curious to mark the similarity thus far existing between the two great ministers, chancellors, and statesmen, combined with such very marked (though perhaps in fact more or less superficial) differences between the two men.

Prince Bismarck has not been thought, even by those who have most thoroughly admired and applauded his *fortiter in re*, to have very successfully combined with it the *suaviter in modo*. The habit of clothing the iron hand with a velvet glove has not been considered to be among his characteristics. And these qualities were very pre-eminently those of the other all-powerful minister.

And the outward and bodily presentment of the two men was as contrasted and as expressive of this difference as that of two high-born gentlemen could well be. I saw recently, in Berlin, a portrait by Lembach of the great North German chancellor. It is one of those portraits which eminently accomplishes that which it is the highest excellence of every great portrait to achieve, in that it gives those who look at it with some faculty of insight, not only that outward semblance of the man, which all can recognize, but something more, which it is the artist's business to reveal to those who have not the gift of reading it for themselves. That portrait, in common with most of those by the great masters in the art of portraiture, reveals to you, with an instantly recognized truthfulness, the interior and intrinsic nature of the man, with a luminousness which your own gaze on the living person would not achieve for you. I have also before me a portrait of Prince Metternich, made at the time of which I am writing, by M. Hervieu, in crayons, for my mother. And without, of course, claiming either for the artist or for the style of work such power as belongs to the portrait of which I have been speaking, I may say that it does very faithfully and expressively give you the presentment of a man in whom strength of will, tenacity of purpose, and high intellectual power are combined with suave gentleness of manner and an air of high-bred courtesy.

That is the man whose lineaments I look on in the sketch, and that is the man with whom I had many opportunities of being in company, and had on several occasions the high honor of conversing. Whether it might be possible for a man devoid of all advantage of feature to produce on those brought into contact with him the same remarkable impression of dignity, the consciousness of high station, and perfection of courtly bearing combined with a pellucid simplicity of manner, I cannot say.

But it is true that all this was rendered more possible in the case of Metternich by great personal handsomeness. He was, of course, when I saw him, what may be called an old man—a white-headed old man—but I doubt if at any time of his life he could have been a better-looking man.

My mother notes in her book on "Vienna and the Austrians" that, as we were returning from a dinner at the house of the English ambassador, Sir Frederic Lamb, where we had just met Metternich for the first time, I observed that he was just such a man as my fancy painted Sir William Temple to have been, and that she thought the illustration a good one. And I don't think that any subsequent knowledge or reflection would lead me to cancel it.

He was a man of middle height, slenderly made rather than thin, though carrying no superfluous flesh; upright, though without the somewhat rigid uprightness which usually characterizes military training to the last, however far distant the training time may have been; and singularly graceful in movement and gesture. He must have been a man of sound body and even robust constitution, but he did not look so at the time of which I am speaking. Not that he had the appearance or the manner of a man out of health; but his extreme refinement and delicacy of feature seemed scarcely consistent with bodily strength. I remember a man—the old Dr. Nott spoken of in the first chapter of this book—who must have been about the same age with Metternich when I first saw him, who equalled him in clear-cut delicacy and refinement of feature, who was certainly a high-bred gentleman, not altogether ignorant of the ways and manners of courts, and who was emphatically a man of intellectual pursuits and habits. But there all equality and similarity between the two men ends. Good, refined, elegant Dr. Nott produced no such impression on those near him as the Austrian statesman did. There must have been therefore a *something* in the latter beyond all those advantages of person and feature with which he was so eminently endowed. And this "something" I take to have been produced partly by native intellectual power, and partly by the long possession of quite uncontested authority.

Upon that first occasion I had no opportunity of hearing any word from Metternich save one gracious phrase on being presented to him. He took my mother in to dinner. I was seated at a far distant part of the huge round table, where I could see, but not hear. And it was the fashion in Vienna for people to leave the house at which they had been dining almost immediately after taking their cup of coffee. But before the party separated it had been arranged that we were to dine at the minister's house on the following Monday.

But all this time I have said no word of the Princess Metternich, who also dined with Sir Frederic Lamb on that, to me, memorable day. In one word, she was one of the most beautiful women I ever looked on. She was rather small, but most delicately and perfectly formed in person, and the extreme beauty of her face was but a part, and not the most peerless part, of the charm of it. To say that it sparkled with expression, and an expression which changed with each changing topic of conversation, is by no means enough. Every feature of her face was instinct with meaning and intelligence. The first impression her face gave me was that of a laughter-loving and *mutine* disposition. But my mother, who saw much of her—more, of course, than it was possible for her to see of the chancellor (especially while the princess was sitting for her portrait by M. Hervieu for her, during which sitting my mother, by her express stipulation, was always with her), and who learned to love her dearly, testified that there was much more behind; that her unbounded affection and veneration for her husband was not incompatible with the formation of thoughtful opinions of her own upon the questions which were then exercising the minds of politicians, as well as all the higher topics of human interest.

I dined at Metternich's table on the day mentioned above as well as on sundry other occasions; on some of which I was fortunate enough to make one of the little circle enjoying his conversation. Of course the dinner-parties at the prince's house were affairs of much magnificence and splendor. But I had, on more than one occasion, the higher privilege of dining with him *en famille*.

On both and all occasions, whether it was a grand banquet of thirty persons or more, or a quite unceremonious dinner *en famille*, the prince's practice was the same, and was peculiar.

He did not in any wise partake of the spread before him. He had always dined previously at one o'clock. But he had a loaf of brown bread and a plate of butter put before him; and, while his guests were dining, he occupied himself with spreading and cutting a succession of daintily thin slices of bread-and-butter for his own repast.

Victor Emmanuel used similarly to dine in the middle of the day, and at his state banquets used to take no more active part than was involved in honoring them with his presence. But Metternich, I think, would not have said what my friend G. P. Marsh, the United States minister, once told me Victor Emmanuel said to him on one occasion. Mr. Marsh, as dean of the diplomatic body (it was before any of the great powers sent ambassadors to the court of the Quirinal) was seated next to his majesty at table. Innumerable dishes were being carried round in long succession, when the king, turning to his neighbor with a groan, said, " Will this *never* come to an end?" I have no doubt Marsh cordially echoed his majesty's sentiments on the subject.

The words of men who have occupied positions in any degree similar to that of Prince Metternich are apt to be picked up, remembered, and recorded, when in truth the only value of the utterances in question is to show that such men do occasionally think and speak like other mortals. And my note-books are not without similar evidences of *gobemoucherie* on my own part. But there is one subject on which I have heard Metternich speak words which really are worth recording. That subject was the Emperor Napoleon Bonaparte.

Of course on such a topic the Austrian statesman might have said much that he was not at liberty to say; and

there was also much that he might have said which could
not have found place in one half-hour's conversation. The
particular point upon which I heard him speak was the
celebrated interview at which the emperor lost his temper because he could not induce Austria to declare war.

Metternich described the way in which the emperor,
with the manners of the guardroom rather than those of
the council-chamber, suddenly and violently tossed his
cocked-hat into the corner of the room, "evidently expecting that I should pick it up and present it to him,"
said the old statesman ; "but I judged it better to ignore
the action and the intention altogether, and his majesty,
after a minute or two, rose and picked it up himself."

He went on to express his conviction that all this display of passion on the emperor's part was altogether affected, fictitious, and calculated ; and said that similar
manifestations of intemperate violence were by no means
infrequently used by the emperor with a view to produce
calculated effects, and were often more or less successful.

It would be a great mistake to suppose that the most
cynical observer could have detected the slightest shade
of bitterness in the words or the manner of Prince Metternich. On *that* field of battle, at all events, the honors
did not fall to the share of Napoleon. And his aged adversary spoke of the encounter with the amused pleasantry
and easy smile of a veteran who recounts passages at arms
in which his part has been that best worth telling.

But with a graver manner he went on to say, that the
most unpleasant part of the circumstance connected with
dealing with Napoleon arose from the fact that he was
not a gentleman in any sense of the word, or anything
like one. Of course the prince, with his unblemished sixteen quarterings, was not talking of anything connected
with Napoleon's birth. And I doubt whether he may
have been aware that Napoleon Bonaparte was technically gentle by virtue of his descent from an ancient Tuscan territorial noble race. Metternich, in expressing the
opinion quoted, was not thinking of anything of the kind.
He was speaking of the moral nature of the man. In these
days, after all that has since that time been published on

the subject, the expression of Metternich seems almost like the enunciation of an accepted and recognized truism. Nevertheless, even now the judgment on such a point, of one who had enjoyed (no, certainly not enjoyed, but we will say undergone) so much personal intercourse with the great conqueror, is worth recording.

My mother has given an account of the same conversation, which I have here recorded, in the second volume of her book on "Vienna and the Austrians." Her account tallies with mine in all essentials (I did not read it—in *this* half-century—till after I had written the above sentences) ; but she relates one or two circumstances which I have omitted ; and she apparently did not hear what the prince said afterwards about Napoleon as a gentleman— or perhaps it was said upon another occasion, which I cannot assert may not have been the case.

One point of my mother's narrative should not be omitted. Metternich, observing that it was impossible for any human being to have heard what passed between him and Napoleon, but that everybody had read all about it, said that Savary relates truly the incident of the hat, *which must have been told him by Napoleon himself.* This is very curious.

Another amusing anecdote recounted by Metternich one evening, when my mother and myself, together with only a very small circle of *habitués* were present, I remember well, and intended to give my own reminiscences of it in this place. But I find the story so well told by my mother, and it is so well worth repeating, that I will reproduce her telling of it.

"During the hundred days of Napoleon's extraordinary but abortive restoration, he found himself compelled by circumstances, *bon gré mal gré,* to appoint Fouché minister of police. About ten days after this arch-traitor was so placed, Prince Metternich was informed that a stranger desired to see him. He was admitted, and the prince recognized him as an individual whom he had known as an *employé* at Paris. But he now appeared under a borrowed name, bringing only a fragment of Fouché's handwriting, as testimony that he was sent by him. His mission he said was of the most secret nature, and, in fact, only extended to informing the prince that Fouché was desirous of offering to his consideration propositions of the most important nature. The messenger declared himself wholly ignorant of their purport, being authorized only to invite the prince to a secret conference through the medium of some trusty envoy, who should be despatched to Paris for the purpose. The prince's reply was, 'You must permit me to think of this.' The agent retired, and the Austrian minister repaired to the emperor, and recounted what had passed. 'And what do you think of doing?' said the emperor.

"'I think,' replied the prince, 'that we should send a confidential agent, not to Paris, but to some other place that may be fixed upon, who shall have no other instructions but to listen to all that the Frenchman, who will meet him there, shall impart, and bring us faithfully an account of it.'

"The emperor signified his approbation; 'And then,' continued the prince, 'as we were good and faithful allies, and would do nothing unknown to those with whom we were pledged to act in common, I hastened to inform the allied sovereigns, who were still at Vienna, of the arrival of the messenger, and the manner in which I proposed to act.' The mysterious messenger was accordingly dismissed with an answer purporting that an Austrian, calling himself Werner, should be at a certain hotel in the town of Basle, in Switzerland, on such a day, with instructions to hear and convey to Prince Metternich whatever the individual sent to meet him should deliver. This meeting took place at the spot and hour fixed. The diplomatic agents saluted each other with fitting courtesy, and seated themselves *vis-à-vis*, each assuming the attitude of a listener.

"'May I ask you, sir,' said the envoy from Paris, at length, 'what is the object of our meeting?'

"'My object, sir,' replied the Austrian, 'is to listen to whatever you may be disposed to say.'

"'And mine,' rejoined the Frenchman, 'is solely to hear what you may have to communicate.'

"Neither the one nor the other had anything further to add to this interesting interchange of information, and after remaining together long enough for each to be satisfied that the other had nothing to tell, they separated with perfect civility, both returning precisely as wise as they came.

"Some time after the imperial restoration had given way to the royal one in France, the mystery was explained. Fouché, *cette revolution incarnée,* as the prince called him, no sooner saw his old master and benefactor restored to power than he imagined the means of betraying him, and accordingly despatched the messenger, who presented himself to Prince Metternich. Fouché was minister of police, and probably all the world would have agreed with him in thinking that if any man in France could safely send off a secret messenger it was himself. But all the world would have been mistaken, and so was Fouché. The argus eyes of Napoleon discovered the proceeding. The first messenger was seized and examined on his return. The minister of police was informed of the discovery, and coolly assured by his imperial master that he would probably be hanged. The second messenger was then despatched by Napoleon himself with exactly the same instructions as the envoy who met him from Vienna, to the effect that he was to listen to all that might be said to him, and when questioned himself, confess, what was the exact truth, that all he knew of the mission on which he came was that he was expected to remember and repeat all that he should hear."

On the 30th of November in that year I witnessed the by far most gorgeous pageant I ever saw—for I was not in Westminster Abbey on the 21st of June, 1887—the installation of eleven Knights of the Golden Fleece. As a pageant, nothing, I think, could exceed the gorgeous and *historic* magnificence of this ceremony; but no "Kings of the Isles brought gifts," nor was the imperial body-guard composed of sovereign princes or their representatives. In *significance,* that show and all others such, even the meeting of the Field of the Cloth of Gold itself, is eclipsed by the ever-memorable day which England has just seen.

But it was not only a very grand but a very interesting sight, the whole details of which may be found by those interested in such matters very accurately described in the volume by my mother which I have so often quoted.

On the very next day I saw another sight which I think it probable no subsequent sight-seer in Vienna during all the half-century that has elapsed since that day has seen, or any will see in the future. It was a sight more monstrously contrasted with the scene I had yesterday witnessed than it could well enter into the human mind to conceive. It was a visit to the vast, long-disused catacombs under the cathedral church of St. Stephen. It was then about sixty years, as I was told—now more than a hundred—since these vaults were used as a place of sepulture. Here, as in many other well-known instances, the special peculiarities of soil and atmosphere prevent all the usual processes of decay, and the tens of thousands of corpses which have been deposited there—very many uncoffined and unshrouded during the visitation of the plague in 1713—have become to all intents and purposes mummies. They retain not only the form of human beings, but in many cases the features retain the ghastly expression which was their last when the breath of life left them. The countless forms, which never apparently from the day they were deposited there had been subjected to any sort of arrangement whatever, lay in monstrous confused heaps, mingled with shattered remains of coffins. The skin in every case had become of the consistency of very thick and tough leather, not quite so thick as that used for the sole of a stout shoe, but a good deal thicker than what is generally used for the upper leather even of the stoutest. There was not the slightest disagreeable odor in any part of the vaults. In the course of a long life I have seen very many strange sights, but never any one to match that in weird strangeness and impressive horror. If any sight on earth merits the degraded epithet "awful," it must be that of those fearsome catacombs.

What I have written here conveys but a very imperfect notion of all that we saw and felt during our progress through that terrible succession of vaults. But I abstain from chronicling the sights of this charnel-house for the same reason that I refrained from any attempt at describing the cloth of gold and the velvets and the silks and satins of the previous day. The detailed description of them may all be found in my mother's book, in the fortieth chapter of which the reader so inclined may sup full of horrors to his heart's content. I will content myself with testifying to the perfect accuracy and absence of exaggeration in the account there given.

My mother expresses disapproval of the authorities who permit such an exhibition, and she is very vague as to the means by which we obtained admission to it. Nor does my memory furnish any clear information upon this point, but I have a strong impression that it was all an affair of bribery managed "under the rose" (what a phrase for such an exploit!) by back-stairs influence in some way. I do not think that the first comer, with however large a fee in his hand, could have caused the door of that chamber of horrors to be opened to him. There are, it is true, sundry words and incidents in my mother's account which seem to indicate that the showman guide who attended us was in the habit of similarly attending others; but I am persuaded that my mother was in error in supposing, if she did suppose, that to be the case. Unquestionably the man was at home in the gruesome place, and well acquainted with all the parts of it, but I have reason to be persuaded that his familiarity with it arose simply from the habit of pillaging the remains of the coffins for firewood!

Not long after this memorable expedition to the catacombs I received a communication from Birmingham which rendered it necessary for me to leave Vienna and turn my face homeward.

CHAPTER XVII.

AT BIRMINGHAM.

I LEFT Vienna by the carriage which carried the imperial mail, shortly before Christmas, in very severe
weather. It would be impossible to construct a more
comfortable carriage for the use of those to whom speed
is no object. It carried only two passengers and the
courier, and was abundantly roomy and well cushioned.
It carried, of course, also all the mails from Hungary and
from Vienna to the north and westward, including those
to Munich and Paris and London. And to the best of my
recollection all these despatches, printed as well as written,
were carried in the hind boot of our conveyance. If they
were not there I can't guess where they were.

I remember that I was tremendously great-coated, having, besides my "box-coat," a "buffalo robe," which I had
brought back with me from America, and I have no recollection of suffering at all from cold. We proceeded in
very leisurely fashion ; and I well remember the reply of
the courier to my question, how long we were to remain
at the place at which we were to dine, given with an air
of mild surprise at my thinking such a demand necessary.
"Till we have done dinner," said the courier—"*Bis wir
gespeist haben*"! The words seem still to echo in my ears!
To me, whose experiences were of the Quicksilver mail!

When we *had* done dinner, and he asked me with leisurely courtesy if I had dined well, he said, in answer to
my confessing that I could have wished nothing more, unless it were a cup of coffee, if perchance there were one
ready, "No doubt the hostess will make us one. It is
best fresh made"! And so, while the imperial mail and
all the Paris and London letters and the post-horses
waited at the door, the coffee *was* made and leisurely
discussed.

I will upon this occasion also spare the reader all guide-book chatter, and pass on to the arrival of myself and the friend who was with me at Dover, which arrival was a somewhat remarkable one.

We had travelled by Antwerp, which I wished to revisit for the sake of the cathedral, and crossed from Ostend, where also I was not sorry to pass a day.

We had a long and nasty passage, but at last reached Dover to find the whole town and the surrounding hills under snow, and to be met by the intelligence that all communication between Dover and London was inter-rupted. Even the boat which used to ply between Do-ver and the London Docks would not face the abomina-ble weather, and was not running. There was nothing for it but to take up our abode at the King's Head (no Lord Warden in those days !), and wait for the road to be opened.

We waited one day, two days, with no prospect of any amelioration of our position. On the third day two young Americans who were in the house, equally weather-bound with ourselves, and equally impatient of their imprison-ment, assured us that in their country the matter would speedily be remedied, and declared their determination of getting to Canterbury on a sledge. We had heard by that time that from Canterbury to London the road was open. The people at the King's Head assured us that no such at-tempt had any chance of succeeding. But, of course, our American friends considered that to be a strictly profes-sional opinion, and determined on starting. We agreed to share the adventure with them. Four of the best post-horses we could find in Dover were hired, a couple of postboys, whose pluck was stimulated by promises of high fees, were engaged, and a sledge was rigged under the per-sonal supervision of our experienced friends.

On the fourth day we got ourselves and our respective trunks on to the sledge, and started among the ill-omened prognostications of our host of the King's Head and his friends. I think the postboys did their utmost bravely, but at the end of about five miles from Dover they dis-mounted from their floundering horses and declared the enterprise an impossible one. It was totally out of the question, they said, to reach Canterbury. It would be quite as much as they could do to get back to Dover.

What was to be done? The boys were so evidently right that the Americans did not attempt to gainsay their decision. A council of war was called, the upshot of which was that our two American allies decided to return to Dover with their and our baggage *and wraps*, while my friend and I determined at all risks to push on to Canterbury on foot. We had eleven miles of bleak country before us, which was simply one uniform undulating field of snow. The baffled postboys gave us many minute directions of signs and objects by which we were to endeavor to keep the road. We had started from Dover about nine o'clock in the morning. It was then not quite noon. The mail would leave Canterbury at ten at night for London, and we had, therefore, ten hours before us for our undertaking.

We thought that four, or, at the outside, five, would be ample for the purpose, if we were ever to get to Canterbury at all. But we did not reach The Fountain in that much-longed-for city till past eight that evening.

It was a terrible walk. Of course at no conceivable rate of progression could we have been eight hours in walking eleven miles if we had continued to progress at all. But we lost the road again and again; sometimes got far away from it, and fought our way back to it by the directions obtained at farmhouses or laborers' cottages, from people who evidently deemed our enterprise a desperate one. Mostly we were struggling knee-deep in snow, once or twice plunging into and out of drifts over our waists. We were not on foot quite all the time; for once we rested in a hospitable cottage for an hour, when we were about six miles from Canterbury. Our host there, who was, I take it, a wagoner, strongly advised us to give it up, and offered to let us pass the night in his cottage. We were already very much beaten, and were sorely tempted to close with his proposal. Perhaps, if we had known that we should never, as was the case, see those Americans again, we should have done so. But much as our bodies needed rest, our

11

souls needed triumph more. So we turned out into the
snow again, and — by eight o'clock did reach the hospitable Fountain.

'But we were in a sad plight, desperately wearied, a good
deal bruised and knocked about, and as thoroughly wet
through literally as though we had been walking in water
instead of snow. Rest was delicious ; a hot supper was
such delight as no "gods" had ever enjoyed. Good beds
would have been Elysium. But — the thought of the
next morning gave us pause. We had no rag of clothing of any sort save the thoroughly soaked things on our
backs. No boots or shoes. And how should we possibly
put on again those on our feet if once they were taken
off ? In London, if once reached, all these troubles would
be at an end.

Finally we decided to go on by the mail at ten that
night. But here a fresh disappointment awaited us.
The mail was booked full inside. There were two outside places, those on the roof behind the driver, available.
But we were dead beat, wet through to the bone, unprovided with any wrap of any kind, and it was freezing
hard.

But on to the mail we climbed at ten o'clock. I believe
the good hostess of The Fountain genuinely thought our
proceeding suicidal, and the refusal of her beds absolutely insane.

That journey from Canterbury to London was by far
the worst I ever made. It really was a very bad business.
But at every change of horses I got down, and, holding on
by the coach behind, ran as far as my breath and strength
would allow me, and thus knocked a little warmth into
my veins. I could not persuade my companion to do likewise. He seemed to be wearied and frozen into apathy.
The consequence was that whereas I was after some
twelve hours in bed not a jot the worse, he was laid up
for a fortnight.

Shortly afterwards I assumed my new duties at Birmingham. The new building had been completed, and
was—or, rather, is, as all the world may see to the present
day—a very handsome one. The head-master, whose as-

sistant I specially was, was Dr. Jeune, who became subsequently Bishop of Peterborough. The second master, Mr. Gedge, had also an assistant named Mason. Our duties were to teach Latin and Greek to any of the sons of the inhabitants of Birmingham who chose to avail themselves of King Edward's benevolent foundation. None of the masters had anything to do with the business of lodging or victualling boys. The boys were all day boys, and our business was to teach them Latin and Greek during certain hours of every day.

I soon became aware, by a strangely subtle process of feeling rather than observation, that my eight years' Winchester experience of schoolboy life and ways had not constituted a favorable preparation for my present work. I felt that I was working in an atmosphere and on a material that was new to me. It would be absurd to imagine that all those sons of Birmingham tradesmen were stupider or duller boys than the average of our Winchester lads. But it appeared to me that it was far more difficult to teach them with any fair amount of success. They were no doubt all, or nearly all, the sons of men who had never learned anything in their lives save the elements of a strictly commercial education. And I felt myself tempted to believe that the results of heredity must extend themselves even to the greater or lesser receptivity of one description of teaching instead of another. I suppose that the descendant of a long line of shoemakers would be more readily taught how to make a shoe than how to build a ship. And it may be in like manner that *ingenuas didicisse fideliter artes* comes more readily to a boy whose forefathers have for generations done the same thing than it would to the descendant of generations unmoulded by any such discipline.

Corporal punishment was used, and naturally had to be resorted to much more frequently by me than by my superior, whose work was concerned with the older and better-conducted portion of the boys. In fact, as far as my recollection at the present day goes, it seems to me that hardly any morning or afternoon passed without the application of the cane. And this corporal castigation, though

devoid of all the judicial formality which might have
made our Winchester "scourging" a really moral punishment if the frequency of it and the prevailing sentiment
upon the subject both of masters and scholars had been
other than it was, was in truth a very much severer infliction as regards the absolute pain to be suffered by the
patient. Three or four strokes with the cane over the
palm of the hand would be very much worse than the
perfunctory swishing with the peculiar Winchester rod.
I do not remember that this caning was ever judicially
used as a sentence to be executed at any future time, or
that it was ever, for the most part, used to punish the idleness which had prevented a boy from learning his lessons
at his home. It was used almost exclusively, as far as I
remember, for the preservation of order and silence during the school hours, and the correction of the offender
followed instantly on the commission of the offence.

And this necessity of enforcing order among a very un-
disciplined crew of some forty or fifty lads, of ages varying from, perhaps, twelve to about fourteen or fifteen, was
by far the most irksome and difficult part of my duty. I
was accustomed to tuition. But the cumulation of the
office of beadle with that of teacher was new to me, and I
did not like it. And still less did I like the constant tendency of the urgent duties of the first office to encroach
upon those of the second.

My scholastic experiences had accustomed me to a state
of things in which idleness, violence, dare-devil audacity,
and neglect of duty had been common enough, but in
which organized trickery and deception had been rarely
seen. And I felt myself unfitted for the duties of a police-
man among these turbulent Birmingham lads. I never
saw the face of any one of them save during school hours;
and I remember thinking at the time that, had this been
otherwise, I might have obtained a moral influence over at
least some of them, which might have been more useful
than all my efforts during school hours to force the rules
and principles of syntax into unwilling brains, accustomed
to the habitual defiance of them during all the remainder
of their lives.

It appeared to me that I was engaged in the perpetual, and somewhat hopeless, task of endeavoring to manufacture silk purses out of sows' ears; and I confess that I never put on my academical gown to go into school without feeling that I was going to an irksome, and, I feared, unprofitable labor. I tried hard to do my duty; but I fear that I was by no means the right man in the right place.

No preparation of any kind, beyond assuming my gown and trencher cap, before going into school was needed, and I had, therefore, abundance of leisure, during which I did a considerable quantity of miscellaneous reading, not, perhaps, altogether so unprofitable as the advocates of regular study devoted to some well-defined end might suppose.

We endeavored—my colleague Mason and I—I remember, to get up a debating society among the few—very few—young men with whom we had become acquainted. But it did not succeed. Young Birmingham, intent on making, and on its way to make, "plums" in hardware, did not think that "debating" was the best way of employing the hours that could be spared from the counting-house.

There might, no doubt, have been found a better element of social intercourse in the younger clergy of the town; but they were all strongly "evangelical," which was at that time quite sufficient to entail an oil-and-vinegar mutual repulsion between them and the young Wykehamist. And this, involving as it does a confession of a discreditable amount of raw young-man's prejudice, I mention as an illustration of the current opinions, feelings, and mental habits of the time, for, after all, I was not more prejudiced and more stupid than the rest of the world around me.

In fact my life at Birmingham was for the most part a very solitary one. I used to come home tired and worn out to my lodgings with Mrs. Clements in New Hall Street; and the prospect of a lonely evening with my book, my teapot, and my pipe was not unwelcome to me, for it was, at least, repose and quiet after noise and tur-

moil. Every now and then I used to dine and pass the
evening with Dr. Jeune; and these were my red-letter
days. Jeune had married the daughter of Dr. Symonds,
the warden of Wadham. She was a tall and very handsome woman, as well as an extremely agreeable one. At
first, I remember, I used to think that if she had been the
daughter of anybody else than the "Head of a House,"
one just emerging from *statu pupillari* might have found
her more charming. But this soon wore off as we got to
know each other better. And long talks with Mrs. Jeune
are the pleasantest—indeed, I think I may say the only
pleasant—recollections of my life at Birmingham.

CHAPTER XVIII.

I HELD my mastership in King Edward's School at Birmingham a year and a half—from shortly after the first day of 1837 to the 19th of June, 1838.

At the end of that time I went back to my mother's house at Hadley. She had in the meantime returned from Vienna, had completed her two volumes on that journey, and published them with such a measure of success as to encourage her in hoping that she might vary her never-ceasing labor in the production of novels by again undertaking other journeys. But for this, and still more for the execution of other schemes, of which I shall have to speak further on, my presence and companionship were necessary to her. And after much consultation and very many walks together round the little quiet garden at Hadley, it was decided between us that I should send in my resignation of the Birmingham mastership, defer all alternative steps in the direction of any other life career, and devote myself, for the present at least, to becoming her companion and squire.

The decision was a very momentous one. As might have been anticipated, the "deferring" of any steps in the direction of a professional career of any sort turned out eventually to be the final abandonment of any such. It could hardly be otherwise in the case of a young man of twenty-eight, which was my age at the time. I was the son of a father who had left absolutely nothing behind him, and I had no prospect whatever of any independent means from any other source. It is true that property settled on my mother before her marriage would in any case suffice to keep me from absolute destitution, but that was about all that could be said of it. And certainly the decision to which my mother and I came during these walks round and round the Hadley garden was audacious rather than prudent.

I have *never* regretted it during any part of the now well-nigh half a century of life that has elapsed since the resolution was taken. I have been, I have not the smallest doubt, a much happier man than I should have been had I followed a more beaten track. My brother Anthony used to say of me that I should never have earned my salt in the routine work of a profession, or any employment under the authoritative supervision of a superior. I always dissented, and beg still to record my dissent, from any such judgment. But, as it is, I can say with sincerely grateful recognition in my heart, that I have been a very happy—I fear I may say an exceptionally happy—man. Despite this, I do not think that were I called upon to advise a young man in precisely similar circumstances to mine at that time, I should counsel him to follow my example; for I have been not only a happy, but a singularly fortunate man. Again and again, at various turning-points of my life, I have been fortunate to a degree which no conduct or prudence of my own merited.

I was under no immediate obligation to work in any way, but I cannot say of myself I have been an idle man. I have worked much, and sometimes very hard.

Upon one occasion—the occasion was that of sudden medical advice to the effect that it was desirable that I should take my first wife from Florence for a change of climate, which I was not in funds to do comfortably—I planned and wrote, from title-page to colophon, and sold a two-volume novel of the usual size in four-and-twenty days. I had a "turn of speed" in writing as well as walking. I could do my five miles and three quarters in an hour at a fair toe-and-heel walk, and I wrote a novel in twenty-four days—it was written indeed in twenty-three, for I took a whole holiday in the middle of the work. Of course it may be said that the novel was trash. But it was as good as, and was found by the publisher to be more satisfactory than, some others of the great number I have perpetrated. And I should like those who may imagine that the arduous nature of the feat I accomplished was made less by the literary imperfection of the work to try the experiment of *copying* six hundred post-octavo pages in the time. I found the register of each day's work the other day. The longest was thirty-three pages. It was no great matter to have written three-and-thirty pages in one day, but I am disposed to think that few men (or even women) could continue for as many days at so high an average of speed. My brother used to say that he could not do the like to save his life and that of all those dearest to him. And he was not a slow writer. Of course when my book was done I was nearly done too. But I do not know that I was ever any the worse for the effort. The novel in question was called "Beppo the Conscript."

No, I have not been an idle man since the day when my mother and myself decided that I was to follow no recognized profession. The long, too long, series of works which have been published as mine will account for probably considerably less than half the printed matter which I am responsible for having given to the world. Nor can I say that I was driven to work "by hunger and request of friends." During all my long career of authorship there was no period at which I could not have lived an idle man —not so well as I wished, certainly; but I was not driven by imperious necessity.

Yet I have a very pretty turn for idleness too. It is as pleasant to me " to smoke my canister and tipple my ale in the shade," as Thackeray says, as to any man. Anthony had no such turn. Work to him was a necessity and a satisfaction. He used often to say that he envied me the capacity for being idle. Had he possessed it, poor fellow, I might not now be speaking of him in the past tense. And still less than of me could it be said of him that he was ever driven to literary work *deficiente crumenâ*. But he labored, during the whole of his manhood life, with an insatiable ardor that (taking into consideration his very efficient discharge of his duties as post-office surveyor) puts my industry into the shade.

Certainly we both of us ought to have inherited, and I suppose did inherit, an aptitude for industry. My father

11*

was, as I have said, a remarkably laborious, though an unsuccessful, man, and my mother left a hundred and fifteen
volumes, written between her fiftieth year and that of her
death.

Shortly after my final return from Birmingham my
mother had a bad illness. It could not have been a very
long one; the record of her published work shows no ces-
sation of literary activity. Whether this illness had anything to do with the resolution she came to much about
the same time to change her residence, I do not remember, but about this time we established ourselves at No. 20
York Street.

Here, as everywhere else where my mother found or
made a home, the house forthwith became the resort of
pleasant people; and my time in York Street was a very
agreeable one. Among other frequenters of it, my diary
makes frequent mention of Judge Haliburton, of Nova
Scotia, better known to the world as Sam Slick, the Clock-
maker. He was, as I remember him, a delightful companion—for a limited time. He was in this respect exactly
like his books—extremely amusing reading if taken in
rather small doses, but calculated to seem tiresomely mo-
notonous if indulged in at too great length. He was a
thoroughly good fellow, kindly, cheery, hearty, and sympathetic always; and so far always a welcome companion.
But his funning was always pitched in the same key, and
always more or less directed to the same objects. His
social and political ideas and views all coincided with my
own, which, of course, tended to make us better friends.
In appearance he looked entirely like an Englishman, but
not at all like a Londoner. Without being at all too fat,
he was large and burly in person, with gray hair, a large
ruddy face, a humorous mouth, and bright blue eyes always full of mirth. He was an inveterate chewer of tobacco, and, in the fulness of comrade-like kindness, strove
to indoctrinate me with that habit. But I was already an
old smoker, and preferred to content myself with that
mode of availing myself of the blessing of tobacco.

" Highways and Byeways " Grattan we also saw occasionally when anything brought him to London. He also

was, as will readily be believed, what is generally called very good company. He, too, was full of fun, and certainly it could not be said that *his* fiddle had but one string to it. His fault lay in the opposite direction. His funning muse "made increment of" everything. He was intensely Irish, in manner, accent, and mind. He had a broken, or naturally bridgeless, nose, and possessed as small a share of good looks or personal advantages as most men. He first urged me to try my hand at a novel. He had seen some of my early scribblings, but repeated that "Fiction, me boy, fiction and passion are what readers want." But I did not at that time, or for many a long year afterwards, feel within myself any capacity for supplying such want.

CHAPTER XIX.

On the 17th of August, in 1838, as I find by my diary, "I went with Henrietta Skerret to see the Baron Dupotet magnetize his patients." This was my first introduction to a subject, and to a special little world of its own, of which subsequently I saw a great deal, and which shortly began to attract an increasing amount of attention from the greater world around it. The Miss Skerret mentioned was the younger of two sisters, the nieces of Mathias, the author of the once well-known, but now forgotten, "Pursuits of Literature." Mr. Mathias and his sister, Mrs. Skerret, had been old acquaintances of my mother from earlier days than those to which any reminiscences of mine run back. And Maryanne and Henrietta Skerret were lifelong friends of my mother's and of mine. They were left at the death of their parents very slenderly provided for, and Maryanne, the elder, became by the interest of some influential person among their numerous friends, received into the service of the queen in some properly menial capacity. But of all those in the immediate service of her majesty, it is probable that there was not one, whether menial or other, equal to Miss Skerret in native power of intellect, extent of reading, and linguistic accomplishment. And this the queen very speedily discovered, the result of which was that to her particular service, which I believe consisted in taking charge of the jewelry which the queen had in daily use, was added that of marking in the volumes which her majesty wished to make some acquaintance with those passages which she deemed worth the queen's attention. She remained with the queen many years, till advancing age was thought to have entitled her to a retiring pension, which she was still enjoying when I saw her, a very old woman, two or three years ago. I know that she found her position in the household, as may be readily understood, an irksome and materially uncomfortable one. But of her royal mistress, and of every member of the royal family she came into contact with, she never ceased to speak with the utmost affection and gratitude.

The younger sister, Henrietta, died some years before her. I had of late years seen much more of her than of her sister; for of course the position of the latter cut her off very much from all association with her friends. Henrietta was as remarkably clever a woman as her sister, but very different from her. She was as good a linguist, but her natural bent was to mathematics and its kindred subjects rather than to general literature. And whereas Maryanne was marked by an exquisite sense of humor, and was always full of fun, Henrietta was, I think, the most judicial-minded woman I have ever known. I have never met the man or woman whom I should have preferred to consult on a matter of weighing and estimating the value of evidence. She was for many years, as was my mother also, an intimate friend of Captain Kater, who was in those days well known in the scientific world as "Pendulum Kater," from some application, I fancy, of the properties of the pendulum to the business of mapping, in which he had been engaged in India. Young, Woolaston, De Morgan, and others *ejusdem farinæ*, were all Miss Skerret's friends, especially the last named. And I was brought into contact with some of them by her means.

This was the lady who, in 1838, invited me to accompany her to a *séance* at the house of Baron Dupotet, a Frenchman, whose magnetizing theories and practice were at that time exciting some attention.

Here is an extract from my diary written the same evening:

"The phenomena I have witnessed are certainly most extraordinary and unaccountable. That one young woman was thrown into a convulsive state is entirely undeniable. Her muscles, which we felt, were hard, rigid, and in a state of tension, and so remained for a longer time than it is possible for any person voluntarily to keep them so—for, I should say, at least twenty minutes. A little girl became to all appearance somnambulous. This, however, might more possibly be imposture. When the little girl and the young woman were placed near each other, the effect on both was increased, and the girl instead of being merely somnambulous, became convulsive. The little girl, *as far as the* CLOSE *observation of the onlookers could detect* [underlining in original], saw the colors of objects, etc., with her eyes closed. This, however, is evidence of a nature easily deceptive. When waked from her magnetic trance, she forgot, or professed to have forgotten, all that she had said or done when in it. But when again put into a state of trance or somnambulism, she again remembered and spoke of what had occurred in the former trance.

"After these patients were disposed of, two young men of the spectators offered themselves as subjects to the magnetizer. He said that they were not good subjects for it, and that it would be difficult to affect them, and would take a long time. He then tried me, and after a short space of time, I think not more than half a minute, he said that I was *very* sensitive to the magnetic influence, and that in two or three sittings he could produce '*des effets extraordinaires*' on me ; but that he was then tired, and that '*rien ne coule plus*' from his fingers."

It is not so stated in my diary, but I remember perfectly well that the general impression left on my mind by the baron was not a favorable one. I find by my diary that I read his book, translated from the French by Miss Skerret, a few days afterwards, and the result was to increase the above impression. But I was far from coming to the conclusion that his pretensions were all chimerical. As regards his dictum about my own impressionability, I may observe that on various occasions at long-distant times I have been subjected to the experiments of several professing magnetizers of reputed first-rate power, but that *never* has the slightest effect of any kind whatever been produced upon me. Sometimes I was pronounced to be physically a bad subject ; sometimes I was accused of spoiling the experiment by wilfully resisting the influence ; sometimes the magnetizer was too tired.

I think I may as well throw together here the rest of my experiences and reminiscences in connection with this subject—or rather some selections from them, for I have at different times and places seen so much of it that I might fill volumes with the reports of my observations.

On the 13th of February, 1839, my mother and I dined with Mr. Grattan to meet Dr. Elliotson, and on the following day we went by appointment to meet him at the house of a patient of his, a little boy in Red Lion Street. I saw subsequently a great deal of Dr. Elliotson, and I may say became intimate with him. It needed but little intercourse with him to perceive that here was a man of a very different calibre from Baron Dupotet. Without at all coming to the conclusion that the latter was a charlatan, it was abundantly evident to me that Elliotson was in no degree such. He was a gentleman, a highly educated and accomplished man, and so genuinely in earnest on this subject of " animal magnetism," as it was the fashion then to call it, that he was ready to spend and be spent in his efforts to establish the truthfulness and therapeutic usefulness of its pretensions.

Here is the account of what we—my mother and I—witnessed on that 14th of February, as given in my diary written the same day :

"He put the little boy to sleep very shortly, then drew him by magnetic passes out of his chair, and caused him, while evidently all the time asleep, to imitate him [Dr. Elliotson] in all his attitudes and movements. We both firmly believed that the boy *was* asleep. We then went to the house of another patient, Emma Melhuish, the daughter of a glazier, sixteen years old, and ill in bed from cataleptic fits."

This was a very remarkable case, and had attracted considerable attention. Emma Melhuish was a very beautiful girl, and she was perhaps the most remarkable instance I ever witnessed of a singular phenomenon resulting from magnetic sleep, which has been often spoken of in relation to other cases—the truly wonderful spiritual beauty assumed by the features and expression of the patient during superinduced cataleptic trance, which has never, I believe, been observed in cases of natural catalepsy. I have seen this girl, Emma Melhuish (doubtless a very pretty girl in her normal state of health, but with nothing intellectually or morally special about her), throw herself during her magnetic trance into attitudes of adoration, the grace and expressiveness of which no painter could hope to find in the best model he ever saw or heard of, while her face and features, eyes especially, assumed a rapt and ecstatic expressiveness which no Saint Theresa could have equalled. It was a conception of Fra Angelico spiritualized by the presence of the breath of life. Never shall I forget the look of the girl as I saw her in that condition! I can see her now! and can remember, as I felt it then, the painfulness of the suggestion that such an apparent outlook of the soul was in truth nothing more than the result of certain purely material conditions of the body. But was it such?

Here is my diary's account of what I saw that first day:

"We found her in mesmeric sleep, she having been so since left by Dr. Elliotson in that condition the day before. We heard her predict the time when her fits would recur, and saw the prediction verified with the utmost exactitude. We heard her declare in what part of the house her various sisters were at the moment, saying that one had just left the counting-house and had come into the next room, all which statements we carefully verified. My mother and myself came home fully persuaded that, let the explanatory theory of the matter be what it might, there had been no taint of imposture in what we had witnessed."

On subsequent visits we assured ourselves of the entire truthfulness of statements to the effect that Emma was conscious of the approach of Dr. Elliotson, while he was still in a different street, and to the punctuality with which she went to sleep and waked, at the hour she had named herself as that when she should do so.

I remember Dr. Elliotson relating to me, as an instance of the utility of the magnetic influence, a curious case to which he had been called. The brother of a young girl had, as a practical joke, suddenly fired off a pistol behind her head. She was of course painfully startled, with the

result of becoming affected by a fit of hiccough so persistent that no means could be found or suggested of
making it cease. It was absolutely impossible for the
girl to swallow anything. She was becoming exhausted,
and the case assumed a really alarming aspect. It was
at this conjuncture that Elliotson was called in. He succeeded in putting her into a magnetic sleep, with of course
perfect calm, after which the hiccough returned no more.

But by far the most curious and interesting of Elliotson's cases was one of which a good deal was, I think,
said and printed in those days, but of which very few persons, probably, saw as much as I did—the case of the two
Okey girls. They were both patients, I believe, for some
form of catalepsy, in a hospital of which Dr. Elliotson
was one of the leading physicians. Dr. Elliotson was
obliged to throw up his position there, because those who
were in authority at the hospital were bitterly opposed to
his magnetizing experiments and practice. And about the
same time, or shortly afterwards, the Okey girls were dismissed for a cause which seems grotesquely absurd, but
the story of which is strictly true. These girls, of, I suppose, about thirteen and fourteen, being in the very extraordinary condition which a prolonged course of magnetizing had produced (of which I shall speak further
presently), were in the habit of declaring that they " saw
Jack " at the bedside of this or that patient in the hospital. And the patients of whom they made this assertion
invariably died ! That the presence of such prophetesses
in the hospital was undesirable is intelligible enough ; but
what are we to think of the motives, presentiments, in-
stincts, intuitions of mental or physical nature which
prompted such guesses or prophecies ?

Much about the same time my brother had a serious and
dangerous illness, so much so that his medical attendants
—of whom Dr. Elliotson was, I know not why, not one,
though we were intimate with him at the time—were by
no means assured respecting the issue of it. Now it is·
within my own knowledge that the Okey girls, especially
one of them (Jane, I think, her name was), were very frequently in the lodgings occupied by my brother at the

time, during the period of his greatest danger, and used constantly to say that they "saw Jack by his side, but only up to his knee," and therefore they thought he would recover—as he did! I am almost ashamed to write what seems such childish absurdity. But the facts are certain, and taken in conjunction with the cause of the girls' dismissal from the hospital, and with a statement made to me subsequently by Dr. Elliotson, they are very curious. I may add that when cross-examined as closely as was possible as to *what* they saw, the girls said they did not know—that they did know that certain persons whom they saw were about to die shortly, and that was their way of saying it. They, on more than one occasion, on reaching our house by omnibus, said that they had seen "Jack" by the side of one of the passengers—of course I cannot say with what issue.

The statement referred to was as follows: Elliotson having been in some sort the cause of the two girls being turned out of the hospital, and being anxious, moreover, to continue his observations on them, took them into his own house. There, looking out one day from an upper window, they saw across the street at the opposite window three fine healthy-looking children. They were, said Elliotson, the children of a hairdresser, who had a shop below. "What a pity," said Jane Okey, "that that child in the middle has Jack at him. He will die!" And so within a day or two—it might have been hours, I am not certain—the child *did* die! Believing, as I do, Dr. Elliotson to have been a truthful and habitually accurate speaker, I confess that it does not satisfy me to dismiss this story, especially when taken in conjunction with the other anecdotes I have related, as mere "coincidence," though I have no shadow of a theory to offer in explanation of it.

The purely physical experiments which were performed with these girls before my eyes were curious and interesting. I have seen those Okey girls, and they were slight, small girls, lift weights which it would be quite impossible for them to lift normally, not by applying the whole strength of the body and back to the task, but by taking the ring of an iron weight in the hand, and so lifting it in obedience to the "passes" of the magnetizer applied to the arm.

But decidedly the most singular and curious part of the case consisted in the abnormal condition of mind and intelligence in which they lived under magnetic influence for many weeks at a time. There were three conditions, or, as it might be said, three stages of condition in which I saw and studied them. Firstly—though it was lastly as regards my opportunities of observation—there was their normal natural condition. Secondly, there was a condition not of trance, or somnambulism, but of existence carried on according to the usual laws and conditions, but resulting apparently from the application of magnetism during prolonged periods of time, during which complete interruption of conscious identity seemed to have taken place. The third state was that of trance. In the first state they were much such as children of that age taken out of a workhouse, say, might be expected to be—awkward, shy, seemingly stupid, and unwilling to speak much when questioned. In the second state they were bright, decidedly clever, apt to be pert, and perfectly self-confident. And in this condition they had no recollection whatsoever of any of the circumstances, persons, or things connected with their previous lives. It was in this state that they talked about "Jack," and in this state that we —my mother and myself—knew them for weeks together. While in this state a very slight accident was sufficient to produce cataleptic rigidity and trance ; often one without the other. I remember one of the girls dining once with us in the middle of the day. A dish of pease was handed round, the spoon in which, it being hot weather, was no doubt heated by the successive hands which had used it. When Jane Okey grasped it in her hand to take some pease her fingers became clinched around it, and she could not open them. But there ensued no trance or other manifestation of catalepsy. On another occasion she was in my mother's house playing on the accordion, which she did very nicely in her magnetic state, but could not do at all in her normal state, and I, sitting at the other side of the room opposite to her, and reading a book, was moving my hand in time to the music, though not thinking of her or of it. Suddenly she fell back in a trance, magnetized unconsciously by me by the "passes" I was making with my hand. I have also produced a similar result by magnetizing her intentionally behind her back, while she was entirely unconscious of what I was doing.

But perhaps the most singular and remarkable scene connected with these girls was that which occurred when, their physical health having been very greatly, if not perfectly, restored, it became necessary to take them out of that "second state" which has been above described, and to restore them to their former consciousness, their former life, and their parents. The scene was a very painful one. The mother only, as far as I remember, was present. Memory seemed only gradually, and, at first, very partially, to return to them. The mother was a respectable, but poor and very uneducated woman, and of course wholly different in intelligence and manners from all the surroundings to which the girls had become habituated. And the expression of repulsion and dismay with which they at first absolutely refused to believe the statements that were made to them, or to accept their mother as such, while she, poor woman, was weeping at what appeared to her this newly-developed absence of all natural affection, was painful in the extreme.

Subsequently the daughter of one of these girls lived for some years, I think, with my brother's family at Waltham, as a housemaid.

The next reminiscences I have in connection with this subject belong to a time a few years later.

We, my mother and I, had heard tidings from America of a certain Mr. Daniel Hume, of whom very strange things were related. It was no longer a question of physical specialties and manifestations, which unquestionably did tend, apart from their medical value, to throw some gleams, or hopes of gleams, of light on the mysterious laws of the connection between mind and matter. The new candidate for the attention of the world claimed (*not* to have the power, as was currently stated at the time, but) to be occasionally and involuntarily the means of producing visitations from the denizens of the spirit world. And before long we heard that he had arrived in England, and was a guest in the house of Mr. Rymer, a solicitor, at Ealing. We lost no time in procuring an introduction to that estimable gentleman and his amiable wife, and were most courteously invited by him to visit him for the purpose of interviewing and making acquaintance with his remarkable guest. We went to Ealing, were most hospitably received, and forthwith introduced to Mr. Daniel Hume, as he was then called, although he afterwards called himself, or came to be called, Home. He was a young American, about nineteen or twenty years of age I should say, rather tall, with a loosely-put-together figure, red hair, large and clear but not bright blue eyes, a sensual mouth, lanky cheeks, and that sort of complexion which is often found in individuals of a phthisical diathesis. He was courteous enough, not unwilling to talk, ready enough to speak of those curious phenomena of his existence which differentiated him from other mortals, but altogether unable or unwilling to formulate or enter into discussion on any theory respecting them. We had tea, or rather supper, I think. There were the young people of Mr. Rymer's family about on the lawn, and among them a pretty girl, with whom, naturally enough, our young "medium" (for that had become the accepted term) was more disposed to flirt—after a fashion, I remember, which showed him to have been a petted inmate of the household—than to attend to matters of another world.

But other guests arrived, Sir David Brewster I remember among them, and Daniel had to be summoned to the business of the evening. This was commenced by our all placing ourselves round a very large and very heavy old-fashioned mahogany dining-table, where we sat in expectation of whatever should occur. Before long little crackings were heard, in the wood of the table apparently. Then it quivered, became more and more agitated, was next raised first at one end and then at the other, and finally was undeniably raised bodily from the ground. At that moment Sir David Brewster and myself, each acting on his own uncommunicated impulse, precipitated ourselves from our chairs under the table. The table was seen to be for a moment or two hovering in the air, perhaps some four or five inches from the floor, without its being possible to detect any means by which it could have been moved.

I said to Sir David, as our heads were close together under the table, and we were on "all fours" on the floor, "Does it not seem that this table is raised by some means wholly inexplicable?" "Indeed it would seem so!" he replied. But he wrote a letter to the *Times* the next day, or a day or two after, in which he gave an account of his visit to Ealing, but ended by denying that he had seen anything remarkable. But it is a fact that he did do and say what I have related.

This was the sum of what occurred. There was no pretence of the presence of any spiritual visitor. I may observe that although an ordinarily strong man might have lifted either end of the table while the other end remained on the ground, I am persuaded that no man could have raised it bodily, unless, perhaps, by placing his shoulders under the centre of it.

After the table exhibition Mr. Hume fell into a sort of swoon or trance. And it was then that he uttered the often-quoted words, "When Daniel recovers give him some bottled porter!" which was accordingly done! It may be observed, however, that he *did* appear to be much exhausted.

Various little fragments of experiences, and the increasing amount of attention which the world was giving to the subject, had kept the matter in my mind, till some years afterwards I had an opportunity of inviting Mr. Hume to visit me in my house in Florence. He came, and stayed with us for a month. And during the whole of that time —every evening as it seems to my remembrance, though I have no diary which records the fact—we had frequent experiments of his "mediumship."

Of course it is (happily for the reader) out of the question for me to attempt to give any detailed record of the proceedings and experiences of those repeated *séances*. I can only select a few facts which appeared to me most striking at the time, and add the general result as to the impression produced on my mind.

All our Florentine friends and acquaintances were eager to have an opportunity of passing an evening with the already celebrated medium. We generally limited our number to about eight persons; but pretty regularly had as many as that every evening. The performance usually began by crackings and oscillations of the round table at which we sat. Then would come more distinct raps; then the declaration that a visitor from the spirit world was present, then the demand for whom the said visit was intended, to which a reply was "knocked out," by raps indicating the letters required to form the desired name as the letters of the alphabet, always on the table, were rapidly run over. Sometimes a mistake was made, and an unintelligible word produced in consequence of too great haste in doing this. And then the process had to be gone through again. The medium never corrected any such mistake at the moment it was made, but seemed to await the completion of the process, as the rest did.

One or more "spirits" came, to the best of my recollection, every evening. Nor could I detect any sort of favoritism, or motive of any sort for the selection of the parties said to be visited. This is the sort of thing that would occur: There was present a well-known and much-respected English banker, established in Florence, a hale, robust, cheery sort of man, and a general favorite—the last man in the world one would say to be credited with nervous impressionability. A "spirit" was announced as having "come for him." Who is it? A name was rapped out in the manner described. The elderly banker declared that he had never had any friend or relative of that name, and had never heard it before. A second time the name was spelled out while the banker sat threshing out his recollections. Suddenly he struck his forehead with his hand, and exclaimed, "By Heaven! it is true! Nanny ——" (I forget the name). "She was my nurse in Yorkshire more than half a century ago!" Of course those who do not understand that scepticism is frequently more credulous than faith, say at once that Mr. Hume, in the exercise of his profession, like the gypsies in the exercise of theirs, had made it his business to discover the former existence of Nanny ——, and her connection with the person he was bent on befooling. But taking into consideration the total severance of the old banker's infancy both as to years and locality from any of his then surroundings; the fact that it was so long since he had heard the name in question mentioned that he had himself entirely forgotten it; and the further fact that there was nobody in Florence who had any connection with him or his family in his early years, and the circumstance that he that evening saw Mr. Hume for the first time, I confess that it seems to me that the improbability of any proposed explanation of the mystery must be incalculably great indeed, for a solution the improbability of which approaches so very near to impossibility to be preferably accepted.

Here is one other case, which I will give both because the person on whose testimony the value of it depends was one on whose accurate veracity I could depend as on my own, and because it illustrates one specialty of Mr. Hume's performances which I have not yet spoken of. This was a sensation of being touched, which was frequently experienced by many of those present. This touching almost invariably took the form of a knee being grasped under the table, or a hand being laid upon it. In the case I am about to relate this was experienced in a more remarkable manner.

A very highly valued old female servant, who had lived in my then wife's family since her birth, and had followed her when she married me, had some months previously died in my house. The affection which had subsisted between her and my wife was a very old and a very strong one. Now there was, it would seem, an old nursery pet name, by which this woman had been, long years before, in the habit of calling my wife. I had never heard it, or of it. My wife herself had never heard it for very many years. She and the old servant had never for years and years spoken on the subject. But one evening this pet name was very distinctly spelled; and my wife declared that she at the same time felt a sort of pressure at her side, as she sat in the circle, as if some person or thing had been endeavoring to find a place by her side. But for all that, my wife, though utterly mystified and incapable of suggesting any theory on the subject, was a strong disbeliever in all Mr. Hume's pretensions. She strongly disliked the man. And were it not that, as we all know, her sex never permits their estimate of facts to be influenced by their feelings, it might be supposed possible that this biassed her mind upon the subject.

I could add dozens of cases to the above two, but they were all very similar; and it is sufficient to say that the same sort of thing occurred over and over again.

I may mention, however, that I observed that any question addressed to the supposed spirits bearing on theology and matters of creed were invariably answered according to the views of the questioner. Catholics, Protestants, materialists, were all impartially confirmed in the convictions of their diverse persuasions.

Also I should not omit to mention that my wife, taking her occasion from Mr. Hume's complaints of his own weakness of lungs, spoke of my brother's death in Belgium and of my life at Ostend, and at a sitting some few days afterwards asked if she could be told where I had last seen my brother on earth. The answer came promptly, "At Ostend." But the truth is, as the reader knows, that I took my leave of him on board the Ostend steamer in the Thames.

My account of these sittings would not be as judicially accurate as I have endeavored to make it, however, were I to omit the statement that Mr. Hume on two or three occasions offered to cause "spirit hands" to become visible to us. The room was darkened for this purpose; and at the opposite side of a rather large table from that at which the spectators were sitting certain forms of hands did become faintly visible. To me they appeared like long kid gloves stuffed with some substance. But I am far from asserting that they were such.

On the whole, the impression left on my mind by my month-long intercourse with Mr. Hume was a disagreeable one of doubt and perplexity. I was not left with the con-

12

viction that he was an altogether trustworthy and sincere man. Nor was I fully persuaded of the reverse. I *saw nothing* which appeared to me to compel the conclusion that some agency unknown to the ascertained and recognized laws of nature was at work. But I *did hear* many communications made in Mr. Hume's presence in the manner which has been described, which seemed to me to be wholly inexplicable by any theory I could bring to bear upon them. It may be observed that no theory of thought-reading will serve the turn, for in many cases the facts, circumstances, or names communicated were evidently *not* in the thoughts of the persons to whom they were so communicated. Of course it may be answered, "Ah! but however '*evident*' that may have seemed to you, the facts *were* in the thoughts of the parties in question." To this I can only reply that to me, my very complete knowledge of the persons in question, and of their veracity—one of them, as in the case above related, being my own wife— renders the explanation suggested absolutely inadmissible.

I have seen at various subsequent periods a great many professors of "mediumship" and their performances. I was present at many sittings given by Mrs. G——, a huge mountain of a woman, very uneducated, apparently good-natured and simple, but with a tendency to become disagreeable when her attempts at communication with the unseen world were declared to be failures.

I will give here the copy of a letter which I wrote to the secretary of "The Dialectical Society," which had applied to me for my "experiences" on the subject. I cannot at the present day sum up any better the conclusions to which they led me.

"FLORENCE, 27*th December*, 1869.

"SIR,—In reply to your letter of the 17th I can only say that I have but little to add to those previous statements of mine, of which you are in possession.

"With regard to the sittings with Mrs. G., I can only say that the greatest watchfulness on the part of those sharing in them failed to detect (as regards the physical phenomena) any trace of imposture. These phenomena, which took place in the dark, such as the sudden falling on the table of a large quantity of jonquils, which filled the whole room with their odor, were extraordinary, and on any common theory of physics unaccountable. The room in which this took place had been completely examined by me, and Mrs. G.'s person had been carefully searched by my wife. With regard to metaphysical phenomena, an attempt to hold communication with intelligences other than those present in the flesh was stated by a lady to whom a communication was addressed to have been extraordinarily successful, and to have been proved by the event. In the case of myself and my wife all such attempts resulted in *total* failure.

"I have recently had a sitting with Dr. Willis of Boston. The physical manifestations (in the dark) were remarkable and perplexing. The attempts at spiritual communication were altogether failures.

"In short, the result of my experience thus far is this—that the physical phenomena frequently produced are, *in many cases*, not the result of any sleight of hand, and that those who have witnessed them with due attention must be convinced that there is no analogy between them and the tricks of professed 'conjurors.' I may also mention that Bosco, one of the most accomplished professors of legerdemain ever known, in a conversation with me upon the subject, utterly scouted the idea of the possibility of such phenomena as I saw produced by Mr. Hume being performed by any of the resources of his art.

"To what sort of agency these results are to be attributed I have no idea, and give no opinion; although (inasmuch as I consider that the word 'supernatural' involves a contradiction in terms) I hold that to admit that the phenomena exist, implies the admission that they are 'natural,' or in accordance with *some* law of nature.

"With regard to the metaphysical phenomena, though I have witnessed many strange things, I have never known any that satisfactorily excluded the *possibility* of mistake or imposture.

"Your obedient servant,   T. ADOLPHUS TROLLOPE."

If I am asked what, upon the whole, is my present state of mind upon the subject, I can only say that it is that unpleasant one expressed in Lord Chancellor Eldon's often-quoted words, "I doubt."

Before, however, quitting the subject, my gossip about which has run to a length only excusable on the ground of the very general interest that has been attracted by it, I will give two more excerpts from my recollections, which relate to cases respecting which I have *no* doubt. They both refer, however, to purely physical phenomena.

A French professor of "animal magnetism" came to Florence. His name, I think, was Lafontaine. He had a young girl with him, his patient. He brought her to my house, in which there was a long room, at one end of which he directed me to stand, then put the girl immediately in front of me, and told me to hold her, so as to prevent her from coming to him, when, standing at the farther end of the room, he should draw her to him. I accordingly placed my arms around her waist, interlacing my fingers in front of her. She was a small, slight girl, and I was at that time a somewhat exceptionally strong man. The operator, then standing at the distance of some twenty feet or more, made "passes," as it were, beckoning her with his hands to come to him. She struggled forward. I held her back with all my force, but was dragged after her towards the magnetizer. This may be accepted as an absolutely accurate and certain fact.

This same Lafontaine had entirely failed in attempts to magnetize me, and in telling me, as he promised to do, what I in my house was doing at a given moment while he was absent.

My second excerpt concerns also my own experience, and shall be given with equally truthful accuracy.

My wife, my wife's sister, and myself had been spending the evening in the house of Mr. Seymour Kirkup, an artist, who, once well known in the artistic world, lived on in Florence to a great age after that world had forgotten him. A girl, his daughter by a servant who lived several years in his house, and who also had pretended to very strongly developed spiritualistic powers, developed, as he asserted, similar powers in a very wonderful degree. And during his latter years the old man absolutely and entirely lived, in every respect, according to the advice and dictates of "the spirits," as oracularly declared by Imogene, for that was her name. In short, she was a clever, worthless hussy, and he was a besotted old man. Our visit to his house was to witness some of Imogene's performances. There was also present a Colonel Bowen, who was a convinced believer.

I, my wife, and sister-in-law detected unmistakably the girl's clumsy attempts at legerdemain, but knew poor old Kirkup far too well to make any attempt to convict her. But as we walked home, with our minds full of the subject, we said, "Let us try whether we can produce any effect upon a table, since that seems the regulation first-step in these mysteries; and, at least, we shall have the

certainty of not being befooled by trickery." So, on
reaching home, we took a table—rather a remarkable one.
It was small, not above eighteen or twenty inches across
the top of it. But it was *very* much heavier than any ordinary table of that size, the stem of it being a massive
bit of ancient chestnut-wood carving which I had adapted
to that purpose.

Well, in a minute or two the table began to move very
unmistakably. We were startled, and began to think that
the ladies' dresses must have, unconsciously to them, pressed
against it. We stood back therefore, taking care that
nothing but the tips of our fingers touched the table. It
still moved! We said that some unconscious exertion of
muscular force must have caused the movement, and,
finally, we suspended our fingers about an inch or so above
the surface of the table, taking the utmost care to touch
it in no way whatever. The table still turned, and that to
such an extent that, entirely untouched, it turned itself
over, and fell to the ground.

I can only observe of this, as the little boy said who
was accused of relating an impossibilty as a fact, " I don't
say it is possible, I only say it is true !"

In Kirkup's case his entire and never-varying conviction
of the truthfulness of Miss Imogene's material manifestations and spiritual revelations was the more remarkable in
that he had for many years—for all his life, for aught I know
to the contrary—entertained and professed the most thorough persuasion of the futility and absurdity of all belief
that the soul of man survived material death. His tenets
on this subject are the more strongly impressed on my
memory by an absurd incident that occurred to my present wife in connection with his materialistic theories.

He and she were one day talking upon the subject, as
they sat *tête-à-tête* on opposite sides of a table. Now
Kirkup was very deaf—worse by a great deal than I am—
and my wife failing to make him hear a question she put
to him, and having no other writing materials at hand,
hastily drew a card from her card-case and pencilled on
the back of it : " What are your grounds for assurance
that the visible death of the body is the death of the spirit

also ?" He read, and addressed himself to reply, letting the card fall on the table between them, which she, thinking only of the matter in discussion, mechanically put back into her card-case, and left at the next house at which she happened to be making a morning-call!

Kirkup's conversion to spiritualism was so complete that, as I have said, his entire life was shaped according to the dictates which Miss Imogene chose to represent as coming from her spiritual visitors. The old man had lived for very many years in Florence. All the interests which still bound him to life were there, and he was much attached to the city in which so large a portion of his long life had been passed. But Imogene one day announced that "the spirits" declared that he must go and live in Leghorn! Of course the blow to the old man was a terrible one, but he meekly and unhesitatingly obeyed, and submitted to be uprooted when he was past eighty and packed off to Leghorn! I discovered subsequently— what I might have guessed at the time—that the good-for-nothing jade had a lover at Leghorn. Kirkup's new faith in the existence of a soul in man, separable from his body, continued firm, I believe, till his death, which occurred shortly afterwards.

I have, at various times and in various countries, been present at the performances of spiritualistic *mediums* (a monstrous word, but one can't write *media*), and always with a uniformly similar result in one respect. No non-material experience whatever has ever been vouchsafed to me myself. *Material* phenomena of a very surprising nature, and altogether unaccountable in accordance with any received physical theories, I have seen in great abundance. And I must in justice say that the performances of Messrs. Maskelyne and Cooke, which attracted so much attention in Piccadilly, masterly as they were as exhibitions of legerdemain, did not by any means succeed in proving the imposture of the pretensions of Hume and others by doing the same things. I think the Piccadilly performances *did* achieve this as regards the tying and loosening of knots in a dark cabinet. But when one of the performers above mentioned proceeded to "float in the air " he only demonstrated the impossibility of doing, by any means known to his art, that which Hume — or Home—was declared, on the most indisputable testimony, to have done. Mr. Maskelyne certainly "floated in the air" above the heads of the spectators, but I saw very unmistakably the wire by which he was suspended. It may not have been *wire*, but I saw the cord, thread, or whatever it may have been, by which he was suspended. Nor is it possible to doubt that the gentlemen who saw, or supposed themselves to have seen, Mr. Hume floating in the air above them would have failed to detect any such artifice as that by which the professor of legerdemain was enabled to do the same. And then we must not lose sight of the all-important difference between the two performances, arising from the fact that the one performer has at command all the facilities afforded by a *locale* in which he has had abundant opportunity of making every preparation which the resources of his art could suggest to him ; whereas the other exhibits his wonders under circumstances absolutely excluding the possibility of any such preparation.

But *I* never saw Mr. Hume float in the air. The only physical phenomena which I saw produced by him consisted in the moving and lifting of tables—in some cases very heavy tables. But I have witnessed, in *very* numerous cases, communications made by the medium to individuals who have declared it to have been absolutely impossible that Mr. Hume should by any ordinary means have known the facts communicated. And it has appeared to me, knowing all the circumstances, to have been as nearly impossible as can well be conceived without being absolutely so.

Here is one more remarkable case—one out of dozens of such. A middle-aged Italian gentleman of the Jewish persuasion asked that the spirit of his father, who, it was stated by the medium, was present, should mention where he and his son, then communicating with him, last met on earth. It should be stated that the inquirer, having abandoned the faith of his fathers, professed entire disbelief in any existence of the soul, or any future life. The answer to his query was spelled out in the manner I have already described, a certain Italian city being named. I watched the face of the sceptical inquirer as the letters were "rapped out" and gradually completed the name required. And I needed no confession of the fact from him to know that the answer had been correctly given. I thought the man would have fallen from his chair. He became ghastly pale, and trembled all over. He was in truth very terribly impressed and affected, but—and the phenomenon is a very curious, though by no means an uncommon one—a few days afterwards the impression had entirely faded from his mind. He continued fully to admit that the fact which had occurred was altogether inexplicable, but wholly refused to believe that it involved any supposition inconsistent with his strictly materialistic creed.

In the above case, as in that of the banker given above, it may of course be said that it was within the bounds of possibility that Mr. Hume should have previously ascertained the fact that he stated. It is, of course, impossible for me here to explain to the reader every detail of the circumstances that seem to me to render such an explanation wholly inadmissible. I can only say that to a mind as entirely open upon the subject as I think my mind is, the supposition in question appears so improbable that it fails to impress me as a possibility.

On the other hand, I have to say that every attempt of a similar kind, whether by Mr. Hume or by any other so-called medium, in which I myself have been the subject of the experiment, has absolutely and wholly failed. Mr. Hume never, to the best of my remembrance, introduced or announced the presence of any spirit "for me." I was like the boy at school whom no relative ever comes to see. The Mrs. G—— who has been mentioned at an earlier page announced upon one occasion the presence of my mother with results which would have sufficed to prove very satisfactorily that my mother's spirit was not there, if I had previously fully believed the case to have been otherwise.

I once went to visit the then celebrated Alexis in Paris. He knew that I was a resident in Florence, and began operations by proposing to describe to me my house there.

Of course such an experiment admitted of almost every conceivable kind of mystification and uncertainty. I told him that the proposed description would necessarily occupy more of his time than seemed to me needed for producing the conviction of the reality of his power which I was anxious to acquire; and that it would be abundantly sufficient for that purpose if he would simply tell me the number composed of four figures which I had written on a piece of paper, and sealed in a (perfectly non-transparent) packet. He refused to make the attempt.

Many years subsequently I attended the *séances* of a gentleman in London, whose performances attracted a good deal of attention at the time—of an unfavorable description, for the most part—and whose chief specialty consisted in enclosing a piece of slate pencil loosely between two ordinary framed slates, securely tied together, and awaiting communications to be made by writing produced on the slate by the pencil thus enclosed acting automatically. I *did* see written words thus produced, where to the best of my observation there had been no words before the slates were (quite securely) tied together. Nor could I form any theory or guess as to the manner in which this writing was produced under circumstances which seemed to make it perfectly impossible that it should be so produced. But the words so written conveyed no remarkable or surprising information—and, indeed, to the best of my recollection had little meaning at all.

Thus once again that portion of the performance which was, or might have been, of the nature of sleight of hand, was done so well as to cause much puzzlement and surprise; while what may be called the spiritual part of the promised phenomenon failed *entirely*.

I have witnessed the performances of sundry other me-di*ums*—I hate to write the word!—always with the same net result. That is to say, the strictly physical phenomena witnessed were in very many cases—not in all—utterly unaccountable and incomprehensible. The statement that the performances of many masters of legerdemain are also unaccountable and incomprehensible appears to

12*

me, while I fully admit the truth of it, to be of very little value. The phenomena produced by these professors are in almost every case totally different in kind, and are in every case placed in a wholly different category by the fact that the performers of them have the assistance of tools and means—the highly-skilled preparation and combination of which constitute a very important (if not the most essential) part of their professional equipment—and of the resources of their own prepared *locale*. Furthermore, I cannot forget the testimony of that "prince of conjurors," Bosco, to the effect that the phenomena which I declared to him I had seen were entirely unachievable by any of the resources of his art.

Above all I have the certain knowledge (resting not only on my own very perfect recollection, but on the unvarying testimony of the two other persons engaged in the experiment) that a table did move much and violently, as recorded above, while wholly and certainly untouched by any human hands or persons, and uncommunicated with—if I may use such an expression—save by the minds of the operators.

The net conclusion, therefore, of my rather extensive experience in the matter is, that as regards phenomena purely physical, such have been and are frequently produced by the practisers of "animal magnetism"—or by whatever name it may be preferred to call it—of a nature wholly inexplicable by any of the theories or suggestions which have been adduced for the explanation of them.

With regard to *non-physical* phenomena—that is to say, such as imply the abnormal exercise of intelligences, whether incarnate or disembodied, outside the intelligence of the individual experimenting—I have to testify that I have *heard* from many highly credible persons the statement of their own experience of such communication with intelligences other than their own. And I have heard such statements immediately on the occurrence of the facts. But I have never in my own person received or been made the subject of any such.

CHAPTER XX.

No! as I said at the end of the last chapter but one, before I was led away by the circumstances of that time to give the world the benefit of my magnetic reminiscences—*valeat quantum!*—I was not yet bitten, despite Colley Grattan's urgings, with any temptation to attempt fiction, and "passion, me boy!" But I am surprised on turning over my old diaries to find how much I was writing, and planning to write, in those days, and not less surprised at the amount of running about which I accomplished.

My life in those years of the thirties must have been a very busy one. I find myself writing and sending off a surprising number of "articles" on all sorts of subjects—reviews, sketches of travel, biographical notices, fragments from the byways of history, and the like, to all kinds of periodical publications, many of them long since dead and forgotten. That the world should have forgotten all these articles "goes without saying." But what is not perhaps so common an incident in the career of a penman is, that *I* had in the majority of cases utterly forgotten them, and all about them, until they were recalled to mind by turning the yellow pages of my treasured but almost equally forgotten journals! I beg to observe, also, that all this pen-work was not only printed but *paid for.* My motives were of a decidedly mercenary description. "*Hic scribit famâ ductus, at ille fame.*" I belonged emphatically to the latter category, and little indeed of my multifarious productions ever found its final resting-place in the waste-paper basket. They were rejected often, but redespatched a second and a third time, if necessary, to some other "organ," and eventually swallowed by some editor or other.

I am surprised, too, at the amount of locomotion which I contrived to combine with all this scribbling. I must have gone about, I think, like a tax-gatherer, with an inkstand slung to my button-hole. And in truth I was industrious; for I find myself in full swing of some journey, arriving at my inn tired at night, and finishing and sending off some article before I went to my bed. But it must have been only by means of the joint supplies contributed by all my editors that I could have found the means of paying all the stage-coaches, diligences, and steamboats which I find the record of my continually employing. "*Navibus atque Quadrigis petimus bene vivere!*" And I succeeded by their means in living, if not well, at least very pleasantly.

For I was born a rambler.

I heard just now a story of a little boy, who replied to the common question, "What he would like to be when he grew up?" by saying that he should like to be either a giant or a *retired* stockbroker! I find the qualifying adjective delicious, and admire the pronounced taste for repose indicated by either side of the alternative. But my propensities were more active, and in the days before I entered my teens I used always to reply to similar demands, that I would be a "king's messenger." I knew no other life which approached so nearly to perpetual motion. "The road" was my paradise, and it is a true saying that the child is father to the man. The Shakespearian passage which earliest impressed my childish mind and carried with it my heartiest sympathies was the song of old Autolycus:

> "Jog on, jog on, the foot-path way,
> And merrily hent the stile-a:
> Your merry heart goes all the day,
> Your sad tires in a mile-a."

Over how many miles of "foot-path way," under how many green hedges, has my childish treble chanted that enlivening ditty!

But that was in much earlier days to those I am now writing of.

During the years between my dreary time at Birming-

ham and my first departure for Italy, I find the record of
many pedestrian or other rambles in England and abroad.
There they are, all recorded day by day—the qualities of
the inns and the charges at them (not so much less than
those of the present day as might be imagined, with the
exception of the demands for beds), the beauty and specialties of the views, the talk of wayfaring companions,
the careful measurements of the churches, the ever-recur-
ring ascent of the towers of them, etc., etc.

Here and there in the mountains of chaff there may be
a grain worth preserving, as where I read that at Haddon
Hall the old lady who showed the house, and who boasted
that her ancestors had been servitors of the possessors of
it for more than three hundred years, pointed out to me
the portrait of one of them, who had been "forester,"
hanging in the hall. She also pointed out the window
from which a certain heiress had eloped, and by doing so
had carried the hall and lands into the family of the present owners, and told me that Mrs. Radcliffe, shortly before
the publication of her "Mysteries of Udolpho," had visited
Haddon, and had sat at that window busily writing for a
long time.

I seem to have been an amateur of sermons in those
days, from the constant records I find of sermons listened
to, by no means always, or indeed generally, complimentary to the preachers. Here is an entry criticising, with
young presumption, a sermon by Dr. Dibdin, whose bib-
liophile books, however, I had much taste for:

"I heard Dr. Dibdin preach. He preached, with much
gesticulation, emphasis, and grimace, the most utterly
trashy sermon I ever heard; words—words—words—without the shadow of an idea in them."

I remember, as if it were yesterday, a shrewd sort of an
old lady, the mother, I think, of the curate of the parish,
who heard me, as we were leaving the church, expressing
my opinion of the doctor's discourse, saying, "Well, it is
a very old story, young gentleman, and it is mighty difficult to find anything new to say about it!"

The bibliomaniacal doctor, however, seems to have
pleased me better out of the pulpit than in it, for I find

that "he called in the afternoon and chatted amusingly
for an hour. He fell tooth and nail upon the Oxford
Tracts men, and told us of a Mr. Wackerbarth, a curate
in Essex, a Cambridge man, who, he says, elevates the
host, crosses himself, and advocates burning of heretics.
It seems to me, however," continues this censorious young
diarist, "that those who object to the persecution, even to
extermination of heretics, admit the uncertainty and dubi-
ousness of all theological doctrine and belief. For if it
be *certain* that God will punish disbelief in doctrines essential to salvation, and *certain* that any church possesses
the knowledge what those doctrines are, does it not follow
that a man who goes about persuading people to reject
those doctrines should be treated as we treat a mad dog
loose in the streets of a city?" Thus fools, when they
are young enough, rush in where wise men fear to tread!

I had entirely forgotten, but find from my diary that it
was our pleasant friend but indifferent preacher, Dr. Dibdin, who on the 11th of February, 1839, married my sister, Cecilia, to Mr., now Sir John, Tilley.

It appears that I was not incapable of appreciating a
good sermon when I heard one, for I read of the impression produced upon me by an "admirable sermon preached
by Mr. Smith" (it must have been Sydney, I take it) in
the Temple Church. The preacher quoted largely from
Jeremy Taylor, "giving the passages with an excellence
of enunciation and expression which impressed them on
my mind in a manner which will not allow me to forget
them." Alack! I *have* forgotten every word of them!

I remember, however, perfectly well, without any reference to my diary, hearing—it must have been much about
the same time—Sydney Smith preach a sermon at St.
Paul's, which much impressed me. He took for his text,
"Knowledge and wisdom shall be the stability of thy
times" (I write from memory—the memory of half a century ago—but I think the words ran thus). Of course the
gist of his discourse may be readily imagined. But the
manner of the preacher remains more vividly present to
my mind than his words. He spoke with extreme rapidity, and had the special gift of combining extreme rapidity

of utterance with very perfect clearness. His manner, I remember thinking, was unlike any that I had ever witnessed in the pulpit, and appeared to me to resemble rather that of a very earnest speaker at the hustings than the usual pulpit style. His sentences seemed to run downhill, with continually increasing speed till they came to a full stop at the bottom. It was, I think, the only sermon I ever heard which I wished longer. He carried me with him completely, for the century was in those days, like me, young. But if I were to hear a similarly fervid discourse now on the same subject, I should surely desire some clearer setting forth of the difference between "knowledge" and "wisdom."

It was about this time, i. e., in the year 1839, that my mother, who had been led, by I forget what special circumstances, to take a great interest in the then hoped-for factory legislation, and in Lord Shaftesbury's efforts in that direction, determined to write a novel on the subject with the hope of doing something towards attracting the public mind to the question, and to visit Lancashire for the purpose of obtaining accurate information and local details.

The novel was written, published in the then newly-invented fashion of monthly numbers, and called "Michael Armstrong." The publisher, Mr. Colburn, paid a long price for it, and did not complain of the result. But it never became one of the more popular among my mother's novels, sharing, I suppose, the fate of most novels written for some purpose other than that of amusing their readers. Novel readers are exceedingly quick to smell the rhubarb under the jam in the dose offered to them, and set themselves against the undesired preachment as obstinately as the naughtiest little boy who ever refused to be physicked with nastiness for his good.

My mother neglected no means of making the facts stated in her book authentic and accurate, and the *mise en scène* of her story graphic and truthful. Of course I was the companion of her journey, and was more or less useful to her in searching for and collecting facts in some places where it would have been difficult for her to look for them.

We carried with us a number of introductions from Lord Shaftesbury to a rather strange assortment of persons, whom his lordship had found useful both as collectors of trustworthy information and energetic agitators in favor of legislation.

The following letter from the Earl of Shaftesbury, then Lord Ashley, to my mother on the subject, is illustrative of the strong interest he took in the matter, and of the means which he thought necessary for obtaining information respecting it :

"MADAM,—The letters to Macclesfield and Manchester shall be sent by this evening's post. On your arrival at Macclesfield be so kind as to ask for Reuben Bullock, of Roe Street, and at Manchester for John Doherty, a small bookseller of Hyde's Cross in the town. They will show you the secrets of the place, as they showed them to me.

"Mr. Wood himself is not now resident in Bradford, he is at present in Hampshire; but his partner, Mr. Walker, carries out all his plans with the utmost energy. I will write to him to-night. The firm is known by the name of ' Wood & Walker.' Mr. Wood is a person whom you may easily see in London on your return to town. With every good wish and prayer for your success, I remain your very obedient servant,

"ASHLEY.

"P.S.—The *Quarterly Review* of December, 1836, contains an article on the factory system which would greatly assist by the references to the evidence before Committee, etc., etc."

It is useless here and now to say anything of the horrors of uncivilized savagery and hopeless abject misery which we witnessed. They are painted in my mother's book, and should any reader ever refer to those pages for a picture of the state of things among the factory hands at that time, he may take with him my testimony to the fact that there was no exaggeration in the outlines of the picture given. What we are there described to have seen, we saw.

And let *doctrinaire* economists preach as they will, and Radical socialists abuse a measure which helps to take from them the fulcrum of the levers that are to upset the whole existing framework of society, it is impossible for one who *did* see those sights, and who has visited the same localities in later days, not to bless Lord Shaftesbury's memory, ay, and the memory, if they have left any, of the humble assistants whose persistent efforts helped on the work.

But the little knot of apostles to whom Lord Shaftesbury's letters introduced us, and into whose intimate *conciliabules* his recommendations caused our admittance, was to my mother, and yet more to me, to whom the main social part of the business naturally fell, a singularly new and strange one. They were all, or nearly all of them, men a little raised above the position of the factory hands, to the righting of whose wrongs they devoted their lives. They had been at some period of their lives, in almost every case, factory workers themselves, but had by various circumstances, native talent, industry and energy, or favoring fortune—more likely by all together—managed to raise themselves out of the slough of despond in which their fellows were overwhelmed. One, I remember, a Mr. Doherty, a very small bookseller, to whom we were specially recommended by Lord Shaftesbury. He was an Irishman, a Roman Catholic, and a furious Radical, but a *very* clever man. He was thoroughly acquainted with all that had been done, all that it was hoped to do, and with all the means that were being taken for the advancement of those hopes, over the entire district.

He came and dined with us at our hotel, but it was, I remember, with much difficulty that we persuaded him to do so, and when at table his excitement in talking was so great and continuous that he could eat next to nothing.

I remember, too, a Rev. Mr. Bull, to whom he introduced us subsequently at Bradford. We passed the evening with this gentleman at the house of Mr. Wood, of the firm of Walker & Wood, to whom also we had letters from Lord Shaftesbury. He, like our host, was an ardent advocate of the ten hours' bill, but, unlike him, had very little hope of legislative interference. Messrs. Walker & Wood employed three thousand hands. At a sacrifice of some thousands per annum, they worked their hands an hour less than any of their neighbors, which left the hours, as Mr. Wood strongly declared, still too long. Those gentlemen had built and endowed a church and a school for their hands, and everything was done in their mill which could humanize and improve the lot of the men, women, and children. Mr. Bull, who was to be the incumbent of the new church, then not quite finished, was far less hopeful than his patron. He told me that he looked forward to some tremendous popular outbreak, and should not be surprised any night to hear that every mill in Bradford was in flames.

But perhaps the most remarkable individual with whom this Lancashire journey brought us into contact was a Mr. Oastler. He was the Danton of the movement. He would have been a remarkable man in any position or calling in life. He was a very large and powerfully framed man, over six feet in height, and proportionally large of limb and shoulder. He would, perhaps, hardly have been said to be a handsome man. His face was coarse, and, in parts of it, heavy. But he had a most commanding presence, and he was withal a picturesque—if it be not more accurate to say a statuesque—figure. Some of the features, too, were good. He had a very keen and intelligent blue eye, a mass of iron-gray hair, lips, the scornful curl of which was terrible, and with all this a voice stentorian in its power, and yet flexible, with a flow of language rapid and abundant as the flow of a great river, and as unstemmable—the very *beau idéal* of a mob orator.

"In the evening," says my diary, "we drove out to Stayley Bridge to hear the preaching of Stephens, the man who has become the subject of so much newspaper celebrity." (Does any one remember who he was?) "We reached a miserable little chapel, filled to suffocation, and besieged by crowds around the doors. We entered through the vestry with great difficulty, and only so by the courtesy of sundry persons who relinquished their places on Doherty's representing to them that we were strangers from a distance and friends to the cause. Presently Stephens arrived, and a man who had been ranting in the pulpit, merely, as it seemed, to occupy the people till he should come, immediately yielded his place to him. Stephens spoke well, and said some telling words in that place, of the cruel and relentless march of the great Juggernaut, Gold. But I did not hear anything which seemed to me

to justify his great reputation. Really the most striking
part of the performance, and that which I thought seemed
to move the people most, was Oastler's mounting the pulpit and giving out the verses of a hymn, one by one, which
the congregation sang after him." So says my diary.
Him I remember well, though Stephens not at all. I remember, too, the pleasure with which I listened to his
really fine delivery of the lines ; his pronunciation of the
words was not incorrect, and when he spoke, as I heard
him on sundry subsequent occasions, his language, though
emphasized rather, as it seemed, than marred by a certain
roughness of Lancashire accent, was not that of an uncultivated man. Yes ! Oastler, the King of Lancashire, as
the people liked to call him, was certainly a man of power,
and an advocate whom few platform orators would have
cared to meet as an adversary.

When my mother's notes for her projected novel were
completed we thought that before turning our faces southward we would pay a flying visit to the lake district,
which was new ground to both of us. I remember well
my intense delight at my first introduction to mountains
worthy of the name. But I mean to mention here two
only of my reminiscences of that first visit to lake-land.

The first of these concerns an excursion on Windermere
with Captain Hamilton, the author of " Cyril Thornton,"
which had at that time made its mark. He had recently
received a new boat, which had been built for him in Nor-
way. He expected great performances from her, and as
there was a nice fresh wind idly curling the surface of the
lake, he invited us to come out with him and try her, and
in a minute or two we were speeding merrily before the
breeze towards the opposite shore. But about the middle
of the lake we found the water a good deal rougher, and
the wind began to increase notably. Hamilton held the
tiller, and not liking to make fast the halyard of the sail,
gave me the rope to hold, with instructions to hold on till
further orders. He was a perfect master of the business
in hand, and so was the new boat a perfect mistress of *her*
business, but this did not prevent us from getting thoroughly ducked. My attention was sufficiently occupied in obey-

ing my orders, and keeping my eye on him in expectation
of fresh ones. The wind meanwhile increased from minute
to minute, and I could not help perceiving that Hamilton,
despite his cheery laughter, was becoming a little anxious.
We got back, however, to the shore we had left after
a good buffeting, and in the condition of drowned rats.
My mother was helped out of the boat, and while she was
making her way up the bank, and I was helping him to
make the boat secure, I said, " Well ! the new boat has
done bravely !" " Between you and me, my dear fellow,"
said he, as he laid his hand on my shoulder with a grip
that I think must have left his thumb-mark on the skin,
" if the boat had not behaved better than any boat of her
class that I ever saw, there would have been a considerable probability of our being dined on by the fishes, instead of dining together, as I hope we are going to do.
I have been blaming myself for taking your mother out ;
but the truth is that on these lakes it is really impossible
to tell for half an hour what the next half-hour may bring
forth."

The one other incident of our visit to lake-land which I
will record was our visit to Wordsworth.

For my part I managed to incur his displeasure while
yet on the threshold of his house. We were entering it
together, when, observing a very fine bay-tree by the door-
side, I unfortunately expressed surprise at its luxuriance
in such a position. " Why should you be surprised?" he
asked, suddenly turning upon me with much displeasure
in his manner. Not a little disconcerted, I hesitatingly answered that I had imagined the bay-tree required more
and greater warmth of sunshine than it could find there.
" Pooh !" said he, much offended at the slight cast on his
beloved locality, " what has sunshine got to do with it ?"

I had not the readiness to reply, that in truth the world
had abundance of testimony that the bay could flourish
in those latitudes. But I think had I done so, it might
have made my peace—for the remainder of that evening's
experiences led me to imagine that the great poet was not
insensible to incense from very small and humble wor-
shippers.

The evening, I think I may say the entire evening, was occupied by a monologue addressed by the poet to my mother, who was, of course, extremely well pleased to listen to it. I was chiefly occupied in talking to my old school-fellow, Herbert Hill, Southey's nephew, who also passed the evening there, and with whom I had a delightful walk the next day. But I did listen with much pleasure when Wordsworth recited his own lines descriptive of Little Langdale. He gave them really exquisitely. But his manner in conversation was not impressive. He sat continuously looking down with a green shade over his eyes even though it was twilight ; and his mode of speech and delivery suggested to me the epithet " maundering," though I was ashamed of myself for the thought with reference to such a man. As we came away I cross-examined my mother much as to the subjects of his talk. She said it had been all about himself and his works, and that she had been interested. But I could not extract from her a word that had passed worth recording.

I do not think that he was popular with his neighbors generally. There were stories current, at Lowther among other places, which imputed to him a tendency to outstay his welcome when invited to visit in a house. I suspect there was a little bit of a feud between him and my brother-in-law, Mr. Tilley, who was the post - office surveyor of the district. Wordsworth as receiver of taxes, or issuer of licenses, or whatever it was, would have increased the profits of his place if the mail-coach had paid its dues, whether for taxes or license, at his end of the journey instead of at Kendal, as had been the practice. But, of course, any such change would have been as much to the detriment of the man at Kendal as to Wordsworth's advantage. And my brother-in-law, thinking such a change unjust, would not permit it.

I cannot say that, on the whole, the impression made on me by the poet on that occasion (always with the notable exception of his recital of his own poetry) was a pleasant one. There was something in the manner in which he almost perfunctorily, as it seemed, uttered his long monologue, that suggested the idea of the performance of a

part got up to order, and repeated without much modification as often as lion-hunters, duly authorized for the
sport in those localities, might call upon him for it. I dare
say the case is analogous to that of the hero and the valet,
but such was my impression.

CHAPTER XXI.

I HAD been for some time past, as has been said, trying my hand, not without success, at a great variety of articles in all sorts of reviews, magazines, and newspapers. I already considered myself a member of the guild of professional writers. I had done much business with publishers on behalf of my mother, and some for other persons, and talked glibly of copyrights, editions, and tokens.

(I fancy, by-the-bye, that the latter term has somewhat fallen out of use in these latter days, whether from any change of the methods used by printers or publishers I do not know. But it strikes me that many youngsters, even of the scribbling tribe, may not know that the phrase " a token" had no connection whatever with signs and wonders of any sort, but simply meant two hundred and fifty copies.)

And being thus equipped, I began to think that it was time that I should attempt *a book*. During a previous hurried scamper in Normandy I had just a glimpse of Brittany, which greatly excited my desire to see more of it. So I pitched on a tour in Brittany as the subject of my first attempt.

Those were happy days, when all the habitable globe had not been run over by thousands of tourists, hundreds of whom are desirous of describing their doings in print —not but that the notion, whether a publisher's or writer's notion, that new ground is needed for the production of a good and amusing book of travels, is other than a great mistake. I forget what proposing author it was, who in answer to a publisher urging the fact that " a dozen writers have told us all about so and so," replied, "But *I* have not told you what *I* have seen and thought about it." But if I had been the publisher I should at

once have asked to see his MS. The days when a capital
book may be written on a *voyage autour de ma chambre*
are as present as ever they were. And "A Summer Afternoon's Walk to Highgate" might be the subject of a delightful book if only the writer were the right man.

Brittany, however, really was in those days to a great
extent fresh ground, and the strangely secluded circumstances of its population offered much tempting material
to the book-making tourist. All this is now at an end;
not so much because the country has been the subject of
sundry good books of travel, as because the people and
their mode of life, the country and its specialties, have all
been utterly changed by the pleasant, convenient, indispensable, abominable railway, which in its merciless, irresistible tramp across the world crushes into a dead level
of uninteresting monotony so many varieties of character,
manners, and peculiarities. And thus "the individual
withers, and the world is more and more!" But *is* the
world more and more in any sense that can be admitted to be desirable, in view of the eternity of that same
individual.

As for the Bretons, the individual has withered to that
extent that he now wears trousers instead of breeches,
while his world has become more and more assimilated to
that of the Faubourg St. Antoine, with the result of losing
all those really very notable and stiff and sturdy virtues
which differentiated the Breton peasant, when I first knew
him, while it would be difficult indeed to say what it has
gained. At all events the progress which can be stated is
mainly to be stated in negatives. The Breton, as I first
knew him, believed in all sorts of superstitious rubbish.
He now believes in nothing at all. He was disposed to
honor and respect God, and his priest, and his seigneur
perhaps somewhat too indiscriminately. Now he neither
honors nor respects any earthly or heavenly thing. These,
at least, were the observations which a second, or, rather,
third visit to the country a few years ago suggested to
me, mainly, it is true, as regards the urban population.
And without going into any of the deeper matters which
such changes suggest to one's consideration, there can be

no possible doubt as to the fact that the country and its people are infinitely less interesting than they were.

My plans were soon made, and I hastened to lay them before Mr. Colburn, who was at that time publishing for my mother. The trip was my main object, and I should have been perfectly contented with terms that paid all the expenses of it. *Di auctius fecerunt*, and I came home from my ramble with a good round sum in my pocket.

I was not greedy of money in those days, and had no unscriptural hankerings after laying up treasure upon earth. All I wanted was a sufficient supply for my unceasing expenditure in locomotion and inn bills—the latter, be it observed, always on a most economical scale. I was not a profitable customer; I took nothing "for the good of the house." I had a Gargantuesque appetite, and needed food of some sort in proportion to its demands. I neither took, or cared to take, any wine with my dinner, and never wanted any description of "nightcap." As for accommodation for the night, anything sufficed me that gave me a clean bed and a sufficient window-opening on fresh air, under such conditions as made it possible for me to have it open all night. To the present day I cannot sleep to my liking in a closed chamber; and before now, on the top of the Righi, have had my bed clothes blown off my bed, and snow deposited where they should have been.

But *quo musa tendis?* I was talking about my travels in Brittany.

I do not think my book was a bad *coup d'essai*. I remember old John Murray coming out to me into the front office in Albemarle Street, where I was on some business of my mother's, with a broad, good-natured smile on his face, and putting into my hands the *Times* of that morning, with a favorable notice of the book, saying as he did so, "There, so *you* have waked this morning to find yourself famous!" And, what was more to the purpose, my publisher was content with the result, as was evidenced by his offering me similar terms for another book of the same description—of which, more anon.

As my volumes on Brittany, published in 1840, are lit-
13

tle likely to come under the eye of any reader at the present day, and as the passage I am about to quote indicates accurately enough the main point of difference between what the traveller at that day saw and what the traveller of the present day may see, I think I may be pardoned for giving it.

"We had observed that at Broons a style of *coiffure* which was new to us prevailed; and my companion wished to add a sketch of it to his fast-increasing collection of Breton costumes. With this view, he had begun making love to the maid a little, to induce her to do so much violence to her maiden modesty as to sit to him for a few minutes, when a far better opportunity of achieving his object presented itself.

"The landlady's daughter, a very pretty little girl about fourteen years old, was going to be confirmed, and had just come down-stairs to her mother, who was sitting knitting in the *salle à manger*, for inspection and approval before she started. Of course, upon such an occasion, the art of the *blanchisseuse* was taxed to the utmost. Lace was not spared; and the most *recherché coiffure* was adopted that the rigorous immutability of village modes would permit.

"It would seem that the fickleness of fashion exercises in constant local variations that mutability which is utterly denied to it in Brittany with regard to time. Every district, almost every commune, has its own peculiar 'mode' (for both sexes), which changes not from generation to generation. As the mothers dress, so do their daughters, so did their grandmothers, and so will their granddaughters." [But I reckoned, when writing thus, without the railroad and its consequences.] "If a woman of one parish marries, or takes service, or for any other cause resides in another, she still retains the mode of her native village; and thus carries about her a mark which is to those among whom she is a sojourner a well-recognized indication of the place whence she comes, and to herself a cherished souvenir of the home which she never ceases to consider her own country.

"But though the form of the dress is invariable, and

every inhabitant of the commune, from the wealthy farmer's wife to the poorest cottager who earns her black bread by labor in the fields, would as soon think of adopting male attire as of innovating on the immemorial *mode du pays*, yet the quality of the materials allows scope for wealth and female coquetry to show themselves. Thus the invariable *mode de Broons*, with its trifling difference in form, which in the eye of the inhabitants made it as different as light from darkness from the *mode de St. Jouan*, was equally observable in the coarse linen *coiffe* of the maid, and the richly laced and beautifully 'got-up' head-dress of the daughter of the house.

"A very slight observation of human nature, under a few only of its various phases, may suffice to show that the instinct which prompts a woman to adorn her person to the best possible advantage is not the hothouse growth of cities, but a genuine wild-flower of nature. No highborn beauty ever more repeatedly or anxiously consulted her wax-lit Psyche on every faultless point of hair, face, neck, feet, and figure, before descending to the carriage for her first ball, than did our young Bretonne again and again recur to the mirror, which occupied the pier between the two windows of the *salle à manger*, before sallying forth on the great occasion of her confirmation.

"The dear object of girlish ambition was the same to both; but the simplicity of the little *paysanne* showed itself in the utter absence of any wish to conceal her anxiety upon the subject. Though delighted with our compliments on her appearance, our presence by no means prevented her from springing upon a chair every other minute to obtain a fuller view of the *tout ensemble* of her figure. Again and again the modest kerchief was arranged and rearranged to show a hair's-breadth more or a hair's-breadth less of her brown but round and taper throat. Repeatedly, before it could be finally adjusted to her satisfaction, was the delicate fabric of her *coiffure* moved with cautious care and dainty touch a *leetle* backwarder or a *leetle* forwarder over her sunburned brow.

"Many were the pokings and pinchings of frock and apron, the smoothings down before and twitchings down behind of the not less anxious mother. Often did she retreat to examine more correctly the general effect of the *coup d'œil,* and as often return to rectify some injudicious pin or remodel some rebellious fold. When all was at length completed, and the well-pleased parent had received from the servants, called in for the express purpose, the expected tribute of admiration, the little beauty took 'L'Imitation de la Vierge' in her hand, and tripped across to a convent of *Sœurs Grises* on the other side of the way to receive their last instructions and admonitions respecting her behavior when she should be presented to the bishop, while her mother screamed after her not to forget to pull up her frock when she knelt down.

"All the time employed in this little revision of the toilet had not been left unimproved by my companion, who at the end of it produced and showed to the proud mother an admirable full-length sketch of her pretty darling. The delighted astonishment of the poor woman, and her accent, as she exclaimed, '*O, si c'était pour moi!*' and then blushed to the temples at what she had said, were irresistible, and the good-natured artist was fain to make her a present of the drawing."

My Breton book ("though I says it as shouldn't") is not a bad one, especially as regards the upper or northern part of the province. That which concerns lower Brittany is very imperfect, mainly, I take it, because I had already nearly filled my destined two volumes when I reached it. I find there, however, the following notice of the sardine fishery, which has some interest at the present day. Perhaps the majority of the thousands of English people who nowadays have "sardines" on their breakfast-table every morning, are not aware that the contents of a very large number of the little tin boxes which are supposed to contain the delicacy are not sardines at all. They are very excellent little fishes, but not sardines ; for the enormously increased demand for them has outstripped the supply. In the days when the following sentences were written, sardines might certainly be had in London (as what might not ?) at such shops as Fortnum & Mason's, but they were costly, and by no means commonly met with.

On reaching Douarnenez in the summer of 1839, I wrote: "The whole population and the existence of Douarnenez depend on the sardine fishery. This delicious little fish, which the *gourmands* of Paris so much delight in, when preserved in oil, and sent to their capital in those little tin boxes whose look must be *familiar to all who have frequented the Parisian breakfast-houses*" [but is now more familiar to all who have entered any grocer's shop throughout the length and breadth of England], "is still more exquisite when eaten fresh on the shores which it frequents. They are caught in immense quantities along the whole of the southern coast of Brittany, and on the western shore of Finisterre as far to the northward as Brest, which, I believe, is the northern limit of the fishery. They come into season about the middle of June, and are then sold in great quantities in all the markets of southern Brittany at two, three, or four sous a dozen, according to the abundance of the fishery and the distance of the market from the coast. I was told that the commerce in sardines along the coast from l'Orient to Brest amounted to three millions of francs annually."

At the present day it must be enormously larger. I remember well the exceeding plentifulness of the little fishes—none of them so large as many of those which now fill the so-called sardine boxes—when I was at Douarnenez in 1839. All the men, women, and children in the place seemed to be feasting upon them all day long. Plates with heaps of them fried and piled up crosswise, like timber in a timber-yard, were to be seen out-doors and in-doors, wherever three or four people could be found together. All this was a thing of the past when I revisited Douarnenez in 1866. Every fish was then needed for the tinning business. They were to be had, of course, by ordering and paying for them, but very few indeed were consumed by the population of the place.

And this subject reminds me of another fishery which I witnessed a few months ago—last March—at Sestri di Ponente, near Genoa. We frequently saw nearly the whole of the fisher population of the place engaged in dragging from the water on to the sands enormously long nets, which had been previously carried out by boats to a distance not more I think than three or four hundred yards from the shore. From these nets, when at last they were landed after an hour or so of continual dragging by a dozen or twenty men and women, were taken huge basketfuls of silvery little fish sparkling in the sun, *exactly* like whitebait. I had always supposed that whitebait was a specialty of the Thames. Whether an ichthyologist would have pronounced the little Sestri fishes to be the same creatures as those which British statesmen consume at Greenwich I cannot say ; but we ate them frequently at the hotel under the name of *gianchetti*, and could find *no* difference between them and the Greenwich delicacy. The season for them did not seem to last above two or three weeks. The fishermen continued to drag their net, but caught other fishes instead of *gianchetti*. But while it lasted the plenty of them was prodigious. All Sestri was eating them, as all Douarnenez ate sardines in the old days. When the net with its sparkling cargo was dragged up on the sand and the contents were being shovelled into huge baskets to be carried up into the town, the men would take up handfuls of them, fresh, and I suppose still living, from the sea, and plunging their bearded mouths in them, eat them up by hundreds. The children, too, irrepressibly thronging round the net, would pick from its meshes the fishes which adhered to them and eat them, as more inland rising generations eat blackberries. I did not try the experiment of eating them thus, as one eats oysters, but I can testify that, crisply fried, and eaten with brown bread and butter and lemon juice, they were remarkably good.

Fortified by the excellent example of Sir Francis Doyle, who in his extremely amusing volume of "Reminiscences" gives as a reason for disregarding the claims of chronology in the composition of it, the chances that he might forget the matter he had in his mind if he did not book it at once, I have ventured for the same reason to do the same thing here. But I have an older authority for the practice in question, which Sir Francis is hardly likely to have lighted on. That learned antiquary and portentously voluminous writer, Francesco Cancellieri, who was well known to the Roman world in the latter years of the last, and the earliest years of the present century, used to compose his innumerable works upon a similar principle. And when attacked by the critics his contemporaries, who, Italian-like, supposed academically correct form to be the most important thing in any literary work, he defended himself on the same ground. " If I don't catch it *now*, I may probably forget it ; and is the world to be deprived of the information it is in my power to give it for the sake of the formal correctness of my work ?"

There is another passage in my book on Brittany respecting which it would be interesting to know whether recent travellers can report that the state of things there described no longer exists. I wrote in 1839 :

" Very near Treguier, on a spot appropriately selected for such a worship—the barren top of a bleak, unsheltered eminence—stands the chapel of *Notre Dame de la Haine!* Our Lady of HATRED ! The most fiendish of human passions is supposed to be under the protection of Christ's religion ! What is this but a fragment of pure and unmixed paganism, unchanged except in the appellation of its idol, which has remained among these lineal descendants of the Armorican Druids for more than a thousand years after Christianity has become the professed religion of the country ! Altars, professedly Christian, were raised under the protection of the.Protean Virgin, to the demon *Hatred;* and have continued to the present day to receive an unholy worship from blinded bigots, who hope to obtain Heaven's patronage and assistance for thoughts and wishes which they would be ashamed to breathe to man. Three *Aves* repeated with devotion at this odious and melancholy shrine are firmly believed to have the power to cause, within the year, the certain death of the person against whom the assistance of Our Lady of Hatred has been invoked. And it is said that even yet occasionally, in the silence and obscurity of the evening, the figure of some assassin worshipper at this accursed shrine may be seen to glide rapidly from the solitary spot, where he has spoken the unhallowed prayer whose mystic might has doomed to death the enemy he *hates*."

I must tell one other story of my Breton recollections, which refers to a time much subsequent to the publication of the book I have been quoting. It was in 1866 that I revisited Brittany in company with my present wife; and one of the objects of our little tour was the Finisterre land's end at the extreme point of the hornlike promontory which forms the department so named. We found some difficulty in reaching the spot, not the least part of which was caused by the necessity of threading our way, when in the immediate neighborhood of the cliffs, among enormous masses of seaweed stacked in huge heaps and left to undergo the process of decay, which turns it into very valuable manure. The odor which impregnated the whole surrounding atmosphere from these heaps was decidedly the worst and most asphyxiating I ever experienced.

We stood at last on the utmost *finis terræ* and looked over the Atlantic not only from the lighthouse, which, built three hundred feet above the sea-level, is often, we were told, drenched by storm-driven spray, but from various points of the tremendous rocks also. They are tremendous, in truth. The scene is a much grander one than that at our own "Land's End," which I visited a month or two ago. The cliffs are much higher, the rocks are more varied in their forms—more cruelly savage-looking, and the cleavages of them are on a larger scale. The spot was one of the most profound solitude, for we were far from the lighthouse, and the scream of the white gulls as they started from their roosting-places on the face of the rocks, or returned to them from their swirling flights, were the only indication of the presence of any creature having the breath of life.

The rock ledges, among which we were clambering, were in many places fearful spots enough—places where a stumble or a divagation of the foot but six or eight inches from the narrow path would have precipitated the blunderer to assured and inevitable destruction. "Here," said I to my wife, as we stood side by side on one such ledge, "would be the place for a husband, who wanted to get rid of his wife, to accomplish his purpose. Done in ten seconds! With absolute certainty! One push would suffice! No cry of any more avail than the screams of those gulls! And no possibility of the deed being witnessed by any mortal eye!"

I had hardly got the words out of my mouth before our ears were startled by a voice hailing us; and after some searching of the eye we espied a man engaged in seeking sea-fowls' eggs, who had placed himself in a position which I should have thought it absolutely impossible to reach, whence he had seen us, as we now saw him!

Let this then, my brethren, be a warning to you!
13*

CHAPTER XXII.

RETURNING from my Breton journey, I reached my mother's house in York Street on the 23d of July, 1839, and on the 26th of the same month left London with her to visit my married sister in her new home at Penrith, where Mr. Tilley had established himself as post-office surveyor of the northern district. His home was a pretty house situated between the town and the well-known beacon on the hill to the north of it.

The first persons I became acquainted with in this, to me, entirely new region, were Sir George Musgrave, of Edenhall, and his wife, who was a sister of Sir James Graham. My brother-in-law took me over to Edenhall, a lovely walk from Penrith, and we found both Sir George and Lady Musgrave at home. We—my mother and I—had not at that time conceived the idea of becoming residents at Penrith. But when, subsequently, we were led to do so, we found extremely pleasant and friendly neighbors at Edenhall, and though not, in strict chronology, due in this place, I may throw together my few reminiscences of Sir George.

He was the *beau idéal* of a country gentleman of the old school. He rarely or never went to London—not, as was the case with some of his neighbors, because the expense of a season there was formidable, for his estate was a fine one, and he was a rich man, living largely within his income, but because his idea was that a country gentleman's proper place was on his own acres, and because London had no temptations for him. He was said to be the best landlord in the county, and really seemed to look upon all his numerous tenants and all their laborers as his born subjects, to whom protection, kindness, assistance, and general looking-after were due in return for their fealty and loyal attachment. I think he would have kicked off his land (and he was a man who could kick) any man who talked in his hearing of the purely commercial relationship between a landlord and his tenants. Of course he was adored by all the country side. No doubt the stout Cumberland and Westmoreland farmers and hinds were good and loyal subjects of Queen Victoria, but for all practical purposes of reverence and obedience Musgrave was king at Edenhall.

Lady Musgrave was a particularly ladylike woman, the marked elegance of whose breeding might, with advantage, have given the tone to many a London drawing-room. I have seen her surrounded by country neighbors, and though she was *velut inter ignes luna minores*, I never saw the country squire's or country parson's wife who was not perfectly happy and at ease in her drawing-room, while, unconsciously, all the time taking a lesson in good-breeding and ladylike manners. She was thoroughly a help-meet for her husband in all his care for his people. I believe that both he and she were convinced, at the bottom of their hearts, that Cumberland and Westmoreland constituted the choicest, best, and most highly-civilized part of England. And she was one of those of whom I was thinking when, in a former chapter, I spoke of highly-educated people whom I had known to affect provincialism of speech. Lady Musgrave always, or, perhaps, it would be more correct to say generally, called a cow a "coo;" and though I suspect she would have left Westmoreland behind if evil fate had called her to London, on her own hillsides she preferred the accents of the native speech.

Sir George had, or affected to have, considerable respect for all the little local superstitions and beliefs which are so prevalent in that "north countree." And the kindness with which he welcomed us as neighbors when we built a house and came to live there was shown, despite a strong feeling which he had, or affected to have, with regard to an incident which fatally marked our *début* in that country.

We bought a field in a very beautiful situation, over-looking the ruins of Brougham Castle and the confluence of the Eden with the Lowther, and proceeded to build a house on the higher part of it. But there was a considerable drop from the lower limit of our ground to the road which skirted the property and furnished the only access to it. There was some difficulty, therefore, in contriving a tolerable entrance from the road for wheel-traffic, and it was found necessary to cause a tiny little spring that rose in the bank by the roadside to change its course in some small degree. The affair seemed to us a matter of infinitesimal importance, but Sir George was dismayed. We had moved, he said, a holy well, and the consequence would surely be that we should never succeed in establishing ourselves in that spot.

And, surely enough, we never did so succeed; for, after having built a very nice little house, and lived in it one winter and half a summer, we—for I cannot say that it was my mother more than I, or I more than my mother— made up our minds that "the sun yoked his horses too far from Penrith town," and that we had had enough of it. Sir George, of course, when he heard our determination, while he expressed all possible regret at losing us as neighbors, said that he knew perfectly well that it must be so, from the time that we so recklessly meddled with the holy well.

He was the most hospitable man in the world, and could never let many days pass without asking us to dine with him. But his hospitality was of quite the old-world school. One day—but that was after our journey to Italy, and when he had become intimate with us—being in a hurry to get back into the drawing-room to rejoin a pretty girl next whom I had sat at dinner, I tried to escape from the dining-room. "Come back!" he roared, before I could get to the door; "we won't have any of your d—d forineering habits here! Come back and stick to your wine, or by the Lord I'll have the door locked."

He was, unlike most men of his sort, not very fond of riding, but was a great walker. He used to take the men he could get to walk with him a tramp over the hill till they were fain to cry "Hold! enough!" But *there* I was his match.

Most of my readers have probably heard of the "Luck of Edenhall," for, besides Longfellow's * well-known poem, the legend relating to it has often been told in print. I refer to it here merely to mention a curious trait of character in Sir George Musgrave in connection with it. The "Luck of Edenhall" is an ancient decorated glass goblet, which has belonged to the Musgraves time out of mind, and which bears on it the legend:

> "When this cup shall break or fall,
> Farewell the luck of Edenhall."

After what I have written of Sir George and the holy well, which we so unfortunately moved from its proper site, it will be readily imagined that he attached no small importance to the safe-keeping of the "Luck;" and, truly, he did so. But, instead of simply locking it up, where he might feel sure it could neither break nor fall, he would show it to all visitors, and, not content with that, would insist on their taking it into their hands to examine and handle it. He maintained that otherwise there was no fair submission to the test of luck which was intended by the inscription. It would have been mere cowardly prevarication to lock it away under circumstances which took the matter out of the dominion of "luck" altogether. I wonder that, under such circumstances, it has not fallen, for the nervous trepidation of the folks who were made to handle it may be imagined.

I made another friend at Penrith in the person of a man as strongly contrasted with Sir George Musgrave as two north-country Englishmen could well be. This was a Dr. Nicholson, who has died within the last few months, to my great regret, for I had promised myself the pleasure of taking him by the hand yet once again before starting on the journey on which we may or may not meet. He was my senior by a few years, but not by many. Nicholson was a man of very extensive reading

---

* Subsequently to the publication of his poem Musgrave asked Longfellow to dine at Edenhall, and "picked a crow" with him on the conclusion of the poem, which represents the "Luck" to have been broken, which Sir George considered a flight of imagination quite transcending all permissible poetical license.

and of profound Biblical learning. It may be deemed surprising by others, as it was and is to me, that such a man should have been an earnest and thoroughly convinced Swedenborgian; but such was the case. And I can conscientiously give this testimony to the excellence of that creed—that it produced in the person of its learned north-country disciple at least one truly good and amiable man. Dr. Nicholson was emphatically such in all the relations of life. He was the good and loving husband of a very charming wife, the unremittingly careful and affectionate father of a large family, a delightful host at his own table, and an excellent and instructive companion over a cigar (hardly correctly alluded to in the singular number !), and a most *jucundus comes* in a tramp over the hills.

Amusing to me still is the contrast between those Cumberland walks with Sir George and my ramblings over the same or nearly the same ground with the meditative Swedenborgian doctor; the first always pushing ahead as if shouldering along a victorious path through life, knowing the history of every foot of ground he passed over, interested in every detail of it, and with an air of continually saying "Ha! ha!" among the breezy trumpets of those hills, like the scriptural war-horse; the second with his gaze very imperfectly turned outward, but very fruitfully turned inward, frequently pausing, with argumentative finger laid on his companion's breast, and smile, half satirical, half kindly, as the flow of discourse revealed theological *lacunæ* in my acquirements, which, I fear, irreparably and most unfairly injured the Regius professor of divinity in the mind of the German graduate. For Nicholson was a theological "doctor" by virtue of a degree from I forget what German university, and had a low estimate, perhaps more justified at that day than it would be now, of the extent and calibre of Oxford theological learning. He was himself a disciple and enthusiastic admirer of Ewald, a very learned Hebraist, and an unflagging student.

I was more capable of appreciating at its due value the extent and accuracy of his knowledge upon another subject—a leg of mutton! It *may* be a mere coincidence, but, certainly, the most learned Hebraist it was ever my

lot to know was also the best and most satisfactory carver
of a leg of mutton.

Nobody knows anything about mutton in these days,
for the very sufficient reason that there is no mutton worth
knowing anything about. Scientific breeding has improved
it off the face of the earth. The immature meat is killed
at two years old, and only we few survivors of a former
generation know how little like it is to the mutton of former
days. The Monmouthshire farmers told me the other day
that they could not keep Welsh sheep of pure breed, because nothing under an eight-foot park paling would confine them. Just as if they did not jump in the days when
I jumped too! Believe me, my young friends, that George
the Third knew what he was talking about (as upon certain other occasions) when he said that very little venison
was equal to a haunch of four-year-old mutton. And the
gravy!—chocolate-colored, not pink, my innocent young
friends. Ichabod! Ichabod!

My uncle, too, Mr. Partington—who married my father's sister, and lived many years chairman of quarter
sessions at Offham, among the South Downs, near Lewes
—was a man who understood mutton. A little silver
saucepan was placed by his side when the leg of mutton, or sometimes two, about as big as fine fowls, were
placed in one dish before him. Then, after the mutton
had been cut, the abundantly flowing gravy was transferred to the saucepan, a couple of glasses of tawny old port
and a *quantum suff.* of currant jelly and cayenne were
added, the whole was warmed in the dining-room, and
then—we ate mutton, as I shall never eat it again in this
world.

Well! *revenir à nos moutons* we never, never shall!
So we must, alas! do the reverse in returning to my Penrith reminiscences.

I remember specially an excellent old fellow and very
friendly neighbor, Colonel Macleod, a bachelor, who having fallen in love with a very beautiful spot, in the valley
of the Lowther, built an ugly brick house, three stories
high, because, as he said, he was so greedy of the view,
forgetful, apparently, that he was providing it mainly for

his maid-servants. Then there was the old maiden lady, with a name that might have been found in north-country annals at almost any date during the last seven hundred years, who mildly and maternally corrected my sister at table for speaking of *vol-au-vent*, telling her that the correct expression was *voulez-vous!* My sister always adopted the old lady's correction in future, at least when addressing her.

Then there were two pretty girls, Margaret and Charlotte Story, the nieces of old De Whelpdale, the lord of the manor. I think he and Mrs. De Whelpdale never left their room, for I do not remember to have ever seen either of them; nor do I remember that I at all resented their absence from the drawing-room when I used to call at the manor-house. One of the girls was understood to be engaged to be married to a far-distant lieutenant, of whom Penrith knew nothing, which circumstance gave rise to sundry ingenious conceits in the acrostic line, based on allusions to "his story" and "mystery." I wonder whether Charlotte is alive. If she is, and should see this page, she will remember. It was for her sake that I deserted, or tried to desert, Sir George's port, as related above.

We left Penrith on that occasion without having formed any decided intention of establishing ourselves there, and returned to London towards the end of August, 1839. During the next two months I was hard at work completing the MS. of my volumes on Brittany. And in November of the same year, after that long fast from all journeying, my mother and I left London for a second visit to Paris. But we did not on this occasion travel together.

I left London some days earlier than she did, and travelled by Ostend, Cologne, and Mannheim, my principal object being to visit my old friend, Mrs. Fauche, who was living at the latter place. I passed three or four very pleasant days there, including, as I find by my diary, sundry agreeable jaunts to Heidelberg, Carlsruhe, etc. My mother and I had arranged to meet at Paris on the 4th of December, and at that date I punctually turned up there.

I think that I saw Paris and the Parisians much more

satisfactorily on this occasion than during my first visit ;
and I suspect that some of the recollections recorded in
these pages as connected with my first visit to Paris belong really to this second stay there, especially I think
that this must have been the case with regard to my acquaintance with Chateaubriand, though I certainly was
introduced to him at the earlier period, for I find the
record of much talk with him about Brittany, which was
a specially welcome subject to him.

It was during this second visit that I became acquainted with Henry Bulwer, afterwards Lord Dalling, and at
that time first secretary of the British legation. My visits
were generally, perhaps always, paid to him when he was
in bed, where he was lying confined by, if I remember
rightly, a broken leg. I used to find his bed covered with
papers and blue-books, and the like. And I was told that
the whole, or at all events the more important part of the
business of the embassy was done by him as he lay there
on the bed, which must have been for many a long hour a
bed of suffering.

Despite certain affectations—which were so palpably affectations, and scarcely pretended to be aught else, that
there was little or nothing annoying or offensive in them
—he was a very agreeable man, and was unquestionably a
very brilliant one. He came to dine with me, I remember,
many years afterwards at my house in Florence, when he
insisted (the dining-room being on the first floor) on being
carried up-stairs, as we thought at the time very unnec-
essarily. But for aught I know such suspicion may have
wronged him. At all events his disability, whatever it
may have been, did not prevent him from making himself
very agreeable.

One of our guests upon that same occasion (I must drag
the mention of the fact in head and shoulders here, or
else I shall forget it) was that extraordinary man, Baron
Ward, who was, or perhaps I ought to say at that time
had been, prime-minister and general administrator to the
Duke of Lucca. Ward had been originally brought from
Yorkshire to be an assistant in the ducal stables. There,
doubtless because he knew more about the business than

anybody else concerned with it, he soon became chief. In that capacity he made himself so acceptable to the duke that he was taken from the stables to be his highness's personal attendant. His excellence in that position soon enlarged his duties to those of controller of the whole ducal household. And thence, by degrees that were more imperceptible in the case of such a government than they could have been in a larger and more regularly administered state, Ward became the recognized and nearly all-powerful head, manager, and ruler of the little Duchy of Lucca. And I believe the strange promotion was much for the advantage of the duke and of the duke's subjects. Ward, I take it, never robbed him or any one else. And this eccentric specialty the duke, though he was no Solomon, had the wit to discover. In his cups the ex-groom, ex-valet, was not reticent about his sovereign master, and his talk was not altogether of an edifying nature. One sally sticks in my memory. "Ah, yes! He was a grand favorite with the women. But *I* have had the grooming of him; and it was a wuss job than ever grooming his hosses was!"

Ward got very drunk that night, I remember, and we deemed it fortunate that our diplomatist guest had departed before the outward signs of his condition became manifest.

Henry Bulwer, by mere circumstance of synchronism, has suggested the remembrance of Ward, Ward has called up the Duke of Lucca, and he brings with him a host of Baths of Lucca reminiscences respecting his serene highness and others. But all these *must* be left to find their places, if anywhere, when I come to them later on, or we shall never get back to Paris.

It was on this our second visit to *Lutetia Parisiorum* that my mother and I made acquaintance with a very specially charming family of the name of D'Henin. The family circle consisted of General le Vicomte D'Henin, his English wife, and their daughter. The general was a delightful old man, more like an English general officer than any other Frenchman I ever met. Madame D'Henin was like an Englishwoman not unaccustomed to courts and wholly unspoiled by them. Mademoiselle D'Henin, very pretty, united the qualities of a denizen of the inmost circles of the fashionable world with those of a really serious student to a degree I have never seen equalled. They were great friends of the Bishop of London, and Mademoiselle D'Henin used to correspond with him. She was earnestly religious, and I remember her telling me of a *démêlé* she had had with her confessor. She had told him in confession that she was in the habit of reading the English Bible. He strongly objected, and at last told her that he could not give her absolution unless she promised to discontinue the practice. She told him that rather than do so she would take what would be to her the painful step of declaring herself a Protestant, whereupon he undertook to obtain a special permission for her to read the English Bible. Whether he did really take any such measures I don't know, and I fancy she never knew; but the upshot was that she continued to read the heretical book, and nothing more was ever said of refusing her absolution.

I have a large bundle of letters from this highly accomplished young lady to my mother. Many passages of them would be interesting and valuable to an historian of the reign of Louis Philippe. She writes at great length, and her standpoint is the very centre of the monarchical side of the French political world of that day. But as I am *not* writing a history of the reign of Louis Philippe, I must content myself with extracting two or three suggestive notices.

In a letter dated from Paris, 19th July, 1840, she writes : "You show much hospitality towards your royal guests. But I assure you it will not in this instance be taken as an homage to superior merit—words which I have heard frequently applied here to John Bull's frenzy about Soult, and to the hospitality of the English towards the Duc de N[emours]. When I told him how much I should like to be in his place (*i. e.*, about to go to England), he protested that he would change places with no one, '*quand il s'agissait d'aller dans un aussi delicieux pays, que cette belle Angleterre, que vous avez si bonne raison d'aimer et d'admirer.*'"

On the 29th of August in the same year she writes at

great length of the indignation and fury produced in Paris by the announcement of the Quadruple Alliance. She is immensely impressed by the fact that "people gathered in the streets and discussed the question in the open air." "Ireland, Poland, and Italy are to rise to the cry of Liberty." But she goes on to say, "Small causes produce great effects. Much of this warlike disposition has arisen from the fact of Thiers having bought a magnificent horse to ride beside the king at the late review." She proceeds to ridicule the minister in a tone very naturally suggested by the personal appearance of the little great man under such circumstances, which no doubt furnished Paris with much fun. But she goes on to suggest that the personal vanity which made the prospect of such a public appearance alluring to him was reinforced by "certain other secondary but still important considerations of a different nature, looking to the results which might follow from the exhibition of a war policy. This desirable end being attained beyond even the most sanguine hopes, the martial fever seems on the decline."

Now all this gossip may be accepted as evidencing the tone prevailing in the very inmost circles of the citizen king's friends and surroundings, and as such is curious.

Writing on the 8th of October in the same year, after speaking at great length of Madame Laffarge, and of the extraordinary interest her trial excited, dividing all Paris into Laffargists and anti-Laffargists, and almost superseding war as a general topic of conversation, she passes to the then burning subject of the fortification of Paris, and writes as follows—curiously enough, considering the date of her letter:

"Louis Philippe, whose favorite hobby it has ever been, from the idea that it makes him master of Paris, lays the first stone to-day. Some people consider it the first stone of the mausoleum of his dynasty. I sincerely hope not; for everything that can be called lady or gentleman runs a good chance of forming part of the funeral pile. The political madness which has taken possession of the public mind is fearful. Foreign or civil war! Such is the alternative. Thiers, who governs the masses, flatters them by promises of war and conquest. The *Marsellaise*, so lately a sign of rebellion, is sung openly in the theatres; the soldiers under arms sing it in chorus. The Guarde Nationale urges the king to declare war. He has resisted it with all his power, but has now, they say, given way, and has given Thiers *carte blanche*. He is, in fact, entirely under his control. The Chambers are not consulted. Thiers is our absolute sovereign. We call ourselves a free people. We have beheaded one monarch, exiled three generations of kings merely to have a dictator, '*mal né, mal fait, et mal élevé.*' There has been a rumor of a change of ministry, but no one believes it. The overthrow of Thiers would be the signal for a revolution, and the fortifications are not yet completed to master it. May not all these armaments be the precursors of some *coup d'état?* A general gloom is over all around us. All the faces are long; all the conversations are sad."

This may be accepted as a thoroughly accurate and trustworthy representation of the then state of feeling and opinion among the friends of Louis Philippe's government, whether *Parceque Bourbon* or *Quoique Bourbon*, and as such is valuable. It is curious too, to find a stanch friend of the existing government, who may be said to have been even intimate with the younger members of the royal family, speaking of the prime-minister with the detestation which these letters again and again express for Thiers.

In a letter of the 19th November, 1840, the writer describes at great length the recent opening of the Chamber by the king. She enlarges on the intensity of the anxiety felt for the tenor of the king's speech, which was supposed to be the announcement of war or peace; and describes the deep emotion with which Louis Philippe, declaring his hope that peace might yet be preserved, called upon the nation to assist him in the effort to maintain it; and expresses the scorn and loathing with which she overheard one republican deputy say to another as the king spoke, "*Voyez donc ce Robert Macaire, comme il fait semblant d'avoir du cœur!*"

A letter of the 14th March, 1842, is written in better spirits and a lighter tone. Speaking of the prevalent hostile feeling towards England, the writer wishes that her countrymen would remember Lamartine's observation that "*ce patriotisme coûte peu! Il suffit d'ignorer, d'injurier et de haïr.*" She tells her correspondent that "if Lord Cowley has much to do to establish the exact line between Lord Aberdeen's *observations* and *objections,* Lady Cowley has no less difficulty in keeping a nice balance between dignity and popularity," as "the embassy is besieged by all sets and all parties; the tag and rag, because pushing is a part of their nature; the *juste milieu* [how the very phrase recalls a whole forgotten world!], because they consider the English embassy as their property; the noble Faubourg, because they are tired of sulking, and would not object to treating Lady Cowley as they treated Colonel Thorn,* viz., establishing their quarters at the Cowley Arms, as they did at the Thorn's Head, and inviting their friends on the recognized principle, ' *C'est moi qui invite, et Monsieur qui paie.*' "

Then follows an account of a fancy *bal monstre* at the Tuileries, which might have turned out, says the writer, to deserve that title in another sense. It was believed that a plot had been formed for the assassination of the king, at the moment when, according to his invariable custom, he took his stand at the door of the supper-room to receive the ladies there. Four thousand five hundred tickets had been issued, and a certain number of these, still blank, had disappeared. That was certain. And it was also certain that the king did not go to the door of the supper-room as usual. But the writer remarks that the tickets may have been stolen by, or for, people who could not obtain them legitimately. But the instantly conceived suspicion of a plot is illustrative of the conditions of feeling and opinions in Paris at the time.

---

* Colonel Thorn was an American of fabulous wealth, who was for a season or two very notorious in Paris. He was the hero of the often-told story of the two drives to Longchamps the same day; first with one gorgeous equipment of *liveries*, and a second time with other and more resplendently clothed retainers.

"For my part," continues Mademoiselle D'Henin, "I never enjoyed a ball so much; perhaps because I did not expect to be amused; perhaps because all the royal family, the Jockey Club, and the fastidious Frenchwomen congratulated me upon my toilet, and voted it one of the handsomest there. They *said* the most becoming (but that was *de l'eau bénite de cour*); perhaps it was because the dukes of Orleans, Nemours, and Aumale, who never dance, and did so very little that evening, all three honored me with a quadrille. You see I expose to you all the very linings of my heart. I dissect it and exhibit all the vanity it contains. But you will excuse me when I tell you of a compliment that might have turned a wiser head than mine. The fame of my huntress's costume [Mademoiselle D'Henin was in those days the very *beau idéal* of a Diana] was such that it reached the ears of the wife of our butcher, who sent to beg that I would lend it to her to copy, as she was going to a fancy ball!"

A letter of the 8th of August, 1842, written from Fulham Palace, contains some interesting notices of the grief and desolation caused by the sad death of the Duke of Orleans.

"Was there ever a more afflicting calamity?" she writes. "When last I wrote his name in a letter to you, it was to describe him as the admired of all beholders, the hero of the *fête*, the pride and honor of France, and now what remains of him is in his grave! The affliction of his family baffles all description. I receive the most touching accounts from Paris. Some ladies about the court write to me that nothing can equal their grief. As long as the coffin remained in the chapel at Neuilly, the members of the family were incessantly kneeling by the side of it, praying and weeping. The king so far mastered his feelings that whenever he had official duties to perform he was sufficiently composed to perform *son métier de roi*. But when the painful task was done he would rush to the chapel and weep over the dead body of his son till the whole palace rang with his cries and lamentations. When the body was removed from Neuilly to Notre Dame, the scene at Neuilly was truly heartrending. My father has

seen the king and the princes several times since the catastrophe, and he says it has done the work of years on their
personal appearance. The Duc de Nemours has neither
eaten nor slept since his brother died, and looks as if walking out of his grave. Mamma wrote him a few lines of
condolence, which he answered by a most affecting note.
Papa was summoned to attend the king to the House, as
grand officier, and says he never witnessed such a scene.
Even the opposition shed their crocodile tears. Placed
immediately near the king on the steps of the throne, he
saw the struggle between kingly decorum and fatherly
affliction. Nature had the victory. Three times the king
attempted to speak, three times he was obliged to stop,
and at last burst into a flood of tears. The contagion
gained all around him. And it was only interrupted by
sobs that he could proceed. And it is in the face of this
despair, when the body of the prince is scarcely cold, that
that horrid Thiers and his associates begin afresh their
infernal manœuvres!"

A letter of the 3d April, 1842, contains among a quantity of the gossip of the day an odd story, which, the
writer says, "is putting Rome in a ferment, and the
clergy in raptures." I think I remember that it made a
considerable stir in ecclesiastic circles at the time. A
certain M. Ratisbonne, a Jew, it seems entered a church
in Rome (the writer does not say so, but, if I remember
rightly, it was the "Gesu") with a friend, a M. de Bussières, who had some business to transact in the sacristy.
The Jew, who professed complete infidelity, meantime
was looking at the pictures. But M. de Bussières, when
his business was done, found him prostrate on the pavement in front of a picture of the Madonna. The Jew, on
coming to himself, declared that the Virgin had stepped
from her frame and addressed him, with the result, as he
said, that having fallen to the ground an infidel, he rose a
convinced Christian! Mademoiselle D'Henin writes in a
tone which indicates small belief in the miracle, but seems
to accept as certain the further facts, that the convert
gave all he possessed to the Church and became a monk.

I have recently—even while transcribing these extracts

from her letters—heard of the death, within the last few years, of the writer of them. She died in England, I am told, and unmarried. Her sympathies and affections were always strongly turned to her mother's country, as indeed may be in some degree inferred from even those passages of her letters which have been given. And I can well conceive that the events which, each more disastrous than its predecessor, followed in France shortly after the date of the last of them, may have rendered, especially after the death of her parents, a life in France distasteful to her. But I, and, I think, my mother also, had entirely lost sight of her for very many years. Had I imagined that she was living in England I should undoubtedly have endeavored to see her.

I have known many women, denizens of *le grand monde*, who have adorned it with equally brilliant talents, equally captivating beauty, equally sparkling wit and vivacity of intelligence. And I have known many, denizens of the studious and the book world, gifted with larger powers of intellect, and more richly dowered with the results of thought and study. But I do not think that I ever met with one who possessed in so large a degree the choice product resulting from conversance with both these worlds. She was in truth a very brilliant creature.

Madame D'Henin I remember made us laugh heartily one evening by telling us the following anecdote. At one of those remarkable *omnium-gatherum* receptions at the Tuileries of which I have spoken in a former chapter, she heard an American lady, to whom Louis Philippe was talking of his American recollections and of various persons he had known there, say to him, " Oh, sire, they all retain the most lively recollections of your majesty's sojourn among them, *and wish nothing more than that you should return among them again!*" The Duke of Orleans, who was standing behind the king, fairly burst into a guffaw.

There was a story current in Rome, in the days of Pius the Ninth, which may be coupled with this as a good *pendant.* His holiness, when he had occupied the papal throne for a period considerably exceeding the legendary twenty-

14

five years of St. Peter, was one day very affably asking an Englishman, who had been presented to him, whether he had seen everything in Rome most calculated to interest a stranger, and was answered : "Yes indeed, your holiness, I think almost everything, except one which I confess I have been particularly anxious to witness—a conclave!"

Here are a few jottings at random from my diary, which may still have some little interest :

"Madame Le Roi, a daughter of General Hoche, told me (22d January, 1840) that as she was driving on the boulevard a day or two ago, a sou piece was thrown with great violence at the window of her carriage, smashing it to pieces. This, she said, was because her family arms were emblazoned on the panel. Most of the carriages in Paris, she said, had no arms on them for fear of similar attacks."

Then we were active frequenters of the theatres. We go, I find, to the Français, to see Mars, then sixty years old, in "Les Dehors Trompeurs" and in the "Fausses Confidences;" to the opera to hear "Robert le Diable" and "Lucia di Lammermuir," with Persiani, Tamburini, and Rubini; and the following night to the Français again, to see Rachel in "Cinna."

I thought her personally, I observe, very attractive. But that, and sundry other subsequent experiences, left me with the impression that she was truly very powerful in the representation of scorn, indignation, hatred, and all the sterner and less amiable passions of the soul, but failed painfully when her *rôle* required the exhibition of tenderness or any of the gentler emotions. These were my impressions when she was young and I was comparatively so. But when, many years afterwards, I saw her repeatedly in Italy, they were not, I think, much modified.

The frequent occasions on which, subsequently, I saw Ristori produced an impression on me very much the reverse. I remember thinking Ristori's "Mirra" too good, so terribly true as to be almost too painful for the theatre. I thought Rachel's "Marie Stuart," upon the whole, her finest performance, though "Adrienne" ran it hard.

Persiani, I note, supported by Lablache and Rubini, had

a most triumphant reception in "Inez de Castro," while
Albertazzi was very coldly received in "Blanche de Cas-
tille." Grisi in "Norma" was "superb." "Persiani and
P. Garcia sang a duet from 'Tancredi;' it was divine! I
think I like Garcia's voice better than any of them. Nor
could I think her ugly, as it is the fashion to call her,
though it must be admitted that her mouth and teeth are
alarming."

Then there were brilliant receptions at the English
embassy (Lord Granville) and at the Austrian embassy
(Comte d'Appony). My diary remarks that stars and
gold lace and ribbons of all the orders in Christendom
were more abundant at the latter, but female beauty at
the former. I remember much admiring that of Lady
Honoria Cadogan, and that of a very remarkably lovely
Visconti girl, a younger sister of the Princess Belgiojoso.
But despite this perfect beauty, my diary notes that it
was "curious to observe the unmistakable superiority as
a human being of the young English patrician." I remember that the "sit-down" suppers at the Austrian embassy—a separate little table for every two, three, or four
guests—were remarked on as a novelty (and applauded)
by the Parisians.

Then at Miss Clarke's (afterwards Madame Mohl) I
find Fauriel, "the first Provençal scholar in Europe," delightful, and am disgusted with Merimée, because he manifested self-sufficiency, as it seemed to my youthful criticism, by pooh-poohing the probability of the temple at
Lanleff in Brittany having been aught else than a church
of the Templars.

Then Arago reads an *Eloge* on "old Ampère," of
which I only remark that it lasted two hours and a half.
Then there was a dinner at Dr. Gilchrist's, whose widow
our old friend Pepe, who for many years had always
called her "Madame Ghee-cree," subsequently married.
My notes, written the same evening, remind me that "I
did not much like the radical old doctor (his wife was an
old acquaintance, but I had never seen him before); he is
eighty, and ought to know better. Old Nymzevitch (I
am not sure of the spelling), the ex-Chancellor of Poland,

dined with us. He is eighty-four. When he said that he had conversed with the Duc de Richelieu, I started as if he had announced himself as the Wandering Jew. But, in fact, he had had, when a young man, an interview with the duc, then ninety. He was, Nymzevitch told me, dreadfully emaciated, but dressed very splendidly in a purple coat all bedizened with silver lace. 'He received me,' said the old ex-chancellor, 'with much affable dignity.'"

Then comes a breakfast with Pepe, at which I met the President Thibeaudeau, "a gray old man who makes a point of saying rude, coarse, and disagreeable things, which his friends call dry humor. He found fault with everything at the breakfast-table."

Then a visit to the Chamber (where I heard Soult, Dupin, and Teste speak, and thought it "a terrible bear-garden ") is followed by attendance at a sermon by Athanase Coquerel, the Protestant preacher whose reputation in the Parisian *beau monde* was great in those days. He was, says my diary, " exceedingly eloquent, but I did not like his sermon ;" for which dislike my notes proceed to give the reasons, which I spare the, I hope grateful, reader. Then I went to hear Bishop Luscombe at the ambassador's chapel, and listened to "a very stupid sermon." I seem, somewhat to my surprise as I read the records of it, to have had a pronounced taste for sermons in those days, which I fear I have somewhat outgrown. But, then, I have been very deaf during my later decades.

Bishop Luscombe may perhaps, however, be made more amusing to the reader than he was to me in the embassy chapel by the following fragment of his experience. The bishop arrived one day at Paddington, and could not find his luggage. He called a porter to find it for him, telling him the name to be read on the articles. The man, very busy with other people, answered hurriedly, "You must go to hell for your luggage." Now Luscombe, who was a somewhat pompous and very *bishopy* man, was dreadfully shocked, and felt, as he said, as if the porter had struck him in the face. In extreme indignation he demanded where he could speak with any of the authorities, and was told that "the board " was then sitting up-stairs.

So to the boardroom the bishop went straightway, and, announcing himself, made his complaint. The chairman, professing his regret that such offence should have been given, said he feared the man must have been drunk, but that he should be immediately summoned to give an account of his conduct. So the porter, in great trepidation, appeared in a few minutes before the august tribunal of "the board."

"Well, sir," said he, in reply to the chairman's indignant questioning, "what could I do? I was werry busy at the time. So when the gentleman says as his name was Luscombe, I could do no better than tell him to go to h'ell for his luggage, and he'd have found it there all right!"

"Oh! I see," said the chairman; "it is a case of misplaced aspirate! We have spaces on the wall marked with the letters of the alphabet, and you would have found your luggage at the letter L. You will see that the man meant no offence. I am sorry you should have been so scandalized, but though we succeed, I hope, in making our porters civil to our customers, it would be hopeless, I fear, to attempt to make them say L correctly." *Solvuntur risu tabulæ.*

I find chronicled a long talk with Mohl one evening at Madame Récamier's. The room was very full of notable people of all sorts, and the tide of chattering was running very strong. "How can anything last long in France?" said he, in reply to my having said (in answer to his assertion that Cousin's philosophy had gone by) that it had been somewhat short-lived. "Reputations are made and pass away. It is impossible that they should endure. It is in such places as this that they are destroyed. The friction is prodigious!"

We then began to talk of the state of religion in France. He said that among a large set religion was now *à la mode*. But he did not suppose that many of the fine folks who *patronized* it had much belief in it. The clergy of France were, he said, almost invariably very illiterate. Guizot, I remembered, calls them, in his "History of Civilization," *doctes et erudits*, but I abstained from quoting him. Mohl went on to tell me a story of a newspaper that had been about to be established, called *Le Democrat.* The shareholders met, when it appeared that one party wished to make it a Roman Catholic and the other an atheist organ. Whereupon the existence of God was put to the vote and carried by a majority of one, at which the atheist party were so disgusted that they seceded in a body.

I got to like Mohl much, and had more conversation, I think, with him than with any other of the numerous men of note with whom I became more or less acquainted. On another occasion, when I found him in his cabinet, walled up as usual among his books, our talk fell on his great work, the edition of the Oriental MSS. in the " Bibliothèque Royale," which was to be completed in ten folio volumes, the first of which, just out, he was showing me. He complained of the extreme slowness of the government presses in getting on with the work. This he attributed to the absurd costliness, as he considered it, of the style in which the work was brought out. The cost of producing that first volume, he told me, had been over £1600 sterling. It was to be sold at a little less than a hundred francs. Something was said (by me, I think) of the possibility of obtaining assistance from the king, who was generally supposed to be immensely wealthy. Mohl said that he did not believe Louis Philippe to be nearly so rich a man as he was supposed to be. He had spent, he said, enormous sums on the chateaux he had restored, and was affirmed, by those who had the means of knowing the fact, to be at that time twelve millions of francs in debt.

My liking for Mohl seems to have been fully justified by the estimation he was generally held in. I find in a recently published volume by Kathleen O'Meara, on the life of my old friend, Miss Clarke, who afterwards became his wife, the following passage quoted from Sainte-Beuve, who describes him as " a man who was the very embodiment of learning and of inquiry, an Oriental *savant*—more than a *savant*—a sage, with a mind clear, loyal, and vast; a German mind passed through an English filter, a cloudless, unruffled mirror, open and limpid; of pure and frank morality; early disenchanted with all things; with a grain of irony devoid of all bitterness, the laugh of a child under a bald head ; a Goethe-like intelligence, but free from all prejudice." "A charming and *spirituelle* Frenchwoman," Miss O'Meara goes on to say, "said of Julius Mohl that Nature, in forming his character, had skimmed the cream of the three nationalities to which he belonged by birth, by adoption, and by marriage, making him deep as a German, *spirituel* as a Frenchman, and loyal as an Englishman."

I may insert here the following short note from Madame Mohl, because the manner of it is very characteristic of her. It is, as was usual with her, undated.

" MY DEAR MR. TROLLOPE,—By accident I have just learned that you are in London. If I could see you and talk over my dear old friend (Madame Récamier) I should be so much obliged and so glad. I live 68 Oxford Terrace, Hyde Park. If you would write me a note to say when I should be at home for the purpose. But if you can't, I am generally, not always, found after four. But if you could come on the 10th or 12th after nine we have a party. I am living at Mrs. Schwabe's just now till 16th this month. Pray write me a note, even if you can't come.

"Yours ever, "MARY MOHL."

All the capital letters in the above transcript, except those in her name, are mine ; she uses none. The note is written in headlong hurry.

Mignet, whom I met at the house of Thiers, I liked too, but Mohl was my favorite.

It was all very amusing, with as much excitement and interest of all kinds crammed into a few weeks as might have lasted one for a twelvemonth. And I liked it better than teaching Latin to the youth of Birmingham. But it would seem that there was something that I liked better still. For on March 30, leaving my mother in the full swing of the Parisian gayeties, I bade adieu to them all and once again " took to the road," bound on an excursion through central France.

CHAPTER XXIII.

My journey through central France took me by Char-
tres, Orleans, down the Loire to Nantes, then through La
Vendée to Fontenay, Niort, Poitiers, Saintes, Rochefort,
La Rochelle, Bordeaux, Angouleme, Limoges, and thence
back to Paris. On looking at the book for the first time
since I read the proof-sheets I find it amusing. The fault
of it, as an account of the district traversed, is that it
treats of the localities described on a scale that would
have needed twenty volumes, instead of two, to complete
the story of my tour in the same proportion. I do not
remember that any of my critics noted this fault. Perhaps they feared that on the first suggestion of such an
idea I should have set about mending the difficulty by the
production of a score of other volumes on the subject! I
could easily have done so. I was in no danger of incurring the anathema launched by Sterne — I think it was
Sterne—against the man who went from Dan to Beersheba
and found all barren. I found matter of interest everywhere, and could have gone on doing so, as it seemed to
me in those days, forever.

The part of France I visited is not much betravelled by
Englishmen, and the general idea is that it is not an interesting section of the country. I thought, and still think,
otherwise. My notion is that if a line were drawn through
France from Calais to the centre of the Pyrenean chain,
by far the greater part of the prettiest country and most
interesting populations, as well as places, would be found
to the westward of it. I do not think that my bill of fare
excited any great interest in the reading world; but I suppose that I contrived to interest a portion of it, for the
book was fairly successful.

I wrote a book in many respects of the same kind many

years subsequently, giving an account of a journey through
certain little-visited districts of central Italy, under the
title of a "Lenten Journey." It is not, I think, so good
a book as my French journeys furnished, mainly, to my
mind, because it was in one small volume instead of two
big ones, and both for want of space and want of time
was done hurriedly and too compendiously. The true
motto for the writer of such a book is *nihil a me alienum
puto*, whether *humanum* or otherwise. My own opinion
is, to make a perfectly clean breast of it, that I could now
write a fairly amusing book on a journey from Tyburn
turnpike to Stoke Pogis. But then such books should be
addressed to readers who are not in such a tearing hurry as
the unhappy world is in these latter days.

It would seem that I found my two octavo volumes did
not afford me nearly enough space to say my say respecting the country traversed, for they are brought to an end
somewhat abruptly by a hurried return from Limoges to
Paris ; whereas my ramble was much more extended, including both the upper and lower provinces of Auvergne
and the whole of the Bourbonnais. My voluminous notes
of the whole of these wanderings are now before me. But
I will let my readers off easy, recording only that I walked
from Murat to St. Flour, a distance of fifteen miles, in five
minutes under three hours. Not bad! My diary notes
that it was frequently very difficult to find my way in
walking about Auvergne, from the paucity of people I
could find who could speak French, the *langue du pays*
being as unintelligible as Choctaw. This would hardly
be the case now.

I don't know whether a knot of leading tradesmen at
Bordeaux could now be found to talk as did such a party
with whom I got into conversation in that year, 1840. It
was explained to me that England, as was well known,
had liberated her slaves in the West Indies perfectly well
knowing that the colonies would be absolutely ruined by
the measure, but expecting to be amply compensated by
the ruin of the French colonies, which would result from
the example, and the consequent extension of trade with
the East Indies, from which France would be compelled

14*

to purchase all the articles her own colonies now supplied her with. One of these individuals told me and the rest of his audience that he had the means of *knowing* that the interest of the English national debt was paid every year by fresh borrowing, and that bankruptcy and absolute smash must occur within a few years. " Ah !" said a much older, gray-headed man, who had been listening sitting with his hands reposing on his walking-stick before him, and who spoke with a sort of patient, long-expecting hope and a deep sigh—" ah ! we have been looking for that many a year, but I am beginning to doubt whether I shall live to see it." My assurances that matters were not altogether so bad as they supposed in England, of course, met with little credence. Still, they listened to me, and did not show angry signs of a consciousness that I was audaciously befooling them, till the talk having veered to London, I ventured to assure them that London was not surrounded by any *octroi* boundary, and that no impost of that nature was levied there.* Then, in truth, I might as well have assured them that London streets were literally paved with gold.

On the 30th of May, 1840, I returned with my mother from Paris to her house in York Street. Life had been very pleasant there to her I believe, and certainly to me during those periods of it which my inborn love of rambling allowed me to pass there. But in the following June it was determined that the house in York Street should be given up. Probably the *causa causans* of this determination was the fact of my sister's removal to far Penrith. But I think, too, that there was a certain unavowed feeling that we had eaten up London, and should enjoy a move to new pastures.

I remember well a certain morning in York Street when we—my mother and I—held a solemn audit of accounts. It was found that during her residence in York Street she had spent a good deal more than she had supposed. She had entertained a good deal, giving frequent "little din-

---

* It may possibly be necessary to tell untravelled Englishmen that the *octroi*, universal on the Continent, is an impost levied on all articles of consumption at the gates of a town.

ners." But dinners, however little, are apt in London to leave tradesmen's bills not altogether small in proportion to their littleness. "The fact is," said my mother, "that potatoes have been quite exceptionally dear." For a very long series of years she never heard the last of those exceptional potatoes. But, despite the alarming deficit caused by those unfortunate vegetables, I do not think the abandonment of the establishment in York Street was caused by financial considerations. She was earning in those years large sums of money—quite as large as any she had been spending—and might have continued in London had she been so minded.

No doubt I had much to do with the determination we came to. But, for my part, if it had at that time been proposed to me that our establishment should be reduced to a couple of trunks, and all our worldly possessions to the contents of them, with an opening vista of carriages, diligences, and ships *ad libitum* in prospect, I should have jumped at the idea. A caravan, which, in addition to shirts and stockings, could have carried about one's books and writing-tackle, would have seemed the *summum bonum* of human felicity.

So we turned our backs on London without a thought of regret and once again "took the road;" but this time separately, my mother going to my sister at Penrith and I to pass the summer months in wanderings in Picardy, Lorraine, and French Flanders, and the ensuing winter in Paris.

I hardly know which was the pleasanter time. By this time I was no stranger to Paris, and had many friends there. It was my first experiment of living there as a bachelor, as I was going to say, but I mean "on my own hook," and left altogether to my own devices. I found, of course, that my then experiences differed considerably from those acquired when living *en famille*. But I am disposed to think that the tolerably intimate knowledge I flatter myself I possessed of the Paris and Parisians of Louis Philippe's time was mainly the result of this second residence. I remember, among a host of things indicating the extent of the difference between those days and these, that I lived in a very good apartment, *au troisième*, in one of the streets immediately behind the best part of the Rue de Rivoli for one hundred francs a month! This price included all service (save, of course, a tip to the porter), and the preparation of my coffee for breakfast if I needed it. For dinner, or any other meal, I had to go out.

"Society" lived in Paris in those days—not unreasonably as the result soon showed—in perpetual fear of being knocked all to pieces by an outbreak of revolution, though, of course, nobody said so. But I lived mainly (though not entirely) among the *bien pensants* people, who looked on all anti‑governmental manifestations with horror. Perhaps the restless discontent which destroyed Louis Philippe's government is the most disheartening circumstance in the whole course of recent French history. That the rule of Charles Dix should have occasioned revolt may be regrettable, but is not a matter for surprise. But that of Louis Philippe was not a stagnant or retrogressive *régime*. "*La carrière*" was very undeniably open to talent and merit of every description. Material well-being was on the increase. And the door was not shut against any political change which even very advanced Liberalism, of the kind consistent with order, might have aspired to. But the Liberalism which moved France was not of that kind.

One of my most charming friends of those days, Rosa Stewart, who afterwards became and was well known to literature as Madame Blaze du Bury, was both too clever and too shrewd an observer, as well as, to me at least, too frank to pretend any of the assurance which was then *de mode*. She saw what was coming, and was fully persuaded that it must come. I hope that her eye may rest on this testimony to her perspicacity, though I know not whether she still graces this planet with her very pleasing presence. For as, alas! in so many scores of other instances, our lives have drifted apart, and it is many years since I have heard of her.

One excursion I specially remember in connection with that autumn was partly, I think, a pedestrian one, to Ami-

ens and Beauvais, made in company with the W——
A—— of whom my brother speaks in his autobiography;
which I mention chiefly for the sake of recording my testimony to the exactitude of his description of that very
singular individual. If it had not been for the continual
carefulness necessitated by the difficulty of avoiding all
cause of quarrel, I should say that he was about the pleasantest travelling companion I have ever known.

In the beginning of April, 1841, after a little episode of
spring wandering in the Tyrol and Bavaria (in the course
of which I met my mother at the chateau of her very old
friend the Baroness de Zandt, who has been mentioned
before, and was now living somewhat solitarily in her huge
house in its huge park near Bamberg), my mother and I
started for Italy. Neither of us had at that time conceived the idea of making a home there. The object of
the journey, which had been long contemplated by my
mother, was the writing of a book on Italy, as she had already done on Paris and on Vienna.

Our journey was a prosperous one in all respects, and
our flying visit to Italy was very pleasant. My mother's
book was duly written, and published by Mr. Bentley in
1842. But the "Visit to Italy," as the work was entitled
(with justly less pretence than the titles of either of its
predecessors had put forward, was in truth all too short.
And I find that almost all of the huge mass of varied recollections which are connected in my mind with Italy and
Italian people and things belong to my second "visit" of
nearly half a century's duration!

We made, however, several pleasant acquaintances and
some fast friends, principally at Florence, and thus paved
the way, although little intending it at the time, for our
return thither.

Our visit was rendered shorter than it would probably otherwise have been by my mother's strong desire to
be with my sister, who was expecting the birth of her first
child at Penrith. And for this purpose we left Rome in
February, 1842, in very severe weather. We crossed the
Mont Cenis in sledges — which to me was a very acceptable experience, but to my mother was one which nothing

could have induced her to face, save the determination not to fail her child at her need.

How well I remember hearing, as I sat in the *banquette* of the diligence which was just leaving Susa for its climb up the mountain amid the snow, then rapidly falling, the driver of the descending diligence, which had accomplished its work and was just about entering the haven of Susa, sing out to our driver—" *Vous allez vous amuser joliment là haut, croyez moi !*"

We did not, however, change the diligence for the sledges till we came to the descent on the northern side. But as we made our slow way to the top our vehicle was supported from time to time on either side by twelve strapping fellows, who put their shoulders to it.

I appreciated during that journey, though I was glad to see the mountain in its winter dress, the recommendation not to let your flight be in the winter.

CHAPTER XXIV.

IN IRELAND.—AT ILFRACOMBE.—IN FLORENCE.

I ACCOMPANIED my mother to Penrith, and forthwith devoted myself heart and body to the preparation of our new house, and the beautifying of the very pretty paddock in which it was situated. I put in some hundreds of trees and shrubs with my own hands, which prospered marvellously, and have become, I have been told, most luxuriant shrubberies. I was bent on building a cloistered walk along the entire top of the field, which would have afforded a charming ambulatory sheltered from the north winds and from the rain, and would have commanded the most lovely views, while the pillars supporting the roof would have presented admirable places for a world of flowering climbing plants. And doubtless I should have achieved it, had we remained there. But it would have run into too much money to be undertaken immediately — fortunately ; for, inasmuch as there was nothing of the sort in all that country-side, no human being would have given a stiver more for the house when it came to be sold, and the next owner would probably have pulled it down. There was no authority for such a thing. Had it been suffered to remain it would probably have been called " Trollope's Folly !"

Subsequently, but not immediately after we left it, the place — oddly enough I forget the name we gave it — became the property and the residence of my brother-in-law.

Of my life at Penrith I need add nothing to the jottings I have already placed before the reader on the occasion of my first visit to that place.

My brother, already a very different man from what he had been in London, came from his Irish district to visit us there ; and I returned with him to Ireland, to his headquarters at Banagher on the Shannon. Neither of this

journey need I say much. For to all who know anything
of Ireland at the present day — and who does not? worse
luck!—anything I might write would seem as *nihil ad
rem* as if I were writing of an island in the Pacific. I remember a very vivid impression that occurred to me on
first landing at Kingstown, and accompanied me during
the whole of my stay in the island, to the effect that the
striking differences in everything that fell under my observation from what I had left behind me at Holyhead
were fully as great as any that had excited my interest
when first landing in France.

One of my first visits was to my brother's chief. He
was a master of foxhounds and hunted the country. And
I well remember my astonishment when the door of this
gentleman's residence was opened to me by an extremely
dirty and slatternly bare-footed and bare-legged girl. I
found him to be a very friendly and hospitable good fellow, and his wife and her sister very pleasant women. I
found too that my brother stood high in his good graces
by virtue of simply having taken the whole work and
affairs of the postal district on his shoulders. The rejected of St. Martin's-le-Grand was already a very valuable and capable officer.

My brother gave me the choice of a run to the Killeries
or to Killarney. We could not manage both. I chose
the former, and a most enjoyable trip we had. He could
not leave his work to go with me, but was to join me subsequently, I forget where, in the west. Meantime he gave
me a letter to a bachelor friend of his at Clifden. This
gentleman immediately asked me to dinner, and he and I
dined *tête-à-tête*. Nevertheless, he thought it necessary to
apologize for the appearance of a very fine John Dory on
the table, saying that he had been himself to the market
to get a turbot for me, but that he had been asked half a
crown for a not very large one, and really he could not
give such absurd prices as that!

Anthony duly joined me as proposed, and we had a
grand walk over the mountains above the Killeries. I
don't forget, and never shall forget—nor did Anthony
ever forget; alas! that we shall never more talk over

that day again—the truly grand spectacular changes from dark, thick, enveloping cloud to brilliant sunshine, suddenly revealing all the mountains and the wonderful coloring of the intertwining sea beneath them, and then back to cloud and mist and drifting sleet again. It was a glorious walk. We returned wet to the skin to Joyce's Inn, and dined on roast goose and whiskey punch, wrapped in our blankets like Roman senators !

One other scene I must recall. The reader will hardly believe that it occurred in Ireland. There was an election of a member for I forget what county or borough, and my brother and I went to the hustings—the only time I ever was at an election in her majesty's dominions. What were the party feelings, or the party colors, I utterly forget. It was merely for the fun of the thing that we went there. The fun, indeed, was fast and furious. The whole scene on the hustings, as well as around them, seemed to me one seething mass of senseless but good-humored hustling and confusion. Suddenly in the midst of the uproar an ominous cracking was heard, and in the next minute the hustings swayed and came down with a crash, heaping together in a confused mass all the two or three hundreds of human beings who were on the huge platform. Some few were badly hurt. But my brother and I being young and active, and tolerably stout fellows, soon extricated ourselves, regained our legs, and found that we were none the worse. Then we began to look to our neighbors. And the first who came to hand was a priest, a little man, who was lying with two or three fellows on the top of him, horribly frightened and roaring piteously for help. So Anthony took hold of one of his arms and I of the other, and by main force dragged him from under the superincumbent mass of humanity. When we got him on his legs his gratitude was unbounded. "Tell me your names," he shouted, "that I'll pray for ye !" We told him laughingly that we were afraid it was no use, for we were heretics. "Tell me your names," he shouted again, "that I'll pray for ye all the more !"

I wonder whether he ever did. He certainly was very much in earnest while the fright was on him.

Not very long after my return from this Irish trip we
finally left Penrith, on the third of April, 1843 ; and I
trust that the nymph of the holy well, whose spring we
had disturbed, was appeased.

My mother and I had now " the world before us where
to choose." She had work in hand, and more in perspective, but it was work of a nature that might be done in
one place as well as in another. So when " Carlton Hill "
(all of a sudden the name comes back to my memory)
was sold, we literally stood with no *impedimenta* of any
sort save our trunks, and absolutely free to turn our faces
in whatsoever direction we pleased.

What we did in the first instance was to turn them to
the house of our old and well-beloved cousin, Fanny Bent,
at Exeter. There after a few days we persuaded her to
accompany us to Ilfracombe, where we spent some very
enjoyable summer weeks. What I remember chiefly in
connection with that pleasant time was idling rambles
over the rocks and the Capstone Hill, in company with
Mrs. Coker and her sister Miss Aubrey, the daughters of
that Major A—— who needs to the whist-playing world
no further commemoration. The former of them was the
wife and mother of Wykehamists (founder's kin), and both
were very charming women. Ilfracombe was in those
days an unpretending sort of fishing-village. There was
no huge Ilfracombe Hotel, and the Capstone Hill was not
strewed with whitey-brown biscuit bags and the fragments
of bottles, nor continually vocal with nigger minstrels and
ranting preachers. The Royal Clarence did exist in the
little town, whether under that name or not, I forget.
But I can testify from experience, acquired some forty
years afterwards, that Mr. and Mrs. Clemow now keep
there one of the best inns of its class that I, no incom-
petent expert in such matters, know in all England.

Then, when the autumn days began to draw in, we returned to Exeter, and many a long consultation was held
by my mother and I, sallying forth from Fanny Bent's
hospitable house for a *tête-à-tête* stroll on Northernhay, on
the question of " What next ?"

It turned out to be a more momentous question than

we either of us imagined it to be at the time; for the decision of it involved the shape and form of the entire future life of one of us, and still more important modification of the future life of the other. Dresden was talked of. Rome was considered. Paris was thought of. Venice was discussed. No one of them was proposed as a future permanent home. Finally Florence came on the *tapis*. We had liked it much, and had formed some much-valued friendships there. It was supposed to be economical as a place to live in, which was one main point. For our plan was to make for ourselves for two or three years a home and way of living sufficiently cheap to admit of combining with it large plans of summer travel. And eventually Florence was fixed on.

As for my mother, it turned out that she was then selecting her last and final home—though the end was not, thank God, for many a long year yet. As for me, the decision arrived at during those walks on Exeter Northernhay was more momentous still. For I was choosing the road that led not only to my home for the next half-century nearly, but to two marriages, both of them so happy in all respects as rarely to have fallen to the lot of one and the same man.

- How little we either of us, my mother and I, saw into the future—beyond a few immediate inches before our noses! Truly *prudens futuri temporis exitum caliginosâ nocte premit Deus!* And when I hear talk of "conduct making fate," I often think—humbly and gratefully, I trust; marvelling, certainly—how far it could have *à priori* seemed probable that the conduct of a man who, without either *œs in presenti*, or any very visible prospect of *œs in futuro*, turns aside from all the beaten paths of professional industry should have led him to a long life of happiness and content, hardly to be surpassed, and, I should fear, rarely equalled. *Deus nobis hæc otia fecit!* —*Deus*, by the intromission of one rarely good mother, and two rarely good, and I may add rarely gifted, wives!

Not that I would have the reader translate "*otia*" by idleness. I have written enough to show that my life hitherto had been a full and active one. And it continued in Italy to be an industrious one. Translate the word rather into "independence." For I worked at work that I liked, and did no task-work. Nevertheless, I would not wish to be an evil exemplar, *vitiis imitabile*, and I don't recommend you, dear boys, to do as I did. I have been quite abnormally fortunate.

Well, we thought that we were casting the die of fate on a very subordinate matter, while, lo! it was cast for us by the Supernal Powers after a more far-reaching and overruling fashion.

So on the 2d of September, 1843, we turned our faces southward and left London for Florence.

We became immediately on arriving in Firenze la gentile (after a little tour in Savoy, introduced as an interlude after our locomotive rambling fashion) the guests of Lady Bulwer, who then inhabited in the Palazzo Passerini an apartment far larger than she needed, till we could find a lodging for ourselves.

We had become acquainted with Lady Bulwer in Paris, and a considerable intimacy arose between her and my mother, whose nature was especially calculated to sympathize with the good qualities which Lady Bulwer unquestionably possessed in a high degree. She was brilliant, witty, generous, kind, joyous, good-natured, and very handsome. But she was wholly governed by impulse and unreasoning prejudice; though good-natured, was not always good-humored; was totally devoid of prudence or judgment, and absolutely incapable of estimating men aright. She used to think me, for instance, little short of an admirable Crichton!

Of course, all the above-rehearsed good qualities were, or were calculated to be, immediately perceived and appreciated, while the less pleasant specialties which accompanied them were of a kind to become more perceptible only in close intimacy. And while no intimacy ever lessened that regard of my mother and myself that had been won by the first, it was not long before we were both, my mother especially, vexed by exhibitions of the second.

As, for instance: Lady Bulwer had for some days been complaining of feeling unwell, and was evidently suffering. My mother urged her to have some medical advice, whereupon she turned on her very angrily, while the tears started to her beautiful eyes, and said, "How *can* you tell me to do any such thing, when you know that I have not a guinea for the purpose?" (She was frequently wont to complain of her poverty.) But she had hardly got the words out of her mouth when the servant entered the room saying that the silversmith was at the door asking that the account which he laid on the table might be paid. The account (which Lady Bulwer made no attempt to conceal, for concealment of anything was not at all in her line) was for a pair of small silver spurs and an ornamented silver collar which she had ordered a week or two previously for the *ceremonial knighting of her little dog Taffy!*

On another occasion a large party of us were to visit the Boboli Gardens. It was a very hot day, and we had to climb the hill to the upper part of the gardens, from whence the view over Florence and the Val d'Arno is a charming one. But the hill, as those who have been at Florence will not have forgotten, is not only an extremely steep, but a shadeless one. The broad path runs between two wide margins of turf, which are enclosed on either side by thick but not very high shrubberies. The party sorted themselves into couples, and the men addressed themselves to facilitating as best they might the not slightly fatiguing work before the ladies. It fell to my lot to give Lady Bulwer my arm. Before long we were the last and most lagging couple on the path. It was hard work, but I did my best, and flattered myself that my companion, despite the radical moisture which she was copiously losing, was in high good-humor, as indeed she seemed to be, when suddenly, without a word of warning, she dashed from the path, threw herself prone among the bushes, and burst into an uncontrollable fit of sobs and weeping. I was horrified with amazement. What had I done, or what left undone? It was long before I could get a word out of her. At last she articulated amid her sobs, "It is TOO hot! It is cruel to bring one here!" Yes, it was *too* hot; but that was all. Fortunately I was not the cruel bringer.

I consoled her to the best of my power, and induced her to wipe her eyes. I dabbled a handkerchief in a neighboring fountain for her to wash her streaked face, and eventually I got her to the top of the hill, where all the others had long since arrived.

The incident was entirely characteristic of her. She was furiously angry with all things in heaven above and on the earth below because she was at the moment inconvenienced.

Here is the beginning of a letter from her of a date some months anterior to the Boboli adventure :

"Illustrissimo Signor Tommaso" (that was the usual style of her address to me), "as your book is just out you must feel quite *en train* for puffs of any description. Therefore I send you the best I have seen for a long while, 'La Physiologie du Fumeur.' But even if you don't like it, *don't* put it in your pipe and smoke it. *Vide* Joseph Fume."

A little subsequently she writes : "Signor Tommaso, the only revenge I shall take for your lecture" (probably on the matter of some outrageous extravagance) "is not to call you *illustrissimo* and not to send you an illuminated postilion" (a previous letter having been ornamented with such a decoration at the top of the sheet), "but let you find your way to Venice in the dark as you can, and then and there, 'On the Rialto I will rate you,' and, being a man, you know there is no chance of my *overrating* you." The following passage from the same letter refers to some negotiations with which she had intrusted me relative to some illustrations she was bent on having in a forthcoming book she was about to publish : "As for the immortal Cruikshank, tell him that I am sure the mighty genius which conceived Lord Bateman could not refuse to give any lady the *werry best*, and if he does I shall pass the rest of my life registering a similar *wow* to that of the fair Sophia, and exclaiming, 'I vish, George Cruikshank, as you vas mine.'"

The rest of the long, closely-written, four-paged letter is an indiscriminate and bitter, though joking attack, upon the race of publishers. She calls Mr. Colburn an "em-

bodied shiver," which will bring a smile to the lips of those
—few, I fear—who remember the little man.

Here are some extracts from a still longer letter written
to my mother much about the same time : "I hear Lady
S—— has committed another novel, called 'The Three
Peers,' no doubt *l'un pire que l'autre !* . . . I have a great
many kind messages to you from that very charming person Madame Récamier, who fully intends meeting you at
Venice with Chateaubriand in October, for so she told me
on Sunday. I met her at Miss Clarke's some time ago,
and as I am a bad *pusher* I am happy to say she asked to
be introduced to me, and was, thanks to you, my kind
friend ! She pressed me to go and see her, which I have
done two or three times, and am going to do again at her
amiable request on Thursday. I think that her fault is
that she flatters a little too much. And flattery to one
whose ears have so long been excoriated by abuse does not
sound safe. However, all is right when she speaks of you.
And the point she most eulogized in you is that which I
have heard many a servile coward who could never go and
do likewise" [no indication is to be found either in this
letter or elsewhere to whom she alludes] "select for the
same purpose, namely, your straightforward, unflinching,
courageous integrity. . . . Balzac is furious at having his
new play suppressed by Thiers, in which Arnauld acted
Louis Philippe, wig and all, to the life ; but, as I said to
M. Dupin, '*C'est tout naturel que M. Thiers ne permetterait
à personne de jouer Louis Philippe que lui-même.*' . . . There
is a wonderful pointer here that has been advertised for
sale for twelve hundred francs. A friend of mine went
to see him, and, after mounting up to a little garret about
the size of a chessboard, *au vingt-septième,* he interrogated
the owner as to the dog's education and acquirements, to
which the man replied, '*Pour ça, monsieur, c'est un chien
parfait. Je lui ai tout appris moi-même dans ma chambre.*'* After this my friend did not sing 'Together let us
range the fields !' . . . Last week I met Colonel Potter

---

* "As for that, sir, the dog is perfect. I have myself taught him everything *in my own room !*"

M'Queen, who was warm in his praises of you, and the great good your 'Michael Armstrong'" (the factory story) " had done. . . . Last Thursday despatches arrived, and Lord Granville had to start for London at a moment's notice. I was in hopes this beastly ministry were out! But no such luck! For they are a compound of glue, sticking-plaster, wax, and vice—the most adhesive of all known mixtures."

Before concluding my recollections of Rosina, Lady Lytton Bulwer, I think it right to say that I consider myself to have perfectly sufficient grounds for feeling certain that the whispers which were circulated in a cowardly and malignant fashion against the correctness of her conduct as a woman were wholly unfounded. Her failings and tendency to failings lay in a quite different direction. I knew perfectly well the person whose name was mentioned scandalously in connection with hers, and knew the whole history of the relationship that existed between them. The gentleman in question was for years Lady Bulwer's constant and steadfast friend. It is quite true that he would fain have been something more, but true also that his friendship survived the absolute rejection of all warmer sentiments by the object of it. It was almost a matter of course that such a woman as Lady Bulwer, living unprotected in the midst of such a society as that of Florence in those days, should be so slandered. And were it not that there were very few if any persons at the time, and I think certainly not one still left, able to speak upon the subject with such *connaissance de cause* as I can, I should not have alluded to it.

She was an admirably charming companion before the footlights of the world's stage—not so uniformly charming behind its scenes, for her unreasonableness always and her occasional violence were very difficult to deal with. But she was, as Dickens' poor Jo says in " Bleak House," " werry good to me !"

CHAPTER XXV.

IN FLORENCE.

AFTER some little time and trouble we found an apartment in the Palazzo Berti, in the ominously named Via dei Malcontenti. It was so called because it was at one time the road to the Florentine Tyburn. Our house was the one next to the east end of the church of Santa Croce. Our rooms looked on to a large garden, and were pleasant enough. We witnessed from our windows the building of the new steeple of Santa Croce, which was completed before we left the house.

It was built in great measure by an Englishman, a Mr. Sloane, a fervent Catholic, who was at that time one of the best-known figures in the English colony at Florence. He was a large contributor to the recently completed façade of the Duomo in Florence, and to many other benevolent and pietistic good works. He had been tutor in the Russian Boutourlin family, and when acting in that capacity had been taken, by reason of his geological acquirements, to see some copper mines in the Volterra district, which the grand duke had conceded to a company under whose administration they were going utterly to the bad. Sloane came, saw, and eventually conquered. In conjunction with Horace Hall, the then well-known and popular partner in the bank of Signor Emanuele Fenzi (one of whose sons married an English wife, and is still my very good and forty-years-old friend), he obtained a new concession of the mines from the grand duke on very favorable terms, and by the time I made his acquaintance had become a wealthy man. I fancy the Halls, Horace and his much-esteemed brother Alfred (who survived him many years, and was the father of a family, one of the most respected and popular of the English colony during the whole of my Florence life), subsequently consid-

15

ered themselves to have been shouldered out of the enterprise by a certain unhandsome treatment on the part of
the fortunate tutor. What may have been the exact history of the matter I do not know. But I do know that
Sloane always remained on very intimate terms with the
grand duke, and was a power in the inmost circles of the
ecclesiastic world.

He used to give great dinners on Friday, the principal
object of which seemed to be to show how magnificent a
feast could be given without infringing by a hair's-breadth
the rule of the Church. And admirably he succeeded in
showing how entirely the spirit and intention of the
Church in prescribing a fast could be made of none effect by a skilfully managed observance of the letter of
its law.

The only opportunity I ever had of conversing with
Cardinal Wiseman was in Casa Sloane. And what I
chiefly remember of his eminence was his evident annoyance at the ultra-demonstrative zeal of the female portion
of the mixed Catholic and Protestant assembly, who *would*
kneel and kiss his hand. A schoolmaster meeting boys in
society, who, instantly on his appearance should begin un-
buttoning their brace buttons behind, would hardly appreciate the recognition more gratefully.

Within a very few weeks of our establishment in Casa
Berti my mother's home became, as usual, a centre of attraction and pleasant intercourse, and her weekly Friday
receptions were always crowded. If I were to tell everything of what I remember in connection with those days,
I should produce such a book as *non dî, non homines, non
concessere volumnæ*—a book such as neither publishers,
nor readers, nor the *columns* of the critical journals would
tolerate, and should fill my pages with names, which, however interesting they may still be for me, would hardly
have any interest for the public, however gentle or pensive.

One specialty, and that not a pleasant one, of a life so
protracted as mine has been in the midst of such a society
as that of Florence in those days, is the enormous quantity of the names which turn the tablets of memory into
palimpsests, not twice, but fifty times written over !—un-

pleasant, not from the thronging *in* of the motley company, but from the inevitable passing *out* of them from the field of vision. One's recollections come to resemble those of the spectator of a phantasmagoric show. Processions of heterogeneous figures, almost all of them connected in some way or other with more or less pleasant memories, troop across the magic circle of light, only, alack! to vanish into uttermost night when they pass beyond its limit. Of course all this is inevitable from the migratory nature of such a society as that which was gathered together on the banks of the Arno.

Some fixtures—comparatively fixtures—of course there were, who gave to our moving quicksand-like society some degree of cohesion.

Chief among these was, of course, the British minister—at the time of our arrival in Florence, and many years afterwards — Lord Holland. A happier instance of the right man in the right place could hardly be met with. At his great *omnium-gatherum* dinners and receptions— his hospitality was of the most catholic and generous sort —both he and Lady Holland (how pretty she then was there is her very clever portrait by Watts to testify) never failed to win golden opinions from all sorts and conditions of men and women. And in the smaller circle, which assembled in their rooms yet more frequently, they showed to yet greater advantage, for Lord Holland was one of the most amusing talkers I ever knew.

Of course many of those who ought to have been grateful for their admission to the minister's large receptions were discontented at not being invited to the smaller ones. And it was by some of these malcontents with more wit than reason that Lady Holland was accused of receiving in two very distinct fashions—*en ménage* and *en ménagerie.* The *mot* was a successful one, and nobody was more amused by it than the *spirituelle* lady of whom it was said. It was too happy a *mot* not to have been stolen by divers pilferers of such articles, and adapted to other persons and other occasions. But it was originally spoken of the time, place, and person here stated to have been the object of it.

Generally, in such societies in foreign capitals, a fruitful source of jealousy and discord is found in the necessary selection of those to be presented at the court of the reigning sovereign. But this, as far as I remember, was avoided in those halcyon days by the simple expedient of presenting all who desired it. And that Lord Holland *was* the right man in the right place as regards this matter the following anecdote will show.

When Mr. Hamilton became British minister at Florence, it was announced that his intention was, for the avoiding of all trouble and jealousy on the subject, to adhere strictly to the proper and recognized rule. He would present everybody and anybody who had been presented at home, and nobody who had not been so presented. And he commenced his administration on these lines, and the grand duke's receptions at the Pitti became notably weeded. But this had not gone on for more than two or three weeks before it was whispered in the minister's ear that the grand duke would be pleased if he were less strict in the matter of his presentations. " Oh !" said Hamilton, " that's what he wants ! *A la bonne heure !* He shall have them all, rag, tag, and bobtail." And so we returned to the *Saturnia regna* of " the good old times," and the duke was credibly reported to have said that he " kept the worst drawing-room in Europe." But, of course, his highness was thinking of the pockets of his liege Florentine letters of apartments and tradesmen, and was anxious only to make his city a favorite place of resort for the gold-bringing foreigners from that distant and barbarous western isle. The pope, you see, had the pull in the matter of gorgeous Church ceremonies, but he couldn't have the fertilizing barbarians dancing in the Vatican once a week !

One more anecdote I must find room for, because it is curiously illustrative in several ways of those *tempi passati, che non tornano più.* Florence was full of refugees from the political rigors of the papal government, who had for some time past found there an unmolested refuge. But the aspect of the times was becoming more and more alarming to Austria, and the *Duchini,* as we called the sovereigns of Modena and Parma ; and pressure was put on the duke by the pontifical government insisting on the demand that these refugees should be given up by Tuscany. Easy-going Tuscany, not yet in any wise alarmed for herself, fought off the demand for a while, but was at last driven to notify her intention of acceding to it. It was in these circumstances that Massino d' Azeglio came to me one morning, in the garden of our house in the Via del Giglio—the same in which the poet Milton lodged when he was in Florence—to which we had by that time moved, and told me that he wanted me to do something for him. Of course I professed all readiness, and he went on to tell me of the critical and dangerous position in which the refugees of whom I have spoken were placed, and said that I must go to Lord Holland and ask him to give them British passports. He urged that nothing could be easier, that no objection could possibly be taken to it; that the Tuscan government was by no means desirous of giving up these men, and would only be too glad to get out of it; that England both at Malta and in the Ionian Islands had plenty of Italian subjects—and, in short, I undertook the mission, I confess with very small hopes of success. Lord Holland laughed aloud when I told my tale, and said he thought it was about the most audacious request that had ever been made to a British minister. But he ended by granting it. Doubtless he knew very well the truth of what d' Azeglio had stated—that the Tuscan government would be much too well pleased to ask any questions; and the passports were given.

It was not long after our establishment in the Via dei Malcontenti that a great disaster came upon Florence and its inhabitants and guests. Arno was not in the habit of following the evil example of the Tiber by treating Florence as the latter so frequently did Rome. But in the winter of the year 1844 a terrible and unprecedented flood came. The rain fell in such torrents all one night that it was feared that the Arno, already much swollen, would not be able to carry off the waters with sufficient rapidity. I went out early in the morning before breakfast, in company with a younger brother of the Dr. Nicholson of Penrith whom I have mentioned, who happened to be visiting

us. We climbed to the top of Giotto's tower, and saw at
once the terrible extent and very serious character of the
misfortune. One third, at least, of Florence was under
water, and the flood was rapidly rising. Coming down
from our lofty observatory, we made our way to the
"Lung' Arno," as the river quays are called. And there
the sight was truly a terrible and a magnificent one. The
river, extending in one turbid, yellow, swirling mass from
the walls of the houses on the quay on one side to those
of the houses opposite, was bringing down with it fragments of timber, carcasses of animals, large quantities of
hay and straw—and amid the wreck we saw a cradle with
a child in it, safely navigating the tumbling waters ! It
was drawn to the window of a house by throwing a line
over it, and the infant navigator was none the worse.

But very great fears were entertained for the very ancient Ponte Vecchio, with its load of silversmiths' and
jewellers' shops, turning it from a bridge into a street—
the only remaining example in Europe, I believe, of a
fashion of construction once common. The water continued to rise as we stood watching it. Less than a foot
of space yet remained between the surface of the flood
and the keystone of the highest arch ; and it was thought
that if the water rose sufficiently to beat against the solid
superstructure of the bridge, it must have been swept
away. But at last came the cry from those who were
watching it close at hand, that for the last five minutes
the surface had been stationary ; and in another half-hour
it was followed by the announcement that the flood had
begun to decrease. Then there was an immense sensation of relief ; for the Florentines love their old bridge ;
and the crowd began to disperse.

All this time I had not had a mouthful of breakfast,
and we betook ourselves to Doney's *bottega* to get a cup
of coffee before going home. But when we attempted
this we found that it was more easily said than done. The
Via dei Malcontenti as well as the whole of the Piazza di
Santa Croce was some five feet under water. We succeeded, however, in getting aboard a large boat, which
was already engaged in carrying bread to the people in

the most deeply flooded parts of the town. But all difficulty was not over. Of course the street door of the Palazzo Berti was shut, and no earthly power could open it.
Our apartment was on the second floor. Our landlord's
family occupied the *primo*. Of course I could get in at
their windows and then go up-stairs. And we had a ladder in the boat; but the mounting to the first floor by
this ladder, placed on the little deck of the boat, as she
was rocked by the torrent, was no easy matter, especially
for me, who went first. Eventually, however, Nicholson
and I both entered the window, hospitably opened to receive us, in safety.

But it was one or two days before the flood subsided
sufficiently for us to be provisioned in any other manner
than by the boat; and for long years afterwards social
events were dated in Florence as having happened "before or after the flood." In those days, and for many
days subsequently to them, Florence did indeed—as I have
observed when speaking of the motives which induced us
to settle there—join to its other attractions that of being
an economical place of residence. Our money consisted
of piastres, pauls, and crazie. Eight of the latter were
equal to a paul, ten of which were equivalent to a piastre.
The value of the paul was, as nearly as possible, equal to
fivepence-halfpenny English. The lira—the original representative of the leading denomination of our own *l. s. d.*
—no longer existed in—the flesh I was going to say, but
rather in—the metal. And it is rather curious that, just
as the guinea remained, and indeed remains, a constantly
used term of speech after it has ceased to exist as current
coin, so the scudo remained, in Tuscany, no longer visible or current, but retained as an integer in accounts of
the larger sort. If you bought or sold house or land, for
instance, you talked of scudi. In more every-day matters
piastre or "francesconi" were the integers used, the latter
being only a synonym for the former. And the proportion in value of the scudo and the piastre was exactly the
same as that of the guinea and the sovereign, the former
being worth ten and a half pauls, and the latter ten. The
handsomest and best preserved coin ordinarily current

was the florin, worth two pauls and a half. Gold we rarely saw, but golden sequins (*zecchini*) were in existence, and were traditionally used, as it was said, for I have no experience in the matter, in the payment by the government of prizes won in the lottery.

Now, after this statement the reader will be in a position to appreciate the further information that a flask of excellent Chianti, of a quality rarely met with nowadays, was ordinarily sold for one paul. The flask contained (legal measure) seven troy pounds weight of liquid, or about three bottles. The same sum purchased a good fowl in the market. The subscription (*abbuonamento*) to the Pergola, the principal theatre, came to exactly two crazie and a half for each night of performance. This price admitted you only to the pit, but as you were perfectly free to enter any box in which there were persons of your acquaintance, the admission in the case of a bachelor, permanently or temporarily such, was all that was necessary to him. And the price of the boxes was small in proportion.

These boxes were indeed the drawing-rooms in which very much of the social intercourse of the *beau monde* was carried on. The performances were not very frequently changed (two operas frequently running through an entire season), and people went four or five times a week to hear, or rather to be present at, the same representation. And except on first nights or some other such occasion, or during the singing of the well-known tid-bits of any opera, there was an amount of chattering in the house which would have made the hair of a *fanatico per la musica* stand on end. There was also an exceedingly comfortable but very parsimoniously lighted large room, which was a grand flirting-place, where people sat very patiently during the somewhat long operation of having their names called aloud, as their carriages arrived, by an official, who knew the names and addresses of us all. We also knew *his* mode of adapting the names of foreigners to his Italian organs. "Hasa" (Florentine for *casa*) "Trolo-pé," with a long-drawn-out accent on the last vowel, was the absolutely fatal signal for the sudden breaking-up of many a pleasant chat.

Florence was also, in those days, an especially economical place for those to whom it was pleasant to enjoy, during the whole of the gay season, as many balls, concerts, and other entertainments as they could possibly desire, without the necessity, or indeed the possibility, of putting themselves to the expense of giving anything in return. There was a weekly ball at the Pitti Palace, and another at the Casino dei Nobili, which latter was supported entirely by the Florentine aristocracy. There were two or three balls at the houses of the foreign ministers, and generally one or two given by two or three wealthy Florentine nobles—there were a few, but very few such.

Perhaps the pleasantest of all these were the balls at the Pitti. They were so entirely *sans gêne*. No court dress was required save on the first day of the year, when it was *de rigueur*. But absence on that occasion in no way excluded the absentee from the other balls. Indeed, save to a new-comer, no invitations to foreigners were issued, it being understood that all who had been there once were welcome ever after. The Pitti balls were not by any means concluded, but rather divided into two, by a very handsome and abundant supper, at which, to tell tales out of school (but then the offenders have no doubt mostly gone over to the majority), the guests used to behave abominably. The English would seize the plates of *bonbons* and empty the contents bodily into their coat pockets. The ladies would do the same with their pocket-handkerchiefs. But the duke's liege subjects carried on their depredations on a far bolder scale. I have seen large portions of fish, sauce and all, packed up in a newspaper, and deposited in a pocket. I have seen fowls and ham share the same fate without any newspaper at all. I have seen jelly carefully wrapped in an Italian countess's laced *mouchoir!* I think the servants must have had orders not to allow entire bottles of wine to be carried away, for I never saw that attempted, and can imagine no other reason why. I remember that those who affected to be knowing old hands used to recommend one to specially pay attention to the Grand Ducal Rhine wine, and remember, too, conceiving a suspicion that certain of these

15*

connoisseurs based their judgment in this matter wholly on their knowledge that the duke possessed estates in Bohemia!

The English were exceedingly numerous in Florence at that time, and they were reinforced by a continually increasing American contingent, though our cousins had not yet begun to come in numbers rivalling our own, as has been the case recently. By-the-bye, it occurs to me that I never saw an American pillaging the supper-table; though, I may add, that American ladies would accept any amount of *bonbons* from English blockade-runners.

And the mention of American ladies at the Pitti reminds me of a really very funny story, which may be told without offence to any one now living. I have a notion that I have seen this story of mine told somewhere, with a change of names and circumstances that spoil it, after the fashion of the people "who steal other folks' stories and disfigure them, as gypsies do stolen children to escape detection."

I had one evening at the Pitti, some years, however, after my first appearance there, a very pretty and naïvely charming American lady on my arm, whom I was endeavoring to amuse by pointing out to her all the personages whom I thought might interest her, as we walked through the rooms. Dear old Dymock, the champion, was in Florence that winter, and was at the Pitti that night. I dare say that there may be many now who do not know without being told, that Dymock, the last champion, as I am almost afraid I must call him—though doubtless Scrivelsby must still be held by the ancient tenure—was a very small old man, a clergyman, and not at all the sort of individual to answer to the popular idea of a champion. He was sitting in a nook all by himself, and not looking very heroic or very happy as we passed, and, nudging my companion's arm, I whispered, "That is the champion." The interest I excited was greater than I had calculated on, for the lady made a dead stop, and facing round to gaze at the old gentleman, said, "Why, you don't tell me so! I should never have thought that that could be the fellow who licked Heenan! *But he looks a plucky little chap!*"

Perhaps the reader may have forgotten, or even never known, that the championship of the pugilistic world had then recently been won by Sayers—I think that was the name—in a fight with an antagonist of the name of Heenan. In fact it was I, and not my fair companion, who was a muff, for having imagined that a young American woman, nearly fresh from the other side of the Atlantic, was likely to know or ever have heard anything about the champion of England.

There happened to be several Lincolnshire men that year in Florence, and there was a dinner at which I, as one of the "web-footed," by descent if not birth, was present, and I told them the story of my Pitti catastrophe. The lady's concluding words produced an effect which may be imagined more easily than described.

The grand duke at these Pitti balls used to show himself and take part in them as little as might be. The grand duchess used to walk through the rooms sometimes. The grand duchess, a Neapolitan princess, was not beloved by the Tuscans ; and I am disposed to believe that she did not deserve their affection. But there was at that time another lady at the Pitti, the dowager grand duchess, the widow of the late grand duke. She had been a Saxon princess, and was very favorably contrasted with the reigning duchess in graciousness of manner, in appearance—for though a considerably older, she was still an elegant-looking woman—and, according to the popular estimate, in character. She also would occasionally walk through the rooms ; but her object, and indeed that of the duke, seemed to be to attract as little attention as possible.

Only on the first night of the year, when we were all in *gran gala*, *i. e.*, in court-suits or uniform, did any personal communication with the grand duke take place. His manner, when anybody was presented to him on these or other occasions, was about as bad and unprincely as can well be conceived. His clothes never fitted him. He used to support himself on one foot, hanging his head towards that side, and occasionally changing the posture of both foot and head, always simultaneously. And he always

appeared to be struggling painfully with the consciousness that he had nothing to say. It was on one of these
occasions that an American new arrival was presented to
him by Mr. Maquay, the banker, who always did that office
for Americans, the United States having then no representative at the grand ducal court. Maquay, thinking to
help the duke, whispered in his ear that the gentleman
was connected by descent with the great Washington;
upon which the duke, changing his foot, said, "*Ah! le
grand Vash!*" His manner was that of a lethargic and
not wide-awake man. When strangers would sometimes
venture some word of compliment on the prosperity and
contentment of the Tuscans his reply invariably was,
"*Sono tranquilli*"—they are quiet. But, in truth, much
more might have been said; for, assuredly, Tuscany was
a Land of Goshen in the midst of the peninsula. There
was neither want nor discontent (save among a very small
knot of politicians, who might almost have been counted
on the hand) nor crime. There was at Florence next to
no police of any kind, but the streets were perfectly safe
by night or by day.

There was a story, much about that time, which made
some noise in Europe, and was very disingenuously made
use of, as such stories are, of a certain Florentine and his
wife, named Madiai, who had been, it was asserted, persecuted for reading the Bible. It was not so. They were
"persecuted" for, *i. e.*, restrained from, preaching to others that they ought to read it, which is, though doubtless
a bad, yet a very different thing.

I believe the grand duke (*gran ciuco*—great ass—as
his irreverent Tuscans nicknamed him) was a good and
kindly man, and, under the circumstances and to the extent of his abilities, not a bad ruler. The phrase which
Giusti applied to him, and which the inimitable talent of
the satirist has made more durable than any other memorial of the poor *gran ciuco* is likely to be, "*asciuga tasche
e maremme*"—he dries up pockets and marshes—is as unjust as such *mots* of satirists are wont to be. The drain-
ing of the great marshes of the Chiana, between Arezzo
and Chiusi, was a well-considered and most beneficent

work on a magnificent scale, which, so far from "drying pockets," added enormously to the wealth of the country, and is now adding very appreciably to the prosperity of Italy. Nor was Giusti's reproach in any way merited by the grand ducal government. The grand duke, personally, was a very wealthy man, as well as, in respect to his own habits, a most simple liver. The necessary expenses of the little state were small, and taxation was so light that a comparison between that of the Saturnian days in question and that under which the Tuscans of the present day not unreasonably groan might afford a text for some very far-reaching speculations. The Tuscans of the present day may preach any theological doctrines they please to any who will listen to them, or, indeed, to those who won't, but it would be curious to know how many individuals among them consider that, or any other recently acquired liberty, well bought at the price they pay for it.

The grand duke was certainly not a great or wise man. He was one of those men of whom their friends habitually say that they are "no fools," or "not such fools as they look," which generally may be understood to mean that the individual spoken of cannot, with physiological accuracy, be considered a *crétin*. Nevertheless, in his case the expression was doubtless accurately true. He was not such a fool as he looked, for his appearance was certainly not that of a wise, or even an intelligent man.

One story is told of him which I have reason to believe perfectly true, and which is so characteristic of the man and of the time that I must not deprive the reader of it.

It was the custom that on St. John's Day the duke should visit and inspect the small body of troops who were lodged in the Fortezza di San Giovanni, or Fortezza da Basso, as it was popularly called, in contradistinction from another fort on the high ground above the Boboli Gardens. And it was expected that, on these occasions, the sovereign should address a few words to his soldiers. So the duke, resting his person first on one leg and then on the other, after his fashion, stood in front of the two or three score of men drawn up in line before him, and, after telling them that obedience to their officers and attachment to duty were the especial virtues of a soldier, he continued, " Above all, my men, I desire that you should remember the duties and observances of our holy religion, and—and—" (here, having said all he had to say, his highness was at a loss for a conclusion to his harangue. But, looking down on the ground as he strove to find a fitting peroration, he observed that the army's shoes were sadly in want of the blacking-brush, so he concluded, with more of animation and significance than he had before evinced) "and keep your shoes clean !"

I may find room further on to say a few words of what I remember of the revolution which dethroned poor *gran ciuco*. But I may as well conclude here what I have to say of him by relating the manner of his final exit from the soil of Tuscany, of which the malicious among the few who knew the circumstances were wont to say—very unjustly—that nothing in his reign became him like the leaving of it. I saw him pass out from the Porta San Gallo on his way to Bologna among a crowd of his late subjects, who all lifted their hats, though not without some satirical cries of " *Addio, sai !*" " *Buon viaggio !*" But a few—a very few—friends accompanied his carriage to the papal frontier, an invisible line on the bleak Apennines, unmarked by any habitation. There he descended from his carriage to receive their last adieus, and there was much lowly bowing as they stood on the highway. The duke, not unmoved, bowed lowly in return, but, unfortunately, backing as he did so, tripped himself up with characteristic awkwardness, and tumbled backwards on a heap of broken stones prepared for the road, with his heels in the air, and exhibiting to his unfaithful Tuscans and ungrateful duchy, as a last remembrance of him, a full view of a part of his person rarely put forward on such occasions.

And so *exeunt* from the sight of men and from history a grand duke and a grand duchy.

CHAPTER XXVI.

CHARLES DICKENS.

IT was not long after the flood in Florence—it seems to me, as I write, that I might almost leave out the two last words!—that I saw Dickens for the first time. One morning in Casa Berti my mother was most agreeably surprised by a card brought in to her with "Mr. and Mrs. Charles Dickens" on it. We had been among his heartiest admirers from the early days of "Pickwick." I don't think we had happened to see the "Sketches by Boz." But my uncle Milton used to come to Hadley full of "the last 'Pickwick,'" and swearing that each number out-Pickwicked Pickwick. And it was with the greatest curiosity and interest that we saw the creator of all this enjoyment enter in the flesh.

We were at first disappointed, and disposed to imagine there must be some mistake. No! *that* is not the man who wrote "Pickwick"! What we saw was a dandified, pretty-boy-looking sort of figure; singularly young-looking, I thought, with a slight flavor of the whipper-snapper genus of humanity.

Here is Carlyle's description of his appearance at about that period of his life, quoted from Froude's "History of Carlyle's Life in London":

"He is a fine little fellow—Boz—I think. Clear-blue, intelligent eyes, eyebrows that he arches amazingly, large, protrusive, rather loose mouth, a face of most extreme mobility, which he shuttles about—eyebrows, eyes, mouth, and all—in a very singular manner when speaking. Surmount this with a loose coil of common-colored hair, and set on it a small, compact figure, very small, and dressed *à la* D'Orsay rather than well—this is Pickwick. For the rest, a quiet, shrewd-looking little fellow, who seems to guess pretty well what he is and what others are."

One may perhaps venture to suppose that, had the second of these guesses been less accurate, the description might have been a less kindly one.

But there are two errors to be noted in this sketch, graphic as it is. Firstly, Dickens' eyes were not blue, but of a very distinct and brilliant hazel—the color traditionally assigned to Shakespeare's eyes. Secondly, Dickens, although truly of a slight, compact figure, was *not a very* small man. I do not think he was below the average middle height. I speak from my remembrance of him at a later day, when I had become intimate with him; but, curiously enough, I find, on looking back into my memory, that, if I had been asked to describe him as I first saw him, I, too, should have said that he was very small. Carlyle's words refer to Dickens' youth soon after he had published "Pickwick"; and no doubt at this period he had a look of delicacy, almost of effeminacy, if one may accept Maclise's well-known portrait as a truthful record, which might give those who saw him the impression of his being smaller and more fragile in build than was the fact. In later life he lost this D'Orsay look completely, and was bronzed and reddened by wind and weather like a seaman.

In fact, when I saw him subsequently in London, I think I should have passed him in the street without recognizing him. I never saw a man so changed.

Any attempt to draw a complete pen-and-ink portrait of Dickens has been rendered forevermore superfluous, if it were not presumptuous, by the masterly and exhaustive life of him by John Forster. But one may be allowed to record one's own impressions, and any small incident or anecdote which memory holds, on the grounds set forth by the great writer himself, who says in the introduction to the "American Notes" (first printed in the biography): "Very many works having just the same scope and range have been already published. But I think that these two volumes stand in need of no apology on that account. The interest of such productions, if they have any, lies in the varying impressions made by the same novel things on different minds, and not in new discoveries or extraordinary adventures."

At Florence Dickens made a pilgrimage to Landor's villa, the owner being then absent in England, and gathered a leaf of ivy from Fiesole to carry back to the veteran poet, as narrated by Mr. Forster. Dickens is as accurate as a topographer in his description of the villa as looked down on from Fiesole. How often—ah, *how* often! —have I looked down from that same dwarf wall over the matchless view where Florence shows the wealth of villas that Ariosto declares made it equivalent to two Romes!

Dickens was only thirty-three when I first saw him, being just two years my junior. I have said what he appeared to me then. As I knew him afterwards, and to the end of his days, he was a strikingly manly man, not only in appearance, but in bearing. The lustrous brilliancy of his eyes was very striking. And I do not think that I have ever seen it noticed that those wonderful eyes which saw so much and so keenly were appreciably, though to a very slight degree, near-sighted eyes. Very few persons, even among those who knew him well, were aware of this, for Dickens never used a glass. But he continually exercised his vision by looking at distant objects, and making them out as well as he could without any artificial assistance. It was an instance of that force of will in him which compelled a naturally somewhat delicate frame to comport itself like that of an athlete. Mr. Forster somewhere says of him, " Dickens' habits were robust, but his health was not." This is entirely true as far as my observation extends.

Of the general charm of his manner I despair of giving any idea to those who have not seen or known him. This was a charm by no means dependent on his genius. He might have been the great writer he was and yet not have warmed the social atmosphere wherever he appeared with that summer glow which seemed to attend him. His laugh was brimful of enjoyment. There was a peculiar humorous protest in it when recounting or hearing anything specially absurd, as who should say "'Pon my soul this is *too* ridiculous! This passes all bounds!" and bursting out afresh as though the sense of the ridiculous overwhelmed him like a tide, which carried all hearers away with it, and which I well remember.   His enthusiasm was boundless.   It entered into everything he said or did.   It belonged doubtless to that amazing fertility and wealth of ideas and feeling that distinguished his genius.

No one having any knowledge of the profession of literature can read Dickens' private letters and not stand amazed at the unbounded affluence of imagery, sentiment, humor, and keen observation which he poured out in them.   There was no stint, no reservation for trade purposes.   So with his conversation—every thought, every fancy, every feeling was expressed with the utmost vivacity and intensity, but a vivacity and intensity compatible with the most singular delicacy and nicety of touch when delicacy and nicety of touch were needed.

What were called the exaggerations of his writing were due, I have no doubt, to the extraordinary luminosity of his imagination.   He saw and rendered such an individuality as Mr. Pecksniff's or Mrs. Nickleby's, for instance, something after the same fashion as a solar microscope renders any object observed through it.   The world in general beholds its Pecksniffs and its Mrs. Nicklebys through a different medium.   And at any rate Dickens got at the quintessence of his creatures, and enables us all, in our various measures, to perceive it too.   The proof of this is that we are constantly not only quoting the sayings and doings of his immortal characters, but are recognizing other sayings and doings as what *they* would have said or done.

But it is impossible for one who knew him as I did to confine what he remembers of him either to traits of outward appearance or to appreciations of his genius.   I must say a few, a very few words of what Dickens appeared to me as a man.   I think that an epithet, which, much and senselessly as it has been misapplied and degraded, is yet, when rightly used, perhaps the grandest that can be applied to a human being, was especially applicable to him. He was a *hearty* man, a large-hearted man that is to say. He was perhaps the largest-hearted man I ever knew.   I think he made a nearer approach to obeying the divine precept, "Love thy neighbor as thyself," than one man in a hundred thousand. His benevolence, his active, energizing desire for good to all God's creatures, and restless anxiety to be in some way active for the achieving of it, were unceasing and busy in his heart ever and always.

But he had a sufficient capacity for a virtue which, I think, seems to be moribund among us — the virtue of moral indignation. Men and their actions were not all much of a muchness to him. There was none of the indifferentism of that pseudo-philosophic moderation which, when a scoundrel or scoundrelly action is on the *tapis*, hints that there is much to be said on both sides. Dickens hated a mean action or a mean sentiment as one hates something that is physically loathsome to the sight and touch. And he could be angry, as those with whom he had been angry did not very readily forget.

And there was one other aspect of his moral nature, of which I am reminded by an observation which Mr. Forster records as having been made by Mrs. Carlyle. "Light and motion flashed from every part of it [his face]. It was as if made of steel." The first part of the phrase is true and graphic enough, but the image offered by the last words appears to me a singularly infelicitous one. There was nothing of the hardness or of the (moral) sharpness of steel about the expression of Dickens' face and features. Kindling mirth and genial fun were the expressions which those who casually met him in society were habituated to find there, but those who knew him well knew also well that a tenderness, gentle and sympathetic as that of a woman, was a mood that his surely never "steely" face could express exquisitely, and did express frequently.

I used to see him very frequently in his latter years. I generally came to London in the summer, and one of the first things on my list was a visit to 20 Wellington Street. Then would follow sundry other visits and meetings—to Tavistock House, to Gadshill, at Verey's in Regent Street, a place he much patronized, etc., etc. I remember one day meeting Chauncy Hare Townsend at Tavistock House and thinking him a very singular and not particularly agreeable man. Edwin Landseer, I remember, dined there the same day. But he had been a friend of my mother's, and was my acquaintance of long, long years before.

Of course we had much and frequent talk about Italy, and I may say that our ideas and opinions, and especially feelings on that subject, were always, I think, in unison. Our agreement respecting English social and political matters was less perfect. But I think that it would have become more nearly so had his life been prolonged as mine has been. And the approximation would, if I am not much mistaken, have been brought about by a movement of mind on his part, which already I think those who knew him best will agree with me in thinking had commenced. We differed on many points of politics. But there is one department of English social life—one with which I am probably more intimately acquainted than with any other, and which has always been to me one of much interest—our public-school system—respecting which our agreement was complete. And I cannot refrain from quoting. The opinion which he expresses is as true as if he had, like me, an eight years' experience of the system he is speaking of. And the passage which I am about to give is very remarkable as an instance of the singular acumen, insight, and power of sympathy which enabled him to form so accurately correct an opinion on a matter of which he might be supposed to know nothing.

"In July," says Mr. Forster, writing of the year 1858-9, "he took earnest part in the opening efforts on behalf of the Royal Dramatic College, which he supplemented later by a speech for the establishment of schools for actors' children, in which he took occasion to declare his belief that there were no institutions in England so socially liberal as its public schools, and that there was nowhere in the country so complete an absence of servility to mere rank, position, and riches. 'A boy there'" (Mr. Forster here quotes Dickens' own words) "'is always what his abilities and personal qualities make him. We may differ about the curriculum and other matters, but of the frank, free, manly, independent spirit preserved in our public schools I apprehend there can be no kind of question.'"

I have in my possession a great number of letters from

Dickens, some of which might probably have been published in the valuable collection of his letters published by his sister-in-law and eldest daughter had they been get-at-able at the time when they might have been available for that publication.* But I was at Rome, and the letters were safely stowed away in England in such sort that it would have needed a journey to London to get at them.

I was for several years a frequent contributor to *Household Words*, my contributions for the most part consisting of what I considered tid-bits from the byways of Italian history, which the persevering plough of my reading turned up from time to time.

In one case I remember the article was sent " to order." I was dining with him after I had just had all the remaining hairs on my head made to stand on end by the perusal of the officially published " Manual for Confessors," as approved by superior authority for the dioceses of Tuscany. I was full of the subject, and made, I fancy, the hairs of some who sat at table with me stand on end also. Dickens said, with nailing forefinger levelled at me, " Give us that for *Household Words*. Give it us just as you have now been telling it to us "—which I accordingly did. Whether the publication of that article was in any wise connected with the fact that when I wished to purchase a second copy of that most extraordinary work I was told that it was out of print, and not to be had, I do not know. Of course it was kept as continually in print as the " Latin Grammar," for the constant use of the class for whom it was provided, and who most assuredly could not have found their way safely through the wonderful intricacies of the confessional without it. And equally, of course, the publishers of so largely circulated a work did not succeed in preventing me from obtaining a second copy of it.

---

* Some of the letters in question—such as I had with me—were sent to London for that purpose. I do not remember now which were and which were not. But if it should be the case that any of those printed here have been printed before, I do not think any reader will object to having them again brought under his eye.

Many of the letters addressed to me by Dickens concerned more or less my contributions to his periodical, and many more are not of a nature to interest the public even though they came from him. But I may give a few extracts from three or four of them.*

Here is a passage from a letter dated 3d of December, 1861, which my vanity will not let me suppress.

"Yes; the Christmas number *was* intended as a conveyance of all friendly greetings in season and out of season. As to its lesson, you need it almost as little as any man I know; for all your study and seclusion conduce to the general good, and disseminate truths that men cannot too earnestly take to heart. Yes, a capital story that of 'The Two Seaborn Babbies,' and wonderfully droll, I think. I may say so without blushing, for it is not by me. It was done by Wilkie Collins."

Here is another short note, not a little gratifying to me personally, but not without interest of a larger kind to the reader :

"*Tuesday, 15th November,* 1859.

"MY DEAR TROLLOPE,—I write this hasty word, just as the post leaves, to ask you this question, which this moment occurs to me.

"Montalembert, in his suppressed treatise, asks, 'What wrong has Pope Pius the Ninth done?' Don't you think you can very pointedly answer that question in these pages? If you cannot, nobody in Europe can.

"Very faithfully yours always,   CHARLES DICKENS."

Some, some few, may remember the interest excited by the treatise to which the above letter refers. No doubt I could, and doubtless did, though I forget all about it, answer the question propounded by the celebrated French writer. But there was little hope of my doing it as "pointedly" as my correspondent would have done it himself. The answer, which might well have consisted of a succinct statement of all the difficulties of the position with which Italy was then struggling, had to confine itself to the limits of an article in *All The Year Round*, and needed, in truth, to be pointed. I have observed that, in all our many conversations on Italian matters, Dickens' views and opinions coincided with my own, without, I think, any point of

---

* I wish it to be observed that any letters, or parts of letters, from Dickens here printed are published with the permission and authorization of his sister-in-law, Miss Georgina Hogarth.

divergence.   Very specially was this the case as regards
all that concerned the Vatican and the doings of the
Curia.   How well I remember his arched eyebrows and
laughing eyes when I told him of Garibaldi's proposal
that all priests should be summarily executed !   I think
it modified his ideas of the possible utility of Garibaldi as
a politician.

Then comes an invitation to "my Falstaff house at
Gadshill."

Here is a letter of the 17th February, 1866, which I will
give *in extenso*, bribed again by the very flattering words
in which the writer speaks of our friendship:

"MY DEAR TROLLOPE,—I am heartily glad to hear from you.   It was such
a disagreeable surprise to find that you had left London [I had been
called away at an hour's notice] on the occasion of your last visit without
my having seen you, that I have never since got it out of my mind.   I felt
as if it were my fault (though I don't know how that can have been), and
as if I had somehow been traitorous to the earnest and affectionate regard
with which you have inspired me.

"The lady's verses are accepted by the editorial potentate, and shall
presently appear.   [I am ashamed to say that I totally forget who the
lady was.]

" I am not quite well, and am being touched up (or down) by the doctors.   Whether the irritation of mind I had to endure pending the discussions of a preposterous clerical body called a Convocation, and whether the
weakened hopefulness of mankind which such a dash of the Middle Ages
in the color and pattern of 1866 engenders, may have anything to do with
it, I don't know.

"What a happy man you must be in having a new house to work at.
When it is quite complete, and the roc's egg hung up, I suppose you will
get rid of it bodily and turn to at another.   [*Absit omen !*   At this very
moment, while I transcribe this letter, I *am* turning to at another.]

" *Daily News* correspondent [as I then for a short time was], Novel,
and Hospitality !   Enough to do, indeed !   Perhaps the day *might* be ad-
vantageously made longer for such work — or say life.   [Ah ! if the small
matters rehearsed had been all, I could more contentedly have put up with
the allowance of four-and-twenty hours.]   And yet I don't know.   Like
enough we should all do less if we had time to do more in.

"Layard was with us for a couple of days a little while ago, and brought
the last report of you, and of your daughter, who seems to have made a
great impression on him.   I wish he had had the keepership of the National Gallery, for I don't think his government will hold together through
many weeks.

"I wonder whether you thought as highly of Gibson's art as the lady did
who wrote the verses.   I must say that I did *not*, and that I thought it of

a mechanical sort, with no great amount of imagination in it. It seemed to me as if he ' didn't find me ' in that, as the servants say, but only provided me with carved marble, and expected me to furnish myself with as much idea as I could afford.

"Very faithfully yours, CHARLES DICKENS."

I do not remember the verses, though I feel confident that the lady who sent them through me must have been a very charming person. As to Gibson, no criticism could be sounder. I had a considerable liking for Gibson as a man, and admiration for his character, but as regards his ideal productions I think Dickens hits the right nail on the head.

In another letter of the same year, 25th July, after a page of remarks on editorial matters, he writes :

"If Italy could but achieve some brilliant success in arms! That she does not, causes, I think, some disappointment here, and makes her sluggish friends more sluggish, and her open enemies more powerful. I fear, too, that the Italian ministry have lost an excellent opportunity of repairing the national credit in London city, and have borrowed money in France for the poor consideration of lower interest, which [*sic*, but I suspect *which* must be a slip of the pen for *than*] they could have got in England, greatly to the re-establishment of a reputation for public good faith. As to Louis Napoleon, his position in the whole matter is to me like his position in Europe at all times, simply disheartening and astounding. Between Prussia and Austria there is, in my mind (but for Italy), not a pin to choose. If each could smash the other I should be, as to those two powers, perfectly satisfied. But I feel for Italy almost as if I were an Italian born. So here you have in brief my confession of faith.

"Mr. Home [as he by that time called himself — when he was staying in my house his name was Hume], after trying to come out as an actor, first at Fechter's (where I had the honor of stopping him short), and then at the St. James's Theatre under Miss Herbert (where he was twice announced, and each time very mysteriously disappeared from the bills), was announced at the little theatre in Dean Street, Soho, as a ' great attraction for one night only,' to play last Monday. An appropriately dirty little rag of a bill, fluttering in the window of an obscure dairy behind the Strand, gave me this intelligence last Saturday. It is like enough that even that striking business did not come off, for I believe the public to have found out the scoundrel; in which lively and sustaining hope this leaves me at present. Ever faithfully yours, CHARLES DICKENS."

Here is a letter which, as may be easily imagined, I value much. It was written on the 2d of November, 1866, and reached me at Brest. It was written to congratulate me on my second marriage, and among the great number which I received on that occasion is one of the most warm-hearted :

"My dear Trollope,—I should have written immediately to congratulate you on your then approaching marriage, and to assure you of my most cordial and affectionate interest in all that nearly concerns you, had I known how best to address you.

"No friend that you have can be more truly attached to you than I am. I congratulate you with all my heart, and believe that your marriage will stand high upon the list of happy ones. As to your wife's winning a high reputation out of your house — if you care for that; it is not much as an addition to the delights of love and peace and a suitable companion for life—I have not the least doubt of her power to make herself famous.

"I little thought what an important master of the ceremonies I was when I first gave your present wife an introduction to your mother. Bear me in your mind then as the unconscious instrument of your having given your best affection to a worthy object, and I shall be the best-paid master of the ceremonies since Nash drove his coach and six through the streets of Bath. Faithfully yours, Charles Dickens."

Among a heap of others I find a note of invitation written on the 9th of July, 1867, in which he says : "My 'readings' secretary, whom I am despatching to America at the end of this week, will dine with me at Verey's in Regent Street at six exact to be wished God-speed. There will only be besides, Wills, Wilkie Collins, and Mr. Arthur Chappell. Will you come ? No dress. Evening left quite free."

I went, and the God-speed party was a very pleasant one. But I liked best to have him, as I frequently had, all to myself. I suppose I am not, as Johnson said, a "clubbable" man. At all events I highly appreciate what the Irishman called a tatur-tatur dinner, whether the gender in the case be masculine or feminine ; and I incline to give my adherence to the philosophy of the axiom that declares "two to be company, and three none." But then I am very deaf, and that has doubtless much to do with it.

On the 10th of September, 1868, Dickens writes :

"The madness and general political bestiality of the general election will come off in the appropriate Guy Fawkes days. It was proposed to me, under very flattering circumstances indeed, to come in as the third member for Birmingham ; I replied in what is now my stereotyped phrase, 'that no

16

consideration on earth would induce me to become a candidate for the representation of any place in the House of Commons.' Indeed, it is a dismal sight, is that arena altogether. Its irrationality and dishonesty are quite shocking. [What would he have said now!] How disheartening it is, that in affairs spiritual or temporal mankind will not begin at the beginning, but *will* begin with assumptions. Could one believe without actual experience of the fact, that it would be assumed by hundreds of thousands of pestilent boobies, pandered to by politicians, that the Established Church in Ireland has stood between the kingdom and popery, when as a crying grievance it has been popery's trump-card.

"I have now growled out my growl, and feel better.

"With kind regards, my dear Trollope,

"Faithfully yours,   CHARLES DICKENS."

In the December of that year came another growl, as follows:

"KENNEDY'S HOTEL, EDINBURGH.

"MY DEAR TROLLOPE,—I am reading here, and had your letter forwarded to me this morning. The MS. accompanying it was stopped at *All The Year Round* office (in compliance with general instructions referring to any MS. from you) and was sent straight to the printer.

"Oh dear, no! Nobody supposes for a moment that the English Church will follow the Irish Establishment. In the whole great universe of shammery and flummery there is no such idea floating. Everybody knows that the Church of England as an endowed establishment is doomed, and would be, even if its hand were not perpetually hacking at its own throat; but as was observed of an old lady in gloves in one of my Christmas books, 'Let us be polite or die!'

"Anthony's ambition [in becoming a candidate for Beverley] is inscrutable to me. Still, it is the ambition of many men; and the honester the man who entertains it, the better for the rest of us, I suppose.

"Ever, my dear Trollope,

"Most cordially yours,   CHARLES DICKENS."

Here is another "growl," provoked by a species of charlatan, which he, to whom all charlatans were odious, especially abominated—the pietistic charlatan:

"Oh, we have such a specimen here! a man who discourses extemporaneously, positively without the power of constructing one grammatical sentence; but who is (ungrammatically) deep in Heaven's confidence on the abstrusest points, and discloses some of his private information with an idiotic complacency insupportable to behold.

"We are going to have a bad winter in England too probably. What with Ireland, and what with the last new government device of getting in the taxes before they are due, and what with vagrants, and what with fever, the prospect is gloomy."

The last letter I ever received from him is dated the 10th of November, 1869. It is a long letter, but I will give only one passage from it, which has, alas! a peculiarly sad and touching significance when read with the remembrance of the catastrophe then hurrying on, which was to put an end to all projects and purposes. I had been suggesting a walking excursion across the Alps. He writes:

"Walk across the Alps? Lord bless you, I am 'going' to take up my alpenstock and cross all the passes. And, I am 'going' to Italy. I am also 'going' up the Nile to the second cataract; and I am 'going' to Jerusalem, and to India, and likewise to Australia. My only dimness of perception in this wise is, that I don't know *when*. If I did but know when, I should be so wonderfully clear about it all! At present I can't see even so much as the Simplon in consequence of certain farewell readings and a certain new book (just begun) interposing their dwarfish shadow. But whenever (if ever) I change 'going' into 'coming,' I shall come to see you.

"With kind regards, ever, my dear Trollope,

"Your affectionate friend,   CHARLES DICKENS."

And those were the last words I ever had from him!

CHAPTER XXVII.

In those days — *temporibus illis*, as the historians of long-forgotten centuries say — there used to be a very general exodus of the English colony at Florence to the baths of Lucca during the summer months. Almost all Italians, who can in any wise afford to do so, leave the great cities nowadays for the seaside, even as those do who have preceded them in the path of modern luxurious living. But at the time of which I am writing the Florentines who did so were few, and almost confined to that inner circle of the fashionable world which partly lived with foreigners, and had adopted in many respects their modes and habits. Those Italians, however, who did leave their Florence homes in the summer, went almost all of them to Leghorn. The baths of Lucca were an especially and almost exclusively English resort.

It was possible to induce the *vetturini* who supplied carriages and horses for the purpose to do the journey to the baths in one day, but it was a very long day, and it was necessary to get fresh horses at Lucca. There was no good sleeping-place between Florence and Lucca—nor indeed is there such now—and the journey from the capital of Tuscany to that of the little Duchy of Lucca, now done by rail in less than two hours, was quite enough for a *vetturino's* pair of horses. And when Lucca was reached there were still fourteen miles, nearly all collar work, between that and the baths, so that the plan more generally preferred was to sleep at Lucca.

The baths (well known to the ancient Romans, of course, as what warm springs throughout Europe were not?) consisted of three settlements, or groups of houses—as they do still, for I revisited the well-remembered place two or three years ago. There was the " Ponte," a considerable village gathered round the lower bridge over the Lima, at which travellers from Florence first arrived. Here were the assembly-rooms, the reading-room, the principal baths, *and* the gaming-tables—for in those pleasant wicked days the remote little Lucca baths were little better than Baden subsequently and Monte Carlo now. Only we never, to the best of my memory, suicided ourselves, though it might happen occasionally that some innkeeper lost the money which ought to have gone to him, because "the bank" had got hold of it first.

Then, secondly, there was the "Villa," about a mile higher up the lovely little valley of the Lima, so called because the duke's villa was situated there. The Villa had more the pretension—a very little more—of looking something like a little bit of town. At least it had its one street paved. The ducal villa was among the woods immediately above it.

The third little group of buildings and lodging-houses was called the "Bagni Caldi." The hotter, and, I fancy, the original springs were there, and it was altogether more retired and countrified, nestling closely among the chestnut woods. The whole surrounding country, indeed, is one great chestnut forest, and the various little villages, most of them picturesque in the highest degree, which crown the summits of the surrounding hills, are all of them closely hedged in by the chestnut woods, which clothe the slopes to the top. These villages burrow in what they live on like mice in a cheese, for many of the inhabitants never taste any other than chestnut-flour bread from year's end to year's end.

The inhabitants of these hills, and indeed those of the duchy generally, have throughout Italy the reputation of being morally about the best population in the peninsula. Servants from the Lucchese, and especially from the district I am here speaking of, were, and are still, I believe, much prized. Lucca, as many readers will remember, enjoys among all the descriptive epithets popularly given to the different cities of Italy, that of *Lucca la industriosa*.

To us migratory English those singularly picturesque villages which capped all the hills, and were reached by

curiously ancient paved mule-paths zig-zagging up among
the chestnut woods, seemed to have been created solely
for artistic and picnic purposes. The Saturnian nature of
the life lived in them may be conceived from the information once given me by the inhabitants of one of these
mountain settlements in reply to some inquiry about the
time of day, that it was always noon there when the priest
was ready for his dinner.

Such were the summer quarters of the English Florentine colony, *temporibus illis*. There used to be, I remember, a somewhat amusingly distinctive character attributed, of course in a general way subject to exceptions, to
the different groups of the English rusticating world, according to the selection of their quarters in either of the
above three little settlements. The "gay" world preferred the "Ponte," where the gaming-tables and ball-
rooms were. The more strictly "proper" people went to
live at the "Villa," where the English Church service was
performed. The invalid portion of the society, or those
who wished quiet, and especially economy, sought the
"Bagni Caldi."

In a general way we all desired economy, and found it.
The price at the many hotels was nine pauls a day for
board and lodging, including Tuscan wine, and was as
much a fixed and invariable matter as a penny for a penny
bun. Those who wanted other wine generally brought it
with them, by virtue of a ducal ordinance which specially
exempted from duty all wine brought by English visitors
to the Baths.

I dare say, if I were to pass a summer there now, I
should find the atmosphere damp, or the wine sour, or the
bread heavy, or the society heavier, or indulge in some
such unreasonable and unseasonable grumbles as the near
neighborhood of fourscore years is apt to inspire one
with; but I used to find it amazingly pleasant once upon
a time. It is a singular fact, which the remembrance of
those days suggests to me, and which I recommend to the
attention of Mr. Galton and his co-investigators, that the
girls were prettier then than they are in these days, or that
there were more of them! The stupid people, who are

always discovering subjective reasons for objective observations, are as impertinent as stupid!

The Duke of Lucca used to do his utmost to make the
baths attractive and agreeable. There is no Duke of Lucca
now, as all the world knows. The Congress of Vienna put
an end to him by ordaining that, when the ducal throne of
Parma should become vacant, the reigning Duke of Lucca
should succeed to it, while his duchy of Lucca should be
united to Florence. This change took place while I was
still a Florentine. The Duke of Lucca would none of the
new dukedom proposed to him. He abdicated, and his
son became Duke of Parma. This son was, in truth, a
great ne'er-do-well, and very shortly got murdered in the
streets of his new capital by an offended husband.

The change was most unwelcome to Lucca, and especially
to the baths, which had thriven and prospered under the
fostering care of the old duke. He used to pass every
summer there, and give constant very pleasant, but very
little royal, balls at his villa. The Tuscan satirist Giusti,
in the celebrated little poem in which he characterizes the
different reigning sovereigns in the peninsula, calls him
the Protestant Don Giovanni, and says that in the roll of
tyrants he is neither fish nor flesh.

Of the first two epithets I take it he deserved the second
more than the first. His Protestantizing tendencies might,
I think, have been more accurately described as non-Cathol-
icizing. But people are very apt to judge in this matter
after the fashion of the would-be dramatist, who, on being
assured that he had no genius for tragedy, concluded that
he must therefore have one for comedy. The duke's Protestantism, I suspect, limited itself to, and showed itself in,
his dislike and resistance to being bothered by the rulers
of neighboring states into bothering anybody else about
their religious opinions. As for his place in the "roll of
tyrants," he was always accused of (or praised for) liberal-
izing ideas and tendencies, which would in those days have
very soon put an end to him and his tiny duchy, if he had
attempted to govern it in accordance with them. As matters were, his "policy," I take it, was pretty well confined
to the endeavor to make his sovereignty as little trouble-

some to himself or anybody else as possible. His subjects were *very* lightly taxed, for his private property rendered him perfectly independent of them as regarded his own personal expenditure.

The "gayer" part of our little world at the baths used, as I have said, more especially to congregate at the "Ponte," and the more "proper" portion at the "Villa," for, as I have also said, the English Church service was performed there, in a hired room, as I remember, when I first went there. But a church was already in process of being built, mainly by the exertions of a lady, who assuredly cannot be forgotten by any one who ever knew the baths in those days, or for many years afterwards—Mrs. Stisted. Unlike the rest of the world, she lived neither at the "Ponte," nor at the "Villa," nor at the "Bagni Caldi," but at "The Cottage," a little habitation on the bank of the stream about half-way between the "Ponte" and the "Villa." Also unlike all the rest of the world, she lived there permanently, for the place was her own, or rather the property of her husband, Colonel Stisted. He was a long, lean, gray, faded, exceedingly mild, and perfectly gentlemanlike old man; but she was one of the queerest people my roving life has ever made me acquainted with.

She was the Queen of the Baths. On one occasion at the ducal villa, his highness, who spoke English perfectly, said, as she entered the room, "Here comes the Queen of the Baths!" "He calls me his queen," said she, turning to the surrounding circle with a magnificent wave of the hand and delightedly complacent smile. It was not exactly *that* that the duke had said, but he was immensely amused, as were we all, for some days afterwards.

She was a stout old lady, with large, rubicund face and big blue eyes, surrounded by very abundant gray curls. She used to play, or profess to play, the harp, and adopted, as she explained, a costume for the purpose. This consisted of a loose, flowing garment, much like a muslin surplice, which fell back and allowed the arm to be seen when raised for performance on her favorite instrument. The arm probably was, or had once been, a handsome one. The large gray head and the large blue eyes and the drooping curls were also raised simultaneously, and the player looked singularly like the picture of King David similarly employed, which I have seen as a frontispiece in an old-fashioned prayer-book. But the specialty of the performance was that, as all present always said, no sound whatever was heard to issue from the instrument! "Attitude is everything," as we have heard in connection with other matters; but with dear old Mrs. Stisted at her harp it was absolutely and literally so to the exclusion of all else.

She and the good old colonel—he *was* a truly good and benevolent man, and, indeed, I believe she was a good and charitable woman, despite her manifold absurdities and eccentricities—used to drive out in the evening among her subjects—*her* subjects, for neither I nor anybody else ever heard him called King of the Baths!—in an old-fashioned, very shabby and very high-hung phaeton, sometimes with her niece Charlotte—an excellent creature and universal favorite—by her side, and the colonel on the seat behind, ready to offer the hospitality of the place by his side to any mortal so favored by the queen as to have received such an invitation.

The poor dear old colonel used to play the violoncello, and did at least draw some more or less exquisite sounds from it. But one winter they paid a visit to Rome, and the old man died there. She wished, in accordance doubtless with his desire, to bring back his body to be buried in the place they had inhabited for so many years, and with which their names were so indissolubly entwined in the memory of all who knew them—which means all the generations of nomad frequenters of the baths for many, many years. The Protestant burial-ground also was recognized as *quasi* hers, for it is attached to the church which she was mainly instrumental in building. The colonel's body, therefore, was to be brought back from Rome to be buried at Lucca Baths.

But such an enterprise was not the simplest or easiest thing in the world. There were official difficulties in the way, ecclesiastical difficulties, and custom-house difficulties of all sorts. Where there is a will, however, there is

16*

a way. But the way which the determined will of the Queen of the Baths discovered for itself upon this occasion was one which would probably have occurred to few people in the world save herself. She hired a *vetturino*, and told him that he was to convey a servant of hers to the baths of Lucca, who would be in charge of goods which would occupy the entire interior of the carriage. She then obtained, what was often accorded without much difficulty in those days, from both the pontifical and the Tuscan governments, a *lascia passare* for the contents of the carriage as *bonâ fide roba usata*—"used up, or second-hand goods." And under this denomination the poor old colonel, packed in the carriage together with his beloved violoncello, passed the gates of Rome and the Tuscan frontier, and arrived safely at the place of his latest destination. The servant who was employed to conduct this singular operation did not above half like the job intrusted to him, and used to tell afterwards how he was frightened out of his wits, and the driver exceedingly astonished, by a sudden *pom - m - m* from the interior of the carriage, caused by the breaking, in consequence of some atmospheric change, of one of the strings of the violoncello.

Malicious people used to say that the Queen of the Baths was innocent of all deception as regarded the custom-house officials; for that if any article was ever honestly described as *roba usata*, the old colonel might be so designated.

The queen herself shortly followed (by another conveyance), and was present at the interment, on which occasion she much impressed the population by causing a superb crimson chair to be placed at the head of the grave, in order that she might be present without standing during the service. The chair was well known, because the queen, both at the baths and at Florence, was in the habit of sending it about to the houses at which she visited, since she preferred doing so to incurring the risk of the less satisfactory accommodation her friends might offer her.

If space and the reader's patience would allow of it, I

might gossip on of many more reminiscences of the baths
of Lucca, all pleasant or laughable ; but I must conclude
by the story of a tragedy, which I will tell, because it is,
in many respects, curiously characteristic of the time and
place.

The duke, who, as I have said, spoke English perfectly
well, was fond of surrounding himself with foreign, and
specially English, dependants. He had, at the time of
which I am speaking, two English—or, rather, one English
and one Irish — chamberlains, and a third, who, though a
German, was, from having married an Englishwoman, and
habitually speaking English, and living with Englishmen,
much the same, at least to the duke, as an Englishman.
The Englishman was a young man ; the German an older
man, and the father of a family. And both were good,
upright, and honorable men ; both long since gone over to
the majority.

The Irishman, also a young man, was a bad fellow ; but
he was an especial favorite with the duke, who was strongly attached to him. It is not necessary to print his name.
He has gone to his account. But it might nevertheless
happen that the printing of my story with his name in
these pages might still give pain to somebody.

There was also that year an extremely handsome and
attractive lady, a widow, at the baths. I will not give
her name either ; for, though there was no sort of blame
or discredit of any kind attached or attachable to her from
any part of my story, as she is, I believe, still living, and
as the memory of that time cannot but be a painful one
to her, it is as well to suppress it. The lady, as I have
said, was handsome and young, and, of course, all the
young fellows who got a chance flirted with her — *en tout
bien tout honneur*. But the Irish chamberlain attached
himself to her, not with any but perfectly avowable intentions, but more seriously than the other youngsters, and
with an altogether serious eye to her very comfortable
dower.

Now during that same summer there was at the Baths
Mr. Plowden, the banker, from Rome. He was then a
young man ; he has recently died an old one in the Eter-

nal City. His name I mention in telling my story because much blame was cast upon him at the time by people in Rome, in Florence, and at the Baths, who did not know the facts as entirely and accurately as I knew them ; and I am able here to declare publicly what I have often declared privately, that he behaved well and blamelessly in the whole matter.

And probably, though I have no distinct recollection that it was so, Plowden may have also been smitten by the lady. Now, whether the Irishman imagined that the young banker was his most formidable rival, or whether there may have been some previous cause of ill-will between the two men, I cannot say, but so it was that the chamberlain sent a challenge to the banker. The latter declined to accept it on the ground that he *was* a banker and not a fighting-man, and that his business-position would have been materially injured by his fighting a duel. The Irishman might have made the most of this triumph, such as it was ; but he was not content with doing so, and lost none of the opportunities, which the social habits of such a place daily afforded him, for insulting and outraging his enemy. And he was continually boasting to his friends that before the end of the season he would compel him to come out and be shot at.

And before the end of the season came his persistent efforts were crowned with success. Plowden, finding his life altogether intolerable under the harrow of the bully's insolence, at length one day challenged *him*. Then arose the question of the locality where the duel was to take place. The laws of the duchy were very strict against duelling, and the duke himself was strongly opposed to it. In the case of his own favorite chamberlain, too, his displeasure was likely to be extreme. But in the neighborhood of the baths the frontier line which divides the Duchy of Modena from that of Lucca is a very irregular and intricate one. A little below the "Ponte" at the baths the Lima falls into the Serchio, and the upper valley of the latter river is of a very romantic and beautiful character. Now we all knew that hereabouts there were portions of Modenese territory interpenetrating that of the Duchy of Lucca, but none of us knew the exact line of the boundary. And the favorite chamberlain, with true Irish impudence, undertook to obtain exact information from the duke himself.

There was a ball that night, at which the whole of the society was present; and, strange as it may seem, I do not think there was a man there who did not know that the duel was to be fought on the morrow, except the duke himself. Many of the women even knew it perfectly well. The chamberlain, getting the duke into conversation on the subject of the frontier, learned from him that a certain highly romantic gorge, opening out from the valley of the Serchio, and called Turrite Cava, which he pretended to take an interest in as a place fitted for a picnic, was within the Modenese frontier.

All was arranged, therefore, for the meeting with pistols on the following morning; and the combatants proceeded to the spot fixed on, some five or six miles, I think, from the Baths. Plowden, who, as a sedate business man, was less intimate with the generality of the young men at the Baths, was accompanied only by his second; his adversary was attended by a whole cohort of acquaintances—really far more after the fashion of a party going to a picnic, or some other party of pleasure, than in the usual guise of men bent on such an errand.

Plowden had never fired a pistol in his life, and knew about as much of the management of one as an archbishop. The other was an old duellist, and a practised performer with the weapon. All this was perfectly well known, and the young men around the Irishman were earnest with him during their drive to the ground not to take his adversary's life, beseeching him to remember how heavy a load on his mind would such a deed be during the whole future of his own. Not a soul of the whole society of the Baths, who by this time knew what was going on to a man, and almost to a woman (my mother, it may be observed, had not been at the ball, and knew nothing about it), doubted that Plowden was going out to be shot as certainly as a bullock goes into the slaughter-house to be killed.

The Irishman, in reply to all the exhortations of his companions, jauntily told them not to distress themselves; he had no intention of killing the fellow, but would content himself with "winging" him. He would have his right arm off as surely as he now had it on!

In the midst of all this the men were put up. At the first shot the Irishman's well-directed bullet whistled close to Plowden's head, but the random shot of the latter struck his adversary full in the groin.

He was hastily carried to a little *osteria*, which stood (and still stands) by the side of the road which runs up the valley of the Serchio, at no great distance from the mouth of the Turrite Cava gorge. There was a young medical man among those gathered there, who shook his head over the victim, but did not, I thought, seem very well up to dealing with the case.

One of my mother's earliest and most intimate friends at Florence was a Lady Sevestre, who was then at the Baths with her husband, Sir Thomas Sevestre, an old Indian army surgeon. He was a very old man, and was not much known to the younger society of the place. But it struck me that *he* was the man for the occasion. So I rushed off to the Baths in one of the *bagherini* (as the little light gigs of the country are called) which had conveyed the parties to the ground, and knocked up Sir Thomas. Of course, all the story came new to him, and he was very much inclined to wash his hands of it. But on my representations that a life was at stake, his old professional habits prevailed, and he agreed to go back with me to Turrite Cava.

But no persuasions could induce him to trust himself to a *bagherino*. And truly it would have shaken the old man well-nigh to pieces. There was no other carriage to be had in a hurry. And at last he allowed me to get an armchair rigged with a couple of poles for bearers, and placed himself in it—not before he had taken the precaution of slinging a bottle of pale ale to either pole of his equipage. He wore a very wide-brimmed straw hat, a suit of professional black, and carried a large white sunshade. And thus accoutred, and accompanied by four stalwart bearers, he started, while I ran by the side of the chair, as queer-looking a party as can well be imagined. I can see it all now ; and should have been highly amused at the time had I not very strongly suspected that I was taking him to the bedside of a dying man.

And when he reached his patient, a very few minutes sufficed for the old surgeon to pronounce the case an absolutely hopeless one. After a few hours of agony the bully, who had insisted on bringing this fate on himself, died that same afternoon.

Then came the question who was to tell the duke. Who it was that undertook that disagreeable but necessary task I forget. But the duke came out to the little *osteria* immediately on hearing of the catastrophe ; also the English clergyman officiating at the Baths came out. And the scene in that large, nearly bare, upper chamber of the little inn was a strange one. The clergyman began praying by the dying man's bedside, while the numerous assemblage in the room all knelt, and the duke knelt with them, interrupting the prayers with his sobs after the uncontrolled fashion of the Italians.

He was very, very angry. But in unblushing defiance of all equity and reason his anger turned wholly against Plowden, who, of course, had placed himself out of the small potentate's reach within a very few minutes after the catastrophe. But the duke strove by personal application to induce the Grand Duke of Tuscany to banish Plowden from his dominions, which, to the young banker, one branch of whose business was at Florence and one at Rome, would have been a very serious matter. But this, poor old *ciuco*, more just and reasonable in this case than his brother potentate, the Protestant Don Giovanni of Lucca, refused to do.

So our pleasant time at the Baths, for that season at least, ended tragically enough ; and whenever I have since visited that singularly romantic glen of Turrite Cava, its deep, rock-sheltered shadows have been peopled for me by the actors in that day's bloody work.

CHAPTER XXVIII.

It was, to the best of my recollection, much about the same time as that visit of Charles Dickens which I have chronicled in the last chapter but one, which turned out to be eventually so fateful a one to me, as the correspondence there given shows, that my mother received another visit, which was destined to play an equally influential part in the directing and fashioning of my life. Equally influential perhaps I ought not to say, inasmuch as one-and-twenty years (with the prospect I hope of more) are more important than seventeen. But both the visits I am speaking of as having occurred within a few days of each other were big with fate, to me, in the same department of human affairs.

The visit of Dickens was destined eventually to bring me my second wife, as the reader has seen. The visit of Mr. and Mrs. Garrow to the Via dei Malcontenti, much about the same time, brought me my first.

The Arno and the Tiber both take their rise in the flanks of Falterona. It was on the banks of the first that my first married life was passed; on those of the more southern river that the largest portion of my second wedded happiness was enjoyed.

Why Mr. and Mrs. Garrow called on my mother I do not remember. Somebody had given them letters of introduction to us, but I forget who it was. Mr. Garrow was the son of an Indian officer by a high-caste Brahmin woman, to whom he was married. I believe that unions between Englishmen and native women are common enough. But a marriage, such as that of my wife's grandfather I am assured was, is rare, and rarer still a marriage with a woman of high caste. Her name was Sultana, I have never heard of any other name. Joseph Garrow, my father-in-law, was sent to England at an early age, and never again saw either of his parents, who both died young. His grandfather was an old Scotch schoolmaster at Hadley, near Barnet, and his great-uncle was the well-known Judge Garrow. My father-in-law carried about with him very unmistakable evidence of his Eastern origin in his yellow skin, and the tinge of the white of his eyes, which was almost that of an Indian. He had been educated for the bar, but had never practised, or attempted to do so, having while still a young man married a wife with considerable means. He was a decidedly clever man, especially in an artistic direction, having been a very good musician and performer on the violin, and a draughtsman and caricaturist of considerable talent.

The lady he married had been a Miss Abrams, but was at the time he married her the widow of (I believe) a naval officer named Fisher. She had by her first husband one son and one daughter. There had been three Misses Abrams, Jewesses by race undoubtedly, but Christians by baptism, whose parent or parents had come to this country in the suite of some Hanoverian minister, in what capacity I never heard. They were all three exceptionally accomplished musicians, and seem to have been well known in the higher social circles of the musical world. One of the sisters was the authoress of many once well-known songs, especially of one song called "Crazy Jane," which had a considerable vogue in its day. I remember hearing old John Cramer say that my mother-in-law could, while hearing a numerous orchestra, single out any instrument which had played a false note—and this he seemed to think a very remarkable and exceptional feat. She was past fifty when Mr. Garrow married her, but she bore him one daughter, and when they came to Florence both girls, Theodosia, Garrow's daughter, and Harriet Fisher, her elder half-sister, were with them, and at their second morning call both came with them.

The closest union and affection subsisted between the two girls, and ever continued till the untimely death of Harriet. But never were two sisters, or half-sisters, or indeed any two girls at all, more unlike each other.

Harriet was neither specially clever nor specially pretty, but she was, I think, perhaps the most absolutely unselfish human being I ever knew, and one of the most loving hearts. And her position was one that, except in a nature framed of the kindliest clay, and moulded by the rarest perfection of all the gentlest and self-denying virtues, must have soured, or at all events crushed and quenched, the individual placed in such circumstances. She was simply nobody in the family save the ministering angel in the house to all of them. I do not mean that any of the vulgar preferences existed which are sometimes supposed to turn some less favored member of a household into a Cinderella. There was not the slightest shadow of anything of the sort. But no visitors came to the house or sought the acquaintance of the family for *her* sake. She had the dear, and, to her, priceless love of her sister. But no admiration, no pride of father or mother fell to *her* share. *Her* life was not made brilliant by the notice and friendship of distinguished men. Everything was for the younger sister. And through long years of this eclipse, and to the last, she fairly worshipped the sister who eclipsed her. Garrow, to do him justice, was equally affectionate in his manner to both girls, and entirely impartial in every respect that concerned the material wellbeing of them. But Theodosia was always placed on a pedestal on which there was no room at all for Harriet. Nor could the closest intimacy with the family discover any faintest desire on her part to share the pedestal. She was content and entirely happy in enjoying the reflected brightness of the more gifted sister.

Nor would, perhaps, a shrewd judge, whose estimate of men and women had been formed by observation of average humanity, have thought that the position which I have described as that of the younger of these two sisters was altogether a morally wholesome one for her. But the shrewd judge would have been wrong. There never was a humbler, as there never was a more loving soul, than that of the Theodosia Garrow who became, for my perfect happiness, Theodosia Trollope. And it was these two qualities of humbleness and lovingness that, acting like invincible antiseptics on the moral nature, saved her from all "spoiling"—from any tendency of any amount of flattery and admiration to engender selfishness or self-sufficiency. Nothing more beautiful in the way of family affection could be seen than the tie which united in the closest bonds of sisterly affection those two so differently constituted sisters. Very many saw and knew what Theodosia was as my wife. Very few indeed ever knew what she was in her own home as a sister.

When I married Theodosia Garrow she possessed just one thousand pounds in her own right, and little or no prospect of ever possessing any more ; while I on my side possessed nothing at all, save the prospect of a strictly bread-and-cheese competency at the death of my mother, and "the farm which I carried under my hat," as somebody calls it. The marriage was not made with the full approbation of my father-in-law; but entirely in accordance with the wishes of my mother, who simply, dear soul, saw in it, what she said, that "Theo" was, of all the girls she knew, the one she should best like as a daughter-in-law. And here again the wise folks of the world (and I among them !) would hardly have said that the step I then took was calculated, according to all the recognized chances and probabilities of human affairs, to lead to a life of contentment and happiness. I suppose it ought not to have done so. But it did. It would be monstrously inadequate to say that I never repented it. What should I not have lost had I not done it !

As usual my cards turned up trumps, but they began to do so in a way that caused me much, and my wife more, grief at the time. Within two years after my marriage poor, dear, good, loving Harriet caught small-pox and died. She was much more largely endowed than her half-sister, to whom she bequeathed all she had.

She had a brother, as I have said above. But he had altogether alienated himself from his family by becoming a Roman Catholic priest. There was no open quarrel. I met him frequently in after-years at Garrow's table at Torquay, and remember his bitter complaints that he was tempted by the appearance of things at table which he ought not to eat. It would have been of no use to give or bequeath money to him, for it would have gone immediately to Romanist ecclesiastical purposes. He had nearly stripped himself of his own considerable means, reserving to himself only the bare competence on which a Catholic priest might live. He was altogether a very queer fish. I remember his coming to me once in tearful but very angry mood, because, as he said, I had guilefully spread snares for his soul! I had not the smallest comprehension of his meaning till I discovered that his woe and wrath were occasioned by my having sent him as a present Berington's "Middle Ages." I had fancied that his course of studies and line of thought would have made the book interesting to him, utterly ignorant or oblivious of the fact that it labored under the disqualification of appearing in the "Index."

I take it I knew little about the "Index" in those days. In after-years, when three or four of my own books had been placed in its columns, I was better informed. I remember a very elegant lady who, having overheard my present wife mention the fact that a recently published book of mine had been placed in the "Index," asked her, with the intention of being extremely polite and complimentary, whether *her* (my wife's) books had been put in the "Index." And when the latter modestly replied that she had not written anything that could merit such a distinction, her interlocutor, patting her on the shoulder with a kindly and patronizing air, said, "Oh, my dear, I am *sure* they will be placed there. They certainly ought to be."

Mrs. Garrow, my wife's mother, was not, I think, an amiable woman. She must have been between seventy and eighty when I first knew her; but she was still vigorous, and had still a pair of what must once have been magnificent, and were still brilliant and fierce black eyes. She was in no wise a clever woman, nor was our dear Harriet a clever girl. Garrow, on the other hand, and *his* daughter were both very markedly clever, and this produced a closeness of companionship and alliance between the father and daughter which painfully excited the jealousy of the wife and mother. But it was totally impossible for her to cabal with her daughter against the object of her jealousy. Harriet, always seeking to be a peacemaker, was ever, if peace could not be made, stanchly on Theo's side. I am afraid that Mrs. Garrow did not love her second daughter at all; and I am inclined to suspect that my marriage was in some degree facilitated by her desire to get Theo out of the house. She was a very fierce old lady, and did not, I fear, contribute to the happiness of any member of her family.

How well I remember the appearance of Mr. and Mrs. Garrow and those two girls in my mother's drawing-room in the Via dei Malcontenti. The two girls, I remember, were dressed exactly alike and very *dowdily*. They had just arrived in Florence from Tours, I think, where they had passed a year, or perhaps two, since quitting "The Braddons" at Torquay; and everything about them from top to toe was provincial, not to say shabby. It was a Friday, my mother's reception-day, and the room soon filled with gayly dressed and smart people, with more than one pretty girl among them. But I had already got into conversation with Theodosia Garrow, and, to the gross neglect of my duties as master of the house, and to the scandal of more than one fair lady, so I remained, till a summons more than twice repeated by her father took her away.

It was not that I had fallen in love at first sight, as the phrase is, by any means. But I at once felt that I had got hold of something of a quite other calibre of intelligence from anything I had been recently accustomed to meet with in those around me, and with a moral nature that was sympathetic to my own. And I found it very delightful. It is no doubt true that, had her personal appearance been other than it was, I should not probably have found her conversation equally delightful. But I am sure that it is equally true that had she been in face, figure, and person all she was, and at the same time stupid, or even not sympathetic, I should not have been equally attracted to her.

She was by no means what would have been recognized by most men as a beautiful girl. The specialties of her

appearance, in the first place, were in a great measure due
to the singular mixture of races from which she had
sprung. One half of her blood was Jewish, one quarter
Scotch, and one quarter pure Brahmin. Her face was a
long oval, too long and too lanky towards the lower part
of it for beauty. Her complexion was somewhat dark,
and not good. The mouth was mobile, expressive, perhaps more habitually framed for pathos and the gentler
feelings than for laughter. The jaw was narrow, the
teeth good and white, but not very regular. She had a
magnificent wealth of very dark brown hair, not without
a gleam here and there of what descriptive writers, of
course, would call gold, but which really was more accurately copper color. And this grand and luxuriant wealth
of hair grew from the roots on the head to the extremity
of it, at her waist, when it was let down, in the most beautiful ripples. But the great feature and glory of the face
were the eyes, among the largest I ever saw, of a deep
clear gray, rather deeply set, and changing in expression
with every impression that passed over her mind. The
forehead was wide, and largely developed both in those
parts of it which are deemed to indicate imaginative and
idealistic power, and those that denote strongly marked
perceptive and artistic faculties. The latter, perhaps, were
the more prominently marked. The Indian strain showed
itself in the perfect gracefulness of a very slender and
elastic figure, and in the exquisite elegance and beauty of
the modelling of the extremities.

That is not the description of a beautiful girl. But it
is the fact that the face and figure very accurately so described were eminently attractive to me physically, as well
as the mind and intelligence, which informed them, were
spiritually. They were much more attractive to me than
those of many a splendidly beautiful girl, the immense
superiority of whose beauty nobody knew better than I.
Why should this have been so? That is one of the mysteries to the solution of which no moral or physical or
psychical research has ever brought us an iota nearer.

I am giving here an account of the first impression my
future wife made on me. I had no thought of wooing

and winning her, for, as I have said, I was not in a position to marry. Meanwhile she was becoming acclimatized to Florentine society. She no longer looked *dowdy* when entering a room, but very much the reverse ; and the little Florentine world began to recognize that they had got something very much like a new Corinne among them. But of course I rarely got a chance of monopolizing her as I had done during that first afternoon. We were, however, constantly meeting, and were becoming ever more and more close friends. When the Garrows left Florence for the summer, I visited them at Lucerne, and subsequently met them at Venice. It was the year of the meeting of the Scientific Congress in that city.

That was a pleasant autumn in Venice. By that time I had become pretty well over head and ears in love with the girl by whose side I generally contrived to sit in the gondolas, in the Piazza in the evening, et cætera. It was lovely September weather—just the time for Venice. The summer days were drawing in, but there was the moon, quite light enough on the lagoons ; and we were a great deal happier than the day was long.

Those Scientific Congresses, of which that at Venice was the seventh and the last, played a curious part, which has not been much observed or noted by historians, in the story of the winning of Italian independence. I believe that the first congress, at Pisa, I think, was really got up by men of science, with a view to furthering their own objects and pursuits. It was followed by others in successive autumns at Lucca, Milan, Genoa, Naples, Florence, and this seventh and last at Venice. But Italy was in those days thinking of other matters than science. The whole air was full of ideas, very discordant all of them, and vague most of them, of political change. The governments of the peninsula thought twice, and more than twice, before they would grant permission for the first of these meetings. Meetings of any kind were objects of fear and mistrust to the rulers. Those of Tuscany, who were by comparison liberal, and, as known to be such, were more or less objects of suspicion to the Austrian, Roman, and Neapolitan governments, led the way in giving the permission asked for ; and perhaps thought that an assembly of geologists, entomologists, astronomers, and mathematicians might act as a safety-valve, and divert men's minds from more dangerous subjects. But the current of the times was running too strongly to be so diverted, and proved too much for the authorities and for the real men of science, who were, at least some of them, anxious to make the congresses really what they professed to be.

Gradually these meetings became more and more mere social gatherings in outward appearance, and revolutionary propagandist assemblies in reality. As regards the former aspect of them, the different cities strove to outdo each other in the magnificence and generosity of their reception of their "scientific" guests. Masses of publications were prepared, especially topographical and historical accounts of the city which played Amphytrion for the occasion, and presented gratuitously to the members of the association. Merely little guide-books, of which a few hundred copies were needed in the case of the earlier meetings, they became in the case of the latter ones at Naples, Genoa, Milan, and Venice, large and magnificently printed tomes, prepared by the most competent authorities and produced at a very great expense.

Venice especially outdid all her rivals, and printed an account of the Queen of the Adriatic, embracing history, topography, science in all its branches, and artistic story, in four huge and magnificent volumes, which remains to the present day by far the best topographical monograph that any city of the peninsula possesses. This truly splendid work, which brought out in the ordinary way could not have been sold for less than six or eight guineas, was presented, together with much other printed matter—an enormous lithographed panorama of Venice and her lagoons, some five feet long, in a handsome roll cover, I remember among them—to every "member" on his enrolment as such.

Then there were concerts and excursions and great daily dinners the gayest and most enjoyable imaginable, at which both sexes were considered to be equally scientific and equally welcome. The dinners were not absolutely gratuitous, but the tickets for them were issued at a price very much inferior to the real cost of the entertainment. And all this, it must be understood, was done not by any subscription of members scientific or otherwise, but by the city and its municipality; the motive for such expenditure being the highly characteristic Italian one of rivalling and outdoing in magnificence other cities and municipalities, or, in the historical language of Italy, "communes."

Old Rome, with her dependent cities, made no sign during all these autumns of ever - increasing festivity. Pity that they should have come to an end before she did so ; for at the rate at which things were going, we should all, at least, have been crowned on the Capitol, if not made Roman senators, *pour l'amour du Grec*, as the *savant* says in the "Précieuses Ridicules," if we had gone to the Eternal City.

But the fact was, that the *soi-disant* 'ologists kicked up their heels a little too audaciously at Venice under Austria's nose ; and the government thought it high time to put an end to "science."

For instance, Prince Canino made his appearance in the uniform of the Roman National Guard ! This was a little too much; and the prince, all prince and Bonaparte as he was, was marched off to the frontier. Canino had every right to be there as a man of science ; for his acquirements in many branches of science were large and real; and specially as an entomologist he was known to be probably the first in Italy. But he was the man who, when selling his principality of Canino, insisted on the insertion in the legal instrument of a claim to an additional five pauls (value about two shillings), for the title of prince which was attached to the possessor of the estates he was selling. He was an out-and-out avowed Republican, and was the blackest of black sheep to all the constituted governments of the peninsula. He looked as little as he felt and thought like a prince. He was a paunchy, oily-looking, black-haired man, whose somewhat heavy face was illumined by a brilliant black eye full of humor and a

17

mouth expressive of good-nature and *bonhomie.* His appearance in the proscribed uniform might have been considered by Austria, if her police authorities could have appreciated the fun of the thing, as wholesomely calculated to throw ridicule on the hated institution. He was utterly unassuming and good-natured in his manner, and when seen in his ordinary black habiliments looked more like a well-to-do Jewish trader than anything else.

As for the social aspects of these scientific congresses, they were becoming every year more festive, and, at all events to the ignoramus outsiders who joined them, more pleasant. My good cousin and old friend, then Colonel, now General, Sir Charles Trollope, was at Venice that autumn. I said, on meeting him, "Now the first thing is to make you a member." "Me, a member of a scientific congress!" said he. "God bless you, I am as ignorant as a babe of all possible 'epteras and 'opteras, and 'statics and 'matics." "Oh, nonsense! we are all men of science here. Come along!"—*i. e.,* to the ducal palace to be inscribed. "But what do you mean to tell them I am?" he asked. "Well, let's see! You must have superintended a course of instruction in the goose-step in your day?" "Rather so," said he. "Very well, then. You are Instructor in Military Exercises in her B. M. Forces. You are all right. Come along!" And if I had said that he was Trumpeter Major of the 600th Regiment in the British Army it would doubtless have been equally all right. So said, so done. And I see his bewildered look now, as the four huge volumes, about a load for a porter, to which he had become entitled, together with medals and documents of many kinds, were put into his arms.

Ah, those were pleasant days! And while Italy, under the wing of science, was plotting her independence, I was busy in forging the chains of that dependence which was to be a more unmixed source of happiness to me than the independence which Italy was compassing has yet proved to her.

Those chains, however, as regarded at all events the outward and visible signs of them, had not got forged yet.

I certainly had not "proposed" to Theodosia. In fact, to the very best of my recollection, I never did "propose" to her—or "pop," as the hideous phrase is—any decisive question at all. We seem, to my recollection, to have come gradually, insensibly, and mutually to consider it a matter of course that what we wanted was to be married, and that the only matter which needed any words or consideration was the question how the difficulties in the way of our wishes were to be overcome.

In the autumn of 1847 my mother and I went to pass the winter in Rome. My sister Cecilia's health had been failing; and it began to be feared that there was reason to suspect the approach of the malady which had already destroyed my brother Henry and my younger sister Emily. It was decided, therefore, that she should pass the winter in Rome. Her husband's avocations made it impossible for him to accompany her thither, and my mother therefore took an apartment there to receive her. It was in a small *palazzo* in that part of the Via delle Quattro Fontane which is now situated between the Via Nazionale and the Church of Santa Maria Maggiore, to the left of one going towards the latter. There was no Via Nazionale then, and the buildings which now make the Via delle Quattro Fontane a continuous line of street existed only in the case of a few isolated houses and convents. It was a very comfortable apartment, roomy, sunny, and quiet. The house exists still, though somewhat modernized in outward appearance, and is, I think, the second, after one going towards Santa Maria Maggiore has crossed the new Via Nazionale.

But the grand question was whether it could be brought about that Theodosia Garrow should be permitted to be my mother's guest during that winter. A hint on the matter was quite sufficient for my dear mother, although I do not think that she had yet any idea that I was minded to give her a daughter-in-law. Theodosia's parents had certainly no faintest idea that anything more than ordinary friendship existed between me and their daughter, or, if they had had such, she would certainly have never been allowed to accept my mother's invitation. As for Theodosia herself and her willingness to come, it seems to me, as I look back, that nothing was said between us at all, any more than anything was said about making her my wife. I think it was all taken for granted, *sans mot dire*, by both of us. But there was one person who knew all about it ; knew what was in both our hearts, and was eagerly anxious that the desire of them should be fulfilled. This was the good fairy, Harriet Fisher. Without the strenuous exertion of her influence on her mother and Mr. Garrow the object would hardly have been accomplished. Of course the plea put forward was the great desirability of taking advantage of such an opportunity of seeing Rome.

My sister, whose health, alas ! profited nothing by that visit to Rome, and could have been profited by no visit to any place on earth, became strongly attached to Theodosia ; and the affection which grew up between them was the more to the honor of both of them, in that they were far as the poles asunder in opinions and habits of thought. My sister was what in those days was called a " Puseyite." Her opinions were formed on the highest High-Church model, and her Church opinions made the greatest part, and, indeed, nearly the whole of her life. Theodosia had no Church opinions at all, High or Low. All her mind and interests were, at all events at that time, turned towards poetry and art. Subsequently she interested herself keenly in political and social questions, but had hardly at that time begun to do so. But she made a conquest of my sister.

Indeed it would have been very difficult for any one to live in the same house with her without loving her. She was so bright, her sympathies so ready, her intelligence so large and varied, that day after day her presence and her conversation were a continual delight; and she was withal diffident of herself, gentle and unassuming to a fault. My mother had already learned to love her truly as a daughter, before there was any apparent probability of her becoming one.

We did not succeed in bearing down all the opposition that in the name of ordinary prudence was made to our marriage, till the spring of forty-eight. We were finally married on the 3d of April in that year, in the British minister's chapel in Florence, in the quiet, comfortable way in which we used to do such things in those days.

I told my good friend Mr. Plunkett (he had then become the English representative at the court of Tuscany) that I wanted to be married the next day. "All right," said he; "will ten o'clock do?" "Could not be better." "Very good. Tell Robbins [the then English clergyman] I'll be sure to be there." So, at ten the next morning we looked in at the Palazzo Ximenes, and in about ten minutes the business was done.

Of Mr. Robbins, who was as kind and good a little man as could be, I may note, since I have been led to speak of him, the following rather singular circumstance. He was, as I have been told, the son of a Devonshire farmer, and his two sisters were the wives of two of the principal Florentine nobles, one having married the Marchese Inghirami and the other the Marchese Bartolomei. What circumstances led to the accomplishment of a destiny apparently so strange for the family of a Devonshire farmer I never heard. The clergyman and his sisters were all much my seniors.

After the expeditious ceremony we all—about half a score of us—went off to breakfast at the house of Mr. Garrow in the Piazza di Santa Maria Novella, and before noon my wife and I were off on a ramble among the Tuscan cities.

CHAPTER XXIX.

My very old friend, Colonel Grant—General Grant many years before he died—used to say that if he wished, without changing his place himself, to see the greatest possible number of his friends and acquaintances, he should stand perpetually at the foot of the column in the Place Vendôme. But it seems to me that at least as advantageous a post of observation for the purpose would be the foot of Giotto's tower in Florence! Who in these days lives and dies without going to Florence; and who goes to Florence without going to gaze on the most perfectly beautiful tower that human hands ever raised?

Let me tell (quite parenthetically) a really good story of that matchless building, which yet, however, will hardly be appreciated at its full value by those who have never seen it. When the Austrian troops were occupying Florence, one of the white-coated officers had planted himself in the piazza in front of the tower, and was gazing at it earnestly, lost in admiration of its perfect beauty. "*Si svita, signore,*" said a little street urchin, coming up behind him—"It *unscrews,* sir!" As much as to say, "Wouldn't you like just to take it off bodily and carry it away?" But, as I said, to apprehend the aptitude of the *gamin's* sneer, one must have one's self looked on the absolute perfection of proportion and harmony of its every part, which really does suggest the idea that the whole might be lifted bodily in one piece from its place on the soil. Whether the Austrian had the wit to answer, "You are blundering, boy; you are taking me for a Frenchman," I don't know.

But I was saying, when the mention of the celebrated tower led me into telling, before I forgot it, the above

story, that Florence was of all the cities of Europe that
in which one might be likely to see the greatest number
of old, and make the greatest number of new, acquaintances. I lived there for more than thirty years, and the
number of persons, chiefly English, American, and Italian, whom I knew during that period is astonishing. The
number of them was of course all the greater from the
fact that the society, at least so far as English and Americans were concerned, was to a very great degree a floating one. They come back to my memory, when I think
of those times, like a long procession of ghosts. Most
of them, I suppose, *are* ghosts by this time. They pass
away out of one's ken, and are lost !

Some, thank Heaven, are *not* lost ; and some, though lost,
will never pass out of ken. If I were writing only for
myself I should like to send my memory roving among
all that crowd of phantoms, catch them one after another
as they dodge about, half eluding one when just on the
point of recovering them, and, fixing them in memory's
camera, photograph them one after another. But I cannot
hope that such a gallery would be as interesting to the
reader as it certainly would to me. And I must content
myself with recording my recollections of those among
them in whom the world may be supposed to take an
interest.

Theodosia Garrow, when living with her parents at "The
Braddons," at Torquay, had known Elizabeth Barrett.
The latter was very much of an invalid at the time ; so
much so, as I think I have gathered from my wife's talk
about those times, as to have prevented her from being a
visitor to "The Braddons." But Theodosia was, I take
it, to be very frequently found by the side of the sofa to
which her friend was more or less confined. I fancy that
Mr. Kenyon, who was an old friend and family connection of Elizabeth Barrett's family, and was also intimately
acquainted with the Garrows and with Theodosia, must
have been the first means of bringing the girls together.
There were assuredly *very* few young women in England
at that day to whom Theodosia Garrow in social intercourse would have had to look *up*, as to one on a higher

intellectual level than her own. But Elizabeth Barrett
was one of them. I am not talking of *acquirements*. Nor
was my wife thinking of such when she used to speak of
the poetess as she had known her at that time. I am talking, as my wife used to talk, of pure native intellectual
power. And I consider it to have been no small indication of the capacity of my wife's intelligence, that she so
clearly and appreciatingly recognized and measured the
distance between her friend's intellect and her own. But
this appreciation on the one side was in no wise incompatible with a large and generous amount of admiration
on the other. And many a talk in long subsequent years
left with me the impression of the high estimation which
the gifted poetess had formed of the value of her highly,
but not so exceptionally, gifted admirer.

Of course this old friendship paved the way for a new
one when the Brownings came to live in Florence. I flatter myself that that would in any case have found some
raison d'être. But the pleasure of the two girls—girls no
more in any sense—in meeting again quickened the growth
of an intimacy which might otherwise have been slower
in ripening.

To say that amid all that frivolous, gay, giddy, and, it
must be owned, for the most part very unintellectual society (in the pleasures and pursuits of which, to speak
honestly, I took, well pleased, my full share), my visits
to Casa Guidi were valued by me as choice morsels of my
existence, is to say not half enough. I was conscious
even then of coming away from those visits a better man,
with higher views and aims. And pray, reader, understand that any such effect was not produced by any talk
or look or word of the nature of preaching, or anything
approaching to it, but simply by the perception and appreciation of what Elizabeth Barrett Browning was; of
the immaculate purity of every thought that passed through
her pellucid mind, and the indefeasible nobility of her
every idea, sentiment, and opinion. I hope my reader is
not so much the slave of conventional phraseology as to
imagine that I use the word "purity" in the above sentence in its restricted, and one may say technical, sense.

I mean the purity of the upper spiritual atmosphere in which she habitually dwelt; the absolute disseverance of her moral as well as her intellectual nature from all those lower thoughts as well as lower passions which smirch the human soul. In mind and heart she was *white*—stainless. That is what I mean by purity.

Her most intimate friend at Florence was a Miss Isabella Blagden, who lived for many years at Bellosguardo, in a villa commanding a lovely view over Florence and the valley of the Arno from the southern side, looking across it therefore to Fiesole and its villa-and-cypress-covered slopes. Whether the close friendship between Mrs. Browning and Isa Blagden (we all called her Isa always) was first formed in Florence, or had its commencement at an earlier date, I do not know. But Isa was also the intimate and very specially highly-valued friend of my wife and myself. And this also contributed to our common friendship. Isa was (yes, as usual, "was," alas, though she was very much my junior) a very bright, very warm-hearted, very clever little woman, who knew everybody, and was, I think, more universally beloved than any other individual among us. A little volume of her poems was published after her untimely death, They are not such as could take by storm the careless ears of the world, which knows nothing about her, and must, I suppose, be admitted to be marked by that mediocrity which neither gods nor men can tolerate. But it is impossible to read the little volume without perceiving how choice a spirit the authoress must have been, and understanding how it came to pass that she was especially honored by the close and warm attachment of Mrs. Browning. I have scores of letters signed "Isa," or rather Sibylline leaves scrawled in the vilest handwriting on all sorts of abnormal fragments of paper, and despatched in headlong haste, generally concerning some little projected festivity at Bellosguardo, and advising me of the expected presence of some stranger whom she thought I should like to meet. Very many of such of these fragmentary scribblings as were written before the Brownings left Florence contain some word or reference to her beloved "Ba," for such was the

17*

pet name used between them, with what meaning or origin I know not.

Dear Isa's death was to me an especially sad one, because I thought, and think, that she need not have died. She lived alone with a couple of old servants, and though she was rich in troops of friends, and there were one or two near her during the day or two of her illness, they did not seem to have managed matters wisely. Our Isa was extremely obstinate about calling in medical advice. It could not be done at a moment's notice, for a message had to be sent and a doctor to come from Florence. And this was not done till the second day of her illness. And I had good reason for thinking that, had she been properly attended to on the first day, her life might have been saved. She would not let her friends send for the doctor, and the friends were unable to make her do so. Unhappily, I was absent for a few days at Siena, and returned to be met by the intelligence that she was dead. It seemed the more sad in that I knew that if I had been there I could have made her call a doctor before it was too late. Browning could also have done so; but it was after the death of Mrs. Browning and his departure from Florence.

How great her sorrow was for the death of her friend, Browning knew, doubtless, but nobody else, I think, in the world save myself.

I have now before me one of her little scraps of letters, in which she encloses one from Mrs. Browning which is of the highest interest. The history and genesis of it is as follows: Shortly after the publication of the well-known and exquisite little poem on the god Pan in the *Cornhill Magazine*, my brother Anthony wrote me a letter venturing to criticise it, in which he says: "The lines are very beautiful, and the working out of the idea is delicious. But I am inclined to think that she is illustrating an allegory by a thought, rather than a thought by an allegory. The idea of the god destroying the reed in making the instrument has, I imagine, given her occasion to declare that in the sublimation of the poet the man is lost for the ordinary purposes of man's life. It has been thus instead of being the reverse; and I can hardly believe

that she herself believes in the doctrine which her fancy
has led her to illustrate. A man that can be a poet is so
much the more a man in becoming such, and is the more
fitted for a man's best work. Nothing is destroyed, and
in preparing the instrument for the touch of the musician
the gods do nothing for which they need weep. The idea,
however, is beautiful, and it is beautifully worked."

Then follows some verbal criticism which need not be
transcribed. Going on to the seventh stanza he says, "In
the third line of it, she loses her antithesis. She must
spoil her man, as well as make a poet out of him—spoil
him as the reed is spoiled. Should we not read the lines
thus :

> " ' Yet one half beast is the great god Pan
> Or he would not have laughed by the river.
> Making a poet he mars a man;
> The true gods sigh,' etc. ?"

In justice to my brother's memory I must say that this
was not written to me with any such presumptuous idea
as that of offering his criticism to the poetess. But I
showed the letter to Isa Blagden, and at her request left
it with her. A day or two later she writes to me : "Dear
friend,—I send you back your criticism and Mrs. B.'s rejoinder. She *made* me show it to her, and she wishes you
to see her answer." Miss Blagden's words would seem
to imply that she thought the criticism mine. And if she
did, Mrs. Browning was doubtless led to suppose so too.
Yet I think this could hardly have been the case.

Of course my only object in writing all this here is to
give the reader the great treat of seeing Mrs. Browning's
"rejoinder." It is very highly interesting.

"DEAREST ISA, — Very gentle my critic is; I am glad I got him out
of you. But tell dear Mr. Trollope he is wrong nevertheless [here it
certainly seems that she supposed the criticism to be mine]; and that
my 'thought' was really and decidedly *anterior* [*sic*] to my 'allegory.'
Moreover, it is my thought still. I meant to say that the poetic organization implies certain disadvantages; for instance an exaggerated general
susceptibility, . . .* which may be shut up, kept out of the way in every-

---

* These dots do not indicate any hiatus. They exist in the MS. as here
given.

day life, and must be (or the man is '*marred*,' indeed, made a Rousseau or a Byron of), but which is necessarily, for all that, cultivated in the very cultivation of art itself. There is an inward reflection and refraction of the heats of life. . . .* doubling pains and pleasures, doubling, therefore, the motives (passions) of life. I have said something of this in A. L. ["Aurora Leigh"]. Also there is a passion for essential truth (as apprehended) and a necessity for speaking it out at all risks, inconvenient to personal peace. Add to this and much else the loss of the sweet unconscious cool privacy among the 'reeds' . . .* which I for one care so much for — the loss of the privilege of being glad or sorry, ill or well, without a 'notice.' That may have its glory to certain minds. But most people would be glad to 'stir their tea in silence' when they are grave, and even to talk nonsense (much too frivolously) when they are merry, without its running the round of the newspapers in two worlds, perhaps. You know I don't *invent*, Isa. In fact, I am sorely tempted to send Mr. Trollope a letter I had this morning, as an illustration of my view, and a reply to his criticism. Only this letter, among many, begins with too many fair speeches. Still it seems written by somebody in earnest and with a liking for me. Its main object is to complain of the cowardly morality in '*Pan*. Then a stroke on the poems before Congress. The writer has heard that I 'had been to Paris, was *fêted* by the emperor, and had had my head turned by imperial flatteries,' in consequence of which I had taken to 'praise and flatter the tyrant, and try to help his selfish ambition.' Well! one should laugh and be wise. But somehow one doesn't laugh. A letter beginning, 'You are a great teacher of truth,' and ending, 'You are a dishonest wretch,' makes you cold somehow, and ill-disposed towards the satisfactions of literary distinction. Yes! and be sure, Isa, that the 'true gods sigh,' and have reason to sigh, for the cost and pain of it; sigh only . . . don't haggle over the cost; don't grudge a crazia, but . . . sigh, sigh . . . while they pay honestly.

"On the other hand, there's much light talking and congratulation, excellent returns to the pocket from the poem in the *Cornhill ;* pleasant praise from dear Mr. Trollope . . . with all drawbacks : a good opinion from Isa worth its gold—and Pan laughs.

"But he is a beast up to the waist; yes, Mr. Trollope, a beast. He is not a true god.

"And I am neither god nor beast, if you please—only a   BA."

It seems that she certainly imagined me to be the critic ; but must have been subsequently undeceived. I will not venture to say a word on the question of the marring or making of a man which results from the creation of a poet ; but if my brother had known Mrs. Browning as well as I knew her, he would not have written that he

---

* These dots do not indicate any hiatus. They exist in the MS. as here given.

could "hardly believe that she herself believes in the doctrine that her fancy has led her to illustrate." At all events, the divine afflatus had not so marred the absolutely single-minded truthfulness of the woman in her as to make it possible that she should, for the sake of illustrating, however appositely, any fancy, however brilliant, put forth a "doctrine" as believing in it which she did not believe. It may seem that this is a foolish making of a mountain out of a molehill; but she would not have felt it to be so. She had so high a conception of the poet's office and responsibilities that nothing would have induced her to play at believing, for literary purposes, any position, or fancy, or imagination which she did not in her heart of hearts accept.

There was one subject upon which both my wife and I disagreed in opinion with Mrs. Browning; and it was a subject which sat very near her heart, and was much occupying all minds at that time—the phases of Italy's struggle for independence, and especially the part which the Emperor Napoleon the Third was taking in that struggle, and his conduct towards Italy. We were all equally "Italianissimi," as the phrase went then; all equally desirous that Italy should accomplish the union of her *disjecta membra*, throw off the yoke of the bad governments which had oppressed her, make herself a nation, and do well as such. But we differed widely as to the ultimate utility, the probable results, and, above all, as to the motives of the emperor's conduct. Mrs. Browning believed in him and trusted him. We did neither. Hence the following interesting and curious letter, written to my wife at Florence by Mrs. Browning, who was passing the summer at Siena. Mrs. Browning felt very warmly upon this subject—so, indeed, did my wife, differing from her *toto cœlo* upon it. But the difference not only never caused the slightest suspension of cordial feeling between them, but never caused either of them to doubt for a moment that the other was with equal sincerity and equal ardor anxious for the same end. The letter was written, as only the postmark shows, on September 26, 1859, and was as follows:

"MY DEAR MRS. TROLLOPE,—I feel doubly grateful to you . . . for the music (one of the proofs of your multiform faculty) and for your kind and welcome letter, which I have delayed to thank you for. My body lags so behind my soul always, and especially of late, that you must consider my disadvantages in whatever fault is committed by me, trying to forgive it.

"Certainly we differ in our estimate of the Italian situation, while loving and desiring for Italy up to the same height and with the same heart.

"For me I persist in looking to *facts* rather than to words official or un-official, and in repeating that, 'whereas we were bound, now we are free.'

"'I think, therefore I am.' *Cogito, ergo sum*, was, you know, an old formula. Italy thinks (aloud) at Florence and Bologna; therefore she *is*. And how did that happen? Could it have happened last year, with the Austrians at Bologna, and ready (at a sign) to precipitate themselves into Tuscany? Could it have happened previous to the French intervention? And could it happen *now* if France used the power she has in Italy *against* Italy? Why is it that the *Times* newspaper, which declared . . . first that the elections were to be prevented by France, and next that they were to be tampered with . . . is not justified before our eyes? I appeal to your sober judgment . . . if, indeed, the Emperor Napoleon *desires the res-toration of the dukes!!* Is he not all the more admirable for being loyal and holding his hand off while he has fifty thousand men ready to 'protect' us all and prevent the exercise of the people's sovereignty? And he a despot (so called) and accustomed to carry out his desires. Instead of which Tuscans and Romagnoli, Parma and Modena, have had every oppor-tunity allowed them to combine, carry their elections, and express their full minds in assemblies, till the case becomes so complicated and strength-ened that her enemies for the most part despair.

"The qualities shown by the Italians—the calm, the dignity, the intelli-gence, the constancy . . . I am as far from not understanding the weight of these virtues as from not admiring them. But the *opportunity* for ex-ercising them comes from the Emperor Napoleon, and it is good and just for us all to remember this while we admire the most.

"So at least I think; and the Italian official bodies have always admitted it, though individuals seem to me to be too much influenced by the suspi-cions and calumnies thrown out by foreign journals—English, Prussian, Austrian, and others—which traduce the emperor's motives in diplomacy, as they traduced them in the war. A prejudice in the eye is as fatal to sight as mote and beam together. And there are things abroad *worse* than any prejudices—yes, worse!

"It is a fact that the emperor used his influence with England to get the Tuscan vote accepted by the English government. Whatever wickedness he meant by *that* the gods know; and English statesmen suspect . . . (or suspected a very short time ago); but the deed itself is not wicked, and you and I shall not be severe on it whatever bad motive may be imput-able.

"So much more I could write . . . about Villafranca, but I won't. The emperor, great man as he is, could not precisely anticipate the high quali-ties given proof of in the late development of Italian nationality. He made the best terms he could, having had his hand forced. In consequence of this treaty he has carried out his engagement to Austria in certain official forms, knowing well that the free will and choice of the Italians are hindered by none of them ; and knowing besides that every apparent coldness and reserve of his towards the peninsula removes a jealousy from England, and instigates her to a more liberal and human bearing than formerly.

"Forgive me for all these words. I am much better, but still not as strong as I was before my attack ; only getting strength, I hope.

"Miss Blagden and Miss Field are staying still with us, and are gone to Siena to-day to see certain pictures (which has helped to expose you to this attack). We talk of returning to Florence by the first of October, or soon after, in spite of the revival of fine weather. Mr. Landor is surprisingly improved by the good air here and the repose of mind ; walks two miles, and writes alcaics and pentameters on most days . . . on his domestic circumstances, and . . . I am sorry to say . . . Louis Napoleon. But I tell him that I mean him to write an ode on my side of the question before we have done.

"I honor you and your husband for the good work you have both done on behalf of this great cause. But his book* we only know yet by the extracts in the *Athenæum*, which brings us your excellent articles. May I not thank you for them ? And when does Mr. Trollope come back ? [from a flying visit to England]. We hope not to miss him out of Florence long.

"Peni's love to Bice.† He has been very happy here, galloping through the lanes on a pony the color of his curls. Then he helps to work in the vineyards and to keep the sheep, having made close friends with the *contadini*, to whom he reads and explains Dall' Ongaro's poems with great applause. By the way, the poet paid us a visit lately, and we liked him much.

"And let me tell *Bice's mother* another story of Penini. He keeps a journal, be it whispered ; I ventured to peep through the leaves the other morning, and came to the following notice : 'This is the happiest day of my *hole* (*sic*) life, because dearest Vittoria Emanuele is really *nostro re !*'

"There's a true Italian for you ! But his weak point is spelling.

"Believe me, with my husband's regards, ever truly and affectionately yours,   ELIZABETH BARRETT BROWNING."

It may possibly enter into the mind of some one of those who never enjoyed the privilege of knowing Mrs. Browning the woman to couple together the stupidly-calumnious insinuations to which she refers in the first letter I have given with the admiration she expresses for the third Napoleon in the second letter. I differed from her wholly in her estimate of the man and in her views of

---

* "Tuscany in 1849 and 1859."   † Browning's boy and my girl.

his policy with regard to Italy. And many an argument
have I had with her on the subject. And my opinions
respecting it were all the more distasteful to her because
they concerned the character of the man himself as well
as his policy as a ruler. And those talks and arguments
have left me probably the only man alive, save one, who
knows with such certainty as I know it, and can assert as
I can, the absolute absurdity and impossibility of the idea
that she, being what she was, could have been bribed by
any amount of imperial or other flattery, not only to profess opinions which she did not veritably hold—this touches her moral nature, perhaps the most pellucidly truthful
of any I ever knew—but to hold opinions which she would
not have otherwise held. This touches her intellectual
nature, which was as incapable of being mystified or modified by any suggestion of vanity, self-love, or gratified
pride as the most judicial-minded judge who ever sat on
the bench. Her intellectual view on the matter *was*, I
thought, mystified and modified by the intensity of her
love for the Italian cause and of her hatred for the evils
from which she was watching the Italians struggling to
liberate themselves.

I heard, probably from herself, of whispered calumnies,
such as those she refers to in the first of the two letters
given. She despised them then, as those who loved and
valued her did, though the sensitive, womanly gentleness
of her nature made it a pain to her that any fellow-creat-
ure, however ignorant and far away from her, should so
think of her. And my disgust at a secret attempt to stab
has impelled me to say what I *know* on the subject. But
I really think that not only those who knew her as she
lived in the flesh, but the tens of thousands who know her
as she lives in her written words, cannot but feel my vin-
dication superfluous.

The above long and specially interesting letter is written in very small characters on ten pages of extremely
small duodecimo note-paper, as is also the other letter by
the same writer given above. Mrs. Browning's handwriting shows, ever and anon, an odd tendency to form
each letter of a word separately—a circumstance which I

mention for the sake of remarking that old Huntingford, the Bishop of Hereford, in my young days, between whom and Mrs. Browning there was one thing in common, namely, a love for and familiarity with Greek studies, used to write in the same manner.

The Dall' Ongaro here spoken of was an old friend of ours—of my wife's, if I remember right—before our marriage. He was a Venetian, or, rather, to speak accurately, I believe, a Dalmatian by birth, but all his culture and sympathies were Venetian. He had in his early youth been destined for the priesthood, but, like many another, had been driven by the feelings and sympathies engendered by Italy's political struggles to abandon the tonsure for the sake of joining the "patriot" cause. His muse was of the drawing-room school and calibre. But he wrote very many charming little poems breathing the warmest aspirations of the somewhat extreme *gauche* of that day, especially some *stornelli* after the Tuscan fashion, which met with a very wide and warm acceptance. I remember one extremely happy, the *refrain* of which still runs in my head. It is written on the newly adopted Italian tricolor flag. After characterizing each color separately in a couplet, he ends:

"E il rosso, il bianco, e il verde,
   E un terno che si giuoca, e non si perde."

The phrase is borrowed from the language of the lottery. "And the red, and the white, and the green, are a threefold combination" [I am obliged to be horribly prosaic in order to make the allusion intelligible to non-Italian ears] "on which we may play and be sure not to lose!"

I am tempted to give here another of Mrs. Browning's letters to my first wife, partly by the persuasion that any letter of hers must be a matter of interest to a very large portion of English readers, and partly for the sake of the generously appreciative criticism of one of my brother's books, which I also always considered to be one of his best. I must add that Mrs. Browning's one bit of censure coincides as perfectly with my own judgment. The letter, as

usual, is dateless, but must have been written very shortly
after the publication of my brother's novel called "The
Three Clerks."

"MY DEAR MRS. TROLLOPE,—I return 'The Three Clerks' with our true
thanks and appreciation.   We both quite agree with you in considering it
the best of the three clever novels before the public.   My husband, who
can seldom get a novel to hold him, has been held by all three, and by
this the strongest.   Also, it has qualities which the others gave no sign
of.   For instance, I was wrung to tears by the third volume.   What a
thoroughly *man's* book it is !   I much admire it, only wishing away, with
a vehemence which proves the veracity of my general admiration, the contributions to the 'Daily Delight '—may I dare to say it ?

"I do hope you are better.   For myself, I have not suffered more than
was absolutely necessary in the late unusual weather.

"I heard with concern that Mrs. Trollope [my mother] has been less
well than usual.   But who can wonder, with such cold ?

            "Most truly yours,   ELIZABETH BARRETT BROWNING.
"CASA GUIDI, *Wednesday.*"

Here is, also, one other little memorial, written, not by
"Elizabeth Barrett Browning," but by "Elizabeth Barrett."   It is interesting on more than one account.   It bears
no date save "Beacon Terrace [Torquay], Thursday."
But it evidently marks the beginning of acquaintanceship
between the two exceptionally, though not equally, gifted girls, Elizabeth Barrett and Theodosia Garrow.   It is
written on a sheet of the very small duodecimo note-paper
which she was wont to use many years subsequently, but
in far more delicate and elegant characters than she used
when much pen-work had produced its usual deteriorating
effect on her caligraphy.

"I cannot return the 'Book of Beauty' [Lady Blessington's annual]
to Miss Garrow without thanking her for allowing me to read in it sooner
than I should otherwise have done those contributions of her own which
help to justify its title, and which are indeed sweet and touching verses.

"It is among the vexations brought upon me by my illness that I still
remain personally unacquainted with Miss Garrow, though seeming to myself to know her through those who actually do so.   And I should venture
to hope that it might be a vexation the first to leave me, if a visit to an
invalid condemned to the *peine forte et dure* of being very silent, notwithstanding her womanhood, were a less gloomy thing.   At any rate, I am
encouraged to thank Miss Fisher and Miss Garrow for their visits of repeated inquiry, and their other very kind attentions, by these written
words rather than by a message.   For I am sure that wherever kindness

can come thankfulness *may*, and that whatever intrusion my note can be guilty of, it is excusable by the fact of my being Miss Garrow's
"Sincerely obliged,   E. BARRETT."

Could anything be more charmingly girlish or more prettily worded? The diminutive little note seems to have been preserved, an almost solitary survival of the memorials of the days to which it belongs. It must doubtless have been followed by sundry others, but was, I suppose, specially treasured as having been the first step towards a friendship which was already highly valued.

Of course, in the recollections of an Englishman living during those years in Florence, Robert Browning must necessarily stand out in high relief and in the foremost line. But very obviously this is neither the time nor the place, nor is my dose of presumption sufficient, for any attempt at a delineation of the man. To speak of the poet, since I write for Englishmen, would be very superfluous. It may be readily imagined that the "tag-rag and bob-tail" of the men who mainly constituted that very pleasant, but not very intellectual society, were not likely to be such as Mr. Browning would readily make intimates of. And I think I see, in memory's magic glass, that the men used to be rather afraid of him. Not that I ever saw him rough or uncourteous with the most exasperating fool that ever rubbed a man's nervous system the wrong way, but there was a quiet, lurking smile which, supported by very few words, used to seem to have the singular property of making the utterers of platitudes and the mistakers of *non-sequiturs* for *sequiturs* uncomfortably aware of the nature of their words within a very few minutes after they had uttered them. I may say, however, that I believe that, in any dispute on any sort of subject between any two men in the place, if it had been proposed to submit the matter in dispute for adjudication to Mr. Browning, the proposal would have been jumped at with a greater readiness of *consensus* than in the case of any other man there.

CHAPTER XXX.

THE Italians, I believe, were "thinking" at a considerably earlier period than that which, in the second letter, transcribed in the preceding chapter, Mrs. Browning seems to have considered as the beginning of their "cogitating" existence, and thinking on the subjects to which she is there adverting. They were "thinking," perhaps, less in Tuscany than in any other part of the peninsula, for they were eating more and better there. They were very lightly taxed. The *mezzeria* system of agriculture, which, if not absolutely the same, is extremely similar to that which is known as "conacre," rendered the lot of the peasant population very far better and more prosperous than that of the tillers of the earth in any of the other provinces. And, upon the whole, the people were contented. The Tuscan public was certainly not a "pensive public." They ate their bread not without due condiment of *compagnatico,** or even their chestnuts in the more remote and primitive mountain districts, drank their sound Tuscan wine from the generous, big-bellied Tuscan flasks, holding three good bottles, and sang their *stornelli* in cheerfulness of heart, and had no craving whatsoever for those few special liberties which were denied them.

Epicuri de grege porci! No progress! Yes, I know all that, and am not saying what should have been, but what was. There *was* no progress. The *contadini* on the little farm which I came to possess before I left Tuscany cultivated it precisely after the fashion of their grandfathers and great-grandfathers, and strenuously resisted any suggestion that it could, should, or might be cultivated

---

* Anything to make the bread "go down," as our people say—a morsel of bacon or sausage, a handful of figs or grapes, or a bit of cheese.

in any other way. But my *contadino* inhabited a large and roomy *casa colonica;* he and his buxom wife had six stalwart sons, and was the richer man in consequence of having them. No, in my early Florentine days the. *cogito, ergo sum,* could not have been predicated of the Tuscans.

But the condition of things in the other states of the peninsula, in Venice and Lombardy under the Austrians, in Naples under the Bourbon kings, in Romagna under the pope, and very specially in Modena under its dukes of the House of Este, was much otherwise. In those regions the Italians were "thinking" a great deal, and had been thinking for some time past. And somewhere about 1849, those troublesome members of the body social who are not contented with eating, drinking, and singing—cantankerous reading and writing people living in towns, who wanted most unreasonably to say, as the phrase goes, that "their souls were their own" (as if such fee-simple rights ever fall to the lot of any man!)—began in Tuscany to give signs that they also were "thinking."

I remember well that Albèri, the highly accomplished and learned editor of the "Reports of the Venetian Ambassadors," and of the great edition of Galileo's works, was the first man who opened my altogether innocent eyes to the fact that the revolutionary leaven was working in Tuscany, and that there were social breakers ahead. This must have been as early as 1845, or possibly 1844. Albèri himself was a Throne-and-Altar man, who thought, for his part, that the amount of proprietorship over his own soul which the existing *régime* allowed him was enough for his purposes. But, as he confided to me, a very strong current of opinion was beginning to run the other way in Florence, in Leghorn, in Lucca, and many smaller cities—not in Siena, which always was, and is still, a nest of conservative feeling.

Nevertheless there never was, at least in Florence, the strength and bitterness of revolutionary feeling that existed almost everywhere else throughout Italy. I remember a scene which furnished a very remarkable proof of this, and which was at the same time very curiously and signifi-

cantly characteristic of the Florentine character, at least
as it then existed.

It was during the time of the Austrian occupation of
Florence. On the whole the Austrian troops behaved
well ; and their doings, and the spirit in which the job they
had in hand was carried out, were very favorably contrasted with the tyranny, the insults, and the aggressive
arrogance with which the French army of occupation
afflicted the Romans. The Austrians accordingly were
never hated in Florence with the bitter intensity of hate
which the French earned in the Eternal City. Nevertheless, there were now and then occasions when the Florentine populace gratified their love of a holiday and testified
to the purity of their Italian patriotism by turning out
into the streets and kicking up a row.

It was on an occasion of this sort that the narrow street
called Por' Santa Maria, which runs up from the Ponte
Vecchio to the Piazza, was thickly crowded with people.
A young lieutenant had been sent to that part of the town
with a small detachment of cavalry to clear the streets.
Judging from the aspect of the people, as his men, coming
down the Lung' Arno, turned into the narrow street, he
did not half like the job before him. He thought there
certainly would be bloodshed. And just as his men were
turning the corner and beginning to push their horses into
the crowd, one of them slipped sideways on the flagstones,
with which, most distressingly to horses not used to them,
the streets of Florence are paved, and came down with
his rider partly under him.

The officer thought, "Now for trouble ! That man will
be killed to a certainty." The crowd—who were filling
the air with shouts of "*Morte !*" "*Abbasso l'Austria !*"
"*Morte agli Austriaci !*" * — crowded round the fallen
trooper, while the officer tried to push forward towards
the spot. But when he got within earshot, and could see
also what was taking place, he saw the people immediately round the fallen man busily disengaging him from his
horse. "*O poverino! Ti sei fatto male? Orsu! Non*

---

* "Death !"   "Down with Austria !"   "Death to the Austrians !"

sara niente! Su! A cavallo, eh ?" And having helped
the man to remount, they returned to their amusement of
"Morte agli Austriaci !" The young officer perceived that
he had a very different sort of populace to deal with from
an angry crowd on the other side of the Alps, or indeed
on the other side of the Apennines.

I remember another circumstance which occurred a few
years previously to that just mentioned, and which was
in its way equally characteristic. In one of the principal
cafés of Florence, situated on the Piazza del Duomo—the
cathedral yard—a murder was committed. The deed was
done in full daylight, when the *café* was full of people.
Such crimes, and indeed violent crimes of any sort, were
exceedingly rare in Florence. That in question was committed by stabbing, and the motive of the criminal, who
had come to Florence for the express purpose of killing
his enemy, was vengeance for a great wrong. Having accomplished his purpose, he quietly walked out of the *café*
and went away. I happened to be on the spot shortly
afterwards, and inquired, with some surprise at the escape
of the murderer, why he had not been arrested red-handed.
" He had a sword in his hand !" said the person to whom
I had addressed myself, in a tone which implied that that
quite settled the matter—that of course it was absolutely
out of the question to attempt to interfere with a man
who had a sword in his hand !

It is a very singular thing, and one for which it is difficult to offer any satisfactory explanation, that the change
in Florence in respect to the prevalence of crime has been
of late years very great indeed. I have mentioned more
than once, I think, the very remarkable absence of all
crimes of violence which characterized Florence in the
earlier time of my residence there. It was not due to
rigorous repression or vigilance of the police, as may be
partly judged by the above anecdote. There was, in fact,
no police that merited the name. But anything in the
nature of burglary was unheard of. The streets were so

---

* "Oh, poor fellow ! Have you hurt yourself ? Up with you ! It will
be nothing ! Up ! Again on your horse, eh ?"

absolutely safe that any lady might have traversed them alone at any hour of the day or night. And I might add to the term "crimes of violence" the further statement that pocket-picking was equally unheard of.

Now there is perhaps more crime of a heinous character in Florence, in proportion to the population, than in any city in the peninsula. I think that about the first indication that all that glittered in the mansuetude of *Firenze la Gentile* was not gold showed itself on the occasion of an attempt to naturalize at Florence the traditional sportiveness of the Roman Carnival. There and then, as all the world knows, it has been the immemorial habit for the population, high and low, to pelt the folks in the carriages during their Corso procession with *bonbons, bouquets*, and the like. Gradually at Rome this exquisite fooling has degenerated under the influence of modern notions till the *bouquets* having become cabbage stalks, very effective as offensive missiles, and the *bonbons* plaster-of-Paris pellets, with an accompanying substitution of a spiteful desire to inflict injury for the old horse-play, it has become necessary to limit the duration of the Saturnalia to the briefest span, with the sure prospect of its being very shortly altogether prohibited. But at Florence on the first occasion, now several years ago, of an attempt to imitate the Roman practice, the conduct of the populace was such as to demand imperatively the immediate suppression of it. The carriages and the occupants of them were attacked by such volleys of stones and mud, and the animus of the people was so evidently malevolent and dangerous, that they were at once driven from the scene, and any repetition of the practice was forbidden.

It is so remarkable as to be, at all events, worth noting, that contemporaneously with this singular deterioration in respect to crime, another social change has taken place in Florence. *La Gentile Firenze* has of late years become very markedly the home of clericalism of a high and aggressive type. This is an entirely new feature in the Florentine social world. In the old time clerical views were sufficiently supported by the government to give rise to the famous Madiai incident, which has been before alluded to. But clericalism in its more aggressive aspects was not in the ascendant either bureaucratically or socially. The spirit which had informed the policy and government of the famous Leopoldine laws was still sufficiently alive in the mental habitudes of both governors and governed to render Tuscany a rather suspected and disliked region in the mind of the Vatican and of the secular governments which sympathized with the Vatican's views and sentiments. The change that has taken place is therefore a very notable one. I have no such sufficiently intimate knowledge of the subject as would justify me in linking together the two changes I have noticed in the connection of cause and effect. I only note the synchronism.

On the other hand there are not wanting sociologists who maintain that the cause of the outburst of lawlessness and crime which has undeniably characterized Florence of late years is to be sought for exactly in that old-time, easy-going tolerance in religious matters which they say is now producing a tardy but sure crop from seeds that, however long in disclosing the true nature of the harvest to be expected from them, ought never to have been expected by wise legislators to produce any other.

Non nostrum est tantas componere lites! But Florence is certainly no longer *Firenze la Gentile,* as she so eminently was in the days when I knew her so well.

When any of the other cities of Italy have in any degree ceased to merit the traditional epithets which so many successive generations assigned to them—how far Genoa is still *la Superba,* Bologna *la Grassa,* Padua *la Dotta,* Lucca *la Industriosa*—I cannot say. Venezia is unquestionably still *la Bella.* And as for old Rome, she vindicates more than ever her title to the epithet *Eterna,* by her similitude to those nursery toys which, throw them about as you will, still with infallible certitude come down heads uppermost.

As for the Florence of my old recollections, there were in the early days of them many little old-world sights and sounds which are to be seen and heard no longer, and which differentiated the place from other social centres.

18

I remember a striking incident of this sort which happened to my mother and myself "in the days before the flood," therefore very shortly after our arrival there.

It was the practice in those days to carry the bodies of the dead on open biers, with uncovered faces, to their burial. It had doubtless been customary in old times so to carry all the dead; but the custom was retained at the time of which I am writing only in the case of distinguished persons, and very generally of the priesthood. I remember, for instance, a poor little humpbacked grand duchess being so carried through the street magnificently bedecked as if she were going to a ball, and with painted cheeks. She had been a beneficent little body, and the people, as far as they knew anything about her, revered her, and looked on her last presentation to them with sympathetic feelings. But it was a sorry sight to see the poor little body, looking much like a bedizened monkey, so paraded.

Well, my mother and I were, aimlessly but much admiringly, wandering about the vast spaces of the cathedral when we became aware of a *funzione* of some sort—a service as we should say—being conducted in a far part of the building. There was no great crowd, but a score or two of spectators, mainly belonging to the *gamin* category, were standing around the officiating priests and curiously looking on. We went towards the spot, and found that the burial service was being performed over the body of a young priest. The body lay on its back on the open bier, clad in full canonicals and with the long tasselled cap of the secular clergy on his head. We stood and gazed with the others, when suddenly I saw the dead man's head slightly move! A shiver, I confess, ran through me. A moment's reflection, however, reminded me of the recognized deceitfulness of the eyes in such matters, and I did not doubt that I had been mistaken. But the next minute I again saw the dead priest slightly shake his head, and this time I was sure that I was not mistaken. I clutched my mother's arm and pointed, and again saw the awful phenomenon, which sent a cold wave through both of us from head to foot. But nobody save ourselves seemed to have seen

anything unusual. The service was proceeding in its
wonted order. Doubting whether it might possibly be
one of those horrible cases of suspended animation and
mistaken death, I was thinking whether it were not my
duty to call attention to the startling thing we had seen,
and had with outstretched neck and peering eyes advanced
a step for further observation, and with the half-formed
purpose of declaring aloud that the man was not dead,
when I spied crouched beneath the bier a little monkey,
some nine or ten years old, who had taken in his hand the
tassel of the cap, which hung down between the wooden
bars which formed the bier, and was amusing himself with
slowly swaying it forward and backward, and had thus
communicated the motion to the dead man's head! It
was almost impossible to believe that the little urchin had
been able to reach the position he occupied without having been observed by any of the clerical attendants, of
whom several were present, and still more difficult to suppose that no one of them had seen what we saw, standing
immediately in front of the corpse while one of them performed the rite of lustration with holy water, the vessel
containing which was held by another. But no one interfered, and none but those who know the Florentines as
well as I know them can feel how curiously and intensely
characteristic of them was the fact that no one did so.
The awful reverence for death which would have impelled
an Englishman of almost any social position to feel indignation and instantly put a stop to what he would consider a profanation, was absolutely unknown to all those
engaged in that perfunctory rite. A certain amount of
trouble and disturbance would have been caused by dis-
lodging the culprit, and each man there felt only this;
that it didn't matter a straw, and that there was no reason
for *him* to take the trouble of noticing it. As far as I
could observe, the amusement the little wretch derived
from his performance was entirely unsocial, and confined
to his own breast; for I could not see that any of the
gamin fraternity noticed it, or cared about it, any more
than their seniors.

I remember another somewhat analogous adventure of

mine, equally illustrative of the Florentine habits of those days. I saw a man suddenly stagger and fall in the street. It was in the afternoon, and there were many persons in the street, some of them nearer to the fallen man than I was, but nobody attempted to help him. I stepped forward to do so, and was about to take hold of him and try to raise him, when one of the bystanders eagerly caught me by the arm, saying, "He is dying, he is dying!" "Let us try to raise him," said I, still pressing forward. "You mustn't, you mustn't! It is not permitted," he added, as he perceived that he was speaking to a foreigner, and then went on to explain to me that what must be done was to call the Misericordia, for which purpose one must run and ring a certain bell attached to the chapel of that brotherhood in the Piazza del Duomo.

Among the many things that have been written of the Florentine Misericordia, I do not think that I have met with the statement that it used to be universally believed in Florence that the law gave the black brethren the privilege and the monopoly of picking up any dying or dead person in the streets, and that it was forbidden to any one else to do so. Whether any such *law* really existed I much doubt, but the custom of acting in accordance with it, and the belief that such practice was imperative, undoubtedly did. And I have no doubt that many a life has been sacrificed to it. The half-hour or twenty minutes which necessarily elapsed before the Misericordia could be called and answer the call must often have been supremely important, and in many cases ought to have been employed in the judicious use of the lancet.

The sight of the black-robed and black-cowled brethren, as they went about the streets on their errands of mercy, was common enough in Florence. But the holiday visitor had very little opportunity of hearing anything of the internal management and rules of that peculiar mediæval society or of the nature of the work it did.

The Florentine Misericordia was founded in the days when pestilence was ravaging the city so fiercely that the dead lay uncared for in the streets, because there was no man sufficiently courageous to bury or to touch them.

The members of the association, which was formed for the performance of this charitable and arduous duty, chose for themselves a costume the object of which was the absolute concealment of the individual performing it. A loose black linen gown drapes the figure from the neck to the heels, and a black cowl, with two holes cut for the eyes, covers and effectually conceals the head and face. For more than five hundred years, up to the present day, the dress remains the same, and no human being, either of those to whom their services are rendered, or of the thousands who see them going about in the performance of their self-imposed duty, can know whether the mysterious weird-looking figure he sees be prince or peasant. He knows that he may be either, for the members of the brotherhood are drawn from all classes of society.

It used to be whispered, and I have good reasons for believing the whisper to have been true, that the late grand duke was a member, and took his turn of duty with his brethren. Some indiscreet personal attendant blabbed the secret, for assuredly the duke himself was never untrue to the oath which binds the members to secrecy.

The whole society is divided into a number of companies, one of which is by turns on duty. There is a large, most melancholy, and ominously sounding bell in the chapel of the brotherhood (not that already mentioned by which anybody can call the attention of the brother in permanent attendance, but a much larger one), which is heard all over the city. This summons the immediate attendance of every member of the company on duty, and the mysterious black figures may any day be seen hurrying to the rendezvous. There they learn the nature of the call, and the place at which their presence is required.

I remember the case of an English girl who was fearfully burned at a villa at some little distance from the city. The injuries were so severe that, while it was extremely desirable that she should be removed to a hospital, there was much doubt as to the possibility of moving her. In this difficulty the Misericordia were summoned. They came, five or six of them, bringing with them their too well-known black-covered litter, and transported the patient to the hospital, lifting her from her bed and placing her in the litter with an exquisitely delicate and skilled gentleness of handling which spared her suffering to the utmost, and excited the surprise and admiration of the English medical man who witnessed the operation. Every part of the work, every movement, was executed in absolute silence and with combined obedience to signalled orders from the leader of the company.

Another case which was brought under my notice was that of a woman suffering from dropsy, which made the necessary removal of her a very arduous and difficult operation. It would probably have been deemed impossible save by the assistance of the Misericordia, who managed so featly and deftly that those who saw it marvelled at the skill and accurately co-operating force, which nothing but long practice could have made possible.

It is a law of the brotherhood, never broken, that they are to accept nothing, not so much as a glass of water, in any house to which they are called. The Florentines well know how much they owe as a community, and how much each man may some day come to owe personally to the Misericordia; and when the doleful clang of their well-known bell is heard booming over the city, women may be seen to cross themselves with a muttered prayer, while men, ashamed of their religiosity, but moved by feeling as well as habit, will furtively do the same.

There is an association at Rome copied from that at Florence, and vowed to the performance of very similar duties. I once had an opportunity of seeing the registers of this Roman Misericordia, and was much impressed by the frequently recurring entry of excursions into the Campagna to bring in the corpses of men murdered and left there!

CHAPTER XXXI.

REMINISCENCES AT FLORENCE — *continued.*

AMONG the other things that contributed to make those Florence days very pleasant ones, we did a good deal in the way of private theatricals. Our *impresario*, at least in the earlier part of the time, was Arthur Vansittart. He engaged the Cocomero Theatre for our performances, and to the best of my remembrance defrayed the whole of the expense out of his own pocket. Vansittart was an exceptionally tall man, a thread-paper of a man, and a very bad actor. He was exceedingly noisy, and pushed vivacity to its extreme limits. I remember well his appearance in some play—I fancy it was in "The Road to Ruin," in which I represented some character, I entirely forget what —where he comes on with a four-in-hand whip in his hand; and I remember, too, that for the other performers in that piece, their appearance on the stage was a service of danger, from which the occupants of the stage-boxes were not entirely free. But he was inexhaustibly good-natured and good-humored, and gave us excellent suppers after the performance.

Then there was Edward Hobhouse, with—more or less with—his exceedingly pretty and clever wife, and her sister, the not at all pretty but still more clever and very witty Miss Graves. Hobhouse was a man abounding in talent of all sorts, extremely witty, brimful of humor, a thorough good fellow, and very popular. He and his wife, though very good friends, did not entirely pull together; and it used to be told of him that, replying to a man who asked him "How's your wife?" he answered, with much humorous semblance of indignation, "Well, if you come to that, how's yours?" Hobhouse was far and away the cleverest and best-educated man of the little set (these dramatic reminiscences refer to the early years of my

Florence life), and, in truth, was somewhat regrettably wasted in the midst of such a frivolous and idle community. But I take it that he was much of an invalid.

Of course we got up "The Rivals." I was at first Bob Acres, with an Irishman of the name of Torrens for my Sir Lucius, which he acted, when we could succeed in keeping him sober, to the life. My Bob Acres was not much of a success. And I subsequently took Sir Anthony, which remained my stock part for years, and which I was considered to do well.

Sir Francis Vincent, a resident in Florence for many years, with whom I was for several of them very intimate, played the ungrateful part of Falkland. He was a heavy actor with fairly good elocution and delivery, and not un-fitted for a part which it might have been difficult to fill without him. He was to a great degree a reading man, and had a considerable knowledge of the byways of Florentine history.

My mother "brought the house down" nightly as Mrs. Malaprop; and a very exceptionally beautiful Madame de Parcieu (an Englishwoman married to a Frenchman) was, in appearance, *manière d'être*, and deportment, the veritable *beau idéal* of Lydia Languish, and might have made *a furore* on any stage, if it had been possible to induce her to raise her voice sufficiently. She was most good-naturedly amenable. But when she was thus driven against her nature and habits to speak out, all the excellence of her acting was gone. The meaning of the words was taken out of them.

Sir Anthony Absolute became, as I said, my stock part. And the phrase is justified by my having acted it many years afterwards in a totally different company—I the only remaining brick of the old edifice—and to audiences not one of whom could have witnessed the performances of those earlier days. Mrs. Richie, an American lady—who had, I think, been known on a London stage under the name of "Mowatt"—was in those latter days, now so far away in the dim past, our manageress. Mrs. Proby, the wife—now, I am sorry to say, the widow—of the British consul, was on that occasion our Mrs. Malaprop, and was an excellent representative of that popular lady, though she will, I am sure, forgive me for saying not so perfect a one as my mother.

Quite indescribably strange is the effect on my mind of looking back at my three Thespian avatars—Falstaff at Cincinnati, Acres and Sir Anthony in Grand Ducal Florence, and Sir Anthony again in a liberated Tuscany. I seem to myself like some old mail-coach guard, who goes through the whole long journey, while successive coachmen "Leave you here, sir?" But then in my case the passengers are all changed too; and I arrive at the end of the journey without one "inside" or "outside" of those who started with me. I can still blow my horn cheerily, however, and chat with the passengers who joined the coach when my journey was half done as if they were quite old fellow-travellers.

It must not be imagined, however, that that pleasant life at Florence was all cakes and ale.

I was, upon the whole, a hard worker. I wrote a series of volumes on various portions of Italian, and especially Florentine history, beginning with "The Girlhood of Catharine de' Medici." They were all fairly well received, the "Life of Filippo Strozzi" perhaps the more so. But the volume on the story of the great quarrel between the Papacy and Venice, entitled "Paul the Pope and Paul the Friar," was, I think, the best. The volumes entitled "A Decade of Italian Women," and dealing with ten typical historic female figures, has attained, I believe, to some share of public favor. I see it not unfrequently quoted by writers on Italian subjects. Then I made a more ambitious attempt, and produced a "History of the Commonwealth of Florence," in four volumes.

Such a work appeals, of course, to a comparatively limited audience. But that it was recognized to have some value among certain Anglo-Saxons whose favorable judgment in the matter was worth having, may be gathered from the fact that it has been a text-book in our own and in transatlantic universities; while a verdict perhaps still more flattering (though I will not say more gratifying) was given by Professor Pasquale Villari (now senator of the

18*

kingdom of Italy), who, in a letter in my possession, pronounces my history of Florence to be in his opinion the best work on the subject extant.

Professor Villari is not only an accomplished scholar of a wide range of culture, but his praise of any work on Italian—and perhaps especially on Tuscan—history comes from no "prentice han'." His masterly "Life of Macchiavelli" is as well known in our country as in his own, through the translation of it into English by his gifted wife, Linda Villari, whilom Linda White, and my very valued friend. All these historical books were written *con amore.* The study of bygone Florentines had an interest for me which was quickened by the daily and hourly study of living Florentines. It was curious to mark in them resemblances of character, temperament, idiosyncrasy, defects, and merits to those of their forefathers who move and breathe before us in the pages of such old chroniclers as Villani, Segni, Varchi, and the rest, and in sundry fire-graven strophes and lines of their mighty poet. Dante's own local and limited characteristics, as distinguished from the universality of his poetic genius, have always seemed to me quintessentially Tuscan.

Of course it is among the lower orders that such traits are chiefly found, and among the lower orders in the country more than those in the towns. But there is, or was, for I speak of years ago, a considerable conservative pride in their own inherited customs and traditions common to all classes.

Especially this is perceived in the speech of the genuine Florentine. Quaint proverbs, not always of scrupulous refinement, old-world phrases, local allusions, are stuffed into the conversation of your real citizen or citizeness of *Firenze la Gentile* as thickly as the beads in the *vezzo di corallo* on the neck of a *contadina.* And, above all, the accent—the soft (not to say slobbering) *c* and *g*, and the guttural aspirate which turns *casa* into *hasa* and *capitale* into *hapitale,* and so forth—this is cherished with peculiar fondness. I have heard a young, elegant, and accomplished woman discourse in very choice Italian with the accent of a market-woman, and, on being remonstrated with for the use of some very pungent proverbial illustration in her talk, she replied with conviction, " That is the right way to speak Tuscan. I have nothing to do with what Italians from other provinces may prefer. But pure, racy Tuscan—the Tuscan tongue that we have inherited—is spoken as I speak it—or ought to be !"

I had gathered together, partly for my own pleasure, and partly in the course of historical researches, a valuable collection of works on *Storia Patria*, which were sold by me when I gave up my house there. The reading of Italian, even very crabbed and ancient Italian which might have puzzled more than one " elegant scholar," became quite easy and familiar to me, but I have never attained a colloquial mastery over the language. I can talk, to be sure, with the most incorrect fluency, and I can make myself understood—at all events by Italians, whose quick, sympathetic apprehension of one's meaning, and courteous readiness to assist a foreigner in any linguistic straits, are deserving of grateful recognition from all of us who, however involuntarily, maltreat their beautiful language.

But the colloquial use of a language must be acquired when the organs are young and lissom. I began too late. And, besides, I have labored under the great disadvantage that my deafness prevents me from sharing in the hourly lessons which those who hear all that is going on around them profit by.

Besides the above-mentioned historical works, I wrote well-nigh a score, I think, of novels, which also had no great, but a fair, share of success. The majority of them are on Italian subjects ; and these, if I may be allowed to say so, are good. The pictures they give of Italian men and women, and things and habits, are true, vivid, and accurate. Those which I wrote on English subjects are unquestionably bad. I had been living the best part of a lifetime out of England; I knew but little comparatively of English life, and I had no business to meddle with such subjects. But, besides all this, I was always writing in periodical publications of all sorts, English and American, to such an extent that I should think the bulk of it, if

brought together, would exceed that of all the many volumes I am answerable for. No, my life in that Castle
of Indolence—Italy—was not a *far-niente* one.

We were great at picnics in those Florence days. Perhaps the most favorite place of all for such parties was
Pratolino, a park belonging to the grand duke, about
seven miles from Florence, on the Bologna road. These
seven miles wave almost all more or less up hill, and when
the high ground on which the park is situated has been
reached, there is a magnificent view over the Val d' Arno,
its thousand villas, and Florence, with its circle of surrounding hills.

There was once a grand-ducal residence there, which
was famous in the later Medicean days for the multiplicity and ingenuity of its water-works. All kinds of surprises, picturesque and grotesque effects, and practical
jokes, had been prepared by the ingenious but somewhat
childish skill of the architect. Turning the handle of a
door would produce a shower-bath, sofas would become
suddenly boats surrounded by water, and such-like more
or less disagreeable surprises to visitors, who were new to
the specialties of the place. But all this practical joking
was at length fatal to the scene of it. The pipes and
conduits got out of order, and eventually so ruined the
edifice that it had to be taken down, and has never been
replaced.

But the principal object of attraction—besides the view,
the charming green turf for dining on, the facility for getting hot water, plates, glasses, etc., from a gardener's house,
and a large hall in the same, good for dancing—was the
singular colossal figure, representing " The Apennine,"
said to have been designed by Michael Angelo. One used
to clamber up inside this figure, which sits in a half crouch-
ing attitude, and reach on the top of the head a platform,
on which four or five persons could stand and admire the
matchless view.

About three miles farther, still always ascending the
slope of the Apennine, is a Servite monastery which is the
cradle and mother establishment of the order. Sometimes
we used to extend our rambles thither. The brethren had

the reputation, I remember, of possessing a large and valuable collection of prints. They were not very willing to exhibit it; but I did once succeed in examining it, and, as I remember, found that it contained nothing much worth looking at.

A much more favorite amusement of mine was a picnic arranged to last for two or three days, and intended to embrace objects farther afield. Vallombrosa was a favorite and admirably well-selected locality for this purpose. And many a day and moonlight night never to be forgotten have I spent there. Sometimes we pushed our expeditions to the more distant convents—or " sanctuaries," as they were called—of Camaldoli and La Vernia. And of one very memorable excursion to these two places I shall have to speak in a subsequent chapter.

Meantime those dull mutterings as of distant thunder, which Signor Albèri had, as mentioned at a former page, first signalized to me, were gradually growing into a roar which was attracting the attention and lively interest of all Europe.

Of the steady increase in the volume of this roar, and of the results in which it eventuated, I need say little here, for I have already said enough in a volume entitled "Tuscany in 1849 and in 1859." But I may jot down a few recollections of the culminating day of the Florentine revolution.

I had been out from an early hour of that morning, and had assisted at sundry street discussions of the question, What would the troops do ? Such troops as were in Florence were mainly lodged in the forts, the Fortezza da Basso, which I have had occasion to mention in a former chapter, and the other situated on the high ground beyond the Boboli Gardens, and therefore immediately above the Pitti Palace. My house at the corner of the large square, now the Piazza dell' Indipendenza, was almost immediately under the walls and the guns of the Fortezza da Basso ; but I felt sure that the troops would simply do nothing ; might very possibly fraternize with the people, but would in no case burn a cartridge for the purpose of keeping the grand duke on his throne.

A short, wide street runs in a straight line from the middle of one side of the Piazza to the fort; and a considerable crowd of people, at about ten o'clock, I think, began to advance slowly up this street towards the *fortezza*, and I went with them. High above our heads, on the turf-covered top of the lofty wall, there were a good number, perhaps thirty or forty soldiers, not drawn up in line, but apparently merely lounging, and enjoying the air and sunshine. They had, I think all of them, their muskets in their hands, but held them idly and with apparently no thought whatever of using them. I felt confirmed in my opinion that they had no intention of doing so.

Arrived at the foot of the fortress wall, the foremost of the people began calling out to the soldiers, "*Abbasso l'Austria! Siete per Italia o per l'Austria?*" I did not — and it is significant — hear any cries of "*Abbasso il Gran Duca!*" The soldiers, as far as I could see at that distance, appeared to be lazily laughing at the people. One man called out, "*Ecco un bel muro per fracassare il capo contro!*"—"That is an excellent wall to break your heads against!" It was very plain that they had no intention of making any hostile demonstration against the crowd. At the same time there was no sort of manifestation of any inclination to fraternize with the revolutionists. They were simply waiting to see how matters would go; and, under the circumstances, they can hardly be severely blamed for doing so. But there can be no doubt that, whichever way things might go, their view of the matter would be strongly influenced by the very decided opinion that that course would be best which should not imply the necessity for *doing* anything. I think that the feeling generally in "the army," if such it could be called, was on the whole kindly to the grand duke, but not to the extent of being willing to fight anybody, least of all the Florentines, in his defence!

How matters *did* go it is not necessary to tell here. If ever there was a revolution "made with rose-water," it was the revolution which deposed the poor *gran ciuco*. I don't think it cost any human being in all Florence a scratch or a bloody nose. It cost an enormous amount of talking and screaming, but nothing else. At the same time it is fair to remember that the popular leaders could not be sure that matters might not have taken another turn, and that it *might* have gone hard with some of them. In any case, however, it would not have gone *very* hard with any of them. Probably exile would have been the worst fate meted out to them. It is true that exile from Tuscany just then would have been attended by a similar difficulty to that which caused the old Scotch lady, when urged to run during an earthquake, to reply, "Ay, but whar wull I run to?"

I do not think there was any bitter, or much even unkind, feeling on the part of the citizens towards the sovereign against whom they rebelled. If any fact or circumstance could be found which was calculated to hold him up to ridicule it was eagerly laid hold of, but there was no fiercer feeling.

A report was spread during the days that immediately followed the duke's departure that orders had been given to the officers in the upper fortress to turn their cannon on the city at the first sign of rising. Such reports were very acceptable to those who, for political purposes, would fain have seen somewhat of stronger feeling against the duke. I have good reason to believe that such orders *had* been given, but I have still stronger reasons for doubting that they were ever given by the grand duke. And I am surest of all that, let them have been given by whom they may, there was not the smallest chance of their being obeyed. As for the duke himself, I am very sure that he would have given or even done much to prevent any such catastrophe.

But perhaps the most remarkable and most singular scene of all that rose-water revolution was the duke's departure from his capital and his duchy. Other sovereigns in similar plight have hidden themselves, travestied themselves, had hairbreadth escapes, or have not escaped at all. In Tuscany the fallen ruler went forth in his own carriage, with one other following it, both rather heavily laden with luggage. The San Gallo gate is that by which the hearse that conveys the day's dead to the cemetery on the slope of the Apennine leaves the city every night.   And the duke passed amid the large crowd assembled at the gate to see him go, as peaceably as the vehicle conveying those whose days in Florence, like his, were at an end, went out a few hours later by the same road.

CHAPTER XXXII.

AMONG the very great number of men and women whom
I have known during my life in Italy—some merely acquaintances, and many whom I knew to be, and a few,
alas! a very few, whom I still know to be trusty friends
—there were many of whom the world has heard, and
some perhaps of whom it would not unwillingly hear
something more. But time and space are limited, and I
must select as best I may.

I have a very pleasant recollection of " Garibaldi's Englishman," Colonel Peard. Peard had many more qualities
and capabilities than such as are essential to a soldier of
fortune. The phrase, however, is perhaps not exactly
that which should be used to characterize him. He had
qualities which the true soldier of fortune should not possess. His partisanship was with him in the highest degree
a matter of conviction and conscientious opinion, and
nothing would have tempted him to change his colors or
draw his sword on the other side. I am not sure, either,
whether a larger amount of native brain power, and (in a
much greater degree) a higher quality of culture, than that
of the general under whom it may be his fortune to serve,
is a good part of the equipment of a soldier of fortune.
And Peard's relation to Garibaldi very notably exemplified this.

He was a native of Devonshire, as was my first wife;
we saw a good deal of him in Florence, and I have before
me a letter written to her by him from Naples on the
28th of January, 1861, which is interesting in more respects than one. Peard was a man who *would* have all
that depended on him ship-shape. And this fact, taken
in conjunction with the surroundings amid which he had

to do his work, is abundantly sufficient to justify the
growl he indulges in.

"MY DEAR MRS. TROLLOPE," he writes, "I am ashamed to think either
of you or of other friends at Florence ; it is such an age since I have written to any of you. But I have been daily, from morning to night, hard at
work for weeks. The *honor* of having a command is all very well, but
the trouble and worry are unspeakable. Besides, I had such a set under
me that it was enough to rile the sweetest-tempered man. Volunteers
may be very well in their way. I doubt not their efficiency in repelling
an attack in their own country, but defend me from ever again commanding a brigade of English volunteers in a foreign country. As to the officers, many were most mutinous, and some something worse. Thank
goodness, the brigade is at an end. All I now wait for is the settlement
of the accounts. If I can get away by the second week in February I at
present think of taking a run as far as Cairo, then crossing to Jerusalem,
and back by Jaffa, Beyrout, Smyrna, and Athens to Italy, when I shall
once more hope to see you and yours.

"Politics do not look well in Southern Italy, I fear. The Mazzinists
have been most active, and have got up a rather strong feeling against
Cavour and what they think the peace party. Now Italy must have a little rest for organization, civil as well as military. They do not give the
government time to do or even propose good measures for the improvement of the country. No sooner are one set of ministers installed than
intrigues are on foot to upset them. I firmly believe that the only hope for
Southern Italy and Sicily is in a strong military government. These districts'
must be treated as *conquered provinces*, and the people educated and taught
habits of industry, whether they like it or not. The country is at present
in a state of barbarism, and must be saved from that. All that those who
are *supposed to be educated* seem to think about is how they can get a few
dollars out of government. [I fear the honest Englishman would find
that those supposed to be educated in those provinces are as much in a
state of barbarism in the matters that offended him as ever.] I never
saw such a set of harpies in my life. One had the assurance to come to
me a few days since, asking if I could not take him on the strength of the
brigade, so as to enable him to get six months' pay out of the government.
As to peculation, read 'Gil Blas,' and that will give you a faint sketch of
the customs and habits of all *impiegati* [civil servants] in this part of Italy. I do not believe that the Southern Italians, taken as a body, know
what honesty is. [All that he says is true to the present day. But the distinction which he makes between the Southern Italians and those of the
other provinces is most just, and must be remembered.] But that is the
fault of the horrid system of tyranny under which they have so long lived.
I do not say that the old system must be reformed ; it must be totally
changed. Solomon might make laws, but so corrupt are all the *impiegati*
that I doubt if he could get them carried out. Poor Garibaldi is made a
tool of by a set of designing intriguers, who will sacrifice him at any moment. He is too honest to see or believe of dishonesty in others. He has

no judgment of character. He has been surrounded by a set of blacklegs and swindlers, many among them, I regret to say, English. How I look forward to seeing you all again! Till we meet, believe me,

"Most truly yours, GIO. [*sic*] PEARD."

The last portion of this letter is highly interesting and historically well worth preserving. It is entirely and accurately true. And there was no man in existence more fitted by native integrity and hatred of dishonesty on the one hand, and close intimacy with the subject of his remarks on the other, to speak authoritatively on the matter than "Garibaldi's Englishman."

The following letter, written, as will be seen, on the eve of his departure for the celebrated expedition to Sicily, is also interesting. It is dated Genoa.

"DEAR MRS. TROLLOPE,—I have been thinking over your observations about *terno*. I don't give up my translation; but would it not be literal enough to translate it, 'the bravest three colors?'

[This refers to the rendering of the lottery phrase *terno* in a translation by my wife of the *stornello* of Dall' Ongaro previously mentioned. In the Italian lottery, ninety numbers, 1–90, are always put into the wheel. Five only of these are drawn out. The player bets that a number named by him shall be one of these (*semplice estratto*); or that it shall be the first drawn (*estratto determinato*); or that two numbers named by him shall be two of the five drawn (*ambo*); or that three so named shall be drawn (*terno*). It will be seen, therefore, that the winner of an *estratto determinato* ought, if the play were quite even, to receive ninety times his stake. But, in fact, such a player would receive only seventy-five times his stake, the profit of the government consisting of this pull of fifteen per ninety against the player. Of course, what he ought to receive in any of the other cases is easily (not by me, but by experts) calculable. It will be admitted that the difficulty of translating the phrase in Dall' Ongara's little poem, so as to be intelligible to English readers, was considerable. The letter then proceeds]:

"I did not start, you will see, direct from Livorno [Leghorn], for Medici wrote me to join him here. Moreover, the steamer by which I expected to have gone did not make the trip, but was sent back to this city. I will worry you with a letter when anything stirring occurs. We sail to-night. Part went off last evening—fifteen hundred. We got in three steamers, and shall overtake the others.

"With kind regards to all friends, believe me,

"Yours very faithfully, JOHN PEARD."

The remarks contained in the former of the two letters here transcribed seem to make this a proper place for recording "what I remember" of Garibaldi.

My first acquaintance with him was through my very old, and very highly valued, loved, and esteemed friend, Jessie White Mario. The Garibaldi *culte* has been with her truly and literally the object (apart from her devoted love for her husband, an equally ardent worshipper at the same shrine) for which she has lived, and for which she has again and again affronted death. For she accompanied him in all his Italian campaigns as a hospital nurse, and on many occasions rendered her inestimable services in that capacity under fire. If Peard has been called " Garibaldi's Englishman," truly Jessie White Mario deserves yet more emphatically the title of " Garibaldi's Englishwoman." She has published a large life of Garibaldi, which is far and away the best and most trustworthy account of the man and his wonderful works. She is not blind to the spots on the sun of her adoration, nor does she seek to conceal the fact that there were such spots, but she is a true and loyal worshipper all the same.

Her husband, Alberto Mario, was—alas! that I should write so ; for no Indian wife's life was ever more ended by her suttee than Jessie Mario's life has practically been ended by her husband's untimely death !—among the, I fear, few exceptions to Peard's remarks on the men who were around Garibaldi. He was not only a man of large literary culture, a brave soldier, an acute politician, a formidable political adversary, and a man of perfect and incorruptible integrity, but he would have been considered in any country and in any society in Europe a very perfect gentleman. He was in political opinion a consistent and fearlessly outspoken Republican. He and I therefore differed *toto cœlo*. But our differences never diminished our, I trust, mutual esteem, nor our friendly intercourse. But he was a born *frondeur*. He edited during his latter years a newspaper at Rome, which was a thorn in the side of the authorities. I remember his being prosecuted and condemned for persistently speaking of the pope in his paper as " Signor Pecci." He was sentenced to imprisonment. But all the government wanted was his condemnation ; and he was never incarcerated. But he used to go daily to the prison and demand the execution of his sentence. The jailer used to shut the door in his face, and he narrated the result of his visit in the next day's paper.

It was as Jessie Mario's friend, then, that I first knew Garibaldi.

One morning at the villa I then possessed, at Ricorboli, close to Florence, a maid-servant came flying into the room, where I was still in bed at six o'clock in the morning, crying out in the utmost excitement, "*C'è il Generale! c'è il Generale! E chiede di lei, signore!*"— "Here's the General! here's the General! And he is asking for you, sir!" She spoke as if there was but one general in all the world. But there was hardly any room in Florence at that time where her words would not have been understood as well as I understood them.

I jumped out of bed, got into a dressing-gown, and ran out to where the "General" was on the lawn before the door, just as I was, and hardly more than half awake. There he was, all alone. But if there had been a dozen other men around him, I should have had no difficulty in recognizing him. There was the figure as well known to every Italian from Turin to Syracuse as that of his own father—the light-gray trousers, the little foraging-cap, the red shirt, the bandana handkerchief loosely thrown over his shoulders and round his neck.

Prints, photographs, portraits of all kinds, have made the English public scarcely less familiar than the Italian with the physiognomy of Giuseppe Garibaldi. But no photograph, of course, and no painting which I have ever seen, gives certain peculiarities of that striking head and face, as I first saw it, somewhere about twenty years ago.

The pose of the head, and the general arrangement and color of the tawny hair (at that time but slightly grizzled), justified the epithet "leonine" so often applied to him. His beard and mustache were of the same hue, and his skin was probably fair by nature, but it had been tanned by wind and weather. The clear blue eyes were surrounded by a network of fine lines. This had no trace or suggestion of *cunning*, as is often the case with wrinkles round the setting of the eyes, but was obviously the result of habitual contraction of the muscles in gazing at very distant objects. In short, Garibaldi's eyes, both in this respect and in respect of a certain steadfast, far-away look in them, were the eyes of a sailor. Seamanship, as is generally known, was his first profession. Another physical peculiarity of his which I do not remember to have seen noticed in print was a remarkably beautiful voice. It was fine in quality and of great range ; sweet, yet manly, and with a suggestion of stored-up power which harmonized with the man. It seemed to belong, too, to the benevolence which was the habitual expression of his face when in repose.

"Jessie [pronounced Jèssee] told me I should find you up ; but you are not so early as I am !" was his salutation. I said he had *dans le temps* been beforehand with others as well as with me. At which he laughed, not, I thought, ill-pleased. And then we talked—about Italy of course. One subject of his talk I specially remember, because it gave rise to a little discussion, and in a great degree gave me the measure of the man.

"As for the priests," said he, "they ought all to be put to death, without exception and without delay."

"Rather a strong measure," I ventured to say.

"Not a bit too strong, not a bit," he rejoined, warmly. "Do we not put assassins to death ? And is not the man who murders your soul worse than the man who only kills your body ?"

I attempted to say that the difference of the two cases lay in the fact that as to the killing of the body there was no doubt about the matter, whereas mankind differed very widely as to the killing of the soul ; and that as long as it remained a moot point whether priests did so or not, it would hardly be practicable or even politic to adopt the measure he suggested.

But he would not listen to me—only repeated with increasing excitement that no good could come to humanity till all priests were destroyed.

Then we talked about the Marios, of both of whom he spoke with the greatest affection ; and of the prospects of "going to Rome," which, of course, he considered the simplest and easiest thing possible.

I saw Garibaldi on many subsequent occasions, but never again *tête-à-tête*, or *a quattro occhi*, as the Italians more significantly phrase it. The last time I ever saw him was under melancholy circumstances enough, though the occasion professed to be one of rejoicing. It was at the great gathering at Palermo for celebrating the anniversary of the Sicilian Vespers. Of course such a celebration would have brought Garibaldi to partake in it, wherever he might have been, short of in his grave. And truly he was then very near that. It was a melancholy business. He was brought from the steamer to his bed in the hotel on a litter through the streets lined by the thousands who had gathered to see him, but who had been warned that his condition was such that the excitement occasioned by any shouting would be perilous to him. Amid dead silence his litter passed through the crowds who were longing to welcome him to the scene of his old triumphs. Truly it was more like a funeral procession than one of rejoicing.

It was very shortly before his death, which many people thought had been accelerated by that last effort to make his boundless popularity available for the propagation of Radicalism.

Peard's words reveal with exactitude the deficiency which lay at the root of all the blunders, follies, and imprudences which rendered his career less largely beneficent for Italy than it might have been. "He had no judgment of character," and was too honest to believe in knavery. It must be added that he was too little intelligent to detect it, or to estimate the consequences of it. Of any large views of social life, or of the means by which, and the objects for which, men should be governed, he was as innocent as a baby. In a word, he was not an intellectual man. All the high qualities which placed him on the pinnacle he occupied were qualities of the heart and not of the head. They availed with admirable success to fit him for exercising a supreme influence over men, especially young men, in the field, and for all the duties of a guerilla leader. They would not have sufficed to make him a great commander of armies ; and did still less fit him for becoming a political leader.

Whom next shall I present to the reader from the portrait-gallery of my reminiscences?

Come forward, Franz Pulszky, most genial, most large-hearted of philosophers and friends!—I can't say "guides," for though he was both the first, he was not the last, differing widely as we did upon—perhaps not most, but at all events—many large subjects.

I had known the lady whom Pulszky married in Vienna many years previously, and long before he knew her. She was the daughter of that highly cultivated Jewish family of whom I have spoken before. When I first knew her she was as pretty and charming a young girl as could be imagined. She was possessed then of all the accomplishments that can adorn a girl at that period of life. Later on she showed that she was gifted with sense, knowledge, energy, firmness, courage, and *caractère* in a degree very uncommon. Since leaving Vienna I had neither seen nor heard more of her, till she came to live with her husband and family of children in Florence. But our old acquaintanceship was readily and naturally renewed, and his villa near the city became one of the houses I best loved to frequent. She had at that time, and even well-nigh I take it in those old days at Vienna, abandoned all seeming of conformity to the practices of the faith she was born in.

I used to say of Pulszky that he was like a barrel full to the bung with generous liquor, which flowed in a full stream, stick the spigot in where you would. He was—is, I am happy to say is the proper tense in his case—a most many-sided man. His talk on artistic subjects, mainly historical and biographical, was abundant and most amusing. His antiquarian knowledge was large. His ethnographical learning, theories, and speculations were always interesting and often most suggestive. Years had, I think, put some water in the wine of his political ideas, but not enough to prevent differences between us on such subjects. He was withal—there again I mean "is," for I am sure that years and the air of his beloved Pesth cannot have put any water in *that* generous and genial wine—a fellow of infinite jest, and full of humor; in a word, one of the fullest and most delightful companions I have ever known. He talked English with no further accent than served to add a raciness to the flavor of his conversation; and every morning of one fixed day in the week he used to come to Ricorboli for what he called a tobacco parliament.

I used frequently to spend the evening at his villa, where one met a somewhat extraordinary cosmopolitan gathering. Generally we had some good music; for Madame Pulszky was—unhappily in her case the past tense is needed—a very perfect musician. Among other people more or less off the world's beaten track I used to meet there a very extraordinary Russian, who had accomplished the rare feat of escaping from Siberia. He was a Nihilist of the most uncompromising type; a huge, shaggy man, with an unkempt head and chest like those of a bear; and by his side—more or less—there was a pretty, *petite*, dainty little young wife—beauty and the beast, if ever that storied couple were seen in the flesh.

Many years afterwards when I and my wife saw Pulszky at Pesth, and were talking of old times, he reminded me of this person; and on my doubting that any man in his senses could believe in the practicability of the extreme Nihilist theories, he instanced our old acquaintance, saying, "Yes, there is a man who in his very inmost conscience believes that no good of any sort can be achieved for humanity till the sponge shall have been passed over *all* that men have instituted and done, and a perfect *tabula rasa* has been substituted for it."

I have many letters from Pulszky, written most of them after his return to Pesth, and for the most part too much occupied with the persons and politics of that recent day to be fit for publication.

Here is one, written before he left Florence, which may be given:

"VILLA PETROVICH.

"MY DEAR TROLLOPE,—I am just returned from a long excursion with Boxall to Arezzo, Cortona, Borgo San Sepolcro, Città di Castello, Perugia, and Assisi. We were there for a week, and enjoyed it amazingly. I am sorry to say that I am not now able to join your party to Camaldoli, since I must see Garibaldi, and do not know as yet what I shall do when the war begins, which might happen during your excursion. I hope you will drink a glass of water to my remembrance at La Vernia from the miraculous well, called from the rocks by my patron saint, St. Francis of Assisi. I shall come to you on Sunday, and will tell you more about him. I studied him at Assisi.   Yours sincerely,   FR. PULSZKY."

The following passages may be given from a long letter, written from Pesth on the 27th of March, 1869. It is for the most part filled with remarks on the party politics of the hour, and persons, many of them still on the scene :

"MY DEAR MRS. AND MR. TROLLOPE,—You don't believe how glad I was to get a token of remembrance from you. It seems to me quite an age since I left Florence, and your letter was like a voice from a past period. I live here as a stranger; you would not recognize me. I talk nothing but politics and business. There is not a man with whom I could speak in the way that we did on Sundays at your villa. I am of course much with old Deak. I often dine with him. I know all his anecdotes and jokes by heart. He likes it, if I visit him; but our conversation remains within the narrow limits of party politics and the topics of the day. Sometimes I spend an evening with Baron Eötvös, the minister of public instruction, my old friend; and there only we get both warm in remembering the days of our youth, and building *châteaux en Espagne* for the future of the country. Eötvös has appointed me director of the National Museum, which contains a library of one hundred and eighty thousand volumes, mostly Hungarian; a very indifferent picture-gallery, with a few good pictures and plenty of rubbish; a poor collection of antiquities; splendid mediæval goldsmith work; arms, coins, and some miserable statues; a good collection of stuffed birds; an excellent one of butterflies; a celebrated one of beetles, and good specimens for geology and mineralogy. But all this collection is badly, if at all, catalogued; badly arranged; and until now we have in a great palace an appropriation of only £1200 a year. I shall have much to do there—as much as any minister in his office, if politics leave me the necessary time for it."

Then follows a quantity of details about the party politics of the day. And then he continues :

"Such a contested election with us costs about £2000 to £3000. I must say I never spent money with more regret than this; but I had to maintain the party interest and my family influence in my electoral district. I have there a fine old castle and a splendid park, but I rarely go to the country, since I have jumped, as you know, once more into the whirlpool of politics, and can't get out again. An agrarian communistic agitation has been initiated, I do not know whether with or without the sanction of S——, but certainly it has spread rapidly over a great portion of the country, and I doubt whether government has the energy for put-

ting that agitation down. It is a very serious question, especially as it
finds us engaged in many other questions of the highest interest."

Then he gives an outline of the position of Hungary in
relation to other states, and then he continues :

"We remain still in opposition with the Wallachians, or, as they now
like to call themselves, Rumanes, and we try to maintain the peace with
Prussia. And now when we should concentrate all our forces to meet the
changes which threaten us, a stupid and wicked opposition divides the nation into two hostile camps [how very singular and unexampled!]. We
fight one another to the great pleasure of Russia and Prussia, who enjoy
our fratricidal feuds as the Romans in the amphitheatre enjoyed the fights
of the barbarians in the arena.

"I must beg your pardon, dear Mrs. Trollope, that I grow so pathetic!
You know it is not my custom when I am with ladies. But you must
know likewise that I live now outside of female society. I do not exactly
know whether it is my fault or that of the ladies of Pesth ; so much is certain that only at Vienna, where I go from time to time, I call upon ladies.
As to my children, Augustus, whom you scarcely know, is a volunteer in
the army according to our law of universal conscription. Charles you may
have seen at Florence. I sent him thither to visit his grandmother.
[Madame Walter, the mother of Madame Pulszky ; the lady who had received us with such pleasant hospitality at Vienna, and who had come to
reside at Florence, where she lived to a great age much liked and respected.] Polixena gets handsome and clever ; little Garibaldi is to go
to school in September next. I grow old, discontented, insupportable
[we found him at Pesth many years afterwards no one of the three!] ; a
journey to Greece and Italy would certainly do me immense good ; but I
fear I must give up that plan for the present year, since after a contested
election it is a serious thing to spend money for amusement. In June I
shall leave my present lodging and go to the museum, which stands in a
handsome square opposite to the House of Parliament. Excuse me for my
long, long talk ; and do not forget your faithful friend, *in partibus infi-
delium,*   FR. PULSZKY."

On the 26th of March, 1870, he writes a letter which
was brought to us by his son, the Augustus mentioned in
the letter I have just transcribed :

"MY DEAR MRS. AND MR. TROLLOPE,—Detained by parliamentary duties
and the management of my own affairs, I am still unable to make a trip
to Italy to visit my friends, who made the time of my exile more agreeable
to me than my own country. But I send in my stead a second edition of
the old Pulszky, revised and corrected *ad usum Delphini,* though I do not
doubt that you prefer the old book, to which you were accustomed. My
son Augustus has now finished his studies, and is D.E.L.—in a few days

lieutenant in the reserve, and secretary at the ministry of finance. Few young men begin their career in a more promising way. As to myself, Augustus will tell you more than I could write. I have remained too long in foreign countries to feel entirely at home at Pesth, where people know how to make use of everybody. I am M.P., belong to the finance committee, am chairman of the committee of foreign affairs in the delegation, director of the museum, chairman of the philological section in the academy of sciences, chairman of the society of fine arts, vice-president of three insurance offices, and member of the council of two railroads. This long list proves sufficiently that my time is taken up from early morning to night. But my health is good, despite of the continuous wear and tear.

"During the summer vacations I wish to go to England. For ten years I have not been there; and I long to see again a highly civilized people; else I become myself a barbarian. Still I am proud of my Hungarians, who really struggle hard, and not without success, to be more than they are now—the first of the barbarians.

"I have for a long time not heard of you. Of course, in our correspondence your letter was the last, not mine. It is my own fault. But you must excuse me still for one year. Then I hope I can put myself in a more comfortable position. For the present I am unable even to read anything but Hungarian papers, bills, reports, and business letters. I envy you in your elegant villa, where you enjoy life! I hope you are both well, and do not forget your old friend,   Fr. Pulszky.

"P.S.—Augustus will give you a good photograph of me."

Here is one other letter of the 13th June, 1872 :

"My dear Trollope,—What a pity that my time does not allow me to visit Italy at any other season than just in summer. We are in the midst of our canvass for the general elections. My son Augustus is to be returned for my old place, Szecseny, without opposition on the 21st. On the following day we go to the poll at Gyöngyös, a borough which is to send me to Parliament. It is a contested election, therefore rather troublesome and expensive, though not too expensive. Parliament meets with us on the first of September. Thus my holidays are in July and August. Shall we never have the pleasure to see you and Mrs. Trollope, to whom I beg you to give my best regards, here at Pesth? Next year is the great exhibition at Vienna. Might it not induce you to visit Vienna, whence by an afternoon trip you come to Pesth, where I know you would amuse yourselves to your hearts' content.

"My children are quite well. Charles is at the university at Vienna. He despises politics, and wants to become professor at the University of Pesth in ten or twelve years.

"As to me, I am well, very busy; much attacked by the opposition since I am a dreaded party man. Besides I have to reorganize the National Museum, from the library, which has no catalogue, to the great collection of mineralogy and plants. We bought the splendid picture-gallery of Prince Esterhazy. This, too, is under my direction, with a most important collection of prints and drawings. You see, therefore, that my time is fully occupied. Yours always, Fr. Pulszky."

My wife and I did subsequently visit our old friend at Pesth, and much enjoyed our brief stay there and our chat of old times. But the work of reorganizing the museum was not yet completed. I do sincerely hope that the task has been brought to an end by this time, and that I may either in England or at Pesth once again see Franz Pulszky in the flesh!

CHAPTER XXXIII.

ACCORDING to the pathetic, and on the face of it accurately truthful, account of the close of his life in Mr. Forster's admirable and most graphic life of him, I never knew Landor. For the more than octogenarian old man whom I knew at Florence was clearly not the Landor whom England had known and admired for so many and such honored years. Of all the painful story of the regrettable circumstances which caused him to seek his last home in Florence it would be mere impertinence in me to speak, after the lucid, and at the same time delicately touched, account of them which his biographer has given.

I may say, however, that even after the many years of his absence from Florence there still lingered a traditional remembrance of him — a sort of Landor legend — which made all us Anglo-Florentines of those days very sure that however blamable his conduct (with reference to the very partially understood story of the circumstances that caused him to leave England) may have been in the eyes of lawyers or of moralists, the motives and feelings that had actuated him must have been generous and chivalrous. Had we been told that, finding a brick wall in a place where he thought no wall should be, he had forthwith proceeded to batter it down with his head, though it was not his wall but another's, we should have recognized in the report the Landor of the myths that remained among us concerning him. But that while in any degree *compos mentis* he had, under whatever provocation, acted in a base, or cowardly, or mean, or underhand manner, was, we considered, wholly impossible.

There were various legendary stories current in Florence in those days of his doings in the olden times. Once—so said the tradition—he knocked a man down in the street, was brought before the *delegato*, as the police magistrate was called, and promptly fined one piastre, value about four and sixpence; whereupon he threw a sequin (two piastres) down upon the table and said that it was unnecessary to give him any change, inasmuch as he purposed knocking the man down again as soon as he left the court. We, *poteri*, as regarded the date of the story, were all convinced that the true verdict in the matter was that of the old Cornish jury, "Sarved un right."

Landor, as I remember him, was a handsome-looking old man, very much more so, I think, than he could have been as a young man, to judge by the portrait prefixed to Mr. Forster's volumes. He was a man of somewhat leonine aspect as regards the general appearance and expression of the head and face, which accorded well with the large and massive build of the figure, and to which a superbly curling white beard added not only picturesqueness, but a certain nobility.

Landor had been acquainted with the Garrows, and with my first wife at Torquay; and the acquaintance was quickly renewed during his last years at Florence. He would frequently come to our house in the Piazza dell' Independenza, and chat for a while, generally after he had sat silent for some little time; for he used to appear fatigued by his walk. Later, when his walks and his visits had come to an end, I used often to visit him in "the little house under the wall of the city, directly back of the Carmine, in a by-street called the Via Nunziatina, not far from that in which the Casa Guidi stands," which Mr. Forster thus describes. I continued these visits, always short, till very near the close; for whether merely from the perfect courtesy which was a part of his nature, or whether because such interruptions of the long morning hours were really welcome to him, he never allowed me to leave him without bidding me come again.

I remember him asking me after my mother at one of the latest of these visits. I told him that she was fairly well, was not suffering, but that she was becoming very deaf. "Dead, is she?" he cried, for he had heard me imperfectly; "I wish I was! I can't sleep," he added, "but I very soon shall, soundly too, and all the twenty-four hours round." I used often to find him reading one of the novels of his old friend G. P. R. James, and he hardly ever failed to remark that he was a "woonderful" writer; for so he pronounced the word, which was rather a favorite one with him.

It was a singular thing that Landor always dropped his aspirates. He was, I think, the only man in his position in life whom I ever heard do so. That a man who was not only by birth a gentleman, but was by genius and culture —and such culture!—very much more, should do this, seemed to me an incomprehensible thing. I do not think he ever introduced the aspirate where it was not needed, but he habitually spoke of 'and, 'ead, and 'ouse.

Even very near the close, when he seemed past caring for anything, the old volcanic fire still lived beneath its ashes, and any word which touched even gently any of his favorite and habitual modes of thought was sure to bring forth a reply uttered with a vivacity of manner quite startling from a man who the moment before had seemed scarcely alive to what you were saying to him. To what extent this old volcanic fire still burned may be estimated from a story which was then current in Florence. The circumstances were related to me in a manner that seemed to me to render it impossible to doubt the truth of them. But I did not *see* the incident in question, and therefore cannot assert that it took place. The attendance provided for him by the kindly care of Mr. Browning, as narrated by Mr. Forster, was most assiduous and exact, as I had many opportunities of observing. But one day when he had finished his dinner, thinking that the servant did not come to remove the things so promptly as she ought to have done, he took the four corners of the table-cloth (so goes the story), and thus enveloping everything that was on the table, threw the whole out of the window.

I received many notes from Landor, for the most part on trifling occasions, and possessing little interest. They were interesting, however, to the race of autograph collectors, and they have all been coaxed out of me at different times, save one. I have, however, in my possession several letters from him to my father-in-law, Mr. Garrow, many passages in which are so characteristic that I am sure my readers will thank me for giving them, as I am about to do. The one letter of his that remains to me is, as the reader will see, not altogether without value as a trait of character. The young lady spoken of in it is the same from whose papers in the *Atlantic Monthly*, entitled "Last Days of Walter Savage Landor," Mr. Forster has gleaned, as he says, one or two additional glimpses of him in his last Florence home. The letter is without date, and runs as follows :

"MY DEAR SIR,—Let me confess to you that I am not very willing that it should be believed desirous [he evidently meant to write either "that I should be believed desirous," or "that it should be believed that I am desirous"] of scattering my image indiscriminately over the land. On this sentiment I forbade Mr. Forster to prefix an engraving of me over my collected works. If Miss Field wishes *one* more photograph, Mr. Alinari may send it to her, and I enclose the money to pay for it. With every good wish for your glory and prosperity,

"I remain, my dear sir,
"Very truly yours,   W. S. LANDOR."

The writing is that of a sadly shaking hand. The lady's request would unquestionably have been more sure of a favorable response had she preferred it in person, instead of doing so through me. But I suspect from the phrase "one more," and the underlining of the word one, that she had already received from him more than one photograph, and was ashamed to make yet another application. But she had led, or allowed, me to imagine that she was then asking for the first time. The care to send the money for the price of the photograph was a characteristic touch. Miss Field was, I well remember, a great favorite with Landor. I remember her telling me that he wished to give her a very large sort of scrap-book, in which, among a quantity of things of no value, there were, as I knew, some really valuable drawings; and asking me whether she should accept it, her own feeling leaning to the opinion that she ought not to do so, in which view I strongly concurred. If I remember right the book had been sent to her residence, and had to be sent back again, not without danger of seriously angering him.

19*

Here are the letters I have spoken of, written by Landor to Mr. Garrow. They are all undated save by the day of the month, but the postmarks show them to have been all written in 1836-1838. The first is a very long letter, almost the whole of which is about a quarrel between husband and wife, both friends of the writer, which it would serve no good purpose to publish. The following passage from it, however, must not be lost:

"What egregious blockheads must those animals have been who discover a resemblance to my style in Latin or other quotations. I have no need of crutches. I can walk forward without anybody's arm; and if I wanted one, I should not take an old one in preference. Not only do I think that quotations are deformities and impediments, but I am apt to believe that my own opinion, at least in those matters of which I venture to treat, is quite as good as any other man's, living or dead. If their style is better than my own, it would be bad policy to insert it; if worse, I should be like a tailor who would recommend his abilities by engrafting an old sleeve on a new coat. . . . Southey tells me that he has known his lady more than twenty years, that the disproportion of their ages is rational, and that, having only one daughter left, his necessary absences would be irksome to her. Whatever he does, is done wisely and virtuously. As for Rogers, almost an octogenarian, be it on his own head! A dry nettle tied to a rose-bud, just enough life in it to sting, and that's all. Lady Blessington would be delighted at any fresh contribution from Miss Garrow. Let it be sent to her at Gore House. I go there to-morrow for ten days, then into Warwickshire, then to Southampton. But I have not given up all hope of another jaunt to Torquay. Best compliments to the ladies.   Yours ever,   W. S. L."

The following is dated the 15th of November, 1837—just half a century ago!

"35 St. James's Square, Bath.

"I should be very ungrateful if I did not often think of you. But among my negligences I must regret that I did not carry away with me the address of our friend Bezzi. [A Piedmontese refugee who was a very intimate friend of Garrow's. I knew him in long subsequent years, when political changes had made it possible for him to return to Italy. He was a very clever and singularly brilliant man, whose name, I think, became known to the English public in connection with the discovery of the celebrated portrait of Dante on a long whitewashed wall of the Bargello, in Florence. There was some little jealousy about the discovery between him and Kirkup. The truth was that Kirkup's large and curious antiquarian knowledge led him to feel sure that the picture must be there, under the whitewash; while Bezzi's influence with the authorities succeeded in getting the wall cleared of its covering.] I am anxious to hear how he endures his absence from Torquay, and I will write to him the moment I hear of him. Tell Miss Garrow that the muses like the rustle of dry leaves almost as well as the whispers of green ones. If she doubts it, entreat her on my part to ask the question of them. Nothing in Bath is vastly interesting to me now. Two or three persons have come up and spoken to me whom I have not seen for a quarter of a century. Of these faces I recollect but one, and it was the ugliest! By the same token—but here the figure of aposiopesis is advantageous to me—old Madam Burridge, of my lodgings, has sent me three large forks and one small, which I left behind. She forgot to send another of each. What is worse, I left behind me a three-faced seal, which I think I once showed you. It was enclosed in a black, rough case. This being of the time of Henry the Eighth, and containing the arms of my family connections, I value far above a few forks, or a few dozens. It cannot be worth six-pence to whoever has it. One of the engravings was a greyhound with an arrow through him, a crest of my grandmother's, whose maiden name was Noble. If you pass by, pray ask about it—not that I am ever disappointed at the worst result of an inquiry. I am afraid the ladies of your house will think me imprudent; and what must be their opinion, if you let it transpire that I have furthermore invested a part of my scrip in the beaver trade. Offer my best regards to them all, and believe me,

" My dear sir, Yours very sincerely, W. S. L."

The following is dated only January 2d, but the post-mark shows it to have been written from Bath on that day, 1838 :

" MY DEAR SIR,—Yesterday there were lying across my fender three or four sheets of paper, quite in readiness to dry themselves, and receive my commands. One of these, I do assure you, was destined for Torquay, but the interruption of visitors would allow me time only to cover half a one with my scrawl. Early last week I wrote a long letter to Bezzi, but wanted the courage to send it. I wish him to remain in England as much almost as you yourself can do. But if after promising his lady [it is noteworthy that such a master of English as Landor should use, now for the second time in these letters, this ugly phrase] to let her try the air of Italy, he should withdraw, she might render his life less comfortable by reproaches not altogether unmerited. When she gets there she will miss her friends; she will hear nothing but a language which is unknown to her, and will find that no change of climate can remove her ailments. I offered my house to Bezzi some time ago, with its two gardens and a hundred acres of land, all for a hundred a year. But I am confident my son will never remain in England, and after the expiration of the year will return to Tuscany. Bezzi cannot find another house, even without garden, for that money. James paid for a worse twelve louis a month, although he took it for eight months. So the houses in Tuscany are very far from inviting to an economist, although vastly less expensive than at Torquay, the rival of Naples in this respect as in beauty. . . . I have found my seal in a waistcoat pocket. I do not think the old woman stole the forks, but she knew they were stolen. . . . Kenyon has something of Falstaff about him, both in the physical and the moral. But he is a friendly man, of rare judgment in literary works, and of talents that only fall a little short of genius.

"God preserve you from your Belial Bishop! [Philpotts]. What an incumbent! I would not see the rascal once a month to be as great a man as Mr. Shedden, or as sublime a genius as Mr. Wise; [word under the seal] would drown me in bile or poison me with blue pills. A society has been formed here, of which the members have come to the resolution of making inquiries at every house about the religion of the inmates, what places of worship they attend, etc., etc. Is it not hard upon a man who has changed a couple of sovereigns into half-crowns for Christmas boxes, to be forced to spend ten shillings for a horsewhip, when he no longer has a horse? Our weather here is quite as mild and beautiful as it can possibly be at Torquay. Miss Garrow, I trust, has listened to the challenges of the birds, and sung a new song. As Bezzi is secretary and librarian, I must apply to him for it, unless she will condescend to trust me with a copy. I will now give you a specimen of my iron seal, brass setting and pewter mending. Yours ever, W. S. L."

The mention of Bishop Philpotts (though not by name) in the foregoing letter, reminds me of a story which used to be told of him, and which is too good to be lost, even though thus parenthetically told. When at Torquay he used to frequent a small church, in which the service was at that time performed by a very young curate of the extra gentle butter-won't-melt-in-his-mouth kind, who had much objection to the phrase in the communion service, "Eateth and drinketh his own damnation," and ventured somewhat tremblingly to substitute "condemnation" for the word which offended him. Whereupon the orthodox bishop reared his head, as he knelt with the rest of the congregation, and roared aloud "*Damnation!*" Whether the curate had to be carried out fainting I don't remember.

The next letter of Landor's that I have is dated 13th April, St. James's Square, Bath. The postmark shows that it was written in 1838.

"MY DEAR SIR,—I have had Kenyon here these last four days. He tells me that he saw Bezzi in London, and that we may entertain some hopes that he will be induced to remain in England. All he wants is some employment; and surely his powerful friends among the Whigs could easily procure him it. But the Whigs, of all scoundrelly factions, are, and have ever been, the most scoundrelly, the most ungenerous, the most ungrateful. What have they done for Fonblanque, who could have kicked them overboard on his toe-nail? Their abilities put together are less than a millionth of his; and his have been constantly and most zealously exerted in their favor. My first conversation with Kenyon was about the publication of his poems, which are just come out. They are in part extremely clever; particularly one on happiness and another on the shrine of the Virgin. He was obliged to print them at his own expense; and his cousin, Miss Barrett, who also has written a few poems of no small merit, could not find a publisher. These, however, bear no proportion to Miss Garrow's.* Yet I doubt whether publishers and the folks they consult would find out that.

"Southey was about to write to me when his brother's death, by which six children came under his care, interrupted him. I wish I possessed one or two of Miss Garrow's beautiful poems, that I might ask his opinion and advice about them. His opinion I know would be the same as mine; but his advice is what I want. Surely it cannot be requisite and advantageous to withhold them from the world so long as you imagine. In one single year both enough of materials and of variety for a volume might be collected and prepared. Would Miss Garrow let me offer one to the 'Book of Beauty'? I shall be with Lady Blessington the last day of the present month. One of the best poems of our days [on death], appeared in the last 'Book of Beauty.' But in general its poetry is very indifferent. With best regards to the ladies,

"I am ever, my dear sir,
"Yours most sincerely,   W. S. L."

The following, dated merely "Gore House, Sunday morning," was written, or at least posted, on the 14th May, 1838 :

"MY DEAR SIR,—It is impossible you should not often have thought me negligent and ungrateful. Over and over again have I redd [*sic*] the incomparably fine poetry you sent me; and intended that Lady Blessington should partake in the high enjoyment it afforded me. I had promised her to be at Gore House towards the end of April, but I had not the courage to face all my friends. However, here I came on Friday evening; and before I went to bed I redd to her ladyship what I promised her. She was enchanted. I then requested her to toss aside some stuff of mine, and to make way for it in the next 'Book of Beauty.' The gods, as Homer says,

---

* To those who never knew Landor, and the habitual limitless exaggeration of his manner of speaking, it may be necessary to observe that he did not really hold any opinion so monstrous as might be supposed from the passage in the text. And a letter given by Mr. Forster expresses earnestly and vigorously enough his high admiration for Miss Barrett's poetry. It must be remembered, also, that at the time this was written Mr. Landor could only have seen some of the earliest of Miss Barrett's writings.

granted half my prayer, and it happened to be (what was not always the case formerly) the better half. She will insert both. It is only by some such means as that that the best poetry in our days comes with mincing step into popularity. Mine being booted and spurred, both ladies and gentlemen get out of the way of it, and look down at it with a touch of horror.

"Now for news, and about your neighbors. Captain Ackland is going to marry a niece of Massy Dawson. Mischievous things are said about Lady M——, all false, you may be sure. Admiral Aylmer, after all his services under Nelson, etc., etc., is unable to procure a commission in the marines for his nephew, Frederick Paynter. Lord A. will not ask. I am a suitor to all the old women I know, and shall fail too, for it is not the thing they want me to ask of them.

"I see two new deputy lord-lieutenants have been appointed for the County of Monmouth. My estate there is larger than the lord lieutenant's; yet even this mark of respect has not been paid me. It might be, safely. I shall consider myself sold to the devil, and for more than my value, when I accept any distinction, or anything else from any man living. The Whigs are growing unpopular, I hear. I hope never to meet any of them. Last night, however, I talked a little with Grantley Berkeley, and told him a bit of my mind. You see, I have not much more room in my paper, else I should be obliged to tell you that the bells are ringing, and that I have only just time to put on my gloves for church.

"Adieu, and believe me, with kindly regards to the ladies,

"Yours,   W. S. L."

The last in this series of letters which has reached my hands is altogether undated, but appears by the postmark to have been written from Bath, 19th July, 1838:

"MY DEAR SIR,—There is one sentence in your letter which shocked me not a little. You say 'The Whigs have not offered you a deputy-lieutenantcy; so cheap a distinction could not have hurt them. But then you are too proud to ask,' etc. Do you really suppose that I would have accepted it even if it had been offered ? No, by God! I would not accept any distinction even if it were offered by honest men. I will have nothing but what I can take. It is, however, both an injustice and an affront to confer this dignity on low people, who do not possess a fourth of my property, and whose family is as ignoble as Lord Melbourne's own, and not to have offered the same to me. In the eleventh page of the 'Letters' I published after the quelling of Bonaparte are these words: 'I was the first to abjure the party of the Whigs, and shall be the last to abjure the principles. When the leaders had broken all their promises to the nation, had shown their utter incapacity to manage its affairs, and their inclination to crouch before the enemy, I permitted my heart after some struggles to subside and repose in the cool of this reflection—Let them escape. It is only the French nation that ever dragged such feebleness to the scaffold.' Again, page 35; 'Honest men, I confess, have generally in the present times an aversion to the Whig faction, not because it is suitable either to honesty or understanding to prefer the narrow principles of the opposite party, but because in every country lax morals wish to be and are identified with public feeling, and because in our own a few of the very best have been found in an association with the very worst.' Whenever the Tories have deviated from their tenets, they have enlarged their views and exceeded their promises. The Whigs have always taken an inverse course. Whenever they have come into power, they have previously been obliged to slight those matters, and to temporize with those duties, which they had not the courage either to follow or to renounce.

"And now, my dear sir, to pleasanter matters. I have nothing in the press, and never shall have. I gave Forster all my works, written or to be written. Neither I nor my family shall have anything to do with book-sellers. They say a new edition of my 'Imaginary Conversations' is called for. I have sent Forster a dozen or two of fresh ones, but I hope he will not hazard them before my death, and will get a hundred pounds, or near it, for the whole.

"If ever I attended a public dinner, I should like to have been present at that which the people gave to you. Never let them be quiet until the Church has gone to the devil, its lawful owner, and till something a little like Christianity takes its place. If parsons are to be lords, it is but right and reasonable that the queen should be pope. Indeed, I have no objection to this, but I have to the other. What a singularity it is that those who profess a belief in Christ do not obey him, while those who profess it in Mahomet or Moses or Boodh are obedient to their precepts, if not in certain points of morality, in all things else. Carlyle is a vigorous thinker, but a vile writer, worse than Bulwer. I breakfasted in company with him at Milman's. Macaulay was there, a clever clown, and Moore too, whom I had not seen till then. Between those two Scotchmen he appeared like a glow-worm between two thistles. There were several other folks, literary and half literary, Lord Northampton, etc., etc. I forgot Rogers. Milman has written the two best volumes of poetry we have seen lately; but when Miss Garrow publishes hers I am certain there will be a total eclipse of them. My friend Hare's brother, who married a sister of the impudent coxcomb, Edward Stanley, has bought a house at Torquay, and Hare tells me that unless he goes to Sicily he shall be there in winter. If so, we may meet; but Bath is my dear delight in all seasons. I have been sitting for my picture, and have given it to Mrs. Paynter. It is admirably executed by Fisher. Yours ever, W. S. L."

These letters are all written upon the old-fashioned square sheet of letter paper, some gilt-edged, entirely written over, even to the turned-down ends, and heavily sealed.

Mr. Forster says no word about the deputy-lieutenantcy, and Landor's anger and disgust in connection with it. He must necessarily have known all about it, but probably

in the exuberance of his material did not think it worth
mentioning. But it evidently left almost as painful an
impression on Landor's mind as the famous refusal of
the Duke of Beaufort to appoint him a justice of the
peace.   .

During the later portion of my life at Florence, and
subsequently at Rome, Mr. G. P. Marsh and his very
charming wife were among our most valued friends for
many years. Marsh was an exception to the prevailing
American rule, which for the most part changes their di-
plomatists with the change of president. He had been
United States minister at Constantinople and at Turin before he came to Florence with the Italian monarchy. At
Rome he was "the dean" of the diplomatic body, and on
many occasions various representative duties fell upon him
as such which were especially unwelcome to him. The
determination of the Great Powers to send ambassadors
to the court of the Quirinal instead of ministers plenipo-
tentiary, as previously, came as a great boon to Mr. Marsh.
For as the United States send no ambassadors, his position
as longest in office of all the diplomatic body no longer
placed him at the head of it.

Mr. Marsh was a man of very large and varied culture.
A thorough classical scholar and excellent modern linguist,
philology was, perhaps, his most favorite pursuit. He
wrote various books, his best I think a very large octavo
volume, entitled not very happily "Man in Nature." The
subject of it is the modifications and alterations which this
planet has undergone at the hands of man. His subject
leads him to consider much at large the denudation of
mountains, which has caused and is causing such calami-
tous mischief in Italy and the south of France. He shows
very convincingly and interestingly that the destruction
of forests causes not only floods in winter and spring, but
drought in summer and autumn. And the efforts which
have recently been made in Italy to take some steps towards the reclothing of the mountain-sides have in great
measure been due to his work, which has been largely circulated in an Italian translation.

The following letter, which I select from many received

from him, is not without interest. It is dated 30th November, 1867.

"DEAR SIR,—I return you Layard's article, which displays his usual marked ability, and has given me much pleasure as well as instruction. I should much like to know what are his grounds for believing that 'a satisfactory settlement of this Roman question would have been speedily brought about with the concurrence of the Italian government and the Liberal party in Rome, and with the tacit consent of the Emperor of the French, had it not been for the untoward enterprise of Garibaldi,' p. 283. I certainly have not the slightest ground for believing any such thing; nor do I understand *to whom* the settlement referred to would have been 'satisfactory.' Does Mr. Layard suppose that any conceivable arrangement would be satisfactory both to the papacy and to Italian Liberals out of Rome? The *government* of Italy, which changes as often as the moon, might have accepted something which would have satisfied Louis Napoleon, Antonelli, and the three hundred *nobili* of Rome, who waited at dinner, napkin on arm, on the Antiboini, to whom they gave an entertainment— but the people?

"I send you one of Ferretti's pamphlets, which please keep. And I enclose in the package two of Tuckerman's books. If you could turn over the leaves of these and say to me in a note that they impress you favorably, and that you are not displeased with his magazine article, I will make him a happy man by sending him the note.

"Very truly yours, GEO. P. MARSH."

I did more than "turn over the leaves" of the book sent, and did very truly say that they had interested me much. It is rather suggestive to reflect how utterly unintelligible to the present generation must be the term " Antiboini " in the above letter, without a word of explanation. The highly unpopular and objectionable " Papal Legion " had been in great part recruited from Antibes, and were hence nicknamed " Antiboini," and not, as readers of the present day might fairly imagine, from having been the opponents of any " boini."

The personal qualities of Mr. Marsh had obtained for him a great and, I may indeed say, exceptional degree of consideration and regard from his colleagues of the diplomatic body, and from the Italian ministers and political world generally. And I remember one notable instance of the manifestation of this, which I cannot refrain from citing. Mr. Marsh had written home to his government some rather trenchantly unfavorable remarks on some portion of the then recent measures of the Italian ministry.

And by some awkward accident or mistake these had found their way into the columns of an American newspaper. The circumstances might have given rise to very disagreeable and mischievous complications and results. But the matter was suffered to pass without any official observation solely from the high personal consideration in which Mr. Marsh was held, not only at the Consulta (the Roman foreign office), but at the Quirinal, and in many a Roman *salon*.

Mr. Marsh died, full of years and honors, at a ripe old age. But the closing scene of his life was remarkable from the locality of it. He had gone to pass the hot season at Vallombrosa, where a comfortable hotel replaces the old *forestieria* of the monastery, while a school of forestry has been established by the government within its walls. Amid those secular shades the old diplomatist and scholar breathed his last, and could not have done so in a more peaceful spot. But the very inaccessible nature of the place made it a question of some difficulty how the body should be transported in properly decorous fashion to the railway station in the valley below—a difficulty which was solved by the young scholars of the school of forestry, who turned out in a body to have the honor of bearing on their shoulders the remains of the man whose writings had done so much to awaken the government to the necessity of establishing the institution to which they belonged.

Mrs. Marsh, for so many years the brightest ornament of the Italo-American society, and equally admired and welcomed by the English colony, first at Florence and then at Rome, still lives for the equal delight of her friends on the other side of the Atlantic. I may not, therefore, venture to say more of "what I remember" of her than that it abundantly accounts for the feeling of an unfilled void, which her absence occasioned and occasions in both the American and English world on the banks of the Tiber.

CHAPTER XXXIV.

It was in the spring of the year 1860 that I first became acquainted with "George Eliot" and G. H. Lewes in Florence. But it was during their second visit to Italy in 1861 that I saw a good deal more of them. It was in that year, towards the end of May, that I succeeded in persuading them to accompany me in a visit to the two celebrated Tuscan monasteries of Camaldoli and La Vernia. I had visited both on more than one occasion previously—once with a very large and very merry party of both sexes, of whom Colley Grattan was one—but the excursion made in company with G. H. Lewes and George Eliot was another-guess sort of treat, and the days devoted to it stand out in high relief in my memory as some of the most memorable in my life.

They were anxious to be moving northwards from Florence, and I had some difficulty in persuading them to undertake the expedition. A certain weight of responsibility, therefore, lay on me—that folks whose days were so sure of being turned to good profit, should not by my fault be led to waste any of them. But I had already seen enough of both of them to feel sure that the specialties of the very exceptional little experience I proposed to them would be appreciated and acceptable. Neither he nor she were fitted by their habits, or, indeed, by the conditions of their health, to encounter much "roughing," and a certain amount of that was assuredly inevitable—a good deal more five-and-twenty years ago than would be the case now. But if the flesh was weak, truly the spirit was willing! I have heard grumbling and discontent from the young of either sex in the heyday of health and strength in going over the same ground. But for my companions on the present occasion, let the difficulties and discomforts be what they might, the continually varied and continually suggestive interest they found in everything around them overrode and overbore all material considerations.

Never, I think, have I met with so impressionable and so delicately sensitive a mind as that of George Eliot! I use "sensitive" in the sense in which a photographer uses the word in speaking of his plates. Everything that passed within the ken of that wonderful organism, whether a thing or combination of things seen, or an incident, or a trait revealing or suggesting character, was instantly reproduced, fixed, registered by it, the operating light being the wonderful native force of her intellect. And the photographs so produced were by no means evanescent. If ever the admirably epigrammatic phrase, "Wax to receive and marble to retain," was applicable to any human mind, it was so to that of George Eliot. And not only were the enormous accumulations of stored-up impressions safe beyond reach of oblivion or confusion, but they were all and always miraculously ready for co-ordination with those newly coming in at each passing moment. Think of the delight of passing, in companionship with such a mind, through scenes and circumstances entirely new to it!

Lewes, too, was a most delightful companion, the cheeriest of philosophers. The old saying of "*Comes jucundus in viâ pro vehiculo est*" was especially applicable to him. Though very exhaustible in bodily force, he was inexhaustible in cheerfulness, and, above all, in unwearied, incessant, and minute care for "Polly." In truth, if any man could ever be said to have lived in another person, Lewes in those days, and to the end of his life, lived in and for George Eliot. The talk of worshipping the ground she trod on, and the like, are pretty lovers' phrases, sometimes signifying much, and sometimes very little. But it is true accurately and literally of Lewes. That care for her, at once comprehensive and minute, unsleeping watchfulness, lest she should dash her foot against a stone, was *never* absent from his mind. She had become his real self, his genuine *ego* to all intents and purposes. And his

talk and thoughts were egoistic accordingly. Of his own
person, his ailments, his works, his ideas, his impressions,
you might hear not a word from him in the intercourse of
many days. But there was in his inmost heart a *naïf* and
never-doubting faith that talk on all these subjects as regarded *her* must be profoundly interesting to those he
talked with. To me, at all events, it was so. Perhaps
had it been otherwise there would have been less of it.

We were to reach Camaldoli the first night, and had
therefore to leave Florence very early in the morning.
At Pelago, a little *paése*—village we should call it—on
the Arno, some fourteen or fifteen miles above Florence,
we were to find saddle-horses, the journey we were about
to make being in those days practicable in no other way,
unless on foot. There was at that time a certain Antonio
da Pelago, whose calling it was to act as guide, and to
furnish horses. I had known him for many years, as did
all those whose ramblings took them into those hills. He
was in many respects what people call "a character," and
seemed to fancy himself to have in some degree proprie-
tary rights over the three celebrated Tuscan monasteries,
Vallombrosa, Camaldoli, and La Vernia. He was well
known to the friars at each of these establishments, and
indeed to all the sparse population of that country-side.
He was a very good and competent guide and courier,
possessed with a very amusingly exaggerated notion of
his own importance, and rather bad to turn aside from
his own preconceived and predetermined methods of doing
everything that had to be done. George Eliot at once
made a study of him.

I am reminded, too, as I write, of the great amusement
with which my old and highly valued friend of many
years, Alfred Austin, who long subsequently was making
the same excursion with me and both our wives, listened
to an oration of the indispensable Antonio. One of his
baggage-horses had strayed and become temporarily lost
among the hills. He was exceedingly wroth, and poured
forth his vexation in a torrent of very unparliamentary
language. "*Corpo di Giuda!*" he exclaimed, among a curious assortment of heterogeneous adjurations—"Body of

Judas !"—stooping to the ground as he spoke, and striking the back of his hand against it, with an action that very graphically represented a singular survival of the classical *testor inferos!* Then suddenly changing his mood, he apostrophized the missing beast with the most tearful reproach, "There! there now! Thou hast made me throw away all my devotions! All! And Easter only just gone!" That is to say, your fault has betrayed me into violence and bad language, which has begun a new record of offences just after I had made all clear by my Easter devotions.

The first stage of our rough ride was to the little hill-town of Prato Vecchio on the infant Arno, and close under the lofty peaks of Falterona, in the flanks of which both the Arno and the Tiber rise. The path, as it descends to the town, winds round the ruins of an ancient castle, beneath the walls of which is still existent that Fontebranda fountain which Adam the forger in the "Inferno" longed for a drop of, and which almost all Dantescan scholars and critics mistake for a larger and nowadays better-known fountain of the same name at Siena. On pointing it out to George Eliot, I found, of course, that the name and the whole of Adam the forger's history was familiar to her; but she had little expected to find his local habitation among these wild hills; and she was unaware of the current mistake between the Siena Fontebranda and the little rippling streamlet before us.

The little *osteria*, at which we were to get some breakfast, was a somewhat lurid dwelling in an uninviting back lane. But the ready and smiling good-humor with which the hostess prepared her coffee and bread, and eggs and bacon, availed much to make up for deficiencies, especially for guests far more interested in observing every minute specialty of the place, the persons, and the things, than they were extreme to mark what was amiss. I remember George Eliot was especially struck by the absence of either milk or butter, and by the fact that the inhabitants of these hills, and indeed the Tuscans of the remoter parts of the country generally, never use them at all—or did not in those days.

But it was beyond Prato Vecchio that the most characteristic part of our ride began.   The hills, into the folds
and gullies of which we plunged almost immediately after
leaving the walls of the little town, are of the most arid
and, it is hardly too much to say, repulsive description.
It is impossible to imagine soil more evidently, to the least
experienced eye, hopeless for any purpose useful to man
than these rolling and deeply water-scored hills.   Nor has
the region any of the characters of the picturesque.   The
soil is very friable, consisting of an easily disintegrated,
slaty limestone, of a pale whitey-brown in prevailing col-
or, varied here and there by stretches of similar material
greenish in tint.   For the most part the hillsides are incapable of nourishing even a blade of grass; and they are
evidently in the process of rapid removal into the Medi-
terranean, for the further extension of the plain that has
been formed between Pisa and the shore since the time,
only a few hundred years ago, when Pisa was a first-class
naval power.   All this, with the varied historical corolla-
ries and speculations which it suggested, was highly interesting to my fellow-travellers.

But the ride, nowhere dangerous, though demanding
some strong faith in the sure-footedness of Antonio's steeds,
is not an easy one.   The sun was beating with unmitigated glare on those utterly shadeless hillsides.   It was
out of the question to attempt anything beyond a walk.
The sides of the gullies, which had to be ascended and descended, though never reaching to the picturesque proportions of precipices, were yet sufficiently steep and rough
to make very fatiguing riding for a lady unaccustomed to
such exercise.   And George Eliot was in no very robust
condition of health at the time.   And despite his well-dis-
sembled anxiety I could see that Lewes was not easy respecting her capability of resisting the heat, the fatigue, and
the unwonted exercise.   But her cheerfulness and activity of interest never failed her for an instant.   Her mind
"made increment of everything."   Nor even while I led her
horse down some of the worst descents did the exigencies
of the path avail to interrupt conversation, full of thought
and far-reaching suggestiveness, as her talk ever was.

At last we reached the spot where the territory of the monastery commences ; and it is one that impresses itself on the imagination and the memory in a measure not likely to be forgotten. The change is like a pantomime transformation scene. The traveller passes without the slightest intermediate gradation from the dreary scene which has been described into the shade and the beauty of a region of magnificent and well-managed forest. The bodily delight of passing from the severe glare of the sun into this coolness, welcome alike to the skin and to the eye, was very great. And to both my companions, but especially to George Eliot, the great beauty of the scene we entered on gave the keenest pleasure.

Assuredly Saint Romuald in selecting a site for his Camaldolese did not derogate from the apparently instinctive wisdom which seems to have inspired the founders of monasteries of every order and in every country of Europe. Invariably the positions of the religious houses were admirably well chosen; and that of Camaldoli is no exception to the rule. The convent is not visible from the spot where the visitor enters the forest boundary which marks the limit of the monastic domain. Nearly an hour's ride through scenery increasing in beauty with each step, where richly green lawns well stocked with cattle are contrasted wonderfully with the arid desolation so recently left behind, has still to be done ere the convent's hospitable door is reached.

The convent door, however, in our case was not reached, for the building used for the reception of visitors, and called the *forestieria*, occupies its humble position by the road-side a hundred yards or so before the entrance to the monastery is reached. There Antonio halted his cavalcade and, while showing us our quarters with all the air of a master, sent one of his attendant lads to summon the *padre forestieraio*—the monk deputed by the society to receive strangers.

Had our party consisted of men only, we should have been received in the convent, where there was a very handsome suite of rooms reserved for the purpose. But females could not enter the precincts of the cloister. The father in question very shortly made his appearance, a magnificent figure, whose long black beard flowing over his perfectly clean white robe made as picturesque a presentment of a friar as could be desired. He was extremely courteous, and seemed to desire nothing better than to talk *ad libitum*. But for my fellow-travellers, rest after their broiling ride was the thing most urgently needed.

And this requirement brought us to the consideration of our accommodation for the night. The humble little *forestieria* at Camaldoli was not built for any such purpose. It never, of course, entered into the heads of the builders that need could ever arise for receiving any save male guests. And for such, as I have said, a handsome suite of large rooms, both sitting-rooms and bedrooms, with huge fireplaces for the burning of colossal logs, is provided. Ordinary brethren of the order would not be lodged there. The magnificence is reserved for a cardinal (Gregory XVI., who had been a Camaldolese, frequently came here), or a travelling bishop and his suite, or a heretic English or American milord. But not for any daughter of Eve ! And the makeshift room over a carpenter's shop, which is called the *forestieria*, has been devoted to the purpose only in consequence of the incomprehensible mania of female English heretics for visiting the disciples of St. Romuald. And there the food supplied from the convent can be brought to them. But for the night? I had warned my friends that they would have to occupy different quarters ; and it now became necessary to introduce George Eliot to the place she was to pass the night in.

At the distance of about twenty minutes' walk above the convent, across a lovely but very steep extent of beautifully green turf, encircled by the surrounding forest, there is a cowhouse, with an annexed lodging for the cowherd and his wife. And over the cow stable is—or was, for the monks have been driven away and all is altered now—a bedchamber with three or four beds in it, which the toleration of the community has provided for the accommodation of the unaccountable female islanders. I have assisted in conveying parties of ladies up that steep

20

grassy slope by the light of a full moon, when all the beds had to be somewhat more than fully occupied. But fortunately George Eliot had the whole chamber to herself—perhaps, however, not quite fortunately, for it was a very novel and not altogether reassuring experience for her to be left absolutely alone for the night, to the protection of an almost entirely unintelligible cowherd and his wife. But there was no help for it. G. H. Lewes did not seem to be quite easy about it; but George Eliot did not appear to be troubled by the slightest alarm or misgiving. She seemed, indeed, to enjoy all the novelty and strangeness of the situation; and when she bade us good-night from the one little window of her chamber over the cows, as we turned to walk down the slope to our grand bedrooms at the convent, she said she should be sure to be ready when we came for her in the morning, as the cows would call her, if the cowherds failed to do so.

The following morning we were to ride up the mountain to the Sagro Eremo. Convent hours are early, and soon after the dawn we had convoyed our female companion down the hill to the little *forestieria* for breakfast, where the *padre forestieraio* gave us the best coffee we had had for many a day. George Eliot declared that she had had an exceptionally good night, and was delighted with the talk of the magnificently black-bearded father, who superintended our meal, while a lay brother waited on us.

The former was to start in a day or two on his triennial holiday, and he was much excited at the prospect of it. His *naïf* talk and quite childlike questions and speculations as to times and distances, and what could be done in a day, and the like, amused George Eliot much. In reckoning up his available hours he deducted so much in each day for the due performance of his canonical duties. I remarked to him that he could read the prescribed service in the diligence, as I had often seen priests doing. "Secular priests no doubt!" he said, "but that would not suit one of *us!*"

Our ride up to the Sagro Eremo was a thing to be remembered. I had seen and done it all before; but I had

not seen or done it in company with George Eliot. It
was like doing it with a new pair of eyes and freshly inspired mind. The way is long and steep, through magnificent forests, with every here and there a lovely enclosed lawn, and fugitive peeps over the distant country.
On our way up we met a singular procession coming down.
It consisted of a low, large cart drawn by two oxen, and attended by several lay brothers and peasants, in the centre of
which was seated an enormously fat brother of the order,
whose white-robed bust with immense flowing white beard,
emerging from a quantity of red wraps and coverings
that concealed the lower part of his person, made an extraordinary appearance. He was being brought down
from the Sagro Eremo to the superior comfort of the convent, because he was unwell.

At the Sagro Eremo—the sacred hermitage—is seen
the operation of the Camaldolese rule in its original strictness and perfection. At the convent itself it is, or has
become, much relaxed in many respects. The Camaldolese, like other Carthusians, are properly *hermits*, that is
to say, their life is not conventual, but eremitical. Each
brother at the Sagro Eremo inhabits his own separately-
built cell, consisting of sleeping-chamber, study, wood-
room, and garden, all of microscopical dimensions. His
food, exclusively vegetable, is passed in to him by a little
turn-table made in the wall. There is a refectory, in which
the members of the community eat in common on two or
three festivals in the course of the year. On these occasions only is any speech or oral communication between
the members permitted. There is a library tolerably well
furnished with historical as well as theological works. But
it is evidently never used. Nor is there any sign that the
little gardens are in any degree cultivated by the occupants of them. I remarked to George Eliot on the strangeness of this abstinence from both the two permitted occupations, which might seem to afford some alleviation of
the awful solitude and monotony of the eremitical life.
But she remarked that the facts as we saw them were just
such as she should have expected to find.

The Sagro Eremo is inhabited by three classes of inmates : firstly, by novices, who are not permitted to come down to the comparative luxury and comfort and milder climate of the convent till they have passed three or four years at the Sagro Eremo; secondly, by those who have been sent thither from the convent below as punishment for some misdoing thirdly, by those who remain there of their own free will, in the hope of meriting a higher and more distinguished reward for their austerities in a future life. One such was pointed out to us, who had never left the Eremo for more than fifty years ; a tall, very gaunt, very meagre old man, with white hair, hollow cheeks, and parchment-skin, a nose like an eagle's beak, and deep-set, burning eyes—as typical a figure, in its way, as the rosy mountain of a man whom we met travelling down in his ox-cart.

Lewes was always anxious lest George Eliot should overtire herself. But she was insatiably interested both in the place and the denizens of it.

Then, before supper at the *forestieria* was ready, our friend, the father *forestieraio*, insisted on showing us the growing crop of haricot-beans, so celebrated for their excellence that some of them were annually sent to Pope Gregory the Sixteenth as long as he lived.

Then followed another night in the cowhouse for George Eliot and for us in the convent, and the next morning we started with Antonio and his horses for La Vernia.

The ride thither from Camaldoli, though less difficult, is also less peculiar, than that from Prato Vecchio to the latter monastery, at least until La Vernia is nearly reached. The *penna* (Cornish, Pen ; Cumbrian, Penrith ; Spanish, Peña) on which the monastery is built is one of the numerous isolated rocky points which have given their names to the Pennine Alps and Apennines. The Penna de la Vernia rises very steeply from the rolling ground below, and towers above the traveller with its pyramidal point in very suggestive fashion. The well-wooded sides of the conical hill are diversified by emergent rocks, and the plume of trees on the summit seems to suggest a Latin rather than a Celtic significance for the "Penna."

It is a long and tedious climb to the convent, but the

picturesque beauty of the spot, the charm of the distant outlook, and, above all, the historical interest of the site, rewards the visitor's toil abundantly. There is a *forestieria* here also, within the precincts of the convent, but not within the technical "cloister." It is simply a room in which visitors of either sex may partake of such food as the poor Franciscans can furnish them, which is by no means such as the more well-to-do Carthusians of Camaldoli supply to their guests. Nor have the quarters set apart for the sleeping accommodation of male visitors within the cloister anything of the spacious old-world grandeur of the strangers' suite of rooms at the latter monastery. The difficulty, also, of arranging for the night's lodging of a female is much greater at La Vernia. There is, indeed, a very fairly comfortable house, kept under the management of two sisters of the order of St. Francis, expressly for the purpose of lodging lady pilgrims to the shrine. For in former days—scarcely now, I think—the wives of the Florentine aristocracy used to undertake a pilgrimage to La Vernia as a work of devotion. But this house is at the bottom of the long ascent—nearly an hour's severe climb from the convent—an arrangement which necessarily involves much additional fatigue to a lady visitor.

George Eliot writes to Miss Sara Hennell, on the 19th of June, a letter, inserted by Mr. Cross in his admirable biography of his wife: "I wish you could have shared the pleasures of our last expedition from Florence to the monasteries of Camaldoli and La Vernia. I think it was just the sort of thing you would have entered into with thorough zest." And she goes on to speak of La Vernia in a manner which seems to show that it was the latter establishment which most keenly interested and impressed her. She was, in fact, under the spell of the great and still potent personality of Saint Francis, which informs with his memory every detail of the buildings and rocks around you. Each legend was full of interest for her. The alembic of her mind seemed to have the secret of distilling from traditions which, in their grossness, the ordinary visitor turns from with a smile of contempt, the spiritual value they once possessed for ages of faith, or at least the poetry with which the simple belief of those ages has invested them. Nobody could be more alive to every aspect of natural beauty than she showed herself during the whole of this memorable excursion. But at La Vernia the human interest overrode the simple æsthetic one.

Her day was a most fatiguing one. And when Lewes and I wearily climbed the hill on foot, after escorting her to her sleeping-quarters, he was not a little anxious lest on the morrow she should find herself unable for the ride which was to take us to the spot where a carriage was available for our return to Florence.

But it was not so. She slept well under the care of the Franciscan nuns, who managed to get her a cup of milk-less coffee in the morning, and so save her from the necessity of again climbing the hill. A charming drive through the Casentino, or valley of the Upper Arno, showing us the aspect of a Tuscan valley very different from that of the Lower Arno, brought to an end an expedition which has always remained in my memory as one of the most delightful of my life.

I had much talk with George Eliot during the time— very short at Florence—when she was maturing her Italian novel, "Romola." Of course, I knew that she was digesting the acquisitions of each day with a view to writing, but I had not the slightest idea of the period to which her inquiries were specially directed, or of the nature of the work intended. But when I read "Romola" I was struck by the wonderful power of absorption manifested in every page of it. The rapidity with which she squeezed out the essence and significance of a most complex period of history and assimilated the net results of its many-sided phases was truly marvellous.

Nevertheless, in drawing the girl Romola, her subjectivity has overpowered her objectivity. Romola is not— could never have been—the product of the period and of the civilization from which she is described as having issued. There is far too much of George Eliot in her. It was a period, it is true, in which female culture trod upon the heels of the male culture of the time, perhaps, more closely than it has ever done since. But, let Vittoria Co-

lonna be accepted, as probably she may be, as a fair expo-
nent of the highest point to which that culture had reached,
and an examination of the sonnets into which she has put
her highest thoughts and aspirations together with a comparison of those with the mental calibre of Romola will,
I think, support the view I have taken.

Tito, on the other hand, gives us, with truly wonderful
accuracy and vigor, "the very form and pressure of the
time." The pages which describe him read like a quintessential distillation of the Florentine story of the time
and of the human results which it had availed to produce.
The character of Savonarola, of course, remains, and must
remain, a problem, despite all that has been done for the
elucidation of it since "Romola" was written. But her
reading of it is most characteristically that which her own
idiosyncrasy—so akin to it in its humanitarian aspects, so
superior to it in its methods of considering man and his
relations to the unseen—would lead one to expect.

In 1869–70 George Eliot and Mr. Lewes visited Italy
for the fourth time. I had, since the date of their former
visit, quitted my house in Florence, and established myself in a villa and small *podere* at Ricorboli, a commune
outside the Florentine Porta San Niccolò. And there I
had the great pleasure of receiving them under my roof,
assisted in doing so by my present wife. Their visit was
all too short a one—less than a week, I think.

But one knows a person with whom one has passed even
that short time under the same roof far better than can
ever be the result of a very much longer acquaintanceship
during which one meets only in the ordinary intercourse
of society. And the really intimate knowledge of her
which I was thus enabled to obtain has left with me the
abiding conviction that she was intellectually by far the
most extraordinarily gifted person it has ever been my
good-fortune to meet. I do not insist much on the uniform and constant tender consideration for others, which
was her habitual frame of mind, for I have known others
of whom the same might have been said. It is true that
it is easy for those in the enjoyment of that vigorous
health which renders mere living a pleasure to be kindly;

and that George Eliot was never betrayed by suffering, however protracted and severe, into the smallest manifestation of impatience or unkindly feeling. But neither is this trained excellence of charity matchless among women. What was truly, in my experience, matchless, was simply the power of her intelligence ; the precision, the promptitude, the rapidity (though her manner was by no means rapid), the largeness of the field of knowledge, the compressed outcome of which she was at any moment ready to bring to bear on the topic in hand ; the sureness and lucidity of her induction ; the clearness of vision, to which muddle was as impossible and abhorrent as a vacuum is supposed to be to nature ; and all this lighted up and gilded by an infinite sense of and capacity for humor—this was what rendered her to me a marvel, and an object of inexhaustible study and admiration.

To me, though I never passed half an hour in conversation with her without a renewed perception of the vastness of the distance which separated her intelligence from mine, she was a companion each minute of intercourse with whom was a delight. But I can easily understand that, despite her perfect readiness to place herself for the nonce on the intellectual level of those with whom she chanced to be brought in contact, her society may not have been agreeable to all. I remember a young lady—by no means a stupid or unintelligent one—telling me that being with George Eliot always gave her a pain in " her mental neck," just as an hour passed in a picture-gallery did to her physical neck. She was fatigued by the constant attitude of looking up. But, had she not been an intelligent girl, she need not have constantly looked up. It would be a great mistake to suppose that George Eliot's mental habits exacted such an attitude from those she conversed with.

Another very prominent and notable characteristic of that most remarkable idiosyncrasy was the large and almost universal tolerance with which George Eliot regarded her fellow-creatures. Often and often has her tone of mind reminded me of the French saying, "*Tout connaître ce serait tout pardonner!*" I think that of all the human

beings I have ever known or met George Eliot would have
made the most admirable, the most perfect father confessor. I can conceive nothing more healing, more salutary
to a stricken and darkened soul than unrestricted confession to such a mind and such an intelligence as hers.
Surely a church with a whole priesthood of such confessors would produce a model world.

And with all this I am well persuaded that her mind
was at that time in a condition of growth. Her outlook
on the world could not have been said at that time to have
been a happy one. And my subsequent acquaintance with
her in after-years led me to feel sure that this had become
much modified. She once said to me at Florence that she
wished she never had been born. I was deeply pained
and shocked ; but I am convinced that the utterance was
the result, not of irritation and impatience caused by pain,
but of the influence exercised on the tone of thought and
power of thinking by bodily malady. I feel sure that she
would not have given expression to such a sentiment when
I and my wife were subsequently staying with her and
Lewes at their lovely home in Surrey. She had by that
time, I cannot but think, reached a brighter outlook and
happier frame of mind.

We had as neighbors at Ricorboli, although on the opposite bank of the Arno, our old and very highly-valued
friends, Mr. G. P. Marsh, the United States minister,
and his charming wife, to whom for the sake of both
parties we were desirous of introducing our distinguished
guests. We thought it right to explain to Mrs. Marsh
fully all that was not strictly normal in the relationship of
George Eliot and G. H. Lewes before bringing them together, and were assured both by her and by her husband
that they saw nothing in the circumstances which need
deprive them of the pleasure of making the acquaintance
of persons whom it would be so agreeable to them to know.
The Marshes were at that time giving rather large weekly
receptions in the fine rooms of their villa, and our friends
accompanied us to one of these. It was very easy to see
that both ladies appreciated each other. There was a large
gathering, mostly of Americans, and Lewes exerted him-

20*

self to be agreeable and amusing—which he always was, when he wished to be, to a degree rarely surpassed.

He and I used to walk about the country together when "Polly" was indisposed for walking; and I found him an incomparable companion, whether a gay or a grave mood were uppermost. He was the best *raconteur* I ever knew, full of anecdote, and with a delicious perception of humor. She also, as I have said—very needlessly to those who have read her books—had an exquisite feeling and appreciation of the humorous, abundantly sufficient, if unsupported by other examples, to put Thackeray's dicta on the subject of woman's capacity for humor out of court. But George Eliot's sense of humor was different in quality rather than in degree from that which Lewes so abundantly possessed. And it was a curious and interesting study to observe the manifestation of the quality in both of them. It was not that the humor, which he felt and expressed, was less delicate in quality or less informed by deep human insight and the true *nihil-humanum-a-mealie-num-puto* spirit than hers, but it was less wide and far-reaching in its purview of human feelings and passions and interests; more often individual in its applicability, and less drawn from the depths of human nature as exhibited by types and classes. And often they would cap each other with a mutual relationship similar to that between a rule of syntax and its example, sometimes the one coming first and sometimes the other.

I remember that during the happy days of this visit I was writing a novel, afterwards published under the title of "A Siren," and Lewes asked me to show him the manuscript, then nearly completed. Of course I was only too glad to have the advantage of his criticism. He was much struck by the story, but urged me to invert the order in which it was told. The main incident of the plot is a murder caused by jealousy, and I had begun by narrating the circumstances which led up to it in their natural sequence. He advised me to begin by bringing before the reader the murdered body of the victim, and then unfold the causes which had led to the crime. And I followed his advice.

The murder is represented as having been committed on a sleeping person by piercing the heart with a needle, and then artistically covering the almost imperceptible orifice of the wound with wax, in such sort as to render the discovery of the wound and the cause of death almost impossible even by professional eyes. And I may mention that the facts were related to me by a distinguished man of science at Florence as having really occurred.

Perhaps, since I have been led to speak of this story of mine, I may be excused for recording an incident connected with it, which occurred some years subsequently at Rome, in the drawing-room of Mrs. Marsh. The scene of the story is Ravenna. And Mrs. Marsh specially introduced me to a very charming young couple, the Count and Countess Pasolini of Ravenna, as the author of "A Siren." They said they had been most anxious to know who could have written that book. They thought that no Englishman could have been resident at Ravenna without their having known him, or at least known *of* him. And yet it was evident that a writer who could photograph the life and society of Ravenna as it had been photographed in the book in question must have resided there and lived in the midst of it for some time. But I never was in Ravenna for a longer time than a week in my life.

It was many years after the visit of George Eliot and Mr. Lewes to my house at Ricorboli that I and my wife visited them at The Heights, Witley, in Surrey. I found that George Eliot had grown. She was evidently happier. There was the same specially quiet and one may say harmonious gentleness about her manner and her thought and her ways. But her outlook on life seemed to be a brighter, a larger, and, as I cannot doubt, a healthier one. She would no longer, I am well assured, have talked of regretting that she had been born. It would be to give an erroneous impression if I were to say that she seemed to be more in charity with all men, for assuredly I never knew her otherwise. But, if the words may be used, as I think they may be understood, without irreverence, or any meaning that would be akin to blasphemy, she seemed to me to be more in charity with her Creator. The ways of God to man had become more justified to her; and her outlook as to the futurity of the world was a more hopeful one. Of course optimism had with her to be long-sighted. But she seemed to have become reconciled to the certainty that he who stands on a lofty eminence must needs see long stretches of dusty road across the plains beneath him.

Nothing could be more enjoyable than the evenings passed by the *partie carrée* consisting of herself and Lewes, and my wife and myself. I am afflicted by hardness of hearing, which shuts me out from many of the pleasures of society. And George Eliot had that excellency in woman, a low voice. Yet, partly no doubt by dint of an exertion which her kindness prompted, but in great measure from the perfection of her dainty articulation, I was able to hear her more perfectly than I generally hear anybody. One evening Mr. and Mrs. Du Maurier joined us. The Leweses had a great regard for Mr. Du Maurier, and spoke to us in a most feeling way of the danger which had then recently threatened the eyesight of that admirable artist. We had music; and Mr. Du Maurier sang a drinking-song, accompanying himself on the piano. George Eliot had specially asked for this song, saying, I remember, "A good drinking-song is the only form of intemperance I admire."

I think also that Lewes seemed in higher spirits than when I had been with him at Florence. But this was no more than an additional testimony to the fact that *she* was happier.

She also was, I take it, in better health, for we had some most delightful walks over the exceptionally beautiful country in the neighborhood of their house, to a greater extent than she would, I think, have been capable of at Florence.

One day we made a most memorable excursion to visit Tennyson at Black Down. It was the first time I had ever seen him. He walked with us round his garden, and to a point finely overlooking the country below, charmingly varied by cultivated land, meadow, and woodland.

It was a magnificent day ; but as I looked over the landscape I thought I understood why the woods, which one
looks down on from a similar Italian height, are called
macchie—stains—whereas our ordinarily more picturesque
language knows no such term and no such image. In
looking over a widespread Italian landscape one is struck
by the accuracy and picturesque truth of the image ; but
it needs the sun and the light and the atmosphere of Italy
to produce the contrast of light and shade which justifies
the phrase.

Our friends were evidently *personæ gratæ* at the court
of the laureate; and after our walk he gave us the exquisite treat of reading to us the just completed manuscript of "Rizpah." And how he read it ! Everybody
thinks that he has been impressed by that wonderful poem
to the full extent of the effect that it is capable of producing. They would be astonished at the increase of
weird terror which thrills the hearer of the poet's own
recital of it.

He was very good-natured about it. It was explained
to him by George Eliot that I should not be able to enjoy
the reading unless I were close to him, so he placed me by
his side. He detected me availing myself of that position to use my good eyes as well as my bad ears, and protested ; but on my appeal *ad misericordiam*, and assurance
that I should so enjoy the promised treat to infinitely
greater effect, he allowed me to look over his shoulder as
he read. After "Rizpah" he read the "Northern Cob-
bler" to us, also with wonderful effect. The difference
between reading the printed lines and hearing them so
read is truly that between looking on a black-and-white
engraving and the colored picture from which it has been
taken. Another thing also struck me. The provincial
dialect, which, when its peculiarities are indicated by letters, looks so uncouth as to be sometimes almost puzzling,
seemed to produce no difficulty at all as he read it, though
he in no wise mitigated it in the least. It seemed the absolutely natural and necessary presentation of the thoughts
and emotions to be rendered. It was, in fact, a dramatic
rendering of them of the highest order.

I remember with equal vividness hearing Lowell read some of his "Biglow Papers" in the drawing-room of my valued friend Arthur Dexter, of Boston, when there were no others present save him and his mother and my wife and myself. And that also was a great treat ; that also was the addition of color to the black-and-white of the printed page. But the difference between reading and hearing was not so great as in the case of the laureate.

When, full of the delight that had been afforded us, we were taking our leave of him, our host laid on us his strict injunctions to say no word to any one of what we had heard, adding with a smile that was half *naïf*, half funning, and wholly comic, "The newspaper fellows, you know, would get hold of the story, and they would not do it as well !"

And then our visit to the Leweses in their lovely home drew to an end, and we said our farewells, little thinking as we four stood in that porch that we should never in this world look on their faces more.

The history of George Eliot's intellect is to a great extent legible in her books. But there are thousands of her readers in both hemispheres who would like to possess a more concrete image of her in their minds — an image which should give back the personal peculiarities of face, voice, and manner, that made up her outward form and semblance. I cannot pretend to the power of creating such an image ; but I may record a few traits which will be set down, at all events, as truthfully as I can give them.

She was not, as the world in general is aware, a handsome, or even a personable woman. Her face was long ; the eyes not large nor beautiful in color — they were, I think, of a grayish blue—the hair, which she wore in old-fashioned braids coming low down on either side of her face, of a rather light brown. It was streaked with gray when last I saw her. Her figure was of middle height, large-boned, and powerful. Lewes often said that she inherited from her peasant ancestors a frame and constitution originally very robust. Her head was finely formed, with a noble and well-balanced arch from brow to crown.

The lips and mouth possessed a power of infinitely varied expression. George Lewes once said to me when I made some observation to the effect that she had a sweet face (I meant that the face expressed great sweetness). "You might say what a sweet hundred faces! I look at her sometimes in amazement. Her countenance is constantly changing." The said lips and mouth were distinctly sensuous in form and fulness.

She has been compared to the portraits of Savonarola (who was frightful) and of Dante (who though stern and bitter-looking was handsome). *Something* there was of both faces in George Eliot's physiognomy. Lewes told us, in her presence, of the exclamation uttered suddenly by some one to whom she was pointed out at a place of public entertainment — I believe it was at a Monday Popular Concert in St. James's Hall. "That," said a bystander, "is George Eliot." The gentleman to whom she was thus indicated gave one swift, searching look and exclaimed *sotto voce*, "Dante's aunt!" Lewes thought this happy, and he recognized the kind of likeness that was meant to the great singer of the *Divine Comedy*. She herself playfully disclaimed any resemblance to Savonarola. But, although such resemblance was very distant— Savonarola's peculiarly unbalanced countenance being a strong caricature of hers—some likeness there was.

Her speaking voice was, I think, one of the most beautiful I ever heard, and she used it *conscientiously*, if I may say so. I mean that she availed herself of its modulations to give thrilling emphasis to what was profound in her utterances, and sweetness to what was gentle or playful. She bestowed great care, too, on her enunciation, disliking the slipshod mode of pronouncing which is so common. I have several times heard her declare with enthusiasm that ours is a beautiful language, a noble language even to the ear, when properly spoken ; and imitate with disgust the short, *snappy*, inarticulate way in which many people utter it. There was no touch of pedantry or affectation in her own measured, careful speech, although I can well imagine that she might have been accused of both by those persons — unfortunately more numerous than could be de-

sired — who seem to take it for granted that *all* difference from one's neighbor, and especially a difference in
the direction of superiority, must be affected.

It has been thought by some persons that the influence
of George Henry Lewes on her literary work was not a
fortunate one, that he fostered too much the scientific bent
of her mind to the detriment of its artistic richness. I do
not myself hold this opinion. I am even inclined to think
that but for his companionship and encouragement she might
possibly never have written fiction at all. It is, I believe, impossible to overestimate the degree to which the sunshine
of his complete and understanding sympathy and his ador-
ing affection developed her literary powers. She has written something to this effect—perhaps more than once; I
have not her biography at hand at this moment for reference—in a letter to Miss Sara Hennell. And no one who
saw them together in anything like intimate intercourse
could doubt that it was true. As I have said before,
Lewes worshipped her, and it is considered a somewhat un-
wholesome experience to be worshipped. Fortunately the
process is not so common as to constitute one of the dangers of life for the average human being. But in George
Eliot's case I really believe the process was not deleterious.
Her nature was at once stimulated and steadied by Lewes's
boundless faith in her powers, and boundless admiration
for their manifestation. Nor was it a case of sitting like
an idol to be praised and incensed. Her own mental attitude towards Lewes was one of warm admiration. She
thought most highly of his scientific attainments, whether
well-foundedly or mistakenly I cannot pretend to gauge
with accuracy. But she also admired and enjoyed the
sparkling brightness of his talk, and the dramatic vivacity
with which he entered into conversation and discussion,
grave or gay. And on these points I may venture to record my opinion that she was quite right. I always used
to think that the touch of Bohemianism about Lewes
had a special charm for her. It must have offered so
piquant a contrast with the middle-class surroundings of
her early life. I observed that she listened with great
complacency to his talk of theatrical things and people.

Lewes was fond of talking about acting and actors, and in telling stories of celebrated theatrical personages would imitate—half involuntarily, perhaps—their voice and manner. I remember especially his doing this with reference to Macready.

Both of them loved music extremely. It was a curious, and, to me, rather pathetic study to watch Lewes—a man naturally self-sufficient (I do not use the word in any odious sense), of a combative turn of intellect, and with scarcely any diffidence in his nature — so humbly admitting, and even insisting upon, "Polly's" superiority to himself in every department. Once when he was walking with my wife in the garden of their house in Surrey, she turned the conversation which had been touching other topics to speak of George Eliot. "Oh," said Lewes, stopping short and looking at her with those bright eyes of his, " *Your blood be on your own head!* I didn't begin it; but if you wish to speak of her, *I* am always ready." It was this complete candor, and the genuineness of his admiring love for her, which made its manifestations delightful, and freed them from offence.

CHAPTER XXXV.

I HAVE a great many letters from G. H. Lewes, and from George Eliot. Many of the latter are addressed to my wife. And many, especially of those from Lewes, relating as they do mainly to matters of literary business, though always containing characteristic touches, are not of sufficient general interest to make it worth while to transcribe them for publication. In no case is there any word in any of them that would make it expedient to withhold them on any other ground. I might, perhaps, have introduced them into my narrative as nearly as possible at the times to which chronologically they refer. But it has seemed to me so probable that there may be many readers who may be glad of an opportunity of seeing these letters without feeling disposed to give their time to the rest of these volumes, that I have thought it best to throw them together in this place.

I will begin with one written from Blandford Square, by George Eliot, to me, which is of great interest. It bears no date whatever, save that of place; but the subject of it dates it with considerable accuracy.

"DEAR MR. TROLLOPE,—I am very grateful to you for your notes. Concerning *netto di specchio*, I have found a passage in Varchi which decides the point according to *your* impression. [Passages equally decisive might be found *passim* in the old Florentine historians. And I ought to have referred her to them. But as she had altogether mistaken the meaning of the phrase, I had insinuated my correction as little presumptuously as I could.]

"My inference had been gathered from the vague use of the term to express disqualification [*i. e.*, NON *netto di specchio* expressed disqualification]. But I find from Varchi, b. viii., that the *specchio* in question was a public book, in which the names of all debtors to the *Commune* were entered. Thus your doubt [no doubt at all!] has been a very useful caveat to me.

"Concerning the Bardi, my authority for making them originally *popolani* is G. Villani. He says, c. xxxix., '*e gia cominciavano a venire possenti i Frescobaldi e Bardi e Mozzi* ma di piccolo cominciamento.' And c. lxxxi., '*e questi furono le principale case de' Guelfi che uscirono di Firenze. Del Sesto d' Oltr' Arno, i Rossi, Nerli, e parte de' Manelli, Bardi, e Frescobaldi de' Popoloni dal detto Sesto*, case nobili *Canigiani*,' etc. These passages corrected my previous impression that they were originally Lombard nobles.

[It needs some familiarity with the Florentine chroniclers to understand that the words quoted by no means indicate that the families named were not of patrician origin. "There walked into the lobby with the Radicals, Lord —— and Mr. ——," would just as much prove that the persons named had not belonged to the class of landowners. But the passage is interesting as showing the great care she took to make her Italian novel historically accurate. And it is to be remembered that she came to the subject absolutely new to it. She would have known otherwise, that the *Case* situated in the Oltr' Arno quarter were almost all noble. That ward of the city was the Florentine *quartier St. Germain*.]

"Concerning the phrase *in piazza*, and *in mercato*, my choice of them was partly founded on the colloquial usage as represented by Sacchetti, whose dialogue is intensely idiomatic. Also *in piazza* is, I believe, used by the historians (I think even by Macchiavelli), when speaking of popular *turnouts*. The ellipse took my fancy because of its colloquial stamp. But I gather from your objection that it seems too barbarous in a modern Italian ear. Will you whisper your final opinion in Mr. Lewes's ear on Monday?

[I do not remember what the ellipse in question was. As regards the use of the phrase *in piazza* she is perfectly right. The term keeps the same meaning to the present day, and is equivalent in political language to *the street*.]

"*Boto* was used on similar grounds, and as it is recognized by the *Voc. della Crusca*, I think I may venture to keep it, having a weakness for those indications of the processes by which language is modified.

[*Boto* for *voto* is a Florentinism which may be heard to the present day, though the vast majority of strangers would never hear it, or understand it if they did. George Eliot, no doubt, met with it in some of those old chroniclers who wrote exactly as not only the lower orders, but the generality of their fellow-citizens, were speaking around them. And her use of it testifies to the minuteness of her care to reproduce the form and pressure of the time of which she was writing.]

"Once more thank you, though my gratitude is in danger of looking too much like a lively sense of anticipated favors, for I mean to ask you to take other trouble yet. Yours very truly, MARIAN E. LEWES."

The following letter, written from Blandford Square on the 5th July, 1861, is, as regards the first three pages, from him, and the last from her:

"MY DEAR TROLLOPE,—We have now read 'La Beata' [my first novel], and must tell you how charmed we have been with it. *Nina* herself is perfectly exquisite and individual, and her story is full of poetry and pathos. Also, one feels a breath from the Val d' Arno rustling amid the pages, and a sense of Florentine life, such as one rarely gets out of books. The critical objection I should make to it, apart from minor points, is that often you spoil the artistic attitude by adopting a critical antagonistic attitude, by which I mean that, instead of painting the thing objectively, you present it critically, *with an eye to the opinions* likely to be formed by certain readers; thus, instead of relying on the simple presentation of the fact of Nina's innocence, you *call up* the objection you desire to anticipate by side glances at the worldly and 'knowing' reader's opinions. In a word, I feel as if you were not engrossed by your subject, but were sufficiently aloof from it to contemplate it as a spectator, which is an error in art. Many of the remarks are delicately felt and finely written. The whole book comes from a noble nature, and so it impresses the reader. But I may tell you what Mrs. Carlyle said last night, which will in some sense corroborate what I have said. In her opinion you would have done better to make two books of it, one the love-story, and one a description of Florentine life. She admires the book very much I should add. Now, although I cannot by any means agree with that criticism of hers, I fancy the origin of it was some such feeling as I have endeavored to indicate in saying you are often critical when you should be simply objective.

"We had a pleasant journey home over the St. Gothard, and found our boy very well and happy at Hofwyl, and our bigger boy *ditto* awaiting us here. Polly is very well, and, as you may imagine, talks daily of Florence and our delightful trip, our closer acquaintance with you and yours being among the most delightful of our reminiscences.

"Yesterday Anthony dined with us, and, as he had never seen Carlyle, he was glad to go down with us to tea at Chelsea. Carlyle had read and *agreed* with the West Indian book, and the two got on very well together; both Carlyle and Mrs. Carlyle liking Anthony, and I suppose it was reciprocal, though I did not see him afterwards to hear what he thought. He had to run away to catch his train.

"He told us of the sad news of Mrs. Browning's death. Poor Browning! That was my first, and remains my constant reflection. When people love each other and have lived together any time they ought to die together. For myself I should not care in the least about dying. The dreadful thing to me would be to live after losing, if I should ever lose, the one who has made life for me. Of course you who all knew and valued her will feel the loss, but I cannot think of anybody's grief but his.

"The next page must be left for Polly's postscript, so I shall only send my kindest regards and wishes to Mrs. Trollope and the biggest of kisses to *la cantatrice* [my poor girl Bice].

"Ever faithfully yours,   G. H. Lewes."

"Dear Mrs. Trollope,—While I am reading 'La Beata' I constantly feel as if Mr. Trollope were present telling it all to me *vivâ voce.* It seems to me more thoroughly and fully like himself than any of his other books. And in spite of our having had the most of his society away from you [on our Camaldoli excursion], you are always part of his presence to me in a hovering, aërial fashion. So it seems quite natural that a letter addressed to him should have a postscript addressed to you. Pray reckon it among the good you do in this world that you come very often into our thoughts and conversation. We see comparatively so few people that we are apt to recur to recollections of those we like best with almost childish frequency, and a little fresh news about you would be a welcome variety, especially the news that you had quite shaken off that spine indisposition which was still clinging to you that last morning when we said our good-byes. We have enough knowledge about you and your world to interpret all the details you can give us. But our words about our own home doings would be very vague and colorless to you. You must always imagine us coming to see you and wanting to know as much about you as we can, and like a charming hostess gratify that want. I must thank you for the account of Cavour in *The Athenæum*, which stirred me strongly. I am afraid I have what *The Saturday Review* would call 'a morbid delight in deathbeds'—not having reached that lofty superiority which considers it bad taste to allude to them.

"How is Beatrice, the blessed and blessing? That will always be a history to interest us—how her brown hair darkens, how her voice deepens and strengthens, and how you get more and more delight in her. I need send no separate message to Mr. Trollope before I say that

"I am always yours, with lively remembrance,

"MARIAN E. LEWES."

It needed George Eliot's fine and minute handwriting to put all this into one page of note-paper.

The next letter that came from Blandford Square, dated 9th December, 1861, was also a joint one, the larger portion of which, however, is from her pen:

"DEAR GOOD PEOPLE,—If your ears burn as often as you are talked about in this house there must be an unpleasant amount of aural circulation to endure! And as the constant *refrain* is, 'Really we must write to them that they may not altogether slip away from us,' I have this morning screwed my procrastination to the writing-desk.

"First and foremost, let us know how you are, and what are the results of the bathing. Then a word as to the new novel, or any other work, will be acceptable. I lend about 'La Beata' in all good quarters, and always hear golden opinions from all sorts of people. Of course, you hear from Anthony. Is he prosperous and enjoying his life? The book will have an enormous sale just now; but I fancy he will find more animosity and less friendliness than he expected, to judge from the state of exasperation against the Britisher, which seems to be general.

"We have been pursuing the even baritone—I wish I could say tenor—of our way. My health became seriously alarming in September, so we went off to Malvern for a fortnight; and there the mountain air, exercise, and regular diet set me up, so that I have been in better training for work than I had been for a long while. Polly has not been strong, yet not materially amiss; but, as she will add a postscript to this, I shall leave her to speak for herself.

"In your (T. A. T.) book huntings, if you could lay your hand on a copy of Hermolaus Barbarus, 'Compendium Scientiæ Naturalis,' 1553, or any of Telesio's works, think of me and pounce on them. I was going to bother you about the new edition of Galileo, but fortunately I fell in with the Milan edition cheap, and contented myself with that. Do you know what there is *new* in the Florentine edition? I suppose you possess it, as you do so many enviable books.

"We heard the other day that Miss Blagden had come to stay in London for the winter, so Polly sent a message to her to say how glad we should be to see her. If she comes she will bring us some account of *casa* Trollope.

"When you next pass Giotto's tower salute it for me; it is one of my dearest Florentines, and always beckoning to us to come back.

"Ever your faithful friend,   G. H. Lewes."

She writes :

"Dear Friends,—Writing letters or asking for them is not always the way to make one's memory agreeable, but you are not among those people who shudder at letters, since you *did* say you would like to hear from us, and let us hear from you occasionally. I have no good news to tell about myself; but to have my husband back again and enjoying his work is quite enough happiness to fall to one woman's share in this world, where the stock of happiness is so moderate and the claimants so many. He is deep in Aristotle's 'Natural Science' as the first step in a history of science, which he has for a long while been hoping that he should be able to write. So you will understand his demand for brown folios. Indeed, he is beginning to have a slight contempt for authors sufficiently known to the vulgar to be inserted in biographical dictionaries. Hermolaus Barbarus is one of those distinguished by omission in some chief works of that kind; and we learned to our surprise from a don at Cambridge that *he* had never heard the name. Let us hope there is an Olympus for forgotten authors.

"Our trial of the water-cure at Malvern made us think with all the more emphasis of the possible effect on a too delicate and fragile friend at Florence. [My wife.] It really helped to mend George. And as I hope the Florentine hydropathist may not be a quack, as Dr. —— at Malvern certainly is, I shall be disappointed if there is no good effect to be traced to 'judicious packing and sitz baths' that you can tell us of. Did Beatrice enjoy her month's dissipation at Leghorn? And is the voice prospering? Don't let her quite forget us. We make rather a feeble attempt at musical Saturday evenings, having a new grand piano, which stimulates musical desires. But we want a good violin and violoncello—difficult to be found among amateurs. Having no sunshine, one needs music all the more. It would be difficult for you to imagine very truthfully what sort of atmosphere we have been living in here in London for the last month — warm, heavy, dingy gray. I have seen some sunshine once — in a dream. Do tell us all you can about yourselves. It seems only the other day that we were shaking you by the hand; and all details will be lit up as if by your very voice and looks. Say a kind word for me sometimes to the bright-eyed lady by whose side I sat in your balcony the evening of the national *Fête*. At the moment I cannot recall her name. We are now going to the British Museum to read — a fearful way of getting knowledge. If I had Aladdin's lamp I should certainly use it to get books served up to me at a moment's notice. It may be better to search for truth than to have it at hand without seeking, but with books I should take the other alterna-tive.   Ever yours,   M. E. LEWES."

The lady in the balcony spoken of in the above letter was Signora Mignaty, the niece of Sir Frederick Adam, whom I had known long years previously in Rome, and who had married Signor Mignaty, a Greek artist, and was (and is) living in Florence. She was, in fact, the niece of the Greek lady Sir Frederick married. I remember her aunt, a very beautiful woman. The niece, Signorina Mar-gherita Albani as she was when I first knew her at eigh-teen years old in Rome, inherited so much of the beauty of her race that the Roman artists were constantly implor-ing her to sit for them. She has made herself known in the literary world by several works, especially by a recent book on Correggio, his life and works, published in French.

The next letter from Lewes, written from Blandford Square on the 2d June, without date of year, but probably 1863, is of more interest to myself than to the public. But I may perhaps be permitted to indulge my vanity by publishing it as a testimony that his previous praise of what I had written was genuine, and not merely the laud-atory compliments of a correspondent.

"MY DEAR TROLLOPE,—Enclosed is the proof you were good enough to say you would correct. When am I to return the compliment?

"I have finished 'Marietta.' Its picture of Italian life is extremely vivid and interesting, but it is a long way behind 'La Beata' in interest of story. I have just finished one volume of Anthony's 'America,' and am immensely pleased with it—so much so that I hope to do something tow-ards counteracting the nasty notice in the *Saturday*.

                   "Ever yours faithfully,   G. H. LEWES."

The next letter is from Lewes, dated "The Priory, North Bank, Regent's Park, 20th March, 1864:

"My dear Trollope,—My eldest boy, who spends his honeymoon in Florence (is not that sugaring jam tart?), brings you this greeting from your silent but affectionate friends. Tell him all particulars about yourselves, and he will transmit them in his letters to us. First and foremost about the health of your wife, and how this bitter winter has treated her. Next about Bice, and then about yourself.

"We rejoice in the prospect of your 'History of Florence,' and I am casting about, hoping to find somebody to review it worthily for the *Fortnightly Review*. By the way, would not you or your wife help me there also? Propose your subjects!

"I hope you will like our daughter. She is a noble creature; and Charles is a lucky dog (his father's luck) to get such a wife.

"We have been and are in a poor state of health, but manage to scramble on. Charles will tell you all there is to tell. With our love to your dear wife and Bice,

"Believe me, ever faithfully yours,　　　　G. H. Lewes."

Shortly after receiving this my wife had a letter from George Eliot, from Venice, dated 15th May, 1864. She writes from the "Hôtel de Ville."

"My dear Mrs. Trollope,—I wonder whether you are likely to be at Lake Como next month, or at any other place that we could take on our way to the Alps. It would make the prospect of our journey homeward much pleasanter if we could count on seeing you for a few hours; and I will not believe that you will think me troublesome if I send the question to you. I am rather discontented with destiny that she has not let us see anything of you for nearly three years. And I hope you too will not be sorry to take me by the hand again.

"My ground for supposing it not unlikely that you will be at one of the lakes, is the report I heard from Mr. Pigott, that such a plan was hovering in your mind. My chief fear is that our return, which is not likely at the latest to be later than the middle of June, may be too early for us to find you.

"We reached Venice three days ago, after a short stay at Milan, and have the delight of finding everything more beautiful than it was to us four years ago. That is a satisfactory experience to us, who are getting old, and are afraid of the traditional loss of glory on the grass and all else, with which melancholy poets threaten us.

"Mr. Lewes says I am to say the sweetest things that can be said with propriety to you, and love to Bice, to whose memory he appeals, in spite of all the friends she has made since he had the last kiss from her.

"I too have love to send to Bice, whom I expect to see changed like a lily-bud to something more definitely promising. Mr. Trollope, I suppose, is in England by this time, else I should say all affectionate regards from us both to him. I am writing under difficulties.

"Ever, dear Mrs. Trollope, very sincerely yours,

"M. E. Lewes.

Here is another from Lewes, which the postmark only shows to have been written in 1865 :

"MY DEAR TROLLOPE,—Thank Signor —— for the offer of his paper, and express to him my regret that in the present crowded state of the *Review* I cannot find a place for it. Don't you, however, run away with the idea that I don't want *your* contributions on the same ground! The fact is ——'s paper is too wordy and heavy and not of sufficient interest for our publication; and as I have a great many well on hand, I am forced to be particular. Originally my fear was lest we should not get contributors enough. That fear has long vanished. But *good* contributions are always scarce; so don't you fail me.

"We have been at Tunbridge Wells for a fortnight's holiday. I was forced to 'cave in,' as the Yankees say—regularly beat. I am not very flourishing now, but I can go into harness again. Polly has been, and, alas! still is, anything but in a satisfactory state. But she is gestating, and gestation with her is always perturbing. I wish the book were done, with all my heart.

"I don't think I ever told you how very much your 'History of Florence' interested me. I am shockingly ignorant of the subject, and not at all competent to speak, except as one of the public; but you made the political life of the people clear to me. I only regretted here and there a newspaper style which was not historic. Oscar Browning has sent me his review, but I have not read it yet. It is at the printer's. Polly sends her love.   Ever faithfully yours,   G. H. L."

He writes again, dating his letter 1st January, 1866, but postmarked 1865. It is singular that the date as given by the writer, 1866, must have been right, and that given by the postmark, 1865, wrong. And the fact may possibly some day be useful to some counsel having to struggle against the evidence of a postmark. The letter commences :

"MY DEAR TROLLOPE,—A happy new year to you and Bice !"

It is quite impossible that Lewes could have so written, while my wife, Theodosia, so great a favorite with both him and his wife, and so constantly inquired for tenderly by them, was yet alive. I lost her on the 13th of April, 1865. It is certain, therefore, that Lewes's letter was written in 1866, and not, as the postmark declares, in 1865. After speaking of some literary business matters, the letter goes on :

"And when am I to receive those articles from you which you pro-
21

jected? I suppose other work keeps you ever on the stretch. But so active a man must needs 'fulfil himself in many ways.'

"We have been ailing constantly without being ill, but our work gets on somehow or other. Polly is miserable over a new novel, and I am happy over the very hard work of a new edition of my 'History of Philosophy,' which will almost be a new book, so great are the changes and additions. Polly sends her love to you and Bice.

"Yours very faithfully,   G. H. Lewes."

Then after a long break, and after a new phase of my life had commenced, Lewes writes on the 14th of January, 1869, from "21 North Bank :"

"Dear T. T.,—We did not meet in Germany because our plans were altogether changed. We passed all the time in the Black Forest, and came home through the Oberland. I did write to Salzburg, however, and perhaps the letter is still there; but there was nothing in it.

"You know how fond we are of you, and the pleasure it always gives us to get a glimpse of you. (Not that we have not also very pleasant associations with your wife,* but she is as yet stranger to us of course.) But we went away in search of complete repose. And in the Black Forest there was not a soul to speak to, and we liked it so much as to stay on there.

"We contemplate moving southwards in the spring, and if we go to Italy and come *near* Florence, we shall assuredly make a *détour* and come and see you. Polly wants to see Arezzo and Perugia. And I suppose we can still get a *vetturino* to take us that way to Rome? Don't want railways, if to be avoided. I don't think we can get away before March, for my researches are so absorbing that, if health holds out, I must go on; if not, we shall pack up earlier. The worst of Lent is that one gets no theatres, and precisely because we never go to the theatre in London we hugely enjoy it abroad. Yesterday we took the child of a friend of ours to a morning performance of the pantomime, and are utterly knocked up in consequence. Somehow or other abroad the theatre agrees with us. Polly sends the kindest remembrances to you and your wife. Whenever you want anything done in London, consider me an idle man.

"Ever yours faithfully,   G. H. Lewes."

And on the 28th February, in the same year, accordingly he writes :

"Touching our visit to Florence, you may be sure we could not lightly forego such a pleasure. We start to-morrow, and unless we are recalled by my mother's health, we calculate being with you about the end of March. But we shall give due warning of our arrival. We both look forward to this holiday, and 'languish for the purple seas;' though the

---

* I had married my second wife on the 29th of October, 1866.

high winds now howl a threat of anything but a pleasant crossing to Calais. *Che! Che!* One must pay for one's pleasure! With both of our
warmest salutations to you and yours,
<blockquote>"Believe me, yours faithfully,   G. H. LEWES."</blockquote>

The travellers must, however, have reached us some
days before the end of March, for I have a letter to my
wife from George Eliot, dated from Naples on the 1st of
April, 1869, after they had left us. She writes:

"MY DEAR MRS. TROLLOPE,—The kindness which induces you to shelter
travellers will make you willing to hear something of their subsequent
fate. And I am the more inclined to send you some news of ourselves
because I have nothing dismal to tell. We bore our long journey better
than we dared to expect, for the night was made short by sleep in our
large coupé, and during the day we had no more than one headache between us. Mr. Lewes really looks better, and has lost his twinges. And
though pleasure-seekers are notoriously the most aggrieved and howling
inhabitants of the universe, we can allege nothing against our lot here
but the persistent coldness of the wind, which is in dangerously sudden
contrast with the warmth of the sunshine whenever one gets on the wrong
side of a wall. This prevents us from undertaking any carriage expeditions, which is rather unfortunate, because such expeditions are among
the chief charms of Naples. We have not been able to renew our old
memories of that sort at all, except by a railway journey to Pompeii; and
our days are spent in the museum and in the sunniest out-of-door spots.
We have been twice to the San Carlo, which we were the more pleased
to do, because when we were here before that fine theatre was closed.
The singing is so-so, and the tenor especially is gifted with limbs rather
than with voice or ear. But there is a baritone worth hearing, and a soprano whom the Neapolitans delight to honor with hideous sounds of
applause.

"We are longing for a soft wind, which will allow us to take the long
drive to Baiæ during one of our remaining days here. At present we
think of leaving for Rome on Sunday or Monday. But our departure will
probably be determined by an answer from the landlord of the Hôtel de
Minerva, to whom Mr. Lewes has written. We have very comfortable
quarters here, out of the way of that English and American society, whose
charms you can imagine. Our private dinner is well served; and I am
glad to be away from the Chiaja, except—the exception is a great one—
for the sake of the sunsets which I should have seen there.

"Mr. Lewes has found a book by an Italian named Franchi, formerly
a priest, on the present condition of philosophy in Italy. He emerges
from its depths—or shallows—to send his best remembrances; and to
Bice he begs especially to recommend Plantation Bitters.

"I usually think all the more of things and places the farther I get
from them, and, on that ground, you will understand that at Naples I
think of Florence, and the kindness I found there under my small mise-

ries. Pray offer my kind regards to Miss Blagden when you seê her, and
tell her that I hope to shake hands with her in London this spring.

" We shall obey Mr. Trollope's injunctions to write again from Perugia
or elsewhere, according to our route homeward. But pray warn him that
when my throat is not sore, and my head not stagnant, I am a much fiercer
antagonist. It is perhaps a delight to one's egoism to hav3 a friend who
is among the best of men with the worst of theories. One can be at once
affectionate and spit-fire. Pray remember me with indulgence, all of you,
and believe, dear Mrs. Trollope,

" Most truly yours,   M. E. LEWES."

It will be seen from the above that George Eliot had
very quickly fraternized—what is the feminine form?—
with my second wife, as I, without any misgivings, fore-
saw would be the case. Indeed, subsequent circumstances
allowed a greater degree of intimacy to grow up between
them than had been possible in the case of my Bice's
mother, restricted as her intercourse with the latter had
been by failing health, and the comparative fewness of
the hours they had passed together. Neither she nor
Lewes had ever passed a night under my roof until I received them in the villa at Ricorboli, where I lived with
my second wife.

What was the subject of the "antagonism" to which
the above letter alludes I have entirely forgotten. In
all probability we differed on some subject of politics,*
by reason of the then rapidly maturing Conservatism
which my outlook ahead forced upon me. Nevertheless,
it would seem from some words in a letter written to me
by Lewes in the November of 1869, that my political heresies were not deemed deeply damning. There was a question of my undertaking the foreign correspondence of a
London paper, which came to nothing till some four years
later, under other circumstances ; and with reference to
that project he writes :

"Polly and I were immensely pleased at the prospect for you. She
was rejoiced that you should once more be giving yourself to public affairs, which you so well understand. . . . We are but just come back from

---

* My wife, on reading this passage, tells me that according to her recollection the differences in question had no reference to politics at all, but
to matters of higher interest, relating to man's ultimate destinies.

the solitudes of a farm-house in Surrey, whither I took Polly immediately after our loss [of his son], of which I suppose Anthony told you. It had shaken her seriously. She had lavished almost a mother's love on the dear boy, and suffered a mother's grief in the bereavement. He died in her arms; and for a long while it seemed as if she could never get over the pain. But now she is calm again, though very sad. But she will get to work, and *that* will aid her.

"For me, I was as fully prepared (by three or four months' conviction of its inevitableness) as one can be in such cases. It is always sudden, however foreseen. Yet the preparation was of great use; and I now have only a beautiful image living with me, and a deep thankfulness that his sufferings are at an end, since recovery was impossible.

"Give my love to your wife and Bice, and believe ever in yours faithfully,   G. H. LEWES."

The following highly interesting letter was written to my wife by Mrs. Lewes, about a year after his death. It is dated "The Priory, 19 December, 1879."

"DEAR MRS. TROLLOPE,—In sending me Dr. Haller's words you have sent me a great comfort. A just appreciation of my husband's work from a competent person is what I am most athirst for; and Dr. Haller has put his finger on a true characteristic. I only wish he could print something to the same effect in any pages that would be generally read.

"There is no biography. An article entitled 'George Henry Lewes' appeared in the last *New London Quarterly*. It was written by a man for whom he had much esteem; but it is not strong. A few facts about the early life and education are given with tolerable accuracy, but the estimate of the philosophic and scientific activity is inadequate. Still it is the best thing you could mention to Dr. Haller. You know perhaps that a volume entitled 'The Study of Psychology' appeared in May last, and that another volume (500 pp.) of 'Problems of Life and Mind' has just been published. The best history of a writer is contained in his writings; these are his chief actions. If he happens to have left an autobiography telling (what nobody else can tell) how his mind grew, how it was determined by the joys, sorrows, and other influences of childhood and youth—that is a precious contribution to knowledge. But biographies generally are a disease of English literature.

"I have never yet told you how grateful I was to you for writing to me a year ago. For a long while I could read no letter. But now I have read yours more than once, and it is carefully preserved. You had been with us in our happiness so near the time when it left me—you and your husband are peculiarly bound up with the latest memories.

"You must have had a mournful summer. But Mr. Trollope's thorough recovery from his severe attack is a fresh proof of his constitutional strength. We cannot properly count age by years. See what Mr. Gladstone does with seventy of them in his frame. And my lost one had but sixty-one and a half.

"You are to come to England again in 1881, I remember, and then, if I am alive, I hope to see you. With best love to you both, always, dear Mrs. Trollope, Yours faithfully, M. E. LEWES."

The " words of Dr. Haller," to which the above letter refers, were to the effect that one of Lewes's great advantages in scientific and philosophical research was his familiar acquaintance with the works of German and French writers, which enabled him to follow the contemporaneous movement of science throughout Europe, whereas many writers of learning and ability wasted their own and their readers' time in investigating questions already fully investigated elsewhere, and advancing theories which had been previously proved or disproved without their knowledge. Dr. Ludwig Haller, of Berlin, in writing to me about G. H. Lewes, then recently deceased, had said, if I remember rightly, that he had some intention of publishing a sketch of Lewes in some German periodical. I am not aware whether this intention was ever carried into effect.

The attack to which the above letter alludes was a very bad one of sciatica. At length the baths of Baden in Switzerland cured me permanently, but after their—it is said ordinary and normal, but very perverse—fashion, having first made me incomparably worse. I suffered excruciatingly, consolingly (!) assured by the doctor that sciatica never kills—only makes you wish that it would! While I was at the worst my brother came to Baden to see me, and on leaving me after a couple of days, wrote to my wife the following letter, which I confiscated and keep as a memorial.

After expressing his commiseration for me, he continues :

"For you, I cannot tell you the admiration I have for you. Your affection and care and assiduity were to be expected. I knew you well enough to take them as a matter of course from you to him. But your mental and physical capacity, your power of sustaining him by your own cheerfulness, and supporting him by your own attention, are marvellous. When I consider all the circumstances, I hardly know how to reconcile so much love with so much self-control."

Every word true! And what he saw for a few hours

in each of a couple of days I saw every hour of the day and night for four terrible months.

But all this is a parenthesis into which I have been led, I hope excusably, by Mrs. Lewes's mention of my illness.

N.B.—I said at an early page of these recollections that I had never been confined to my bed by illness for a single day during more than sixty years. The above-mentioned illness leaves the statement still true. The sciatica was bad, but never kept me in bed. Indeed, I was perhaps in less torment out of it.

Here is the last letter of George Eliot's which reached us. It is written by Mrs. Lewes to my wife, from " The Priory, 30 December, 1879 :"

" DEAR MRS. TROLLOPE,—I enclose the best photograph within my reach. To me all portraits of him are objectionable, because I see him more vividly and truly without them. But I think this is the most like what he was as you knew him. I have sent your anecdote about the boy to Mr. Du Maurier, whom it will suit exactly. I asked Charles Lewes to copy it from your letter with your own pretty words of introduction.

" Yours affectionately, M. E. LEWES."

It is pretty well too late in the day for me to lament the loss of old friends. They have been well-nigh some time past all gone. I have been exceptionally fortunate in an aftermath belonging to a younger generation. But they too are dropping around me ! And few losses from this second crop have left a more regretted void than George Henry Lewes and his wife.

CHAPTER XXXVI.

MY MOTHER.—LETTERS OF MARY MITFORD.—LETTERS OF
T. C. GRATTAN.

I HAVE thought that it might be more convenient to
the reader to have the letters contained in the foregoing
chapter all together, and have not interrupted them therefore to speak of any of the events which were meantime
happening in my own life.

But during the period which the letters cover the two
greatest sorrows of my life had fallen upon me—I had
lost first my mother, then my wife.

The bereavement, however, was very different in the
two cases. If my mother had died a dozen years earlier I
should have felt the loss as the end of all things to me—
as leaving me desolate and causing a void which nothing
could ever fill. But when she died at eighty-three she
had lived her life, upon the whole a very happy one, to
the happiness of which I had (and have) the satisfaction
of believing I largely contributed.

It is very common for a mother and daughter to live
during many years of life together in as close companionship as I lived with my mother, but it is not common for
a son to do so. During many years, and many, many
journeyings, and more *tête-à-tête* walks, and yet more of
tête-à-tête home hours, we were inseparable companions
and friends. I can truly say that, from the time when
we put our horses together on my return from Birmingham to the time of my marriage, she was all in all to me.
During some four or five days in the early time of our
residence at Florence I thought I was going to lose her,
and I can never forget the blank wretchedness of the prospect that seemed to be before me.

She had a very serious illness, and was, as I had subsequently reason to believe, very mistakenly treated. She was attended by a practitioner of the old school, who had at that time the leading practice in Florence. He was a very good fellow, and an admirable whist-player ; and I do not think the members of our little colony drew a sufficiently sharp line of division between his social and his professional qualifications. He was, as I have said, essentially a man of the (even then) old school, and retained the old-fashioned general practitioner's phraseology. I remember his once mortally disgusting an unhappy dyspeptic old lady by asking her, " Do we go to our dinner with glee ?" As if the poor soul had ever done anything with glee !

This gentleman had bled my mother, and had appointed another bleeding for the evening. I believe she would assuredly have died if that had been done, and I attribute to Lord Holland the saving of her. Her doctor had very wrongly resisted the calling in of other English advice, professional jealousy, and indeed enmity, running high just then among us. Lord Holland came to the house just in the nick of time ; and overruling authoritatively all the difficulties raised by the Esculapius in possession of the field, insisted on at once sending his own medical attendant. The result was the immediate administration of port wine instead of phlebotomy, and the patient's rapid recovery.

My mother was at the time far past taking any part in the discussion of the medical measures to be adopted in her case. But I am not without a suspicion that she too, if she could have been consulted, would have sided with phlebotomy and whist, as against modern practice unrelieved by any such alleviation. For the phlebotomist had been a constant attendant at her Friday night whist-table; and as it was she lost him, for he naturally was offended at her recovery under rival hands.

What my mother *was* I have already said enough to show, as far as my imperfect words can show it, in divers passages of these reminiscences. She was the happiest-natured person I ever knew—happy in the intense power of enjoyment, happier still in the conscious exercise of the

21*

power of making others happy ; and this continued to be the case till nearly the end. During the last few years the bright lamp began to grow dim and gradually sink into the socket. She suffered but little physically, but she lost her memory, and then gradually more and more the powers of her mind generally. I have often thought that this perishing of the mind before the exceptionally healthy and well-constituted physical frame in which it was housed may have been due to the tremendous strain to which she was subjected during those terrible months at Bruges, when she was watching the dying bed of a much-loved son during the day, and, dieted on green tea and laudanum, was writing fiction most part of the night. The cause, if such were the case, would have preceded the effect by some forty years ; but whether it is on the cards to suppose that such an effect may have been produced after such a length of time, I have not physiological knowledge enough to tell.

She was, I think, to an exceptional degree surrounded by very many friends, mostly women, but including many men, at every period of her life. But the circumstances of it caused the world of her intimates during her youth, her middle life, and her old age to be to a great degree peopled by different figures.

She was during all her life full of, and fond of, fun ; had an exquisite sense of humor ; and at all times valued her friends and acquaintances more exclusively, I think, than most people do, for their intrinsic qualities, mainly those of heart, and not so much perhaps intellect, accurately speaking, as brightness. There is a passage in my brother's " Autobiography " which grates upon my mind, and, I think, very signally fails to hit the mark.

He writes (pp. 19, 20): " She had loved society, affecting a somewhat Liberal *rôle*, and professing an emotional dislike to tyrants, which sprung from the wrongs of would-be regicides and the poverty of patriot exiles. An Italian marquis who had escaped with only a second shirt from the clutches of some archduke whom he had wished to exterminate, or a French *prolétaire* with distant ideas of sacrificing himself to the cause of liberty, were always

welcome to the modest hospitality of her house. In after-years, when marquises of another cast had been gracious to her, she became a strong Tory, and thought that
archduchesses were sweet. But with her politics were
always an affair of the heart, as indeed were all her convictions. Of reasoning from causes I think that she knew
nothing."

Now there is hardly a word of this in which Anthony
is not more or less mistaken ; and that simply because he
had not adequate opportunities for close observation. The
affection which subsisted between my mother and my
brother Anthony was from the beginning to the end of
their lives as tender and as warm as ever existed between
a mother and son. Indeed, I remember that in the old
days of our youth we used to consider Anthony the Ben-
jamin. But from the time that he became a clerk in the
post-office to her death, he and my mother were never
together but as visitors during the limited period of a
visit. From the time that I resigned my position at Birmingham to the time of her death, I was uninterruptedly
an inmate of her house, or she of mine. And I think that
I knew her as few sons know their mothers.

No regicide, would-be or other, ever darkened her doors.
No French *prolétaire*, or other French political refugee
was ever among her guests. She never was acquainted
with any Italian marquis who had escaped in any degree
of distress from poverty. With General Pepe she was
intimate for years. But of him the world knows enough
to perceive that my brother cannot have alluded to him.
And I recollect no other marquis. It is very true that in
the old Keppel Street and Harrow days several Italian
exiles, and I think some Spaniards, used to be her occasional guests. This had come to pass by means of her
intimacy with Lady Dyer, the wife and subsequently widow of Sir Thomas Dyer, whose years of foreign service
had interested him and her in many such persons. The
friends of her friend were her friends. They were not
such by virtue of their political position and ideas. Though
it is no doubt true, that caring little about politics, and in a
jesting way (how jesting many a memorial of fun between

her and Lady Dyer, and Miss Gabell, the daughter of Dr.
Gabell of Winchester, is still extant in my hands to prove),
the general tone of the house was "Liberal." But nothing can be farther from the truth than the idea that my
mother was led to become a Tory by the "graciousness"
of any "marquises" or great folks of any kind. I am inclined to think that there was *one* great personage, whose
(not graciousness, but) intellectual influence *did* impel her
mind in a Conservative direction. And this was Metternich. She had more talk with him than her book on Vienna would lead a reader to suppose ; and very far more of
his mind and influence reached her through the medium
of the princess.

To how great a degree this is likely to have been the
case may be in some measure perceived from a letter which
the princess addressed to my mother shortly after she had
left Vienna. She preserved it among a few others, which
she specially valued, and I transcribe it from the original
now before me.

"Vous ne pourriez croire, chère Madame Trollope, combien le portrait
que vous avez chargé le Baron Hügel de me remettre m'a fait de plaisir !

"Il y a longtemps que je cachais au fonds de mon cœur le désir de pos-
séder votre portrait, qui, interressant pour le monde, est devenu précieux
pour moi, puisque j'ai le plaisir de vous connaître telle que vous êtes, bonne,
simple, bienveillante, et loin de tout ce qui effroie et eloigne des reputations
litéraires. Je remercie M. Hervieu de l'avoir fait aussi ressemblant. Et
je vous assure, chère Madame Trollope, que rien ne pouvait me toucher
aussi vivement et me faire autant de plaisir que ce souvenir venant de
vous, qui me rappelera sans cesse les bons moments que j'ai eu la satisfaction de passer avec vous et qui resteront à jamais chères à ma mémoire.
                "MELANIE, PRINCESSE DE METTERNICH."

I think that the hours passed by the princess and my
mother *tête-à-tête*, save for the presence of the artist occupied by his work during the painting of the Princess Melanie's portrait for my mother, were mainly the cause of
the real intimacy of mind and affection which grew up
between them—though, of course, the painting of the
portrait shows that a considerable intimacy had previously
arisen. And it had been arranged that the portrait of my
mother, which was the occasion of the above letter, should
be exchanged for that of the princess. But there had

been no time, amid the whirl of the Vienna gayeties, to get it executed. It was, therefore, sent from England by Baron Hugel when he called on my mother, on visiting this country shortly after her return from Austria.

It occurs to me here to mention a circumstance which was, I think, the first thing to begin—not the acquaintance but—the intimacy in question; and which may be related as possessing an interest not confined to either of the ladies in question.

The Archduchess Sophie had graciously intimated her desire that my mother should be presented to her, and an evening had been named for the purpose. But a few days before — just three, if I remember rightly — my mother caught a cold, which resulted in erysipelas, causing her head to become swollen to nearly double its usual size. Great was the dismay of the ladies who had arranged the meeting with the archduchess, chief among whom had been the Princess Melanie. She came to my mother, and insisted upon sending to her an old homœopathic physician, who was her own medical attendant, and had been Hahnemann's favorite pupil. He came, saw his patient, and was told that what he had to do was to make her presentable by the following Friday! He shook his head, said the time was too short—but he would do his best. And the desired object was *fully* attained.

I have no doubt that my mother returned from her Vienna visit a more strongly convinced Conservative in politics than she had hitherto been. And it does not seem to me that the modification of her opinions in that direction, which was doubtless largely operated by conversation with the great Conservative statesman and his *alter ego*, the princess, needs to be in any degree attributed to the "graciousness" of people in high position, either male or female. Is it not very intelligible and very likely that such opinions, so set forth, as she from day to day heard them, should have honestly and legitimately influenced her own?

But I think that I should be speaking, if perhaps presumptuously, yet truly, if I were to add that there was also one very far from great personage, whose influence in the same direction was greater than even that of Prince Metternich or of any other great folks whatever; and that was the son in daily and almost hourly communion and conversation with whom she lived. I also had begun life as a "Liberal," and was such in the days when Mr. Gladstone was a high Tory. But my mind had long been travelling in an inverse direction to his. And far too large a number of my contemporaries, distinguished and undistinguished, have been moving in the same direction for it to be at all necessary to say that most assuredly my slowly maturing convictions were neither generated nor fostered by any "graciousness" or other influence of dukes or duchesses or great people of any sort.

That my mother's political ideas were in no degree "an affair of the heart," I will not say, and by no means regret not being able to say. But I cannot but assert that it is a great mistake to say that they were uninfluenced by "reasoning from causes," or that the movement of her mind in this respect was in any degree whatever due to the caresses which my brother imagines to have caused it.

She was not a great or careful preserver of papers and letters, or I might have been able to print here very many communications from persons in whom the world feels an interest. Among her early and very dear friends was Mary Mitford.

I have a very vivid remembrance of the appearance of Mary Russell Mitford as I used to see her on the occasions of my visits to Reading, where my grandfather's second wife and then widow was residing. She was not corpulent, but her figure gave one the idea of almost cubical solidity. She had a round and red full-moon sort of face, from the ample forehead above which the hair was all dragged back and stowed away under a small and close-fitting cap, which, surrounding her face, increased the effect of full-blown rotundity. But the gray eye and even the little snub nose were full of drollery and humor, and the lines about the generally somewhat closely-shut mouth indicated unmistakable intellectual power. There is a singular resemblance between her handwriting and that of my mother. Very numerous letters must have passed between them. But of all these I have been able to find but four.

On the 3d of April, 1832, she writes from the " Three Mile Cross," so familiar to many readers, as follows :

" MY DEAR MRS. TROLLOPE,—I thank you most sincerely for your very delightful book, as well as for its great kindness towards me ; and I wish you joy, from the bottom of my heart, of the splendid success which has not merely attended but awaited its career—a happy and, I trust, certain augury of your literary good-fortune in every line which you may pursue. I assure you that my political prejudices are by no means shocked at your dislike of Republicanism. I was always a very aristocratic Whig, and since these reforming days am well-nigh become a stanch Tory, for pretty nearly the same reason that converted you—a dislike to mobs in action. . . . Refinement follows wealth, but not often closely, as witness the parvenu people in dear England. . . . I heard of your plunge into the Backwoods first from Mr. Owen himself, with whom I foregathered three years ago in London, and of whom you have given so very true and graphic a picture. What extraordinary mildness and plausibility that man possesses ! I never before saw an instance of actual wildness—madness of theory accompanied by such suavity and soberness of manner. Did you see my friend, Miss Sedgwick ? Her letters show a large and amiable mind, and a little niece of nine years old, who generally writes in them, has a style very unusual in so young a girl, and yet most useful and natural too. . . . Can you tell me if Mr. Flint be the author of ' George Mason, or the Young Backwoodsman ' ? I think that he is ; and whether the name of a young satirical writer be Sams or Sands ? Your answering these questions will stead me much, and I am sure that you will answer them if you can.

" Now to your kind questions. I am getting ready a fifth and last volume of ' Our Village ' as fast as I can, though with pain and difficulty, having hurt my left hand so much by a fall from an open carriage that it affects the right, and makes writing very uncomfortable to me. And I am in a most perplexed state about my opera, not knowing whether it will be produced this season or not, in consequence of Captain Polhill and his singers having parted. This would not have happened had my coadjutor the composer kept to his time. And I have still hopes that when the opera be [shall, omitted probably] taken in (the music is even now not finished), a sense of interest will bring the parties together again. I hope that it may, for it will not only be a tremendous hit for all of us, but it will take me to London and give me the pleasure of a peep at you, a happiness to which I look forward very anxiously. I know Mr. Tom, and like him of all things, as everybody who knows him must, and I hear that his sisters are charming. God bless you, my dear friend. My father joins me in every good wish, and

" I am ever most affectionately yours,
" M. R. MITFORD."

A few weeks later she writes a very long letter almost entirely filled with a discussion of the desirability or non-desirability of writing in this, that, and the other "annual" or magazine. Most of those she alludes to are dead, and there is no interest in preserving her mainly unfavorable remarks concerning them and their editors and publishers. One sentence, however, is so singularly and amusingly suggestive of change in men and women and things that I must give it. After reviewing a great number of the leading monthlies, she says, " as for *Fraser's* and *Black-wood's*, they are hardly such as a lady likes to write for !"

After advising my mother to stick to writing novels, she says :

" I have not a doubt that that is by far the most profitable branch of the literary profession. If ever I be bold enough to try that arduous path, I shall endeavor to come as near as I can to Miss Austen, my idol. You are very good about my opera. I am sorry to tell you, and you will be sorry to hear, that the composer has disappointed me, that the music is not even yet ready, and that the piece is therefore necessarily délayed till next season. I am very sorry for this on account of the money, and because I have many friends in and near town, yourself among the rest, whom I was desirous to see. But I suppose it will be for the good of the opera to wait till the beginning of a season. It is to be produced with extraordinary splendor, and will, I think, be a tremendous hit. I hope also to have a tragedy out at nearly the same time in the autumn, and *then* I trust we shall meet, and I shall see your dear girls.

" How glad I am to find that you partake of my great aversion to the sort of puffery belonging to literature. I hate it ! and always did, and love you all the better for partaking of my feeling on the subject. I believe that with me it is pride that revolts at the trash. And then it is so false ; the people are so clearly flattering to be flattered. Oh, I hate it ! ! !

" Make my kindest regards [*sic*] and accept my father's.

" Ever most faithfully and affectionately yours,

" M. R. MITFORD.

" P.S.—I suppose my book will be out in about a month. I shall desire Whittaker to send you a copy. It is the fifth and last volume."

The following interesting letter, franked by her friend Talfourd, and shown only by the postmark to have been posted on the 20th of June, 1836, is apparently only part of a letter, for it is written upon one page, and the two "turnovers " only; and begins abruptly :

" My being in London this year seems very uncertain, although if Mr.

Sergeant Talfourd's "Ion" be played, as I believe it will, for Mr. Macready's benefit, I shall hardly be able to resist the temptation of going up for a very few days to be present upon that occasion. But I scarcely ever stir. I am not strong, and am subject to a painful complaint which renders the service of a maid indispensable not only to my comfort but to my health; and that, besides the expense, has an appearance of fuss and finery to which I have a great objection, and to which, indeed, I have from station no claim. My father, too, hates to be left even for a day. And splendid old man as he is in his healthful and vigorous age, I cannot but recollect that he is seventy-five, and that he is my only tie upon earth —the only relation (except, indeed, a few very distant cousins, Russells, Greys, Ogles, and Deans, whom I am too proud and too poor to hook on upon), my only relation in the wide world. This is a desolate view of things; but it explains a degree of clinging to that one most precious parent which people can hardly comprehend. You can scarcely imagine how fine an old man he is; how clear of head and warm of heart. He almost wept over your letter to-day, and reads your book with singular delight and satisfaction, in spite of the difference in politics. He feels strongly, and so, I assure you, do I, your kind mention of me and my poor writings—a sort of testimony always gratifying, but doubly so when the distinguished writer is a dear friend. Even in this desolation, your success—that of your last work ["Paris and the Parisians"] especially must be satisfactory to you. I have no doubt that two volumes on Italy will prove equally delightful to your readers, while the journey will be the best possible remedy for all that you have suffered in spirits and health.

"I am attempting a novel, for which Messieurs Saunders & Ottley have agreed to give £700. It is to be ready some time in September—I mean the MS.—and I am most anxious upon every account to make it as good as possible, one very great reason being the fair, candid, and liberal conduct of the intended publishers. I shall do my very best. Shall I, do you think, succeed? I take for granted that our loss is your gain, and that you see Mr. Milman and his charming wife, who will, I am sure, sympathize most sincerely in your present * affliction.

"Adieu, my dear friend. I am tying myself up from letter-writing until I have finished my novel, while I cannot but hope for one line from you to say that you are recovering. Letters to me may always be enclosed to Mr. Sergeant Talfourd, M.P., 2 Elm Court, Temple. Even if he be on circuit, they will reach me after a short delay. God bless you all. My father joins heartily in this prayer, with

"Your faithful and affectionate
"M. R. MITFORD."

The next, and last which I have found, is entirely undated, but postmarked 20th April, 1837:

---

* Mr. Milman had resigned recently the incumbency of a parish in Reading. My mother's affliction alluded to was the death of her youngest daughter, Emily.

"MY DEAR FRIEND,—I don't know when a trifle has pleased me so much as the coincidence which set us a-writing to each other just at the same time. I have all the north-country superstition flowing through my veins, and do really believe in the exploded doctrine of sympathies. That is to say, I believe in all *genial* superstitions, and don't like this steam-packet railway world of ours, which puts aside with so much scorn that which for certain Shakespeare and Ben Jonson held for true. I am charmed at your own account of yourself and your doings. Mr. Edward Kenyon—(whose brother, John Kenyon, of Harley Place, the most delightful man in London—of course, you know him—is my especial friend)—Mr. Edward Kenyon, who lives chiefly at Vienna, although, I believe, in great retirement, spending £200 upon himself, and giving away £2000—Mr. Edward Kenyon spoke of you to me as having such opportunities of knowing both the city and the country as rarely befell even a resident, and what you say of the peasantry gives me a strong desire to see your book.

"A happy subject is in my mind, a great thing, especially for you whose descriptions are so graphic. The thing that would interest me in Austria, and for the maintenance of which one almost pardons (not quite) their retaining that other old-fashioned thing, the state prisons, is their having kept up in their splendor those grand old monasteries, which are swept away now in Spain and Portugal. I have a passion for Gothic architecture, and a leaning towards the magnificence of the old religion, the foster-mother of all that is finest and highest in art; and if I have such a thing as a literary project, it is to write a romance of which Reading Abbey in its primal magnificence should form a part, not the least about forms of faith, understand, but as an element of the picturesque, and as embodying a very grand and influential part of bygone days. At present I have just finished (since writing 'Country Stories,' which people seem so good as to like) writing all the prose (except one story about the fashionable subject of Egyptian magicians, furnished to me by your admirer, Henry Chorley; I wish you had seen him taking off his hat to the walls as I showed him your father's old residence at Heckfield), all the prose of the most splendid of the annuals, Finden's 'Tableaux,' of which my longest and best story—a Young Pretender story—I have been obliged to omit in consequence of not calculating on the length of my poetical contributors. But my poetry, especially that by that wonderful young creature Miss Barrett, Mr. Kenyon, and Mr. Procter, is certainly such as has seldom before been seen in an annual, and joined with Finden's magnificent engravings ought to make an attractive work.

"I am now going to my novel, if it please God to grant me health. For the last two months I have only once crossed the outer threshold, and, indeed, I have never been a day well since the united effects of the tragedy and the influenza . . . [word destroyed by the seal]. What will become of that poor play is in the womb of time. But its being by universal admission a far more striking drama than Rienzi,' and by very far the best thing I ever wrote, it follows almost, of course, that it will share the fate of its predecessor, and be tossed about the theatres for three or four years to come. Of course, I should be only too happy that it should be brought out at Covent Garden under the united auspices of Mr. Macready and Mr. Bartley.* But I am in constitution and in feeling a much older person than you, my dear friend, as well as in look, however the acknowledgment of age (I am 48) may stand between us; and belonging to a most sanguine and confiding person, I am, of course, as prone to anticipate all probable evil as he is to forestall impossible good. He, my dear father, is, I thank Heaven, splendidly well. He speaks of you always with much delight, is charmed with your writings, and I do hope that you will come to Reading and give him as well as me the great pleasure of seeing you at our poor cottage by the roadside. You would like my flower-garden. It is really a flower-garden becoming a duchess. People are so good in ministering to this, my only amusement. And the effect is heightened by passing through a laborer's cottage to get at it, for such our poor hut literally is.

"You have heard, I suppose, that Mr. Wordsworth's eldest son, who married a daughter of Mr. Curwen, has lost nearly, if not quite, all of his wife's portion by the sea flowing in upon the mine, and has now nothing left but a living of £200 given him by his father-in-law. So are we all touched in turn.

"I have written to the Sedgwicks for the scarlet lilies mentioned by Miss Martineau in her American book. Did you happen to see them in their glory? of course they would flourish here; and having sent them primroses, cowslips, ivy, and many other English wild flowers, which took Theodore Sedgwick's fancy, I have a right to the return. How glad I am to hear the good you tell me of my friend Tom. His fortune seems now assured. My father's kindest regards.

"Ever, my dear friend,
"Very faithfully yours,   M. R. MITFORD.

"P.S.—Mr. Carey, the translator of Dante, has just been here. He says that he visited Cowper's residence at Olney lately, and that his garden room, which suggested mine, is incredibly small, and not near so pretty. Come and see. You know, of course, that the 'Modern Antiques' in 'Our Village' were Theodosia and Frances Hill, sisters of Joseph Hill, cousins and friends of poor Cowper."

What the "good" was by which my "fortune was assured" I am unable to guess. But I am sure of the sincerity of the writer's rejoicing thereat.

Mary Mitford was a genuinely warm-hearted woman, and much of her talk would probably be stigmatized by the young gentlemen of the present generation, who consider the moral temperature of a fish to be "good form," as "gush." How old Landor, who "gushed" from cradle to grave, would have massacred and rended in his wrath such talkers! Mary Mitford's "gush" was sincere at all events.

---

* This gentleman was an old and highly valued friend of my mother.

But there is a " hall-mark " for those who can decipher it, " without which none is genuine."

A considerable intimacy grew up between my mother and the author of "Highways and Byeways" during the latter part of his residence in England, and subsequently, when returning from Boston on leave, he visited Florence and Rome. Many letters passed between them after his establishment as British consul at Boston, some characteristic selections from which will, I doubt not, be acceptable to many readers.

The following was written on the envelope enclosing a very long letter from Mrs. Grattan, and was written, I think, in 1840 :

"I cannot avoid squeezing in a few words more just as the ship is on the point of sailing or steaming away for England. . . . 'The President' has been a fatal title this spring. Poor Harrison, a good and honest man, died in a month after he was elected, and this fine ship, about which we have been at this side of the Atlantic so painfully excited ever since March, is, I fear, gone down with its gallant captain (Roberts, with whom we crossed the Atlantic in the *British Queen*) and poor Power, whom the public cannot afford to lose.

"Since I wrote my letter three days ago—pardon the boldly original topic —the weather has mended considerably. Tell Tom that every tree is also striving to turn over a new leaf, and it is well for you that I have not another to turn too. God bless you.   T. C. G."

I beg to observe that the exhortation addressed to me had no moral significance, but was the writer's characteristic mode of exciting me to new scribblements.

The following, also written on the envelope enclosing a letter from Mrs. Grattan, is dated the 30th of July, 1840:

"I cannot let the envelope go quite a blank, though I cannot quite make it a prize. . . . In literature I have done nothing but write a preface and notes for two new editions of the old " Highways and Byeways," and a short sketchy article in this month's number of the *North American Review* on the present state of Ireland. I am going to follow it up in the next number in reference to the state of the Irish in America, and I hope I shall thus do some good to a subject I have much at heart. I have had various applications to deliver lectures at lyceums, etc., and to preside at public meetings for various objects. All this I have declined. I have been very much before the public at dinners for various purposes, and have refused many invitations to several neighboring cities. I must now draw back a little. I think I have hitherto done good to the cause of peace and friendship between the countries. But I know these continued public appearances will expose me to envy, hatred, and malice. I hope to do something historical by and by, and perhaps an occasional article in the *North American Review*. But anything like light writing I never can again turn to."

From a very long letter written on the 13th of May, 1841, I will give a few extracts :

"MY DEAR AND VALUED FRIEND,—Your letter from Penryth [*sic*], without date, but bearing the ominous postmark, 'April 1st,' has completely made a fool of me, in that sense which implies that nothing else can excuse a gray head and a seared heart for thinking and feeling that there are such things in the world as affection and sincerity. Being fond of flying in the face of reason, and despising experience, whenever they lay down general rules, I am resolved to believe in exceptions, to delight in instances, and to be quite satisfied that I have 'troops of friends '—you being one of the troopers—no matter how few others there may be, or where they are to be found.

" You really must imagine how glad we were to see your handwriting again, and I may say, also, how surprised; for it passeth our understanding to discover how you *make* time for any correspondence at all. We have followed all your literary doings step by step since we left Europe, and we never cease wondering at your fertility and rejoicing at your success. But I am grieved to think that all this is at the cost of your comfort. Or is it that you wrote in a querulous mood when you said those sharp things about your gray-goose quill? Surely composition must be pleasant to you. No one who writes so fast and so well can find it actually irksome. I am aware that people sometimes think they find it so. But we may deceive ourselves on the dark as well as on the bright side of our road, and more easily because it *is* the dark. That is to say, we may not only cheat ourselves with false hopes of good, but with false notions of evil, which proves, if it proves anything just now, that you are considerably mistaken when you fancy writing to be a bore, and that I know infinitely better than you do what you like or dislike."

It is rather singular to find a literary *workman* talking in this style. Grattan was not a fertile writer, and, I must suppose, was never a very industrious one. But he surely must have known that talk about the pleasures of "composition" was wholly beside the mark. *That* may be, often is, pleasant enough, and if the thoughts could be telephoned from the brain to the types it would all be mighty agreeable, and the world would be very considerably more overwhelmed with authorship than it is. It is the "gray-goose quill" work, the necessity for incarnating the creatures of the brain in black and white, that is the world's protection from this avalanche. And I, for one, do not understand how anybody who, eschewing the sunshine and the fields and the song of birds, or the enjoyment of other people's brain-work, has glued himself to his desk for long hours, can say or imagine that his task is, or has been, aught else than hard and distasteful work, demanding unrelaxing self-denial and industry. And, however fine the frenzy in which the poet's eye may roll while he builds the lofty line, the 'work of putting some thousands of them on the paper, when built, must be as irksome to him as the penny-a-liner's task is to *him*—more so, in that the mind of the latter does not need to be forcibly and painfully restrained from rushing on to the new pastures which invite it, and curbed to the packhorse pace of the quill-driving process.

"You must not," he continues, "allow yourself to be, or even fancy that you are, tired, or tormented, or worn out. Work the mine to the last. Pump up every drop out of the well. Put money i' thy purse; and add story after story to that structure of fame, which will enable you to do as much to that house by the lake-side where I *will* hope to see you yet."

He then goes on to speak at considerable length of the society of Boston, praising it much, yet saying that it is made more charming to a visitor than to a permanent resident. "In this it differs," he says, "from almost all the countries I have lived in in Europe except Holland."

Speaking of a visit to Washington during the inauguration of General Harrison, which seems to have delighted him much, he says he travelled back with a family,

"At least with the master and mistress of it, of whom I must tell you something. Mr. Paige is a merchant, and brother-in-law of Mr. Webster; Mrs. Paige a niece of Judge Story. From this double connection with two of the first men in the country their family associations are particularly agreeable. Mrs. Paige is one of three sisters, all very handsome, spirited, and full of talent. One is married to Mr. Webster's eldest son. Another, Mrs. Joy, has for her husband an idle gentleman, a rare thing in this place. Mrs. Paige was in Europe two years ago with Mr. and Mrs. Webster, senior (the latter, by-the-bye, is a *most* charming person), and had the advantage of seeing society in England and France in its best aspect, and is one who can compare as well as see. . . . Among the men [of the Boston society] are Dr. Channing, a prophet in our country, a pamphleteer in his own;

Bancroft, *the* historian of America, a man of superior talents and great agreeability, but a black sheep in society, on account of his Van Buren politics, against whom the white sheep of the Whig party will not rub themselves; Prescott, the author of 'Ferdinand and Isabella,' a handsome, half-blind shunner of the vanities of the world, with some others who read and write a good deal, and no one the wiser for it. Edward Everett is in Italy, where you will surely meet him [we saw a good deal of him]. He is rather formal than cold, if all I hear whispered of him be true; of elegant taste in literature, though not of easy manners, and, altogether, an admirable specimen of an American orator and scholar. At Cambridge, three miles off, we have Judge Story, of the Supreme Court, eloquent, deeply learned, garrulous, lively, amiable, excellent in all and every way that a mortal can be. He is, decidedly, the gem of this western world. Mr. Webster is now settled at Washington, though here at this moment on a visit to Mrs. Paige. Among our neighboring notabilities is John Quincy Adams, an ex-President of the United States, ex-minister at half the courts in Europe, and now, at seventy-five, a simple member of Congress, hard as a piece of granite and cold as a lump of ice."

Speaking of his having very frequently appeared at public meetings during the first year of his consulship, and of his having since that refrained from such appearances, he continues :

"I was doubtful as to the way my being so much *en evidence* might be relished *at home*. Of late public matters have been on so ticklish a footing that all the less a British functionary was seen the better.

"In literature I have done nothing, barring a couple of articles on Ireland and the Irish in America, a subject I have much at heart. But, much as I feel for them and with them, I refused dining with my countrymen on St. Patrick's Day because they had the *gaucherie* (of which I had previous notice) to turn the festive meeting into a political one by giving 'O'Connell and success to repeal' as one of their 'regular' toasts, and by leaving out the Queen's health, which they gave when I dined with them last year."

Then, after detailed notices of the movements of his sons, he goes on :

"We have many plans in perspective—Niagara, Canada, Halifax, the mountains, the springs, the sea—the result of which you shall know as soon as we receive a true and faithful account of your adventures in just as many pages as you can afford; but Tom must, in the meantime, send me a long letter. . . . Tell Tom I have half resolved to give up punning and take to repartee. A young fellow said to me the other day, 'Ah! Mr. Consul (as I am always called), I wish I could discover a new pleasure.' 'Try virtue!' was my reply. A pompous ex-governor said, swaggeringly, to me, at the last dinner-party at which I assisted, 'Well, Mr. Consul, I suppose you Europeans think us semi-civilized here in America?' 'Almost!' said I. Now ask Tom if that was not pretty considerable smart. But assure him, at the same time, it is nothing at all to what I *could* do in the way of impertinence! Need I say how truly and affectionately we all love you?

"T. C. GRATTAN."

I wrote back that I would enter the lists with him in the matter of impertinence, and, as a sample, told him that I thought he had better return to the punning.

I could, I doubt not, find among my mother's papers some further letters that might be worth printing or quoting. But my waning space warns me that I must not indulge myself with doing so.

CHAPTER XXXVII.

THEODOSIA TROLLOPE.

I SAID at the beginning of the last chapter that, during the period, some of the recollections of which I had been chronicling, the two greatest sorrows I had ever known had befallen me. A third came subsequently. But that belonged to a period of my life which does not fall within the limits I have assigned to these reminiscences. Of the first, the death of my mother, I have spoken. The other, the death of my wife, followed it at no great distance, and was, of course, a far more terrible one. She had been ailing—so long, indeed, that I had become habituated to it, and thought that she would continue to live as she had been living. We had been travelling in Switzerland in the autumn of 1864; and I remember very vividly her saying, on board the steamer by which we were leaving Colico, at the head of the Lake of Como, on our return to Italy, as she turned on the deck to take a last look at the mountains, " Good-bye, you big beauties!" I little thought it was her last adieu to them; but I thought afterwards that she probably may have had some misgivings that it was so.

But it was not till the following spring that I began to realize that I must lose her. She died on the 13th of April, 1865.

I have spoken of her as she was when she became my wife, but without much hope of representing her to those who never had the happiness of knowing her as she really was, not only in person, which matters little, but in mind and intellectual powers. And to tell what she was in heart, in disposition—in a word, in soul—would be a far more difficult task.

In her the æsthetic faculties were probably the most markedly exceptional portion of her intellectual constitu-

22

tion. The often-cited dictum, *les races se feminisent*, was not exemplified in her case. From her mother, an accomplished musician, she inherited her very pronounced musical* faculty and tendencies, and, I think, little else. From her father, a man of very varied capacities and culture, she drew much more. How far, if in any degree, this fact may be supposed to have been connected in the relation of cause and effect, with the other fact, that her mother was more than fifty years of age at the time of her birth, I leave to the speculations of physiological inquirers. In bodily constitution her inheritance from her father's mother was most marked. To that source must be traced, I conceive, the delicacy of constitution, speaking medically, which deprived me of her at a comparatively early age; for both father and mother were of thoroughly healthy and strong constitutions. But if it may be suspected that the Brahmin Sultana, her grandmother, bequeathed her her frail diathesis, there was no doubt or difficulty in tracing to that source the exterior delicacy of formation which characterized her. I remember her telling me that the last words a dying sister of her mother's ever spoke, when Theodosia, standing by the bedside, placed her hand on the dying woman's forehead, were, "Ah, that is Theo's little Indian hand." And, truly, the slender delicacy of hand and foot which characterized her were unmistakably due to her Indian descent. In person she in no wise resembled either father or mother, unless it were, possibly, her father, in the conformation and shape of the teeth.

I have already, in a previous chapter of these reminiscences, given a letter from Mrs. Browning in which she speaks of Theodosia's "multiform faculty." And the phrase, which so occurring, might in the case of almost any other writer be taken as a mere epistolary civility, is in the case of one whose absolute accuracy of veracity never swerved a hair's-breadth, equivalent to a formal certificate of the fact to the best of her knowledge. And she knew my wife well both before and after the marriage of either of them. Her faculty was truly *multiform*.

---

* But this she might, also, have got from her father, who was passionately fond of music, and was a very respectable performer on the violin.

She was not a great musician ; but her singing had for
great musicians a charm which the performances of many
of their equals in the art failed to afford them. She had
never much voice, but I have rarely seen the hearer to
whose eyes she could not bring the tears. She had a spell
for awakening emotional sympathy which I have never
seen surpassed, rarely, indeed, equalled.

For language she had an especial talent, was dainty in
the use of her own, and astonishingly apt in acquiring—
not merely the use for speaking as well as reading purposes, but — the delicacies of other tongues. Of Italian,
with which she was naturally *most* conversant, she was
recognized by acknowledged experts to be a thoroughly
competent critic.

She published, now many years ago, in the *Athenæum*,
some translations from the satirist Giusti, which any intelligent reader would, I think, recognize to be cleverly
done. But none save the very few in this country who
know and can understand the Tuscan poet's works in the
original can at all conceive the difficulty of translating
him into tolerable English verse. And I have no hesita-
tion in asserting that any competent judge, who is such
by virtue of understanding the original, would pronounce
her translations of Giusti to be a masterpiece, which very
few, indeed, of contemporary men or women could have
produced. I have more than once surprised her in tears
occasioned by her obstinate struggles with some passage of
the intensely idiomatic satirist, which she found it almost
—but eventually not quite — impossible to render to her
satisfaction.

She published a translation of Niccolini's "Arnaldo da
Brescia," which won the cordial admiration and friendship
of that great poet. And neither Niccolini's admiration
nor his friendship were easily won. He was, when we
knew him at Florence in his old age, a somewhat crabbed
old man, not at all disposed to make new acquaintances,
and, I think, somewhat soured and disappointed, not certainly with the meed of admiration he had won from his
countrymen as a poet, but with the amount of effect which
his writings had availed to produce in the political senti-

ments and then apparent destinies of the Italians. But he was conquered by the young Englishwoman's translation of his favorite, and, I think, his finest work. It is a thoroughly trustworthy and excellent translation; but the execution of it was child's play in comparison with the translations from Giusti.

She translated a number of the curiously characteristic *stornelli* of Tuscany, and especially of the Pistoja mountains. And here again it is impossible to make any one who has never been familiar with these *stornelli* understand the especial difficulty of translating them. Of course the task was a slighter and less significant one than that of translating Giusti, nor was the same degree of critical accuracy and nicety in rendering shades of meaning called for. But there were not—are not—many persons who could cope with the especial difficulties of the attempt as successfully as she did. She produced also a number of pen-and-ink drawings illustrating these *stornelli*, which I still possess, and in which the spirited, graphic, and accurately truthful characterization of the figures could only have been achieved by an artist very intimately acquainted *intus et in cute* with the subjects of her pencil.

She published a volume on the Tuscan revolution, which was very favorably received. The *Examiner*, among other critics — all of them, to the best of my remembrance, more or less favorable—said of these "Letters" (for that was the form in which the work was published, all of them, I think, having been previously printed in the *Athenæum*), "Better political information than this book gives may be had in plenty; but it has a special value which we might almost represent by comparing it to the report of a very watchful nurse, who, without the physician's scientific knowledge, uses her own womanly instinct in observing every change of countenance and every movement indicating the return of health and strength to the patient. . . . She has written a very vivid and truthful account." The critic has very accurately, and, it may be said, graphically, assigned its true value and character to the book.

I have found it necessary in a former chapter, where I have given a number of interesting and characteristic letters from Landor to my wife's father, to insert a deprecatory *caveat* against the exuberant enthusiasm of admiration which led him to talk of the probability of her eclipsing the names and fame of other poets, including in this estimate Elizabeth Barrett Browning. The preposterousness of this no human being would have felt more strongly than Theodosia Garrow, except Theodosia Trollope, when such an estimate had become yet more preposterous. But Landor, whose unstinted admiration of Mrs. Browning's poetry is vigorously enough expressed in his own strong language, as may be seen in Mr. Forster's pages, would not have dreamed of instituting any such comparison at a later day. But that his critical acumen and judgment were not altogether destroyed by the enthusiasm of his friendship, is, I think, shown by the following little poem by Theodosia Trollope, written a few years after the birth of her child. I don't think I need apologize for printing it.

The original MS. of it before me gives no title ; nor do I remember that the authoress ever assigned one to the verses.

I.

"In the noonday's golden pleasance,
    Little Bice, baby fair,
With a fresh and flowery presence,
    Dances round her nurse's chair,
In the old gray loggia dances, haloed by her shining hair.

II.

"Pretty pearl in sober setting,
    Where the arches garner shade!
Cones of maize like golden netting,
    Fringe the sturdy colonnade,
And the lizards pertly pausing glance across the balustrade.

III.

"Brown cicala dryly proses,
    Creaking the hot air to sleep,
Bounteous orange-flowers and roses,
    Yield the wealth of love they keep,
To the sun's imperious ardor in a dream of fragrance deep.

IV.

"And a cypress, mystic hearted,
    Cleaves the quiet dome of light
With its black green masses parted
    But by gaps of blacker night,
Which the giddy moth and beetle circle round in dubious flight.

V.

"Here the well-chain's pleasant clanging,
    Sings of coolness deep below;
There the vine leaves breathless hanging,
    Shine transfigured in the glow,
And the pillars stare in silence at the shadows which they throw.

VI.

"Portly nurse, black-browed, red-vested,
    Knits and dozes, drowsed with heat;
Bice, like a wren gold-crested,
    Chirps and teases round her seat.
Hides the needles, plucks the stocking, rolls the cotton o'er her feet.

VII.

"Nurse must fetch a draught of water,
    In the glass with painted wings,*
Nurse must show her little daughter
    All her tale of silver rings,
Dear sweet nurse must sing a couplet—solemn nurse, who *never* sings.

VIII.

"Blest Madonna! what a clamor!
    Now the little torment tries,
Perched on tiptoe, all the glamour
    Of her coaxing hands and eyes!
May she hold the glass she drinks from—just one moment, Bice cries.

IX.

"Nurse lifts high the Venice beaker,
    Bossed with masks, and flecked with gold,
Scarce in time to 'scape the quicker
    Little fingers overbold,
Craving, tendril-like, to grasp it, with the will of four years old.

---

* Those unacquainted with the forms of the old decorated Venetian glass will hardly understand the phrase in the text. Those who know them will feel the accuracy of the picture.

X.

"Pretty wood-bird, pecking, flitting,
  Round the cherries on the tree,
Ware the scarecrow, grimly sitting,
  Crouched for silly things, like thee!
Nurse hath plenty such in ambush. 'Touch not, for it burns,'* quoth she.

XI.

"And thine eyes' blue mirror widens
  With an awestroke of belief;
Meekly following that blind guidance,
  On thy finger's rosy sheaf,
Blow'st thou softly, fancy wounded, soothing down a painless grief.

XII.

"Nurse and nursling, learner, teacher,
  Thus foreshadow things to come,
When the girl shall grow the creature
  Of false terrors vain and dumb,
And intrust their baleful fetish with her being's scope and sum.

XIII.

"Then her heart shall shrink and wither,
  Custom-straitened like her waist,
All her thought to cower together,
  Huddling, sheeplike, with the rest,
With the flock of soulless bodies on a pattern schooled and laced.

XIV.

"Till the stream of years encrust her
  With a numbing mail of stone,
Till her laugh lose half its lustre,
  And her truth forswear its tone,
And she sees God's might and mercy darkly through a glass alone!

XV.

"While our childhood fair and sacred,
  Sapless doctrines doth rehearse,
And the milk of falsehoods acrid,
  Burns our babe-lips like a curse,
Cling we must to godless prophets, as the suckling to the nurse.

XVI.

"As the seed time, so the reaping,
  Shame on us who overreach,

---

* "*Non toccare che brucia*," Tuscan proverb.

While our eyes yet smart with weeping,
Hearts so all our own to teach,
Better they and we lay sleeping where the darkness hath no speech!"

It is impossible for any but those who know—not Florence, but—rural Tuscany well to appreciate the really wonderful accuracy and picturesque perfection of the above scene from a Tuscan afternoon. But I think many others will feel the lines to be good. In the concluding stanzas, in which the writer draws her moral, there are weak lines. But in the first eleven, which paint her picture, there is not one. Every touch tells, and tells with admirable truth and vividness of presentation. In one copy of the lines which I have, the name is changed from Bice to "Flavia," and this, I take it, because of the entire non-applicability of the latter stanzas to the child, whose rearing was in her own hands. But the picture of child and nurse—how lifelike none can tell but I—was the picture of her "baby Beatrice," and the description simply the reproduction of things seen.

I think I may venture to print also the following lines. They are, in my opinion, far from being equal in merit to the little poem printed above, but they are pretty, and I think sufficiently good to do no discredit to her memory. Like the preceding, they have no title.

I.

"I built me a temple, and said it should be
    A shrine, and a home where the past meets me,
    And the most evanescent and fleeting of things,
    Should be lured to my temple, and shorn of their wings,
        To adorn my palace of memories.

II.

"The pearl of the morning, the glow of the noon,
    The play of the clouds as they float past the moon,
    The most magical tint on the snowiest peak,
    They are gone while I gaze, fade before you can speak,
        Yet they stay in my palace of memories.

III.

"I stood in the midst of the forest trees,
    And heard the sweet sigh of the wandering breeze,

And this with the tinkle of heifer bells,
As they trill on the ear from the dewy dells,
   Are the sounds in my palace of memories.

IV.

"I looked in the face of a little child,
With its fugitive dimples and eyes so wild,
It springs off with a bound like a wild gazelle,
It is off and away, but I've caught my *
   And here's mirth for my palace of memories.

V.

"In the morning we meet on a mountain height,
And we walk and converse till the fall of night,
We hold hands for a moment, then pass on our way,
But that which I've got from the friend of a day,
   I'll keep in my palace of memories."

The verses which Landor praised with enthusiasm so excessive were most, or I think all of them, published in the annual edited by his friend Lady Blessington, and were all written before our marriage. I have many long letters addressed to her by that lady, and several by her niece Miss Power, respecting them. They always in every instance ask for "more."

Many of her verses she set to music, especially one little poemlet, which I remember to this day the tune of, which she called the "Song of the Blackbird," and which was, if I remember rightly, made to consist wholly of the notes uttered by the bird.

Another instance of her "multiform faculty" was her learning landscape sketching. I have spoken of her figure-drawing. And this, I take it, was the real bent of her talent in that line. But unable to compass the likeness of a haystack myself, I was desirous of possessing some record of the many journeys which I designed to take, and eventually did take with her. And wholly to please me she forthwith made the attempt, and though her landscape was never equal to her figure drawing, I possess some couple of hundred of water-color sketches done by her from nature on the spot.

---

* Word here illegible.

22*

I used to say that if I wanted a Sanscrit dictionary, I had only to put her head straight at it, and let her feel the spur, and it would have been done.

We lived together seventeen happy years. During the first five I think I may say that she lived wholly and solely in, by, and for me. That she should live for somebody other than herself was an absolute indefeasible necessity of her nature. During the last twelve years I shared her heart with her daughter. Her intense worship for her "Baby Beatrice" was equalled only by—that of all the silliest and all the wisest women, who have true womanly hearts in their bosoms, for their children. The worship was, of course, all the more absorbing that the object of it was unique. I take it that, after the birth of her child, I came second in her heart. But I was not jealous of little Bice.

I do not think that she would have quite subscribed to the opinion of Garibaldi on the subject of the priesthood, which I mentioned in a former chapter—that they ought all to be forthwith put to death. But all her feelings and opinions were bitterly antagonistic to them. She was so deeply convinced of the magnitude of the evil inflicted by them and their Church on the character of the Italians, for whom she ever felt a great affection, that she was bitter on the subject. And it is the only subject on which I ever knew her to feel in any degree bitterly. Many of her verses written during her latter years are fiercely denunciatory or humorously satirical of the Italian priesthood, and especially of the pontifical government. I wish that my space permitted me to give further specimens of them here. But I must content myself with giving one line, which haunts my memory, and appears to me excessively happy in the accurate truthfulness of its simile. She is writing of the journey which Pius the Ninth made, and describing his equipment, says that he started "with strings of cheap blessings, like glass beads for savages."

With the exception of this strong sentiment my wife was one of the most tolerant people I ever knew. What she most avoided in those with whom she associated was, not so much ignorance, or even vulgarity of manner, as pure native stupidity. But even of that, when the need arose, she was tolerant. I never knew her in the selection of an acquaintance, or even of a friend, to be influenced to the extent of even a hair's-breadth by station, rank, wealth, fashion, or any consideration whatever, save personal liking and sympathy, which was, in her case, perfectly compatible with the widest divergence of views and opinions on nearly any of the great subjects which most divide mankind, and even with divergence of rules of conduct. Her own opinions were the honest results of original thinking, and her conduct the outcome of the dictates of her own heart—of her heart rather than of her reasoning powers, or of any code of law—a condition of mind which might be dangerous to individuals with less native purity of heart than hers.

As a wife, as a daughter, as a daughter-in-law, as a mother, she was absolutely irreproachable. In the first relationship she was all in all to me for seventeen years. She brought sweetness and light into my life and into my dwelling. She was the angel in the house, if ever human being was.

Her father became an inmate of our house after the death of his wife at a great age at Torquay, whither they had returned after the death of my wife's half-sister, Harriet Fisher. He was a jealously affectionate, but very exacting father ; and few daughters, I think, could have been more admirable in her affection for him, her attention to him, her care of him. And I may very safely say that very few mothers of sons have the fortune of finding such a daughter-in-law. My mother had been very fond of her before our marriage, and became afterwards as devotedly attached to her as she was to me, of whom she knew her to be an indivisible part, while she was to my mother simply perfect. Her own mother she had always been in the habit of calling by that name. She always spoke to and of my mother as "mammy." What she was to her own daughter I have already said. There was somewhat of the tendency towards "spoiling" which is mostly inseparable from the adoration which a young mother, of the right sort, feels for her first-born child, but she never made any attempt to avert or counteract my endeavors to prevent such spoiling. When little Bice had to be punished by solitary confinement for half an hour, she only watched anxiously for the expiration of the sentence.*

But that her worth, her talent, her social qualities, were recognized by a wider world than that of her own family, or her own circle of friends, is testified by the recording stone which the municipality placed on my house at the corner of the Piazza dell' Independenza, where it may still be seen. Indeed, the honor was not undeserved. For during the whole of her residence in Italy, which nearly synchronized with the struggle of Italy for her independence and unity, she had adopted the Italian cause heart and soul, and done what was in her to do, for its advancement. The honor was rendered the more signal, and the more acceptable, from the fact that the same had recently been rendered by the same body to Elizabeth Barrett Browning.

---

* I do not remember that little Bice ever consoled herself under the disgrace of such captivity as my present wife has confessed to me that she did when suffering under the same condemnation. *Her* method of combining the maintenance of personal dignity with revenge on the oppressor was to say to the first person who came to take her out of prison, "No, you can't come into *my* parlor!"

CHAPTER XXXVIII.

THE house in the Piazza dell' Independenza which was
known in the city as " Villino Trollope," and of which I
have spoken at the close of the last chapter, was my property, and I had lived in it nearly the whole of my married
life. During that time four deaths had occurred among
its inmates.

The first to happen was that of the old and highly valued servant of whom I had occasion to speak when upon
the subject of Mr. Hume's spiritualistic experiences at my
house. She had been for many years a much trusted and
beloved servant in the family of Mr. Garrow at Torquay,
and had accompanied them abroad. Her name was Elizabeth Shinner. Her death was felt by all of us as that of
a member of our family, and she lies in the Protestant
cemetery at Florence by the side of her former master,
and of the young mistress whom she had loved as a child
of her own.

The next to go was Mr. Garrow. His death was a very
sudden and unexpected one. He was a robust and apparently perfectly healthy man. I was absent from home
when he died. I had gone with a Cornishman, a Mr. Tre-
whella, who was desirous of visiting Mr. Sloane's copper
mine, in the neighborhood of Volterra, of which I have
before spoken. We had accomplished our visit, and were
returning over the Apennine about six o'clock in the morning in a little *bagherino*, as the country cart-gigs are called,
when we were hailed by a man in a similar carriage meeting us, whom I recognized as the foreman of a carpenter
we employed. He had been sent to find me, and bring
me home with all speed, in consequence of the sudden illness of Mr. Garrow. As far as I could learn from him,

there was little probability of finding my father-in-law alive. I made the best of my way to Florence. But he had been dead several hours when I arrived. He had waked with a paralytic attack on him, which deprived him of the power of moving on the left side, and, drawing his face awry, made speech almost impossible to him. He assured his servant—who was almost immediately with him—speaking with much difficulty, that it was nothing of any importance, and that he should soon get over it. But these were the last words he ever spoke, and in two or three hours afterwards he breathed his last.

Then, in a few years more, the *crescendo* wave of trouble took my mother from me at the age of eighty-three. For the last two or three years she had entirely lost her memory, and for the last few months the use of her mental faculties. And she did not suffer much. The last words she uttered were " Poor Cecilia !"—her mind reverting in her latest moments to the child whose loss had been the most recent. She had for years entertained a great horror and dread of the possibility of being buried alive, in consequence of the very short time allowed by the law for a body to remain unburied after death; and she had exacted from me a promise that I would in any case cause a vein to be opened in her arm after death. In her case there could be no possible room for the shadow of doubt as to the certainty of death ; but I was bound by my promise, and found some difficulty in the performance of it. The medical man in attendance, declaring the absolute absurdity of any doubt on the subject, refused to perform an operation which, he said, was wholly uncalled for, and argued that my promise could only be understood to apply to a case of possible doubt. I had none; but was none the less determined to be faithful to my promise. But it was not till I declared that I would myself sever a vein, in however butcher-like a manner, that I induced him to accompany me to the death-chamber and perform under my eyes the necessary operation.

My mother, the inseparable companion of so many wanderings in so many lands, the indefatigable laborer of so many years, found her rest near to the two who had gone from my house before, in the beautiful little cemetery on which the Apennine looks down.

But it was not long before this sorrow was followed by a very much sorer one—by the worst of all that could have happened to me. After what I have written in the last chapter it is needless to say anything of the blank despair that fell upon me when my wife died, on the 13th of April, 1865. She also lies near the others.

My house was indeed left unto me desolate, and I thought that life and all its sweetness was over for me.

I immediately took measures for disposing of the house in the Piazza dell' Independenza, and before long found a purchaser for it. I had bought it when the speculator, who had become the owner of the ground at the corner of the space which was beginning to assume the semblance of a "square" or "piazza" had put in the foundations, but had not proceeded much further with his work. I completed it, improving largely, as I thought, on his plan; adapted it for a single residence, instead of its division into sundry dwellings; obtained possession of additional ground between the house and the city wall, sufficient for a large garden; built around it, looking to the south, the largest and handsomest "stanzone"* for orange and lemon plants in Florence, and gathered together a collection of very fine trees, the profits from which (much smaller in my hands than would have been the case in those of a Florentine to the manner born) nevertheless abundantly sufficed to defray the expenses of the garden and gardeners. In a word, I made the place a very complete and comfortable residence. Nearly the whole of my first married life was spent in it. And much of the literary work of my life has been done in it.

I used in those days, and for very many years afterwards, to do all my writing standing; and I strongly recommend the practice to brother quill-drivers. Pauses, often considerable intervals, occur for thought while the

---

* " Stanzone " is the term used in Tuscany to signify the buildings destined to shelter the " Agrumi," as the orange and lemon plants are called generically, in the winter; which in Florence is too severe to permit of their being left in the open air,

pen is in the hand. And if one is seated at a table, one remains sitting during these intervals. But if one is standing, it becomes natural to one, during even a small pause, to take a turn up and down the room, or even, as I often used to do, in the garden. And such change and movement I consider eminently salutary both for mind and body.

I had specially contrived a little window immediately above the desk at which I stood, fixed to the wall. The room looking on the " loggia," which was the scene of the little poem transcribed in the preceding chapter, was abundantly lighted, but I liked some extra light close to my desk.

In that room my Bice was born. For it was subsequently to her birth that the destination of it was changed from a bedroom to a study.

Few men have passed years of more uncheckered happiness than I did in that house. And I was very fond of it.

But, as may readily be imagined, it became all the more odious and intolerable to me when the " angel in the house " had been taken from me.

CHAPTER XXXIX.

CONCLUSION.

ASSUREDLY it seemed to me that all was over, and the future a dead blank; and for a time I was as a man stunned.

But in truth it was very far otherwise. I was fifty-five; but I was in good health, young for my years, strong and vigorous in constitution, and before a year had passed it began to seem to me that a future, and life and its prospects, might open to me afresh; that the curtain might be dropped on the drama that was passed, and a new phase of life begun.

I had had and vividly enjoyed an entire life, according to the measure that is meted out to many, perhaps I may say to most men. But I felt myself ready for another. And—thanks this time also to a woman—I have *had* another, *in no wise* less happy, in some respects, as less checkered by sorrows—more happy than the first. I am in better health too, having outgrown, apparently, several of the maladies which young people are subject to.

Of this second life I am not now going to tell my readers anything. "What I remember" of my first life may be, and I hope has been, told frankly, without giving offence or annoyance to any human being. I don't know that the telling of the story of my second life would necessarily lead me to say anything which could hurt anybody. But, mixed up as its incidents and interests and associations have been with a great multitude of men and women still living and moving and talking and writing round about me, I should not feel myself so comfortably at liberty to write whatever offered itself to my memory.

Ten years hence, perhaps ("Please God, the public lives!" as a speculative showman said), I may tell the reader, if he cares to hear it, the story of my second life. For the present we will break off here.

But not without some words of parting kindness—and, shall we say, wisdom!—from an old man to readers, most of whom probably might be his sons, and many doubtless his grandsons.

Especially, my young friends, don't pay overmuch attention to what the Psalmist says about "the years of man." I knew *dans le temps* a fine old octo- and nearly nonogenarian, one Gräberg de Hemsö, a Swede (a man with a singular history, who passed ten years of his early life in the British navy, and was, when I knew him, librarian at the Pitti Palace in Florence), who used to complain of the Florentine doctors that "Dey doosen't know what de nordern constitooshions is!" and I take it the same may be said of the Psalmist. Ten years beyond threescore and ten need not be all sorrow and trouble. Depend upon it, kindly nature—*prudens*, as that jolly old fellow, fine gentleman, and true philosopher, Horace, says in a similar connection—kindly nature knows how to make the closing decade of life every whit as delightful as any of the preceding, if only you don't balk her purposes. Don't weigh down your souls, and pin your particles of divine essence to earth by your yesterday's vices; be sure that when you cannot jump over the chairs so featly as you can now, you will not want to do so; tell the girls, with genial old Anacreon, when the time comes, that whether the hairs on your forehead be many or few, you know not, but do know well that it behooves an old man to be cheery in proportion to the propinquity of his exit, and go on your way rejoicing through this beautiful world, which not even the Radicals have quite spoiled yet.

And so *à rivederci—au revoir—auf Wiedersehn*—why have we no English equivalent better than "Here's to our next pleasant meeting!"

INDEX.

23*

THE END.